A More
Perfect
Union

VOLUME 8

A More
Perfect
Union

A NOVEL BY
RON CARTER

BOOKCRAFT

SALT LAKE CITY

PRELUDE TO GLORY

Volume 1: Our Sacred Honor
Volume 2: The Times That Try Men's Souls
Volume 3: To Decide Our Destiny
Volume 4: The Hand of Providence
Volume 5: A Cold, Bleak Hill
Volume 6: The World Turned Upside Down
Volume 7: The Impending Storm
Volume 8: A More Perfect Union

Library of Congress Cataloging-in-Publication Data

Carter, Ron, 1932-
  A more perfect union / Ron Carter.
    p. cm. — (Prelude to glory ; v. 8)
  Includes bibliographical references.
  ISBN 1-59038-308-7 (alk. paper)
    I. United States—History—Confederation, 1783-1789—Fiction. 2. United
States. Constitutional Convention (1787)—Fiction. 3. Philadelphia
(Pa.)—Fiction. I. Title. II. Series

  PS3553.A7833M67 2004
  813'.54—dc22
  2004002864

Printed in the United States of America   72076
Publishers Printing, Salt Lake City, UT

10   9   8   7   6   5   4   3   2

This volume is most humbly dedicated to the fifty-five men who met in the old Philadelphia Statehouse between May 14, 1787, and September 17, 1787, in the last attempt to save the United States from oblivion. The north and the south, big states and small, each with their own agenda, fought it out with threats and compromise, give and take, and the core conviction that they must succeed. The document they created, the Constitution of the United States of America, changed the world forever.

It was their last great hope.

They had won the war with Britain, and lost the peace among the thirteen states. Thirteen separate countries, each with its own history, constitution, court system, money, commerce, laws, identity, biases, and prejudices. The Articles of Confederation that had bound them together through the war years had proven worthless in their heartbreaking attempts to hold the states together, while petty differences over borders, river rights, tariffs, money, and bankruptcies erupted into armed conflicts. In quiet desperation the leaders in the country sent word to all thirteen states. Send delegates. Philadelphia. Monday, May 14, 1787.

In the insufferable summer heat, they fought and threatened and quarreled, and they learned to compromise and give and take, and in the end they drafted a document the like of which had never been conceived of before.

They changed the world forever. This is their story.

PREFACE

Following the *Prelude to Glory* series will be substantially easier if the reader understands the author's approach.

The Revolutionary War was not fought in one location. It was fought on many fronts, with critical events occurring simultaneously in each of them. It quickly became obvious that moving back and forth from one event which was occurring at the same moment as another, would be too confusing. Thus, the decision was made to follow each major event through to its conclusion, as seen through the eyes of selected characters, and then go back and pick up the thread of other great events that were happening at the same time in other places, as seen through the eyes of characters caught up in those events.

Volume I, *Our Sacred Honor*, follows the fictional family of John Phelps Dunson from the beginning of hostilities in April 1775, through to the sea battle off the coast of England in which the American ship *Bon Homme Richard* defeats the British ship *Serapis*, with Matthew Dunson navigating for John Paul Jones. In volume 2, *The Times That Try Men's Souls*, Billy Weems, Matthew's dearest friend, survives the terrible defeats suffered by the Americans around New York and the disastrous American retreat to the wintry banks of the Delaware River. Volume 3, *To Decide Our Destiny*, leads us across the frozen Delaware River on Christmas night, 1776, with Billy Weems and his friend Eli Stroud, to take the town of Trenton, then Princeton. Volume 4, *The Hand of Providence*, addresses the tremendous, inspiring events of the campaign for possession of the Lake Champlain–Hudson River corridor, wherein British General John Burgoyne, with an army of eight thousand, is defeated by the Americans in one of the most profoundly moving stories in the history of America, at a place on the Hudson River called Saratoga. Volume 5, *A Cold, Bleak Hill*, leads us through two heartbreaking defeats in the summer of 1777, one at Brandywine Creek, the other at

Germantown, and then into the legendary story of the terrible winter at Valley Forge, Pennsylvania.

Volume 6, *The World Turned Upside Down*, brings us through the realization by the British King and Parliament that they have underestimated the strength of the Americans in the northern colonies. Upon the resignation of the commander in America, General William Howe, they order General Sir Henry Clinton to take command and move the war effort to the South. The French and Spanish join forces with the United States, and the entire course of the war changes.

Away from the battles, we find General Benedict Arnold and his wife, Peggy, entering into their treason with British Major John André, resulting in the arrest and death of John André, while Benedict Arnold escapes to become a British officer.

In that volume, the British conquer Savannah, Georgia, then Charleston, South Carolina, and General Cornwallis, given command of the British forces in the South by General Clinton, begins his march north. Crucial battles are fought at Camden, then King's Mountain, and at Guilford Courthouse, with General Nathanael Greene commanding the American forces in a delay-hit-run-delay tactic that slowly exhausts the British forces. General Cornwallis moves his beleaguered army to Yorktown, Virginia, protected by the guns of the British navy while he refits his men. But when the French navy engages them and drives the British ships away, General Cornwallis is landlocked, and General Washington makes his historic march from New York to Yorktown. With French soldiers assisting, the Americans place the British under siege, and ultimately General Cornwallis must surrender his entire command.

The war is over. It remains only to quell a few British who will not accept defeat, before moving on to the signing of the peace treaty.

In volume 7, *The Impending Storm*, we discover that the defeat of the British at Yorktown results in a horrendous split in the British government, with King George III determined to hold the American colonies, while his cabinet is divided on the question, and Parliament is against him. The result is the most dramatic housecleaning in the history of English politics, when the entire cabinet is dismissed and a new one appointed. Instantly the cabinet and parliament vote to abandon

America, and peace negotiations commence, with a resulting treaty in 1783. America has become a free and independent nation.

It is then the new nation is shocked by the harsh reality of their victory. The United States are bankrupt, with a congress that is powerless to raise revenue or compel unity among the states. Immediately the several states begin bickering over border tariffs, river rights, and money. Most states print their own currency, as does Congress, and within months the paper money is valueless. Veterans are discharged from the Continental Army without the pay they had been so ardently promised and must return home penniless. Without money they cannot pay the debts they have accumulated over the years they were serving their country, and bank foreclosures and bankruptcies reach horrifying levels. Robert Morris and Haym Salomon, the two financial geniuses to whom George Washington turns for help, quickly understand that without taxing powers being vested in Congress, the United States is doomed.

Slowly but steadily the United States is descending into a chaos that will destroy everything the Americans fought for. The best and brightest among them realize something must be done, but as yet, no one has dreamed what it will be. Then, in August of 1786, an event occurs that puts the issue squarely before the entire country. A discharged army captain named Daniel Shays leads 1,200 veterans against the courthouse in Northampton to stop the court from entering more bankruptcies and putting the debtors in prison. Concurrently, others storm the courthouses in Worcester, Concord, Taunton, and Great Barrington. Men are shot dead and wounded.

In this volume, a fundamental change has to occur, or all is lost. James Madison of Virginia begins writing letters. There will be a gathering of representatives from all states at Philadelphia on the second Monday of May 1787. This assembly will address the ills that must now be resolved.

Seventy-four of America's best and brightest were commissioned to attend for the purpose of amending the failed Articles of Confederation. Fifty-five came. Nineteen did not bother. Rhode Island ignored it altogether. With the doors and windows of the East Room of the old Statehouse locked against the news reporters and the public, and the drapes drawn against inquisitive eyes, they elected George Washington of

Virginia to serve as president of the Grand Convention and Nathaniel Gorham of Massachusetts as chairman of the Committee of the Whole. They swore an oath that what occurred in that closed room would remain secret, and in the unbearable heat of a Philadelphia summer they bowed their backs and took stock of the Articles of Confederation, and commenced.

Forty-eight hours later the Articles were dead, abandoned forever, and the convention plunged into the unauthorized creation of a new government the like of which no man had ever dreamed, and for which the history of mankind provided no pattern, no polar star, no guidelines. A bicameral congress, a president, and a system of courts, vested with the power to override every state law, every state constitution, every state court system, and the power to tax. The big states demanded voting power based on population, and the small states hotly demanded one vote for each state, regardless of population, or they would walk out, despite the fact it would wreck the convention and dissolve the Union. The hard-headed Yankees of the north looked down long Puritan noses at the decadent southern delegates and their fine linens and bows and slaves, and the southern gentlemen peered suspiciously at the devious Yankees in their brown homespun.

Their differences exploded. Debate became hot, then angry, then accusatory. A vote was taken, and for one day the existence of the United States hung by the tiniest thread, and was saved only by the absence of two delegates, and the vote of one big state delegate in favor of the small states. The war in the insufferably hot room continued, and the delegates learned to compromise, to give and take, or fail. July 16, 1787, the great compromise came to a final vote, and the Union was saved by the vote of five states to four, two divided and not voting. And what was the compromise? The House of Representatives would be elected by popular vote, which favored the large states. The Senate would provide one vote per state, which favored the small states. The slaves? They were never referred to as slaves, but as "other persons," and they were included in the voting power of the states, on the basis of sixty votes per one hundred slaves.

Then they attacked the details, one at a time. How many persons would compose the "president"? One? Three? How much power would be vested in the "president"? Should he be empowered like a king? Should he have veto power over state laws? If not the president, then who? How long should a representative or a senator serve? How much should they be paid, if they were to be paid at all? Who or which institution should have the power to tax? And if the taxes are not paid, how are they to be collected? By armed force? Send armed troops into a state that refuses to pay? What court system should this new national government have? One supreme court? Lower courts? Appellate courts? What powers should the courts have? How long should judges be appointed? Or should they be elected? Who has the power to remove them for misconduct? Who has the right to remove the "president" for misconduct? Or a representative, or a senator?

The delegates wiped at the sweat in the steamy, enclosed room, and hammered out the details one at a time. July became August, then September, and then the day come that they stopped and looked at what they had done. To the best and highest wisdom that was in them, they had created a government with checks and balances that would prevent despots, and they had vested the power on which the entire structure was built in the people. Not a king. Not a parliament. Not congress. Not the courts. The people. The last great repository.

September 17, 1787, they signed the final draft. June 21, 1788, in their ratification convention, New Hampshire became the ninth state to ratify the document, and the new U.S. Constitution became the overriding law of the land.

The work was done. The new nation was born. The world was changed forever.

CHRONOLOGY OF IMPORTANT EVENTS
RELATED TO THIS VOLUME

1787

May 14. The first delegates arrive for what became known as the Grand Convention, or the Continental Convention, to be held in the Statehouse in Philadelphia, Pennsylvania. The Grand Convention was seen as the last great hope to save the United States from dissolving. On this date, delegates from only two states arrive. Lacking a quorum, the convention cannot begin.

May 25. Delegates from the seventh state arrive. The convention has a quorum, and convenes. George Washington is unanimously elected president of the convention. Nathaniel Gorham is elected chairman of the Committee of the Whole.

July 16. The Grand Convention votes on the question of representation in the new congress. With a bicameral legislature, that is, a house and a senate, the issue is how will representatives and senators be elected? The more populous states demand it be by popular vote, which would give them the advantage of greater numbers in both the house and the senate, and hence control of the smaller states. The smaller states threaten to walk out, which would put an end to the convention and result in the thirteen states aligning themselves into two or more separate nations. In the face of this dilemma, a compromise is proposed. Let the number of representatives to the house be determined on the basis of population, but let each state have two senators. Further, no bill will become law until approved by both the house and the senate, providing equal strength to the states. This became known as The Great Compromise, which saved the Grand Convention, and the United States. The vote on the Great Compromise is five in favor, four against. The United States survives by one vote.

August 24. The second great issue that threatens to end the convention is that of slavery. At least three southern states threaten to walk out if the delegates presume to interfere with the practice of slavery as it currently exists. A committee is appointed to propose a solution. There is none that can be found. The committee therefore recommends that the issue of slavery be set aside and not considered until at least the year 1800. The compromise is accepted and again the United States survives. The vote to postpone the question is seven in favor, two against.

September 17. The Constitution is finished and signed by delegates from all thirteen states; however, for differing reasons, three of the leading delegates refuse to sign: Elbridge Gerry of Massachusetts and George Mason and Edmund Randolph of Virginia. To become the law of the land, the Constitution, by its own terms, requires ratification by nine of the thirteen states. The Grand Convention directs that ratification conventions be convened in each state. It work complete, the Grand Convention is adjourned, *sine die*, by George Washington.

1788

June 21. New Hampshire becomes the ninth state to ratify the Constitution, and the document becomes the law of the United States of America.

PART ONE

CHAPTER I

★ ★ ★

*S*leep came slowly and troubled for Matthew Dunson, twisting and turning while disconnected fragments of sentences and the thunder of cannon and the terrible sounds of men locked in mortal combat
and wind whistling in the ship's rigging mixed to echo in his head.
Distorted faces and jumbled scenes from the past danced before his eyes,
surging, fading, one on top of the other. The faint rumble of thousands
of distant cavalry at full gallop rose and held, and then the horses crested
a green rise and swept down like a tidal wave toward him, and the red-
coated riders with the black tricorns were hunched low over the necks of
their sweated mounts with their drawn sabers flashing in the bright New
England sun. They were grinning, and there was no one beside Matthew,
and he drew his saber and faced them alone, hopeless, and then from the
recesses of his brain he heard himself mumble, *it's only rain, not cavalry, not
cavalry, it's raining.* He jerked awake and waited while the British horses and
riders faded and were gone and he was in his bed, hearing a soft, warm
spring rain that had come quietly in the night to murmur on the
rooftops of Boston Town, and leave the trees and grass and flower beds
in the white-fenced yards dripping, and the cobblestones in the crooked,
narrow streets glistening.

For a time he lay still in the blackness of his bedroom to let con-
sciousness sort dream from reality, and then he closed his eyes to listen to
the deep, slow breathing of his wife, Kathleen, next to him. She was

asleep; he had not wakened her. He pondered the time—how close to five o'clock and how long before dawn. At seven o'clock Adam would be at the front door, and at eight o'clock the two of them were to be on the quarterdeck of a tough, heavy-keeled, thick-hulled, three-masted, six-hundred-ton merchantman named *Adonis,* owned by the Dunson & Weems Shipping Company, tied to the Lewis docks, loaded and low in the water, undulating heavily on the roll of the outgoing Atlantic tides.

The *Adonis* was scheduled to sail south from a rain-drenched Boston harbor to the mouth of the Delaware, then west up the river to the deep-water port of Philadelphia to deliver eleven hundred barrels of dried Maine cod to the warehouse of Terrell & Company. From Philadelphia, she was to continue south to the Chesapeake, thence west to the York River where she was to dock at the small, battle-scarred tobacco trading hamlet of Yorktown to take on three hundred tons of prime, cured Virginia tobacco for delivery to the Dutch brokerage firm of Van Der Mein in New York, and then return to her home port of Boston for her next cargo. Adam Dunson, Matthew's youngest brother, was to be her navigator, but Matthew would not be with the *Adonis* when she tied up to the old, battered dock at Yorktown. He was to leave the ship at Philadelphia, where he would remain for at least fifteen days, mingling with and interviewing delegates commissioned by each state in the Union, who would be gathering in the Statehouse on May 14, in one last, desperate effort to save the United States from self-destruction.

Matthew flinched at the distant, muffled sound of the rattle-watchman on his nightly one-hour rounds in the Boston streets. "Three o'clock. Rain. All's well." For several moments he listened for a change in Kathleen's breathing, and there was none; only the blackness, and the quiet sound of the rain. He turned onto his back and silently laid his forearm across his closed eyes while his thoughts reached back twelve years, and came in bits and pieces.

April nineteenth, 1775—Lexington—Concord—the British—the shooting—the near total destruction of the American Continental Army at Long Island. Trenton—Princeton—the battle on Lake Champlain—Saratoga—the French joining the Americans—the Nassau raid—the

British invasion of the southern states—the sea battle of Chesapeake Bay—the siege of the British at Yorktown—the surrender of General Cornwallis and his army—the end of the shooting war—the 1783 Treaty of Paris with the British.

And then the shock of discovering that the government of the United States, established by the Articles of Confederation, was fatally flawed. There was no power provided to levy taxes—no way to raise revenue or control interstate disputes. Bankruptcies ran rampant—land foreclosures by the thousands—good men thrown into debtor's prison—border wars between states—the rise of Daniel Shays and his small army in rebellion, closing courthouses to stop court proceedings—Americans killing Americans at three pitched battles on January 25, February 4, and February 27, 1787—a civil war.

Frantic leaders saw the collapse of the Union looming. Washington, Madison, Adams, Jefferson, Jay, Hamilton, arranged conferences for belligerent states to meet and settle their differences short of shooting. Those conferences failed.

The bright, hot memory wrenched Matthew's heart, and he could not lie still. He turned in his bed, listening to the murmur of the rain, waiting for the next call of the rattle-watch, unable to stem the dark memories. He remembered the driving compulsion to do something—anything—to stop the fragmenting of the country, and recalled the bleak realization of his own limitations. He had served six years as an officer in the United States Navy, which had prevented him holding public office. He was limited—needing more than he had. He resolved he would find Thomas Jefferson; he would know what to do.

He recalled as if it were yesterday their meeting in April of 1784, beneath a dull, slate-gray overcast at Annapolis, Maryland, at Jefferson's boardinghouse quarters near the Statehouse, in a room jammed with books and writings. Matthew had sat in awe, saying little and listening much as Jefferson led him into his world of lofty thought and concept. Their time together awakened in Matthew the vision. History and circumstance had brought together as never before, a limitless land, rich beyond imagination, and an idea, and a gathering of men with the wisdom and the vision and the daring to change the world forever.

Scarcely breathing, he had inquired, "What can I do?"

Jefferson's eyes narrowed, and he spoke with quiet intensity. "In each state there is a committee. A Committee of Correspondence, or a Committee of Merchants. Their purpose is to tell the world what's happening here and lift it to action. Find the committee in Boston. If there is none, create one. Write letters. Publish articles. Stir your people. Raise them. Will you do it?"

It was not a question. It was a commission.

Matthew returned to Boston and plunged in. Billy and Caleb and the others ran the Dunson & Weems shipping company while Matthew sat at his desk, early and late, writing letters and articles to newspapers and leaders in all thirteen states. Responses came flooding, many from men of consequence—Washington, Madison, Hamilton, Rutledge, Pinckney, Gerry, Mason, Jefferson, Adams, Jay. But by 1786 the common thread in all of it was stark dread that the United States was on the brink of disunion, and no one man among them could conceive of a workable plan to save it.

Then, through James Madison, one last appeal went out to all thirteen states: commission and send delegates to one final convention to be held the second Monday in May of 1787 at Independence Hall in Philadelphia, to amend the Articles of Confederation sufficient to save the United States. Should this convention fail, the six years of bitter, tortuous war, at a cost of tens of thousands of lives on both sides, followed by six tragic years of watching the thirteen infant states sink toward oblivion, would have been for nothing.

The rattle-watch call came again, nearer, louder. "Five o'clock. Raining. All's well."

Matthew opened his eyes and waited while the dreamworld faded, then he listened to the breathing of Kathleen; it was too shallow, too measured. He turned his head and whispered.

"Awake?"

"Yes."

Matthew kept a lamp on the night table beside the bed with the wick trimmed to a tiny pinpoint of light, enough to let him find it should their son, John, awaken in the night, but not enough to bring any sense of light to the room. Kathleen was an indistinct blur in the darkness, but he saw her in his mind—tall, striking, long dark hair tumbled on her pillow and around her face, and he felt the rise in his heart.

"Five o'clock," he said.

"I heard the rattle-watch," she said.

From down the long hall came the muffled sound of five timed strikes of the mantel clock, distant, yet loud in the still blackness. Matthew took a deep breath and shifted his feet.

"I have to get moving. Today's the day."

Her hand reached to touch his arm and she said quietly, "Hold me for a minute." There was a sense of need in her low voice. In silence they reached for each other, and for a little time they lay entwined in the warmth and security of their bed, the world forgotten as their souls gave and received that which would sustain them for the time of their coming separation.

Matthew kissed her and released her. "I have to go. Adam will be here soon."

"You go," she said. "I'll get breakfast. Try to not wake John."

He pushed back the comforter and swung his bare feet to the braided oval rug on the floor, stood, picked up the lamp, and twisted the wheel to adjust the wick. The room became a mix of yellow light and misshapen shadows as he took the three steps to the door into the hallway, and silently walked shivering down the cold, polished hardwood floor to the parlor. In his long nightshirt, he set the lamp on the mantel and knelt beside the banked coals in the great fireplace, took the leather bellows, and gently worked the handles until the coals glowed. He dropped pine shavings onto them, then pumped the bellows until tiny flames came licking. They caught, and he added kindling. Then he lit the large lamp on the mantel beside the beautifully carved clock and, scooping the small brass shovel full of burning coals and walked into the shadowy kitchen, to the black cast-iron stove. With his toes curled against the cold of the floor, he opened the two fireboxes and dumped the glowing coals inside, followed by pine shavings and kindling from the woodbox beside the stove. He adjusted the damper in the stovepipe for draw, watched the kindling catch, closed the doors, and set two kettles of water on the stove to heat for shaving and washing. He was turning when Kathleen walked through the archway with her robe tied about her waist, and her woollen slippers moving silently on the floor. She had brushed her long hair back and caught it behind her head with a bit of ribbon, and for a moment Matthew studied her in the pale lamplight, stirred in his soul as always.

"Need anything from the root cellar? Potatoes? Sausage?" he asked.

She was tying her apron as she shook her head. "No. Got them last night. And eggs."

He nodded. "I'll go start packing."

She watched his back as he walked through the archway into the parlor, lifted the bedroom lantern from the mantel, and padded down the hall to their bedroom. For a moment she listened to the faint sounds of him working with his seaman's bag in the bedroom. She was seeing him—tall, dark-haired, eyes dark and serious, features tending toward delicate but also manly, with the three-inch scar on his left cheek, received in the sea battle near Valcour Island on Lake Champlain.

The sound of water coming to a full rolling boil in the kitchen brought Kathleen back from her reveries to the gentle sound of rain on the roof in the blackness outside, and the reality of a household to run, and a husband leaving at seven o'clock for three weeks in Philadelphia. Beyond the dread of watching Matthew walk out into the rain to be gone for nearly a month, this was Tuesday in Boston, and she had a week's ironing waiting her. On Monday in Boston town, the backyard clotheslines of every virtuous Puritan citizen was a patchwork of white laundry stirring in the breeze, and on Tuesday the worthy righteous women sweated in the kitchen with at least four flatirons, which they rotated on the stove while they labored through ironing Monday's wash. Failure to observe the entrenched Monday–Tuesday washing-ironing ritual would raise indignant neighborhood noses, while fingers pointed and quiet whispers were exchanged over white picket fences.

Kathleen reached a small bowl of last fall's shriveled potatoes from the cupboard, quickly plucked the sprouts from the eyes, peeled the potatoes, and sliced them sizzling into butter melted in a large black skillet on the stove. She salted them, peppered them, turned for a sausage that she laid in the butter beside the potatoes, then wiped her hands on her apron as she walked silently down the dark hall to the dull light in the bedroom. Matthew, in his nightshirt and a pair of trousers, was setting his packed bag on the floor beside their bed. She spoke softly.

"Water's hot."

He nodded and followed her silently past the bedroom where John slept, out to the kitchen. He used a heavy cloth to lift the black kettle from the stove and carry it through the door into the washroom. He poured steaming water into the deep porcelain basin on the washstand, mixed it with cold water from the wooden bucket next to it, and pulled his long nightshirt over his head to hang it on a wall peg. With cloth and soap he washed himself, opened the door into the blackness of the backyard, threw the water into the rain, and returned the basin to the washstand to fill it once more with a mix of hot and cold water. He used the cloth to rinse himself, then took his razor from the wall cabinet, opened it, seized the end of a long strop made from the hide of a pig and fastened to the wall, and pulled it taut. Carefully he stroked the razor back and forth, first on the rough side of the strap, then the smooth, to hone the delicate edge. Satisfied, he soaped his face and carefully shaved. After rinsing the remaining lather from his face and wiping it dry, he dried the razor and folded it closed before throwing the water from the basin out the door. With his nightshirt draped over his shoulder and with his razor in one hand and the kettle of hot water in the other, he walked back into the kitchen, set the kettle back on the stove, and went on to the bedroom to pack his razor, tie the drawstrings on his bag, and dress in traveling clothes.

When he silently walked back into the dining room in his stockinged feet, carrying his square-toed shoes with the polished brass buckles, a heavy china plate was smoking at his place at the breakfast table, piled with fried potato slices, sausage, two fried eggs, and a thick piece of homemade bread. There was only a cup at Kathleen's place; she preferred to eat with John when he awakened later in the morning. Matthew set his shoes beside his chair and waited while Kathleen poured steaming chocolate into the cup next to his plate. She poured for herself before both knelt beside their chairs, and with bowed heads sought the blessings of the Almighty on their food, their family, their home, and the day. Then they rose and sat at the table, Matthew at the head, Kathleen to his right. With pleasure known only to a wife and mother, Kathleen watched him begin with his knife and fork, savoring the breakfast she had prepared for him. She picked up her cup of steaming chocolate and held it between her hands, blowing gently before she sipped. She let him eat in silence for a time before she spoke.

"This business in Philadelphia. You're concerned?"

He nodded and continued eating.

She sipped. "You didn't sleep well. Worried those men won't come?"

He put down his knife and fork and reached for his cup. "Yes."

"George Washington? Is he coming?"

Matthew sipped, then nodded. "He wasn't at first. Said he had a prior commitment to the Society of the Cincinnati. Madison and Hamilton wrote him and he relented. He'll be there."

"Who else? Have you seen the lists?"

Matthew reflected for a moment. "Some. Not all."

"Who from Massachusetts?"

"Nathaniel Gorham. Caleb Strong. Elbridge Gerry. Rufus King."

Kathleen studied the cup between her hands. "I've heard of Elbridge Gerry and Rufus King. Not the other two. Will Thomas Jefferson be there?"

"Can't. He's in Paris, serving as American Minister."

"John Adams?"

"In London as American Minister."

Kathleen's eyes narrowed. "Who's coming from the south? Slavery is bound to come up."

Matthew set his cup down and for a moment stared at his plate, then spoke slowly, softly. "Slavery could split the convention and the United States with it."

Kathleen repeated her question. "Who's coming from the south?"

Matthew held his cup between his hands for a moment, then spoke in measured words. "The south will be led by three men from South Carolina. Charles Pinckney, John Rutledge, and Charles Cotesworth Pinckney. The two Pinckneys are cousins. All three are powerful men. All united in their stand on slavery. If slavery is abolished, I think they'll walk out, and if they do, the Union is finished."

"That serious?"

"That serious."

For a time Kathleen worked on her hot chocolate while Matthew finished his plate, then picked up his own cup.

She spoke. "Any other serious problems?"

Matthew drew and released a great breath. "I think one more. Big states are starting to say they should have more power than small states. New York has ten times the population of Rhode Island, and some think that entitles them to ten times more power. The small states won't stand for it. If the small states find themselves doormats for the big ones, they'll likely leave."

Kathleen straightened and for a moment stared at Matthew in the silence before she put her cup down. "The rain has stopped."

Matthew nodded. "I hope it clears before we sail." He gestured toward the door leading to the backyard. "There's enough wood cut and stacked for four weeks. I left six twenty-dollar gold pieces on the dresser. Is that enough house money?"

"Yes. Too much."

"If anything should happen and you need more money, go ask Billy."

She nodded. "I know."

"If you need anything done here at the house, find Caleb."

Again she nodded, but remained silent.

He paused for a moment. "The root cellar is well stocked. I can't think of anything else you might need."

"We'll be fine."

"I'll write when I can."

He raised his cup, finished it, and set it down. "I'd better get my bag. Adam will be here soon." He started to rise when Kathleen laid her hand on his arm, and he settled.

"Did I forget something?" he asked.

"No. I wasn't going to tell you until you returned, but I think I'd better." He saw the look on her face and waited.

"It's possible we are going to have another child."

For a moment he sat still, wide-eyed. For six years they had waited, hoping, wanting their family to grow. "Are you sure?"

"Not certain. I'll see Doctor Soderquist while you're gone. I'll write when I know."

He rounded his mouth and blew air softly for a moment in thought. "I'd better stay here. I'll cancel this Philadelphia trip."

She scoffed. "That's nonsense. I'm fine. You go. If anything happens, your mother's only two blocks away, and the doctor can be here in ten minutes. You go."

"Sure?"

"I'm sure."

He took her hand in his, and raised it to press it against his cheek, and for a moment they sat quietly, saying nothing. He released her hand and rose, and silently strode down the hall to their bedroom while she began clearing the breakfast table. Minutes later he returned to set his large seaman's bag beside the front door and hang his cape and tricorn on the pegs next to the door. He was seated at the table putting on his shoes when movement in the great archway to the hall brought his head up. John was standing in his nightshirt, toes raised from the cool floor, with his dark, straight, unruly hair awry, one eye clenched shut, digging at the other one with a knotted fist. In the yellow lamplight, Matthew could see much of his father in the boy, with his blocky face and the miniature cleft in his chin. John dropped his hand and opened one eye to a slit, squinted at Matthew, and spoke.

"Where's Mother?"

"Kitchen."

"You bring me something when you come back?"

"If you mind your mother and take care her."

"I'll take care of her."

"And the house."

"And the house."

Matthew worked with the buckles on his shoes. "Keep the kindling boxes full. Both parlor and kitchen."

"I will."

"Keep your room straight."

"I will. I'm hungry."

"Mother has breakfast ready, but it's early."

"I smell hot chocolate. Can I have some hot chocolate?"

"Ask your mother."

Kathleen walked in from the kitchen and smiled at her son, and he turned his squinted eye to her. "Can I have some hot chocolate?"

"Half a cup. Breakfast later. Get your robe. And your slippers. Floor's cold."

John bobbed his head and turned on his heel and they heard him trot down the hall. Matthew glanced at Kathleen and smiled as he finished with his shoe buckles. John came trotting back down the hall and into the room, working to tie the cord to his robe. He went to the table and sat down, waiting for hot chocolate, and Matthew turned to him.

"I'll be gone for a while. A long time. You'll have to be the man of the house. If you need help with anything, get Uncle Caleb, or Billy. Understand?"

John nodded as Kathleen came through the door with a half-cup of steaming chocolate and set it on the table before him.

Matthew continued. "Don't play with the ax. Don't climb on the stacked firewood. You could get hurt if it fell. Help pull weeds from the flower beds and the vegetable garden. The weeds, not the flowers and vegetables. Say your prayers every day. Understand?"

John bobbed his head and reached for the cup with both hands.

Matthew leaned forward. "If you're good, you can sit at my place at the head of the table while I'm gone. That's where men sit when they're the man of the house."

The boy stopped with the cup halfway up. "Honest? I can sit in your place?"

Matthew turned to Kathleen. "What do you say?"

"If he does the work of the man of the house, he should sit there."

John turned incredulous eyes back to Matthew. "I'll do it."

Matthew bobbed his head. "Then you sit at my place while I'm gone. That's fair."

The boy raised the cup to his mouth, blew for several seconds, then sipped gingerly, only to jerk the cup back while he licked violently at singed lips. Kathleen turned her head to stifle a laugh and was on her way back to the kitchen when a quiet rap came at the door.

Matthew stood. "That's Adam." He walked quickly across the room, turned the key and swung the door open to let the yellow lamplight flood outward. It cast an irregular yellow shape on the wet grass and dripping shrubbery, and framed Adam standing with tricorn in his hand, seaman's bag at his side, and cape latched about his shoulders. The youngest of the three Dunson brothers, Adam was the quiet one, dark-eyed, dark-haired, regular features, not as tall as Matthew, taller than Caleb, thoughtful, mature beyond his years, a Harvard College-trained navigator after his brother Matthew, and a born leader among men. The sound of rainwater dripping from eaves and trees sounded behind him, but there was no rain falling.

"Come in, come in," Matthew exclaimed.

Adam nodded and stepped inside where he set his seaman's bag beside Matthew's.

Matthew gestured toward the table. "Had breakfast?"

"Yes, thank you."

"Hot chocolate?"

"No, thanks."

Kathleen walked in from the kitchen and Adam smiled as he spoke. "You're looking well, Kathleen." He gestured toward Matthew. "Can you spare him for a while?"

Kathleen laughed and tossed one hand in the air. "Take him. He's yours."

Adam grinned back. "We'll try to deliver him back safely."

John spoke up from the table. "Uncle Adam, are you going to sail the ship, or is Father?"

"I will navigate. That means I pick the direction the ship goes. The captain is Neil Sturman. He's a very good captain. Your father is our passenger."

"What does he do?"

Adam grinned, "Whatever the captain tells him."

John turned pained eyes to Matthew. "I thought you were captain."

"I'm just a passenger this time. Maybe I'll be captain next time." Matthew turned to Kathleen. "Anything we've forgotten?"

She shook her head. "No. You two better go. It's seven o'clock."

Matthew snapped his cape about his shoulders and took his tricorn in hand as Kathleen walked to the open door, arms folded in front of her in the way of women. She motioned to John who dropped from his chair and came to stand beside her. Matthew reached for her and they held each other close for several moments before Matthew kissed her and released her. He looked down at John, and the boy thrust his hand upward to shake that of his father, but Matthew swept him off his feet into his arms. The boy threw his arms about his father's neck and locked his legs about him and clung to him for a time before he let go, and Matthew set him on the floor. Kathleen looked at Adam, and reached to hold him for a moment, and kiss him on the cheek.

"You two be careful," she said.

"We will," Adam answered.

The two men hefted their bags and stepped out the door into the wet world, dim beneath the deep purple of heavy rain clouds moving southeast over the Boston Peninsula. The rising sun was but a faint impression in the blue-black of the eastern rim as they walked to the front gate, turned back to wave to the two silhouettes in the door, and were gone, striding briskly east in the clean, chill air, through the narrow, winding streets toward the Boston waterfront.

Notes

The Boston custom of men called the "rattle-watch," patrolling the streets at night and calling out the hour and the weather is described in Earle, *Home Life in Colonial Days*, p. 362.

Hot chocolate was a drink commonly used in America at the times in question. Earle, *Home Life in Colonial Days*, p. 165.

The Articles of Confederation, which formed the first Continental Congress and served as the first inclusive form of government between the thirteen states, was fatally flawed, since it granted the government no power to tax and almost no powers of enforcement. Bernstein, *Are We to Be a Nation?* pp. 81–82, 85–91; Warren, *The Making of the Constitution*, pp. 6–7.

Merchants and other interested persons in the various states and major cities set up what was called a Committee of Merchants or a Committee of Correspondence, intending that the committees work together to resolve the conflicts that were becoming epidemic between the states. Bernstein, *Are We to Be a Nation?* p. 90.

The references to Daniel Shays, an honorably discharged captain in the Continental Army, and his leading of thousands of other discharged soldiers in what was eventually called "Shays' Rebellion," are accurate, including the closing of courthouses in many cities to prevent bankruptcy proceedings and debtors' prison for thousands of unpaid veterans, as well as the three open battles of January 25, 1787, at Springfield, Massachusetts; February 4, 1787, at Petersham; and finally at Sheffield on February 27, 1787. Bernstein, *Are We to Be a Nation?* pp. 93–95; Freeman, *Washington*, p. 534; Higginbotham, *The War of American Independence*, pp. 447–48; Warren, *The Making of the Constitution*, pp. 30–33; Rossiter, *1787: The Grand Convention*, p. 44; Berkin, *A Brilliant Solution*, pp. 27–29.

Nathaniel Gorham, Caleb Strong, Elbridge Gerry, and Rufus King comprised the Massachusetts delegation to the Grand Convention. John Rutledge, Charles Cotesworth Pinckney, Charles Pinckney (second cousins), and Pierce Butler comprised the South Carolina delegation. A complete list of all delegates from all participating states may be found in Bernstein, *Are We to Be a Nation?* p. 284. A description of the background and general physical appearance of the delegates is found in Rossiter, *1787: The Grand Convention*, pp. 79–156.

George Washington was President of the Society of Cincinnati, an organization dedicated to honoring the officers of the Revolutionary War, membership in which was to pass from father to son. Washington opposed the bloodline membership requirement, and it was abandoned. At the time of the Grand Convention, Washington was to preside at the annual Convention of Cincinnati meetings scheduled in Philadelphia concurrent with the Grand Convention, but after receiving many letters from leaders begging him to represent Virginia at the Grand Convention instead (including a very persuasive letter from James Madison), Washington excused himself from the Convention of the Society to attend the Grand Convention. Bernstein, *Are We to Be a Nation?* pp. 124–27; Warren, *The Making of the Constitution*, pp. 62–63, 88; Rossiter, *1787: The Grand Convention*, pp. 44–45.

The question of states with large populations having voting powers greater than those with small populations very nearly split and destroyed the Grand Convention. Resolution of the conflict became known as "The Great Compromise," and it will be discussed in later chapters of this volume. Bernstein, *Are We to Be a Nation?* p. 167.

The slavery issue nearly divided the northern states from the southern states and ended the Grand Convention. Bernstein, *Are We to Be a Nation?* pp. 175–77.

At the time of the Grand Convention in Philadelphia, Thomas Jefferson was serving as the American minister to France, while John Adams was serving the same function in England. Rossiter, *1787: The Grand Convention*, pp. 83, 138.

Boston

May 8, 1787

CHAPTER II

★ ★ ★

*R*ainwater stood in the streets and in low places on the narrow sidewalks as the two men made their way through the gathering morning traffic toward the familiar scent of salt sea air. Storekeepers and workers and merchants, clad in coats and capes and tricorns rustled from their homes to walk hunch-shouldered, staring down to avoid puddles as they hastened toward the small shops and taverns and offices they owned, or the places where they were employed. They offered a perfunctory "Good morn'" to acquaintances they passed in their hurry to be about the business of another unremarkable rainy Tuesday in Boston.

Old, weathered wagons and great, two-wheeled carts rattled from the farms and gardens on the peninsula and from the mainland, heavy with fresh and salted meat, milk in cans and jars, forty-pound cheeses, chickens complaining in coops, sacks of milled flour, and the first of the year's vegetables. Milk carts drawn by huge dogs stopped before homes while the drivers patiently dipped milk, still warm and frothy into buckets and exchanged them at the door for copper and silver coins before moving to the next stop. Some wagons stopped at the small shops with lamps glowing in the windows to cast odd-shaped patterns of light into the streets, where drivers in old, patched coats and trousers and worn shoes haggled price with the shopkeepers who wore shawls about their shoulders. Bargains were struck, goods were exchanged for coins, and the wagons and carts rolled on.

Some traveled on Fruit Street to pass through the town to the clamor and bustle of the Boston waterfront, where ships under flags from most of the ports of the world were tied to wharves and docks, being loaded and unloaded by men who wore dress strange to the Puritan Bostonians and spoke languages and dialects from lands and peoples that, for many, existed only in fables and storybooks. The wagons and carts creaked slowly past the wall-to-wall offices of shipping companies and brokerage firms on the north side of the waterfront, through the jostling crowd on the wharves, while the drivers read the names carved on the bows of the ships tied to the docks on the south side until they found the one they sought, where they hauled their loads to a stop to inquire after the quartermaster. Contracts were read, heads nodded, and men unloaded the wagons and carts into great nets spread on the black timbers of the dock, to be hoisted by the yardarm onto the ship's deck, emptied, and lowered for the next load of flour, potatoes, salted meat, or cheeses, other goods. The outbound tides were running, and ship's crews with schedules and contracts to meet in ports all over the world were intent on clearing Boston harbor, steering out into the Atlantic, before the moon changed and reversed them; none wanted the frustration of bucking incoming tides.

For Matthew and Adam, the sights and smells and sounds of the waterfront were like a second home. They picked their way past the weathered buildings with peeled paint and lamplight glinting dull through grimy windows, and the rattle of wagons and carts, and the loud, coarse confusion of the voices and languages of the crews unloading them. Seagulls with black heads and wingtips, and terns and cranes and pelicans wheeled, squawking overhead, plummeting down to pluck dead fish and carrion and garbage from the sea or the shore, then battling other winged thieves to keep it. The two men angled left to the large sign with black block letters "DUNSON & WEEMS SHIPPING COMPANY" high above the door and pushed inside. They set their seamen's bags against the inside wall and Matthew closed the door behind them.

The room was large, rectangular, with two windows in the front wall, and one in the rear wall, next to the backdoor. The two sidewalls were common with the offices next door, and without windows. There were six heavy, plain desks in two rows, each covered with books and ledgers, divided by an aisle down the center. Half a dozen scarred chairs stood against the front wall, three on either side of the door. On the wall beside the first desk on the left hung a large calendar with penciled notations on various dates, and next to it was a chart of contracts and dates for the company ships to carry freight all over the eastern seaboard, through the month of December. On the wall to the right was a huge map of the east coast of the North American Continent, from Greenland to the West Indies, with the Gulf Stream, the Horse Currents, known reefs, islands, channels, water depths, deep-water ports, and rivers marked. Past the great map was an American flag. Four lamps were mounted on each wall, and all were burning. A large black stove stood in the front left corner, and another in the right rear corner of the room, both with fires in their potbellies, and the quiet sound of air sucking through the slitted settings in the doors. A pot of tea steamed on the top of the stove at the rear of the room, and behind it were a dozen heavy pewter mugs on a wall shelf, next to an open box of India tea, and an open three-pound canister of sugar. A two-ton iron safe, painted gray, stood opposite the stove at the rear of the room, and above it, on the rear wall, hung an old, plain clock that struck off the hours. There was nothing else. The office of the Dunson & Weems Shipping Company was solid, sparse, no-nonsense, in the fashion of men of the sea.

Four men stood in the aisle between the desks, handling papers between them, and at the sound of the door they stopped to look. All four had arrived at the office while it was still raining, and the pungent odor of wet wool hung heavy in the room. None spoke while Matthew and Adam hung their capes and tricorns on the row of pegs beside the door, next to the damp coats and capes already in place.

Matthew led the way to the group, Adam following, and they nodded and exchanged a perfunctory greeting with Billy Weems, Thomas Covington, Neil Sturman, and Theodore Pettigrew. With Matthew and Adam, these four men managed the affairs of the company. Billy handled the books. Thomas Covington, gray-haired, round-shouldered, slightly stooped with years, a widower, had sold his failing shipping company to Matthew and Billy more than two years earlier, and they had invited him to stay on. Theodore Pettigrew, plain, long upper lip, straightforward, honest to a fault, had hired on as captain of one ship, then was given charge of handling all captains for the six ships purchased from Covington, and the two added since. Neil Sturman, short, rotund, balding, heavy-jowled, a tough, seasoned, capable ship's captain, had been trained at Marblehead under John Glover. Each man recognized and respected the competence of the others, and none wasted words.

Matthew spoke to Sturman. "Crew on board? Ship's surgeon?"

"All aboard."

He turned to Billy. "Contracts and manifest?"

Billy gestured to Sturman. "The captain has them," and Sturman raised a sealed packet of papers to show.

"Signed off on them?" Matthew asked.

Sturman nodded, and Matthew continued.

"Insurance papers?"

"With the manifest," Billy pointed.

Adam was silent, watching, absorbing from these men what Harvard College had never taught him.

Matthew continued. "War chest?"

Billy hooked a thumb over his shoulder. "Behind my desk."

Matthew turned to Sturman. "Signed off on it?"

Sturman bobbed his head. "Half an hour ago."

Matthew turned to Adam. "Maps? Charts?"

"On board, in my quarters."

Matthew glanced at Thomas Covington, whose old, blue-gray, watery eyes were missing nothing. "We forget anything?" Matthew asked.

Covington turned to Sturman, eyes narrowed. "When you unload those three thousand barrels in Philadelphia, get a representative from the insurance company to certify the count. The Terrell representative has counted short a few times in the past. Be careful."

"I understand," Sturman said.

Matthew paused for a moment, then asked Pettigrew, "Anything about our other ships or crews that you can't handle for the next six weeks or so?"

"Nothing I know of."

Matthew turned back to Sturman. "Whenever you're ready, Captain. We're at your orders."

Sturman turned. "Let's get the war chest. Tide's running, and there's no time to waste."

Billy led Pettigrew to the war chest behind Billy's desk and seized the handle on one end, Pettigrew the other, and the two lifted the one-hundred-forty-pound coffer and carried it to the front desk to set it down. It was crafted from oak one inch thick, bound together by two broad, heavy iron straps and a huge latch, all bolted and riveted in place. The latch was sealed by a great iron lock. Inside were one thousand six hundred dollars in gold, earmarked for unforeseen emergencies, together with a roster showing the name of every crew member, and sealed copies of the maps, manifest, shipping contracts, and insurance contracts necessary for the voyage. If the ship and crew were lost, the contents would be vital to establish ownership, as against the laws of salvage at sea. Captain Sturman was responsible for the war chest, which would be locked in his private quarters on board the ship. He had but two keys, one of which he would keep on his person, the other to be delivered to his first mate once the ship cleared the harbor.

"Let's go," Sturman said, and they all reached for their coats, capes, and tricorns. While they were working with buttons and snaps, Billy spoke quietly to Matthew.

"I intend talking to Brigitte while you're gone."

Matthew's hands stopped for a moment while thoughts flashed. His sister Brigitte, beautiful, hotly independent, and all too sure of herself at age eighteen, had foolishly given her heart to the British Captain Richard Arlen Buchanan shortly after the shooting erupted in 1775. Two years later, on the darkest day of her life, she had received a letter informing her that Richard was dead, killed at the battle of Saratoga, thirty miles north of Albany on the Hudson River. Seven years after the surrender of the British at Yorktown, and as Congress began discharging the Continental army, Billy, plain, homely, solid, sensible, had confided to Matthew that he had secretly admired Brigitte for years—had written letters to her but had never sent them—had held his feelings inside because he knew he was not handsome nor dashing nor attractive. A stunned, angry Matthew told him, go to her, tell her. In time, Billy shocked Brigitte speechless when he quietly spoke of his feelings to her, and gave to her more than twenty letters, tattered and faded, that he had written to her over the years and carried with him, refusing to mail them. Brigitte recoiled in blank bewilderment. Love? Marriage? With Billy? Incomprehensible!

Months passed before she began to see Billy for the man he was and realized that she had never considered him other than the boy who had become as another brother to her. That he could love her, and she him, was beyond anything she had ever dreamed. The day came when the girl she had been was gone forever, and the curtain of youthful fantasy was lifted from her eyes as she came into the full woman. She saw the world as it is, and Billy became something she had never expected. At age 27, a spinster by all Bostonian standards, she sought him out and told him Richard Buchanan would always have a place in her heart, but that her feelings for him were such that she would consider marriage if he so chose. He asked for time, and she granted it.

Matthew squared with Billy and looked him in the eye. "Marriage."

"If she'll have me. I thought I should get your blessing. You're the senior man in her family. I'll talk to Margaret too, before I talk to Brigitte."

The thought that Billy would seek his permission caught Matthew by surprise. "My blessing? You have it. The sooner the better."

Billy nodded and the two men continued fastening their capes and coats. Matthew and Adam shouldered their seamen's bags while Covington opened and held the door, and they all filed out into the dull gray overcast, Sturman leading. They clustered around Billy and Pettigrew and the war chest, and picked their way rapidly through the morass of dockhands and carts and wagons on Lewis dock, conscious of all movement and all men they passed. A few wore strange garb from distant ports, and swarthy beards and pigtails or turbans, and slowed in their work to cast hard, covetous eyes on the passing war chest. The would-be thieves licked at their lips as they measured the six men with it, and then reluctantly turned back to their work.

The top of the gangplank reaching from the dock to the deck of the *Adonis* rose and fell with the ship as she rode the tide-swells when Sturman led his little column thumping upward, and at the top they stopped, facing the first mate, Ulysses Faulkner. Burly, bearded, direct, wise to the ways of the sea and the men who venture, Faulkner carried a heavy scar on the left side of his face, and his left ear was partly missing, partly deformed. Years earlier a knife stroke from a wild, drunken deckhand had cut most of the ear from his head and laid the scalp open to the bone before Faulkner struck back. The ship's surgeon had sewed what he could find of the ear back in place the best he could, and put an additional twenty-one stitches in the scalp. The deckhand was nine weeks recovering.

Faulkner stood to one side as the six men came on board, while the crew that was on deck stopped where they were to watch and listen. Sturman led Billy and Pettigrew to his quarters where they set the war chest in a small corner closet, bolted the door, and returned to those waiting on deck. Billy said his goodbyes and walked back down the gangplank to the dock and to stop and watch.

Sturman fronted Faulkner. "All hands aboard?"

"Yes, sir."

"Ready to cast off?"

"Ready."

"Carry on."

Faulkner turned and barked orders to the crew, and in the gray overcast, men burned brown by wind and sun trotted to their duty stations. Two pounded down the gangplank onto the dock, and went opposite directions, one to the bow, the other to the stern of the ship to unwind the three-inch hawsers from the cleats and cast them free, while men above them on deck hauled them upward to coil them on the worn planking. The two men on the dock trotted back up the gangplank, and with two others hauled it clattering aboard as the *Adonis* slowly drifted away from the wharf. Others climbed rope ladders to the two arms on the mainmast where the great sails were furled tight, and worked their way outward on a one-inch rope, spaced themselves, and stood waiting spread-legged, chests against the heavy timber, arms hooked over it, peering downward, waiting for Faulkner's hand signal. Sturman took his place at the wheel on the quarterdeck and nodded to Faulkner, who waved to the men overhead. Hands rough from hawsers and ropes and salt water jerked knots free, and the canvas, dripping from the rain in the night, dropped free to send a shower onto the deck below. Within seconds the lower edges of the sails were secured. They caught the morning breeze quartering in from the northwest, and Sturman spun the wheel as the sails popped full and billowing.

It was as though the wood and the iron and the canvas of the *Adonis* suddenly became a free, living thing. The squat, blunt-nosed ship slowly turned from the dock, angling away south toward the deep-water channel, obedient to the wind and the rudder, running with the tide. Sturman brought her into the wake of the small pilot boat that was to guide them out of Boston Harbor, and the tiny craft spilled her sails to slow and wait for the huge, heavy ship to gain speed. Faulkner raised a hand to the men spaced on the arms of the foremast, and two minutes later the canvas on the foremast popped full. The big ship plunged forward and the bow began to cut a six foot curl as she plowed on. The small pilot boat added sail and speed, and all hands on both ships watched the small islands in Boston harbor slip past, and then the pilot boat turned due east out into Massachusetts Bay. She spilled her sails to let the *Adonis* pass, and then set them to turn north and tack into the wind as she returned to Boston. Sturman waved to the pilot boat as it passed, and Faulkner raised a hand to the men in the rigging. They unfurled the sails on the aftermast, and they snapped full, and the big ship was running with the wind. Faulkner strode to the bow where men waited for his order to unfurl the spankers, and within three minutes all canvas on the ship was filled and the curl beneath the bowsprit was a full ten feet.

Adam gave a new heading to Sturman, and the captain turned the wheel to the right, bearing east-south-east, to pass the Provincetown lighthouse on the northern tip of the giant hook of Cape Cod, forty-five miles distant. Sturman gave the wheel to Faulkner, who checked the compass bearing, and held the ship steadily on course, while the crew settled into the established routine of four-hour shifts, with Sturman and Faulkner and Adam handling the wheel.

The *Adonis* was running in open waters, all canvas out, full, tight, and straining. She was loaded heavy, with the stubby bow cutting a ten foot curl hissing, rising and settling with the gentle sea swells. A deep, unspoken sense of rightness rose in the breast of every man on board at the feel of it. For them, the ship was a living thing, to be cared for and nurtured and protected. In return, for the days they were at sea with her, their world was the *Adonis*, small, simple, understandable, predictable.

At noon the overcast thinned. By two o'clock, shafts of sunlight were reflecting like jewels off the Atlantic waters. Adam brought his sextant from his quarters and carefully took a reading before giving Faulkner a course correction, due south. The sun was setting in a clear sky when the crew paused in their labors to peer two miles due west at the familiar sight of the eastern shores of Cape Cod sliding past. Evening mess was in progress on the thick, scarred table in the small mess hall below decks when they passed the Chatham lighthouse on the southeastern tip of the cape. They were in full darkness when the crewman in the crow's nest, eighty feet up the mainmast, called out, "Landfall due west—Monomoy Island," and the lights on shore passed and slipped behind them and disappeared as they continued due south with the open waters of Nantucket Sound to the west. It was past midnight when the call came from the crow's nest, "Lighthouse ahead to the port side," and Sturman held the wheel steady on the course due south. The night crew had just rung two bells when the lights of Nantucket Island with its Sianconset lighthouse passed on the starboard side, and Adam came to the wheel to give Sturman a new heading, south by southwest, following the westerly slant of the coast. If the winds held, and no spring storms swept in from the Atlantic, they would hold that course for the next four days, past the coastlines of Rhode Island, Connecticut, New York, and New Jersey, to Delaware Bay, which separated New Jersey from Delaware. The bay narrowed at the northwest tip, where the Delaware River flowed into it.

At daybreak on the fourth day, the eastern horizon clouded, and at midmorning a rain squall caught them and held for half an hour before the purple clouds moved on west, leaving the ship and most of the crew drenched and the sky clear. Half an hour after the one o'clock mess, Adam turned the wheel over to Faulkner and went belowdecks to the tiny quarters reserved for the officers. He stopped before Matthew's door, bowed his head to listen for a moment, then rapped.

"Who's there?" came the voice.

"Me. Adam."

"It isn't locked."

Adam raised the latch and pushed the thick door inward, with the heavy iron-strap hinges quietly complaining. Matthew was seated before his small table facing the door, with two stacks of documents before him. His long-sleeved, white shirt was open at the throat, and it was obvious to Adam that he had been working with the papers. Matthew leaned back in his chair, waiting, and Adam spoke.

"You've been down here a while. Anything wrong?"

Matthew shook his head and gestured, and Adam sat down facing him. Matthew tapped the top of the nearest stack of papers. "In two days I'll be meeting with the delegates to the big convention in Philadelphia. I've been going over the letters and papers I've gathered over the past two years—the ones written between the leaders. Some to me. I have to be ready."

Adam sat focused, studying Matthew. "I know a little about what's happening. Not enough. How do you see it?"

"You were away at college for most of it." A smile flitted across Matthew's face and was gone. "You sure you want to hear all this?"

"Yes. I'd like to know."

Matthew's brows raised. "From the beginning?"

"From the beginning."

Matthew shrugged. "All right." He paused for a moment to order his thoughts.

"We could lose it all—everything we've fought for since 1775. There are kings in Europe right now who are waiting for the states to go to war with each other." He rummaged to pick a copy of a letter from the stack and laid it before Adam.

"George Washington. June, 1780. 'Our measures are not under the influence and direction of one Council, but thirteen, each of which is actuated by local views and politics . . . we are attempting the impossible.'"

Adam quickly read the letter and laid it back on the table. His expression did not change. Matthew continued, his voice restrained as he plucked up a copy of another letter.

"Washington again. Six months later. December, 1780." Matthew read aloud, "'. . . there are two things (as I have often declared) which, in my opinion, are indispensably necessary to the well-being and good government of our public affairs; these are greater powers to Congress and more responsibility and permanency in the Executive bodies.'"

Matthew dropped the paper back on the stack and for a moment did not raise his eyes. Then he went on. "That was in 1780, seven years ago. He saw it coming as far back as 1780. A government that was going to die because it lacked the power to raise revenue to maintain itself and had no head."

Adam shifted in his chair but remained silent. Matthew reached for the next copied document.

"Washington. 1783. A letter to all thirteen governors." He scanned the paper for a moment, then once more read aloud.

"'There are four things . . . essential . . . to the existence of the United States, as an independent power. First. An indissoluble union of the States under one Federal head; secondly. A sacred regard to public justice; thirdly. The adoption of a proper peace establishment; and fourthly. The prevalence of that pacific and friendly disposition among the people of the United States, which will induce them to forget their local prejudices and policies; . . .'"

Adam studied his brother—the timbre of his voice, the flitting expressions on his face, and he saw the first hint of fear rising. Matthew shuffled for more copied documents and held them up one at a time as he spoke.

"John Jay of New York. September twenty-fourth of 1783, to Gouverneur Morris of New York. 'I am perfectly convinced that no time is to be lost in raising and maintaining a National spirit in America . . . In a word, everything conducive to union and constitutional energy of government should be cultivated, cherished, and protected . . .'"

He dropped the copied letter and read from the next one.

"John Hancock of Massachusetts to the Massachusetts legislature. September. 1783. Our Massachusetts John Hancock—the one who so boldly signed the Declaration of Independence. 'How to strengthen and improve the union so as to render it completely adequate, demands the immediate attention of these states. Our very existence as a free nation is suspended on it.'"

Adam was aware that Matthew's voice was rising as Matthew went on with the next document.

"Thomas Jefferson to James Madison. 1784. Jefferson shared these letters with me. 'I find the conviction growing strongly that nothing can preserve our Confederacy unless the bond of union, their common council, can be strengthened.' Matthew dropped the letter and referred to the next one. "Jefferson again, to James Monroe. 1785. 'The interests of the states ought to be made joint in every possible instance, in order to cultivate the idea of our being one Nation.'"

Matthew paused to take a deep breath and release it slowly while he brought his thoughts under control. He raised his eyes to Adam and spaced his words.

"The country's coming to pieces, but that's not the worst of it." He laid the next document on the table. "From Stephen Higginson—remember him? Former Congressman from our own state? To John Adams. December, 1785. 'Experience and observations most clearly evince that in their habits, manners, and commercial interests, the

Southern and Northern States are not only very dissimilar, but in many instances directly opposed . . .' "

He laid the papers on the table and leaned back in his chair. His face was a blank, his eyes without expression. "The north against the south. It could mean war."

For the first time Adam dropped his eyes and leaned forward, studying the floor while he worked with his thoughts. Matthew sighed and straightened in his chair.

"You didn't come to hear all this. You've got a ship to navigate."

Adam raised his head. "No. I need to hear it. Go on."

Matthew shrugged and picked up the next document. "The Higginson letter shook Congress. They appointed a committee. Rufus King, Charles Pinckney, James Monroe, John Kean, and Charles Pettit. They were to investigate and report."

Adam raised a hand. "I recognize Rufus King and James Monroe, but not Pinckney, Kean, or Pettit. Who are they?"

"Pinckney and Kean are from South Carolina. Pettit's from Pennsylvania. All Congressmen."

Adam nodded, and Matthew reached for a thick document. "Here's the report they made to Congress on February sixteenth of last year. 1786. I'll read part of their conclusion. ' . . . the crisis has arrived when the people of the United States . . . must decide whether they will support their rank as a nation, by maintaining the public faith at home and abroad; or whether for want of a timely exertion in establishing a general revenue and thereby giving strength to the Confederacy, they will hazard not only the existence of the Union, but of those great and invaluable privileges for which they have so arduously and so honorably contended."

Again Matthew paused, slowly lowered the document to the tabletop, and quietly said, "There it is. We change, or we die."

For a time the only sound was the creaking of the ship, and then Adam spoke. "Did Congress do anything about it?"

Matthew picked up the next document. "May thirteenth, last year. Pinckney moved Congress for the appointment of a general Committee to propose a plan to save us. August seventh the Committee reported. They had a long list of acts Congress had to approve, or they predicted that the Union would dissolve into chaos. The list was too long. Congress did nothing. The report was tabled and the whole project died."

Adam was incredulous. "Congress ignored it?"

Matthew nodded. "They did. Facing a prediction of dissolution of the thirteen states, they ignored it. North against the south. That's when talk began in the backrooms of Congress about appointing a king. When Washington heard of it, no one could remember fury like they saw in him. He wrote, 'What astonishing changes a few years are capable of producing! I am told that even respectable characters speak of a monarchial form of government without horror!'"

Adam's eyes widened. "Washington? He wrote that?"

Matthew laid a paper before him. "There it is."

For fifteen seconds Adam studied the paper, then shook his head and laid it down while Matthew went on.

"Backroom whispers became open talk in Congress. The State legislatures. Leaders everywhere were shaken." Matthew sorted out two more documents and scanned them for a moment. "Here. Last August. August nineteenth. James Monroe to Thomas Jefferson. 'I am sorry to inform you that our affairs are daily falling into a worse situation . . .' And here. Monroe again, this time to Patrick Henry. Governor Patrick Henry. 'Certain it is that Committees are held, in this town, of Eastern men and others of this State upon the subject of a dismemberment of the States east of the Hudson from the Union and the erection of them into a separate government.'"

Matthew stopped and for a time said nothing. Then he quietly continued. "That was nine months ago. Leaders getting ready to break up the Union. The leaders!"

Adam saw the pain and the fear, and he did not know what to say or what to do.

Matthew dropped his eyes to the tabletop and put his hands together, working them one with the other, thoughtful, sorting out his thoughts. Then he raised his head.

"Is this what Father died for? Father and thousands of other good men? Valley Forge. Trenton. Morristown. Saratoga. Yorktown. Is this what they died for? Suffered for? Mother. You. Brigitte. Prissy. Six years of it. Is this what we bought with all the blood and tears and suffering?"

For a time the two brothers sat in silence, each remembering, each deep in his own thoughts. Then Adam spoke. "I heard about a convention— maybe two conventions—of leaders trying to find a way to stop all this."

Matthew nodded. "Madison organized one between Virginia and Maryland to settle arguments about the Potomac and Pocomoke Rivers. In Alexandria, Virginia. March twenty-first of 1785. Madison and the Virginia delegates came, but none of the Maryland delegates appeared. George Washington heard about it and quickly sent an invitation for all of them to come to Mt. Vernon. They did. Most of their disputes were handled, but it didn't stop the talk about splitting the union."

Adam drew a breath and asked. "Was there a second convention? Do I remember a second one?"

"One was arranged for 1786 on September eleventh in Annapolis. All states were invited to send a delegation. Connecticut, South Carolina, Georgia—all failed to send any delegates at all. The delegations from Massachusetts, New Hampshire, Rhode Island, North Carolina—all arrived too late to participate. A total of twelve men—twelve men— from New York, New Jersey, Pennsylvania, Delaware, and Virginia appeared. It was a disaster. They met for three days, then appointed Alexander Hamilton and James Madison to write a report of the failure. They did, and it was a thing of pity. The report ended with one last, final request. Every state was requested to send a delegation to Philadelphia on the second Monday in May of this year—May fourteenth—in one last try to save the country. I have their report here." For a moment Matthew handled papers, then laid one on the top of the stack.

"Let me read the last three lines. ' . . . to devise such further provisions as shall appear to them necessary to render the constitution of the Federal Government adequate to the exigencies of the Union.'"

Matthew looked up and then asked, "Any question about what Madison and Hamilton meant by that?"

Adam shook his head. "None. One last try. Do or die."

"Are you aware of how Congress reacted to that?"

"Not good."

"Ignored it. And things got worse. Here." Matthew extracted another document from the stack. "October twenty-seventh, 1786. Benjamin Rush from Philadelphia to Richard Price in London. 'Some of our enlightened men who begin to despair of a more complete union of the States in Congress have secretly proposed a Northern, Middle, and Southern Confederacy.'"

Adam rounded his lips and gently blew air. "Benjamin Rush? Of Pennsylvania? He wrote such a thing?"

"Yes. Dr. Benjamin Rush of Pennsylvania."

"Hard to believe."

"Washington heard of it, and November fifth last year—five months ago, wrote to James Madison. His letter is very nearly a prophecy. Here." He picked up a copy of a letter and read. "'. . . Let prejudices, unreasonable jealousies, and local interests, yield to reason and liberality . . . No morn ever dawned more favorably than ours did; and no day was ever more clouded than the present . . . We are fast verging on anarchy and confusion . . . Thirteen sovereignties pulling against each other, and all tugging at the Federal head, will soon bring ruin on the whole.'"

Adam interrupted. "Ruin on the whole? When did Daniel Shays rise up? Wasn't it about then?"

"December of last year. Forced courthouses to close, because if judges couldn't get inside to sign orders, they couldn't foreclose farmers from their land, or send men to debtor's prison. Shays and the Massachusetts Militia fought a pitched battle at the Springfield armory on January twenty-fifth, and another one on February fourth at Petersham, and their last one on February twenty-seventh. Altogether about forty-five men were killed. Think of it! Americans killing Americans! I was there. With Billy and Eli Stroud. Trying to stop it. It broke my heart."

Adam took a deep breath. "If I understand it right, Shays lost, but his rebellion put enough pressure on Congress to do something."

"James Madison saw the value of the rebellion and began writing letters to leaders all over the country. They put pressure on Congress. February twenty-first, Congress passed a resolution. I have a copy." Matthew read from another document. "' . . . That in the opinion of Congress, it is expedient that on the second Monday in May next, a Convention of delegates who shall have been appointed by the several states, be held at Philadelphia, for the sole purpose of revising the Articles of Confederation . . . adequate to the exigencies of Government, and the preservation of the union.'"

Adam asked, "And the states responded?"

"Some did, some didn't. New York and the four New England states rejected it. They claimed the Articles of Confederation had its own provision for amendments, and they had to originate in Congress, not in the states. They said any amendments would be illegal if they originated with the states."

"What changed their minds?"

"Madison persuaded George Washington to attend. At first Washington was reluctant, but when he realized what was at stake, he consented. And when he did, it turned the dissenters around. They're coming, or at least most of them."

"Have any states refused?"

"We don't yet know about Rhode Island."

Adam shook his head in puzzlement, then pointed to a second large stack of papers on the table. "More letters?"

"No. Notes and documents on the background of most of the men who will be attending the convention. I'll need that if I intend talking with them."

"Any appear to be the leaders?"

Matthew reflected for a few moments. "Hamilton. Madison. Mason. Washington. Randolph. Morris. Rutledge. Maybe Pinckney. A few others. One never knows."

"Which Morris? Robert? The financier?"

"No, Gouverneur Morris. New York. Strong thinker. Writes well. Robert Morris will be there, but I don't know how effective he'll be."

Matthew smiled. "Gouverneur Morris has one wooden leg. Rumor is he lost the leg jumping from the second floor window of a lady's boudoir. It isn't true—he lost it in a carriage accident—but it made a good story. I think he enjoyed it while it lasted. Looks to be a typical politician."

Adam grinned, then sobered. "Any others? Perhaps some from Massachusetts?"

"Gorham, Strong, Gerry, and King. Any one of them could be a surprise. On paper, Gerry appears to be an eternal pessimist. Everything is wrong if he wasn't the one that thought of it."

Adam shifted in his chair, then stood to stretch muscles that had set. "I've taken too much of your time. I better go shoot the sun and check the chart."

Matthew stood. "I'll go up with you. How many times've you navigated the Delaware?"

"Twice. This is my third."

Matthew followed his brother out into the narrow passageway to Adam's tiny quarters where he opened the scarred case to pick up his sextant, and in those moments Matthew quickly scanned the charts on the small table nearby. He recognized them as the standard charts, created from the best available drawings of cartographers and mariners on two continents, and from eleven years of hard experience he knew that in some details, the charts were flawed. His eyes narrowed as he saw the great number of notes and the tiny drawings that Adam had carefully made on the thick parchments, correcting them, adding to them, making them complete, correct, his own. For a moment he was seeing his own charts, his own notes, and he felt a shock when he realized that Adam— little Adam—the youngest brother—had become a rare navigator.

Adam turned with his sextant in hand, and Matthew ducked to follow him out into the passage and up the stairway so narrow two men could not pass. They both hunched low to clear the doorframe at the head of the stairs, and soon were out on the deck, wind at their backs, the late afternoon sun on their shoulders, hearing the whisper of the rigging and the canvas overhead, and the creaking of the masts, and the quiet hiss of the ten-foot curl being cut by the bow of the ship. For a moment they stood still, caught up in the sounds, and the feeling of the immensity of the sea, and the power of nature, and the slow rise and fall of the deck beneath their feet, and knew once again the humbling truth of their own smallness. Adam again stood still while he took the position of the sun, and nodded in satisfaction.

From the crow's nest, eighty feet up the mainmast, came the call, "Weather. Due east," and wherever men were at their work stations, all heads swiveled to peer. Matthew, Adam, and Sturman slowly walked to the portside railing and studied the horizon, but there was nothing. Faulkner, at the wheel, tipped his head back to call the question upwards, "What do you see?"

The lean, bearded, barefooted seaman overhead cupped both hands about his eyes to limit his vision, and seconds later came his answer.

"Fog. Maybe rain."

Faulkner responded. "Wind?"

"No sign. Fair seas so far."

Fifteen minutes passed before those on deck could see the thin gray line rising on the eastern horizon, and two minutes later Sturman and Matthew exchanged glances. Within two hours the *Adonis* would be locked in fog, and fog hid the sea and all that was in it. Everything upon which seamen depended became changed, nearly useless, at times a deadly threat. Sounds were muffled, queer, distorted. Time became warped, meaningless, incalculable. Lights were but a blur, always closer than they appeared. An infinity of invisible water droplets hung in the air to cling to beards, brows, faces, clothing, and make the deck, the wheel, and the sails slick. The ship became swallowed up in a world where there was no sun or star to guide. Subtle shifts in the currents of the sea, or miscalculations of position or speed, could bring disaster on reefs and rocks.

How thick the fog, and for how long it would hold them, was yet to be seen, but of one thing the entire crew was certain. Not far to the south of them, and then due west, was the entrance to Delaware Bay; Cape May on the New Jersey side, and Cape Henlopen on the Delaware side. Ships entering the Bay divided the twenty-mile distance between the two lighthouses equally, to hold to the safety of the deep-water channel, then corrected course from due west to northwest and held steady for forty-two miles before they corrected again, slightly west, up the ever nar-rowing Bay past Salem on the starboard side and into the mouth of the Delaware River. From there it was a matter of holding to the center of the river, where deep-water ships could pass, on to Chester, then Philadelphia, both on the port side. Making passage from the Atlantic to Philadelphia on a clear night required seasoned navigators and sea-men. Making it in a night shrouded in fog required something more. Some captains of the sea refused to risk such passage in fog, choosing rather to drop anchor and wait for the safety of clear skies. All men on the *Adonis* went back to their duty stations, peering east through slitted eyes as they worked, making their own calculations as the gray line rose in the blue sky, and rolled on toward them.

The towering fog bank was a quarter-mile to the east and rapidly approaching when Adam took his last shot of the western sun, and immediately went belowdecks to his charts. Ten minutes later he returned to the deck with rolled parchments in his hand and beckoned Sturman and Matthew to the wheel of the ship, where Faulkner stood. He spread the charts before them.

"We are exactly here," he said, and tapped a place three miles off the New Jersey shore, and twenty-six miles north of the point where the ship was to change course to due west to pass between Cape May and Cape Henlopen to enter Delaware Bay.

He continued. "Right now the tides are beginning to run west, into the Bay. I calculate that if the winds hold and we maintain our present speed running with the tide, we can make a course change to due west at about seven-forty this evening, and pass just about center between the two lighthouses into the Bay."

He went on, calm, efficient, contained. "Once inside the bay we furl all canvas except the mainmast to reduce speed. We make a course cor-rection about nine o'clock to the northwest. That will take us through the bay to where it narrows to the river. About one o'clock we enter the river." He was slowly moving his finger on the chart, up the Delaware Bay, as he spoke. "The river will be running against us and slow us a little.

Sometime around five o'clock tomorrow morning we should be about here"—he tapped the chart—"here the river makes its bend back to the northeast." He paused and lifted his finger. "We should pass Chester about ninety minutes later, and be at the Philadelphia docks about eight o'clock tomorrow morning. Sunday. I repeat, this all depends on the winds."

He turned to Sturman. "Or we can drop anchor and wait for the fog to clear."

Sturman did not hesitate. "What do you recommend?"

"If we keep men at the bow, both port and starboard, to make depth soundings as we go, and correctly judge the winds and the tide running with us, and the flow of the Delaware against us, we should be able to calculate pretty close where we are. It can be done."

The crew moved closer on the smooth deck, knowing that the four men who held their lives in their hands were struggling. They turned an ear away from the wind and breathed lightly to listen. Matthew and Faulkner remained silent, eyes on the charts, giving Sturman time to consider all that could go right, and wrong, weigh it, and make the decision that was his and his alone to make. For a time he studied the maps and the notes made by Adam, then turned to stare, first eastward at the incoming fog, then west as though he could see the coast, while thoughts and questions came rushing. Once they cleared Cape May, control of the ship would be given to Adam. Young, lacking in experience, did he have the instincts and the gift of dead reckoning that would move the *Adonis* through the channel into the Bay, then correct course to the north for the forty-two mile run to the mouth of the river, and then the tricky, twisting, turning course upstream? Would he feel shifts in the currents, or changes in the winds, and could he correctly calculate the speed of the tides and the drag of the river current against them in a world blinded by fog? Could the seamen accurately handle the thin lines and the lead balls to make the depth soundings that would keep them in the deep-water channels, away from the reefs and shoals and sandbars and rocks that could ground them or rip open the hull? How long would the fog hold? Hours? Days? Was it worth the risk of a ship and a cargo and a crew to arrive in Philadelphia on schedule?

Sturman took a deep breath and made his decision. "For now, we'll keep moving. If need arises we'll stop and drop anchor."

Adam nodded. "Yes, sir."

The seamen began to breathe again, and once more turned their heads toward the fog bank, now minutes away and closing. They licked at dry lips and set their jaws and returned to their duties.

Sturman turned to Matthew. "For now, you take the wheel and follow Adam's orders."

"Yes, sir." Faulkner stepped back and Matthew took the wheel, checked the compass heading, and held the ship steady.

Sturman spoke to Faulkner. "We'll need two experienced men with lines for depth soundings on the bow, port, and starboard. All other hands to duty posts for fog. See to it."

"Yes, sir." Faulkner pivoted and gave orders to the waiting crew.

Sturman hesitated for a moment, then turned to Adam. "You be available to the wheel whenever you're needed. I'll be at the bow most of the time, and you join me when you can. Understand?"

"Yes, sir." The murmur of the curl being cut by the bow could tell an experienced ear much about the speed of the ship, and tides, and currents.

The thick, gray wall rolled over the ship, and the crew silently settled into their four-hour rotation, every instinct, every nerve alive as they stood to their posts for running in the twilight of fog. Men standing amidship could see neither bow nor stern. Those who walked the wet, slick footropes in the rigging tied safety ropes around their chests, then to the heavy, wooden arms, and talked to each other as they moved. The man in the crow's nest became invisible—a voice from above. At six o'clock the first shift took their fifteen-minute turn in the tiny mess hall belowdecks, then hurried back to their duty posts while the next shift disappeared to bolt their food and return. By seven-thirty the dusk had turned to full blackness, and all lamps on the ship were burning. At seven-forty Adam gave orders to Faulkner at the wheel, and the crew felt the ship lean to port as Faulkner corrected, and she made her turn to starboard, due west. The crew on deck quieted and listened while the two men at the bow threw the lead balls on the thin lines into the sea and called out the count of the knots in the ropes as they drew them up, one knot for each fathom. Seven fathoms—six fathoms—five fathoms—four—five. For one hour the crew listened to the calls, which were never less than four fathoms—twenty-four feet—before their breathing eased. They were inside the Bay. It appeared that Adam had split the entrance near center.

Standing beside Faulkner at the wheel, Adam nodded, and Faulkner called orders. Men disappeared into the rigging to furl all sails except the mainmast, and minutes later the heavy ship eased and slowed, and the creaking lessened. With a lamp in one hand and his chart in the other, Adam once again gave Faulkner a new heading, and the *Adonis* swung to a course northwest, up the Bay, to where the Bay steadily narrowed to meet the Delaware River.

The winds held, and at midnight, with Matthew at the wheel, the crew on deck went below to their gently swinging hammocks while the next shift who had rested and tried to sleep went above to take control. At one o'clock they felt the ship gradually slow, and Faulkner, Sturman, and Adam walked to the bow to listen. The sound of the curl had not diminished. Adam spoke quietly to Sturman, with Faulkner listening.

"We're entering the river."

Both men nodded but said nothing, and the silence held as they listened to the men making the calls of the depths as they drew the lines and lead balls from the water and counted the knots. With a lantern casting yellow light on his chart, Adam listened to every call, referencing it against the depth lines printed on the parchment, and his own notes, tracking both shorelines of the river every yard of the way. Four times in the next four hours he called minute corrections to Matthew, at the wheel, following the bends of the river, first to the left, then to the right, then back to the left. "Six degrees left rudder." "Five degrees left rudder." "Eight degrees right rudder." "Nine degrees left rudder."

It was fifteen minutes past five o'clock when he called, "Twenty-two degrees right rudder." By his calculations they were into the last turn of the river before Chester, with Philadelphia beyond. At this turn the river narrowed rapidly; if there was to be trouble, it would be in the next thirty minutes. Faulkner had taken the wheel from Matthew at four o'clock, and under the dull light of the wheel lantern turned the wheel and watched the compass needle swing twenty-two degrees, to a heading just east of true north. Matthew was at the port bow, listening, watching, with Sturman at the starboard bow, pacing, with every man listening to the depth soundings being called from the bow. Adam tracked the calls against his charts, steady, intense, missing nothing as he calculated the position of the ship between the two banks of the river. Ten minutes became fifteen, twenty, thirty, and the black fog slowly became deep purple as a hidden sun rose in the east, to their right.

Suddenly from the crow's nest came the shout, "Fog clearing! Sun in the east!"

Fifteen minutes later the skies were gray, and then sunlight and blue showed through in tiny patches. Soon, through lingering wisps of gray, the shorelines of the river could be seen, and from overhead came the call, "Clear skies. Steady as she goes."

In full morning sunlight Sturman rounded his lips and blew air. Matthew took a deep breath and released it and reached to rub his jaw-line. At the wheel, a tight grin showed in Faulkner's beard. Crewmen glanced at Adam, and shook their heads in wonder, and turned back to their duties.

Twenty minutes later the man in the crow's nest pointed and called, "Lighthouse ahead on the port side."

Adam tapped his map. "Chester. We'll make Philadelphia about twenty minutes past eight o'clock."

During the last hour, while the crew made ready to dock and tie up the ship, the small settlement of Gloucester City passed on the starboard side, one mile east of the river bank, and then the town of Camden came into view on the starboard side. Across the river, on the port side of the *Adonis*, the city of Philadelphia sprawled more than two miles along the shore, extending inland more than one mile west. The crew stood to their stations as the ship slowed and worked her way past two sloops anchored just out of the deep channel. Then, on Faulkner's order, they spilled the sails on the aftermast, and the big vessel slowed and settled as they brought her in to the dock, next to a large, weather-stained sign, "TERRELL" bolted to a piling. The ship thumped against the heavy black timbers, and the coiled, three-inch hawsers came arcing down from the deck, where expert hands jerked them tightly around the great cast-iron cleats and looped them back once, twice, three times, and the *Adonis* was secure. Seamen on board raised the hinged section of the ship's railing, shoved the gangplank forward through the opening and set the lower edge slamming onto the dock, while below, busy men slowed for a moment in their work to stare up in wonderment at the ship and the crew, unable to believe the *Adonis* had crossed the Bay and navigated the river at night, in a fog bank that had stopped all other watercraft.

It was Sunday morning, the Sabbath, but it made little difference on the docks of one of the busiest ports in America. The sounds and the smells and the bustle of men on the wharves and piers working with cargoes coming and going on ships of many, many flags, were as on every other day. The crew of the *Adonis* lined the rail to lean forward on their forearms, peering down at the jumbled business, then beyond, at what they could see of the shops and taverns and pubs of the town. They would help the Terrell crew unload three thousand barrels of dried Maine cod, but they would also have some free time. Captain Sturman would give them a few dollars against their pay, and they would wash and change into their best, and visit the Red Rooster or the Black Horse or some other nearby tavern, where a plump lady with a stained apron and hair loosely balled on top of her head and a laugh that was too loud would bring them a pewter mug of hot rum with cinnamon and floating chunks of butter melting. They would sit at plain, scarred tables and tell anyone who would listen that they were the ones who had made passage from the Atlantic into Delaware Bay, crossed the Bay, worked their way up the twisting, crooked river, and docked in Philadelphia. Done it all on the night when the fog was so thick the cook had gathered a kettleful of it, added potatoes, and made soup. Right tasty, too, since the fog was so thick the shad and salmon were all swimming thirteen feet above the water and the cook got six of 'em in the pot when he gathered the fog. Nary a bump nor a snag, nor another ship the whole night, because no other ship dared try to do what they done. Best captain, best first mate, best navigator, best crew, best ship on the coast. Yes, sir, it was the *Adonis* done it, and they were the men of the *Adonis*. And then they would sit and work on their hot rum and grin while seamen from another ship would spin a tale taller, and more artfully filled with lies, and swear it was so.

On board, Matthew shook Faulkner's hand, then turned to Adam. Neither of the brothers spoke as they shook hands, eyes locked for a moment. Matthew bobbed his head, and Adam understood, and Matthew stooped to shoulder his seaman's bag, and spoke to Sturman, who stood waiting with a packet of papers clutched in one hand.

"Ready when you are, sir."

Without a word Sturman led Matthew marching down the gangplank to the bustle on the dock with the May sunshine on their shoulders. The two worked their way through the shipping crates and the great nets hanging from yardarms, and the shouts and clamor, and the bearded men, to the office with the word "TERRELL" on the sign above the door. The rotund, balding man behind the counter glanced up, then laid his quill on the ledger in which he had been making entries, rose, and approached. For one second his eyes narrowed and then recognition struck, and his eyes opened wide.

"Cap'n Sturman! When did you . . . you docked this morning?"

Sturman laid his packet of paperwork on the counter. "'Morning, Gibbs. Yes. Fifteen minutes ago."

"You came . . . the Bay? Up the river? Last night?"

"God willing we made it. We're ready to unload. Which warehouse? We'll need your crew to take first shift unloading. Mine needs about six hours rest. We have to be in Yorktown and loaded in five days and on our way. Tobacco for New York."

Gibbs was incredulous. "Through that fog? You came in the fog?"

"Yes." He waited a moment while Gibbs stared, then pushed the papers toward him. "The manifest, insurance, and our contract. We'll need to get an insurance representative to certify the count."

Gibbs shook his head, still unable to accept the arrival of the *Adonis.* "It'll take maybe two hours. We weren't . . . we didn't think you'd try the Bay and the river last night. We expected you late today, or tomorrow morning. No one else tried it last night, either direction."

"We noticed. If you'll get your crew and the insurance man down to the ship in two hours, they can start."

Gibbs started through the paperwork. "Give me a minute." He scanned the manifest, then the insurance papers, and finally the contract between Terrell and the Dunson & Weems Shipping Company.

"Seem to be in order. Harbor master arrived at your ship yet?"

"No. Mr. Faulkner will handle that. First Mate."

Gibbs looked up at Matthew. "Mr. Dunson, isn't it? I think we met before once or twice. You're a navigator. Part owner of the shipping line."

Matthew shook his offered hand. "Matthew Dunson. Yes. Part owner."

"You navigated last night?"

"No. My youngest brother. Adam Dunson."

Gibbs grinned and his jowls moved. "Family tradition? Big brother watched over little brother last night?"

Matthew smiled as he shook his head. "No. Adam didn't need help."

Gibbs straightened the papers and returned them to Sturman. "I'll get our crew together. See you at the ship in about two hours."

Sturman nodded, turned on his heel, and Matthew followed him out the door back onto the wharf, where Sturman stopped and faced him.

"I'll go back to the ship. You go on with your business here."

"You'll give the men some time to rest? Last night was tense. A drain."

"On all of us. They'll have eight hours rest before they take their shift unloading. You see to it you get some rest too."

Matthew saw the concern in the hazel eyes. "I will, sir. If anything happens—if you need me—I'll be at Asher's Boardinghouse on Thirteenth Street, just off Market."

Sturman repeated it. "Asher's. All right. Be on your way."
Matthew reached to shake the thick, strong hand, then shouldered
his seaman's bag and was gone.

Notes

A multitude of quotations from letters and other documents written by
political leaders of the time are set forth in this chapter, defining the fact that
the Articles of Confederation had been adequate to bind the states together in
their common need to throw off British rule, but lacked the power or provisions to hold the union together in the peace that followed the British surrender. The quotations are verbatim selections from Warren, *The Making of the
Constitution*, as follows, with support from some other sources:

Washington's reference to the changes that even a short period of time can
produce, changing minds to accept notions of restoring a king, p. 18. Rufus
King to Jonathan Jackson, September 3, 1786—conditions existing in the
United States had caused the overthrow of prior governments, p. 19. John Jay
to George Washington, June 27, 1786—conditions might drive men into anti-
republican views of government, p. 17. Congress was alarmed at the mounting
dissention among the states, February, March, 1786, p. 20. Congressman
Charles Pinckney of South Carolina moved Congress to appoint a committee
to investigate and report, May 13, 1786, p. 20. Congress appointed a sub-
committee headed by Pinckney, and the committee reported with vital recommendations on August 7, 1786; Congress did nothing, and the report died,
p. 21. The failure of Congress to take action on the Pinckney committee report
triggered the effort to convene a convention at Annapolis, Maryland, between
several states, and that convention was set for September 11, 1786. That convention convened on time, but only five states sent delegates who appeared. The
convention concluded September 14, and produced but one document—a
bleak warning written by James Madison and Alexander Hamilton that the
union of states would disintegrate if actions were not taken to prevent it,
pp. 22–23. Talk of splitting the Union into three separate confederacies—
north, middle, and south—became common among leaders, as defined in the
letter from James Monroe to James Madison, August 14, 1786, pp. 24–25.
James Monroe wrote to Governor Patrick Henry in August, 1786, that there
were leaders openly advocating splitting the Union into three confederacies,
p. 25. August 6, 1786, Theodore Sedgwick of Massachusetts wrote to Caleb
Strong, warning that talk of breaking the United States into three confederacies

had evolved into detailed discussions, p. 27. Shays' Rebellion erupted in September, 1786, causing great alarm that the dissolution of the Union had begun, p. 30. In the last months of 1786, and in January and February of 1787, in great fear of losing the Union, several states began preparations for a great convention to address the approaching disaster of the destruction of the United States, without Congressional consent or approval, pp. 40–41. February 21, 1787, yielding to horrendous pressure, Congress approved the convening of the Convention, to be held at Independence Hall, Philadelphia, the second Monday in May, 1787, with delegates from all thirteen states, p. 42. In support, see also Bernstein, *Are We to Be a Nation?* p. 106; Berkin, *A Brilliant Solution,* p. 29.

James Madison was among the key figures arranging the Philadelphia Convention, and wrote the pivotal letter to persuade George Washington to lend the indispensable weight and prestige of his presence by attending, thus giving the Convention legitimacy, p. 61. In support, see also Bernstein, *Are We to Be a Nation?* pp. 109, 149–50.

The route followed by the ship *Adonis,* from Boston to Philadelphia, including the names of all islands, lighthouses, etc., can be found in Donley, Marton, Palmedo, *National Geographic Picture Atlas of Our Fifty States,* see foldout map.

Matthew Dunson and all characters in this chapter connected with the fictional shipping company of Dunson & Weems are fictional.

Philadelphia
May 13, 1787

CHAPTER III

★ ★ ★

*P*ast the docks, Matthew hailed a hack, shouldered his heavy bag into the floor of the open coach, and climbed in. He sat on the weathered, cracked leather seat as the driver looked back over his shoulder inquiringly.

"Asher's Boardinghouse. Thirteenth Street, just off Market," Matthew directed.

The old, hunch-shouldered driver nodded, clucked to the horse, popped the buggy whip, and slapped the reins on the brown rump. The hack lurched forward, then settled into a steady, swaying motion with the iron shoes of the trotting horse and the iron rims of the large wheels clattering on the smooth, rutted cobblestones of Market Street, the grand thoroughfare that ran due west from the Delaware River past the Schuylkill River and divided Philadelphia in half, north and south. The coach rolled past great hotels and elegant shops and tall buildings that housed banks and the offices of lawyers and merchants and business accounting offices on both sides of the street. The financial heart of the city gave way to smaller shops with locked doors and drawn blinds, and windows staring back like dead eyes, with small signs in one corner, "CLOSED." This was Sunday, the Sabbath, and Philadelphia was giving the day its due.

Traffic dwindled, and the business district yielded to streets lined with trees heavy with the green of summer. White picket fences enclosed square homes built of bricks painted white, surrounded by yards alive with reds and yellows of flowers and the white blossoms of fruit trees. Men in powdered wigs and black, low-crowned, broad-brimmed felt hats, dressed in black suits with white lace and black ties at their throats, and white, knee-length stockings, walked ramrod straight, chins high, with women dressed in ankle-length, soft colored Sunday gowns and bonnets that covered most of their faces, clinging to one arm. Behind marched their children, silent, the boys dressed like their fathers, the girls like their mothers, winding their way to the nearest red brick church with a white steeple and a clanging bell calling all God-fearing Philadelphians to their Sunday duty.

The coach rattled on west, and Matthew settled into the seat, casually aware of the trimmed trees casting shade on the narrow sidewalks and streets, and the neatly kept yards and houses and the people passing in their Sunday finery, calling greetings. Weariness settled over him, and he removed his tricorn to lean back against the brittle leather to let thirty sleepless hours filled with the unrelenting tension of moving a huge ship blind in fog and the black of night, through a bay, and up a narrow, crooked river, make its claim on him. The driver drew on the right rein and the coach turned from Market Street north onto Thirteenth Street, where the coach came to a stop before a large, white, two-storied home with a small sign above the door, "Asher's Boarding." Matthew stepped to the street, handed coins to the driver, and offered his "Thank you." The driver tipped his high-topped hat while Matthew lifted his seaman's bag from the floor of the coach, waved once more to the driver, and strode up the flower-lined, brick-paved walk to the large, maple wood front door of the home. He raised the great brass knocker and dropped it three times and waited while rapid footsteps approached from the inside.

As the door swung open, Matthew lowered his head to peer down at a stout woman in a gray, ankle-length dress with sleeves to her elbows, partly covered by a figured apron with dustings of flour and specks of stain. Her hair was gray and covered with a white net, her face round, jowled, and double-chinned, lips a narrow line, and eyes that were startlingly blue. She clapped her hands together and exclaimed, "You are Matthew Dunson! You're here for the Grand Convention."

Matthew removed his tricorn. "Yes, I am. I believe I have a room reserved."

The blue eyes twinkled and the thin lips smiled broadly. "I'm Sarah Asher. Named after Sarah in the Old Testament. The one that was married to Abraham. You call me Mother Asher. Or just Mother. I'm so glad you got here safe. Last night we had fog, you know. Couldn't see a thing. Worried all night about the boats and things on the river. Oh, me! Excuse my bad manners—can't stop talking. Got that from my mother, you know. Come in, come in, come in." She reached to take his arm. "You wanted a room on the corner of the second floor. I've held it for you. Good bed—changed the sheets last night so they're fresh." She led him onto the flowered carpet in the parlor. A sofa and great chair, worn, comfortable, faced a large stone fireplace with arms bolted on the inside walls from which kettles could be hung to heat water or cook. Unremarkable paintings hung on three walls. A guest sat on a straight, wooden chair, intent on reading a one-page newspaper from two days earlier. The aroma of ham roasting in the kitchen oven hung in the air, mingled with the pungent smells of relishes and mince pie.

She pointed to the staircase against one wall. "You can take your bag right up there and get unpacked. The only room in the corner. Just down the hall is a washroom with water and soap and towels. You can shave there if you want. I serve dinner at one o'clock—beef soup and bread and tarts. Supper's at six o'clock—ham and potatoes and pie—do you like ham? But if you're hungry now, I've got bread and cold mutton, and I can have hot chocolate ready in a minute to get you through to one o'clock. My late husband, Horatio, he loved my hot chocolate, died eight years ago, you know. Would you like some hot chocolate?"

Matthew stifled a grin. "Thank you, no, Mrs. Asher. I had breakfast aboard the ship not long ago."

She looked disappointed. "Mother. Not Mrs. Asher," she corrected him.

Matthew could no longer conceal the grin. "Mother."

"That's better. Now you go on up and get your things in the wardrobe. You look all worn out. Take your shoes off and lie down a while. I'll come get you in time for dinner."

"Could I pay now?" Matthew asked.

"Oh, now or later. Doesn't matter. Why don't we work that out tonight after supper?"

"As you wish." Matthew shouldered his bag once more and walked up the worn wooden stairs, paused at the door of the corner room, then pushed in, onto a large, braided oval rug. The room was large yet modest enough, dominated by a tall bed with a goosedown quilt and two pillows. A painting of an ancient mariner hung on one wall, and a smaller one of a pastoral scene of spotted Holstein cows in a field on another. There was a small fireplace in one wall, a desk and chair in one corner, and a large upholstered chair opposite. Between the two chairs was a tall dresser with six drawers, and a mirror. A wooden wardrobe occupied one of the corners. Two windows afforded a view of the intersection of Market Street and Thirteenth. Matthew parted the lacy curtains and peered down at both streets, then lifted his bag onto the bed and opened it to hang clothing in the wardrobe and lay shirts and linen in the dresser drawers, then set his papers on the desk. Finished, he took razor and soap to the washroom down the hallway, shaved and washed, and returned to the quiet confines of the room. He opened the Market Street window halfway and went back to sit on the bed to unbuckle his shoes and put them on the floor next to the nightstand with the lamp. He sat for several moments, working his stockinged feet against the texture of the braided rug, feeling his muscles and his brain beginning to let go of the tensions that had ridden him heavy for over thirty-six sleepless hours. Weariness came, and he swung his legs up onto the bed and laid back against the pillows, then turned on his side, and drifted into a deep, dreamless sleep.

Too soon the knocking came and he slowly came from a world of black, thoughtless silence to a world where Mother Asher was calling, "Mr. Dunson! Mr. Dunson! Dinner is served in ten minutes." He licked at dry lips and tried to speak and could not, then forced it and croaked,

"Thank you, Mrs. Asher, I'll be down," and heard the reply, "Mother Asher." He waited his turn at the washroom, rinsed his face in cold water, smoothed his long hair and re-tied it behind his head, and went back to his room to change into fresh clothing.

There were ten at the midday meal. Two elderly married couples along one side of the table, a dour, thin, hatchet-faced, hunch-shouldered widower with a cane and a limp at one end, Matthew and three other men facing the couples, and a quiet, timid woman with a nervous twitch in one eye at the other end. Mother Asher made introductions, and each nodded as their name was called. The timid woman at one end flushed red and diverted her eyes when her name—Maude Chidester—was called, and the elderly man at the other end of the table sat expressionless as his name was given—Ira Bouchard. They all bowed their heads while one of the married men said grace, and the meal began. The soup was heavy with chunks of beef and carrots and potatoes, the bread was sliced thick, the home-churned butter was rich, and the tarts sweet and light. Talk was at first hesitant, then more generous as strangers became acquainted. They finished their meal, paid their compliments to Mother Asher, excused themselves, and left the dining room. Matthew followed one of the elderly couples upstairs and entered his own room.

At ten minutes past two o'clock, he walked back downstairs where Mother Asher was finishing the washing and drying of the dinner dishes.

"Is there a church nearby? Perhaps one you attend?"

"You wish to attend services?"

"If I can."

"I'm going to attend the three o'clock service. Lasts one hour. Reverend Becker—Augustus Becker—a Presbyterian—preaches so well. You'll come with me."

The small white church with the traditional belled steeple was three blocks distant, and Mother Asher was puffing when they walked through the doors and took a place in one of the front pews. The Reverend Becker, a ponderous man in a black robe, with a booming voice, made it clear that when Jehovah gave Moses those ten very succinct commandments cut in stone on Mount Sinai, he meant exactly what he had said.

The human race was to have no other gods before him! And those who spent their lives, their talents, their ambitions, their substance, seeking wealth, fame, and fortune, were without question worshipping gods other than Jehovah, and woe be unto them in the day of final judgment. On that day they would receive their just rewards: suffering the fires of the eternal pit!

Mother Asher hooked her arm inside Matthew's for the walk back to the boardinghouse, rehearsing for him the entire sermon, expanding on it considerably with her own observations, comments, and wisdom. They entered the boardinghouse, where she thanked Matthew for escorting her and excused herself. She had supper to prepare.

Matthew walked upstairs to his room, hung his coat, slipped out of his shoes, opened the windows, and for a moment peered down at the street while a breeze moved the curtains and stirred the stale air. Then he took his place at his desk, and for more than an hour reviewed notes and documents, reading again and again the background and history of the seventy-four men who had been commissioned by the thirteen states to attend the convention that was to begin the next morning at the State-house. Once again he felt the grab in the pit of his stomach at the realization that close to ten of them had already stated their refusal to waste the states' money and their time in such a hopeless attempt to do what could not be done. Would there be others? Would the convention fail for lack of a quorum? Would it?

He drew a deep breath and scanned his notes on the men, their similarities, differences, characters, professions, education, public service histories. Thirty-nine of them had already served in the Confederation Congress. Eight had been signers of the Declaration of Independence. Eight had been instrumental in forming and drafting the Constitutions of their own states. Five had attended the Annapolis Convention in September of 1786. Seven had been governors of their states. Twenty-one had borne arms in battle to win their freedom from Britain.

Not less than thirty-three had been lawyers. Ten had served as state judges. Eight were engaged in business, most of them mercantile. Six were planters—large land owners. Three were physicians. About half were college graduates, nine from Princeton. Others had attended Yale, Harvard, Columbia, the University of Pennsylvania, and William and Mary College.

Six of the men were under thirty-one years of age. Only twelve were over fifty-four years: Read, Washington, Blair, Dickinson, Carroll, Johnson, Wythe, Mason, Livingston, Jenifer, Sherman, and Franklin. Benjamin Franklin. Eighty-one years of age. The Dean of them all. What would his contribution be?

In thoughtful silence Matthew slowly went over the names of those he had listed as the obvious leaders: Washington, Franklin, Madison, Hamilton, Randolph, King, Sherman, Robert Morris, Gouverneur Morris, Dickinson, Mason, Wythe, Gerry, Rutledge, and the two Pinckneys from South Carolina. Would there be others? Strange things happen in the heat of debate. Quiet men sometimes become warriors. Who would they be?

He paused at the remembrance of the sharp criticism Elbridge Gerry and Rufus King had loudly and publicly made of the very idea of a Grand Convention when it was first proposed in 1785. Their writing appeared in every major newspaper in the states:

"Plans have been artfully laid and vigorously pursued which, had they been successful, we think would inevitably have changed our Republican Governments into baleful aristocracies. Those plans are frustrated, but the same spirit remains in their abettors. And the Institution of the Cincinnati, honourable and beneficent as the views may have been of the officers who compose it, we fear, if not totally abolished will have the same fatal tendency . . ."

Gerry and King of Massachusetts, always suspicious, seeing danger in all shadowy places, stood solid against any convention convened by anyone for any purpose, fearing that such gatherings were the breeding ground for men seeking power that would corrupt. And of all such gatherings they most feared the Society of Cincinnati. The Society had been established by General Henry Knox with the purpose of honoring those men who had served as officers in the Continental Army, such honor to be passed from father to son. Washington had been the unanimous choice for president of the Society, only to endure first subtle, then open criticism of the organization, or any organization, which tended toward creating an aristocracy by limiting membership to blood descendants. America had just beaten a country wherein the power of monarchy was by law conferred upon the eldest male descendant, regardless that the man might be a fool, an imbecile, or a despot. To suggest such a principle be allowed to spread its poison in America was beyond all toleration, and it made no difference that the purpose was to honor men who had earned it, or that the President of the Society was George Washington himself. Gerry and King had early and vigorously condemned the organization.

Then, by pure chance, the Society of the Cincinnati had set their annual gathering in Philadelphia for the same time as the convening of the Grand Convention, and Washington had excused himself from attending the Society's convention, claiming, among other things, ill-health. All thoughtful men knew that if the Grand Convention were to succeed, it demanded the presence and the endorsement of George Washington and a deluge of letters poured in to his Mt. Vernon home, pleading for him to attend. Thus Washington found himself in the embarrassing position of having rejected the invitation to attend the convention of the Society of Cincinnati in Philadelphia in the second week in May, only to realize that all he had fought for in the past twelve years would be at stake in the Grand Convention, which was to be held in the same city at the same time. He could find no socially acceptable way out. Then a letter from James Madison brought him to his decision. Madison wrote:

"It was the opinion of every judicious friend whom I consulted, that your name could not be spared from the Deputation to the Meeting in May at Philadelphia . . ."

Washington ignored the social embarrassment and accepted the appointment of the State of Virginia and made arrangements to attend.

Matthew sat back in his chair and rounded his mouth and gently blew air as he pondered. It was true that since their publicly declared position against conventions in general and the Society of Cincinnati in 1785, both Gerry and King had been persuaded to modify their thinking about conferences sufficiently to accept a commission to represent Massachusetts at the Grand Convention. They would be here. But had they modified their thoughts about the Society of the Cincinnati? Would they attack George Washington for being president of that organization? Would they divide the convention? Matthew shook his head in frustration. Only time would tell.

He felt his mind begin to wander, and he straightened the papers and his ledger, stretched, rose, and went to the bed to take off his shoes. Within minutes he was asleep in the softness of the thick quilt, with rich smells of roasting ham and mince pie drifting up from Mother Asher's kitchen and the soft murmur of people moving in the streets below. He was awakened by the rap at the door and looked at his watch on the nightstand, disbelieving he had slept for an hour.

After washing his hands and face in the washroom, he retied his tie, shrugged into his coat for Sunday dinner, and walked downstairs to greet the other guests as they gathered again around the dining table. Mother Asher came from the kitchen with a sugared ham steaming on a large platter, then made a hurried second trip to return with a heaping bowl of smoking mashed potatoes, then gravy, and condiments. On her nod they took their places, the long-faced bachelor at the end of the table growling out grace before they began. The ham was as good as any they had ever tasted, the potatoes fluffy, and the gravy rich and thick. The relishes and condiments were sweet, the bread warm from the oven. All talk stopped when Mother Asher brought out the warm mince pie, and the silence held while all ten guests slowly savored every mouthful. They pushed back from the table, laid their napkins beside their plates, groaned as they stood, thanked Mother Asher, and made their way from the dining room. Matthew remained for a moment.

"May I help clear the table? Do the dishes?"

She smiled as she shook her head vigorously. "Heavens, no. That's for me to do. You go back—"

She got no further. The thunder of cannon less than one mile away was followed by the faint rattling of the windows and the floor vibrations as the concussion waves passed. Instantly the ringing of bells in church steeples filled the air, and seconds later a second volley of cannon blasts came rolling. Matthew stopped dead still and turned inquiring eyes toward Mother Asher. She stood white-faced, wide-eyed, one hand clasped over her mouth, trembling. Matthew was moving toward the door when he asked, "Any idea what that is?"

Mother Asher could only shake her head.

"Stay here," Matthew exclaimed. "Tell the others not to leave—do not go out into the streets."

Mother Asher bobbed her head, and Matthew bolted out of the kitchen, through the front door and turned onto Market Street sprinting east, back toward the waterfront. He slowed at the roar of the third cannon volley and the pandemonium of the bells, then ran on. People opened their doors and stood staring down the street, hesitant, fearful, confused. Some came through their white picket gates to peer toward the rising tumult. Matthew had passed Ninth Street when he saw the mob filling the street, and then he saw the white haze of burned gunpowder in the evening sunlight and the clear blue of the sky, and then he heard the shouts and cheering from the people. He slowed to a trot, and went on, working his way through the crowd until he broke into the open at the intersection of Market and Third Street, and only then could he see, more than two blocks away, the great, open carriage drawn by four matched gray geldings, under escort of a large troop of uniformed Philadelphia City Light Dragoon Cavalry led by Colonel Henry Miles. Beyond the prancing horses Matthew could see twelve cannon aligned on each side of the street, wisps of white smoke still drifting from the muzzles. Shouting, cheering people jammed the sidewalks and the street, opening to allow a dark, brass-studded, burnished carriage to pass. The tall figure in the forward-facing seat sat ramrod straight, nodding acknowledgement and waving first to the pressing crowd on one side of the street, then the other. Beside him sat a fleshy man, and in the seat facing them sat uniformed generals with the gold stars on their shoulder epaulets glinting in the sun low in the west. Matthew was still one hundred yards from the carriage and the cavalry escort, when he caught his breath in recognition.

Citizen George Washington had arrived from Chester for the Grand Convention, and the Philadelphians had opened their city and their hearts to him with a cannonade salute and a company of cavalry as an honorary escort. Seated beside Washington was Robert Morris, the richest man in America, and the financial wizard who had used every device his genius could create, including much of his own fortune, to amass enough money to save the revolution from failure. Matthew stepped from the street onto the cobblestone sidewalk to wait and watch as the coach came steadily on, moving west on Market Street, with the cheering crowd jostling to get a glimpse of Washington. Matthew moved back, further from the street to let the leading edge of the crowd pass, and watched closely as the coach and the cavalry escort clattered by, peering intently at Washington to see what time and the crushing burden of the war and the terrible crises of the peace had done to the man he remembered from their meeting those many years ago. The setting sun caught the Roman nose that dominated, and Matthew saw the deepening lines in the face. The head was still high, proud, and the shoulders square. The brows were slightly more shaggy, but the blue-gray eyes were as they had always been, dominant, probing, penetrating, commanding. Matthew watched the coach pass and stood still to let the crowd go by, then turned to walk behind, following them up Market Street.

The coach stopped momentarily at Fifth Street, then continued west on Market, to stop at the greatest and grandest mansion in Philadelphia. Brick, three stories, many windows, large, exquisitely furnished rooms, stables for twelve horses, and vacant lots on both sides filled with sculpted flower beds and decorative trees and fruit trees and a great garden filled with growing vegetables, the entire estate enclosed in a high, white picket fence. The name Robert Morris was beautifully scrolled in black cursive on a small sign beside the high white gate. Matthew watched four cavalrymen dismount and loosen the straps on the baggage rack at the rear of the coach, then carry the trunks and bags of Washington through the high gate, up the broad brick walk, and through the great, polished double doors into the house. They returned to remain standing, holding the bridles of their horses. The throng of people stepped back respectfully to allow Washington to step down from the coach, followed by Robert Morris, and the four dismounted cavalrymen escorted them to the front door. Washington turned, waved once more, bowed slightly, and stepped into the cavernous entryway of the Morris mansion while Robert Morris closed the doors. The coach rolled on with the cavalry escort, and the milling crowd began to drift away, pausing to look back, then moving on, talking loudly among themselves, pointing, gesturing. Matthew waited for a time before he continued west on Market Street into the golden glow of a sun half set, exulting in the growing realization of the pivotal meaning of what he had witnessed.

Washington is here and he's staying at the Robert Morris mansion! He came. He came. He came—he will be a Virginia delegate at the Grand Convention—not at the gathering of the Society of the Cincinnati. With him at the convention, we have a chance. Maybe. Maybe.

He turned onto Thirteenth Street and returned to the boarding-house. Mother Asher and the guests were out in the yard talking loudly, and they came to meet him as he opened the gate and came up the walk. Mother Asher exclaimed, "People said all the noise was about George Washington. He came for the Grand Convention. Did you see him?"

"I did."

Instantly they all gathered around, silent, waiting, alive with anticipation.

"He came in a carriage. A large, polished carriage. Four matched gray horses. A troop of mounted cavalry escorted him. Robert Morris was beside him, and they went to the Morris mansion on Sixth Street. They took all the baggage inside. I believe that's where Washington will be staying during the Convention."

"Were there people? A lot of people?"

"The streets were filled."

"Cannon?" Mother Asher exclaimed. "Was it cannon we heard?"

"Twenty-four of them. Twelve on each side of the street."

She clasped her hands. "Oh, I wish I could have seen it. Do you know Washington? Did he see you?"

"About eleven years ago I met him. During the war. We talked. I was a navigator for the Continental Navy. He didn't see me today—too many people. I doubt he'd remember."

The dour, long-faced guest with the crippled leg asked, "You talked with Washington eleven years ago? Face-to-face?"

"Yes."

"You were an officer in the navy?"

"I was. Six years."

"That where you got that scar?" He gestured toward Matthew's cheek.

"Yes. At the battle of Lake Champlain."

The old man straightened. "October of '76? You were with Arnold?"

"Yes. On his boat. The *Congress.*"

A look of recognition crossed the aged man's face, and for the first time a light came into his eyes. "I was there—helped build those boats that summer. Got this crippled leg when we was sunk in the fight. Nearly lost it when we had to walk out. More'n a hundred miles. They wanted to take it off, but I wouldn't let 'em." A wry, crooked smile came as he continued. "Said I'd die if they didn't take it off, but I wouldn't let 'em, and I didn't die." He stopped, and his face settled, and the light faded from his eyes.

For a moment the ten people around him stared in silence, and then Mother Asher put her hand to her mouth and uttered a quiet "Ohhhh."

Matthew asked, "Which boat were you on?"

"*Washington.*"

For a few seconds Matthew stared at the ground, reaching back in his memory before he spoke, loudly enough for all of them to hear. "The *Washington* survived the first day. When fog settled that night and the hole opened in the British fleet, it was the *Washington* and the *Congress* that covered the escape of the other boats that were still afloat."

The gray head nodded, and Matthew went on. "We were seventeen small boats, and the British were twenty-eight, some of them three-decked battleships. We lost the battle, but we damaged the British so badly they had to return to their ports in the north. They were unable to come on down the Hudson to cut the United States in two as they had planned." He faced the old man directly. "You helped save the revolution in that fight. I am honored to know you, Mr. Bouchard."

Matthew stepped forward and thrust out his hand. For a moment the old eyes opened wide in surprise, and then the man extended his bony hand with the too-large knuckles, and looked up into Matthew's eyes. He attempted to speak, and could not, and he swallowed and nodded. For a moment all eyes looked elsewhere, then back to Ira Bouchard. Mother Asher broke the awkward silence.

"Come on back into the dining room. We still have two mince pies that need attention. Come on."

Dusk fell as they sat at the table savoring the sweet, spicy pies while Mother Asher scurried about, lighting the lamps. It was dark before the married couples and the three men seated opposite them placed their forks on their plates, exclaimed about the pie, and made their way to their separate rooms. Bouchard grasped his cane and started to rise to leave when Matthew spoke to him quietly.

"Sir, Mother Asher mentioned you are a widower?"

Bouchard settled back into his chair and the craggy old face turned, surprised. "Yes."

"How long?"

"Agnes—my wife—passed on twenty-four years ago. August of 1763. Died giving birth to our daughter, Caroline."

Matthew saw the pain. "Your only child?"

Bouchard shook his head. "No, we had a son in 1760. Chad. Chad Bouchard. I lost him in 1781. October. He was at Yorktown. He was twenty-one—seventeen when he joined and fought Burgoyne at Saratoga. Fought most battles after that, on through to Yorktown. Died when we stormed Redoubt Number Ten, there on the river."

There was a silence as the old man worked his jaw, and swallowed hard. Matthew spoke quietly. "I was there. At Yorktown. I had a brother there, too, and a friend." Matthew could think of nothing more to say, and quiet held for a moment.

Then the old man drew and released a great breath, and asked, "Did they live?"

"Yes. Both. I lost my father at Concord in '75."

Bouchard nodded his head gently, but said nothing, and Matthew asked, "Your daughter—is she living?"

"Yes. Married a minister from South Carolina. They're fine."

"You hear from her?"

He shook his head. "Not often. She writes sometimes. Someday I'm going down to visit her. Four grandchildren. I've got to see my grandchildren. When I get enough money."

"You live here? In this boardinghouse?"

He shook his head. "In Reading. I'm a cobbler—make shoes. Owned a farm before I got hurt, but I couldn't keep it after. Saved my money for more'n a year to come here to see the start of the convention. I want to see the men when they get here tomorrow. Got to find out if they can fix the country. Need to know if this leg and my only son was worth it."

"That's why I'm here, too, sir. To find out."

The old man struggled to his feet. He paused for a moment, and it was plain he wanted to say something but could not find the words. He turned, and Matthew watched him put most of his weight on the cane as he hobbled down the hall to his room. Matthew rose and was pushing his chair in when Mother Asher walked through the archway from the kitchen.

"Matthew—may I call you Matthew? I heard part of it. About Mr. Bouchard. That dear, dear man! That leg, his son, a daughter with four grandchildren he's never seen—and him coming here to see if it was all worth it."

Matthew stared at the tabletop for a moment before he answered. "I wonder how many more there are like him. The ones who faced the British when there was little hope. If it was all for nothing. . . ."

Mother Asher was firm. "No, sir, the Almighty isn't going to let that happen. You hear? It's going to be all right!"

Matthew looked into the determined blue eyes, and said, "I hope you're right, Mother."

He climbed the stairs, lighted the lamp on his desk, and once more checked his papers to be certain they were in order. He unbuckled his shoes and dropped them beside the bed, worked his toes against the carpet, then went back to his desk to sit down in the steady yellow light of the lamp. With quill in hand, he set a clean sheet of paper on the desk, dipped the feather in the inkwell, and thoughtfully wrote.

May 13, 1783.
Phila. Penn.
My Dearest Kathleen,

I must first say that you have scarce been out of my mind since I left Boston. I am not complete without you. My greatest concern is that you are well and happy. You, and John.

There are many things you will want to hear. First, we made a safe passage, although the last night was a challenge. We crossed Delaware Bay and made our way up the river to Philadelphia in heavy fog. Adam did a master's job navigating. I did nothing to help him.

I am staying with a Mrs. Asher at her boardinghouse. You can write me here, at Market Street and Thirteenth Street, Phila. Penn. I must smile as I tell you, I now have a new mother. Mrs. Asher insists on being called Mother Asher and has ordered me to call her Mother, while she calls me Matthew. She is an excellent cook and most gracious hostess. She is a widow. The other guests staying here—there are ten of us—are all good people and we get along well.

Today, Sunday, George Washington arrived in a grand coach, escorted by a company of light cavalry. He was greeted by a cannonade and people crowding the streets, cheering him on. He will be staying at the home of Robert Morris, the financier of whom I have often spoken, who resides in the finest estate in Philadelphia. It is late, and I am going to bed soon. I will add to this letter tomorrow after I have attended the opening of the Grand Convention.

I worry about you. If need arises, see Billy for money, or Caleb for help at the house. If John obeys, let him sit at my place at the table. I miss you all.

Your loving and obd't husband,
Matthew Dunson.

He read the letter slowly, laid the quill down, knelt beside his bed, and with bowed head and hands clasped before him, finished his day.

Notes

Market Street was a great thoroughfare dividing Philadelphia from east to west, from the Delaware River on the east, past the Schuylkill river on the west. See maps appearing in F. E. Compton Company Division of Encyclopedia Britannica, Inc., *Compton's Encyclopedia and Fact-Index*, volume 19, pp. 251a, 251b.

Robert Morris, the richest man in America in May of 1787, owned and lived in the greatest mansion in Philadelphia, on Market Street, just west of Fifth Street. Morris insisted Washington stay with him in his mansion during the convention, and Washington did so. Washington arrived in Philadelphia on Sunday early evening, May 13, 1787, having traveled the short distance from the small town of Chester, just southwest of Philadelphia. He was greeted by a cannon salute and a company of Philadelphia City Light Dragoon cavalry commanded by Colonel Miles, which escorted him into the city amid ringing church bells and cheering crowds that filled the streets. He was to have stayed at the boarding residence of Mrs. House on Fifth Street, at Market. However, as above indicated, he excused himself to Mrs. House and stayed at the residence of Robert Morris, who had invited him to do so as early as April 23, and constantly thereafter. The Morris estate was the greatest estate in Philadelphia, which is accurately described herein. Rossiter, *1787: The Grand Convention*, p. 159; Warren, *The Making of the Constitution*, pp. 99–101, and see especially the footnote on page 100, describing the Morris estate.

The background of the delegates who participated in the convention of May, 1787, as recited by Matthew Dunson, i.e., thirty-nine had served in

Congress, eight had signed the Declaration of Independence, eight had helped form their state constitutions, etc., is accurate. Warren, *The Making of the Constitution,* p. 55.

The battle between 17 small, hastily built, flat-bottomed boats and 28 British warships on Lake Champlain, as recounted in this chapter between Matthew Dunson and the fictional Ira Bouchard is accurate. The British ordered their ships down Lake Champlain to carry enough infantry to continue down the Hudson past Albany, to New York, to cut the American states in two, and thus divided, conquer them. Benedict Arnold was ordered to do what he could to stop them long enough to let the oncoming winter force them back north into Canada. The lopsided battle took place October 11 and 12, 1776, with the result that the Americans lost every boat, and the survivors of the crews had to walk home. However, they damaged the British fleet severely enough that they were forced back to Canada for repairs, essentially saving the Revolution. The night of October 11, following the battle of the first day, a fog set in, and the Americans were able to find a hole sufficient for their remaining boats to slip through, with the American boats *Congress* and *Washington,* covering their maneuvers. Leckie, *George Washington's War,* pp. 297–306.

Hot chocolate was a drink commonly used in America at the times in question. Earle, *Home Life in Colonial Days,* p. 165.

In 1785, Rufus King and Elbridge Gerry of Massachusetts both made public statements opposing the Grand Convention, and the quotation herein set forth is taken verbatim from a letter written by them in 1785, and published in many newspapers, in which they were highly critical of the proposal for the Convention, insisting it would lead to a "baleful aristocracy." Rossiter, *1787: The Grand Convention,* p. 87; Warren, *The Making of the Constitution,* p. 88.

CHAPTER IV

★ ★ ★

n the night, a strange, uneasy mix of excitement and anxiety had settled over the city. This was the day that seventy-four duly commissioned men were to convene in the Pennsylvania Statehouse to make a nation from thirteen independent, infant states. They were to make a nation, or admit they could not, then stand helplessly by while they and a waiting world watched one hundred sixty-seven years of blood and sweat and tears, wins and losses, joys and sorrows, and priceless inner awakenings of thoughts and concepts, dwindle and fade and die. From the day in 1620 when the tiny *Mayflower* dropped her anchor off the Massachusetts coast, until 1787—all for nothing? Today would be the day.

In the gray before dawn, Matthew swung his legs from beneath the thick goosedown quilt in his boardingroom and sat hunched forward, staring at the dim blur of his bare feet on the braided oval rug, arms down stiff on either side, palms flat on the bed, head bowed in the deep darkness of his room. In less than four hours he would be among the men into whose hands nature and history had delivered the awful burden of a land and a people and a principle, which if they could be melded, could change the history of the world forever. It had all come down to here, and now, or lose it forever. Thoughts came in the dead silence, and Matthew carefully defined them, weighed them, put them in order.

The land? In the treaty that formally ended the war between America and the British, signed in Paris in 1783, England had grudgingly conceded to the United States all claims westward past the Appalachian Mountains, on beyond the reaches of the pristine Ohio Valley, to the Mississippi River! Overnight, the size of the United States had more than doubled; sprawling from the Atlantic to the Mississippi, and from the Great Lakes to the West Indies. A land mass large enough to swallow up France, Italy, Spain, Germany, Britain, and Ireland, with ground to spare. Endless forests, so thick with timber of every description, that one standing on the forest floor could not see the blue sky overhead. Beneath the green canopy was an abundance of animals and creatures of every shape, there for the taking for furs and food. In and above the canopy were birds and waterfowl of every size and hue, flocks at times so dense they darkened the noonday sun in their flight. Coal, iron, copper, and silver lay buried in the mountains and valleys, waiting for those with the nerve and sinew to come digging. Soil that had lain fallow for millennia, made rich and fertile by the cycle of nature that dropped leaves and ancient forest giants to Mother Earth, there to molder and return tenfold the strength they had received.

Great rivers abundant with fish flowed from west to east, and from north to south—the Potomac, Delaware, Hudson, Connecticut, Santee, PeeDee, Broad, Yadkin, Schuylkill, Raritan, Richlieu, Savannah, Mississippi, York, James, and more—giant water highways to carry the freight and the people of a nation. The rivers gathered sweet water from ten thousand creeks and streams that networked the unending forests, which would sustain those with the heart and the will to carve out farms and homesteads. And in the negotiations preceding the treaty with England, the stubborn, recalcitrant John Adams had bullied the British until they granted New England fisherman the immeasurable gift of rights to fish the rich waters of the Grand Banks, off the coast of Nova Scotia.

Matthew shifted his weight and for a few moments listened to the stirrings in the kitchen on the first floor below. A faint smile passed as he thought of plump Mother Asher in her apron and kerchief, humming a spontaneous bit of something known only to her, bustling about in the kitchen, preparing breakfast for her ten boarding guests. He sobered at the thought—ten ordinary Americans, representatives of the nearly four million other Americans living in the cities and towns and hamlets and on the homesteads in the forests. These were the people who bore the nation on their bowed shoulders as they silently accepted the relentless grind of eking out daily existence in a world where but three things were certain: they would work for what they wore on their backs and the shelter over their heads and their daily food; they would live their entire lives in the constant, bewildering uncertainty of life that is the common denominator of all humanity; and no matter what they did, or how they believed, sooner or later they would die. Matthew slowly shook his head in reverent awe at the terrible faith and courage and endurance of the faceless, nameless masses that bear the burden while they build nations, neither asking nor expecting much beyond their daily bread. For a time he pondered and then his thoughts deepened.

What great secrets had the Americans learned that had driven them to the absurdity of defying Mother England? What thoughts, what principles, had become common to all of them and were so dearly held that they were willing to risk everything—even blood and suffering—to possess and maintain them?

Matthew felt the rise in his heart as the answers came.

Nature, and the Almighty, intended men, no matter their talents or intellect, to be equal in the one fundamental on which all else finally comes to rest: no man has the right of dominion over another. The world, both political and social, was meant to be governed by natural laws as certain as those that govern the physical world, and those natural laws are unalienable and essential to meaningful existence. The three basic natural laws are: the right to life, the right to enjoy individual liberty, and the right to own property acquired by honest industry. The purpose of government is to ensure men the enjoyment of these natural rights. Such a government must be built on a framework of morality and goodness and repudiate evil. Natural law requires that that government be plain, simple, limited, constitutional, and kept as near the people as possible.

The essence of government is trust, by which those who are chosen to govern never forget they are servants, not masters. And always, always, the citizenry must remember that nothing corrupts men more readily and completely than the taste and touch of political power.

Seconds passed before Matthew carefully reduced the whole of it to its simplest elements. It's all here—a land so huge and rich it sets men dreaming wild dreams; a people who cherish liberty; and a convocation of wise men who understand the true principles of government, gathered now to make it all come together as a nation.

Then he framed the fearful question. Can they do it? The north and the south? The large and the small? Can they? Can they? Despite the monarchs in Europe, who predict failure?

He took a deep breath and felt the frustration of not knowing and spoke softly to himself as he stood. "Well, today we start. We'll know before long." He put on his robe and slippers, gathered his soap and washcloth, razor and strop, and softly walked down the hall to the washroom.

The house was filled with the aroma of scrambled eggs mixed with great chunks of diced ham and hot chocolate and warm bread. At eight o'clock all ten guests were at the table with heads bowed while one said grace, and the bowls and pitchers and platters began their rounds. Excited talk flowed, marveling about the gathering of famous men at the Statehouse, anxiously speculating about the shape and powers of the government they would create, and fearing the divisions and differences between northern and southern, and the big and small states, might disembowel the entire process. Matthew finished his breakfast first, complimented Mother Asher on her splendid victuals, asked to be excused, and quickly climbed the stairs to his room. One minute later he came rapidly back down with a large packet of papers under his arm and his tricorn on his head. He paused to nod briefly to those still in the dining room and was out the door.

The air was still and warm and filled with the sweet scent of fruit trees and tulips and roses in full bloom. The streets were alive with color and sound and movement as Matthew pushed through the front gate, hurried to the intersection, and turned east onto Market Street. Overhead, swallows did their morning pirouettes beneath a cloudless, sunlit sky in pursuit of tiny, invisible flying things. Robins stood like statues inside the fenced yards, heads cocked and turned sideways, somehow knowing an earthworm was moving just beneath the grassy surface. Then came the blurred strike, the pointed beak driving down, the rearing back, and the battle between the robin stretching the earthworm upward while it struggled to cling to Mother Earth, and to life. One would win, and one would lose, and the eternal cycle would go on.

Matthew moved east on Market toward the heart of the city, which reached from Tenth Street eastward to the wharves on the Delaware River. In his years as a navigator, and then part owner of the Dunson & Weems Shipping Company, he had docked ships on the Philadelphia waterfront many times and walked the city streets to the plush offices of banks and corporations in the financial district, always preoccupied with the business at hand, seldom noticing the wonders about him.

But not today. Today he was seeing the city as though for the first time. He walked with every nerve alive, watching in the heavy bustle of pedestrian and carriage traffic to catch a glimpse of any of the seventy-four men who were to assemble at the Statehouse at nine o'clock. He knew well the narrow, crooked, winding streets of Boston and New York and Charleston and Savannah, and now he marveled at the wide, level streets laid out in a square grid by Philadelphia's founding fathers, who had named the streets running east to west and numbered those running north to south. With rare insight and vision they had arranged the wharves and docks of the Delaware River on the east side of town to be easily accessible to the merchants, and then had done all in their power to promote their city as the American hub of worldwide commerce. The result was waterfront docks stacked high with goods from ports around the civilized world: silks from India and China, woollens from Ireland, silverware from workshops in England, cutlery from Solingen, Germany, and Sheffield, England, teas and herbs from Canton, China, porcelains and art from Italy, wines from France. They early saw the potential of the printing press, and now ten newspapers—more than in any other

American city—scrambled to print the more sensational news of the day, including natural disasters, funerals, sales of every imaginable product that might be desired by Philadelphian housewives, marriages, political harangues, editorials on morality, preachments by local ministers, advertisements for meetings, performances at the opera houses, and the goings-on at the Indian Queen, the sumptuous hotel-restaurant on Fourth Street near Market that was the unofficial clearing house for just about everybody and everything occurring in Philadelphia. Matthew glanced upward at the street intersections to admire the posts with lamps at the top that kept the streets lighted at night, while constables walked their beats to maintain peace and security.

Only too well had Matthew studied the leading citizenry of the city, which proudly claimed the world-renowned Doctor Benjamin Franklin as her own, as well as Robert Morris, the richest man in the United States, Doctor Benjamin Rush of medical and political fame, Charles Willson Peale who had captured the men and the most memorable events of the Revolution with his paintings, oils on canvas, and David Rittenhouse, who had invented his own telescope to survey and settle ancient boundary disputes. As Matthew walked in the warmth of the morning sun, amidst the cleanliness and orderliness of the streets and felt the spirit of the city, he understood why it had been chosen for the gathering of men that were expected to construct a nation. The cultural, intellectual, financial, social, scientific, and political leader among all major cities in the United States, it was here the rebellious colonies had declared their independence in July of 1776, and it was here, in the same assembly hall eleven torturous years later, they would finish the work they had begun.

He had just reached Sixth Street when he saw a crowd gathering one block south, to his right, toward the Statehouse. He stood tall for a moment, peering, then strode hurriedly on Sixth Street to Chestnut and was entering the intersection when he saw four wagons in the street with bareheaded men in coarse clothing standing in the huge wagon boxes, feet braced as they shoveled loose brown dirt over the high sides of the wagons while the drivers held the four-horse teams back, moving the wagons slowly as the dirt piled in the street. On the cobblestones, twelve men moved slowly with the wagons, spreading the dirt evenly, eight inches deep. Matthew stopped in disbelief, then walked on until he reached the first bearded man working with a shovel, sweating, intent on making an even spread.

Matthew asked, "Dirt? In the streets? What's the purpose?"

The man stopped long enough to wipe perspiration from his forehead onto his shirtsleeve. "If I been asked that once this mornin' I been asked a hunnerd times." He grinned. "About nine o'clock the convention starts right over there in that building." He pointed. "Those gennelmen is supposed to fix the gov'ment, and a few of us got orders that they aren't to be disturbed. We was told to spread dirt in the streets around the buildin' to stop the noise of all the buggies and wagons and such, and all the people who're gonna be dead set on gettin' as close as they kin to what's goin' on over there." He stopped and once again wiped at the sweat, then pointed at the old Independence Hall, now renamed the Statehouse, and continued. "Over there, about noon, they'll have a passel of constables with orders to watch ever'body that stops to take a look. Well, after they had one look, them constables will tell 'em to keep movin'. They don't want nobody interruptin' those proceedin's." The man spat into the dirt, wiped at his beard, and bobbed his head at Matthew. "Anyway, that's why we're spreadin' dirt."

Matthew shook his head in amazement. "I never would have guessed."

The man chuckled and gestured to the other crews. "Funny thing. Me'n the others spend most of our time keepin' the streets in this fair city clean. Feels right confusin', sweepin' 'em clean one day and throwin' dirt on 'em the next." He shrugged. "But isn't that the way of it? Undoin' one day what you done the day before?"

Matthew smiled back at him. "That's the way of it."

The man winked and resumed spreading the dirt, moving the high places to the low, while Matthew looked at his pocket watch— 8:33 A.M.—and walked on toward the Statehouse. He slowed as he approached, studying the simple, classic lines of the square, two-storied structure and took his place in the loose line of those entering the building. He was conscious of a sense of excited anticipation as he passed through the door, and he stepped to one side for a moment while his eyes adjusted from the bright morning sunlight to the lesser light in the interior of the building.

The entry and the hallways were filled with men, some gathered in clusters talking, gesturing, others striding rapidly to disappear through doors, or into the moving, milling crowd. Voices and clicking heels echoed off the stone walls and granite floor, and resounded from the high ceiling. Five lawyers clad in black robes and powdered white wigs, with large, leatherbound books clutched beneath one arm made their way through the throng to pass between large columns and high arches into an austere courtroom with an oak bench elevated at one end. Before the bench were two heavy, dark tables and chairs. One side of the room was sectioned behind a banister with chairs for a jury, the other side for spectators. It was here the three judges, clad in distinctive scarlet robes, conducted the business of the Pennsylvania Supreme Court, and Court was in session.

Matthew stood still for a time, scanning faces, searching for those who would be gathering in the large hall on the east side of the building, opposite the Supreme Court.

There were none.

He walked on to a broad cross-aisle and turned east to the chamber where the Constitutional Convention was to convene in less than fifteen minutes. A man stood at the locked door, stocky, formidable, silently watching everyone who approached or passed. Matthew stopped, facing the man, who coolly measured Matthew as Matthew spoke.

"Sir, I understood the Grand Convention was to convene this morning."

The man's voice was firm. "That is correct, sir. In about twelve minutes."

Matthew gestured. "Are some of the delegates inside?"

"No, sir."

"Are they meeting at some other place before coming here?"

"That I do not know, sir. Earlier I saw members of the Virginia dele-gation, and most of the Pennsylvania delegation, but no others. They must enter through this door, so I can check their credentials. Only delegates can enter, and none have done so yet."

Matthew asked, "You are the doorman for the convention?"

"Yes, sir. Once I'm officially appointed."

Matthew thrust out his hand. "I am Matthew Dunson, of Boston. I'm here to follow the proceedings."

The man, shorter and older than Matthew, grasped his hand. "I am Joseph Fry. I'm here to help if I can."

"Thank you. Did you mention that none of the delegates have arrived? None? No one?"

"I don't know if they've arrived in Philadelphia. I only know they have not arrived here, at this door."

"Is it all right if I stand nearby?"

"Yes."

Matthew nodded and stepped to one side, close to the wall, away from those in the broad hallway, where he stood bewildered, searching for an explanation that would not come. A sudden quiet near the build-ing entrance held for a few seconds, followed by a great, spontaneous outburst of voices that brought him up short, and he raised his head, searching. For a time he could see only a crowd of men gathered and moving slowly toward him, and then he saw one head above the others, and recognition struck. The gray hair caught behind the head, the large Roman nose, the set of the chin—he was looking at Citizen George Washington of the Virginia delegation. Matthew remained where he was as those gathered about the Virginians opened a path, and the delegation moved steadily toward the entrance into the east hall. Relief flooded through Matthew as they approached, and he studied their faces, their build, their dress, identifying each in turn. George Washington, John Blair, George Mason, George Wythe, and James McClurg. Two were missing, and it was not until they were abreast of him that he saw the diminutive James Madison in the mix, nearly hidden on the far side of George Washington, who towered over him. It was Madison, the smallest among them, who carried a thick leather case. There was still one missing—Governor Edmund Randolph—and Matthew strained to find him in the crowd, but he was not there. The delegation stopped before Joseph Fry and each produced a paper. Fry read each in turn, nodded, opened the door and held it while six of the Virginia delegation entered the chamber before he closed it.

The crowd clustered in the hall remained for a time, excited, pointing, exclaiming, and then began to move away in twos and threes, and the echoing talk subsided. Matthew drew and slowly released a great breath. *It's begun. The General is here. Madison is here. And Mason and Wythe. Randolph—where's Randolph? And the delegates from the other states? Where are they?* He drew his watch from his vest pocket and studied the delicate hands. *Ten minutes past nine. And only one state represented. What's happened?*

With growing concern he remained where he was, near the wall, not far from the door into the Convention chamber, waiting, watching, listening. At nine-forty, without fanfare or notice, five more men presented their credentials at the door, and Matthew studied them carefully. Thomas Mifflin, George Clymer, Thomas Fitzsimmons, James Wilson, and Jared Ingersoll, all of Pennsylvania.

Matthew's breathing slowed. *The Pennsylvania delegation. Only five out of eight. Where are the other three? Franklin, and Robert Morris and Gouverneur Morris? Critical to the convention—where are they?* By ten minutes past ten o'clock, another delegate had been cleared and given entrance, John Dickinson of Delaware. Matthew stood with teeth set, mouth a straight line. *Two states with a majority of their delegates—enough to be recognized. Virginia and Pennsylvania. One state with one man. Ten states with no one here. Not one delegate. What's happening? What's happening?*

He remained where he was with dark forebodings growing steadily. He was unable to find, or invent, an explanation, a reason, why ten states had failed to have even one of their delegates present, and one other had failed to have a quorum. Had they misunderstood? How? How could they misunderstand the letters from Madison and Hamilton? How could they fail to see that this convention was the final desperate hope for the United States? Some of the greatest men on the face of the earth—

Washington, Franklin, Morris, Mason, Randolph, Pinckney, Gorham, Wythe, Rutledge, and others—knew! Either this convention succeeds, or the last great hope for America, and the world, is doomed! What had gone wrong?

Matthew paced, and waited.

It was just past eleven o'clock when the door into the chamber rattled, and then opened. Matthew turned and stood, braced, not breathing, watching the delegates file out. Thomas Mifflin and Jared Ingersol of Pennsylvania led, with George Clymer and James Wilson following, and the others bunched behind. Their faces were set, void of expression, as they passed into the broad corridor, speaking only rarely to each other, while the late-morning hall traffic slowed to watch and point and exclaim.

Shock hit Matthew and he stood transfixed, numb as he watched them pass. General Washington, toward the rear with James Madison, was less than six feet from him when Matthew forced some semblance of reason to his scattered thoughts.

Is it over? With ten states making no showing of any kind, did they decide it was hopeless? A waste? Have they adjourned sine die?

He fell in behind the group and followed them out the large front doors of the building into the bright sunlight, and came in beside James Madison, stride for stride. Madison glanced at him, and Matthew exclaimed, "Sir, I am Matthew Dunson of the Committee of Merchants in Boston. We've exchanged correspondence."

Madison slowed, shifted his heavy leather carrying case, and turned his head to look Matthew full in the face. He stopped, and Washington stopped with him. Madison thrust out his hand.

"I recall your letters. Exceptional. I am honored to meet you, sir."

"The honor is mine," Matthew returned. "I formed the Boston Committee of Merchants at the direction of Thomas Jefferson. It was his opinion, and mine, that this convention must succeed. I am here to learn what I can about the progress, and report to the other states."

"A worthy cause." Madison nodded, then turned toward Washington. "Mr. Dunson, may I present General George Washington."

Washington offered his hand, and Matthew reached for it as Washington spoke. "Have we met before?"

"Yes, sir. I served as a ship's navigator during the war. I had the honor of meeting you three times. The last was at Yorktown."

Washington's eyes narrowed. "Were you the officer that led the French ships out of the York River into the Chesapeake to engage the British? Admiral Graves?"

"Yes, sir. I had the honor."

Washington's handshake was firm, sure. "That was a remarkable act, Mr. Dunson. Remarkable. Many times I have wished to extend my personal thanks. It is a privilege to do so now."

Matthew nodded. "I am humbled, sir. I shall never forget your great victory at the surrender of General Cornwallis."

For a moment a faraway look came into Washington's eyes at the remembrance of the relentless blasting of American cannon that filled Yorktown with white smoke during the days and lighted the skies at night as they placed the British under siege. "A good soldier. Great man. We were fortunate."

Matthew turned back to Madison. "I apologize for interrupting you here in the street, but I need to know. Can you tell me what happened this morning?"

Instantly Madison saw the discouragement in Matthew's eyes. He smiled tiredly. "Nothing. It appears the delegates from some states are a bit tardy in making an appearance." He shrugged. "So we've adjourned until tomorrow morning. We'll meet again. And if they don't appear then, we'll adjourn until Wednesday. We'll meet every day until we have a quorum. Seven states."

Relief was nearly a physical thing in Matthew. "I'm happy to know that. I was concerned."

Madison smiled. "So were we. But we'll see it through."

"Would you mind if I talk with you from time to time?"

"Not at all."

"Thank you. I'll be here tomorrow morning."

Madison nodded. "Good. I'll look forward to seeing you then."

The three men shook hands, and Madison and Washington took their leave, walking west on Chestnut Street. Matthew watched until they disappeared in the crowd, then turned back toward the Statehouse, anxious to see if other delegates had arrived. It was well past one o'clock when he watched the delegation from South Carolina gather at the door into the East Room to have their credentials checked, and Joseph Fry studied each of the four men. John Rutledge, Charles Cotesworth Pinckney and his much younger cousin Charles Pinckney, and Pierce Butler—the entire delegation. All too well Matthew understood that these four men, together with the delegation from North Carolina, had set their heels on the question of slavery: they would not tolerate change. The overt threat loomed as a great, black, ominous cloud. At best it might be settled by hot debate; at worst, it would divide the convention and destroy it, and with it, the hope of a United States. He watched as Fry explained the convention had not formally convened, for lack of a quorum of states. The South Carolinians talked for a moment among themselves, then walked down the corridor and left the building.

It was past three o'clock when Matthew walked out the doors into the afternoon sunshine and strode hastily to the Indian Queen Hotel on Fourth Street. He entered the lavish foyer with great oak columns reaching the high ceiling, and a gigantic fireplace with a great, delicately carved mantel of dark maple covering most of one wall. A massive, cut glass chandelier hung on gold chains from the frescoed ceiling to dominate the entire vast room. Matthew stopped, astonished at the Monday midafternoon swarm of people. The cushioned chairs at every table were filled. Men dressed in black suits and white shirts with lace at their throats and breasts, and women demure in the latest silken finery stood in groups, chattering, some caught up in the accepted social sport of being obvious and impressive in luxurious, sophisticated places, while the men had papers spread at random on the tables and were locked eye-to-eye in heated political, or mercantile, or religious exchanges. He worked his way through the crowd, begging the pardon of those he jostled, until he reached the alcove where expensive, high-topped beaver hats, and gloves, and colorful parasols were neatly arranged on shelves and in small compartments. He stood to one side intently listening to the muddle of talk, and studying faces, searching for delegates. Minutes passed before he understood that the Grand Convention was not the only significant gathering in town. One large table in the corner of the vast lobby-restaurant was surrounded by devout Baptists, with offended expressions on their faces at the opulence they were witnessing, which in their opinion could only be termed "decadent." Two tables to their right was a convocation of Presbyterians, competing with the Baptists in their revulsion at the sin around them. In another corner a collection of abolitionists stared judgmentally down raised noses at the slave-owning multitude. In the furthest corner sat twelve men, stiff in full military regalia, gold and stars in obvious abundance on their shoulder epaulets. Matthew studied them for more than a minute before he understood they were of the Society of Cincinnati—the military society for revolutionary war officers fostered by General Henry Knox, membership in which was to be perpetuated by blood lines only, father to son. George Washington was the most prominent member of the society but had excused his presence from their gathering to attend instead the Grand Convention.

It was approaching four o'clock when Matthew worked his way back through the crowd, out the huge, etched, glass-paneled double doors, into the street, and slowed while his eyes adjusted to the blinding glare of a late spring sun in a clear blue sky. He made his way to Market Street and turned west toward Thirteenth Street and Mother Asher's boardinghouse. He walked slowly, thoughtfully watching the faces and feeling the mood of those he passed. They seemed alive, outgoing, optimistic, caught up in the excitement and pivotal importance of their times. And he marveled once more at the cleanliness and orderliness of the streets and the pride the Philadelphians clearly took in their city.

The sun was gone, the western sky was golden, and twilight was creeping when Matthew finished his fig pudding at the boardinghouse table, paid his compliments to Mother Asher, and climbed the stairs up to his room. He lighted his desk lamp, removed and hung his coat, dropped his cravat on the bed, and rolled his shirtsleeves two turns before he sat down, leaned slightly forward, hands clasped before him on the desktop. For a time he remained silent, ordering his recollections of the day before he reached for his journal and quill. Then for twenty minutes the only sound in the room was the quiet scratching of the split end of the feather on the paper until he finished his entry for that day.

He laid the quill down, read what he had written, then closed the book and pushed it over to the corner of the desk. Behind him the room had grown dark, and the lamp was casting long, misshapen shadows on the floor and walls. He drew a fresh piece of paper from the drawer, squared it on the desktop, dipped the quill, and began to write again.

> May 14, 1787
> My Dear Family,
>   I must first say that you are foremost in my thoughts
> as I sit alone in my room. Mother Asher is a gracious
> hostess, the room is fine, and the meals have been
> excellent. However, the world over, there is no place
> more dear, nor persons more precious, than home, and
> yourselves.

He paused and reflected, weighing whether he should tell of the disturbing failure of most of the delegates to appear at the Statehouse on the first day of the convention. He dipped his pen and continued.

> Today was the appointed day for convening at the
> Statehouse, however, I am saddened and alarmed to
> report that of the 74 men expected, only sixteen
> appeared, from four states. Virginia, Pennsylvania,
> Delaware, and South Carolina. It was my privilege to pass
> a few words with James Madison and George Washington
> as they left the East Room of the Statehouse after they
> adjourned their first meeting. They had accomplished
> nothing, since they can not commence the official
> business until a quorum of the states are represented.
> They will meet again tomorrow morning, and I shall be
> there. I dearly hope that enough other delegates will
> appear to permit the conference to proceed. It is very

disquieting to realize that it is possible this convention could fail from apathy or hopelessness on the part of those appointed to save this nation.

I will continue this letter tomorrow evening, and I pray the news will be more encouraging. Know that both of you are in my heart, and my prayers, always.

In the yellow lamplight he read the half-page, then placed it in the drawer. He rose and walked to the window to pull back the curtain and peer down at the intersection of Thirteenth Street and Market, eyes widened in surprise. Lamps on tall posts on both sides of the street shone in the night, and nearby a constable tended his beat, nodding amiably to passersby who walked the night streets unafraid, unconcerned, chatting as they moved on. Half an hour later, Matthew hung his clothing in the wardrobe, pulled on his nightshirt, and knelt beside his bed with his hands clasped before his bowed head.

He was up with the sun, washed, shaved, and at the breakfast table with the other guests when Mother Asher bustled in with a large steaming bowl of cooked oatmeal laced with raisins, bread hot from the oven, berry jam, and buttermilk. By half-past eight he was at the Statehouse, standing at the door into the East Room, intently watching the heavy flow of men moving about in the corridor. At ten minutes before nine o'clock, the Virginia delegation, led by Washington and Madison, worked its way to the door, where Madison turned to Matthew as the others filed into the chamber.

"Good morning, sir. Mr. Dunson, as I recall. Matthew Dunson."

Matthew nodded deeply. "Good morning, Mr. Madison. I believe you are the first this morning. Do you know if others have arrived in town?"

Madison thought for a moment. "A few. Not many."

Matthew continued. "Is there an explanation for their failure?"

Madison shrugged. "The rains last week may have slowed some who have a long distance to come. Stopped others. I think they'll get here sooner or later. In the meantime we're doing what we can." A light came into his eyes as he patted the heavy leather carrying case beneath his arm.

Matthew asked, "Your delegation is working on something?"

"A few things we think will be helpful. We'll meet daily until the convention begins." He gestured to the door. "I should go in with my colleagues. Nice seeing you again, Mr. Dunson."

"The pleasure is mine."

Madison submitted his credentials to Joseph Fry, and Matthew studied the delegate as he disappeared into the East Room, aware that there was something in the little man that somehow silently drew respect. There was an unmistakable aura about Madison, a confidence that he knew who he was, why he was here, and where he was going.

For a few moments Matthew reflected on his notes of Madison. *Born March 16, 1731, at Port Conway, Virginia—childhood spent on a 5,000 acre tobacco and grain plantation in Orange County, Virginia, with one hundred slaves—schooled first at home, then preparatory school, then Princeton College in New Jersey—a dedicated student—plunged into the writings of Locke, Newton, Swift, Hume, Voltaire, Cicero, and a dozen other great philosophers from all ages—graduated Princeton 1771 with a Bachelor of Arts Degree—continued studies under the tutorship of Princeton President John Witherspoon, a strict Scottish moralist and pragmatist—entered the ministry, then the law, but soon realized his future was in the study of human nature and government and spent eleven years refining his conclusions—his brilliant and creative mind were legendary—a member of the Virginia Assembly that created the first Virginia Constitution—elected to the Confederation Congress from 1780 to 1784—then the Virginia Assembly from 1784 to 1787—unequaled in his powers of logic and reason—of him Fisher Ames of the Confederation Congress said: "He is a thorough master of almost every public question that can arise or he will spare no pains to become so—well-versed in public life, was bred to it—it is rather a science than a business with him"—small in stature and delicate of bone and structure, heart-shaped face of refined features, a voice that was rather high and soft, and dark blue eyes that penetrated.*

Joseph Fry closed the door into the East Room, and Matthew reflected on what he knew of James Madison. *He lacks the physical stature of George Washington and the sagacious wit of Franklin, but neither of them can touch his mind or his grasp on government. Madison is the one to watch.*

At ten o'clock Matthew nervously fingered his watch from his vest pocket, then replaced it. By his count, there were but three more delegates inside than yesterday. At eleven o'clock the doors opened, and the small entourage walked out, stone-faced, paying little attention to the traffic in the huge corridor. Matthew fell in stride with Madison.

"Adjourned for the day?"

Madison tossed up his free hand. "Nothing else we could do. We'll reconvene again in the morning."

The delegates reconvened the following morning, May sixteenth, and the following two mornings, May seventeenth and eighteenth, still lacking a quorum, able to do nothing more than adjourn and wait and hope. On Friday evening, May eighteenth, Matthew sat alone in his room, the lamp casting distorted shadows on the walls. His chair was turned away from the table, and he sat hunched over with his elbows on his knees, slowly rubbing the palms of his hands together in despair, staring at them unseeing, his thoughts dark and foreboding.

Five days, and only half enough delegates to convene with a quorum. Is this how it ends? Nothing? No one?

He did not know how long he had sat thus before he opened the drawer to the table, drew out the unfinished letter to Kathleen and John, squared it on the tabletop, and picked up his quill.

> May 18, 1787
>
> My Dearest Family,
>
> For the fifth consecutive day there are not enough delegates for the convention to commence its business. In fact, there are less than half enough to make a quorum. I do not know the reason. I only know that I cannot recall the last time I felt such blackness inside. I will remain here until a quorum convenes, or until the convention is abandoned. I am no longer able to determine if I expected too much, or they expected too little to come of such a convention.
>
> How I wish I could be home with both of you. The center of my life is there, not here. Aside from my discouragement, I am well; do not fear for my health. But I ask that each night you seek the blessing of the

Almighty upon this effort. I will post this letter
tomorrow.

I send my love,
Your obd't husband and father,
Matthew Dunson.

Notes

The description of the enlightened plan by which the city fathers laid out
the city of Philadelphia, as detailed in this chapters is factual. See F. E.
Compton Company Division of Encyclopedia Britannica, Inc., *Compton's
Encyclopedia and Fact-Index*, volume 19, pp. 251a and 251b. With a population of
45,000, Philadelphia was the largest city in the United States and had become
the center of commercial, scientific, financial, social, political, and cultural
affairs, boasting residency of such leading citizens as Benjamin Franklin, Robert
Morris, Charles Willson Peale, David Rittenhouse, and others. Rossiter, *1787:
The Grand Convention*, pp. 25–26, 33; Leckie, *George Washington's War*, pp. 247–48.

The size of the United States, and the wealth therein, as herein described,
is accurate. The western lands lying between the thirteen states and the
Mississippi River were hotly contested by both the adjacent states and land
speculators, who saw and coveted the wealth. Rossiter, *1787: The Grand
Convention*, pp. 24–25, 50–51; Bernstein, *Are We to Be a Nation?* pp. 39–40.

The realization by the leaders of the time that they stood at a singular
crossroads in history and their fear that failure to seize the moment would result
in a disunion among the thirteen states are generally set forth in Warren, *The
Making of the Constitution*, chapter one, which consists of 54 pages and is titled
"Fears of Disunion."

Matthew Dunson's reflections on the "great secrets" the Americans had
learned concerning the "laws of nature" and that the Almighty intended man to
be free, with rights to life, liberty and property earned by honest industry, is
set forth in excellent detail in Rossiter, *1787: The Grand Convention*, pp. 59–61, as
is the fact that skeptical European monarchs predicted the United States would
fail, p. 24.

The Indian Queen Hotel on Fourth Street was Philadelphia's most sumptuous hostelry and the gathering place for just about any event of note. Rossiter,
1787: The Grand Convention, p. 181; Warren, *The Making of the Constitution*, p. 118.

In consideration of the anticipated Grand Convention and in an effort to minimize outside noise, the City of Philadelphia did in fact haul in dirt which was spread over the cobblestone paved streets adjacent to the Statehouse. Farrand, *The Framing of the Constitution of the United States,* p. 55; Rossiter, *1787: The Grand Convention,* p. 160; Warren, *The Making of the Constitution,* p. 304; Bernstein, *Are We to Be a Nation?* p. 155.

Joseph Fry is an historical figure who served as doorman for the Grand Convention. Farrand, *The Records of the Federal Convention,* volume I, p. 2.

The description herein of James Madison is accurate. Rossiter, *1787: The Grand Convention,* pp. 124–26. Madison was once described as being as big as "half a piece of soap." Moyers, *Report from Philadelphia,* page dated Wednesday May 23, 1787. (This resource book by Moyers identifies the pages by dates, not numbers.)

The Grand Convention was scheduled to convene May 14, 1787, but on that day only two delegations appeared, Virginia and Pennsylvania, five short of the seven states required to form a quorum. The available delegates met only to adjourn until a quorum of states appeared. Warren, *The Making of the Constitution,* p. 101.

CHAPTER V

★ ★ ★

*S*ix-year-old John Matthew Dunson glared at his image in the
mirror that hung on the wall just above the porcelain basin in the washroom next to his bedroom, teeth set in angry frustration as he tried once
more to conquer the rooster tail that stood up at the back of his head.
He had used water until his hair was dripping and plastered it down four
times, only to have it stand straight up again, stubborn, refusing to die.
He had washed his hands and face for breakfast, and had somewhat succeeded in establishing a part in the left side of his hair, albeit the part
more closely resembled a winding country road than a straight line. It
was the rooster tail that he could not subdue. It seemed to him it had a
mind of its own and was defying him with gleeful vengeance. As the
battle climaxed, he felt the sick realization that he was going to lose. For
one brief moment a vision of scissors flashed in his mind, and he felt
the evil temptation to sneak to his mother's sewing room, find the shears,
creep back to the washroom, and assassinate the rooster tail. Reluctantly,
he abandoned the idea, dropped the comb beside the basin on the washstand, and stalked out the door and down the hallway to the dining
room.

The rooster tail was forgotten at the scent of cooked oatmeal mixed
with dried apple slices steaming on the kitchen stove and the sight of his
mother standing at the table pouring buttermilk into a glass beside his
bowl. A can of brown sugar, a small cutting board with slices of warm

bread, a pitcher of milk, and a saucer with a large pat of home-churned butter surrounded his glass of buttermilk. Today was Monday in Boston, and that meant washtubs and scrub boards and water buckets and clothes hanging on the line in the backyard. His mother was dressed in an ankle-length gray work dress, high-topped leather shoes, and a thick blue apron. Her long, dark hair was pulled back and tied behind her head. Though he had given it no conscious thought, for him, she was the most beautiful woman in the world.

She glanced at him as he approached the table, and he saw her make a mother's instant appraisal. He was wearing old, hand-me-down leather shoes that were too big and made a clomping sound as he walked on the hardwood floors, a worn, tan cotton work shirt, and his heavy brown trousers with the broad straps over his shoulders. The look of approval came into her eyes for a moment, and he knew he had passed inspection for the day's work.

"Take your place," she said, and he climbed onto Matthew's chair at the head of the table to peer at her place to his left, where there was no bowl or glass. He looked up at her, worry in his wide eyes.

"Don't you want any buttermilk?" he asked, "or breakfast?"

She shook her head. "Not hungry."

He asked no further. In the past ten days she had not eaten breakfast five times, and had only picked at her midday dinner and supper. It had caused him worry, and he had asked why. She had only shrugged and smiled and said, "Just not hungry. You're not to worry."

She brought the pot from the stove to scoop twice into his breakfast bowl with the large wooden spoon, then spoke as she returned the smoking pot to the stove and set the lid on it, clanging. "Butter your bread while it's hot," she called to him.

He reached for a slice of warm bread with one hand and his knife with the other as she walked back from the kitchen to sit down next to him. He smoothed the butter thickly on the bread then laid the knife down.

"Grace," she said, and he bowed his head and clasped his hands beneath his chin and repeated, "Almighty Father, we thank thee for this food and ask thee to bless it and may we do good always and bless father to be safe and to come home soon, Amen."

He raised his face to peer into hers for approval, she nodded slightly, and he reached for the large, decorated can of sugar. She sat unmoving to watch him sprinkle the brown sugar, then reach for the milk pitcher. He carefully added the milk, slowly so it would not splash, then set the pitcher down and reached for his spoon and the buttered bread at the same time. The rooster tail swayed slightly each time he leaned forward for the next spoonful of sweet, warm oatmeal, and again when took the next bite of the bread. He did not see the mix of emotions in his mother's eyes as she watched him eat, nor would he have understood the love, and the fear, and the fierce, selfless need to protect him in the innocence and trust of his childish world.

He finished, wiped his face on his napkin, gathered his bowl and utensils, and carried them to the kitchen to set them on the cupboard while Kathleen took the milk, buttermilk, and butter out the backdoor into the bright sunlight of a calm, warm, beautiful May morning in Boston. The outer door to the root cellar was already open as she had left it, leaned against its post, and she descended the six steps to the inner door and entered the deep shadows and the dank coolness to store the food. John was in the kitchen, waiting, and he faced her as she entered, waiting for her to speak.

"Let's get the sheets off our beds," she said, and led him through the archway into the hall where she turned left to her bedroom while he turned right, to his. Three minutes later they were back in the kitchen with a large woven-reed basket filled with the week's wash on the floor between them. Without a word Kathleen turned and John followed her out to the woodyard where they dragged the low, heavy bench from beneath the lean-to that covered the woodyard, out to its place near the backdoor, followed by the three wooden washtubs, which they wrestled onto the bench. Ten minutes later they had the nine-foot, iron tripod in place with the black, cast-iron kettle dangling from the chain, and a fire crackling beneath it. John walked to the well and lowered the bucket into the black hole while Kathleen came behind, a wooden bucket with a rope handle in either hand.

Twenty minutes later, water was steaming in the kettle, and Kathleen used a long-handled, wooden dipper to scoop it into the first two wash-tubs—one for scrubbing, one for hot rinse, the third for cold rinse. She dipped a clean rag in the hot water and walked to the clotheslines strung outward from the woodyard to a heavy pole frame, and walked rapidly back and forth, clutching the wet, hot rag over the lines to wipe them clean. Then she and John half-dragged, half-carried the clothes basket from the kitchen, and Kathleen carved curls from the large, brown bar of homemade soap into the first washtub and stirred the water with a peeled oak stick until the soap had mostly dissolved. Then she lifted the first sheet into the hot water and poked it down. Dropping the corrugated, wooden washboard into the tub, she gathered the sopping sheet in her hands, hunched over, and began the monotonous, arduous labor of bearing down hard as she rubbed the sheet up and down, up and down the board. Finished, she wrung what soapy water she could from the dripping sheet, dropped it into the hot water rinse, poked it down, plucked up the next sheet and poked it into the soapy water, then wrung out the rinsed sheet and dropped it into the cold water rinse. She poked it down, worked it with her hands, then lifted it out, handed one end to John, and the two of them twisted in opposite directions until it quit dripping. Then they carried it to the clotheslines where John handed her the clothes-pegs while she hung the sheet, and then they both walked back to the washtub to start the second sheet through the rinse, wring, and hang process.

By half-past ten o'clock, Boston was sweltering in the heat of a humid spring day. John watched his mother wipe with her long sleeve at her forehead and blot the tiny beads of sweat that hung from the end of her nose and the point of her chin. He stood nearby, trousers and shoes damp, rooster tail forgotten, eyes squinted against the bright sun, wishing he could go into the cool of the house, thinking of his two armies of toy soldiers in the big box under his bed, one clad in red coats, one in blue, wishing he could once again pit them against each other at the

Battle of Yorktown the way Father and Billy Weems had told him, or at the fight at Cowpens when old Daniel Morgan had tricked the terrible British Colonel Banastre Tarleton and beat him so badly, according to Uncle Caleb.

But he could not leave the work and go into the house. Father had told him he could sit in his place at the table as long as he did the work of man of the house, and he had to do it. He did not think about why, he only knew he had to do it, no matter what. He stood near his mother, perspiring, shifting his weight, moving his feet, ready to do the things he had been taught should be done by the man of the house, to help her.

The sun was directly overhead when John watched his mother hang the last of the clothes that were finished, place her hands on her hips, and lean back for a moment before she spoke.

"Time for dinner," she said, and John gratefully followed her into the house. She set two places at the table along with sliced bread and plum jam, then disappeared into the root cellar for milk, strips of cooked mutton, and the remainder of a small block of cheese. They said grace, and John silently began to eat. He nodded when his mother said, "Chew it well," and for a few seconds slowed before her order was forgotten, and he chewed on. He was aware when Kathleen reached for a small piece of cheese and broke a tiny corner off a slice of bread to put into her mouth and work at it indifferently.

John looked at her in silent question.

She forced a smile and shrugged. "Just not hungry."

For a moment he stared into her eyes, and she broke it off before he could speak. "Want any more cheese or meat? Milk?"

He shook his head.

She stood and gathered the food and started for the door. "When I get back from the root cellar we'll clear the table and rest a while. You can play with your soldiers if you like."

He brightened and reached for his milk glass.

With dinner finished, John trotted down the hall to his room, dropped to his knees, and drew out the large box of soldiers. He had the British soldiers inside the imaginary Redoubt Number Ten on the banks of the imaginary York River at the imaginary Yorktown, and was lining the Americans in a semicircle for their predawn attack when he heard his mother in the hall, and turned to look. She stopped in the doorframe.

"I'm going to lie down for half an hour. We need to finish before four o'clock. I'm expecting Doctor Soderquist."

John's eyes widened and he blurted defensively, "I don't feel sick."

"Not for you. I just need to talk with him for a few minutes. Leave your soldiers out. You can play with them while he's here."

It was twenty minutes past three o'clock when they leaned the last washtub against the wall beneath the lean-to and walked into the kitchen. Their clothes were damp from the washing and wringing of the laundry, and they were both sweating in the heat and humidity. By five minutes before four o'clock they were both washed and wearing clean, dry clothes. At ten minutes past four o'clock a rap came at the door, and John watched his mother stride across the parlor and swing the large door open. Facing her was Doctor Walter Soderquist, large, shambling, heavyjowled, a great shock of white hair, large nose, bushy white brows, and gray eyes that said he had seen and survived most of what mortal life had to offer. In his left hand was a small black leather bag.

For John, Doctor Soderquist was part of Boston, like the waterfront and the North Church and the great grassy green. He had been there for every sickness or ailment of the Thorpe family and the Dunson family since John could remember. He did not know why his mother wanted to talk with him, nor did he question it. He knew that grown-ups had secrets that they kept from children, although he was not clear as to why. All he knew was that his father and his mother and his Grandmother Margaret had at different times each held his chin in their hand while they looked him in the eye and said, "Someday you'll understand." It left him struggling with the question, "When is someday?" He was already six and acting as the man of the house. Wasn't that someday?

"Do come in, Doctor," his mother said.

John watched the large man move himself inside the door, and for the first time saw that he moved slowly, with a heavy, crooked, oak cane supporting his right side. Never before had the doctor relied on a cane. John silently stared.

"Thank you, Kathleen," the doctor said and moved awkwardly through the door. He shook his head in disgust. "Can't get used to this blessed cane," he growled.

"Come into the parlor and take a seat. Would you care for some cider?"

Soderquist brightened. "That sounds good, if it's not too much trouble."

Within two minutes they were seated across the table from each other, each with a cup of cider at hand. Kathleen looked at John.

"There's a cup of cider on the kitchen cupboard for you. You can take it to your room and play with your soldiers. The doctor and I will be finished shortly."

John spun on his heel and trotted into the kitchen, then down the hallway to his room. He stopped long enough to drink long at the sweetness of the apple juice, then put the cup on the nightstand beside his bed. For several moments he stared at his soldiers, weighing which was most important: storming Yorktown's Redoubt Number Ten or sneaking back down the hall to listen to why his mother had asked Doctor Soderquist to come visiting.

Doctor Soderquist won.

Silently, slowly, he crept down the hall, avoiding the two places that squeaked if stepped on. He could hear their voices in hushed conversation as he came nearer, and he stopped a scant six feet from the archway into the parlor, listening to the voice of Doctor Soderquist.

". . . how long since? Six weeks? Eight?"

"Four."

"Been regular before that?"

"Yes."

"Smells give you nausea? Food?"

"Yes. Sometimes I can't eat."

"Well, child," the doctor said with finality, "I don't think there's a question. It sticks out all over you like the plague. That look in your eye.

Your face. Give it about seven more months—around Christmas or maybe New Year's—and it'll take care of itself. I'll be back in about a month to give you an examination to confirm it. In the meantime, my condolences for your discomfort and my congratulations for the blessing that's coming. Seems the Almighty tried to keep things in balance when he saw to it the greatest blessings come with the heaviest price."

He drained his cider cup and smacked his lips. "That was sure worth the trip." He handed her his empty cup then shrugged and heaved his frame back onto his feet. "John's looking more like his grandfather every day. Stout little fellow. I can see some of Matthew in him, too. And you."

Kathleen stood to face him, smiling. "He's a good boy."

"I need to get started for home," Soderquist said. "Can't move like I used to. You schedule with my wife. We'll do the examination next month."

"How much do I owe you?"

"Wait 'til it's over."

John listened to the footsteps across the hardwood parlor floor, then the door opening and closing, and his mother walked back to the kitchen with the two empty cups. John waited for a few seconds before he walked through the archway.

"Is Doctor Soderquist gone?"

"Yes."

"Why was he here?"

"You'll know in a while."

John shook his head. *What was so secret? When was a while?*

After the supper table had been cleared, and he had dried some of the dishes while Kathleen washed, John sat close to his mother on the sofa, facing the great fireplace as she read to him from the Bible, letting him follow each word with his finger. Then they knelt for prayer, and Kathleen took him back to his room where she tucked him into bed, turned down the lamp to a faint light, and left the door half open as she walked back into the hall. John waited until the house was quiet, then crept back down the dimly lighted hallway to the library. Through the crack in the doorway he saw his mother seated at the writing table in the corner, a piece of paper before her, and a quill in her hand. For a time she sat with her head tilted slightly back, then leaned forward, and for several minutes the quiet scratching of the quill was the only sound. She laid the quill down, read what she had written, folded it, sealed it with wax, and laid it on the writing table.

When she stood, John quickly vanished back down the hallway to his room and was buried beneath the comforter when Kathleen silently opened his bedroom door to study him before she retreated across the hall. He heard her bedroom door open as she wearily entered to go to her rest, and he lay for a time in the dark shadows, deep in thought about what the secret was that he would learn about at Christmas. Slowly John's thoughts drifted, and the work and worries of the day faded. His muscles relaxed, and his eyes closed, and then he was at Redoubt Number Ten with the Americans, and the British were losing.

Note

John Matthew Dunson is the six-year-old son of Matthew and Kathleen Dunson, all of whom are fictional characters.

CHAPTER VI

★ ★ ★

A scatter of wispy clouds flamed red and yellow at sunrise, and by eight o'clock fluffy balls of cotton speckled the bright blue Philadelphia skies. On the waterfront, men of the sea cast narrowed eyes at the heavens, reading the signs, making calculations. At Mother Asher's Boardinghouse, Matthew Dunson parted the curtains in his bedroom and leaned forward to peer upward through the half-open window. His practiced eye told him the isolated, fluffy cottonballs would soon collect into huge, white, billowing clouds. The thunderheads would turn to gray, then purple, and when the tons of water inside them became too heavy, Philadelphia would enjoy a spring cloudburst. He could smell it and feel it. It was coming. Late today. Maybe tonight. Without conscious thought it became part of his plan for the day.

He knotted his cravat, then descended the stairs down to the kitchen where Mother Asher was scurrying about to bring the bread to a golden brown at the same time a huge omelet filled with diced ham, chopped onions, and green peppers reached perfection. She smiled her good morning to Matthew.

"Three more minutes. Take your place at the table."

For a time, silence held as the nine guests settled into their portions of the morning's offerings. The omelet was a work of art, the bread without fault, the apple cider sweet. The usual morning pleasantries began only after they had tasted each, and they were halfway through the meal before Matthew noticed that the place at the far end of the table was empty. The crippled Ira Bouchard was missing.

He spoke to Mother Asher. "Is Mr. Bouchard ill?"

She shook her head and there was a sadness in her eyes as she answered. "He left early to make arrangements to leave Philadelphia. He'll be back sometime today, but I believe he plans to leave Monday." For a moment the guests looked at each other in question, and the hush held for a few moments before they continued with their eating.

With breakfast finished, Matthew went to his room to gather his paperwork for the walk down Market Street to the Statehouse. At the bottom of the stairs he stepped into the kitchen and observed to Mother Asher, "I'm surprised at Mr. Bouchard's leaving. I thought he was here to observe the convention."

Mother Asher stopped piling dirty dishes into the basin of hot, soapy water. "He was. But this is the tenth day, and it hasn't even started and only heaven knows when it will. Maybe never. Anyway, I think it's money. I don't think he has the money to stay."

"I'm sorry to hear that," Matthew said as he started through the archway.

Mother Asher followed him, speaking as they went. "So am I. That poor, dear man—hurt in the war, wife and son gone on, daughter down south, grandchildren he's never seen." She shook her head then paused at the front door to watch Matthew hurry to the corner and turn west onto Market Street before she returned to her kitchen.

Matthew was halfway to the Statehouse on Sixth Street when the sun disappeared behind a small gather of billowing white clouds, and a faint stir of breeze came in from the waterfront. Then the clouds passed, the breeze died, and the city once again brightened in the sunlight as Matthew walked on. *Tonight. The rain will come in the night.*

At Sixth Street he turned south to Chestnut, then entered the now familiar Statehouse, and worked his way through the usual morning multitude of judges in scarlet robes, lawyers in black robes, contestants gathering in the Supreme Court chambers to learn if they had won or lost in their lawsuits, and a host of others hurrying between offices on both floors of the building to conduct the affairs of the State of Pennsylvania.

Joseph Fry smiled his greeting as Matthew approached, and Matthew spoke. Fry could not miss the anxiety in his voice.

"Any more delegates this morning?"

"Not yet, Mr. Dunson. A few more arrived late yesterday. I think Alexander Hamilton is here for New York. And Rufus King for Massachusetts."

Quickly Matthew made calculations, and his face fell. "Still not a quorum. Anyone inside? The Virginians? Mr. Madison?"

"No, sir."

Matthew inquired, "Has Mr. Madison ever mentioned to you what it is he carries in that leather case?"

"Not Mr. Madison, but I recall them standing here for a minute after they adjourned two or three days ago. George Mason talked about it. Mr. Madison came to Philadelphia with a written plan. Has apparently worked on it for months. He's been meeting with the Virginia delegation every day since they got here, going over the plan point by point. Mr. Mason said Mr. Madison makes a written record of everything." He smiled. "He's the smallest of the delegation, but when Mr. Madison speaks, they listen. Even General Washington."

Fry's eyes diverted from Matthew, and he turned to face Nathaniel Gorham, Elbridge Gerry, and Rufus King, from Massachusetts. Each held a parchment in his hand on which the great seal of the State of Massachusetts was prominently stamped, together with the few lines of beautiful cursive handwriting, and the signature, that declared their authority to attend the Grand Convention.

"Good morning, gentlemen," Fry said, quickly scanning their documents as they passed into the convention hall. The door closed behind them, and within seconds other delegates began to arrive in twos and threes. For fifteen minutes the sporadic appearances continued— Madison and Washington and Mason, the two cousins Pinckney, Rutledge, Butler—and then the arrivals ended. Matthew made a mental calculation and shook his head.

"Still two states short of a quorum."

The doorman sobered and looked him in the eye. "Ten days overdue. I'm starting to wonder. Worry."

"Anyone suggested what they'll do if they can't raise a quorum?"

There was a pause before Fry answered. "Nothing. They'll go home, and that will be the end of it."

"And what of the country?"

"Sectionalize is my guess. North, Middle, South. Three separate countries."

Matthew softly blew air for a moment. "We'll have destroyed ourselves."

Fry's face was a blank, his eyes dead. "Like Europe. Fragmented. Disputes. Wars."

Within fifteen minutes the doors opened and the entire assembly filed out. There was little talk among them, and the delegates did not linger, but made their way directly out of the building. Matthew followed them out into the overcast light to watch them separate and merge into the Thursday morning Philadelphia traffic and disappear. He pondered a moment, then walked quickly to the Indian Queen. With the conventions of the Presbyterians, Baptists, and the Society of the Cincinnati concluded and their crowds gone, the great, lavish foyer was nearly vacant at this hour of the morning. A few of the delegates were scattered about at tables, talking, waiting for their orders of a late breakfast. Matthew saw none that he shared familiarity with. He walked back out into the street, turned north, and hurried to the huge boardinghome of Mrs. House. Inside, he climbed the stairs to the second floor and walked down the hall to the room of James Madison. He knocked, waited, knocked again, and there was only silence. He was turning to leave when the light sound of steady footsteps on the hardwood staircase reached him, and he stopped to wait. James Madison appeared at the head of the stairs, alone.

The little man with the piercing blue eyes nodded a greeting. "Mr. Dunson! Have you come to see me?"

"Yes."

Madison worked the key in the lock. "Come in." They entered the small room, Madison set his leather case on the writing table heaped with papers and books, gestured, and they sat down in facing chairs.

"What can I do for you?"

Matthew took a moment to compose his thoughts before he spoke. "I was at the Statehouse this morning. This is the tenth day and still no quorum. I'm concerned."

Madison's brows peaked, and he spoke in his high, soft, quiet voice. "With good reason. All of us are—those of us who are here. George Mason is irritated at the pomp and ceremony of Philadelphia. General Washington is showing impatience with those who don't understand the meaning of punctuality. I'm discouraged at the lack of preparation I sense in the others. If we don't soon reach a quorum, I am fearful of what will happen."

Matthew put the pivotal question to him. "Would those here go home?"

"They very well could. All these men bear heavy responsibilities. They're willing to give time for their country, but not to waste it on a failed project. If they do go home, I doubt they will return."

"General Washington?"

"Concerned."

"Can anything be done? Anything I can do?"

"Nothing. Wait. Be patient."

"Are you meeting with the Virginia delegates again this afternoon?"

"The usual. Three o'clock at the home of Robert Morris. Little remains for us to do until we reach a quorum and convene."

For several seconds the two sat in silence, searching for a way to force what could not be forced. Finally, Matthew stood and gestured to the leather carrying case on the writing table.

"I'll leave you to your work. I appreciate your time."

Madison stood, nearly a foot shorter than Matthew, and raised a hand. "Wait. Would it ease your mind if you came to our three o'clock meeting at the Morris mansion?"

Matthew stopped in surprise. "Wouldn't my presence interfere?"

Madison reflected for a moment. "I doubt it. They know who you are—why you're here. Might be a good thing."

"Are you certain?"

"Yes. Come along."

"Thank you. I'll be there."

Matthew said little during the midday meal at Mother Asher's table, and at three o'clock, beneath a gray overcast that hid the afternoon sun, he was at the huge set of double doors in the front of the Robert Morris mansion at Sixth and Market Streets. A gray-haired, round-shouldered, uniformed servant answered his knock.

"May I tell Mr. Morris who is calling?"

"Matthew Dunson. I was invited to be here by Mr. James Madison."

The servant bowed slightly and gestured Matthew inside. The entry was massive. An oak stairway spiraled upward two floors. A great stone fireplace with a matching, carved oak mantel nearly filled one wall. Paintings, great and small, graced the walls. A figure sculpted from marble of a biblical woman holding a water pitcher on her shoulder dominated one corner. Matthew listened to the fading click and the echo of the heels of the elderly servant on the hardwood floor as he disappeared down a broad hallway to his right. A door opened, closed, opened again, and the servant reappeared.

"This way, sir."

Matthew followed him back down the hallway rich with murals on both walls and gold-gilded lamp fixtures. The servant pushed open a massive, dark door, and held it while Matthew entered the library of the great Morris mansion.

Before coming to Philadelphia for the convention, he had created in his mind an imaginary library befitting the grandest mansion and the richest man in America. But never had his imaginings approached the reality. The ceiling reached two stories. Two walls were lined with oak book shelves filled with books of every description. Interspaced between the volumes were bronze and marble sculptures of all the gods of the pagan and eastern and Christian worlds and busts of the great philosophers and historical figures reaching back to the dim beginnings of the

Old Testament. One entire wall was a fireplace of cut and matched stonework, crowned with a massive, delicately hand-carved oak mantel, in the center of which was a hand-crafted clock with a twenty-inch face, mounted in carved, stained maple. A silver chandelier with three tiers of hundreds of candles hung from the heavy, overhead ridgebeam. Thick, intricately woven India carpets covered the polished hardwood floors. Original paintings by the world's masters were prominent on the walls. The faint scent of furniture oil and cleaning compound was light in the air.

On one side of the spacious room was a long, heavy oak table with sculpted legs, surrounded by twelve matching, upholstered chairs. As Matthew entered, the seven men seated at the table rose and turned to face him. Nearest was James Madison, then George Mason and George Wythe. At the head of the table was Governor Edmund Randolph, and on the far side, George Washington, James McClurg, and John Blair. The entire Virginia delegation, and some of the most prominent men in America. For an instant Matthew's eyes swept the group, and then he walked directly to James Madison.

"It is good to see you again, sir."

Madison nodded. "Nice that you could come." He turned and his hand slowly made a gesture that included all the others. "I believe you have met these gentlemen on previous occasions."

Matthew bowed. "Indeed I have. It is my great pleasure to renew their acquaintance."

Madison gestured to the chair next to his. "Would you care to be seated?"

Matthew stepped to the chair, waited for a moment, and they all sat down together. For the first time, Matthew noticed that documents and letters lay on the tabletop, some in stacks, some at random. Madison's leather carrying case lay before him, empty; the documents were in a large stack directly in front of him.

Madison's soft voice reached out. "Gentlemen, months ago Mr. Dunson counseled with Thomas Jefferson. Mr. Jefferson advised him to work through the committees of merchants in the states to form a network, as it were, of men whose primary purpose is to promote the mending of the flaws that now threaten the union. Mr. Dunson has done so. He is in Philadelphia for the convention and is much concerned that the ten-day delay bodes ill for this entire affair. I invited him here today that he may inquire of you." He turned back to Matthew. "Do you have specific questions?"

Ill at ease to suddenly be the center of attention in such a gathering, Matthew cleared his throat, then responded, nervous, halting. "Yes. Seventy-four men were commissioned—"

"Excuse me, Mr. Dunson, but you'll have to speak up if I'm to hear you," John Blair said, leaning forward and cupping an ear.

"I'm sorry," Matthew said, then in a stronger voice began again. "Seventy-four men were commissioned from the thirteen states to meet May fourteenth. This is May twenty-fourth. Less than twenty-five delegates have appeared, and less than seven states are represented. Is this convention doomed to fail?"

Matthew studied each man in turn. There was instant surprise in their eyes that he had not attempted to be solicitous, and then the surprise was hidden by a veil that dropped to shield their innermost thoughts from this tall, direct, dark-haired man who had taken a scar on his left cheek at the battle of Lake Champlain, but who was yet largely a stranger to most of them. For a few seconds the room was caught in silence. Then Madison drew a breath and spoke.

"It could be, but I do not think it will."

Madison turned to George Mason, but said nothing. Mason, high forehead, dark hair, leaned back in his chair, his round, slightly jowled face a mask, mouth drawn slightly in deep thought. Then he broke the silence.

"It will not fail for lack of delegates or states. They'll get here eventually. That isn't the problem. We have some issues between the states that are far weightier than tardy delegates."

Edmund Randolph moved in his chair, and George Wythe snorted softly under his breath, then spoke. "Population. Northern versus southern interests. Slavery. Economics. Westward expansion. River navigation rights. Tariffs." He clamped his mouth shut.

Randolph shook his head. "Those are symptoms. The fundamental fault is that the Articles of Confederation are fatally flawed. I don't know if they can be amended sufficiently to meet the need. I just don't know."

George Washington quietly said, "They can't." All eyes turned to him, waiting for him to finish his thoughts, but the fifty-five-year-old man who had carried his beloved country on his shoulders for eight long, terrible years said no more.

John Blair pointed to the stack of documents before Madison. "We've been working on those since May fourth. We can only hope our work is of some use."

Matthew straightened and stared at the pile of papers for a moment, then locked eyes with Madison, silently asking the question. Madison tapped the papers.

"These are some recommendations that we hope to present to the convention. We've gathered the best principles on government we can find from every source available and organized them in anticipation of the debates that are surely coming."

Mason cut him off. "Correction. *You* have gathered the best that can be learned about sound government, clear back to the Garden of Eden. We have only made suggestions."

Matthew saw the faint smile form on Madison's face, then pass. Madison responded, "We will offer this at the convention to those who will listen." Matthew leaned forward, and his boldness stopped every man at the table as he spoke to Madison. "General Washington has declared the Articles of Confederation cannot be amended adequate to the need." He pointed at Madison's papers. "Then these are not proposed amendments? Is this a new plan?"

In that instant a tension leaped through the room like something alive. Not one man moved, or spoke, and then Madison smiled. "These are only suggestions. We have no idea how they will be received." The others at the table stirred in their seats but remained silent as Madison's young face settled, and an intensity Matthew had not seen came into the dark blue eyes. "It was our intent that our suggestions would remain with us until they are presented at the convention."

Matthew could not miss Madison's meaning. He nodded. "I presume once they are introduced on the convention floor they will become available to the public."

"That," Madison replied, "will be decided by the delegations."

Matthew dropped his eyes in thought for a moment. "I understand. I'll wait."

The masked expressions on the faces of the six other men did not change, but the tension that had charged the room began to drain. Hunched shoulders relaxed and quiet remarks began to flow among them. Madison let a little time pass before he turned back to Matthew.

"I invited you here this afternoon for two reasons. First, I thought the resolve of this delegation would interest you. We believe the convention will occur. We're prepared. Second, you have helped create a network of committees that has the potential of being a tremendous help in doing what we think must be done later. When the time comes, your work will be as vital as ours."

Madison stopped, and Matthew's breathing slowed as the weight of Madison's words settled in. Madison's face brightened with a smile that was at once sincere and engaging. "So, Mr. Dunson, we will do our work and trust you to do yours when your time comes. Is there anything else we can do for you now?"

Matthew looked into the face of each man briefly. Their expressions were of men who understood the intricate and complex workings of human nature and had learned the necessity and the art of wearing expressions on their faces that said what they wanted at any given time. At this moment, their expressions were bland, amiable, noncommittal, and Matthew knew it. There was nothing to be gained by going further. The meeting was over.

He smiled at Madison. "No, not at this moment. If I can be of any use, will you let me know?"

"Rest assured."

Madison stood and Matthew also arose. He bowed slightly to those still seated at the table. "Gentlemen, I'm honored to be in your presence. Thank you for your time."

There were murmured responses as he turned, and Madison followed him out into the hall and down to the lavish entry. He swung the heavy door open and offered his hand to Matthew.

"Will I see you in the morning?"

"I'll be there."

Matthew stepped out through the massive front door, which quietly closed behind him, and he stood for a moment on the porch of the mansion, beneath a gigantic overhead portico supported by six tall, white columns. By ingrained habit he glanced at the gray sky, as seamen do. *It's coming. Tonight.*

He left behind the clipped, rolling grass and the fruit trees covered with white blossoms and the manicured flower beds of the Morris estate and turned west on Market, deep in thoughts and reflections on the time he had spent with the seven men from Virginia.

Suggestions. Madison said they were suggestions. Worked on them since May fourth—all seven of them—twenty days—that pile of papers was near four inches deep—and they're suggestions? Washington—the Articles of Confederation can't be amended—four inches of suggestions? Suggestions for what?

He walked on, oblivious to those he passed in the streets, watching only for buggies and carts as he crossed the streets.

Madison has the papers—not Washington, not Mason, not Randolph. Madison. It has to be a plan. A new plan.

It struck him with such force that he stopped, staring straight ahead, unseeing.

They have a new plan! For a new government! Madison couldn't say it outright, but he expects me to reach that conclusion from what he let me see and hear today! And if those men succeed in the convention, he knows he'll need the help of our committees when the new plan—whatever it is—reaches the people. That's what this meeting was all about this afternoon!

He began walking slowly. *A new plan? Why do they refuse to talk about it? Can it be that startling? Shocking? Risky? Can it?*

He took charge of his wild, racing thoughts. *Those seven? Maybe startling, but it will be solid—no foolish dream. Not those men.*
He was not prepared for the fresh leap of hope that rose in his heart.

Notes

Ira Bouchard and Mother Asher and the Asher Boardinghouse are fictional.
James Madison had taken residence in a boardinghouse owned by Mrs. House, on Fifth and Market Streets and had arrived there at least ten days before the Grand Convention was to convene to work on his notes and plan and to confer with the other members of the Virginia delegation. At the time of the Grand Convention, there were four other conventions being held in Philadelphia: Baptists, Presbyterians, Society of Cincinnati, and the abolitionists. Rossiter, *1787: The Grand Convention*, pp. 159–60; Warren, *The Making of the Constitution*, p. 100.

The mansion owned by Robert Morris on Market Street just east of Sixth Street was the most sumptuous and finest in Philadelphia, as described herein. Warren, *The Making of the Constitution*, p. 100.

On May 24, 1787, eleven days after its call, there were still not enough states to constitute a quorum. Those present met and adjourned. Warren, *The Making of the Constitution*, p. 101.

CHAPTER VII

★ ★ ★

A chill, pelting rain began in the night. By 4:00 A.M. many of the Philadelphia street lamps were dark, drowned by the steady downpour. By half-past six Matthew was in the second floor washroom of Mother Asher's, shaving. He returned to his room to sit at his writing table, hunched forward, studying his list of the seventy-four delegates to the convention. In the yellow lamplight he went over them one at a time, silently reading the notes he had made of the history of each man, his strengths, weaknesses, habits, accomplishments. At eight o'clock he was seated at the breakfast table. He took breakfast with the other guests, then set his tricorn on his head, latched his cape about his shoulders, and walked out into the rain, hunched forward, picking his way around growing puddles on the cobblestones in the light morning street traffic.

He entered the Statehouse and stopped to throw the rainwater from his dripping tricorn and cape, then walked down the nearly deserted hall to the entrance of the East Room, where he hung his wet cape and tricorn in the cloakroom and approached Fry.

"Good morning, Mr. Fry."

"Good morning, sir."

"Any arrivals?"

"None yet, sir. Might be a while in this rain."

At ten-forty the Virginia delegation arrived, dripping, hung their cloaks and hats, and came to the door digging their credentials from inner pockets. Madison, cheerful, smiling, paused to greet Matthew.

"Good morning. Rumor at the Indian Queen is that we have a quorum. New Jersey has arrived. Worst weather in two weeks, and we have a quorum."

Matthew brightened. "I hope so."

Fry glanced at their well-known credentials, checked their names on his list, and closed the door behind them. At ten minutes before eleven o'clock a few others had arrived, but far short of anything resembling a quorum, and Matthew's hopes dimmed. Then, with only minutes to spare, the Pennsylvania delegation arrived in force, and Matthew watched them admitted, to be led into the East Room by Gouverneur Morris, thumping on his wooden leg. It was exactly eleven o'clock when the front door of the building opened and more than twelve men entered, talking, condemning the weather, shaking out their cloaks and tricorns. They came to Fry who checked their credentials, and Matthew silently identified each in turn. Among them were the two second cousins from South Carolina, Charles Pinckney and Charles Cotesworth Pinckney, and behind them came John Rutledge and Pierce Butler. He watched the two Pinckneys enter the East Room, and moments later, Rutledge and Butler followed.

Matthew caught his breath. Twenty-seven in all. Six states represented. One more state would make it seven—a quorum! He stood tall, scarcely breathing as he searched the hall for enough delegates to complete the representation of one more state, and suddenly they were there. William Paterson and William Churchill Houston, both of New Jersey, walked through the doors and began peeling off their dripping capes and hats as they hurried to the cloakroom.

Matthew watched their every move, and was standing next to Fry when he checked their credentials, opened the door, and ushered them into the East Room.

Matthew spoke. "Didn't that make seven states? A quorum?"

A look of hope mixed with fear came into Fry's eyes. "Seven. They can convene."

Matthew shifted his feet, nervous, before he responded. "I wonder what they're doing in there. How they're organizing."

Fry scratched at his chin. "Time will tell. We wait."

Inside the chamber, the delegates took seats at random, with the exception of James Madison. No one paid attention when he quietly sought the table and the chair at the front of the room, facing the elevated podium on which the large desk and the upholstered chair prepared for the presiding officer had been placed. He set his large leather case on the table and sat down, a small man in a large room filled with larger men. He laid fresh, blank paper on his desk, reached for the quill on the far edge, dipped it, carefully wrote the date in the upper left corner of the first sheet of paper, and laid the quill down.

The East Room was rectangular in shape, with a high ceiling and tall curtained windows spaced in the two long, opposing walls. The entrance faced the far end of the room where the raised platform, or dais, was placed. The wall behind the dais was oak paneled with hand-carved, unremarkable adornment at the top. There was an exit door in either corner. Immediately flanking the dais on either side were two rather small marble-faced fireplaces. Little had been done to break the austere appearance; there were no paintings, nothing to interrupt the plainness of the walls except the lamps and candleholders. The bare, polished hardwood floors accented the click of leather heels, and sounds echoed slightly. An aisle led from the entrance door to the dais, with plain desks on either side prepared for the delegates, arranged at angles so that each desk faced the dais and the presiding officer, directly. On each desk was a quill, inkwell, and small fixed box for odds and ends. It was a solid, no-nonsense, practical room, intended for use in handling the business of the State of Pennsylvania.

Talk buzzed until Robert Morris, at once the financial savior of the American Revolution and entrepreneur whose risky empire of land speculation made prudent men skeptical, stood and tapped on his desk. All eyes turned to him, talk ceased, and the only sound in the room was the quiet hum of rain outside. Morris cleared his throat and began.

"Gentlemen, by the instruction and in behalf of the deputation of

Pennsylvania, I have the honor to propose George Washington, Esquire, late Commander in Chief, for president of the convention."

Loud talk filled the room and held for a time. Every soul in the room knew. George Washington was the most admired man in the nation. There was no other who symbolized everything this infant nation stood for, aspired to become. Virtuous, respected, honorable, successful, principled. It was inconceivable that any other man alive could sit in the presiding chair without diminishing the convention—tarnishing it, detracting from its luster, damaging its legitimacy.

Instantly John Rutledge of South Carolina was on his feet, thumping his desk, waiting for the talk to subside.

"With every confidence that the choice will be unanimous," he exclaimed, "I second the motion."

"Hear, hear!" Strong voices filled the room.

Without hesitation Morris and Rutledge walked to either side of Washington, who stood, and the two men escorted him to the front of the room, up onto the raised dais, to the chair from which he would preside. Washington raised a hand, the room fell silent, and every man present hung on each word the tall Virginian spoke.

"I am deeply moved by the honor you have bestowed upon me. I have long pondered the novelty of the scene of business in which I am now to act, with you. I am keenly conscious of my lack of qualifications in the position I will now occupy, since the past many years of my life have been devoted to matters far removed from those now before us. I have no doubt that I will commit error from time to time, and in those occasions I can only beg of you to be patient and indulge me in my inexperience."

Few noticed that James Madison, at his desk directly in front of Washington, was quietly but rapidly writing, catching the essence of the utterances of Washington. Citizen George Washington concluded his remarks, Rutledge and Morris returned to their chairs, and Washington took charge.

Most of those present knew that only one other man had been briefly considered for the position now filled by Washington: Benjamin

Franklin. Eighty-one years old, plagued daily by gout and failing health, the fires of youth dwindling, it was Franklin himself who made it clear the mantle of leadership must fall on Washington. He had prepared to take the floor of the convention himself to make the nomination so no one would question who was to preside, but the rain and the chill had made swinging his legs out of bed a matter of torture. He could not attend the session. He had summoned Robert Morris to his bedside and given him the high honor of nominating George Washington.

Washington sat down, scanned the desk before him, raised his face, and began.

"We will now entertain nominations for a secretary to the convention."

Nearly every man present understood that Major William Jackson of Philadelphia, not a delegate to the convention, had let it be known more than two weeks previous that he intended serving as secretary, and had campaigned openly for the position. His nomination was almost automatic, but as soon as it was seconded, a New Jersey delegate came to his feet. The room quieted, Washington recognized him, and the man spoke.

"I rise to nominate William Templeton Franklin of New Jersey to serve as secretary. Indeed, it was he who endured the lengthy and arduous task of serving as secretary to the American delegation which negotiated the Treaty of Paris with the British, which delegation included his grand-father, Benjamin Franklin."

Caught by surprise, the delegates turned to each other in question, and a buzz started. Talk held for a moment, then quieted, and they waited for a second to the nomination. It did not come. A delegate stood and said, "I call for the vote."

There was but one man whose nomination had been seconded, and the vote was obvious. William Jackson became the secretary. Hastily the men who had nominated him, and seconded the nomination, left the chamber and marched to the small room nearby where Jackson was nervously pacing. They escorted him back inside where Washington congratulated him, and directed him to take his seat. A beaming Jackson settled onto the chair at one side of the dais, surveyed his surroundings, and nodded to Washington, who moved on.

"Our next order of business will be the reading and recording of credentials."

Each delegate took his turn in standing to read the commission and credentials granted him by his home state, authorizing his actions as a delegate.

Washington waited until Jackson finished his notes, then went on.

"We shall now appoint a messenger and a doorman for the duration of the convention."

A delegate promptly stood. "I nominate Nicholas Weaver to become the official messenger and Joseph Fry to become the doorman."

It was unanimous. Weaver took his position at a desk near Jackson, and Fry remained at his post, standing at the door.

Washington nodded his approval and continued. "Nominations are now in order for a committee to prepare standing rules and orders for the conduct of our business."

Nominations were made in rapid order, seconds were made, the vote taken, and three delegates became the committee: George Mason of Virginia, Alexander Hamilton of New York, and young Charles Pinckney of South Carolina.

Washington glanced at the top of the desk, then back at the delegation. "The committee on rules is requested to have their proposals at the earliest time possible, tomorrow if they can." He paused for a moment, then went on. "I believe that concludes the business we can properly address this morning. This convention is adjourned until ten o'clock A.M. Monday next, May twenty-eighth."

It seemed everyone stood simultaneously, and talk rolled freely between the delegates. They began a slow migration toward the door, and out into the hallway, still talking among themselves. Matthew waited and watched and listened, and relief came in a rush when he heard that George Washington had been unanimously elected President. William Jackson serving as secretary came as no surprise, since Jackson's campaign for the position had been open and ongoing. Fragmented sentences about a committee of three who had a vaguely defined assignment to do something about rules brought questions in Matthew's mind, and he waited and watched for Madison. The little man was in the last three to exit the hall, his leather case tucked under one arm. Matthew approached, and Madison stopped as Matthew spoke.

"General Washington presides?"

Madison smiled immensely. "Unanimous vote. No one else was nominated."

"William Jackson?"

"Secretary. There was a suggestion about William Templeton Franklin—Benjamin's grandson—but it failed."

Matthew's forehead wrinkled in puzzlement. "Is William Jackson a delegate?"

"No. It was not required that he be a delegate. Secretary is a salaried position."

Matthew moved on. "A committee? Three men? To do what?"

"Messrs. Mason, Hamilton, and Pinckney—Charles Pinckney—assigned to draft rules of procedure."

"When do you meet next?"

"Monday morning, ten A.M."

"Anything I can do to help?"

Madison shrugged. "Wait. See what Monday brings." He drew out his pocket watch. "I should go to my room. Some writing I need to finish."

Madison pocketed his watch, and he and Matthew walked to the cloakroom, where small drippings of water had collected on the floor from the wet capes and coats, and the thick smell of wet wool hung in the air like a pall. Matthew breathed lightly while they buckled their capes over their shoulders and pushed their damp tricorns onto their heads, with the leather hatbands cold on their foreheads. They walked out the doors together, heads forward, shoulders hunched into the rain, each to go his own direction.

Matthew stopped at the door into Mother Asher's boardinghouse to shake his cape and tricorn, then stepped inside where his landlady was waiting. "Here, let me hang those for you." She did not wait for a response, but took them from him and hung them in the small cloak-room before she turned back to Matthew.

"Well?" She stood still, plump and motionless, eyebrows raised expectantly.

"They convened. Seven states were represented."

She clasped her hands to her breast. "Thank the Almighty! Did they do anything?"

"George Washington is President. William Jackson is secretary. Three men are assigned to draft rules of procedure. They reconvene Monday morning, ten A.M."

"When will they finish? When will we know?"

Matthew smiled at her impetuousness. "No one knows. Soon, I hope."

She bobbed her head. "Come to the kitchen. I held some dinner for you."

Matthew carried the covered platter of warm bread, currant jam, hot sliced mutton and steamed cabbage, with a cup of cider, up to his room and set it on his writing table while he took off his wet shoes and put on thick wool house stockings. He finished the meal, took the platter and utensils downstairs, thanked Mother Asher, and returned to his room. At his writing table, he drew the unfinished, two-page letter he had been adding to each day from its drawer, and scanned it. He dipped the quill into the ink bottle, and thoughtfully added the final entries.

> 25th May 1787
> Philadelphia
> My Dearest Family:
> Today ended the long wait. Seven states were
> represented, and the Convention was officially opened.
> George Washington was unanimously elected president,
> with William Jackson of Pennsylvania appointed
> secretary. Mr. Jackson is not a delegate. They appointed
> three men, George Mason, Charles Pinckney, and
> Alexander Hamilton as a committee to draft rules of

procedure. They adjourned and will meet again Monday next.

The weather here is cold, and a steady rain has been falling since about three o'clock this morning. My health continues good. My landlady, Mother Asher, cannot refrain from mothering me. You would enjoy her very much.

I am unable to tell you the relief I felt at the opening of the convention this morning. Mr. James Madison has recently predicted to me personally that the convention will take care of its business, although he does not presume to know what the results will be.

I close this letter by telling you that there is no time you two are not in my mind, and my heart. Tell John that if he will continue to act for me as the man of the house, it is possible I will find something to bring him. And you.

You have my love as always,

Your obd't husband and father
Matthew Dunson

He folded the letter, heated the wax over the chimney of the lamp, and sealed it, and walked quietly down the stairs to Mother Asher, bustling about the kitchen as always, preparing the supper meal. She looked at him as he entered.

"A letter?"

"For my wife."

She wiped her hands in her apron as she walked to him. "Here. I'll see it gets posted."

He handed her the letter, and coins for postage. "Thank you."

Matthew returned to his room to sit at his table, deep in thought, listening to the gentle undertone of rain falling outside. It was late in the afternoon when he heard the outside door open downstairs, and the uneven footsteps of Ira Bouchard move across the parlor entry. A few minutes passed before Matthew slipped on his shoes, took coins from the leather purse in his traveling bag, and walked steadily downstairs to the room of the crippled man. He knocked, listened, and the door swung open.

The old man raised his eyes in surprise. "I didn't expect a visitor."

"Do you have a minute?"

"Come in. I'm packing. The room is in disorder."

"That's all right." Matthew waited until Bouchard gestured to the only chair in the little room, and the two men sat down—Matthew in the chair, Bouchard on the edge of his bed.

"Is there something I can do for you?" the old man inquired.

Matthew came directly to it. "I understand you're leaving."

"Got to go home. Get back to work. I came to see the convention, but it hasn't even started, and I can't stay longer."

"It started today, but nothing will happen until next week."

The old man started, then settled. "What happened today?"

"George Washington will preside. They appointed a committee to make rules. Nothing else."

The old man's eyes shined. "Gen'l Washington? Then it will be all right. It will be all right."

Matthew nodded. "I think so."

The old man's head tilted forward, and he stared at the floor. "That's good, but I can't stay longer."

"You live in Reading?"

"Yes. A long day's ride."

"Horseback?"

"Freight wagon. I talked with a man leaving Monday with a load of freight."

"Your daughter is in South Carolina?"

Surprise came into the aged face. "Just outside Charleston. Why?"

Matthew stacked the coins on the table. "There's enough here for sea passage to Charleston, and back, and on to Reading. And forty pounds British sterling to spare. I want you to take it. Go see your daughter. Stay for a while. Then go home. Will you do it?"

Matthew could not recall ever seeing such an expression in the face of an aged man. Ira Bouchard tried to speak and could not, and he waited and cleared his throat and tried again.

"Why? Why are you doing this?"

"You earned it. Your country can't pay, but I can. Do this for me. Will you do it?"

The old voice cracked. "I can't repay."

"I didn't expect it. Will you do it?"

Ira Bouchard swallowed at the lump in his throat and could only nod his head.

Matthew stood and his words were forceful. "Not a word to anyone. Not Mother Asher, not the guests, not your daughter, not anyone. Just book your passage and go. Agreed?"

There was wonder in the old eyes as he nodded again, and Matthew turned and walked out the door and closed it.

Notes

The Statehouse, formerly Independence Hall, and the East Room, where the Grand Convention was held, are accurately described herein. Warren, *The Making of the Constitution*, pp. 303–5.

On Friday, May 25, 1787, Philadelphia was drenched with rain. Finally, twelve days after the call, a quorum of states was present, and the delegates convened. Matters went forward as described herein, including the details about Benjamin Franklin, who was to have nominated George Washington to preside as President, but being bedridden with gout, Franklin had extended that privilege to Robert Morris. James Madison did in fact select the seat directly in front of the dais on which the presiding officer would sit, so he could hear and record all that was said. Rossiter, *1787: The Grand Convention*, pp. 161–65.

CHAPTER VIII

★ ★ ★

*E*very green and flowering thing in Philadelphia was in full glory as the Saturday morning sun rose in a clear blue sky on a city still dripping from the spring rain that had stopped only one hour earlier. Spirits soared. There was a lift in the air, and a special swing in the stride of those in the streets. Greetings were called with unusual gusto, and hats were tipped a bit higher than social custom required. The words *convened* and *committee* dominated conversations, and the name *Washington* was everywhere spoken.

The Convention had begun and would convene again on Monday! The gathering that was expected to be the salvation of America was under way. The ten newspapers that collectively scoured the city unceasingly for every savory scrap of news, or gossip, or calamity, or blessed event, had pounced on the proceedings. The lamps and candles in their offices glowed all night as the reporters compiled every bit of information they could on each delegate and every tidbit about the brief proceedings of the preceding day. Feverishly they reduced their findings to writing, while the typesetters scrambled, and the operators spun the wheels on the tops of their printing presses. By breakfast, Saturday newspapers were everywhere, headlines declaring Washington as the presiding and dominant presence. With him were twenty-seven more of America's finest sons, abundantly blessed with every virtue known to the human race. Never had there been such a gathering. Who could doubt the success of the venture, with venerable Benjamin Franklin in the mix? And Robert Morris and Gouverneur Morris, Alexander Hamilton, James Madison, George Mason—the list went on and on. Philadelphians seized the newspapers, and excitement mushroomed at the Indian Queen and in the taverns. Opinion and speculation ran wild over what the first order of business should be on Monday morning.

At one o'clock, Pierce Butler of South Carolina sat alone at a table in the Indian Queen, away from the stream of traffic coming and going, quietly sipping at hot tea. Before him were three newspapers, with the *Herald* on top. Around him were citizens from the upper level of society, newspapers on the tables, thumping them with stiff index fingers as they exclaimed their views, their biases, their prejudices, their judgments on what had been done, and on what was yet to come. Butler watched, and he listened, and he thoughtfully sipped at his steaming tea.

At three o'clock, eight blocks to the west, with a copy of all ten newspapers clutched under his arm, Matthew Dunson turned from Market Street onto Thirteenth, entered Mother Asher's boardinghouse, hung his tricorn in the cloakroom, ascended the stairs two at a time, and barged into his room. He drew back the window curtains to let sunlight flood the room, then set the stack of newspapers on his table, sat down, and began studying them. He interrupted his second reading for supper, then returned to his room to finish. He had studied them all a third time before he pulled his nightshirt on over his head, blew out the table lamp, and knelt beside his bed with bowed head.

Sunday morning breakfast at the boardinghouse was alive with talk, opinions, speculation. The text chosen by the Reverend Becker for his sermon was taken from the New Testament, the book of Matthew, Chapter 22, verse 21, "Render therefore unto Caesar the things which are Caesar's; and unto God the things that are God's." With a resounding amen, the congregation filed out of the white church to linger, gathered in groups on the grass and cobblestones to chatter and gesture about what belonged to Caesar and what belonged to God, and exactly which had claim on the United States. Matthew returned from church to the boardinghouse, sat down at his table, reached for quill and fresh paper, and spent the afternoon writing a two-page letter to Kathleen and John. He spent the evening writing a second letter to Billy Weems, and a third letter to his mother and Caleb and Prissy.

By nine-thirty Monday morning he was striding east on Market in brilliant sunlight, then over to Chestnut, making his way toward the Statehouse, when he slowed. The entry was jammed, with people backed up fifty yards into the streets in both directions, and he could hear the rumble of their exclamations over something in their midst that he could not yet make out. It broke in his mind that someone was down, hurt, and instantly there was a grab in his stomach. Could it be one of the delegates had been assaulted? Assassinated? He broke into a trot and pushed his way through the crowd to the center, and stopped in his tracks, stunned into silence. His jaw dropped open and he stared at an apparition that reached beyond his wildest imagination.

Benjamin Franklin had arrived. While his arrival was noteworthy in any event, his arrival in a swaying sedan chair, carried on poles by four husky convicts from the nearby Walnut Street jail was sensational beyond belief. Until that moment, no one in America had ever seen a sedan chair. It was something that existed only in books written about strange people in exotic lands and was a truly foreign device to the practical, isolated Americans. To see Benjamin Franklin arrive at the Grand Convention inside such a conveyance was a scene none of them would forget so long as they lived.

Franklin thrust his arm out the window, the four convicts stopped, the sedan chair settled onto its four stubby legs, and two of the prisoners came to his door to open it. The old man slowly worked one leg out, and the convicts reached inside to help support his aging body as he struggled until both feet were out and he was standing on the cobblestones. He heaved a great sigh, stood still until he could straighten his back, then took a tentative step on one gout-ravaged leg. It trembled but held, and he took a step with the other. He wore a plain brown suit with an unremarkable shirt and a tie at his throat and a sparse fall of wispy, long gray hair hanging down from under an aged tricorn.

A path opened to the front doors of the Statehouse, and the old man slowly made his way, swaying slightly from side to side as his pain-wracked legs took the load. He smiled and raised a hand to those on each side as he passed, ever mindful of drama, politics, and an opportunity to enhance his already legendary reputation among both the elite and the common folk. Women gasped and exclaimed, and men pointed and murmured as he approached the door. Someone opened it for him, and he continued down the hall to the entrance into the East Room. He fumbled for his credentials, but Joseph Fry waved him on in before he found them. Benjamin Franklin was his own best credential.

Matthew clacked his mouth closed, stood for a few seconds recovering from the unprecedented scene he had just witnessed, then worked his way through the throng of people gathered to watch the other delegates arrive. He jostled his way through the hall, hung his tricorn in the cloakroom, and peered about, searching for delegates. Five more elbowed their way toward the door, and the doorkeeper was hard put to keep the entrance free enough for the delegates to approach. More arrived, and Matthew helped keep a corridor open for them to have their credentials checked and enter the East Room. Madison arrived alone with his ever present leather case and paused at the door only long enough to nod to Matthew before he entered. At exactly ten o'clock the last of the delegates arrived and were admitted. Matthew turned to Fry.

"I counted twenty-nine. Gorham and Strong are here from Massachusetts, and Ellsworth from Connecticut."

Fry ran his finger down the list. "Twenty-nine."

Within minutes the buzzing crowd began to thin, and Matthew stood close to the door, listening intently. The only sounds from within were the opening of the windows. Matthew looked at Fry and shook his head.

"This could take some time. I think I'll get a chair to wait it out."

Inside the chamber, Washington mounted the dais, took his place behind his desk, and scanned the room, finally looking down at the eager face of Madison, directly in front of him. All talk ceased and every eye was on Washington as he sat down.

"Mr. Secretary, is there a quorum present?"

"Yes, Mr. President."

"Thank you. We are now in session. Our first order of business is a report from the committee assigned to rules. Does the committee have a spokesman?"

Charles Pinckney rose. By any fair reckoning, young Pinckney, twenty-nine years of age, had earned his seat at the convention. Born to wealth and power, he had risked it all when he took up arms as an American officer in defense of his beloved Charleston. Captured by the British, he had suffered their reprisals and survived. He studied law, became a competent lawyer, served three years in the United States Congress to become an active, vital force in politics and an avid supporter of changes in the Articles of Confederation to heal the fatal ills of his country. Handsome, popular, vain, a dandy, he harbored a few ideas of his own concerning the direction this convention should go. And, in a not-so-covert attempt to gain notoriety, he had calmly claimed to many to be "twenty-four years of age," and the youngest member of the convention. The others winked and smiled and said nothing.

"I have the honor," Pinckney said.

"Very well. Proceed."

Pinckney cleared his throat, raised a document to reading level, took a deep breath and began.

"The committee is agreed upon the following propositions. First, as it has always been in the Confederation Congress, the voting on all matters properly before the convention shall be by the states, and not by the individual delegates."

He paused, fully aware that the next sentence could draw debate so violent that the convention could deadlock and end before it had begun. He continued.

"Each state, regardless of size or population, shall have one vote." He stopped.

The intake of breaths could be heard throughout the room. The large and populous states had quietly made it known in casual conversations at the Indian Queen and in the taverns and the boardinghouses, that they had grown bone-weary of conventions and congresses where small states with small populations had the same voting powers as the large and populous states. The Pennsylvanians had been adamant that they intended correcting the obvious inequity at first opportunity, and this was the opportunity. In their view, fairness required that states should have voting power commensurate with their population; the larger the state, the greater the power. After all, who could argue in favor of a state such as Georgia, with a population of 56,000 having the same voting power as Virginia, with 650,000—more than ten times larger. On that principle, the small states could block the big ones at will, for any reason convenient to the small state, no matter the consequence to its larger neighbor. Understandably, the small states took the opposite view. Why should they be forever subject to the big states, who could abuse them and their welfare at will if granted voting power based on population? Only days before the convention convened, the Virginians had poured oil on the troubled waters by urging the large states to remain silent in the opening days, to avoid a collision that could wreck the convention before it got started. Be patient.

Now Pinckney had boldly made it the first issue to come before the delegation. He stood with eyes straight ahead, waiting for the explosion. Seconds ticked by in silence. Men glanced at each other, and some set their jaws, but no one spoke. Washington's face was a mask of discipline as his eyes worked the room. Franklin leaned back and flicked imaginary breakfast crumbs from his vest. Madison remained hunched over his journal, quill poised in hand, holding his breath, waiting for the storm.

Silence held until it was clear that this issue, which could split the states and end the convention in bitterness, would be raised and debated on some future day when it could be framed cleanly, with nothing else on the calendar to detract.

Pinckney took his cue and moved on.

"Each delegate will scrupulously conduct himself befitting a gentlemen. Proper decorum in this august body shall be observed at all times. Delegates will receive permission from the President to speak and shall stand when speaking. At all times when a delegate is recognized by the President and is speaking, all others will refrain from whispering, reading, or passing notes. Further, should anyone offend in this particular, any other delegate may call him to order, as may the President. Further, all delegates shall show deference and due respect to the President in all matters, and his powers and dignity shall be recognized and maintained. When the house shall adjourn, every member shall stand in his place until the President pass him."

Pinckney paused for a moment before concluding. "Any member of the delegation shall have the right to call for the yeas and nays and have them entered on the minutes." He continued by setting forth, one at a time, the standard rules of protocol that had been used for thirteen years in the Confederation Congress, and with slight modifications in most state legislatures. Finished, he raised his eyes to Washington.

"That is the report of the committee."

Washington nodded. "Is there debate?"

A delegate rose. "Permission to speak."

"Granted."

"I object to the rule allowing any member to call for the yeas and nays and have them recorded. That could become a device to delay proceedings indefinitely by simply calling for the yeas and nays every few minutes. I move that rule be stricken." He sat down.

Washington looked about. "Any debate?"

There was none.

"Is there a second?"

Another delegate spoke up. "Seconded."

"All in favor say yea."

The response was firm, loud.

"All against say nay."

No one spoke.

"Motion carried. The rule is stricken. Any other debate?"

Richard Dobbs Spaight of North Carolina rose. "Permission to speak."

"Granted."

Spaight spoke with conviction. "I propose a rule to provide that, on the one hand, the house may not be precluded by a vote upon any question from revising the subject matter of it, when they see cause; nor, on the other hand, be led too hastily to rescind a decision which was the result of mature discussion."

Thoughtful men fell silent as they considered. Spaight's proposal provided a way to go back and change a prior vote if it became obvious that it was wrong. And in this business of inventing a government, one thing was imminently clear. What they decided today could be a stumbling block tomorrow. If they lacked the power to correct their own prior mistakes, only mischief could result.

Heads nodded vigorously. Washington went on.

"Any debate?"

The silence held.

"Very well. The committee will reduce the proposed rule to writing for a vote tomorrow."

Again Washington looked about. "Is there further debate?"

There was none.

"All in favor of the rules offered by the committee, as amended, say yea."

The yeas were unanimous.

"All against say nay."

There were no nays.

"The rules are approved and are binding upon this convention."

Washington referred to the paper on his desk. "Are there any other motions at this time?"

There were none.

"Are there any other matters of business to come before us at this time?"

Pierce Butler of South Carolina rose. "Permission to speak."

"Granted."

Tending to be rash, outspoken on occasion, Butler was nevertheless a man of judgment and value, both to his state and the convention. He wasted no time.

"I am sure we are all aware that this fair city enjoys the blessing of ten separate newspapers, each one committed to delivering news superior to the other nine. I shared with many of you all ten special editions that were published Saturday last and was staggered to learn of the profound and magnificent strides we made last Friday. My recollection is that we elected our President, his Excellency George Washington, our secretary, and appointed a committee to draft our rules, and adjourned. The entire proceeding lasted but a few minutes. Yet, I was sorely taxed to match the glorious and glowing account in the newspapers with the facts as I know them."

He paused, and there were chuckles and nods throughout the chamber. He sobered, the hall quieted, and he went on.

"These newspapers reach far and wide in this land, very quickly. Our constituents in our various states will hear of these proceedings within a few days of the event. And, given the nature of the human race, it is clear to me we will be subjected to an onslaught of opinion and pressure from our own people that can only be destructive of our aims here."

Again he paused, shifted his feet, and there was the sound of others moving in their chairs. The hall quieted, and he went on.

"I therefore suggest there would be great wisdom in guarding against licentious publications of these proceedings. Should our debate become grist for the newspapers, this convention can, and likely will, quickly reduce to a battlefield of regional opinion that will end in disaster. The proceedings within these walls ought to remain here until we are finished."

Butler stopped, waiting for a response.

For several moments no one spoke. Few had considered what the newspapers could do to such a convention. Fewer still had reckoned that if the newspapers had the power to wreck it, it was only a matter of time until one tried. And almost none of them had thought to the bottom of it. If one newspaper tried, the dark side of human nature would pounce on it. The circulation of that newspaper would skyrocket, the other nine would follow to protect their share of the market, and every great and noble hope for success in the convention would be forever buried and lost in an avalanche of perverted sensationalism.

Washington broke the silence. "Very well. The committee will prepare a written motion for consideration tomorrow."

Butler answered, "Very well, sir," and sat down.

"Is there other business?"

The secretary, William Jackson stood with a document in his hand. "Yes, sir. I have a letter received this date from various leading citizens in the state of Rhode Island."

Rhode Island! The state that had made such a study of obstinacy, nonconformance, and disruption that newspapers had begun to call it "Rogue Island." The Articles of Confederation that bound the thirteen states together required that all thirteen states must concur in matters affecting the United States at large. No one could remember how many times Rhode Island had used that as a weapon to single-handedly wreck what the other twelve states proposed. For reasons that left wise men shaking their heads in absolute wonder, Rhode Island had for years steadfastly used that veto power to deny the United States what was desperately needed in commerce, trade, paper money, tariffs, border disputes, and international trade. Worse, it had never paid its share of the costs of the war. The ultimate insult came when Rhode Island refused to send delegates to the Grand Convention and made it clear they did not intend to.

Rhode Island? Instantly muffled laughter could be heard. Only Washington's icy stare silenced it. Jackson went on.

"If I may summarize, the letter states that the citizens deplore the failure of Rhode Island to send delegates to the Convention, owing to a nonconcurrence of the upper and the lower houses of their legislature. They believe that the well-informed through their state are in favor of giving Congress full power over commerce, and they sincerely hope that the absence of Rhode Island will not result in action unfavorable to the commercial interests of that state. They request that this convention make such provisions as have a tendency to strengthen the Union, promote commerce, increase the power, and establish the credit of the United States."

Jackson pursed his mouth, thumped the paper onto his desk, and looked up at Washington.

Washington looked down at him. "The letter shall be placed on file."

Jackson bobbed his head. "Yes, sir." He took his seat.

Murmuring was heard on the floor, and then it subsided.

Once again Washington scanned the delegates. "Is there any other business to be brought before us at this time?"

The delegates looked at each other, shaking their heads.

"We stand adjourned until ten o'clock tomorrow morning."

All stood and held their places while Washington left the dais and walked from the room. It was only then that the others began gathering their papers, and open talk flowed as they made their way out while Madison remained at his desk, writing rapidly to complete his notes of the proceedings of the day. Others glanced at him, hunched forward, quill scratching furiously, and they began to realize the little man with the soft voice had voluntarily taken upon himself the gargantuan task of creating a record that was detailed, inclusive, and objective to a fault. It occurred to a few that such a record, if made public when their work was finished, could prove to be an embarrassment to some, a great compliment to others, depending on their conduct.

Finished writing, Madison laid down his quill, capped the ink bottle, gathered his papers, and drew his watch from his pocket. It was three minutes past 2:00 P.M. He thrust the watch back into its place, tucked his case beneath his arm, and walked out.

Matthew was waiting, and Madison stopped in the hall as Matthew spoke.

"I take it the rules were approved."

"A few modifications. Nothing significant. Walk with me."

They moved down the hall side by side, Matthew looking down, Madison looking up as they talked.

"Anything else of significance that I may know?" Matthew inquired.

Madison pondered for a moment. "Yes. It appears we'll be able to reconsider a vote if we later see it was wrong. Sounds trivial, but in this business it could be critical."

"Who proposed it?"

"Mr. Spaight. North Carolina."

They pushed through the front doors out into the uncommon beauty of a late spring day and turned toward Madison's boardinghouse.

"Anything else?"

Madison smiled. "We filed a letter from Rhode Island."

Matthew exclaimed, "Rhode Island? They wrote a letter?"

"Yes. Some good citizens voiced their strong disapproval of their legislature. Wanted us to know they hoped we would solve all their problems with commerce, tariffs, credit, and the rest of the civilized world."

Matthew chuckled out loud. "Would it be a big surprise to anyone if this convention excluded that state from the Union?"

Madison grinned at him. "Only to Rhode Island."

"Anything else of significance?"

Madison slowed and stopped, organizing his thoughts, making a decision. He looked at Matthew.

"Yes. It was proposed we keep the newspapers and the public out of this. Newspapers being what they are, and human nature being what it is, that combination could stop this convention permanently."

Madison stared into Matthew's eyes, waiting for him to grasp the portent of the thought. For five seconds Matthew struggled before the light of understanding burst in his mind.

"Wait a moment. Keep the newspapers out? What of the rest of us who have an interest in this? A deep interest. If you keep the newspapers out, you'll have to keep us out, too. Who proposed this?"

"Mr. Pierce Butler. South Carolina." Madison slowly shook his head. "He's right. Newspapers live on sensationalism. This convention must live on hard, cold realism. Our debate must be honest, straightforward, uninhibited, the best we have in us. We must be free to admit our errors, change our position, and move on. That will not happen if the newspapers and the public are given free access because none of us will be willing to appear foolish. We cannot be compromised, diverted, by public reaction or the slanted views of the newspapers or the public gadflies who feast on such things. Sensationalism and hardheaded reality do not mix well, and given a choice, most people prefer the sensational. That gives the newspapers and the nabobs the power to enflame the public in any direction they choose, and once that starts, it is only a matter of time until all we say, all we do, will be lost in a country divided against itself. I despise it, but Mr. Butler is right. We have to protect this convention. The newspapers and the public will be excluded."

Matthew persisted. "And the rest of us?"

For a moment Madison dropped his eyes. "It appears you will be unintended casualties along with them."

Matthew groaned and his head rolled back for a moment. "When will we know?"

"Tomorrow. Mr. Butler will present a written motion. There will be a vote."

"What is your prediction?"

"It will pass."

Madison saw the bitter disappointment in Matthew, and placed a hand on Matthew's arm. "Can you see the wisdom in it?"

"Yes. In part. But I'm conflicted. I see the need for it, but I also see the need for the people to know. To deliberate. Decide."

"So do we. But weigh them in the scales of wisdom. There is no question which is the greater need."

Matthew drew a great breath. "Well, it's useless to fret. The convention was called to handle such matters, and all we can do is trust you men. We'll know soon enough."

Madison stepped back. "I have to go now—an appointment."

"I will see you in the morning."

Matthew walked steadily back to the boardinghouse, struggling with his thoughts and the anguish following Madison's advice of excluding the proceedings from public scrutiny. He was hanging his tricorn in the cloak room when Mother Asher appeared in the archway to the kitchen.

"Mr. Bouchard left today." She drew a small sealed letter from her apron pocket. "He left this for you."

She saw the surprise in Matthew's face as he accepted it. He thanked her and climbed the stairs to his room. He dropped the letter on his table, sat down, and for a time stared out the window, going over again and again the report from Madison.

Close the convention to the public? My purpose in being here—gone. What can be done about it? Nothing. Nothing.

He picked up the letter, broke the seal, and spread it on the table. The penmanship was crude, and the few lines were brief.

> 28th May '87
> Philadelphia
> Dear Sir:
>
> I am a cobbler and unskilled in writing. I will see my daughter and her husband, and my grandchildren, soon. Then I will return to Reading. I do not believe anyone ever gave me such a gift. I will remember you. God bless you.
>
> Y'r obd't servant,
Ira Bouchard

Matthew read the lines again, then raised his head to peer out the window. He was seeing ten thousand more Ira Bouchards who had answered the call and offered their all for their country. Then he was seeing the East Room of the Statehouse, where twenty-nine men had met twelve hours earlier to begin the impossible process of creating a new nation to be certain the Ira Bouchards had not fought in vain.

Notes

Philadelphia had ten newspapers during the time portrayed, one of which was the *Herald.* Rossiter, *1787: The Grand Convention,* p. 26; Warren, *The Making of the Constitution,* p. 123.

Benjamin Franklin's arrival at the Grand Convention on Monday morning, May 28, 1787, was sensational, since he arrived in a sedan chair as described. Though a familiar form of conveyance in other lands, sedan chairs were unknown in America prior to that time. Moyers, *Report from Philadelphia,* page dated Monday, May 28, 1787.

The commencement of the Grand Convention with its setting, participants, the order of business, and conclusions reached are accurately portrayed, including the tenor of the letter sent by certain citizens of Rhode Island, which because of its prior obstinacy had for years been cynically referred to by many as "Rogue Island."

A motion was made to close the Grand Convention to everyone except the delegates, in the fear newspaper reports would politicize the proceedings beyond hope. The motion passed and later proved to be the salvation of the entire effort. Rossiter, *1787: The Grand Convention*, pp. 132–33, 166–68; Warren, *The Making of the Constitution*, pp. 130–31; Moyers, *Report from Philadelphia*, page dated May 28, 1787; Bernstein, *Are We to Be a Nation?* pp. 154–55.

CHAPTER IX

*T*he convention will come to order."

Half a dozen delegates checked their pocket watches. It was exactly 10:00 A.M., and President George Washington was standing behind his desk. All talk ceased, and each man took his seat.

"Mr. Secretary, do we have a quorum present?"

"Yes, sir. We do."

Washington looked at Spaight. "Mr. Spaight, I believe you have a motion."

Spaight stood. "Yes, sir, I do." He raised a document, scanned it for a moment, then read slowly.

"I propose that a motion to reconsider a matter that has been determined by a majority, may be made with leave unanimously given, on the same day on which the vote passed; but otherwise not without one day's previous notice, in which last case, if the House agree to the reconsideration, some future day shall be assigned for that purpose."

He stopped, and for several seconds silence held as each man considered the language.

Then Washington asked. "Second?"

Several spoke simultaneously to second the motion.

Washington continued. "Debate?"

There was none, and the vote was unanimous.

Washington next turned to George Mason, a fellow Virginian. "Sir, do you have a motion prepared?"

Chancellor George Mason rose to represent the three-man committee on rules. Sixty-one years of age, he entered life in the noted Mason family of plantation owners. He had attended William and Mary College, studied law with Stephen Dewey, was admitted to the Virginia Bar in 1746, served in the Virginia House of Burgesses and the Second Continental Congress and later as judge of the court of chancery and member of the elite committee composed of Thomas Jefferson and George Mason, among others, to revise and codify the laws of the state of Virginia. He made a profound impression with his dedication and had earned the title "Mason the Just."

"I do." Mason read carefully. "I propose a motion that no copy be taken of any entry on the journal during the sitting of the house without leave of the house; that members only be permitted to inspect the journal; that nothing spoken in the house be printed or otherwise published or communicated without leave."

Dead silence seized the room for a full five seconds.

"Is the motion seconded?"

Several voices raised to second the motion.

"Debate?"

Men looked about, but none spoke. The startling proposal made by Butler in the previous session, had been debated overnight by nearly every man present, in their boardinghouses, or the Indian Queen, and each understood that it must pass, or the convention would almost certainly become a hopeless tangle of bitterness. George Mason had thoughtfully reduced it to the written proposal that was now before the delegates.

"There being no debate, all in favor say yea."

The vote was unanimous.

Washington spoke in measured words. "The motion passes and is now binding on every man who attends this convention. It is to be enforced without exception. Nothing written or spoken in this chamber between this time and the adjournment *sine die* shall leave this room. Nothing in your letters to business associates, your families, nothing in the journals you keep outside this room. I trust each of you understands that by taking your oath as a delegate, you have also taken your oath to the secrecy required by this rule, which is effective as of this minute."

He paused for a moment, then continued. "By the powers that I believe are vested in the office of President of this convention, I intend to issue an order that while we are in session, the door is to be locked. Further, the windows shall be closed, and the blinds drawn. I have no illusions about the skill of curious newspaper reporters and some members of the general public to utilize such things to gain access to what goes on in here. Are there objections?"

Stunned silence held for a few moments before open talk began. Lock the door? Close the windows? Draw the blinds? In the heat of a Philadelphia summer? Ridiculous! Beyond any need!

Washington let the tumult continue for several seconds before he called them to order.

"If we are to protect our work, I see no other way. Is there debate?"

The talk dwindled and died as the delegates accepted the hard truth: Washington was right.

Washington turned to the secretary. "Hearing nothing to the contrary, I direct that you draft such an order today for my signature."

"Yes, sir."

"Very good. We shall now move on to the heavier business of the day." He turned his head to look at Edmund Randolph of Virginia. Thirty-three years of age, striking in appearance, six feet tall, Randolph was of the celebrated Randolph family of Virginia. A graduate of William and Mary College, he had early become a lawyer, served on the staff of General Washington, become the youngest member of the Virginia convention of 1776, served as attorney general for his native Virginia, then three years in the Confederation Congress before he was elected governor to succeed Patrick Henry. A gifted and forceful speaker, his strong reputation preceded him to Philadelphia.

Washington said to him, "Mr. Randolph, I understand you are prepared to address the convention."

Randolph rose, his long, unpowdered brown hair flowing and for a few seconds straightened a thick stack of documents on his desk. He took the top one in hand and raised his voice.

"I am, sir."

For more than one hour he spoke. His discourse began calmly with a description of the form of government all patriots had dreamed of and fought for—a government that derived its power from the consent of the people. His voice rose as he counted on his fingers the fatal defects of the Articles of Confederation: powerless to raise money to pay its own expenses, powerless to resolve disputes between states, powerless to regulate treaties with foreign sovereigns. He reached the peak of his argument when he listed the fruits of the flawed Articles, including the rebellion and war between Shays' followers and the United States military; the horrendous commercial havoc inflicted on the United States by the issuing of paper money by the states; the humiliation and ridicule heaped on the country by foreign banks and merchants; the treaties between United States and foreign sovereigns that had been breached by the Americans because they could not meet their obligations; the disputes between states over rights to the navigable rivers, westward expansion, and tariffs, that had come perilously close to destroying the union altogether. Randolph invited them to envision America as three separate nations: north, central, and south. Should that occur, he declared, we are lost forever. Murmurs broke out. Some shuddered at the thought.

He stopped, asked for and was given a glass of water, drank, and set the glass on his desk.

Madison laid a fresh sheet of paper on his table and dipped his quill in the ink bottle.

Washington leaned back in his chair, glanced down at Madison, then at George Mason and George Wythe. All six of the Virginia delegation turned their eyes to their seventh member, Edmund Randolph, and waited in strained silence. Over the previous three weeks, they had all helped with the address Randolph was presenting. James Madison had been the chief architect and the others had helped with the polish. They knew that Madison, with his soft voice and manner was not the one to deliver it with the force and fire it demanded. It would need the voice and the figure and the power and the flair of Edmund Randolph. Madison the architect, Edmund the deliverer.

They settled into their chairs and their breathing shortened as Randolph moved into it.

"I therefore propose the following as essentials for completing our work of establishing a durable government:

"First, that the Articles of Confederation be corrected and enlarged to accomplish the objects proposed by their institution."

Other delegates glanced out the windows in disinterest, wondering what it would be like to sit in the hall with the windows closed, the curtains drawn, and the door locked. There was a disquieting sense that it sounded much like prison. Few were paying more than casual attention as Randolph continued.

"Second. A scheme of representation be devised, based on contributions or population.

"Third. A bicameral legislature."

Delegates were letting their minds wander, mentally composing letters home to wives, families, legislatures, their businesses.

"Fourth. Election of the first branch by the people.

"Fifth. Election of the second branch by the first, out of a proper number of persons nominated by the state legislatures."

Words began to catch in the minds of a few. Representation by population? Bicameral legislature? Election? People vote? They pulled their thoughts together and began to listen.

"Sixth. Authority in the national legislature to pass laws superior to those of any state, with power to override state laws that contravene laws of the union, and to use force against recalcitrant states."

Suddenly there was a rustle in the room, and the sound of chairs squeaking as men sat bolt upright in utter shock.

"Seventh. An executive to be elected by the legislature, to be compensated, and ineligible for reelection, and possessed of general authority to execute the laws."

Men were turning, looking at each other with astonished stares, unable to grasp what they were hearing. An executive with supreme powers to execute laws that would override any state law? A king? We just got rid of a king!

"Eighth. A council of revision consisting of the executive and selected judges who shall have a qualified veto over acts of the legislature.

"Ninth. A judiciary consisting of one supreme tribunal with lesser tribunals as needed, each empowered with jurisdiction national in scope."

National? What is national? We have a *federal* government, not national! A *national court* with *national* jurisdiction? What of our *state* courts? Abolished?

"Tenth. Admission of new states with less than a unanimous vote in the legislature.

"Eleventh. A guarantee to each state of its republican institutions and its territory."

No one was moving. There was no sound. Eyes were wide in shock.

"Twelfth. A provision for the continuance of the Confederation Congress until a day certain after the reform of the Articles of union."

The Confederation Congress *terminated?* Impossible!

"Thirteenth. Provision for the amendment of the new constitution without the assent of the legislature."

New constitution? Constitution of what? Each state has its own constitution. Are we to have one new constitution that applies to all states? Revoke all thirteen state constitutions? Are the states to be dissolved, done away with, eliminated?

"Fourteenth. A requirement that all state officers be bound by oath to support the new constitution."

The death knell of the states?

"Fifteenth. Ratification of these proposals once they are approved by the Convention by state conventions expressly chosen by the people."

Randolph laid his paperwork down, stood to his full six feet, and turned his face to Washington to speak firmly.

"These, Mr. President, are the proposals that I wish to place before this body for debate and approval."

"Thank you, Mr. Randolph."

Not one of the Virginia delegation—not Madison, Washington,

Randolph, Mason, Wythe, Blair, nor McClurg—had even the faintest idea of what the reaction of the convention would be. Madison's work had begun years before when he had made government and the principles on which true government is based, the center of his life study. It was he who in those years had first set pen to paper to begin the labor of reducing those principles to a plan, one at a time, organizing them, making the complex simple, finally reducing the fruits of his labor to the fifteen recommendations Randolph had delivered. It was the other six men in the Virginia delegation who had labored for weeks with Madison behind closed doors, nudging the plan, laboring with one word here, another there, polishing, adding, discarding.

They knew what they had done. Their first recommendation—to "correct and enlarge" the familiar but fatally flawed Articles of Confederation—was intended to, and did, suggest to the Convention that they were attempting to preserve the Articles, because the commission granted by each state to each delegate was to amend those Articles. Their next fourteen recommendations did not amend the Articles. They demolished them. They left no vestige, no part, of the Articles standing. Rather, they launched the entire convention into uncharted waters never dreamed of, with no compass, no North Star, no lighthouses, and no chart showing the shoals and reefs and rocks that could rip the bottom clear out of their foundling ship of state.

Randolph sat down. For a few moments not one word was heard. The delegates sat white-faced, immobilized, thoughts fragmented, wild, disorganized, minds lurching about, reeling, unable to focus.

National? Bicameral? Executive? Elections? Veto? Constitution? Supreme Tribunal? States subservient? Force against nonconforming states? Confederation Congress abolished? In the name of all under heaven that is holy, *what are they proposing?*

The seven men in the Virginia delegation sat without moving, watching, trying to gauge how violently they had stirred the convention, waiting for the volcano to erupt. Murmuring started among the others, and the Virginians waited.

No one stood. No one pounded his desk and shouted, "Blasphemy!"

The Virginians were stunned. Why had not someone—Lansing or Yates or Ellsworth or Dickinson—particularly the pacifist Dickinson—leaped to his feet and shouted, "Treason!" Clearly, the proposals fathered by the genius of Madison and delivered by the eloquent Randolph had breached the commission of every delegate in the room. Not one state had authorized one delegate to utterly destroy the Articles of Confederation, and none had even dreamed of creating the government Randolph had described. It could not be more clear that the framework of government now before them was shot through and through with just about everything they thought had led to the war and the throwing off of the yoke of England! A *national* government, with one *executive,* to which every state was subservient at the risk of destruction for disobedience? What, pray tell, was the difference between *that* proposal, and a *king,* with an army to crush anyone who disagreed with him?

Mutterings began, with no one rising to make a coherent response, because no one could spontaneously decide where to begin to attack the avalanche that just buried them all. They were all jolted when Charles Pinckney rose.

"Permission to speak."

"Granted."

The room silenced and all eyes were on the young delegate from South Carolina.

"Gentlemen, I have presumed to reduce some of my ideas on a new government to a system, which I prepared in writing prior to my arrival in Philadelphia. In review, I must confess that it is grounded on much the same principles as the proposal of Mr. Randolph. Nonetheless, I request permission to present this proposed draft of a federal government at this time. I have a copy to be delivered to the secretary."

"Very well. Your proposal shall be filed with the secretary."

Pinckney recoiled slightly. "It was my intent to read the proposal."

"The hour is late. It shall be filed with the secretary for those who wish to obtain it."

With a flourish, Pinckney picked up a copy of his writing, passed it to William Jackson, then sat down. His proposal was ignored, never again to be mentioned, throughout the entire convention.

Washington quickly moved on. "We have the proposal of Mr. Randolph before us. The floor is open for debate."

Debate? Where does one start with a proposal that point blank sets forth fourteen propositions that systematically sweep an entire government into oblivion? The delegates turned to one another befuddled, unable to spontaneously organize their thoughts into a workable plan of debate. Finally one of them stood.

"Permission to speak."

"Granted."

"I move that we adjourn for the day in favor of beginning debate tomorrow."

Another stood.

"Permission to speak."

"Granted."

"For the debate, I move that we dissolve the entire delegation into a committee of the whole. I further move that the presiding officer of such committee be Nathaniel Gorham of the State of Massachusetts."

For a moment all eyes shifted to Washington, concerned at how he would receive the implication that Gorham, not he, would best serve as the presiding officer of the committee of the whole. A few saw the relief in Washington's face.

Nathaniel Gorham celebrated his forty-sixth birthday as he traveled to Philadelphia to attend the convention. The son of a packet boat operator in Charlestown, across the harbor north from Boston, his formal education was sketchy; at age fifteen he was apprenticed as a mechanic to New London. He became a reasonably successful merchant and politician until 1775, when most of his property was destroyed by the invading British. Without hesitation he turned to privateering against the British and selling his prizes on the open market, to emerge at the end of the war with enough wealth to live comfortably, despite his failures at investing wisely. He served in political capacities ranging from a representative to town meetings in Charlestown, to the Congress of the

United States, where he was speaker of the lower house for three years, as well as a member of the board of war, and a judge in the Middlesex court of common pleas. None, including Washington, questioned his mastery of parliamentary procedure, nor his qualifications to preside over the committee of the whole.

Debate was brief and unanimous. The vote on both motions was in the affirmative.

Washington concluded. "This convention will reconvene at ten o'clock A.M. tomorrow and immediately dissolve into a committee of the whole. Mr. Nathaniel Gorham of Massachusetts shall be the presiding officer of the committee. I remind each of you that this delegation is sworn to secrecy. Nothing of what we have said or written is to leave this room. We stand adjourned until tomorrow morning." He stood and walked down the aisle while the convention waited until the doors closed behind him.

Color had returned to the faces of most delegates as they stood and gathered their papers. Loud talk filled the chamber, and as they opened the door to begin their exit, it spilled out into the hallway to echo and reecho for a moment. Persons in the building on other business slowed and stopped to stare at the outburst, the like of which had never before been heard coming from the East Room. As though by a signal, each suddenly remembered Washington's admonition of secrecy, and the delegates clamped their mouths shut to exit in near total silence.

Instantly Matthew was at the door, groping to understand the silence and the flat expressions on their faces as the delegates marched down the hall and out into the sunlight. Madison slowed and gestured for Matthew to walk with him, and they made their way out without a word, then slowed in question at the crowd gathered at street's edge, excited and exclaiming at the sight of Benjamin Franklin laboriously stepping into his sedan chair and closing the door. The four burly convicts seized the poles, hoisted the sedan off the cobblestones, and walked north on Chestnut.

Madison looked up at Matthew and smiled. "Only Benjamin

Franklin," he said, and the two of them turned toward the Indian Queen. They were halfway there before Madison stopped, and Matthew spoke.

"Something momentous happened in the convention today."

Madison nodded, and in his quiet voice said, "Yes. It did. The entire delegation was sworn to total secrecy. No one can utter a word of what occurs in the convention. Nothing. We cannot speak of it in letters, even to our families. No written document is to leave the hall. No one outside is to hear a single word."

Matthew's eyes narrowed. "Newspapers?"

"Particularly newspapers."

"For how long?"

"Until we finish and adjourn *sine die.*"

"Effective when?"

"Five hours ago."

For several seconds Matthew stood silent while he accepted the fact that his stay in Philadelphia, and his overpowering need to be part of the effort to save his country were gone, vanished. For a moment he set his teeth before he spoke.

"Doesn't that end it for me, for now?"

Madison answered. "It does. Do you see the good sense in it?"

Matthew's response was slow, reluctant. "Yes. I do. I wish it were otherwise, but I do see the need."

Madison shifted his leather case. "I should join my delegation at the Indian Queen."

Matthew asked, "Would you agree to let me write to you on occasion?"

"Absolutely, so long as you understand I cannot say a word about the convention."

"I understand that. My only purpose would be to find out when you expect it to end. I plan to be here for that."

"Write me. I'll give you what I can."

Matthew offered his hand to Madison and felt the surprising strength in the grip as Madison's small hand took his. The two locked eyes for a moment, then turned and went their separate ways—Madison to a meeting in which no one could speak of the revolution that had been touched off in the convention that morning, Matthew to the waterfront to find a ship on which he could arrange passage to Boston and Kathleen and John and a shipping business.

───────────

Notes

The business of the Grand Convention for May 29, 1787, as described in this chapter is historically accurate. Delegate Edmund Randolph's list of fifteen essentials needed to correct the fatal flaws in the existing government did not merely correct the defects in the Articles of Confederation but obliterated them, setting the entire Grand Convention adrift. Their minds boggled by the scope of the proposal, the delegates did in fact adjourn, hoping to recover by the next day. Rossiter, *1787: The Grand Convention*, pp. 84, 169–71; Warren, *The Making of the Constitution*, pp. 136–46; Berkin, *A Brilliant Solution*, pp. 66–67; Farrand, *The Framing of the Constitution of the United States*, pp. 68–82; Bernstein, *Are We to Be a Nation?* pp. 158–59.

Boston

May 30, 1787

CHAPTER X

*T*he first arc of the rising sun had cleared the flat eastern sky-line to set the tops of the trees that lined the streets and filled the white-fenced yards of Boston aglow against the clear blue sky. The masts of the ships anchored in the harbor and tied to the waterfront wharves were slender, brilliant yellow spires pointed into the still heavens. Carts and wagons rumbled through the streets, bringing the morning milk and cheese and produce from the farms on the Boston Peninsula, and from the mainland, through the Neck, to market. Dockhands and seamen handling the freight of the world on the docks, and merchants preparing to open their bakeries and taverns and mercantile shops could feel it coming. It was going to be a hot, sultry day.

In her modest home south of the bustling business district, Dorothy Weems stood in the archway that separated her kitchen from the dining room and parlor, arms folded in the manner of women, studying her son. Plain, stocky, quiet by nature, Billy sat at the breakfast table, hunched forward, finishing griddle cakes and sausages. There was concern in Dorothy's face as she watched him lay his fork on his plate, wipe his mouth on his napkin, and pick up his plate and empty cup. He rose to walk into the kitchen, and she moved to let him pass. He set the utensils on the cupboard and without a word walked back out into the parlor. She spoke as she followed him.

"You're spending too much time at your office. You're not sleeping at night. You hardly talk any more. Do you have too much on you?"

He stopped. "I'm all right. You're not to worry."

"Is something wrong at the business?"

He drew a great breath and shook his head. "I don't know. We've got eight ships out, from Nova Scotia to the West Indies. One of those up north was due back five days ago. The one in the Indies, six days. There was a storm—a bad one—down in the Caribbean. We might have lost that ship. Maybe the crew." He stopped for a moment, and she saw the sick, controlled fear leap in his eyes. "Adam's the navigator."

She started, and her breath came short. Losing a ship was a disaster. Losing a crew could break his heart. He might never recover if anything were to happen to Adam Dunson. She held her silence, and he continued.

"I haven't heard of any storms up north. There's no reason I know of that our ship up there should be five days overdue."

Trudy walked into the kitchen from the hall into the bedrooms, where she had been straightening beds. Plain and stout like her mother, wearing an ankle-length dress that was gray, plain, and durable, she was now in her twentieth year. No man had ever come to the door with his hat in his hand asking permission to see her, and she had accepted the reality that probably none ever would. According to Boston custom, she was just entering the age of spinsterhood, and she was doing so stoically, with the growing realization that she must harbor all her natural instincts for husband, home, and family in a private chamber in her heart, there to be sealed away for the remainder of her life. She had learned the harsh truth that inner beauty too often remains unperceived for the lack of outer beauty. She stopped and listened in silence as her mother continued.

"Billy, it's too much. You've got too much on you."

"I'll be all right. It will work out."

Dorothy was hearing echoes of her husband, Bartholomew. Huge, strong, he had served as first mate on a fishing boat plying the waters off the Grand Banks, far to the north, where the violence of sudden storms is legendary. Bartholomew had also smiled at her and said, "I'll be all right. It will work out." But it hadn't worked out. In this life, she would never forget the day a stranger came to her door—a fishing boat captain with his hat in his hand and eyes that would not look into hers—came to inform her that Bartholomew's boat had been lost at sea, and the crew with it.

"You can't keep this up forever," Dorothy scolded. "Matthew away. Captain Pettigrew away. Caleb. You and Tom Covington trying to do the work of five men. You'll ruin your health."

He masked his impatience. "Things are fine. I'll be home early today."

Her eyes widened. "Something's happening?"

He spoke as Trudy stepped to her mother's side. "I intend on speaking with Brigitte tonight."

Trudy started and Dorothy gasped and brought her hand to her mouth. "You didn't tell me!"

"I meant to. Just too much going on right now. I spoke with Margaret last Sunday. She gave permission."

"The ring?"

"I get it this afternoon. From Simon."

"Oh!" Dorothy exclaimed. "The one he drew on paper?"

He nodded, and he saw a hint of pain pass in Trudy's eyes.

"I'll be home early. By six. Brigitte gets home from the millinery around then, and I'm to see her at seven."

"I'll have supper ready."

"I doubt I'll have time to eat before I see Brigitte. Better wait 'til I'm back."

The two women followed him to the door and watched him pass through the gate into the cobblestoned street before they turned back and set about their day's work.

Within two winding blocks, Billy had his coat off, hooked on one finger, tossed over his shoulder. Within another block he had his cuffs unbuttoned and sleeves rolled back and his collar open. Sweating in the humid heat, he arrived at the offices of DUNSON & WEEMS

SHIPPING on the waterfront, and with the black-eyed, yellow-beaked gulls wheeling and quarreling over the carrion left by the tides, worked his key in the lock and entered. He hung his coat on the pegs near the door and went directly to the hardbacked chair at his desk. He had begun organizing the month-end bills and payroll when the door rattled and Thomas Covington entered, speaking as he closed the door.

"Mornin'. Goin' to be a hot one."

Billy paused to study Tom for a moment. Aging, gray-haired, in the past three months Tom had become forgetful, and from time to time his hand trembled so that his journal entries and letters were misshapen, unclear. He had to be watched.

Billy spoke. "Hot." He gestured to a stack of letters on Tom's desk. "Anything there that looks good?"

Tom spoke as he hung his coat. "A few. Charbonnet Company wants a one year contract. Want French porcelain-ware carried from Quebec to Charleston and Savannah. Indigo and tobacco on the return. Looks good. We got two offers from Europe. Irish silverware and Italian wine." He took his chair and picked up the top letter, then turned to face Billy. "Think we'll ever start crossing the Atlantic for the European trade?"

Billy shook his head. "Likely not. Too much risk. We have all we can handle right here."

Tom nodded and fell silent, reading the correspondence, sorting out the offers to contract that met the criteria of Dunson & Weems. By 10:00 A.M. the two men had both doors of the office open, hoping for a breeze to stir the dead air, but none came. They wiped at the sweat beads on their foreheads and continued the monotonous, grinding, unending paperwork that was the backbone of the shipping company. Four times their suppliers came in with bills that had fallen due—for rope and canvas and food for the crews, and Billy patiently wrote out bank drafts for them. Two bearded men came inquiring about work and Billy took their names and where they could be reached; Dunson & Weems was not hiring at the moment. Billy and Tom locked the office at noon to walk down four doors to a waterfront eatery where they had boiled cod and sauce and cider, then returned to their paperwork. At 2:00 P.M., Tom walked up six doors to the Red Heron tavern where the daily mail was held and returned with eight sealed documents. Billy met him at the door, and they silently went through the letters together. There were five bank drafts in payment for shipping contracts, and three new signed shipping contracts, but nothing from either of the overdue ships. Both men went back to their desks.

At 3:00 P.M. Billy stood and stretched, and Tom sat back in his chair, arms raised over his head to relax set muscles. Billy broke the silence.

"You worried about the *Belle?* Down in the Indies?"

Tom lowered his arms. "A little."

"Six days. I wonder where they rode out the storm."

"A lot of ports down there. I'm more worried about privateers. Pirates."

Billy sat down. "Think pirates could've taken her?"

"Possible. It's a worry."

Tom handled the three seamen who came looking for work at three-thirty, and the two men who came to negotiate contracts to supply salted beef for the ship crews. At four o'clock Billy paused in his work to rotate his head to stretch tight muscles in his neck, peered through the front window, and suddenly stood.

"I'll be right back."

Tom glanced at him. "Need something?"

Billy pointed out at the docks. "I think the *Bethany* just tied up. One of the Weston ships. Back from the Caribbean. Maybe she has news of the *Belle.*"

Tom walked to the door and watched as Billy hurriedly worked his way through the bustle of the waterfront, down to a merchantman just lowering her gangplank. He saw Billy stop on the dock, cup his hands about his mouth, and call up to the first mate. There was an answer, an exchange, Billy nodded and turned back to the office. Tom retreated to his desk, waiting in silence.

Billy spoke as he entered the door. "Strong gale. They came through all right. One ship on a reef. Not one of ours. Others anchored in ports to ride out the blow. They don't know about the *Belle.*"

Tom fingered his quill for a moment, then both men continued with their book work. At five o'clock Billy closed his ledgers, stood, stretched, and spoke as he walked to his coat by the front door.

"I need to leave. You'll be here for a while?"

"Six o'clock. A little after."

"Lock up?"

"Sure. Yes."

"See you in the morning then."

Billy made his way through the familiar waterfront jumble and sounds of men and crates and nets filled with goods loading and unloading and the screeching of gulls and terns and grebes, past the business district, to a white frame home with a small, delicately carved sign hanging from a white post in the front yard. SIMON. SILVERSMITH & JEWELER. He passed through the gate and rapped on the door.

A slender, gray-haired woman met him, smiling. "Mr. Weems! Do come in. Friedrich is expecting you."

Billy followed her to a room off the parlor where Friedrich Simon— short, paunchy, bald, heavily jowled—rose from the stool at his workbench to greet Billy. The Swiss accent was strong as he hooked his thumbs in the straps of his work apron and tilted his head forward to peer over his spectacles and speak.

"So good to see you again. You are coming to get the ring. Nein?"

Billy grinned. "Yes."

"It is finished. Yesterday. It is looking nice. Wait one little moment."

He used a key to open a square metal box on the corner of his workbench. His eyes glistened with pride as he drew out a tiny box made of oak, with a single beautiful rose engraved on the top. He removed the top, pursed his mouth to give his work one last inspection, then handed it to Billy. He turned his round face upward to watch Billy's expression as he took the box and peered at the ring.

Simple, elegant, the engagement ring was one diamond clustered in four tiny ones, set in silver. The wedding band matched, etched with eight roses on stems. Billy's eyes sparkled, and Friedrich beamed.

Billy nodded his approval and pressed the top back onto the small box. "It's beautiful. Thank you."

"For that girl—Dunson—Brigitte Dunson. Nein?"

"Yes. Brigitte."

"She is a fortunate girl."

Billy shook his head. "I'm the fortunate one."

Friedrich's paunch moved when he laughed. "Nein. You do not understand. She is fortunate that she is getting her wedding rings from Simon. Getting you for a husband, well, that is a different story."

Billy laughed as he reached for the leather purse in his pocket. "What do I owe you?"

Friedrich fumbled with some papers on his desk, removed one, and showed it to Billy. Billy opened his purse and counted coins while Friedrich marked the bill paid and signed it. They exchanged the paid bill for the coins, Billy pocketed the precious rings, and Friedrich followed him to the front door.

"You are telling her—Miss Dunson—that Friedrich wishes her long life and great happiness. You will do that?"

"I will. Thank you for everything."

Friedrich hooked his thumbs in his apron straps and peered over his spectacles to watch Billy disappear down the street.

It was five minutes past six o'clock when Billy walked through the gate in front of his mother's home. Dorothy and Trudy were waiting inside the open door, faces alive with anticipation, and Dorothy called to him, "Will you have time for supper?"

He shook his head as he entered the door. "No time. I have to get washed and change clothes."

The two women stepped aside as he strode through the parlor, down the hall to his bedroom, poured tepid water from the large pitcher into the basin, stripped to the waist, and washed. He dried with a towel and then sat down on his bed for a few moments towel in hand, to mop at the perspiration until it stopped. Unexpected thoughts came, and he sat for a moment, head tipped while he stared down at the towel in is hands.

I am going to marry a woman whose heart is divided. Part of it still belongs to her

English officer—Richard Arlen Buchanan—and he is dead and I can do nothing about it. Nothing. Will he always be there, between us? One day will it do harm?

He sighed and rose and went to the wooden wardrobe to reach for his Sunday suit, shirt, cravat, and trousers. He laid them on the bed, then returned to reach his best square-toed shoes with the silver buckles from the wardrobe floor, and clean white stockings from a dresser drawer. By force of will he dressed slowly to avoid perspiring. He spent a little time brushing back his damp, sandy red hair, inspected himself in the small mirror above the wash basin, started for the door, and stopped short. He spun around, thrust his hand into the pocket of his workpants on the bed, and drew out the small ring box. Opening it to admire the ring once more, he then closed the lid and carefully put it in his coat pocket, took a deep breath, and walked out into the parlor where both women were waiting.

He passed them for the door before it hit him. He stopped, turned, and came back to them.

"Do I look all right?"

Dorothy's eyes shone. "You look fine."

"Mother, I'm going to ask a woman to marry me, and I don't know what to say."

Dorothy raised a hand to stop him. "Be yourself, Billy. Say what's in your heart. I'm so proud of you."

"Would you like to see the rings?"

Trudy exclaimed, "Oh, could we?"

Billy drew the box from his coat pocket and handed it to his sister. Her hands were trembling as she removed the top, and both women gazed at the simple beauty of the set. For a few moments neither spoke, and then both exclaimed at once.

" . . . precious . . . beautiful."

"Think she'll like them?"

Trudy closed the lid. "She'll love them, Billy. Oh, Billy!" Impulsively the plain girl threw her arms about her brother, and he wrapped his arms about her and she held him for a few seconds with all her strength before she released him and stepped back. Instantly Dorothy buried her round, homely face in his shoulder and for a time held him close. Then she pushed herself back and smiled as she raised her apron to wipe at her tears.

"Look at me! A happy time, and I'm crying. You go now. We'll be waiting."

The two women were standing in the door when Billy opened the front gate and turned left, and they were standing at the front fence watching as he walked slowly away, moving more like a man going to the gallows than on his way to make a proposal of marriage to a woman he had secretly loved for as far back as he could remember.

As he walked, thoughts rose to crowd his mind. Marriage. Children. Responsibilities. He slowed in the stifling, humid, late afternoon heat, at a loss to know what he was going to say to Brigitte. For eleven years he had lived with the dream that this day would come, never really believing that it would. He could not remember how many times he had invented perfect scenes in his mind of cool moonlight and the sweet scent of honeysuckle and roses for his proposal of marriage, and he had composed perfect sentences that he would speak. And now, walking to her home in the oppressive late-afternoon heat, the scene was all wrong, and every word, every sentence he forced to his mind sounded ridiculous, flat, contrived. He could not recall how many times he had faced musket, bayonet, and cannon in his six years of war, nor how many times he had stared into the terrible face of death. But for one flitting moment a battlefield seemed a very desirable place to be.

Arriving at the Dunson home, he paused before opening the gate and making his way up the countersunk cobblestone walkway to the front door. This had been his second home since the day he was born, yet he was seeing things in the carefully kept yard that he had never noticed before—daisies with heads drooping in the heat, and branches in the fruit trees that needed to be pruned.

He used his handkerchief to swab at the perspiration on his face, then thrust it back into his coat pocket. He felt for the ring box, squared his shoulders, and knocked. It seemed an eternity before footsteps sounded on the hardwood floor inside, and Margaret swung the door open to face him.

"Billy!" she exclaimed. "Do come in."

She stepped aside to let him pass, as she had done a thousand times before, and he stepped into the entryway, looking about for some sign of Brigitte and Prissy. There was nothing, and he turned to Margaret as she closed the door.

"I wondered if this might be a good time to talk with Brigitte."

Margaret masked her need to laugh. "Of course. She's in her bedroom changing. Just got home from the millinery shop. She won't be a minute. Would you like something? Cider? It's cool, in the cellar."

"No, thank you," Billy croaked and followed as Margaret led him to the library where he nervously took the chair she offered. She remained standing.

"Been hot today," Margaret observed.

"Yes. It has." *Hot? You don't know how hot it is.*

"How are things at the shipping company?"

"Waiting for word on arrival of two of our ships. Fine."

"Any news from Adam? Or Matthew?"

"Not for a while. Adam's on the way home. Matthew's still in Philadelphia, so far as I know."

"I'm worried about Adam. His ship is overdue. Six days."

Billy slowly rubbed his hands together for a moment, then raised his eyes to hers. "I wouldn't start to worry yet. I learned today that there was a storm down in the West Indies last Thursday. Not a hurricane—wrong season for hurricanes—just a strong blow. Adam likely put into a port down there to ride it out. Philadelphia got the last of the storm two days ago. Monday. Rain. No wind. No reason to think Adam's in trouble. He's a good navigator, and Rittenhouse is a good captain. They'll be all right."

"How do you know about the storm? In Philadelphia."

"A ship that came in from the Caribbean today. I talked to them. Their first mate."

There was relief in Margaret's face. "Oh. I've been worried." She glanced at the door and said, "I can't imagine what's keeping Brigitte. Wait here. I'll just go see." She left the room and Billy heard the footsteps in the hall that served the bedrooms. Seconds later footsteps returned, slower, more deliberate, and then Brigitte came through the library door and closed it behind her.

Billy stood.

She was wearing an ankle-length, simple blue dress with a small white band at the waist. Her auburn-brown hair was curled and brushed, held back by a white ribbon tied into a bow. Never had he seen the depth of expression that he now saw in her hazel eyes.

He bowed slightly. "How are you?"

"Well." Her eyes did not leave his.

"It . . . I spoke with Matthew before he left for Philadelphia. And with your mother last Sunday. They gave permission for me to . . . to be here." Self-conscious, he stopped for a moment, then went on. "You remember that we talked a few months ago. . . . About marriage. That's my purpose in being here."

"I know."

Billy remained motionless for a moment, took a deep breath, then said, "There are so many things I thought I could say—I wanted to say. Now, here, looking at you as you are, none of them seems right." He dropped his eyes and tried to put his thoughts in order. Then he raised his eyes back to hers. He shook his head and said in a quiet voice, "Brigitte, I love you. I have loved you ever since I can remember. There is nothing in this life I want more than to have you for my wife. Will you have me?"

She looked at him steadily. Sandy hair, a round, plain face, thick shoulders, a barrel chest, legs like tree stumps, steady, solid, tested, tried. She smiled at the sheer sturdiness of him and the earnest goodness reflected in his face.

"I love you, Billy. Yes, I will be your wife."

He knew he would never again feel what rose in his chest at that moment.

He drew the box from his coat pocket and removed the lid. "I would

be honored if you would wear this ring." He could think of nothing
more that needed to be said, and he handed the box to her. She took it
and her eyes shone as she gazed at the simple beauty of Simon's work.
For a time she stood still, tenderly touching the ring with her fingers, face
glowing, and then she raised her face.

"I've never seen such a beautiful thing. I will be proud to wear it
wherever I go. Always."

She handed the box back to him, and he removed the engagement
ring with his thick, strong fingers and reached for her left hand. Gently,
he slipped it onto her ring finger, held her hand for a moment while he
studied it and the ring, then nodded and released her hand. She raised it
to peer at it, and he could not miss the radiance in her face. He put the
lid back on the box and replaced it, with the wedding band still inside, in
his coat pocket.

"Brigitte, I don't know how to tell you . . . my gratitude—"

She suddenly stepped close and wrapped her arms about him, and
she kissed him, and he closed her inside those arms that could lift a cannon, and he held her to him and kissed her. Neither knew how long they
stood in the embrace, nor did they care.

He released her, and she stepped back, face flushed, eyes glowing. "I
didn't expect it to feel this way," she said. "I didn't know what it would
be, but I did not expect it to feel so calm, so right. I shall never forget it."

"Nor will I."

Her eyes were glistening but she was smiling. "Could we tell mother?
I know she and Prissy are waiting somewhere, dying to hear it all."

Billy grinned and nodded. "Yes. We should."

He took her hand and they walked to the library door and Brigitte
opened it. Standing there, startled, wide-eyed, caught unashamedly eaves-
dropping, were Margaret and Prissy. Billy chuckled, then laughed, and
Brigitte laughed, and the two red-faced women laughed.

"Well?" Margaret exclaimed. "What happened? Did she say yes?"

Billy nodded as Brigitte held out her left hand, and Billy said. "She did."

At the sight of the ring, Margaret clapped a hand over her mouth.
"Oh! Oh! Did you ever see such a thing of beauty?"

She seized Brigitte's hand and Prissy reached, and the three women stood huddled, exclaiming, excited, sharing. Billy stood to one side, forgotten, ignored, grinning.

Prissy grasped Brigitte's arm and exclaimed, "Did you kiss him?"

Brigitte blushed. "Oh, Prissy, you don't ask such things."

"Well," Prissy blurted, "I do."

"Of course she kissed him," Margaret declared. She looked up at Billy. "Didn't she? And you kissed her."

Billy ducked his head, grinning, and remained silent, and Margaret reached up to embrace him. "Oh, Billy, I'm so happy for you two. So happy."

He held her for a moment and then she stepped back and spoke.

"Have you two picked the time for the wedding?"

Brigitte shook her head. "I thought our families should work that out. We'll have to find a time when Matthew's home. And Adam and Caleb."

Margaret thought for a moment. "Billy, can you work that out at the shipping company?"

"Yes."

"Make it soon. Not good to let these things go on too long."

"As soon as we know when Matthew's coming back from Philadelphia we can arrange it."

"Good. I'll talk with Dorothy. We'll take care of everything else." She turned to Prissy. "Come with me. We have things to do in the kitchen."

Prissy's eyebrows arched in question. "What to do? We're finished in the kitchen."

There was an edge in Margaret's voice. "No we're not. Come on."

Prissy looked at Margaret, then glanced at Brigitte and Billy, and raised a hand to cover her mouth. "Oh." She followed Margaret out of the library and closed the door without another word.

Billy turned to Brigitte, grinning, head shaking slightly. "Sometimes I wonder how long your mother has known this day would come."

Brigitte laughed. "I don't know. Probably longer than we can guess."

He took her hands. "I want you to know—I will cherish this little time always."

"As will I."

He drew her close and held her, and he kissed her.

"I should go. My mother and Trudy are waiting. Can I see you tomorrow?"

"Of course."

"I'll come after supper."

"Come early. Share supper with us."

"Would Margaret mind?"

"Mind? Has she ever?"

Neither could remember how many times over thirty years Billy had been at their supper table, or Matthew at the Weems's supper table.

"No, she hasn't. Tell her I thank her."

"For supper?"

"Yes. . . . And for you."

He took her by the hand and walked from the library to the front door, opened it, lingered for a moment looking at her, then walked out into the early purple of oncoming dusk. He paused at the front gate to raise one hand, and she waved back with her left hand, and then clasped her two hands to her breast, her right hand firmly pressed over her ring.

The heat of the day was passing, and dusk was deepening when Billy pushed through his gate and entered his house. Dorothy and Trudy were waiting in the parlor. Dorothy took one look at her grinning son and exclaimed, "You asked her, and she said yes!"

Billy couldn't help laughing. "It worked out."

Dorothy pointed. "Supper's on the table. Sit down and tell us while we eat. Everything."

They sat, Billy said grace, and the talk began.

Note

Billy Weems, Brigitte Dunson, and other characters and events in this chapter are fictional.

Philadelphia

May 30, 1787

CHAPTER XI

*T*hey came tentative, quiet, subdued, to gather in the East Room of the building on Chestnut, glancing at each other, saying little, their brains swamped, staggered by the four-hour thunderbolt Governor Edmund Randolph of Virginia had delivered that second day. In a single stroke he had blasted the Articles into oblivion forever and plunged the convention into a wild concoction of untried notions such as the world had never seen, or dreamed. Worse, they were now sworn to speak not one word of the proceedings outside the East Room! They could not gather at the Indian Queen, or one of their boardinghouse rooms, to thrash out what each thought he had heard from Randolph. Many, perhaps most of them, had spent a sleepless night in the privacy of their own rooms, pacing, running their hands through rumpled hair, mumbling to themselves, pacing again in their desperate effort at making their mind stretch far enough to grasp and understand the foundations on which Randolph's ramblings had finally come to rest. Some had caught it, to stand stock-still, mesmerized when it burst inside them like a bomb in the darkness. Others recoiled in shock, aghast at what they saw. The one common bond that bound them together as they took their seats was that none of them were sure. Of anything.

With the convention doors locked, the windows closed, and the shades drawn, every eye tracked Washington in total silence as he walked to the dais, took his chair, raised those blue-gray eyes, and said, "The convention will come to order."

No one moved.

Washington turned to William Jackson. "Mr. Secretary, is a quorum present?"

"It is, sir."

"Following the address of Mr. Randolph of Virginia yesterday, this convention elected to dissolve into a committee of the whole for the purpose of giving the delegates wider latitude and ease in debating the issues. Mr. Nathaniel Gorham of Massachusetts was elected to chair the committee of the whole. I now yield the chair to Mr. Gorham to conduct the business of the committee."

Washington rose, took his seat as a delegate, and Gorham took the chair on the dais. He took a few moments to organize the desk, then spoke.

"As a committee of the whole, our first item is to consider the fifteen proposals made by Governor Randolph yesterday. Debate is open."

Instantly Randolph rose and spoke. "I move that the first resolution be adopted, that is, that the Articles of Confederation be corrected and enlarged to accomplish the objects proposed by their institution."

His words were still echoing when Gouverneur Morris, the Pennsylvania delegate who was in truth from New York, but who by masterful political maneuvers had wrangled a seat as a delegate from Pennsylvania, was on his one foot, and his wooden leg. His voice was firm, strong.

"The first resolution is not consistent with the other fourteen! Are we to begin our work with obvious inconsistencies?"

Randolph's mind leaped ahead and he turned to look at the big man with the Roman nose and the wooden leg. *Morris intends laying this whole thing wide open! Now! Without prologue, without foundation!* For one fraction of a second Randolph hesitated while he decided whether he dared put the whole of it before the delegation, raw, head-on, unvarnished. Then he turned back to Gorham and spoke with resolve.

"I request that my previous motion be put aside and that we adopt the following three resolutions.

"One. That a union of the states merely federal will not accomplish the objects proposed by the Articles of Confederation, namely common defense, security of liberty, and general welfare.

"Two. That no treaty or treaties among the whole or part of the states, as individual sovereignties, would be sufficient.

"Three. That a national government ought to be established consisting of a supreme legislative, executive, and judiciary."

A collective gasp bounced off the walls. Some minds stalled and for a moment ceased functioning.

National? Supreme? What of the states? Their constitutions? Their courts? Is this man proposing the states and all they have fought for be surrendered? Abandoned? Abolished? Only the states are prepared to remain close enough to the people to know their will. A national government? Never can it be reached by the people! Not in ten thousand years!

With their thoughts scattered like autumn leaves in the first winds of winter, young Charles Pinckney of South Carolina stood, struggling to form the right words. Ben Franklin turned to study him, his old eyes narrowed as he concentrated.

Pinckney's voice was clear, his inquiry straight and direct. "Mr. Randolph, how far do you propose going in reducing the power of the states?"

Pinckney remained standing for a moment, then sat down, and Pierce Butler of South Carolina quickly arose.

"I rise to pose one question to Mr. Randolph. Can he show us that the existence of the states cannot be preserved by any other mode than a national government?"

There it was! In the first twenty minutes of the first session that addressed the real issues that had brought them all to Philadelphia, they had cut to the heart of the issue that had crippled America for twelve long, frustrating years.

Without moving, Franklin shifted his eyes from Pinckney to Butler, then to Randolph. Did Randolph have the political acumen to understand the opening these two delegates had just delivered?

Randolph licked dry lips. "It is not my intent to attack the sovereignty of the states." He stopped and looked first at Pinckney, then Butler, allowing time for his words to settle in. "Far from it. It was only my intent to replace the Confederation. Can we agree that the Confederation has proven itself fatally flawed? Unresponsive to the needs of our country today? I see no way to remedy it except to abolish it. By proposing a national government, I do not in the least suggest that it will, or should, directly or indirectly, abolish the state governments. I use the term *national* in the sense of the *form* of government which we so desperately need, not the *powers* with which it shall be vested. Those powers will be as this convention chooses to define them, and not one whit more."

Franklin relaxed. Randolph had survived, very well.

Charles Cotesworth Pinckney, twice the age of his young cousin and with twice the respect, rose. "Do we dare? Do we dare conduct a discussion of a system of government founded on principles so different from the federal constitution that now exists? In short, what authority does this convention actually enjoy, to even consider replacing the legitimate government of the United States?"

Again Gouverneur Morris rose, and his wooden leg thumped on the hardwood floor. His reply was blunt, strong, loud.

"Let us be honest. The clear choice facing this convention is this: Shall we have a confederation, or a nation? A federal government such as the Articles of Confederation created is a mere compact, resting on the good faith of the parties. A national or supreme government, however, has complete and compulsive operation on both the states and the citizens." Morris paused for a moment to order his thoughts and select his words. "One supreme government is better calculated to prevent wars or render them less expensive or bloody. We had better take a supreme government now than a despot twenty years hence—for come he must. What Mr. Randolph proposes is not for the fainthearted. But, I beg you to consider the simple truth that there can be but *one* supreme power, and only one!"

The words struck deep, and for a moment silence held as the delegates' minds slowly accepted the fundamental truth Morris had thrust before them, and they realized the issue was framed, finally, fully, and staring the entire convention in the face: would they attempt to amend the old government and the Articles of Confederation from which it sprang and struggle on, or would they sweep it aside and create an entirely new one?

Morris pursed his mouth for a moment and sat down.

Instantly Roger Sherman of Connecticut stood. Sixty-Six years of age, born to a poor farm family in Massachusetts, he later walked to a new life in Connecticut where he became a jack-of-all-trades for a time before he became a self-taught lawyer and storekeeper, publisher of almanacs, and successful treasurer of Yale University, which awarded him an honorary Master of Arts degree for his unselfish service. So impressed was Connecticut with this honest, plain, homely, shambling man with a large family that it sent him to the Confederation Congress for years, where he labored with distinction, serving on the five-man committee of which Franklin and Jefferson were members, to draft the Declaration of Independence.

"I rise to remind us all of our commissions, or rather, the limitation of our commissions. I agree that the Confederation lacks sufficient power to be an effective government. I do not quarrel with that. I also agree that the jurisdictions of the federal and the state governments must not overlap. But I do question—challenge if you will—the right of this convention to make great inroads on the existing system."

Washington remained silent, while his thoughts raced. *He's trying to be cautious—too cautious. If the first act of this convention is to abolish the Confederation, he fears the states will never consider whatever comes later—he's saying go slow—think reform, not revolution. Will the other states follow him? Or will they follow Randolph and Morris?*

Some delegates rose to condemn the proposition that the old Articles of Confederation must fall, while others stood to loudly declare there was no other way.

"The idea of a *national* government as contradistinguished from a *federal* one, never entered into the mind of any state in sending delegates! And may I be so bold as to suggest that it never entered the mind of one in ten thousand of the citizens of the United States, either!"

"Not so! From the outset, those who have seriously contemplated the subject have been fully convinced that a total change of the system is necessary!"

"What, pray tell, are we considering? Precisely what is the difference between a *national* government, and a *federal* government, in the context now before us?"

"It is very simple. No one need be mistaken. A *federal* government is what we now have. It consists of a Confederation Congress convened under the authority of the thirteen states, which Congress is empowered to create acts that affect the states, and the states *only*. It has no power to act upon *one single citizen* of the United States. Further, the Congress is totally dependent on the good faith and will of the states to comply with all acts legally created by it. Should any state refuse to comply with any act of Congress, Congress is absolutely powerless to require the obedience of that state. Congress is *powerless* to enforce its own acts! Is there any question why we find the United States on the brink of oblivion?

"However, a *national* government, as contemplated in this committee, is empowered to pass acts that are obligatory upon the states, and in addition, to pass acts that operate directly upon the individual citizens of the states. Thus it is that in the case of a renegade state that refuses to comply, a *national* government is empowered to *require* compliance, since it can *require* the individual citizens to comply with its acts by any means necessary, including the force of arms.

"And there we have it, gentlemen. We speak of ourselves as a nation. But we have not yet accepted the hard truth that if we are indeed a *nation*, we *must* have a *national* government."

"What? What? How can we have a *national* government without destroying our *state* governments? If the national government you describe is to exist, the state governments must yield!"

"Not true! Not true! Cannot the *national* government be limited to issues that address matters of *national* interest, and leave the states to address matters that are limited to purely *state* issues?"

"Are you suggesting, sir, that Americans are going to be citizens of *two* governments? One state, the other national? And do so at the same time?"

"That is *exactly* what is being suggested."

"How, sir, can one man answer to two masters at the same moment?"

"Quite easily. Limit the authority of the two masters to the extent that one cannot be in conflict with the other! In the case before us, let the *national* government limit itself to *national* affairs. Let the *state* governments limit themselves to *state* affairs."

"You propose that can be done?"

"You propose that it cannot? Should we fail, the shame is upon *us!*"

James Madison had turned in his chair in front of the dais to peer into the faces of the delegates as the tempo of the argument heated. He turned back to his desk repeatedly, his quill scratching furiously to keep pace with the essence of the arguments, and those who rose to speak. Washington sat to one side like a statue, face passive, only his eyes moving as he absorbed the temper and the quality of each man's contribution. *It's coming—the fundamentals of the plan are surviving—the dissenters are beginning to see—truth and right are stubborn—they're getting it.*

Franklin was sitting bent forward, slowly massaging his gout-ridden leg. From time to time he glanced at the speakers, then back at his leg, from all appearances more interested in getting a little relief from the relentless ache than the fact that this gathering was locked in mortal combat over an issue that could change the world forever. *The pendulum's swinging—many—maybe most—had no notion what they were walking into when they came here—they're past the shock—starting to find the ground—not quite ready yet—but soon—is Randolph capable—will he know when?*

George Mason sat erect in his chair, every nerve, every instinct alive, racing to stay abreast of the swift change of spirit, of attitude in the hall. Sixty-two years of age, the son of Virginia wealth and aristocracy, his wife an heiress of Maryland wealth and aristocracy, he had reluctantly served in the House of Burgesses in 1759, only to flee at first opportunity from what he saw in the hypocrisy and intrigues of politics. He was appointed to the Virginia convention, and Virginia found in him a man gifted and eloquent in his contributions to the Virginia Constitution, and later in the famous Virginia Declaration of Rights the same year, 1776. Indeed, the historic Declaration was very nearly the sole work of George

Mason. He, with Thomas Jefferson and James Madison, formed a triumvirate without peer in their native Virginia. Slowly but steadily he had built Gunston Hall, a vast wheat and tobacco plantation of national reputation, on which he kept and maintained three hundred slaves—an irony and enigma on which he had thus far chosen to remain silent.

Mason turned slightly to judge the speakers as the debate raged on. *The nabobs are beginning to falter—beginning to sense that the Confederation is gone— beginning to see that the only issue before us is whether we have the vision and the courage to declare it dead right here, right now, or watch it die within the next five years and the United States with it—do they have the eyes to see—and the courage to act? Do they?*

Slowly Randolph rose to his feet, eyes turned to Nathaniel Gorham, waiting. The murmuring slowed and stopped, and all other delegates eased back into their chairs, staring, waiting.

Gorham gestured. "Mr. Randolph? Do you rise to speak?"

"I do."

An unexpected spirit came stealing into the hot, closed hall—as though every man in the room sensed that a time had arrived which had been preparing for hundreds of years. The silence was electric as Governor Randolph continued.

"I do not intend multiplying words for the sake of multiplying words. Rather, I am compelled to speak simply. I have it in my heart that the matter before us should be resolved now. Here. By us. It is for this reason we have come to this chamber." He paused for a moment and his eyes dropped to his desktop, then lifted again. "I therefore move that the three resolutions I previously made now be brought to a vote. Yea or nay. All else we do here will finally come to rest on what we now do."

A delegate stood. "May I request, Mr. Chairman, that the text of those resolutions be read once again, that we not be mistaken in our recollections?"

Gorham nodded. "Mr. Secretary?"

William Jackson stood and droned through the resolutions.

"First . . . a union of the states merely federal will not accomplish the objects . . .

"Second . . . no treaties among the whole or part of the states would be sufficient . . .

"Third . . . a national government ought to be established consisting of a supreme legislative, executive, and judiciary."

Jackson turned his face to Gorham, set his ledger on his desk, and sat down.

Gorham straightened in his chair. "You've heard the resolutions again. Now, do we have a second to Mr. Randolph's motion for a vote?"

"Second."

"The motion passes. The vote will be taken by delegation."

Madison was sitting erect, breath coming short. Washington did not change the expression on his face. There was a light in Franklin's eyes.

Gorham stared down at Jackson. "Mr. Secretary, take the vote."

"Massachusetts."

"Aye."

"New York."

"The delegates are divided. New York abstains."

"Delaware."

"Aye."

"Pennsylvania."

"Aye."

"Virginia."

"Aye."

There was an audible release of breath in the room. Eight states represented, and New York had abstained. Four states of seven had voted in the affirmative. The resolutions were passed! Jackson went on.

"Connecticut."

"Nay."

"North Carolina."

"Aye."

"South Carolina."

"Aye."

Six affirmative, one negative, and one abstention. No one had believed the vote would be so overwhelmingly one-sided.

Open talk filled the hall, and Gorham let it run for several moments. For one second Madison closed his eyes as relief flooded through his being. They had crossed the mountain! They had shown the courage— reckless as it might be—to ignore the limited commissions each had from his home state to amend the Articles and had instead abandoned them altogether. The old, fatally flawed government was dead. They had now set a course to create a new government, the shape and character of which was known only to the Almighty.

Slowly Madison rose above his euphoria and turned his thoughts to the realities his plan had brought on, and for a split second a shudder seized him. *Big states against small states—how will they do—slavery—can they rise above it—how will they structure a new national government—will they follow the plan?*

He did not know.

Gorham's voice settled the hall. "Gentlemen, we have accomplished the business of the day."

Men glanced at the clock on the wall, startled that they were deep into the afternoon.

Gorham continued. "Are there any other matters that ought to be placed before this committee at this time?"

No one spoke.

"Then this committee is adjourned for the day. The convention shall continue under the authority of its president, George Washington."

Gorham left the dais, and Washington stepped to the chair behind the desk.

"Is there further business to be brought before this convention?"

There was none.

"I remind each of you of the oath of secrecy we have all taken. This convention is adjourned until ten o'clock tomorrow morning."

Notes

The proceedings of the Convention for May 30, 1787, were as they have been set forth in this chapter, including the nicety of the delegates conducting their business as a committee of the whole with Gorham acting as chair.

Following debate, matters were reduced to a vote on the three resolutions, which were approved six states to one, with one abstention, as described, thus abolishing the Articles of Confederation without anyone knowing what they were going to do to replace them. Rossiter, *1787: The Grand Convention,* pp. 172–73; Warren, *The Making of the Constitution,* pp. 146–56; Berkin, *A Brilliant Solution,* pp. 68–71; Bernstein, *Are We to Be a Nation?* p. 160.

Gouverneur Morris, Pierce Butler, Charles Cotesworth Pinckney, and Roger Sherman are all accurately described. Rossiter, *1787: The Grand Convention,* pp. 90–92, 107–8, 131–32, 133.

Philadelphia

May 31, 1787

CHAPTER XII

★ ★ ★

*J*oseph Fry swung the big door closed, twisted the key, and quickly passed down both sides of the hall, closing all the windows and drawing the drapes before he returned to the door to stand facing the dais. The stifling buildup of heat began immediately. George Washington took his place behind the desk, opened the session, dissolved the convention into a committee of the whole, and delivered the desk to Nathaniel Gorham. Gorham spent scant time on formalities before he reached the heart of the day's agenda.

"Resolved, that the national legislature ought to consist of two branches."

Madison laid down his quill for a moment and turned to watch and listen. *This could be very quick or very lengthy—one of the branches is the senate, and the qualifications for senators in the state legislatures is that they must be property owners—the elite—and worse yet, in some states those selected by the legislature to elect the senators are the greatest of the property owners—the elite electing the elite to represent the elite—to the ignoring of the common folk. The Confederation Congress is a single house legislature—Pennsylvania also—but eleven of the thirteen states already have bicameral legislatures—two houses—they'll vote aye on this resolution—what will Pennsylvania do?*

Pennsylvania did nothing.

It was the cautious Roger Sherman of Connecticut who stood to speak against the resolution. "I see no necessity for a legislature consisting of two branches. The complaints so often voiced against the Confederation Congress have not been of the lack of wisdom of its acts, but of the insufficiency of its powers."

George Mason of Virginia rose. "I disagree. While the minds of the people of America are unsettled as to some points, in two points I am sure they are settled: first in attachment to the republican form of government, and second, in an attachment to more than one branch in the legislature. Only thus do we have one chamber acting as a check on the other."

Mason sat down and Madison waited, but no others stood to speak. Gorham shrugged, called for the vote, and the resolution passed with but one "nay"—Pennsylvania. Madison glanced at Benjamin Franklin, then turned back to his quill and ledger, smiling to himself. *The Pennsylvania "nay" was for Franklin—they all know he's partial to a unicameral legislature.*

Gorham picked up the next paper from his desk. "We shall take up our next order of business. Resolved, that the members of the first branch of the National Legislature ought to be elected by the people of the several states."

A hush settled as each delegate struggled to come to a focus. Within the past twenty-four hours the convention had buried the only government the United States had ever known, and started construction of a new one by establishing a bicameral legislature. Most felt they were riding a cyclone, streaking into blank, uncharted space, wildly groping for familiar landmarks, and finding none.

The people elect the members of the lower house? Common people? Uneducated? Ignorant in the business of government and business affairs? People who could be swayed by eloquent scoundrels, or cowed by despots? Are not the property owners in the state legislatures—who have education and the wisdom of experience in political and business affairs—better qualified to select the new national congress?

Or, is the nature of a national government such that it ought to be established by the direct vote of the people at large, not state legislatures? And if by the direct vote of the common people, what is to be done about the chicanery and deception of the power mongers, for nothing is more certain than that they will come, as they have since the dawn of time, and they will corrupt the government to their own gain, on the backs of the common people.

The issue was framed: is the lower house of the national congress to be elected by the people, or by the state legislatures? While it sounded simple and mundane when   en, there were those in the hall who recognized that they were now facing the second momentous vote of the convention. In recorded history, no government of consequence had ever gambled its existence on the will of the common people. Would this delegation dare?

Mason of Virginia rose. "The lower house is to be the grand depository of the democratic principles of government. It ought to know and sympathize with every part of the whole republic. We ought to attend to the rights of every class of people. I have often wondered at the indifference of the superior classes of society to this dictate of humanity and policy; considering that, however affluent their circumstances or elevated their situations might be, the course of a few years not only might but certainly will distribute their posterity through the lowest classes of society. Every selfish motive, therefore, every family attachment, ought to recommend such a system of policy as would provide no less carefully for the rights and happiness of the lowest than of the highest orders of citizens."

He had not yet sat down when Elbridge Gerry of Massachusetts was on his feet, slight, frail, sharp-faced, bony finger pointing.

"To place the government at the whim of the common man would lead only to the demise of the entire structure. The evils we experience flow from the excess of democracy, and while I am firm in my commitment to the republican form of government, I have been taught by experience the danger of the leveling spirit. I do not suppose that the common man is by nature evil, or destructive—far from it. But I do propose that the affairs of government—complex and intertwined as they are—are far beyond the experience and grasp of the common man. The people simply are not prepared, nor qualified, to make the judgments upon which governments survive. I do not distrust the heart of the common man, but I do distrust his judgment in the matters of government which are so clearly beyond his abilities. Far better that all powers of the national government we propose be derived from the state legislatures." Gerry pursed his mouth for a moment, then sat down.

Madison was motionless, breathing lightly, waiting to see how the remainder of the delegates would divide on the question. They had come to the second decisive fork in the road. Would they follow Mason or Gerry?

The cautious, reluctant Roger Sherman stood. "It is clear that the people immediately should have as little to do as may be about the government. They want information constantly and are indiscriminate in the sources from which they get it. They are ever subject to the likelihood of being misled on the most crucial of issues, and in time, likely sooner than later, there is no doubt they will be, to their own wounding."

Sherman was barely seated when James Wilson rose. Born in Scotland in 1742, Wilson was an able and learned lawyer who had served in Congress. An eager signer of the Declaration of Independence, he stood in highest repute in his city of residence, Philadelphia. Washington had declared him to be one of the most able, candid, and honest members of the convention. Thoughtfully Wilson spoke.

"It appears obvious to me that there is great wisdom in giving the federal pyramid as broad a base as possible. Let the people learn the business of government, to become competent, and collectively become the base on which this government rests."

Madison let Wilson be seated before he stood. He took a deep breath, and in his quiet voice, succinctly laid out his logic.

"Experience and study leave but one conclusion. I have long considered the popular election as essential to every plan of free government. To the extent we vest the electoral powers in less than all the people, we have reduced free government. The great fabric to be raised would be more stable and durable if it should rest on the solid foundation of the people themselves, than if it should stand merely on the pillars of the legislatures."

Madison sat down. Franklin sensed the time had arrived for the vote, and looked at Gorham. Washington's eyes moved, first to Madison, then to Gorham, waiting.

Gorham spoke. "There being no further debate, the ballot will be taken."

A charged, hushed silence held while Jackson called for the votes.

Six states voted "aye." Two, South Carolina and New Jersey, voted "nay." Two, Connecticut and Delaware, were divided, and abstained. The power in the new nation would be vested in the common people, not just the elite.

Franklin shifted his feet and gritted his teeth at the pain in his legs. He moved them until they were more comfortable, then settled with his thoughts running. *A landmark! The common man won!* He paused for a moment, then his thoughts continued. *But no one defined the term. Who is the "common man"? What color is he? White? Red? Yellow? Black? We've got "common men" of all those colors. Do we mean to let them all vote?* He pursed his mouth for a moment, and then a wry smile came. *I think we haven't seen the last of the debate on the "common man."*

Large white handkerchiefs were in rich abundance as the delegates mopped at the sweat glistening on their faces. The air inside the closed room had become stagnant, stifling, and they peered longingly at the drawn drapes covering the closed windows. The hardheaded Yankees from the north silently cursed their wool suits, while the southern gentlemen sat more easily in their light linens. Gorham, at the desk, reached for the next document, and the room quieted as he scanned it. He read it aloud.

"The national legislature shall enjoy the legislative rights vested in congress by the confederation, and moreover to legislate in all cases to which the separate states are incompetent or in which the harmony of the United States may be interrupted by the exercise of individual legislation."

Washington glanced at the faces of the delegates he could see. The eyes of many, perhaps most of them, were glazed, their expressions a near total blank. Every man in the room knew that the old confederation had failed because it lacked the power to enforce its own acts. They also knew that if this government they were now trying to invent one piece at a time were to succeed, they could not make the same fatal error. They *must* give it the power to enforce what it enacted. But few of them had ever dreamed of granting Congress the broad, all-inclusive, sweeping powers that were now on the floor for debate. Such powers in the wrong hands could destroy the states!

Pierce Butler of South Carolina was the first to collect his wits and stand. "I confess that yesterday I stated my willingness to go to great lengths to establish a government that had the power to succeed. But as I now contemplate the language in the resolution before us, I believe we are running into an extreme in taking away the powers of the states. That we cannot—must not—do!"

John Rutledge of North Carolina was on his feet before Butler was seated. "I rise to object—strongly—to the use of the term *incompetent*. How are we to understand that word in the context of this resolution? In what particulars is a state to be considered 'incompetent'? Who makes that decision? The state? Or the national government? And if it be the national government, then it is only a matter of time before the individual states are rendered not only incompetent, but for all practical purposes, nullities!"

Charles Pinckney was moving in his chair, nervous, impatient, and stood the moment Rutledge sat down.

"I agree with Mr. Rutledge. The term *incompetent* can mean whatever a man, or an entire congress, wants it to mean. Before we find ourselves trapped in such a circumstance, we *must* define what we are taking away from the states, and what we are giving to this new, untried, unproven national government. We must have a detailed enumeration of those powers."

Randolph turned to Rutledge. "I disdain any intention to give indefinite powers to the national legislature. That was never in the contemplation of this resolution. Once again may I say, these resolutions are merely intended to propose the *form* of the national government. The detail is for this body to resolve."

Madison stood, and the hall quieted. The delegation was beginning to understand that the resolutions so boldly proclaimed by the eloquent Randolph were in fact part of a much larger, radical, startling new plan for the national government. And while from all appearances the entire Virginia delegation had become the champion for the new plan, all the delegates, or nearly all of them, were rapidly learning that the plan was the product of the years of study and preparation by James Madison, not Randolph. It was Madison who, largely unnoticed, had spent years gathering the best he could garner from the great minds of America—Jefferson, Washington, Mason, Wythe, Adams, Hamilton, Jay—the list was nearly inexhaustible—and reduced the kernel of it to the plan now being fed to the convention one resolution at a time. And it was Madison who had harassed the Virginia delegation to appear in Philadelphia days before the convention was to gather, and insisted they meet daily to polish and refine his plan.

Madison turned from his position directly in front of the dais to face the entire convention, and no man stirred.

"I have brought with me into the convention a strong bias in favor of an enumeration and definition of the powers necessary to be exercised by the national legislature; but I have also brought doubts concerning the practicability of such an enumeration and definition. My wishes have remained unaltered, but my doubts have become stronger."

The delegates nearest him were intent on every word. Those furthest were beginning to sit straighter in their chairs, turning their heads to hear the quiet voice. The call came from the rear of the room, "Would you speak a bit louder, Mr. Madison? We cannot hear you."

Madison smiled and nodded his understanding, and raised his voice to continue. "What my opinion on the question might ultimately be, I cannot tell. But I will shrink from nothing which should be found essential to such a form of government as will provide for the safety, liberty, and happiness of the community."

It was enough. No one rose to speak further on the resolution. Gorham called for the vote, and William Jackson recorded it. All states present voted "aye," except Connecticut, which was divided, and abstained.

Gorham did not hesitate. "We shall address the next resolution. 'Resolved, that Congress shall have authority to negate all laws passed by

the states which contravene in its opinion the articles of union.' "
Gorham looked out at the committee. "Open for debate."

A delegate stood. "I move to amend the resolution to include a provision that the national congress be empowered to negative state laws
contravening national treaties."

"Seconded."

"Moved and seconded. Further debate?"

There was none. Gorham droned on. "On the motion to amend,
Mr. Jackson will record the vote."

It was unanimous.

"On the resolution as now amended, open for debate."

Most of the delegates were all too well aware that the debate on this
issue had been opened years before the notion of the Grand Convention
entered the minds of the delegates. The sins of the state legislatures were
legion, against other states, the Union, and their own citizenry, and few
thinking men hesitated in delivering broadsides. George Mason caught
the bitter sum of it in 1783, in a letter written to William Cabell, in
which he said:

"A strict adherence to the distinctions between right and wrong for
the future is absolutely necessary to restore that confidence and reverence
in the people for the Legislature which a contrary conduct has so greatly
impaired, and without which their laws must remain little better than a
dead letter. Frequent interferences with private property and contracts,
retrospective laws destructive of all public faith as well as confidence
between man and man, and flagrant violations of the Constitution, must
disgust the best and wisest part of the community, occasion a depravity
of manners, bring the Legislatures into contempt, and finally produce
anarchy and public convulsion."

Early in the convention Madison had laid it bare. "Effectual provision for the security of private rights and the steady dispensation of
justice are essential, since interferences with these, perhaps more than
anything else, produced this Convention. The state legislatures have tres-
passed on each other, giving preference to their own citizens, and to
aggressions on the rights of other states by emissions of paper money

and kindred measures; also, the retaliating acts passed by the states pose a threatened danger not in the harmony only, but the tranquility of the union. Experience in all the states has evinced a powerful tendency in the legislature to absorb all power into its vortex. This is the real danger to the American constitution."

Gouverneur Morris had been vociferous. "The public liberty is in greater danger from legislative usurpations than from any other source. Legislative instability and legislative tyranny are the great dangers to be apprehended."

Many men now sitting in the heat of the East Room had joined in the wholesale condemnation of the errant legislatures. Thus it was that when Gorham called for formal debate, none saw need to utter a single word. The matter had long since been decided. Silence held for ten seconds before Gorham straightened, surprise clear on his face, and asked, "Is there debate?"

A few heads shook in the negative, and a startled Gorham said, "There being no debate, is there a second?"

"Seconded."

"Mr. Jackson will record the vote."

The vote was unanimous.

Both Franklin and Washington moved slightly in their chairs, then settled, each caught up in reckoning what was happening on this last day in May 1787.

Gorham took up another document. "We now take up our last matter of business. 'Resolved, that the national legislature be empowered to call forth the force of the union against any member of the union failing to fulfill its duty under the articles thereof.'"

With no exception, every man in the hall understood that the fundamental flaw that finally doomed the old Confederation congress was the fact it was powerless to enforce its own acts. Without question, the entire committee knew they could not allow the same error to exist in the new government. It *must have* power to enforce its acts, including force of arms if necessary.

To the surprise of the entire committee, it was Madison who stood first.

"I have had time to reflect on the use of force as implied in this resolution, and the more I have considered it, the more I doubt the practicability, the justice, and the efficacy of it, when applied to people collectively, and not individually."

Pinckney's thoughts were running. *He sees that punishing an entire state is excessive—punishing an individual or an institution is more to be desired—and he's right.*

Madison finished. "Accordingly, I move that debate and vote on this resolution be postponed to a date to be determined at a future time."

The second came instantly, and the vote was unanimous. The issue was postponed.

Gorham glanced at his pocket watch, wiped at the sweat on his forehead, and declared, "The committee has concluded the business of the day. If there is nothing else to properly come before us, we are adjourned, and I deliver the chair back to General Washington for the concluding affairs of the convention."

Handkerchiefs were in abundance as Gorham stepped down from the dais and Washington started from his chair. Men moved in their chairs, and small talk held for a few moments. A half-sheet of paper fluttered unnoticed from one table to the aisle floor as Washington mounted the two steps up onto the dais and took his chair.

"Is there further business for this convention?"

There was none.

"We stand adjourned until ten o'clock tomorrow morning, June first." Washington began gathering his papers from his desk.

For a moment George Mason leaned back in his chair, eyes narrowed in thought while he took stock of what the day had brought. *Yesterday we struck down the only government this country ever had—today we set up a two-house congress—gave it power over everything it thinks the states are incompetent to handle—without a hint of a listing of what that means—gave the vote to the common man—whoever he is—and very nearly authorized the new national congress to march the whole Continental army into a disobedient state and take it over! If anyone outside this room hears all this, I expect the doors will be smashed down within minutes, and incensed citizens will adjourn our grand convention* sine die, *forthwith.*

He straightened, then rose with the other delegates, and they all began gathering up their notes and papers, when one of them noticed the half-sheet of paper lying in the aisle. For a moment he stared, then picked it up and walked forward to the dais to face Washington.

"Mr. President, this paper was found on the aisle floor. I have not examined it, but I thought it ought to be brought to.your attention." Washington took the paper, and while the delegate turned on his heel and marched back to his seat, Washington unfolded it. Those nearest had witnessed the entire episode and were watching when the lightning came into Washington's eyes, and the muscles in his jaw began working. Instantly the entire convention became motionless, silent, while their President read the document again to be certain, and then he raised his eyes and held up the paper.

"One of you allowed this document to be left on the aisle floor. On it are notes regarding some of the work done today by the committee of the whole."

Not one man moved a hand, or a handkerchief, in the stifling, stale air. Sweat was left running as Washington continued.

"I must entreat you gentlemen to be more careful, lest our transactions get into the newspapers and disturb the public repose by premature speculations. I know not whose paper it is, but there it is."

He turned and threw it down on the desk behind him. "Let him who owns it take it!"

Every eye was locked on Washington as he picked up his hat. He bowed slightly from the waist, straightened to his full height, stepped down from the dais, and marched down the aisle in dead silence, looking neither right nor left, the sound of his clicking boot heels echoing from the walls. Those standing on the aisle shrank slightly as he passed, and for several moments no one moved or spoke. Talk and movement began hesitantly, and then the delegates quietly filed out of the hall, each peering down at the aisle floor, and around every desk as they went.

The incriminating half-sheet of paper was never claimed.

Notes

On May 31, 1787, the committee of the whole addressed the issue of who shall elect the first house of the bicameral legislature—the state legislatures or the people—which placed the question squarely before the committee: Could they trust common people to be responsible for their own government? It had never been done before in history, and the issue was hotly debated before the vote was taken. It passed, six to two, with two states abstaining. The next issue proposed granting power to the newly proposed national government to legislate in all matters in which the various states were incompetent—which is to say, the national government had to have power to legislate on national affairs, and the states were to have power to legislate on state affairs. It passed unanimously. The proposed vesting of power in the new national government to punish disobedient states was postponed and they adjourned. The Grand Convention was now creating a totally new government, unheard of, undefined, one step at a time. Warren, *The Making of the Constitution*, pp. 158–72; Rossiter, *1787: The Grand Convention*, pp. 72–73; Moyers, *Report from Philadelphia*, see page dated Thursday, May 31, 1787.

James Wilson, George Mason, John Rutledge, and Elbridge Gerry are correctly described. Rossiter, *1787: The Grand Convention*, pp. 85–86, 104–5, 120–21, 130–31.

The incident herein recited of the delegate who allowed a piece of paper to be left on the floor of the convention room, which was given to George Washington as President of the Convention, prompting him to warmly reprimand whoever dropped it, is true. No one ever claimed the paper. Farrand, *The Framing of the Constitution of the United States*, p. 65; Warren, *The Making of the Constitution*, p. 139.

CHAPTER XIII

★ ★ ★

*I*t was not yet ten o'clock when Benjamin Franklin slowly set his feet on the cobblestones in front of the Statehouse and eased his eighty-one-year-old body out of the coach to see if his gout-ridden legs would take the load. One of the coachmen was at his side, an arm about his waist, the other beneath his elbow to take some of the weight until the legs stopped trembling and Franklin could straighten. The heat had held through the night, and the morning sun had turned Philadelphia into a sweltering sauna of dead air so heavy the streets seemed locked in a hazy mist.

Franklin set his cane and smiled at the coachman. "Thank you. I think I can manage from here."

The man nodded and released his hold and took one step back, watching intently as Franklin took the first few faltering steps. The stride of the old statesman in the plain brown suit and the long gray hair became stronger as he walked up to the door of the Statehouse, and he nodded his thanks to the person who opened it for him to enter.

He made his way down the hall with his thoughts reaching back to a time that not one other man in the building could recall. Born in Boston in 1706, the youngest of twelve children, he left home at age seventeen for Philadelphia to seek his fortune. Now, this morning, the first day of June of 1787, he could not remember the plethora of high positions he had held, both in America and in Europe, nor all the inventions that had come from his genius, nor all the honors and laurels that the world had heaped on him as a scientist, statesman, inventor, philosopher. Nor did he care. None knew better than he that the world cannot give that which is most precious in life. That is earned, not given. He could not reckon the number of kings and monarchs who had it in their hearts and hands to do great and grand works, only to sacrifice the dream to the insidious seduction of power and adulation. Great works are reserved for those with the strength and the vision to hold to a loftier view. None knew it better than Franklin.

He fumbled inside his rumpled coat for his credentials, smiled at Joseph Fry as the doorman waved him into the chamber, and walked slowly to his desk. He took his time in backing up to his chair and easing his body down, then heaved a great sigh while he smiled and nodded to those who paused to pay him silent respect. With his cane laid across his desk, he moved his feet to ease the ache. For a moment his jowled face sobered.

Today we find out the shape of the executive office of the United States. Will it be one man, with the risk of him becoming a corrupted despot? Or will it be a council, with the risk of jealousies and greed between them destroying the office altogether? And what powers will the executive have? A puppet? A king? He shrugged and settled back to listen.

Nathaniel Gorham took his chair on the dais, Jackson reported a quorum present, and Gorham scanned his agenda.

"The first business to come before this committee today is the following resolution." He tracked with his finger as he read in a voice devoid of emotion: "'Resolved, that a national executive be instituted; to be chosen by the national legislature; for a term of years to be determined; to receive punctually at stated times a fixed compensation for the services rendered; in which no increase or diminution shall be made so as to affect the magistracy existing at the time of such increase or diminution; and to be ineligible a second time; and that besides a general authority to execute the national laws, it ought to enjoy the executive rights vested in Congress by the Confederation.'"

He finished reading and peered out into the faces of the delegation.

A strange silence held, as though the delegates were reluctant to speak. Franklin straightened his left leg and sat upright, concern creeping into his face as he waited. Gorham wiped at sweat on his forehead, looked at Washington in question, then Madison, waiting for someone to rise. No one moved or spoke.

Gorham's voice sounded too loud in the silence and stifling heat. "Is there debate?"

Slowly James Wilson of Pennsylvania rose, and every eye in the room was on him. "I propose that a national executive to consist of a single person be instituted."

The delegates struggled with the temptation to turn and stare at George Washington, the only living man on earth in whom they would dare place such power. Every delegate had lived part of his life under the hand of a king and had learned the bitter truth. Power corrupts. Some were remembering King George II of England who died insane, and some were remembering King George III whose lust for power had cost England the thirteen colonies, and some were remembering the Governor of Pennsylvania who had turned his high position into an open and notorious extortion business. And a few were remembering that Robert Morris, seated among them as a delegate from Pennsylvania, had become a despot in his office of Superintendent of Finance for the United States. For his alleged abuse of power, he had been removed from office and a committee appointed to replace him. His salvation as a politician and financial wizard rested on the fact that despite his excesses, he had rescued the country from the vortex of financial ruin and most likely civil war.

Franklin allowed the strained, odd quiet to continue for a time, then thumped the floor with his cane. Gorham acknowledged him, and Franklin spoke without rising.

"Gentlemen. The form of the office of the presidency of this government, and the powers with which it is to be vested, are a point of great importance. We ought not hesitate, but speak out boldly. I urge you all to deliver your sentiments on it."

The delegates covertly glanced about before John Rutledge of South

Carolina rose. "Am I in error in my perception that there is a sense of shyness among us regarding this resolution, and other resolutions as well? And am I in error in concluding that it is a result of most of us having previously openly and frankly taken a hard position on the issues, that we now feel we are precluded from changing our minds? I do not take that to be the case at all. Quite the reverse. Only by taking a position and then engaging in lively debate to defend it do we find its weaknesses and flaws. And once such flaws are discovered, prudent men change their minds accordingly. On the question before us, it is my opinion that the chief executive should be one person, and one only, although I do not favor giving him the power of war and peace. A single man would feel the greatest responsibility and administer the public affairs best."

Rutledge stopped and the robust voice of Gouverneur Morris boomed, "Hear, hear!"

Charles Pinckney was on his feet instantly. "I recommend that the proposition of Messrs. Rutledge and Wilson and Gouverneur Morris is correct. The executive should be but one person. Only then can we expect that office to be executed with energy and dispatch."

Roger Sherman of Connecticut tossed his quill on his notes and stood. "I disagree." He leaned forward, one index finger thrust upward for emphasis. "The traditional view of such an executive, and the view I urge us to take, is very simple. The executive is nothing more than an institution for carrying the will of the legislature into effect." He paused to let murmuring grow, then decline, and he went on. "The number of persons serving in the executive office should be determined by the legislature, and the legislature should select them and appoint them."

James Wilson rose again, and all eyes turned to him. "I perceive that the only powers strictly executive in nature are those of executing the laws passed by the legislature and appointing officers other than those to be appointed by the legislature. May I repeat. This being true, one single executive will certainly bring more efficiency and dispatch to the office than two or more."

At the front of the room, James Madison rose. Heads craned to see the small man, and men strained to hear his soft voice.

"Respectfully may I suggest that we are approaching the question of the office of the executive in reverse of its proper order. How can we determine whether the executive office should consist of one person, or more than one, until we decide on the extent of the duties and authority of the office?"

He stopped, reflected for a moment, then sat down.

Governor Edmund Randolph came to his feet and waited for the room to quiet. "I strenuously oppose the proposition of an executive consisting of one man." He paused to let the murmuring stop. "One man in that position of power is the fetus of monarchy. I have no motive to be governed by the British government as our prototype. Nor do I mean to throw censure on that excellent fabric. If we were in a situation to copy it, I do not know that I should be opposed to doing it. But the fixed genius of the people of America requires a different form of government. I do not see why the great requisites for the executive department, which are vigor, dispatch, and responsibility, could not be found in three men, as well as in one man. The executive ought to be independent. It ought therefore to consist of more than one."

George Mason rose and the room fell silent. "I concur with my colleague Governor Edmund Randolph. The executive office ought to consist of three persons, and further, such persons should have access to a Council of Revision composed of members of the judiciary whereby they shall increase the strength of the executive in defending itself against the encroachments of the legislature."

He stopped to organize his thoughts, and to look into the startled, blank faces of the delegates before he went on.

"If strong and extensive powers are vested in the executive, and that office consists of only one person, the government will of course degenerate into a monarchy—a government so contrary to the genius of the people that they will reject even the appearance of it."

The delegates broke off staring at him and exchanged glances as he continued.

"To allay state jealousies I propose that one member of the executive be chosen from the Northern states, one by the Middle, and one by the Southern."

For a few moments, Mason studied the faces of his colleagues, trying to gauge their acceptance—or rejection—of his proposal. Then he sat down and waited.

Elbridge Gerry stood and his grim hatchet face was drawn. "I favor the policy of annexing a council to the office of the executive. It will give weight and inspire confidence."

James Wilson stood once again, and the flat of his hand smacked on his desk. "Though the thirteen states agree on scarcely anything else, they are agreed on placing a single magistrate at the head of the government. No state has accepted the idea of three heads. Among three equal persons in one office, I can see nothing but uncontrolled, continued, and violent animosities which would not only interrupt the public administration, but diffuse their poison through the other branches of government, throughout the states, and at length throughout the people at large."

Franklin leaned back in his chair, yawned, flexed his legs, and closed his eyes. *They're into the nut of the thing. The devil is in the detail. How do we select the executive, and for how long?*

By noon the handkerchiefs of the delegates were damp with sweat. By two o'clock the arguments were growing strained, direct, abrasive. Motions were made to delete some words from the resolutions, change others, add to, delete from. How long should the executive serve? James Wilson insisted seven years. Pinckney was abrupt—three years only. And what of a reappointment? "Yes," argued Sherman, "to reap the benefit of experience." "No," insisted Mason, "since uninterrupted tenure would invite intrigues between the legislature and the executive, and eventually corrupt the entire government."

By mid-afternoon a delegation of sweated-out, exhausted men put the question, how long shall the executive serve, and the vote was taken on the proposition of seven years.

New York, New Jersey, Pennsylvania, Delaware, Virginia, and North Carolina—"Aye."

Connecticut, Georgia, and South Carolina—"Nay."

Massachusetts, divided.

Six "ayes," three "nays," one state divided. The executive, whoever or whatever that was to be, would serve for seven years.

Gorham droned on. "What compensation shall be granted for the services of the executive?"

Franklin stirred and came erect in his chair. "I respectfully move that the question of compensation for the services of the executive be postponed in order to make a substitution in the proposal as it now stands. The substitution should be that the executive shall receive such compensation as to defray all necessary expenses, but he shall receive no salary, stipend, fee, or reward whatsoever for his services."

All murmuring ceased and all eyes came to Franklin. He took a paper from his desk and continued. "I am very sensible of the effect of age on my memory and have been unwilling to trust it for the observations which seem to support my motion. So I have reduced my thoughts to writing, and I request permission of the committee to have James Wilson read it."

The paper was passed to Wilson, and for several seconds he scanned the writing, then nodded to Franklin, and began.

"In this particular of salaries to the executive branch I happen to differ; and as my opinion may appear new and chimerical, it is only from a persuasion that it is right, and from a sense of duty that I hazard it.

"Sir, there are two passions which have a powerful influence on the affairs of men. These are ambition and avarice, the love of power and the love of money. Separately each of these has great force in prompting men to action; but when united in view of the same man, they have in many minds the most violent effects. . . . And of what kind are the men that will strive for this profitable preeminence? It will not be the wise and moderate, the lovers of peace and good order. It will be the bold and the violent, the men of strong passions and indefatigable activity in their selfish pursuits. These will thrust themselves into your government and be your rulers."

Wilson paused for a moment, and in that instant Franklin turned his head far enough to see George Washington, seated to his left, stoic, noncommittal, and then Wilson went on.

"To bring the matter nearer home, have we not seen the great and most important of our officers, that of General of our armies executed for eight years together without the smallest salary, by a patriot whom I will not now offend by any other praise; and this through fatigues and distress in common with the other brave men his military friends and companions, and the constant anxieties peculiar to his station? . . . I think we shall never be without a sufficient number of wise and good men to undertake and execute well and faithfully the office in question."

Wilson finished reading and for a time stood gazing at the paper. Seconds passed before anyone stirred, and then Gorham broke the silence.

"Mr. Franklin moved for time to amend the executive compensation clause as it now exists, and that motion is granted." He looked down at his agenda and continued. "The next question is the mode of appointing the executive."

A weary James Wilson rose. "I once again declare for appointment by the people, along with both houses of the legislature. Only in that way can the executive and the legislature be as independent of each other as possible, as well as independent of the states. To allow the legislature to appoint the executive invites intrigues."

John Rutledge shook his head. "The executive should be elected by the second branch of the national legislature. Not by the people. Their lack of experience and judgment in matters of government will only defeat it."

George Mason raised a hand of caution. "The executive ought to be responsible to the people, not the legislature. I strongly urge that Mr. Wilson be given time to digest his proposal into a form acceptable to him."

Gorham rapped for order. "Mr. Wilson shall have his time. This committee is adjourned until tomorrow morning, Saturday, June 2, at ten o'clock A.M."

Saturday morning broke sweltering and by ten o'clock the men seated in the sealed East Room were mopping sweat. George Washington took the dais, called the convention to order, immediately resolved it into the committee of the whole and turned the platform over to Nathaniel Gorham. As Washington stepped down to his desk, he was suddenly aware that for a few moments a strange quiet had settled. He sat down and studied the faces and the demeanor of the delegates, and then it came to him.

Reality had seized them. It had finally broken clear in their minds that they were far, far beyond amending their failed Articles of Confederation; they were deep into a task that was profound beyond anything they had imagined. They were inventing a new government like nothing any of them had ever seen before, and there was a growing awareness that what they were creating might forever decide the fate of republican government. Each was reaching deep inside himself, seeking new inner wells of vision and determination for the journey.

On the dais, Nathaniel Gorham scanned the assembly and spoke.

"Mr. Secretary, let the record show that delegate James McHenry of Maryland received a dispatch informing that his brother lay dangerously close to death and has taken leave to return to Baltimore."

"Yes, sir." Jackson nodded and his quill scratched in the convention ledger.

Gorham pursed his mouth while he reviewed the agenda, then continued. "We will take up the debate on the unresolved issues of yesterday, June first. Debate is open on the question of the mode of appointing the executive."

Slowly and guardedly at first, then more swiftly and obviously as the heat inside the East Room raised perspiration and tempers, the division of the delegation into two opposing camps clarified.

One camp followed the thinking first presented by James Wilson, that the executive ought to be one man.

The other camp doggedly followed the thought first presented by Roger Sherman, insisting that the executive had to be comprised of at least three men. And further, if the recalcitrant Elbridge Gerry had his way, that committee of three would have an advisory council to be certain the three did not wreck the office of executive by intrigue, conspiracy, or infighting!

Debate raged. Delegates wiped at sweat and battled to control nerves frayed raw by the stifling heat and the bulldog obstinacy of those who lacked the common sense to agree with them. By late afternoon a frustrated and exhausted Gorham adjourned the muddled convention until Monday, June fourth.

Monday arrived, but neither the sweltering heat in the East Room, nor the fervor of the debate had cooled when they reconvened. Nathaniel Gorham braced himself, took the dais after George Washington called the convention to order, and plowed into the agenda of the committee of the whole once more.

Pinckney rose. "I move that we resume debate on the question of whether the executive be a single person."

James Wilson raised his hand. "Seconded."

Gorham declared, "On the motion made and seconded, the committee will continue on the question of the executive. Shall it be one single person, or three, and shall a council be appointed to advise the executive?"

James Wilson stood and was recognized. "I again strongly urge that the executive *must* be a single person. The idea of three heads for one government can only lead to uncontrolled, continued, and violent animosities. The result would not only interrupt the public administration, but diffuse their poison through the other branches of government, then through the states, and at length through the people at large. Should the executive be constituted by three separate men, it is possible that all three might adopt a separate view on a given subject, and never reach accord on any of it. May I repeat my statement of two days ago? While we may differ on nearly everything else, it is my position that all thirteen states have learned that a single executive is essential to a unified government."

Roger Sherman stood. "While it is true that the thirteen states each has one man at its head, it is also true that they have an advisory council. Even in Great Britain, the King has a council. It is true that he is the one that appoints it, but nonetheless, the advice of the council has weight with him and attracts confidence of the people."

Obstreperous and crusty Elbridge Gerry arose. "I am at a loss to discover the wisdom in having an executive composed of three persons. In military matters, we would have one general with three heads!"

Gorham took a deep breath. "If there is no more debate, does anyone call for the vote?"

The vote was called. Ayes, seven. Nays, three.

The executive of the United States would be one single man without an advisory council.

Jackson recorded the vote and Gorham moved on.

"Next issue. Shall the executive have power to negate any laws enacted by the legislature?"

Once again James Wilson arose. "If the legislative, executive, and judiciary are to be distinct and independent, the executive ought to have an absolute negative power. Without such a means of self-defense, the legislature can at any moment sink the executive into nonexistence!"

Elbridge Gerry rose, shaking his head. "I see no necessity for so great a control over the legislature, as the best men in the community would be comprised in the two branches of it."

Benjamin Franklin thumped his cane on the floor and all eyes swung to him. "I am sorry to differ from my colleague for whom I have a very great respect, but I have had some experience on this check in the executive, on the legislature, under the government in Pennsylvania." He paused to weigh his words, then went on, blunt, candid. "The negative power in the Governor has constantly been used to extort money! No good law whatever can be passed without a private bargain with the governor, and a sizeable contribution to his pocket by way of salary increase, or donation. It became such an open practice that finally no bill that had been passed by the legislature came to the Governor's desk for signature without a Treasury Order attached to it, in his favor. When the Indians were scalping American citizens in the western reaches of the state, the concurrence of the Governor in means of self-defense could not be got until it was agreed that the Governor's estate would be exempted from taxation!"

The room was deadly silent as Franklin continued.

"I greatly fear that if an absolute negative should be given to the executive as proposed, more money and more power would be demanded until at last enough of both would be gotten by the executive to influence and bribe the legislature into a complete subjection to the will of the executive."

Franklin pursed his mouth for a moment, then nodded his head. He had finished.

Roger Sherman stood. "I am against giving the executive such absolute negative powers. No one man should have the power to stop the will of the whole. We ought to avail ourselves of his wisdom in revising the laws, but not permit him to overrule the decided and cool opinions of the legislature."

Gorham waited for a moment, then called for the vote. All voting states, "Nay." The executive would not have absolute power to negate, or veto, a bill passed by the legislature.

It was then moved that the executive should have the power to negate, or veto, any bill passed by the legislature, but that the legislature could override the negative by a two-thirds vote in the affirmative.

Once again Gorham called for the vote. The motion passed *sub silentio.* Any veto by the executive could be overridden by a two-thirds vote in the legislature.

Elbridge Gerry, face sour, glanced at Franklin, then Madison, then Gorham. *A one man executive who has the power to override the entire legislature—no compensation for the executive, which means only rich men can serve—no definition and no limitation on his duties—some want him elected by the common people who know nothing about government—a perfect arrangement for a disaster. What lunacy!*

Franklin glanced at Madison. The little man was bent over his desk, quill in hand, writing steadily in the shorthand method he had invented to keep as complete a record as humanly possible of the proceedings. Franklin's gaze drifted to Washington, whose face was a study in masked thought. Franklin moved his legs, gritted his teeth at the pain, then settled back. *It's going the right direction. Checks. Balances. The power divided between a legislature and a single executive—neither has it all. It is not as I would wish it to go, necessarily, but this is a new generation of Americans, and they need to be free to make their own mistakes just as we all did as younger men. And who knows? Perhaps these younger men can see farther because they stand on our shoulders. So much yet to be done. But we'll get there. We'll get there.*

Gorham looked up at the clock, then down at the unfinished agenda and shook his head. *Too much—too many heavy issues—never finish today.* He scanned the room and saw sweltering men who had no more to give without an overnight reprieve.

"This committee is adjourned for the day. We'll meet again in the morning."

Notes

The proceedings of the Grand Convention from June first through June fourth, 1787, as they appear in this chapter, were taken from the following historical records and books.

Farrand, *The Records of the Federal Convention*, Volume One, pp. 63–141.

Bernstein, *Are We to Be a Nation?* pp. 152–62.

Warren, *The Making of the Constitution*, pp. 173–88.

Rossiter, *1787: The Grand Convention*, pp. 171–74.

Moyers, *Report from Philadelphia*, pages named Friday, June 1, 1787, Monday June 4, 1787.

Farrand, *The Framing of the Constitution of the United States*, pp. 73–79.

Berkin, *A Brilliant Solution*, pp. 77–95.

The issues handled by the Grand Convention were more numerous than appear in this book and cannot all be included because of their volume. The central issues are set forth herein. Further, the speeches made by the individuals in the debates were often of great length, as can be seen in Farrand, *The Records of the Federal Convention*, which work is itself an abridgement of the actual debates and proceedings, and still includes three volumes, totaling over 1,800 pages. Farrand's work includes most of the best records kept of the debates, including those of James Madison, whose contribution to the history of the Grand Convention is heroic. Thus, though some debate presented herein is verbatim as it appears in the above referenced sources, much of it is abbreviated, and some of it is adjusted by this writer to language more understandable at the time of this writing, since the language and figures of speech used in 1787 are often not readily understood today. Every effort has been made to preserve the clarity and intent of the debates, and any errors are the result of abbreviating and adjusting by this writer.

James Madison invented his own method of shorthand writing to facilitate rapid recording of the proceedings. Bernstein, *Are We to Be a Nation?* p. 152.

CHAPTER XIV

★ ★ ★

y midmorning, the sun was a brass ball in the heavens, and dead, sultry air hung heavy on the Boston waterfront, punishing the crews working the ships and wharves and piers, sucking their strength, slowing them. By midafternoon the crew bosses were giving their men time to find shade and sit, heads down, salt-sweat dripping from their noses and chins while they gathered the will and the strength to finish their shift.

Inside the offices that lined the docks, those who managed the shipping companies had long since opened all doors and windows, praying for a stir of air from the Atlantic. None came, and they shed their tunics, removed their ties, loosened their collars, and rolled up their sleeves as they continued with the endless paperwork that keeps shipping companies running.

In the austere office of Dunson & Weems, Tom Covington, seated at his desk, raised an arm to wipe his damp face with his sleeve, then used his quill to make a large check mark on a three page contract proposal, and toss it onto a stack of rejects on the right side of his old, worn desk. The fledgling firm of Dunson & Weems was not yet ready to enter the world of transatlantic shipping trade. He picked the next document from the stack on his left and heaved a weary sigh. The price of salt beef from their New Jersey supplier had gone up two cents per pound, and salt beef was a necessary staple for the crews that sailed the company ships. He reached for a ledger and for several minutes searched for other suppliers of salt beef. Two cents per pound on 8,000 pounds was one hundred sixty dollars. Not a lot, but if ignored, slowly rising prices on food supplies could eat deep into profits. How many shipping companies had failed because they did not keep an iron control on fixed costs?

To Tom's left, across the open aisle, Billy Weems was hunched over his ledger, face drawn as he struggled to finish the profit and loss sheet for the month of May. June first had arrived on the previous Friday, and Billy had used that day, and part of his Saturday seated at his desk with his quill in hand, running the totals of all costs—crews, repairs, maintenance of ships, food, insurance, taxes, rent, office supplies, harbor fees, and incidentals, against all money they had received and banked from customers. He would finish in the early evening and have a statement ready by morning with a final figure that would reveal whether the company had made a profit or sustained a loss.

Behind Billy, Caleb Dunson concentrated on a map of the east coast of the United States, and a ledger for each of their ships. The ledgers were filled with the ships' logs of each voyage they made, to which was added the cargoes they carried from one port to another, as well as the names of every man on board, his assignment, and his pay. The estimated date for the return of each ship was carefully noted, and not a day passed that they did not check the schedule. Nothing in the business of men at sea rode them heavier than an overdue ship. A few days overdue—that could mean anchored to make repairs, or locked in a harbor riding out a storm, or docked in a port to find a doctor for an injured crewman that the ship's surgeon was incapable of handling, or stopped to take on fresh water, or any number of ordinary incidents that would slow the return of a ship. But more than a few days? With a ship and a cargo and the lives of a crew at stake, a ship too long overdue would not let go of those at the home office. It was a worry that sat heavily on them, day and night.

And the *Belle*, one of their ships, was now twelve days overdue. Her captain was Einar Stengard, first mate, Christian Dodds, navigator, Adam Dunson. Her outward destination was San Salvador far to the south, in the West Indies. Her cargo going down was all manufactured goods from the New England states—needles, pins, nails, bolts, flatirons, and pig iron—all merchandise that could not be made in the islands. Her return cargo was to be rum and brown sugar. There had been a strong blow down in the Indies three weeks earlier, with some ships beached and some damaged. Other ships that had weathered the storm had since arrived back in port, or sent word, but nothing had been heard from the *Belle.* According to their office practice, and with dark foreboding, Tom had pulled the office copies of the insurance contracts covering loss of ship, crew, and cargo, checked them to be certain they were in order, then returned them to the file.

At the sound of men entering the office front door, Caleb and Billy raised their heads, and Tom stood. The bright sunlight streaming through the two front windows and the open door had turned the visitors into two silhouettes standing side by side, one with his tricorn in his hand; even in silhouette it was clear they were men of the sea. Tom stepped out into the aisle and spoke.

"Is there something we can do for you?"

The leader was short, stocky, powerful, with a full beard and a brass ring in his left ear. His voice came raspy. "We came about the *Belle.* Harbormaster said she was one of yours."

Was?

Instantly Billy and Caleb were on their feet, moving toward the three men as Tom exclaimed, "Yes, what about her?"

The stocky man cleared his throat. "We was on the *Bonnet* bound for Port Royal. A blow come in from sou'sou'east, and we put in at New Providence to ride it out. When we could we went on down towards the Windward Channel to get to our port, and on the way we seen three ships run aground on reefs. One was the *Belle.*"

The man paused and Tom blurted, "Did you stop?"

"Stopped and sent a longboat. No one on board the *Belle.* Cargo gone. Demasted. Burned bad."

Caleb was scarcely breathing. His voice was low. "The crew dead?"

The man shook his head. "Don't know. There was no bodies. We looked. She was hulled four times on the port side by cannon. Mainmast shot in half, and down. Marks and holes from musket balls. Railings all broke. She'd had a bad fire." The man paused before he went on. "She had no cannon. Couldn't defend herself."

Tom exclaimed, "Pirates? Pirates had taken her?"

The man nodded. "Had to be."

Tom's brow furrowed. "In a storm?"

"The way we saw it, she'd been taken just before the storm broke. They took the war chest and most of the cargo and set her afire and left her when the storm come in. She was burning when the wind and rain hit and the rain got the fire." The man paused to gather his thoughts. "As for the crew, there was no longboats left on the *Belle.* We spent half a day moving as close to the island beaches as we dared, usin' our telescopes, but we didn't see a longboat or a body or a signal fire or a sign of the crew. It looked like them that survived the fight was left on the *Belle* when she was set afire and the storm hit, and they launched the longboats and tried for the island. No way to know if any made it."

Billy cut in. "When? When did you see all this?"

"Ship's log on the *Bonnet* says it was Sunday, the twentieth day of May."

"Where is the *Bonnet?* Who is her captain?"

"Tied up at the pier used by the Hubert company, unloading. A little way up the docks. Cap'n is Horace Messina. He sent us here. I'm Stuart McDaris, First Mate." He turned to the taller man next to him, slender, cavernous eyes, dark, swarthy. "This is Ulysses Waltman. Bos'n."

Caleb spoke as he turned to the great map on the right wall of the room. "Come show us exactly where you were when all this happened."

A moment later all five men were clustered at the wall, staring at the detailed map of the east coast of the United States, reaching south far past the West Indies, far south of the state of Florida, to Trinidad. It took McDaris three seconds to orient himself and drop his stubby finger, pointing.

"Right here. Just making landfall on the north islands of the Bahamas." His finger moved as he spoke. "The blow came and we put in here, at New Providence and rode her out. When the worst of it was past, we moved southeast towards the island of San Salvador, here, holding as close to the islands as we dared. We found the *Belle* here"— he tapped the map—"on a reef, wrecked." He looked up at Caleb. "Like I said, we hunted for any sign of the crew but there was none. We went on down and turned starboard through the Windward Channel to Port Royal, here, where we unloaded our cargo and took on a load of rum." He dropped his hand back to his side, finished.

Caleb's eyes were glowing. "You're certain?"

A faint smile crossed Bos'n Ulysses Waltman's taciturn face, but he said nothing. He could not remember how many times McDaris had sailed among the countless islands in the Bahamas, and the Caribbean, and south into the Antilles, into every port, including Trinidad, less than five miles from South America. Few seamen knew the Bahamas and the Caribbean better than McDaris.

McDaris nodded. "Certain."

Caleb asked one more question. "The storm was moving from south to north?"

McDaris' finger traced a line. "Sou'sou'east to nor'nor'west. Right up the coast."

Caleb fell silent, and McDaris continued. "I figured the *Belle* might have been bound for San Salvador."

Tom nodded. "She was."

McDaris drew a breath and made a guess. "Any of you have family on board?"

Caleb nodded. "Brother. Navigator."

McDaris' face fell for a moment, and the pain showed, but he said nothing.

Billy straightened and turned. "You'll be in port here for a while?"

"Probably four, five more days. We have to finish unloading, and then load."

"We might need you. Verify the loss for insurance and paperwork."

"Anytime."

McDaris and Waltman turned and the five men moved to the front door where Tom, Caleb, and Billy stopped, and Billy reached to shake McDaris's hand.

"We appreciate what you did down there, and for coming here to tell us."

McDaris bobbed his head once. "No thanks necessary." He was referring to the unwritten law of the sea. Ships did what they could for those less fortunate, and reported disasters to the owners if they could.

Billy, Tom, and Caleb watched the two disappear into the crowd on the waterfront before they turned back into the office, silent for a moment, each lost in his own bleak thoughts. They gathered at the wall map to stare for a moment, as though somehow it would tell them where to find Adam and the others.

Caleb broke the strained silence. "I'm going down there."

Instantly Tom exclaimed, "You can't! If the British or the Spanish found you down there in those islands, you *know* what they'd do! You'd rot in a jail if they could find an excuse."

Caleb ignored it, and Billy broke in. "Tom's right." He raised a finger to Caleb. "You've read that order issued by the British government. That Orders In Council paper. We've got a copy in a file. They lost the shooting war, but they're not going to lose the commercial war down there. American ships and American goods are banned from British ports, and as far as they're concerned, from all waters south of Florida. The Spanish are none too friendly down there either, and even the French are jealous about their trade."

Tom's voice was too high, too loud. "The only way we dared send the *Belle* down there in the first place was to find a Dutch dealer in a neutral harbor at San Salvador. Clear up at the north end of the Caribbean and the Bahamas. You go down there—Haiti, Puerto Rico, Jamaica, Tahiti—you're right in the middle of islands and ports owned by all three—Britain, France, Spain. You start snooping for the crew of a lost American ship, you won't stand a chance!"

Billy interrupted. "We better take a little time on this. Wait for Matthew. He owns half this company. He has a right to have his say before we start risking another ship and crew."

Tom was reaching his limits, and plunged on, hating his own words. "It's near certain that the crew is dead. Including Adam. You heard McDaris. No trace. A ship hit by pirates, shot-up, burned, wrecked on a reef, and not one body, not one longboat. If any of them did survive, they're bound to be in a British or French prison right now! If they are, you'll be right there with them the minute the British or the French or the Spanish find out who you are. Is that what you want?"

Caleb was struggling between the soul-wrenching need to find his brother and bring him home, his smoldering hatred of the British, and the truth he was hearing from Tom and Billy. For five seconds filled with hot tension, the three men stared at each other, and then Caleb shook his head and answered. "Time's against us. We don't know when we'll see Matthew. I'm going."

Tom recoiled. "How? How are you going down there?"

Caleb's eyes were points of light as he jabbed a finger toward the huge calendar on the left wall that listed all ships, and the dates and destinations of their voyages through the month of December. "The *Zephyr.* She's the lightest and fastest schooner we've got, and she's due in from Nova Scotia on Thursday. Two days. I'll need a crew and a navigator."

Tom exploded. "The *Zephyr!* The *Zephyr's* due out again on the sixteenth! For Savannah. You can't take her. We need her."

Caleb shook his head with finality. "I'm taking her south as soon as we can get supplies and a crew onboard. Some other ship will have to carry the freight to Savannah."

Tom was nearly shouting. "We don't have another one free on the sixteenth."

Caleb's words were sharp, clipped, final. "Lease one. Buy one. That's your problem. Adam is mine." He turned to Billy. "We got enough money to buy supplies for this trip? Hire a crew? Or do we have enough men already?"

Billy raised both hands, palms flat against Caleb. "Slow down. Get hold of yourself. There's more to this than a lost crew. I'm going to take a little time to think this one through."

Billy turned on his heel and walked deliberately to his desk and sat down. Tom settled and took his chair at his desk, working his quill between his hands, raising his eyes to glance at Billy from time to time. Caleb studied the big map on the wall. Twenty minutes passed before Billy spoke, and both men listened from where they were.

"We have the money for supplies, and some of the men. We can get others. The *Zephyr* is probably our best chance—light, fast, maneuverable. We can hire a ship from another line for the Savannah cargo—there are at least two in the harbor now that are idle. We can have Caleb on the way by the end of this week."

Tom was incredulous. "Risk another ship and crew? Think of the cost of insurance!"

Thoughtfully Billy locked eyes with Tom. "There won't be any insurance, because the *Zephyr* won't be carrying cargo." He paused for a moment and studied his thick, broad hands on the desk before him. "This isn't altogether about the shipping business. It's about what we won and what we didn't win in the war. We won our independence. Now it looks like we have to win our survival. A different kind of war. If we let the British and the Spanish and the French stop our shipping, how long will we last? I mean the United States. They banned us from what should be open trade down in the Caribbean, and they did it to cripple us, get rid of us if they can. They're the ones who have picked this fight." Again Billy paused to gather his thoughts. "What would have happened if we had not stood up back in 1775? Where would we be today?"

Tom slowly eased back in his desk chair, and his eyes began to widen. He said nothing.

Caleb was staring at Billy as though he had never seen him before. Too well he knew Billy had faced British cannon and musket from Lexington in 1775, through every major battle to Yorktown in 1781, and never faltered. But in his own quiet way Billy had never declared his innermost thoughts until now.

Billy leaned forward, his thick forearms on his desk. "I think we better go down there and get our men, if they're alive." He turned his head directly to Caleb. "We'll need an extra day to mount some cannon on the *Zephyr*, and your crew better include a few men who understand a fight."

Notes

The characters in this chapter are fictional.

For a map of the southeastern seaboard of the United States, down to Trinidad, as they are discussed in this chapter, see Mackesy, *The War for America, 1775–1783,* p. 226.

Following the formal Treaty of Paris of 1783, by the terms of which England granted the United States their independence and made concessions regarding both land and fishing rights, England nonetheless severely criticized the United States for failing to comply with the terms of the treaty, which required the United States to remove all legal barriers from British and Loyalist creditors recovering property and debts due them. In retaliation for the American failure, the British retained some of their forts in the Great Lakes region to cut off American access to the wealth and trade in that sector. In addition, and of great significance, Britain reasoned that they were entitled to reclaim their shipping trade in the Bahama Islands—The West Indies. Consequently, the British government issued its ORDERS IN COUNCIL, which rescinded Lord Shelburne's proposed plan, which granted American ships the same privileges of shipping as British ships. Said ORDERS also barred American shipping, from Canada to the north down to the West Indies to the south. The ORDERS also banned the export from England and its possessions of machine tools to the United States, a blow aimed at crippling America's ability to manufacture goods for the marketplace. Bernstein, *Are We to Be a Nation?* p. 83.

CHAPTER XV

★ ★ ★

*A*nd please bless Father to come home soon. In thy holy name, amen."

John Matthew Dunson unclasped his hands and rose from his knees to stand beside his bed in his long nightshirt while Kathleen rose from beside him and turned down the sheet. In the yellow lamp light she leaned over, and he wrapped his arms about her neck for a moment to give her a peck on the cheek, then scrambled into his bed while she pulled the sheet up to his chin.

"I'll come cover you later," she said. "You go to sleep." He saw the tenderness and the soft glow in her eyes as she reached to touch his cheek, and he nodded and turned toward her as she lifted the lamp from the night table and walked out of the room. She left the door half open, and he listened to the whisper of her woollen house slippers and the faint rustle of her long nightshirt fade down the hall. For a few moments he lay in silence while his six-year-old heart struggled with anxiety.

Earlier in the day, while they were tending the fires and carrying water to the washtubs in the backyard, she had talked too little, and he sensed she was troubled, even fearful. While she was hanging clothes on the lines, she had stopped twice to walk through the house, out through the front yard to the gate in the white picket fence and shade her eyes with one hand to look up and down the street, and he knew she was looking for father. In his young heart he did not know his world was built on his mother and his father. He only knew that when she showed fear about his father, he felt it too. It filled him, pushed everything else aside, left him unable to take it away, to make it all better. He could only stand by in silence, watching her eyes, her every expression, gauging her pain, and consequently his own. These were the unexpressed feelings in his heart as he drifted into troubled sleep.

In the kitchen Kathleen kept her hands busy with the day's dishes in the hot water, washing, rinsing, methodically working the heavy plates and cups into the cupboards. She threw the water out the backdoor into the darkness, wiped the pans dry, and hung the damp towels on the rods attached to the cupboards. She passed through the dining room where the week's wash stood on the table in two large woven reed baskets, dry from the sun and breeze, sheets and towels stiff and protruding. She had reached the large upholstered chair before the fireplace in the parlor and placed the lamp on the side table, and was picking up the Bible when she heard a soft rap at the front door, and then the sound of the key working in the lock and the latch being quietly drawn. She jerked erect and her breath came short as she hurried through the gloom of the unlighted parlor toward the door. It opened, and she saw the tall, shadowy image, and she saw and heard the heavy seaman's bag being dropped to the hardwood floor, and she threw herself against Matthew and clutched him to her and buried her face against his neck as he wrapped her inside his arms. For a time they stood in their embrace, each lost in the other, neither speaking.

Then she murmured, "Matthew, oh, Matthew."

He held her until the trembling stopped, and he said quietly, "What's wrong? Are you all right?"

She tipped her head back and he saw the tears. "Now. I'm all right now. I've been so scared. So scared."

His eyes widened. "About what?"

"You. We saw in the newspapers two weeks ago that the convention was to be secret and we knew you'd come home. And then you didn't."

"I wrote. Didn't you get the letter?"

"No. Not yet."

"I couldn't get passage home until five days ago. No ships coming to Boston." He peered down at her. "I didn't. . . . This isn't like you . . . I've been late before."

"It's what's happened to Adam. All I could see was . . ."

Matthew came to an instant focus. "What's happened to Adam?"

She pushed herself back. "His ship was wrecked. Down in the Bahamas. Two men came to the office. They saw the ship on a reef. All smashed. Burned."

She felt the tension leap in Matthew. "Adam? Where's Adam?"

She shook her head, helpless. "Missing. All of them. When you didn't come home, that's all I could see. You on a ship that was wrecked. You gone."

He led her back to the dining table and pushed the two baskets aside, and sat her down facing him.

"Who were the two men?"

"I don't know their names. They were on a ship that came. They stopped at the office and told Billy and Tom and Caleb what they saw."

"Exactly what did they see?" Matthew was leaning forward, intense, missing nothing.

"The ship—the *Belle*—on a reef down in the Indies. Bahamas. It was wrecked."

"Wrecked? How wrecked?"

"Billy said the masts were gone, and she had holes."

"Holes from what?"

"Cannon. Muskets. Tom says it had to be pirates."

Matthew came to his feet. "The longboats?"

"Gone. No sign of them."

"When? When did those two men come into the office?"

"Last week. Tuesday I think. The fifth."

"When did they sight the *Belle?* Did they say?"

"Sometime the last of May. Billy knows."

"Has anything been done about it? To find them?"

She hesitated. "Yes. Caleb's gone down there."

"Caleb!" he exclaimed. "How? How did he go down?"

"One of the company ships."

Matthew recoiled, voice too loud, too demanding. "Caleb's gone down to the Bahamas in one of our ships? An American ship?"

"Yesterday."

Matthew was on his feet. He took two steps, then spun and returned to the table, leaned forward on stiff arms, palms flat on the table.

"Did Billy say anything about the British? Their Orders in Council? If the British find Caleb, they'll impound the ship and put the crew in prison! Tom and Billy know that. Did they let Caleb take that ship and go?"

"You'll have to ask Billy." Kathleen's chin began to tremble, and for a moment she covered her mouth with her hand, then murmured, "Matthew, I'm so sorry."

He tipped his head back and she watched all the air go out of him. He straightened and sat down once again, facing her, voice withdrawn, quiet.

"There's nothing you could do about it. It's just that I didn't expect this. Coming home—I didn't expect this." For a moment he studied his hands, then raised his head. "These things happen if you're in the shipping business. We've been lucky until now. We're going to lose ships . . . but Adam. . . ." His eyes dropped and he shook his head slowly.

She saw the terrible wrenching in his heart, and she reached to cover his hand with hers. For a time they sat in silence, not needing words. Then Matthew drew a deep breath and took charge of himself.

"Does Mother know all this?"

"Yes. She's beside herself with worry, but she'll be all right."

Matthew nodded and forced a smile.

"This hasn't been much of a homecoming for you. I'm sorry. Its good to be home. I missed you. It's hard to be away. There's a lot I have to tell."

Her dark eyes shone as she answered. "Tell me. Now."

"We'll have time for that. Did you see Doctor Soderquist?"

She smiled and he was lost in the beauty that came into her face. "Next January. We're going to have a little girl."

Matthew straightened, eyes wide in feigned surprise. "A girl? Soderquist said that? He's a better doctor than I thought!"

Kathleen laughed. "He didn't say that. I did. Mothers are entitled to know some things."

A sound at the archway into the hall brought both their heads around, and John stood facing them, bare toes curled up, digging at his eyes with clenched fists. He moved one hand enough to squint at the dining table, then dropped both hands, still squinting. For two seconds he studied his father, whom he had not seen for nearly a month, and he labored with a shyness for a moment before he marched to him and climbed into his lap.

Matthew wrapped his arms about the stout little body and held him close for a moment before he spoke.

"I'm home. Daddy's home."

The boy, both eyes still closed, nodded, but said nothing.

"You all right?" Matthew asked.

Again John nodded, and then asked, "Bring me something?"

Matthew looked stern. "Have you been good? Did you mind mother?"

"Uh-huh."

"Keep the kindling stacked?"

"Uh-huh?"

Kathleen was glowing, watching.

"Did you sit at the head of the table every day?"

"Uh-huh. Did you bring me something?"

Matthew raised his head to look at Kathleen. "Is it true? Did he obey? Has he earned it?"

"Yes. He's been my little man."

"Then I think I have something in that bag by the front door."

The boy leaned back and peered up at his father. "Get it."

The two walked across the dim parlor to the seaman's bag, and Matthew brought it back to the dinner table in the dining room. The boy watched as Matthew unlaced the ties on the end of the bag and rummaged inside for a moment, then stopped. In alarm he peered down at his son, who was standing wide-eyed in anticipation.

"I must have forgot it."

John's face drew down. "That isn't fair. I was good."

"Well, maybe I'd better look again." Once more Matthew's hand disappeared in the bag and then it stopped and he grinned broadly. "There it is!"

He drew out his hand and set a wrapped package on the table. "For you."

The boy reached for it and tugged at the strings and dropped them on the floor, then laid it on the table to fold the paper back until he saw the round, three-inch leather pouch with the hand-stitching and the tab holding it closed. He looked up at Matthew in question, and Matthew said, "Open the pouch."

The tab lifted from its clasp, and the boy carefully drew out a navigator's hand compass, cased in steel, with the legend engraved on the outer edge giving all points of the compass, and all the degrees. For a moment he stood in silence, then looked up at his father.

"A real one? For me?"

"One of the best. Read on the back of it."

The boy turned it, and there on the back, engraved in beautiful cursive scroll he slowly read, "JOHN MATTHEW DUNSON."

He raised unbelieving eyes. "Mine? Forever?"

"Just like mine, and Adam's. Yours forever. But you've got to earn it."

"I already did. I was good."

"I don't mean that. You've got to go with me on a ship and tell me what direction we're going."

The boy's mouth dropped open. "Honest? On a ship?"

Matthew bobbed his head. "Absolutely."

"When?"

"Soon."

The boy laid the compass on the table and watched the delicately balanced needle turn, pivot back, and slowly settle. He looked up at

Matthew proudly and exclaimed, "It says that's south. Well, pretty much south."

Matthew grinned. "No, the needle always points north. Turn the compass until the needle is on the big 'N.'"

Slowly the boy turned the steel case until the "N" and the needle point were aligned, and then looked up, face split with a great grin. He pointed. "That's north."

"You'll always know where north is, and if you know that, you know where every other direction is."

Instantly the boy was lost in moving his compass, watching the needle swing, turning it on the tabletop. Suddenly he stopped and looked up once more, eyes wide. "What makes it point that direction all the time?"

"We'll get out a book tomorrow and find the answer."

That was enough for John. If father said they'd find out tomorrow, they would find out tomorrow. He began working with his new treasure again, and Matthew thrust his hand once more into the seaman's bag.

"Maybe there's something in here for your mother, too."

In a moment he placed a small package in Kathleen's hands, and she worked through the wrappings to hold up a single strand of matched pearls. She gasped and clapped her hand to her breast. "Oh, Matthew! They're beautiful." John watched his mother throw her arms about his father and kiss him then step back and inspect her gift with eyes bright in the lamplight.

The sound of the clock on the mantle in the library striking half-past nine gave them pause, and Matthew reached to pick up his son. "Time you were asleep."

"Can I take my compass with me in bed?"

Matthew started for the archway. "Navigators don't do that. They take good care of compasses. Put them on a table or a shelf for the night."

The boy nodded, and Matthew picked the compass and the leather case from the table, and with the boy on one arm and the compass in the other hand, walked down the hall to John's bedroom, Kathleen following with the lamp. They set the compass and case on his night-stand and Matthew spoke.

"Let's kneel for night prayers."

John said, "We already did."

"Then we'll do it again."

They knelt and clasped their hands before bowed heads and closed eyes, and Matthew thanked the Almighty for protecting his family and for safe passage home. They finished, John got back into his bed, and Matthew pulled the sheet up to his chin and spoke softly.

"Thank you for taking care of your mother while I was gone. Now you go to sleep."

John nodded, and Matthew led Kathleen from the room and closed the door halfway. They walked quietly back to the parlor, and Matthew carried his seaman's bag to their bedroom to unpack while Kathleen warmed ham and potatoes. They sat at the dining table talking while Matthew ate and drank buttermilk, and when he finished they remained, talking, mindless of the passing time. Kathleen was spellbound with the stories of Matthew's meeting with Madison who carried the leather case in which he kept his writings that were guiding the entire convention, and she laughed at the thought of old Benjamin Franklin arriving in a covered chair bolted to four poles, carried by four convicts from the local jail. She fell in love with Mother Asher in her boardinghouse and resolved that some day she would visit Philadelphia to thank her for taking such good care of Matthew.

Matthew listened intently as she chattered about the little things. John struggling against temptation to be sure he did everything Matthew had instructed. The kindling, don't play with the ax, help mother with the wash, take care of your room. He grinned at the story of the little boy getting a stick of kindling wood to chase a stray dog out of the yard because the dog had barked at Kathleen, and he chuckled out loud when Kathleen told of John's battle in learning to comb his own stubborn, unruly hair.

The clock struck eleven before they cleared the table, picked up the lamp, and walked hand in hand to their bedroom. Matthew pulled his nightshirt over his head and turned to Kathleen. "Prayer?"

"I've had two already tonight."

"That should be enough."

He turned the lamp until only the faintest gleam of light remained, and they slipped beneath the sheet. He reached for her and she came into his arms, and their separation and their troubles faded as they entered their own little world of peace and completeness and fulfillment.

Twice in the night Kathleen wakened to see the dark shape of Matthew sitting on his side of the bed, feet on the floor, elbows on his knees, head bowed forward. In her heart she knew he was suffering from fear for Adam, and she knew he needed time to himself, so she remained silent and motionless until he quietly lay back down.

He was up at dawn and had split and stacked kindling by the time she had steaming oatmeal and fried sausages on the breakfast table. He helped clear the breakfast dishes then walked quietly to John's bedroom to silently lean over the slumbering boy and kiss his forehead before he returned to the parlor. He embraced Kathleen for a moment, then quietly walked out the front door. In twenty minutes he was on the Boston waterfront, working his key in the front door of the office of Dunson & Weems, and half an hour later he greeted Tom Covington and Billy as they walked in. At the sight of Matthew, Billy stopped short and spoke.

"Glad you're back. You had us worried. When did you get in?"

"Last night. You two all right?"

Tom nodded, and Billy wasted no time. "We're fine, but things are not good here."

Matthew picked it up. "Kathleen told me. How does it stand now?"

The three sat down around Billy's desk and Billy laid it out. "You know about the *Belle?* Shot up, burned, wrecked on a reef down near San Salvador? Longboats and crew gone?"

"I know. Caleb?"

"He went down to find Adam and the crew, or learn what happened to them."

Matthew pointed at a filing cabinet. "You know about the British

Orders in Council? What they'll do if they find Caleb down there with an American ship?"

"We talked about it."

"You let him go anyway?"

"Not much choice. He was going, one way or another."

"One of our ships?"

"The *Zephyr.*"

Matthew paused to reflect. "Light and fast, but she won't have a chance if British gunboats catch her in a harbor. A ship and a crew at serious risk. I'm surprised you let it happen."

Tom cut in. "We told Caleb about the British. And the French and Spanish. Any one of them will take him if they can."

Matthew shook his head as Tom went on.

"For what it's worth, we mounted twelve cannon—thirty-two pounders—on the *Zephyr,* and we picked a crew that have been in sea battles before. Some were with you at the fight on the Chesapeake."

Matthew nodded. "That might help a little, but not enough if two or three gunboats trap the *Zephyr* in a harbor, or even against some island."

Tom cracked a smile, and Matthew looked at him, puzzled. "You know something you're not telling me?"

"Probably," Tom answered. "Caleb took some flags with him. British, French, Spanish. He intends flying whichever one he needs to get into the harbors down there. He took along a British seaman who was first mate on a British merchantman before the war, and fought on our side from 1777 on. He'll let that man do all the talking when they tie up to a British dock in San Salvador, or wherever the hunt takes them."

Matthew looked at Billy. "He could be hanged for flying a false flag."

Billy shrugged. "We told him."

Tom cut them off. "He left here with the hold of the *Zephyr* empty. No cargo. Nothing. Riding high and moving fast. When he gets down there he's going to open the seacocks and flood the hold with about three feet of seawater. She'll settle in the water and look like a merchantman with a load. If he finds Adam and the others, he'll pump the hold empty, get them on board, and make a run for it."

Matthew shook his head. "Wild. Risky. Dangerous."

Billy cut in. "Nearly impossible. But I have to tell you, there was no talking him out of it. He means to find his brother. I wish you had been here. You'd have let him go. Maybe even gone with him. I offered to go, but he said no. He knows about the promise I made my mother when my father died."

Matthew looked at Billy. "You notify the insurance companies?"

"They're on notice. They haven't decided yet if they want to send people down there to verify the loss. I doubt they will."

Tom smiled and stood. "I can tell you one thing, Matthew. I wouldn't fancy the idea of having Caleb Dunson mad at *me.*" He shook his head violently. "No, sir. Not Caleb Dunson. I don't know if he'll find Adam, or get him home, but I can tell you one thing. No matter what happens, the British, or the French, or the Spanish, or whoever has him, are going to do some suffering."

Notes

The characters and events in this chapter are fictional.

The British Orders in Council were explained in the endnotes of chapter 14.

Philadelphia

June 5–9, 1787

CHAPTER XVI

★ ★ ★

*A*n overnight shift in the winds from north to southwest, and a filmy cloud cover that turned the sun into a hazy ball, brought blessed relief from the wilting heat that had beleaguered Philadelphia. Shortly before nine o'clock the embattled delegates to the Grand Convention arrived at the Statehouse with a bit of a spring in their stride and a glint in their eye. The heat that had sapped them, wearied them, frazzled their tempers, was gone at least for this one blessed day, and they were starting to get the heft and feel of the Herculean task in which history and circumstance had buried them. They had killed the old Articles of Confederation in the first two days and cut the United States adrift from every vestige of government they had ever known. Over the next nine days they had conjured up a bicameral legislature and a one-man executive, and although not one man among them knew the shape of what lay ahead, there were some things they had learned that gave them the faintest beginnings of hope.

First, they were beginning to sense the direction in which they were moving. Exactly where it was leading they did not know, but in their bones was the instinct that said it was right. And every man could remember that just such an instinct was all they had had on that bright spring morning of April nineteenth of 1775, when their citizen-army met the British redcoats at the North Bridge in Concord and the shooting began. It had led them to independence.

Second, they were seeing the beginnings of a sorting of the delegates into two camps. One camp was pushing the entire convention toward retaining the power of government in the state legislatures, and the other was pulling it away from the state legislatures because of distrust of the turbulent, factious, and inconsistent actions taken by the states. Were it left to one camp, national power would be in the state legislatures— made up of men of property and substance and education, obviously better qualified in such matters than the common man. Left to the other camp, the power would vest in the citizenry.

And third, there was an emerging feeling that the small man who sat directly in front of the dais and meticulously recorded everything— James Madison—was the real force behind the fifteen shocking proposals so eloquently delivered in the four-hour, monumental speech given by Governor Edmund Randolph that first day. With some allowances for temporary departures, and errant and unrelated speeches by some delegates, the drift the entire convention had taken was noticeably consistent with that of Randolph's pronouncements. With the oath of secrecy that blanketed the entire proceeding, no one dared speak of it outside the room; but it was becoming difficult for those inside the room not to see that the startling plan Randolph had so powerfully delivered was not his own, but the product of the genius of the quiet little man in front.

The delegates took their seats, Jackson noted a quorum, and Gorham framed the first issue for the day.

" 'It is proposed that the national judiciary, including the supreme tribunal and all inferior tribunals, be chosen by the national legislature.' "

Wilson nudged his spectacles back up his nose and rose. "Experience has shown the impropriety of such appointments by numerous bodies. The consequence of such procedure can only be intrigue, partiality, and concealment. A principal reason for unity in the Executive was that officers might be appointed by a single, responsible person. So it should be with the judiciary. Let the judges be appointed by one person."

John Rutledge of South Carolina was shaking his head before he was on his feet, one hand high, a finger pointed to the ceiling. "I find it dangerous to grant so great a power to any single person. Not the least of the troubles such a thing would stir is the hard fact that the people will think we are leaning far too much towards monarchy! And I can find no sound reason to establish more than one single national tribunal. One supreme judiciary. The state tribunals are both capable and proper to decide in all cases in the first instance."

Pinckney rose when Rutledge sat down. "I hereby give notice that when the clause respecting the appointment of the judiciary shall again come up before this committee, I shall move to restore the 'appointment by the national legislature.'"

Rutledge smiled his approval of Pinckney's good sense.

Madison rose and the room fell silent so his quiet voice could be heard.

"I dislike the election of judges by the legislature, or any numerous body. The danger of intrigue and partiality is necessarily present in such elections, because many members of the political bodies are not sensitive to the requisite qualifications of a judge. Legislative talents are very different from those needed by a judge, and all too often legislators are not cognizant of it." He paused for a moment, and the other delegates shifted in their chairs, then became silent as he continued. "Nor am I satisfied with referring the appointment to the executive. My preference would be the senate, however, may I move that the words '. . . appointed by the legislative . . .' be struck out and a blank left to be hereafter filled on more mature reflection."

Relieved at Madison's motion to postpone the argument to another day, Wilson seconded the motion, the vote was taken, and it passed, nine to two. Who, or what institution, would appoint the court system of the new government would wait.

Franklin thumped his cane on the floor, and Gorham recognized him.

The elder statesman of the entire convention rocked forward in his chair, adjusted his right leg, and took a moment to settle his spectacles. Those nearest saw the signs and knew something outlandish was coming. They fell silent and waited.

Franklin cleared his throat and began. "Gentlemen, perhaps some of you have heard rumor that my errant life has led me to many places, here and abroad."

Instantly half the delegates were smiling in anticipation.

"In those wasted years of rambling, I was once pleasantly surprised to find myself in Scotland." He stopped, eyebrows raised as if something had just occurred to him. "For those of you who have not been privileged to know, Scotland is abroad, somewhere near England, as I recall."

Men strained to maintain their composure.

"While I was there, attempting my escape . . ."

Someone chuckled.

" . . . I chanced to find myself strenuously engaged with a Scottish court."

There were sounds of muffled sniggering.

"To my utter astonishment, the judge correctly ruled they had no cause to hold me, and ordered my release!"

Gorham was grinning.

"I could not help inquiring how it was they had managed to place such an excellent judge of character and the law on the bench."

Men had their hands covering their mouths, and Madison was steadily writing.

"I was informed of their system of selecting judges, and I now share that bit of Scottish wisdom with this august body. You see, in Scotland, they vest the power of selecting judges in the lawyers. And for very good reason. The lawyers meticulously determine which among them is the most capable and ablest in the profession, and that is the man they elevate to the bench."

The room fell silent as they waited for whatever it was Franklin intended dropping on them in his conclusion.

"The result is, the judges who grace the Scottish bench are the best they have. As for the lawyer whom they have elevated to the judgeship, they are now rid of him, and they most happily divide up his practice among themselves."

Laughter filled the room. Men jabbed each other in the ribs, letting it roll, reveling in the momentary release from the tension and the snarled matters that were daily crushing them. Of those attending the convention, over thirty had spent part of their lives in the field of law; thirteen were practicing lawyers, and none relished Franklin's irreverent jab at the legal system more than they.

Gorham leaned back in his chair and waited until the room quieted and some modicum of decorum returned before he pressed on.

"'Such judges to hold their offices during good behavior, and to receive punctually at stated times, a fixed compensation for their services, in which no increase or diminution shall be made so as to affect the persons actually in office at the time of such increase or diminution.'"

The clause was put to the vote and passed. Judges would be held to a standard of performance, and be paid.

An adventurous, aggressive spirit seemed to creep into the room, and as the day wore on, Gorham moved the committee forward in rapid order. Three propositions were presented, argued briefly, and postponed to a future date. First, that new states could be created; second, that they should be guaranteed republican government; third, that the system now being established ought to be subject to amendment without requiring the assent of the national legislature.

He stopped at the next proposition, scanned it carefully, and read it slowly. "'It is recommended that conventions under appointment of the people of the various states be empowered to ratify the constitution.'"

Roger Sherman came to his feet. "I conclude that popular ratification of the new constitution is unnecessary, since the Articles of Confederation provide for changes and alterations with the assent of Congress and ratification of state legislatures."

Madison was on his feet the moment Sherman sat down. "We must remember the Articles of Confederation are no longer in force, and in any event, even as a model, those articles were flawed regarding ratification, since in many states the acceptance rested with the legislatures only. Hence in conflicts between acts of the states and Congress, an uncertainty prevailed. Further, since the Articles of Confederation were in effect a treaty between the states, they were subject to attack on the grounds that a breach of any one article, by any state, absolved all other parties from the entire document. For these reasons, the new constitution must, I repeat *must*, be ratified in the most unexceptionable form, by the supreme authority of the people themselves."

For a moment, silence held, and then Gerry was on his feet, sharp face dour. "I disagree in the strongest terms. The constitutions of the eastern states have been sanctioned by the people, and I am certain this committee is aware they have the wildest ideas of government in the world! Massachusetts is now for abolishing the senate, and giving all the powers of government to the other branch of legislature! The people can not be trusted with ratification of the constitution."

Rufus King rose and there was a tone of conciliation toward the remarks of his fellow Massachusetts delegate, Elbridge Gerry. "I observe that the ratification of the Articles of Confederation was effected in the southern states by the legislatures only, and I further observe that after the ratification, they were impliedly given full sanction by the people. But it seems to me, a convention of people appointed to effect such ratification—being a single house—may be more easily conducted than the legislatures, since the legislatures consist of several branches, and many more persons."

James Wilson shook his head. "Regardless of the process, one thing needs to be observed. We must not approve a system which will cause a plurality of states to suffer if a minority chooses to be selfish or obstinate."

Pinckney took the floor. "In case the ratification experiment should not unanimously take place, then a combination of nine states should be authorized to unite under the constitution."

For a moment a hush settled over the room. Nine states? Out of thirteen? Four states disenfranchised and lost? They sensed the need to postpone the proposition, let it mature, and upon motion, the entire question of ratification of the new constitution, should they ever produce one, was set over to a future, unnamed date, when perhaps their heads would be clearer.

Gorham peered up at the clock. "It's late in the day. This committee is adjourned until tomorrow."

★ ★ ★ ★ ★

The sixth day of June dawned cool, with a fair breeze coming down the Delaware. The delegates came to the Statehouse with their coattails flapping and their tricorns clamped firmly onto their heads. Washington called the convention to order and delivered the dais to Gorham, who wasted no time in getting through the required formalities of opening and recognized Pinckney to open debate.

The young man stood. "According to notice previously recorded by myself, I move that the first branch of the national legislature be elected by the state legislatures, and not by the people, for the following reasons." He paused for effect, then continued. "First, the people are simply not qualified to judge which candidates are fit for the national legislature, and second, the state legislatures will be much less likely to promote the adoption of the new government if they are excluded from all share in it."

Gouverneur Morris shifted his bulk in his chair and bit down on the terrible urge to stand and in terms raw and cutting declare that this convention was charged with creating a new government that was built on the character, the spirit, the common sense and will of the *people!* How could they not see that America was a nation, and a nation deserves a national government. They had already established that the house of representatives should be elected by the vote of the people. Why, then, should not the members of the senate—the first house of the new Congress—be elected on the same principle? Why could they not be consistent in following this vital principle?

It was Elbridge Gerry who rose to his feet to be recognized. Washington glanced at him, and those nearest Washington saw the muscles in his jaw tighten for a moment. Franklin took a deep breath, exhaled, and tipped his head forward to close his eyes as though to nod off to a nap.

Gerry launched into a major speech. "Much depends on the mode of election of our legislature. In England, the people will probably lose their liberty from the smallness of the proportion having a right to elect their government." He paused for a moment, and his voice raised when he continued. "Our danger in this country arises from the opposite extreme. Our people will most likely lose their liberty *because of the tremendous number of them allowed to participate in electing their own government.*" Again he paused, and thoughtful men were listening as he continued. "In Massachusetts the worst men get into the legislature." Chairs squeaked as men moved and glanced at each other, and Gerry went on. "Several members of that body have lately been convicted of infamous crimes. Men of indigence, ignorance, and baseness spare no pains, however dirty, to carry their point against men who are superior to the artifices practiced. I am not disposed to run into extremes. I am as much principled as ever against aristocracy and monarchy. It is necessary on the one hand that the people should appoint one branch of the government in order to inspire them with the necessary confidence, and we have already provided them that opportunity in electing the house of representatives. However, the election of the senate should be such as to secure more effectually a just preference of merit. It seems clear to me that the people should *nominate* persons in certain districts, but that the state legislatures should make the appointment from those persons, for the national senate."

Gouvernor Morris shifted his wooden leg to stand, but James Wilson was already on his feet.

"I dearly wish for vigor in the government, but also earnestly wish that vigorous authority to flow immediately from the legitimate source of all authority—the people. The government ought to possess not only the *force*, but also *the mind and sense* of the people at large. The national legislature ought to be the most exact transcript of the whole society. Representation is made necessary only because it is impossible for the people to act collectively without it. The people will be rather more attached to the national government than to the state government. There is no danger of improper elections if made by large districts. Bad elections proceed from the smallness of the districts, which give an opportunity to bad men to intrigue themselves into office."

Roger Sherman rose. "If it is in view to abolish the state governments, the elections for national government ought to be by the people.

But if the state governments are to be continued with the national government, then it is necessary for harmony between the two that the national government be elected by the state government, and not directly by the people. The rights of the people to participate in the national government would be secured by their right to elect the state governments, who shall in turn select the national government. The purposes for which we are laboring to form a new national government are few: national defense, disputes between states, treaties, regulation of foreign commerce, and drawing revenue from it. All other matters will be better handled by the state governments. It is true that in states too small, and states too large, improprieties do arise, but they can be dealt with. It seems obvious we should clearly define the limited scope of the proposed new government, and give it only so much power as is necessary."

George Mason took the floor. "Under the existing confederacy, the congress represents the states, and not the people of the states. The acts of the confederacy congress operate on the states, not the individuals." He stopped for a few moments to change directions. "The case will be changed with the new plan of government. The *people* will be represented! They ought therefore to choose the representatives who represent them!"

Madison's blue eyes were narrowed in deep concentration. *We have arrived at the fulcrum. We stand or fall on the issue of who has the power—the states or the people.* He cleared his throat and came to his feet, Gorham recognized him, and Madison began.

"I consider an election of at least one branch of the national legislature by the people as a clear principle of free government. This mode, under proper regulations, has the additional advantage of securing better representatives, as well as of avoiding too great an agency of the state governments in the national government. I differ with my colleague from Connecticut in that I believe that in addition to all the obvious functions of a national government, there are less noticeable objects which are vital to peace and tranquility. Among these are the securing of private rights to the citizens, and a steady dispensation of justice. Interferences with these were evils which had more perhaps than anything else, produced this convention."

The room was silent as the delegates concentrated to lift their thoughts to the level of Madison's. He continued.

"Do we suppose that republican liberty can long exist under the abuses of it practiced in some states? The gentleman from Connecticut has admitted that in a very small state, faction and oppression will prevail. It is true that the abuses have also prevailed in the largest states, but to a markedly lesser degree, with the result that we are led to conclude we should enlarge the sphere as far as the nature of government would admit. The factor of size is the only defense against the inconveniences of democracy, and at the same time consistent with the democratic form of government."

Again he paused in the silence before continuing.

"Lacking the restraint of size, all civilized societies would be divided into different sects, factions, and interests, as they happen, to consist of rich and poor, debtors and creditors, the landed and the manufacturers, the commercial interests, the inhabitants of one district or another, the followers of one political leader or another, the disciples of this religious sect or that one. In all cases where a majority are united by a common interest or passion, the rights of the minority are in danger. What motives are to restrain them?

"A prudent regard to the maxim that honesty is the best policy is found by experience to be as little regarded by bodies of men as by individuals. Respect for character is always diminished in proportion to the number among whom the blame or praise is to be divided. Conscience, the only remaining tie, is known to be inadequate in individuals. In large numbers, little is to be expected from it. Besides, religion itself may become a motive to persecution and oppressions."

He paused again, and there was a rustle and a squeaking of chairs in the room as men shifted, then settled.

"These observations are verified by the histories of every country, ancient and modern. In Greece and Rome, the rich and the poor, the creditors and debtors, as well as the patricians and plebeians alternately oppressed each other with equal unmercifulness. What a source of oppression was the relation between the parent cities of Rome, Athens, and Carthage, and their respective provinces! The former possessed the power and the latter were sufficiently distinguished to be separate objects of such power. Why was America so justly apprehensive of parliamentary injustice? Because Great Britain had a separate interest, real or supposed, and if her authority had been admitted, Britain could have pursued that interest at our expense."

Madison stopped, and for several seconds the delegates watched him reach a decision before he continued.

"We have seen the mere distinction of color made in the most enlightened period of time, a ground of the most oppressive dominion ever exercised by man over man."

There was an intake of breath, then stony silence. Rutledge's brow furrowed, and his eyes narrowed. *Slavery! He's into slavery!*

Madison continued unruffled. "What has been the source of those unjust laws complained of among ourselves? Has it not been the real or supposed interest of the major number? Debtors have defrauded their creditors. The landed interest has borne hard on the mercantile interest. The holders of one species of property have thrown a disproportion of taxes on the holders of another species. The lessons we are to draw from the whole is that where a majority are united by a common sentiment and have an opportunity, the rights of the minor party have become insecure. In a republican government the majority, if united, have always an opportunity."

He stopped again to marshal his thoughts, find the fewest right words to drive home the fundamental principle of the entire discourse. He selected his words and his soft voice rang as he delivered them, slowly, emphatically.

"The only remedy is to enlarge the sphere of government, and thereby divide the community into so great a number of interests and parties, that in the first place a majority will not be likely at the same moment to have a common interest separate from that of the whole, or of the minority, and in the second place, that in case they should have such an interest, they may not be apt to be united in the pursuit of it. It is incumbent on us then to try this remedy, and with that view to frame a republican system on such a scale and in such a form as will control all the evils which have been experienced."

The little man stopped, and for a moment his eyes swept the delegation before he resumed his seat.

Washington had not moved until Madison sat down, and then he leaned forward, forearms on his desk, reflecting for a moment to be certain he understood what Madison had labored so hard to define. *Madison proposes that the existence of a true republican government is dependent on creating a large enough mass of citizens that their competing interests will be so numerous that no one faction with one interest will be able to control the majority because there are too many other, diverse interests dividing the entire population. He favors having both the house of representatives and the senate elected by the people, and neither one appointed by the state legislatures.* Washington studied the faces of the delegates, probing for some sign of their thoughts.

Gerry, face drawn, mouth pursed, was shuffling paper to convey his contempt of Madison's discourse. Sherman was drumming his fingers on his desk in boredom. Wilson was whispering to the delegate next to him, gesturing, nodding vigorously. Mason was leaning back, confident, satisfied. Franklin's eyes were half-closed, as though he were either nodding off into one of his naps, or waking from one.

John Dickinson of Delaware rose to his feet. There was the slightest hint of hesitancy in his voice.

"I consider it essential that one branch of the legislature be drawn immediately from the people, and just as expedient that the other branch be chosen by the state legislatures. This combination of state governments with the national government is as politic as it is unavoidable. In the formation of the senate we ought to carry it through such a refining process as will assimilate it as near as may be to the House of Lords in England."

House of Lords in England? Is Dickinson suggesting we follow the British model of government? Can we not improve on it?

The hall fell into instant silence as Dickinson continued. "I have the utmost admiration for the British Constitution. I wholly support a strong national government, but it is obvious that we must leave the states a considerable position of power in the system."

George Read, a companion delegate with Dickinson from Delaware rose. "We are showing far too much attachment to the state governments. We must look beyond their continuance. A national government must soon of necessity swallow them up—all of them. They will soon be reduced to the mere office of electing the national senate. I am strongly against patching up the old federal system, and I hope that idea will be very soon dismissed altogether. To patch it up with the new government we are now creating will be like putting new cloth on an old garment. The Confederation was founded on temporary principles, and it cannot last, nor can it be amended. If we do not establish a good government on new principles, we must either go to ruin, or have the work to do over again."

Read sat down and the debate dragged on. William Pierce spoke for the state legislatures appointing the senate, and Pinckney rose to support Pierce. Wilson stood once again and doggedly championed the common people—let them elect both houses in their new national government. A motion was made and seconded for the vote on the issue of whether the state legislatures should choose the new national senate. One by one the states answered Jackson, who recorded their vote. Aye: three. Nay: eight. At this point the state legislatures would not elect the new national senate.

Weary men grimaced when James Wilson once more took the floor. "I move to reconsider the vote excluding the judiciary from a share in the revision of the laws, and to add to the resolution the words 'with a convenient number of the judiciary' following the words 'national executive.'"

Wilson had just proposed an idea originated by Madison—the "Council of Revision," which Madison had borrowed from the New York Constitution of 1777. Madison seconded the motion, arguing that judges would need such powers to defend their decisions.

Then the debate disintegrated into shadings and positions that became an impossible tangle. Gerry left no doubt that the executive would be more impartial in his judgment of the laws if he were not subject to being seduced by the sophistry of the judges. King was convinced that if the unity of the executive was preferred for the sake of responsibility, the policy of it was as applicable to the revisionary as to the executive powers. Pinckney had retreated from his original proposal of a council of revision, and Mason was adamant that the executive ought to remain unattached to any such council—the purse and the sword ought never to get into the same hands, whether legislative or executive. Dickinson had no question but that the executive had to remain independent, and Williamson was for substituting a clause requiring a two-thirds majority for every effective act of the legislature, rather than any such revisionary provisions.

A motion for the vote was seconded, and Jackson recorded the results. Aye: three. Nay: eight.

On the business of joining the judges with the executive on revisionary matters, the answer was a resounding *no.* The executive and the judicial branches would remain independent of each other, altogether.

Pinckney immediately rose to state that tomorrow he would move for the reconsideration of the clause.

Gorham took the measure of the temper of the delegation and without hesitation adjourned for the day.

The cooling southwest winds held overnight, and at ten o'clock the following morning the delegates were once more in their chairs, sorting papers and reviewing notes, when Washington called the convention to order. He yielded the dais to Gorham, and the committee settled in.

Pinckney arose and moved to reconsider the clause respecting the negative, or veto power, in the national government against state laws, and waited. There was no second.

In the quiet that followed, Dickinson rose, coughed, and moved that the members of the national senate ought to be chosen by the state legislatures, and not the people. Sherman seconded, and once again, the debate heated.

Sherman insisted that if the state legislatures were responsible for appointing national senators, it would obviously tend to bind the two governments together harmoniously. Pinckney raised the question of how many senators was each state to have? After all, if the small states were given one, and the balance were given senators according to population, there would be in excess of eighty senators—far too many for the senate to fulfill its purpose of balancing the great number of representatives in the house.

Wilson shook his head. If the house was elected by the people and the senate appointed by the state legislatures, the bicameral government they were talking about would have two chambers resting on different foundations, and mischief would occur. The only remedy was to have both chambers, house and senate, elected by the people.

A tiny buzz began in the far reaches of the minds of Washington, Franklin, Madison, Mason, Randolph, and a few others. The big states with triple the power of the small states in the senate? The large states already had the power in the house of representatives, since that chamber was elected by the common people. If the large states were also to have the balance of power in the senate, what was to restrain the large states from making the small states their pawns, or worse, nonentities? The buzz held and began to grow, and those who heard it cringed and remained silent. They said nothing, but in their hearts they knew that sooner or later that single issue was going to ignite a war inside the East Room. The only question was when.

Debate quieted, a motion for the vote was seconded, and Jackson recorded the results. On the issue of having the state legislatures appoint the national senate: Aye: ten. Nay: zero. The national senate would be appointed by the state legislatures.

Gorham, with his years of experience in the old Confederation Congress, including his time as president, correctly read the mood of the delegates. It was enough for the day.

"This committee is adjourned until ten o'clock tomorrow morning, Friday, June eighth."

The winds died in the night, and Friday broke with a clear, cloudless sky, calm and cool. By shortly after nine o'clock most delegates were out in the streets, striding to the Statehouse, gathering their inner selves for whatever Gorham and the delegates divined should be the next issue that would have them battering at each other's views.

David Brearly of New Jersey paused at the breakfast table of his boardinghouse before he walked out the door to casually glance at the headlines on the four-page newspaper, *Herald.* His head dropped forward in disbelief, and wide-eyed, he read the printed line again.

"RHODE ISLAND EJECTED FROM UNION."

For a moment he stood stock-still, mind reeling. Dismissed? By whom? How? Why? When?

He snatched up the paper and silently read the column, astonished by the harsh, scathing accusations against the tiny state. The article declared the delegates to the Grand Convention had deeply resented Rhode Island, often referred to as "Rogue Island," for her blind, insulting refusal to send representatives to the Convention. Worse, her leaders had openly stated they wanted no part of this attempt to form a national government.

It continued, "Rhode Island still perseveres in that impolitic, unjust, and scandalous conduct which seems to have marked all her public councils of late. Consequently, no representation is yet here from thence."

The article ripped the tiny state from one end to the other. Rhode Island had from earliest times been a pigheaded rogue. She was the only state to be established without a state religion and quickly became a haven for the radicals, the atheists, and the disbelievers. Her freethinking on religion spilled over into her freethinking on spending. With the end of the war, it was Rhode Island that printed cheap, nearly valueless paper money to pay its debts, and forced creditors to accept it as payment. Then the tiny state repudiated its debt to the federal government! It never paid its share of the horrendous costs of winning the war with Britain!

Deep into the article came the only favorable commentary, written by the businessmen and merchants of the state to George Washington, confessing their embarrassment at the conduct of their state and apologizing for the state's behavior and its absence from the convention. The letter to Washington said:

"The merchants, tradesmen, and others of this place, deeply affected with the evils of the present unhappy times, have thought proper to communicate in writing their approbation of your meeting. It is the general opinion here that full power for the regulation of the commerce of the United States ought to be vested in the National Council."

Brearly suddenly raised his head, jerked out his pocket watch, and tucked the newspaper under his arm as he hurried out the door into the streets. Within the first two blocks of his rapid walk to the Statehouse, he realized the article was either a great hoax or blatantly wrong, since it was doubtful that the Confederation could exclude Rhode Island, or any other state, from the union, because the Articles of Confederation made no such provision. To the contrary, the Articles referred to a "perpetual union."

At ten minutes before ten o'clock, Joseph Fry checked Brearly's credentials and admitted him into the East Room where delegates were gathered in groups. They held newspapers and were reading to each other, heartily laughing, outdoing each other with slanderous and comic remarks about the little state that had thumbed its nose at them. It never occurred to them that someone ought to send a stern warning to the *Herald* that any further articles claiming to have information of what was being done inside the East Room would be dealt with by the law, and, in any event, the article was a blatant lie, slanderous against Rhode Island, and ought to result in a gigantic lawsuit against the newspaper!

Nothing ever came of it.

But with all the excitement, and the uproarious field day the delegates enjoyed poking pins and needles in Rhode Island, a vague shadow arose in the recesses of the mind of every man. If the tiniest state of all has already said no to the whole concept of trying to unite thirteen separate states, with thirteen separate constitutions and governments, how fragile were the chances of ever tying them together forever?

At ten o'clock George Washington convened the convention and yielded the dais to Nathaniel Gorham, who wasted no time.

Pinckney moved that the national legislature should have authority to negative all laws passed by the state legislatures, which the national legislature should judge to be improper, since to vest the national legislature with less than that would be its undoing. Madison seconded the motion, and the debate flowed.

Williamson argued against giving the national legislature a power that might restrain the states from regulating their internal police. Gerry could not see the outer extent of such power, and was against granting the national legislature any power that was not necessary, but had no definition of what was meant by "necessary." Sherman argued that the negative powers should be defined, but could not describe how. The day wore on with no one yet able to find concept or language that would put the question squarely on the ground in understandable form, and the vote was called for.

Aye: three. Nay: seven. They weren't yet ready to grant the veto power to the national legislature.

A tired Gorham adjourned until the next morning, Saturday, June ninth, and at ten o'clock the frustrated delegates were once more in their places when Gorham called the committee to order and Gerry took the floor.

"I renew my prior motion, namely, that the national executive should be elected by the executives of the states whose proportion of votes should be the same with that allowed to the states in the election of the senate."

The buzz that had started in the back of their heads within the past forty-eight hours was still there. Are the big states to have more power in electing the executive branch of the new government than the small states? Will the small states stand for it? Or will it wreck the entire convention?

Randolph rose. "I strongly urge the inexpediency of Mr. Gerry's mode of appointing the national executive. The small states would lose all chance of an appointment from within themselves. Bad appointments would be made, since the executives of the states are obviously not conversant with conditions, or with men, outside their own small spheres. Worse, the states will select an executive who is sympathetic and partial to the affairs of their separate state, and not the national affairs. If a vacancy occurs, how is it to be filled?"

The vote was called for, and Jackson recorded the result. Aye: zero. Nay: ten. The state executives would not be electing or appointing the national executive.

There was a pause before Paterson of New Jersey stood. "I move that the committee resume debate on the clause relating to the issue of voting for the national legislature."

Brearly quickly seconded and launched into a discourse in favor of the small states. Had not this same issue been thrashed out in the old Confederation, with the result that each state, regardless of size, was given one vote? Should any scheme be contrived granting large states greater voting power, the smaller states would suffer. Judging by the disparity of the states by the quota of congress, Virginia would have sixteen votes, and Georgia one. Three states—Massachusetts, Pennsylvania, and Virginia—could outvote all the rest of the states combined, and if they had that power, human nature being what it is, it would only be a matter of time until they did so, to the wounding of all lesser states.

Then Brearly made a proposal that stunned the entire delegation. The remedy, he proposed, was simple. Spread out a map of the United States, erase all existing state borders and boundaries, and partition the entire United States into thirteen equal parts!

Paterson rose and entered into a long, verbose discourse that boiled to one simple proposition. Reconfiguring the United States was impracticable, and, if states were given voting power by population, it could only be seen as a strike at the smaller states. It would eventually defeat itself.

It was not stated in words, but the thinly veiled innuendo could not be missed. For the first time, it was implied that if the small states were to find themselves at the mercy of the voting power of the large ones, they would have no reason to maintain their place in the union. The conclusion was inevitable: they would sever from the United States.

Sobered, alarmed, the delegates maintained their silence, and

Paterson concluded. "There is so much depending on this issue, it might be thought best to postpone the decision until tomorrow."

Gorham declared debate concluded for the day, and since tomorrow was Sunday, the tenth day of June, adjourned the committee until Monday, June eleventh, at ten o'clock.

The delegates rose and began gathering their papers, eyes narrowed in thought as they concentrated on what they now sensed was an issue that could erupt at any time to destroy not only the convention, but tear the union into pieces. How tremulous, how frail was the union? Could they lose it all, over the question of big states versus little ones? It was clear that to give a small state the same voting powers as large ones would be to vest in a citizen of a small state more power than a citizen of a large one. Conversely, to give citizens in all states the same voting powers would favor the large states. Manifestly they could not make big states smaller, nor small ones larger. How, then, could they untie the Gordian knot?

As they filed out of the East Room, not one of them could conceive of an answer. But each of them could conceive of the result if they failed to find one.

Notes

The proceedings set forth in this chapter are found as follows:
Bernstein, *Are We to Be a Nation?* pp. 160–62.
Farrand, *The Records of the Federal Convention*, Volume I, pp. 115–91.
Moyers, *Report from Philadelphia*, pages designated Tuesday, June 5, 1787, through Saturday, June 9, 1787.
Warren, *The Making of the Constitution*, pp. 189–204.
Berkin, *A Brilliant Solution*, pp. 90–95.
Farrand, *The Framing of the Constitution of the United States*, pp. 76–83.
Rossiter, *1787: The Grand Convention*, pp. 173–75.
The humorous anecdote of Benjamin Franklin regarding the system used by Scotland in selecting judges and the story of the Philadelphia newspapers reporting an intent to eject Rhode Island from the United States, are found in the above reference from Moyers, *Report from Philadelphia*, as well as other places.

PART TWO

CHAPTER XVII

★ ★ ★

*M*ost of the delegates sensed the collision that was coming between the large states and the small and shuddered. In the first seventeen days of the convention, the issue had slowly risen and defined itself until it eclipsed all others. The question was simple. In the new national congress, how would the power be divided among the states? If done by population, three states—Virginia, Pennsylvania, and Massachusetts—could collectively control the entire nation, and with the power to do so, it would only be a matter of time until they did. If done by vesting the voting power equally among all the states, then the small states could conceivably control the larger ones.

The small states had openly declared that they would not become the pawns and the doormats for the larger states. Before they would allow it, they would break from the union and go their own way. The large states had indignantly made it known that they would not allow their citizenry to be crippled by the interests of the small states. Before they would allow such a thing, they likewise would secede from the union to form their own governments. The deadly collision was coming, sooner than later, and it could rip the convention, and the United States, into small republics, or kingdoms, or monarchies, that would inevitably degenerate into the abysmal pattern of European history: bickering, then contentions, and finally the inevitable descent into the unending wars that would sap them until the dream of the revolution was forever lost.

Recognizing the oncoming threat was one thing. Recognizing that they faced the burden of inventing a workable solution to it was another. With almost nothing in the history of mankind to serve as their polar star, they were beginning to understand that they would have to create a new government from their own native genius, and it was this that filled them with apprehension as they gathered at the Statehouse and took their places at ten o'clock on Monday morning, June eleventh, 1787. They sat nervously while Washington went through the now familiar and somewhat boring procedure of calling the convention to order and turning the dais over to Gorham to conduct the business of the committee of the whole. They had hardly drawn a breath when Roger Sherman rose.

"I propose that the proportion of votes in the house of representatives should be according to the respective numbers of free inhabitants in each state, and that in the senate, each state should have one vote and no more. Since each state will remain possessed of certain individual rights, each state ought to be able to protect itself. If it is not so, then a few large states will rule the rest. The House of Lords in England have certain particular rights under their constitution, and thus they have an equal vote with the House of Commons that they may defend their rights."

Gunning Bedford rose abruptly. "Will not these large states crush the small ones whenever they stand in the way of their ambitions or interested views? It seems as if Pennsylvania and Virginia wish to provide a system in which they will have an enormous and monstrous influence."

The quiet words, "Hear, hear," came from somewhere, and then David Brearly of New Jersey rose. "The large states—Massachusetts, Pennsylvania, and Virginia—will carry everything before them. Virginia with her sixteen votes will be a solid column indeed, while Georgia with her solitary vote and the other little states will be obliged to throw themselves constantly into the scale of some large one in order to have any weight at all."

They were into it up to their fetlocks, and every man in the room was focused, intense, waiting, watching for the first signs of a schism between the large and the small states. It came when William Paterson of New Jersey, with her small population, rose, defiant, loud.

"I declare that I *will never consent! Myself or my state will never submit to tyranny or despotism!*"

Wide-eyed, James Wilson of Pennsylvania recoiled in disbelief. Tyrant? Despot? Had Patterson implied that the state of Pennsylvania was a tyrant? A despot? Hot, white-faced in outrage, Wilson rose and his voice was too high, too loud.

"Let it be understood! New Jersey should not have the same strength in congress as the state of Pennsylvania, since it has much fewer numbers in its citizenry. It is unjust! I will never confederate on this plan. *If no state will part with any of its sovereignty, it is in vain to talk of a national government!*"

They were there. The single greatest issue that could rip the country into pieces was on the floor of the convention. One small state had sworn it would never submit to the will of large ones. One large state had declared there was no other way. The battle lines were drawn, clear, final.

For several seconds that seemed an eternity no one spoke, and then John Rutledge rose, shaking his head. "I propose that the proportion of votes in the house should be according to the amount of money contribution of each state. In my view, the justice of this rule cannot be contested."

Pierce Butler loudly called, "Second the motion."

Rufus King was on his feet. "I move that the power to vote for membership in the house of representatives of the national legislature ought not be according to the rule established in the Articles of Confederation, one vote for each state. It should be according to some equitable ration of representation."

Some delegates were sitting with narrowed eyes, brains straining to comprehend the proposals that were now starting to swirl, and to calculate the principles on which the proposals finally came to rest.

John Dickinson's voice cut in. "If the money contributions are to be the basis for the voting power of the states, then it must be based on the actual contributions of each state, and not on what the rule indicates they *should* pay!"

Rufus King took the floor again. "It is uncertain what mode might be used in levying a national revenue, but it is probably that imports would be one source of it. If the actual contributions are to be the rule, then the nonimporting states, such as Connecticut and New Jersey, will be in dire circumstances indeed. With almost no imports, it could well be that neither of those states will have representation at all!"

Benjamin Franklin raised a hand and spoke. "I have anticipated this debate by putting some of my thoughts on paper, which my colleague Mr. James Wilson has agreed to read."

Wilson rose, took a deep breath, and launched into a discourse that rambled and reached and touched many issues. It commenced with Franklin's attempt to raise the delegation above pettiness and faction before it fragmented.

"Until this point the debates have generally been cool and tempered—if anything contrary has on this day appeared, it should not be repeated—we are sent here to *consult* and not to *contend*—declarations of fixed opinions and of resolutions to never change them neither enlighten nor convince—positiveness and warmth beget the same reactions from others and tend to promote harmony and union which are extremely necessary to our councils."

Wilson took a breath and went on.

"Whereas my original opinion was that members of the national congress would deem themselves representatives of the whole, and not of a particular state, it is obvious by now that such was not to be. That being so, members of the national congress ought to be selected by the vote of the people, but that would give larger states power over the smaller ones, and that seems now to be the impasse. However, on close analysis I do not see the advantage the greater states would have in swallowing up the smaller nor do I think they would attempt it—rather, I think it would come to the same result we observe in the arrangement between Scotland and England—you will recall Scotland was fearful that with inferior representatives in the English parliament they would be ruined by the greater number of English representatives—but history has shown the fears to be unfounded—Scotland remains and is satisfied.

"Lacking a workable arrangement for sharing the power in congress, I beg leave to provide one that I believe practical and equitable. Let the weakest state among us say what proportion of money or force it is able and willing to furnish for the general purposes of the union. Then let all other states oblige themselves to match such contribution in equal proportion. Grant Congress power to make any necessary adjustments. You will recall this is the arrangement which the United States shared with England when we were still colonies."

Wilson finished the discourse, shuffled the papers together, and announced, "I move that we add to the pending motion the words 'in proportion to the whole number of white and other free citizens and inhabitants of every age, sex, and condition, including those bound to servitude for a term of years and three-fifths of all other persons not comprehended in the foregoing description, except Indians not paying taxes, in each state.'"

A startled hush settled. Three-fifths of all other persons? There was but one category of other persons. The African slaves! Were the slaves going to be "other persons," and not called out for what they were? Slaves?

Then Elbridge Gerry rose and in his own cryptic, acrid style opened the slavery wound. "I cannot agree that property should be the rule governing representation in the national congress. Why should blacks, who are property in the south, be considered in the rule of portioning out the voting power, any more than the cattle and horses in the north? After all, the cattle and horses in the north are simply property, like the blacks in the south!"

Stunned delegates sucked air, trying to believe what Gerry had just done. With the volcanic issue of big states versus small states framed not thirty seconds earlier, Gerry had chosen to plunge the already muddled convention into the second issue that could smash the entire union. Slavery! The tension became like a living thing. The delegates from the southern states set their jaws and stared their defiance, while those of the northern states glared back their condemnation of the practice.

Gerry had laid out the raw, garish truth in terms that could not be misunderstood. Slaves not human beings? Property, like cattle, horses? For a few moments, sick, unbearable silence settled in the room like a pall. It seemed the air was charged with electricity. Strong men, wracked by consciences seared by white-hot torment as never before, dropped their eyes and refused to raise them.

Washington sat like a statue, face a blank, studying the delegates with an intensity unnoticed by most. *Will they survive it? Will they recognize that either they rise above their regional differences and compromise? Or will they let their differences destroy the United States?*

Roger Sherman of tiny Connecticut brought it to a head.

"I move that the question be taken whether each state shall have one vote in the senate. It is clear that everything depends on this. The smaller states will never agree to the plan on any other principle than an equality of voting power in this branch of the national congress."

Sherman's colleague from Connecticut, Oliver Ellsworth, exclaimed, "Second the motion."

Gorham called for the vote, and the only sounds were Jackson calling the names of the states, and the response of the spokesmen.

Connecticut, New York, New Jersey, Delaware, Maryland. Aye.

Massachusetts, Pennsylvania, Virginia, North Carolina, South Carolina, Georgia. Nay.

Five "Ayes," six "Nays."

The big states had won by the narrowest margin possible. The house of representatives and the senate in the new bicameral congress were to be elected by the people on the basis of popular vote. For a brief moment Washington watched the delegates from the small states. *Will they walk out, as they implied?*

The small state delegates sat firm, silent, jaws clenched, but they did not rise, nor did they utter a word of condemnation against the large states. Rather, they raised their eyes to Gorham, waiting for the next issue to come before the committee.

The day wore on with smaller, less significant issues being debated, some hotly, some with near disinterest. Should there be a guarantee of republican government, and for territory, for each state—how was the constitution to be amended—should oaths of loyalty toward the national government be required of members of the state governments? The small states debated the issues without rancor and cast their votes when Gorham made the calls.

It was deep in the afternoon when the session adjourned, to convene the next day, June twelfth. At 10:00 A.M. Washington called the convention to order and delivered the dais to Gorham, and took his place among the delegates, relieved that the delegates from the smaller states were in their places. They had not bolted.

With the startling events of the previous day bright in their minds, the committee gingerly avoided the unsettled and explosive question of dividing the voting power and moved steadily into the question of how long men should serve in the house of representatives, and how long in the senate.

Elbridge Gerry took the floor, and several delegates leaned back in their chairs, heads tipped back, eyes closed in resignation as Gerry launched into it. It was not by accident he was often referred to as the "Grumbletonian." He grumbled about everything that he himself had not thought of or introduced on the floor.

"We in New England propose a term of one year for the representatives. They are accustomed to annual town meetings where local officials must answer to their neighbors." He thrust a bony finger toward the ceiling as he finished. "We in New England look on elections every year as the only defense the citizens have against tyranny, and we will never give them up!"

So far as Gerry was concerned, he had put the entire matter of tenure at rest. The representatives would serve one year at a time and be accountable to the people at the end of each year.

Madison rose. In his quiet manner he explained, "If the opinions of the people are to be our guide, it will be difficult to say what course we ought to take. No member of the convention can say what the opinions of his constituents are at this time. We ought to consider what is right and necessary in itself for the attainment of a proper government. Might I recommend that representatives serve for three years? A three-year term would allow them to learn of the interests of the other states and become familiar with the national scene. I further suggest that seven years would be an appropriate term for senators. With seven years to become competent in their office, they should be able to check the passions of the lower house elected directly by the people."

The vote was called. The longer terms won. Three years for representatives, seven for senators. Gerry grumbled.

On the question of how much to pay the representatives and the senators, Benjamin Franklin cleared his throat, and the hall became silent with anticipation.

"I move to change the compensation provision from 'liberal compensation' to 'moderate compensation.'"

For the first time in forty-eight hours chuckles were heard. The vote was called, and it came down a resounding, unanimous affirmative. The members of the new congress would be paid a "moderate" compensation. Not a "liberal" one.

Washington stifled a smile. *He's pulled them back together.*

The proceedings inside the East Room ground on. On June thirteenth, the delegates learned of a Massachusetts newspaper that had published an editorial begging the people to be patient.

"Ye men of America, banish from your bosoms those demons, suspicion and distrust. Be assured, the men whom ye have delegated to work out your national salvation are men in whom ye may confide—their extensive knowledge, known abilities, and approved patriotism warrant it."

The delegates read the words, and wished mightily they had as much faith in themselves as that Massachusetts editor.

On Tuesday, June fourteenth, in stifling heat, Gorham opened the floor to debate only to have William Paterson of New Jersey rise abruptly.

"It is the wish of several deputations, particularly that of New

Jersey, that further time might be allowed them to contemplate the plan reported from the committee of the whole, and to digest one purely federal, and contradistinguished from the reported plan. It is our hope to have such a plan ready tomorrow to be laid before the Convention."

Franklin scanned the delegation. *Mr. Paterson has deceived no one. He's offered a direct challenge to the plan of Randolph and the Virginians. Well, we'll see. We'll see.*

Gorham closed his ledger. "Adjourned until tomorrow morning, June fifteenth, at this same hour."

The delegates heaved a sight of relief before they rose, gathered their papers, and walked out of the building, most of them due east toward the taverns and restaurants lining the Delaware River, hoping for a cooling breeze to relieve the relentless heat. But the delegates of the small states turned east towards the Indian Queen hotel and a closed-room caucus, to lay their plans for their all-out assault on the Virginia Plan of James Madison that had overwhelmed the convention from the first day.

Friday, June fifteenth, a curious, focused committee of the whole took their places at ten o'clock, and all eyes were intently turned on William Paterson when Gorham gave him the floor.

"I came here not to speak my own sentiments, but the sentiments of those who sent me. If the sovereignty of the states is to be maintained, the representatives must be drawn from the states, not from the people. And we have no power to vary the idea of equal sovereignty."

Large state delegates leaned back in their chairs, eyes narrowed as they braced for the battle they saw coming.

Paterson plucked up a stack of papers from his desktop, scanned them briefly, then began his delivery.

"The plan I propose is set forth in sections, which I request shall be substituted for those in the Virginia Plan already voted in the committee of the whole." Mutterings were heard, and he paused and waited for silence before he delivered the shock.

"Section One. That the Articles of Confederation ought to be so revised, corrected, and enlarged as to render the federal constitution adequate to the exigencies of government and the preservation of the union."

Chairs groaned as men shifted their weight and shook their heads in disgust. *Amend the Articles of Confederation? That was settled two weeks ago when we abandoned them. Are we going to thrash it out again?*

Paterson ignored the obvious and laid it out, one section at a time. The Articles of Confederation to be amended and remain the controlling document of government; congress to be granted new powers to raise money through import duties and stamp taxes; to regulate commerce; to compel delinquent states to honor requisitions; an executive composed of more than one man to be elected by congress; a supreme court to be appointed by the executive and added to the machinery of the confederation; the executive be authorized to call forth the power of the confederated states to enforce the laws and treaties of the United States in the face of state opposition.

As they listened, the faces of the delegates subtly changed from listening, to questioning, then to puzzlement. Who had drafted this document that seemed to meander about from one subject to another, sometimes in conflict with itself? They thought they could hear and smell Paterson, Brearly, Sherman, Lansing, and Luther Martin in some of it, but who was responsible for the rest of it? They puzzled and conjectured, but could not decide.

Paterson finished his discourse, and John Lansing of New York stood. "It is my earnest desire, and that of some other gentlemen, that the convention not go into the committee of the whole on the subject until tomorrow. Clearly, we are to decide between a *national* government that is without precedent in the history of mankind, and which vests power in the people, and a *federal* government based on the Articles of Confederation, that vests power in the *states.* In the delay of one day, the supporters of this new plan will be better prepared to explain and support it, and more important, copies will be available to all delegates."

Heads nodded. Gorham shifted in his chair and adjourned the meeting for one more day, to June sixteenth at 10:00 A.M.

At ten o'clock the following morning, the delegates each took their seat with a copy of the plan of the small states and now championed by William Paterson of New Jersey and John Lansing of New York, locked in deep concentration as they worked with the proposals one at a time, trying to force them into a coherent, consistent document. Within minutes they were calling it the "New Jersey" plan, as opposed to the "Virginia" plan of Randolph and Madison.

Washington convened the delegates and turned the dais to Gorham to preside over the committee of the whole. Lansing stood, Gorham recognized him, and instantly the East Room was plunged into the collision that had held the entire convention in fear from the beginning. Large states against small, with the pending threats from each that they would walk out and destroy the union if the other won, and no one able to conceive a way to avoid it.

"I call for reading of the first resolution of each plan," Lansing declared, "which are in direct conflict. The plan of Mr. Paterson sustains the sovereignty of the states, and that of Mr. Randolph destroys it."

There could be no clearer definition of the battle lines, but few expected what Lansing did next. He did not attack the merits of either plan. Rather, he attacked the power of the convention to even *consider* the Virginia plan. Delegates sat mesmerized as he ripped into it.

"I point out emphatically we who are delegates in this convention and this committee are *not empowered by the terms of our commissions to even discuss, or propose, the plan of Mr. Randolph—the Virginia plan.*"

He stopped and for a few moments stared defiantly into the eyes of the supporters of the Virginia plan, then others. Their faces were set, noncommitttal, defensive.

He plowed on, his voice rising. "Further, it is clear to me that it is highly improbable it will not be adopted in any event!" He stopped, then continued. "The commissions the various states have issued to its delegations to this convention have specifically limited the powers vested in us to the amendment of the confederacy! We can amend the Articles of Confederation, but we can not go one step further!" Murmuring rose and subsided. He waited for silence, then rose onto his toes, with one hand thrust high to go on.

"I can assure you, New York would never have concurred in sending deputies here if she had supposed the deliberations were to turn on a consolidation of the states, and a national government. Is it probable that the various states will adopt and ratify a scheme of government which they have never authorized us to propose? The states will never give a national government the power to veto their own state laws. At this time, if our vote some two weeks ago for the Virginia plan did away with the confederacy, then all states here today stand on equal footing as sovereign states, which gives each state, large or small, equal standing. If that be true, then why do we not vote so right now?"

He paused to let the logic sink in, then continued.

"On the other hand, if the vote two weeks ago did not kill the confederation under the Articles of Confederation, then we are still bound by the articles, and if we are, that document dictates that we are absolutely bound under article five that gives each state one vote, and further, under article thirteen which dictates that no alteration can be made of the articles without unanimous consent."

He stopped to allow the delegates to digest his reasoning. There was a rustle and some whispered remarks, and then he finished.

"What is unanimously done, must be unanimously undone. If the sovereignty of the states is to be maintained, the members of the federal congress must be elected by the states, not the people, since we have no power other than to maintain equal sovereignty among the states. To abandon that power by giving it to the people will throw the states into hotchpot!"

Then Paterson shifted his argument so abruptly that some delegates cast their eyes about, trying to follow it.

"The Virginia plan will also be enormously expensive! Allowing Georgia and Delaware two representatives in congress, the aggregate number of all representatives from all states in the house of representatives will be one-hundred-eighty! Add to it half that number for the senate, and you will have two-hundred-seventy members in the new national congress! In the present deranged state of our finances, can so expensive a system be seriously considered? The New Jersey plan will save most of this unthinkable expense, and all purposes of good government will be observed." He stopped and waited for total silence before he leaned forward and ended his discourse. "At least a trial ought to be made of it."

For a few moments he straightened the sheaf of papers he held in his hand, bobbed his head, and sat down.

James Wilson was on his feet instantly. "Multiplying words is to be avoided in what is now before us, so I beg leave to enter at once into a comparison of the two plans—Virginia and New Jersey—point by point without further prologue."

For hours, with deadly precision, Wilson launched into the comparison, his voice and his arguments gaining strength as he demolished the New Jersey plan one step at a time. The Virginia plan included a bicameral congress, the New Jersey plan but one; the people have the power in the Virginia plan and therefore the people can prevail, while the states have it in the New Jersey plan, and rob the people of their voice. In the Virginia plan there is one executive, removable on impeachment and conviction; laws can be checked; there are lower national courts; the laws extend to all cases affecting the national peace and harmony; and finally, ratification is to be by the people themselves. All of which provisions do not exist in the New Jersey plan!

He paused and tapped his desktop with his index finger. "With regard to the question raised by Mr. Paterson that this convention is not empowered to depart from the Articles of Confederation, but only to amend them, I declare that I consider myself authorized to *conclude nothing, but I am at liberty to propose anything.*"

There was a moment of silence, and then an audible intake of breath at how deftly Wilson had undercut Paterson's dogged adherence to the Articles of Confederation.

With the momentum gathering in his favor, Wilson pressed on. "Further, regarding Mr. Paterson's fears regarding the sentiments of the people and their purported fear of a new government not grounded in the Articles of Confederation, I suggest that it is difficult, if not impossible, to know what those sentiments are. It is error to reckon that the sentiments of one segment of the people in one location is the sentiment of the whole. I do not believe that a federal government selected by the states is irrevocably endeared to the people, nor do I believe that one selected by the people is so obnoxious to them. I do not fear the outcome if the choice is given to the people at large, and not to the state legislatures!"

Clearly exhausted by his earnest and lengthy treatise, Wilson sat down, and young Charles Pinckney rose. In abrupt, succinct terms he said, "The whole of it comes to this. Give New Jersey an equal vote, and she will dismiss her scruples and concur in the national system set out in the Virginia plan." He paused and changed direction. "I must also state that in my view of it, this convention is authorized to go to any length in recommending any form of government, so long as we find it necessary to remedy the evils which produced this convention in the first place."

Randolph came to his feet and all eyes turned to him, some fearful he was about to embark on another odyssey as he had that first day, others fearful that he might provide the spark that would set off the powderkeg. He did neither.

"In the strongest language of which I am capable, I again point out the imbecility of the existing confederacy and the imminent danger of delaying a substantial reform. We must abandon what has proven itself to be a fatally flawed government and create a new one which we believe will bring peace and harmony among the states, and the people. To do otherwise would be an act of treason against our trust. Only a national government will answer all our needs, and I beg this august body to consider that the present moment is the last one for establishing such a government. Should we fail in doing so, the people will yield to ultimate despair."

Gorham stood. "It is obvious this debate will not be concluded today. It is equally obvious that a Sunday recess will be beneficial. This committee is adjourned until Monday morning, June eighteenth, same hour."

The weary, embattled delegation stood and began gathering their papers from their desks when Dickinson made his way to Madison's side, and the two looked at each other for a moment before Dickson delivered his blunt warning. "You see the consequence of pushing things too far. Some of the small states are friends to a good national government. But we would sooner submit to a foreign power than submit to be deprived of an equality of voting power and thereby be thrown under the domination of the larger states."

The two of them, champions of two opposing causes that were imminently to collide head-on, stared at each other for a moment, and then Dickinson walked back to his desk. The diminutive Madison watched Dickinson's rigid back as he went, masking his shock at the audacity of the delegate from Delaware. Hot, impassioned debate on the floor of the convention was one thing; thinly-veiled threats off the floor were quite another. Madison turned back to the business of gathering his papers.

On that bright Monday morning of June eighteenth, not one member of the delegation had the slightest suspicion of the odd, bizarre proceeding that awaited them. Gorham called the committee of the whole to order and was startled when Alexander Hamilton stood. The slender, handsome, thirty-two-year-old New York delegate had achieved monumental recognition since his arrival in America before the revolution, from his native West Indies origins, where he was thought to be an illegitimate child. Brilliant, charismatic, he had risen through the ranks of the Continental Army during the war to become an officer and had performed spectacularly when the sick and tattered remnants of the shattered Continental Army crossed the frozen Delaware River and stormed Trenton. He had survived the unparalleled misery of Valley Forge, then been promoted to the staff of General Washington from 1777 to 1781. His boldness and overconfidence in his own views had brought him at odds with the General briefly, but the rift had healed, and Hamilton was leading his fighting command when the Americans stormed the British Redoubt Number Ten at Yorktown. At war's end, Hamilton was a bright and shining star of the revolution. He studied law, and by 1787 his keen mind and boundless energy quickly brought him to the top of the legal profession in New York. He had entered the world of politics with pamphlets he composed, had printed, and were distributed, in which he loudly and publicly declared his strongly nationalist views on government.

Hamilton faced Gorham, waiting to be recognized, and Gorham declared, "The delegate from New York wishes to be heard." Hamilton glanced at his papers and then spoke.

"I have been hitherto silent on the business before the convention, partly from respect to others whose superior abilities, age, and experience rendered me unwilling to bring forward ideas dissimilar to theirs, and partly from my delicate situation with respect to my own state, to whose sentiments as expressed by my colleagues I can by no means accede."

He paused, and other delegates quickly understood that Hamilton had just leveled a scathing indictment against John Lansing, his fellow delegate from New York, for Lansing's support of the Articles of Confederation. The New York delegation was split on the single-most explosive issue in the convention!

Hamilton rapidly continued. "The crisis which now marks our affairs is too serious to permit any scruples whatever to prevail over the duty imposed on every man to contribute his efforts for the public safety and happiness. I have examined both the Virginia and the New Jersey plans, and I am friendly to neither of them."

Every delegate in the room stared in surprise, mystified at what was too quickly taking shape before them.

For one second Hamilton cast his eyes about, and then entered upon a six-hour presentation that touched every point of both the Virginia Plan and the New Jersey plan, picking each to pieces one clause at a time, his voice rising and falling with drama, his command of the language and selection of words enthralling. He was well past the fifth hour of his lecture-harangue when he caught everyone by surprise.

"It is my firm belief that the British government is the best in the world, and I doubt very much whether anything short of it will do in America. I accept the fact that my ideas reach far beyond those of most of the members of this body, but they do embody the principles necessary to check and control the evils in this country, which is the purpose of our being here."

For one brief moment there was silence, and then every other man in the East Room shut out Hamilton, ignoring the remainder of his discourse. Each had at one time been a British subject, and each knew that the British constitution and form of government was seen in the international world of politics as providing the most liberty and justice for its subjects. Their separation from England came not because the British form of government was untenable, but because the British had abandoned and violated their own principles of liberty and justice in their harsh treatment of their thirteen colonies.

It was later that William Samuel Johnson of Connecticut undid Hamilton's magnificent but badly misconceived effort with one cryptic sentence. "The gentleman from New York is praised by all, but supported by none."

Hamilton sat down, and for a few moments no one spoke as the delegates puzzled over what Hamilton had hoped to accomplish. That he had attempted to shred both the Virginia and the New Jersey plans was evident, but was there more? Did he expect someone to construe his discourse as a proposal, to be seconded and voted upon?

There was no second, no comment. Hamilton's efforts died on the floor.

Gorham shook his head and took charge. "We are adjourned for the day to reconvene tomorrow morning, June nineteenth, at ten o'clock."

At 9:55 A.M. the following morning, Joseph Fry admitted the last of the delegates into the East Room, closed the doors, and sat down on his chair. Washington called the convention to order and delivered the dais to Gorham.

"I understand Mr. Madison wishes to address the committee of the whole."

Madison stood, small, immaculate, disciplined. The representatives glanced at each other inquisitively, then settled, focused on Madison as he picked up a sheaf of his own notes. Silence gripped the hall as the men strained to hear his soft voice.

"Much stress has been laid by some gentlemen on the want of power in the convention to propose any other than a *federal* plan, connected with the Articles of Confederation. I can only say that neither of the characteristics attached to a federal plan will support that proposition. In the ordinary transactions between persons, breach by one party of an article with another sets both parties free from the article, unless in the article itself is language defining the remedy for such breach. This rule shows that we are not to consider the federal union as analogous to a social compact between individuals, for if it were so, a majority would have a right to bind the rest, and even to form a new constitution for the whole."

He paused. No one moved, and he continued.

"If the current federal plan, founded on the Articles of Confederation, is not analogous to the ordinary transactions between persons, but instead is analogous to the compacts between states, what is the result? Clearly, under the law of nations, a breach of any one article by any one party, leaves all the other parties at liberty to consider the entire convention dissolved. That being so, I now point out that New Jersey herself breached the Articles of Confederation when she expressly refused to comply with a requisition issued to her by the Confederation Congress. In so doing, she has released all other states from the binding effect of the Articles of Confederation. Further, there is not one word in the said Articles that addresses what shall be done in the event one state does such a thing, as was done by New Jersey."

Paterson sat transfixed, sensing for the first time that Madison was on the fringe of destroying his New Jersey plan. And for the first time men moved, and chairs scraped on the floor. Madison went on.

"May we now examine the New Jersey plan one proposition at a time."

With a sense of calm dignity, facts known to every man in the room, and logic beyond reproach, Madison disassembled the entire plan.

"1. Will it prevent violations of international laws and treaties which will lead us into the calamities of war with foreign nations? The Articles of Confederation are silent on the question.

"2. Will it prevent encroachments by the states on federal authority? No! Virginia and Maryland have already entered into treaties that breach the authority of the confederation congress, and Pennsylvania and New Jersey have done the same, all without prior consent from congress, and with no apology after. Massachusetts has raised a standing army without even apprising congress of her intentions.

"3. Will it prevent trespasses of the states on each other? The records are clearly to the contrary. Virginia and Maryland have both given their own citizens unfair and unjust advantages over citizens of the other state in transactions. Creditors from one state who have brought suit in the other to collect debts justly owed have been denied any sense of justice.

"4. Will it secure tranquility and peace between the states? The recent insurrections in the state of Massachusetts have taught all states that they are exposed to such violence, and that the confederation congress is powerless to prevent it.

"5. Will it secure good laws and administration in the particular states? One need only study the multiplicity of laws in the various states, many in conflict with the laws in neighboring states, the mutability of their laws, the injustice that is manifest in them, and the impotence of the laws.

"6. Will it secure the union against the influence of foreign powers? History teaches that the intrigues practiced among the Amphictyonic Confederates, first by the Kings of Persia, and then by Philip of Macedon, then Achaeans, then Rome, followed by France, England, Spain, and Russia, can, and eventually will, develop between the states themselves, and the Articles of Confederation are powerless to prevent it.

"7. The smaller states would be well advised to examine the situation in which they would find themselves if Mr. Paterson's New Jersey plan is adopted. They would have all the expense of maintaining their representatives in the new national congress, knowing all the time that they will be dominated by the larger states in all matters whatsoever."

Madison stopped to adjust the papers in his hand before he concluded.

"I beg the smaller states to consider the situation in which they will remain in the event their commitment to an inadmissible plan prevents them from adopting any other plan."

Again he stopped and this time he raised those piercing blue eyes to scan the faces of the entire delegation. His words came slow, measured, in the hushed room.

"Let the union of the states be dissolved and one of two consequences must happen. Either the states must remain individually independent and sovereign, or two or more confederacies must be formed among them. In the first event would the small states be more secure against the ambition and power of their larger neighbors than they are now? In the second event, can the smaller states expect their larger neighbors to confederate with them as equals, as it now stands under the Articles of Confederation?"

He paused to clear his throat and went on.

"Mr. Paterson has stated that 'it would not be *safe* for Delaware to allow Virginia sixteen times as many votes as Delaware, although Virginia has sixteen times more citizens than Delaware.' May I respectfully suggest that in so saying, Mr. Paterson has implicitly acknowledged that it is not *just* to grant Delaware equal voting power with Virginia, since Virginia has sixteen times more citizens than Delaware."

The silence held as the delegates examined the logic of Madison's thoughts, and then he finished.

"If New Jersey and Delaware conceive that an advantage can be had by both by an equalization of the power, why might not this right be granted to each of them by a constitution that that leaves them at liberty to do whatever they please?"

Men straightened in their chairs, overwhelmed by the rare power, and the logic, and the masterful delivery of Madison's discourse. For a time Madison stood still, looking into the eyes of the delegates, watching their thoughts come together, sensing the set of their minds. Then he sat down. His presentation had taken most of the day.

Gorham broke the spell. He called for action on two or three small matters, then announced the vote would be taken on whether the convention would support the New Jersey Plan of Paterson, or the Virginia plan of Madison and Randolph. Not a man in the room moved as Jackson called out the names of the states and recorded the votes in favor of the Virginia plan.

Aye: Massachusetts, Connecticut, Pennsylvania, Delaware, Virginia, North Carolina, South Carolina, Georgia. Total, eight.

Nay: New York, New Jersey, Delaware. Total, three.

Maryland, divided, no vote.

The Virginia plan had survived; the New Jersey plan had failed.

Paterson and Lansing dropped their eyes and began setting their desks in order. Their New Jersey plan was lost; the battle of the day had gone against them. But they also knew that the issue was not forever settled. Madison had left the door open to raise the same question for another fight, another day. As the delegates filed from the hall, most realized that the eloquence and the knowledge and genius of James Madison had saved the union, at least for the moment. As for tomorrow, none could predict.

Notes

The dates, issues, participants, and results of the convention appearing in this chapter are taken from the following:

Farrand, *The Records of the Federal Convention*, pp. 192–333.

Warren, *The Making of the Constitution*, pp. 207–33.

Rossiter, *1787: The Grand Convention*, pp. 173–79.

Berkin, *A Brilliant Solution*, pp. 92–103.

Farrand, *The Framing of the Constitution of the United States*, pp. 84–93.

Moyers, *Report from Philadelphia*, pages designated Monday, June 11, 1787, through Tuesday, June 19, 1787.

The description of Alexander Hamilton is found in Rossiter, *1787: The Grand Convention*, pp. 94–96.

Elbridge Gerry of Massachusetts was called the "Grumbletonian" because of his habitual grumbling at just about everything he did not originate. Bernstein, *Are We to Be a Nation?* p. 179.

The reader is reminded that speeches have been abstracted because it is impossible to include every address in its entirety in this volume. Wording has been changed where it was felt necessary to make the language and figures of speech understandable today. Every effort has been made to preserve the intent and meaning of the original transcripts, and wherever possible, direct quotations have been included. Errors and misrepresentations are the sole responsibility of this writer.

The Bahamas

June 20, 1787

CHAPTER XVIII

*T*he tense, shrill shout came down from the crow's nest, sixty feet up the mainmast of the small schooner *Zephyr* as she sped south through the clear, blue-green waters, two-hundred-eighty miles due east of the southern coast of East Florida.

"Landfall, sou'west!"

One second later the voice of the sweating, bearded seaman cracked out again, "Ship! Due west. Two ships! Two!"

Below, on the rolling deck, Caleb Dunson and half a dozen crewmen trotted to the railing of the starboard bow and wiped salt-sweat from their eyes to peer westward, hands raised to shade their eyes against the glare of the setting sun, straining to see the irregularity on the flat horizon that would be another of the myriad of tiny islands approaching the Bahamas, and the tall specks that would be two ships. They were not there.

Caleb turned to the first mate, Miles Young, standing next to him. "Get Tunstall and his charts!"

"Yes, sir." Average height, thin, angular, bearded, dark-haired, pale green eyes, fourteen years in the British navy before abandoning England to become part of the fledgling United States Navy, Young pivoted, bare feet slapping the wet planking of the deck. He jerked open the small door at the quarterdeck and disappeared down four steps into the cramped passage leading to the officer's quarters, and stopped to hammer on the first door.

The deep, muffled voice of Nathan Tunstall, navigator, called, "Enter," and Young barged in. Tunstall, stripped to the waist, barefooted and sweating in the heaviness of the tropical heat, stood hunched over his tiny table, piled high with maps. His sextant, alidade, compass, calipers, and other equipment were on a shelf at his left elbow.

Young exclaimed, "Cap'n says bring your maps. Now!"

Taller, red-haired, flaming red beard, jutting chin that gave his face a fierce cast, Tunstall turned narrowed eyes to Young. "What's happened?"

"Landfall. Sou'west. Two ships due west. *Move!*"

Tunstall grabbed up two maps and as the two hunched down to hurry through the restricted passageway asked, "How near?"

"Can't see 'em yet from the deck. Bartolo sees 'em from the nest."

Bartolo was the tiny, swarthy Portuguese seaman with scraggly beard and bowed legs and the black eyes that Tunstall swore could see ships and land fifteen miles beyond the curvature of the earth. In these waters, open and international by all rules of the sea, but claimed by the British and French and Spanish, and pirates, it was Bartolo the ship's crew wanted in the crow's nest.

The two trotted to where most of the crew was clustered at the starboard bow, and the seamen opened a lane to let them take their places beside Caleb. All were barefooted and bearded. Most were stripped to the waist, clad only in pants that reached midway between their knees and ankles, though a few wore a light, striped cotton shirt against the ravages of a blistering tropical sun. All were burned brown, some with dead skin peeling.

In Boston, before they sailed, Caleb had thought hard on the question of a crew, and then sent out word, first to all seamen in the employ of Dunson & Weems Shipping Company, then to any on the Boston waterfront who wished to listen. He was going to take a schooner south into the Bahamas and maybe beyond, into waters legendary for sudden storms, wrecked ships, and lost crews, and now infested with ships from just about every other competing foreign country in the world: Britain, France, Spain, and the Dutch most prominent among them. His purpose was to find any survivors of the crew of a merchantman ship that had been plundered and burned by pirates and driven onto a reef by a storm, if there were any such survivors. Chances of a fight were excellent, and chances of safe return to Boston were not. They would travel fast, go in, get out, and do it under any flag necessary—British, French, Dutch, Spanish, or pirate. They would be armed with muskets, swords, knives, and twelve, thirty-two-pound cannon, concealed by canvas and lashed against the main-deck railings next to the gun ports, which had been newly cut in the small schooner and would be kept closed until they were needed. They would carry twenty extra kegs of gunpowder in the hold for whatever eventualities might be required. Pay would be standard sea-man's wages if they survived to return to Boston, with an additional ten pounds sterling for all who came back. The crew was to be volunteers, and men with families were urged not to apply. Ninety-three volunteers appeared at the Dunson & Weems office; fourteen were chosen, in addi-tion to Caleb, Miles Young to serve as first mate, Nathan Tunstall to navigate, and a ship's surgeon.

Caleb spoke to Tunstall. "How close are we to the north end of the Bahamas?"

Quickly Tunstall spread a map on the hatch behind them, scanned it, then tapped it with his finger. "We're about here. About eighty miles north of the first big island. There's more'n seven hundred islands down there, most small, a lot of them uncharted. I think Bartolo is seeing one of the uncharted ones."

"Where's the reef McDaris said has the wreck of the *Belle?*"

Tunstall pointed to a distinctive "X" he had made on the map. "Right there. About two-hundred-eighty miles south by sou'east. The island is likely uncharted."

Caleb cupped his hands to shout up to Bartolo, "Can you see the two ships?"

The little man's arm shot up, pointing. "There. Due west."

"Use your telescope. What flag?"

Seconds passed while the little man adjusted his telescope and squinted. "Cannot tell."

"What heading are they on?"

"Due east. T'ord us."

Suddenly Young pointed. "There!"

Instantly Caleb, Young, and Tunstall raised their telescopes, adjusted them, and picked up the two tiny flecks on the horizon. For several seconds they watched them coming on, growing in size, cutting a course directly for the *Zephyr*. Caleb lowered his telescope and reflected for a moment before he called to the seaman at the wheel.

"Steady as she goes." He turned back to Young and Tunstall. "We get ready to put on all canvas, and then we wait until we see their flag." He glanced up at the flag they were flying—the British Union Jack— and nodded to Young. "Get the crew into the rigging, ready with the water buckets, but wait until we know who those ships are."

"Aye, sir."

Young gave orders and a few seamen with hot wind blowing their hair and beards scrambled up the rope ladders to the spars on the two masts, then worked their way outward on the hawsers, bare feet and toes clinging as they leaned forward to loop their arms over the spars with their chests against them while peering at the two ships quartering in from the west. Other seamen walked the ropes to control the spankers and the jibs at the bow and stern, which would give more sail to the slender little schooner. Those still on deck seized heavy wooden buckets and stood by barrels of seawater, ready to dip them full and pass them up the rope ladders to the men in the rigging.

Minutes passed before Bartolo shouted down, "French flags! Both French!"

Caleb and Young felt the relief and rounded their mouths and blew air. A French ship would not be anxious to attack a British ship in these open waters. The British, French, Dutch, and Spanish had long since made their competing claims to most of the string of lush, tropical islands arcing southeast for more than fifteen hundred miles—the Bahamas, Greater Antilles, and Lesser Antilles. The British had ports in the Bahamas, Jamaica, Barbuda, Antigua, Dominica, Barbados, Tobago, and others, while the Spanish laid claim to Trinidad, Puerto Rico, Saint Domingo, and Cuba, and the French to Martinique, Marie-Galande, Guadeloupe, and Saint Lucia, and the Dutch to Saint Eustatius and Curacao. While each country jealously hovered over their ships and their islands and ports, none was eager to provoke an incident that could start a naval war with the others. But an American ship? None of them was reluctant to take an American ship if they thought they could conjure up some claim of right to justify it, and avoid retaliation from the United States. Pirate ships were another matter altogether. Seldom seen, they flew any flag, or none at all, and they struck anyone they could from coves and inlets hidden among the hundreds of tiny islands.

The three men on deck had telescopes focused to watch the two ships loom ever larger, their colorful French fleur-de-lis flags blowing in the wind. They were one mile away when Caleb asked Young and Tunstall, "See any cannon ports?"

Both men shook their heads and Young answered, "None. They look like merchantmen."

At one-half mile Young lowered his telescope and a quizzical look crossed his face, and he turned to Tunstall. "Look at the quarterdeck. The officers. Do they look right?"

Tunstall answered, his voice low. "I been watchin' them. They don't look French to me."

Caleb came alive and turned to the two of them, both with years of experience on the sea far beyond his own. "You mean their dress?"

Young nodded. "French seamen don't wear dark clothes this close to the equator. And did you ever see the captain of a French merchantman with a sword at his side and a pistol in his belt?" He pointed. "Both ships are riding too high, cutting too big a curl. They aren't loaded. What's a merchantman doing coming at us empty? Look how the crew's standing, spread down both the port and starboard railings. What are they doing? Getting cannon ready?"

Tunstall shook his head. "I don't like it."

Caleb turned to the crew, tense, waiting, and barked orders. "Stand by to unfurl the jibs and spankers! Fill the water buckets!" He turned back to Young and Tunstall. "If they haven't declared themselves at two hundred yards, we make a run."

At four hundred yards, every man on the *Zephyr* was at his station, standing like statues in the wind, eyes locked onto every detail of the approaching ships. At three hundred yards the two vessels began a slow turn to their starboard, which would soon show their port side to the schooner and bring them into near collision with the *Zephyr* if she held her course. At two hundred yards Caleb and his crew stood stock-still to watch the French flag lowered from the mainmasts of the looming ships, and none were sent up to replace them. Two seconds later eight gun ports yawed open on the port side of both ships, and the black snouts of heavy cannon were jammed outward.

"*Pirates,*" bellowed Young, and the crew of the *Zephyr* exploded into action even as Caleb shouted orders. "All canvas out! Get the water buckets moving! Helmsman, hard to port, NOW!"

Within one minute, dripping, sloshing buckets of seawater were being relayed up to the men in the rigging, and they threw it drenching on the sails to capture more wind, and dropped the buckets to waiting hands below to be filled and sent up again. On the bow and stern, nimble fingers jerked the lashings from the spanker and jib sails, and they dropped and snapped tight in the wind and within seconds were dripping water from the buckets. The helmsman wrenched the wheel to port, the schooner leaned violently to starboard with Bartolo crouched, clinging in the crow's nest, and instantly leaped skimming ahead, throwing a forty foot curl and leaving a wake two hundred yards long, like a living thing born to the sea, distancing the larger ships as though they were standing still. The helmsman spun the wheel starboard, and the *Zephyr* corrected to a course due east.

Caleb ran to the stern to grasp the rail and peer west toward the last arc of the sun, telescope to his eye, tense, watching as the two ships corrected course to follow, and he held his breath as two black gun ports opened in the bow of each ship, and then the muzzles of cannon came thrusting through, and he watched the gun crews lining the heavy guns on the *Zephyr*. He counted five seconds, then turned to shout at the helmsman, "Hard to port!"

In one second the little ship answered the rudder and swung hard left, and two seconds later Caleb saw the white smoke belch from all four cannon. Four geysers erupted from the sea, straddling the wake where the *Zephyr* had been, and then the blasting boom swept past the speeding schooner. The gun muzzles disappeared, and one minute later came back into view, reloaded, at the ready.

Caleb judged the interval between the flying schooner and the heavier ships behind at one thousand yards and growing every second, and settled. He glanced at Young, beside him, then back at the rapidly fading ships, and quietly said, "Catch us if you can." Young grinned and licked at parched, dried lips and said nothing. The big guns blasted one more time, and the crew of the *Zephyr* watched the geysers leap ninety yards behind to blow spray thirty feet in the air.

With the sun gone, and the western horizon rapidly becoming a line of dwindling yellow against the dark sea, the crew of the schooner watched as the two heavy ships slowed, then swung to starboard. They held their turn until they were but a small silhouette traveling west, from whence they had come, and then faded into the deep dusk.

Caleb gave orders to the men on the first four-hour duty, and the cook went below to prepare the evening mess. Then Caleb led Tunstall and Young down to the captain's cramped quarters where they spread the charts on a table with a lamp dangling, undulating overhead, casting oblique, moving shadows.

"Where are we now?" Caleb asked.

Tunstall turned the chart to coordinate north, then tapped with his finger. "Right about here."

Caleb studied the position, then asked, "How far from the wreck of the *Belle?*"

"We lost about twenty miles running from those ships. We're close to three hundred miles from the place McDaris said, more or less. Sou'west."

"Any major islands between?"

"Three big ones." His finger traced the chart as he spoke. "Grand Bahama here, Great Abaco here, Eleuthera here. The *Belle* is on an island about here, just south of Eleuthera, north of San Salvador."

"Can you set the course by the stars?"

Tunstall grinned. "I can set it without the stars."

The trade winds held steady through the night, and the *Zephyr* sped south, cutting a great curl that hissed and left a long, straight wake behind, ghostly under the stars and quarter moon. The crew took their four-hour intervals on duty, eyes straining to see hidden, uncharted reefs, and then four hours off duty, curled in their canvas hammocks, swinging lightly with the gentle roll of the little ship. Caleb awoke at the sound of the bells that signaled crew changes and came on deck to watch one man descend from the crow's nest and another climb up the treads bolted to the mainmast. He paused at the bow railing both times to marvel at the clarity of the blue-green water under the stars, and the occasional glow from luminescent coral that cast a dull, eerie light for thirty yards in all directions. Sunrise found Bartolo back in the crow's nest, and the great ball seemed to fill the entire eastern horizon as it rose, turning the tops of the masts and then the sails on fire with the golden glow. It was during morning mess that Bartolo's voice came from the crow's nest.

"Landfall. West sou'west."

Within seconds Caleb, Young, and Tunstall and his charts were at the bow, adjusting their telescopes, waiting for the rise of the land dead ahead. It came and soon covered much of the western horizon.

"Grand Bahama," Tunstall said. He pointed south. "Down there is Great Abaco, then Eleuthera, and then the place the *Belle* should be. We should be there by late tomorrow morning if the wind holds."

Caleb asked, "Can you find it?"

"If McDaris was right, I can."

Caleb stroked his beard for a moment. "The British claim the Bahamas?"

"Yes."

Caleb pointed up the mainmast. "Do we fly the Union Jack?"

Young cut in. "Best chance we have."

Caleb nodded. "Carry on."

By noon they had passed four ships far to the west, near the erratic line of islands, three flying British colors, one flying the horizontal orange, white and blue bars of the Dutch. None slowed nor came inquiring. At two o'clock Young pointed east, toward a low, flat cloud, gathering purple, and the crew hung sail canvas sagging from the railings to the hatches, and waited. Just after three o'clock a squall passed over to dump rain so thick the men bowed their heads to breathe. It disappeared to the west as quickly as it had come, leaving the little ship drenched, and the makeshift canvas catch-basins filled with fresh water. The crew used buckets to fill their water barrels while the deck steamed and they dripped with sweat under the unrelenting tropical sun.

The sun dipped to touch the western rim of the world then disappear, and the crew of the *Zephyr* went on with the monotony of the unending, unchanging routines that filled most of the lives of men who choose the sea. They held their southward course as the quarter moon rose, with men in the crow's nest and on the starboard railing, watching the distant lights of a few tiny, scattered harbors and small villages on the shores of the islands. The starry night yielded to approaching dawn, and Tunstall came to the port railing to shoot the risen sun with his sextant and take his bearings.

Caleb squinted up at the crow's nest. "Any ships moving?"

"Far to the west. None towards us, sir."

Caleb walked to Tunstall. "Can you calculate when we should see the island where the *Belle* is beached?"

"Sometime after ten o'clock. Ever searched for a ship wrecked on rocks or a reef?"

Caleb shook his head. "No."

"Sometimes you're right on top of them before you see them. We're going to have to move closer to the islands."

"How close?"

"As close as the reefs and the rocks and the sandbars will let us. The man in the nest is going to have to look sharp."

"Shouldn't be hard to see rocks and reefs and sandbars in this water. Why is it so clear?"

"There are no rivers on these islands. Nothing to wash silt down to the sea to dirty it."

Caleb's eyes widened in surprise. "No rivers? How do the people get fresh water?"

"Dig cisterns and put out barrels and canvas to catch rain. Distill sea-water. Any way they can. Ships bring water to some islands and sell it."

Caleb asked, "What do we do about other ships while we're close to the islands?"

Tunstall shrugged. "We take our chances."

Caleb sobered and paused for a moment. "Better mount our cannon?"

"Your decision. Speed's your best weapon. Speed and maneuver-ability."

Caleb took a deep breath. "No cannon. When do we start?"

"Now."

"All right. I'll get the crew to their posts. You take your charts to the helmsman and give him his heading. The ship is yours. Who do you want in the nest?"

"Bartolo."

Caleb gave orders, and every crewman took his place on the railing, some scanning the beaches and inlets for ships, others for any sign of life in the tangle of lush growth on the land. Tunstall charted her course, the helmsman spun the wheel, and the *Zephyr* cut sharply to starboard and bore in toward the islands with Bartolo sixty feet up the mainmast, watch-ing every riffle, every change of color in the clear blue-green water, every rock or spine of coral beneath the surface, judging depth, calculating whether the small schooner could pass over them or must avoid them, shouting down orders to the helmsman who made instant adjustments.

The bowsprit of the ship was a scant forty yards from the white-sand beach of a small, uncharted island when Tunstall gave orders and the helmsman brought her hard to port. She leaned, then straightened on a course that took her south, parallel to the white strip of sand and the deep emerald green of the forest behind.

Caleb gave orders, and seamen climbed the ropes to the spars and furled all the sails on the aftermast and the top sails on the mainmast. The ship slowed and continued south, with the crew studying every outcrop of rock, every reef for anything that resembled a wrecked, burned ship. They cleared the south tip of the small island and continued on, Bartolo guiding them through the tricky jumble of coral and volcanic rocks that lay submerged, leading to the next small rise of land. The crew stared in silence as they passed the ancient remains of two ships that had been driven onto the sharp, jutting death traps. All that remained were the blackened pieces of their broken keels, and the stubbed ends of a few of the ribs, covered with two hundred years of coral growth and sea slime. Few things affect men of the sea like a ship, once alive and proud, now dead with its back broken and its naked ribs crumbling.

They had passed the second small island when Caleb came to Tunstall's side. "Which of these islands are we looking for?"

Frustration showed in Tunstall's face as he tapped the chart. "Right where we are. McDaris couldn't say which one—only that it was here among the others."

Caleb drew a breath. "We keep looking."

It was past one o'clock, with the sun directly overhead and beating down to sweat every man dripping, when they approached the north end of the third island. Forty minutes passed before Bartolo's voice sang out, high, excited.

"There!" His arm was stretched, pointing. "Past the cove! The mast! See the mast!"

Within seconds every man on deck was at the starboard rail, hands shielding their eyes as they squinted to the left of a tiny cove. There on the rocks was the broken, shattered mast of a ship, partially hidden.

Young shouted up, "Can you see the ship?"

"Not yet but it must. . . . NO . . . There! It is there, further down, south, in the rocks. Do you see the quarterdeck? And the bow?"

Instantly all eyes shifted left and strained and then arms shot up, pointing, and excited voices exclaimed, "There! I see it. There!"

Within minutes they were thirty yards from the broken remains of a ship, and while some crewmen dropped the anchor, others jammed their shoes on and worked to launch a longboat. Caleb and Young took their places, and six crewmen settled onto the plank cross-members, shoved the oars into the oarlocks, and bent their backs to drive the blades deep. They beached the boat, then worked their way through the rocks to the wreck.

She had been demasted by cannon and the storm before she slammed into the volcanic lava, hard enough to shatter the keel at mid-ship, where the notch had been cut for the mainmast. With her spine broken, the hull had cracked amidship, to let the bow and the stern thrust upward, leaving the deck at the center of the ship awash. They saw the three black, gaping holes in the hull where cannonballs had passed through. The fourth was below the waterline. She lay in the rocks, the grotesque remains of a once proud thing.

Men of the sea spend their years locked within the sure laws of nature. The monstrous power of a hurricane has taught them of their own awful smallness. Cholera, or dysentery, or the black plague that can kill the entire crew of a ship at sea has taught them the frailties of all living things. Strange and unexplainable happenings in exotic places, of men driving knives into their bodies without blood, and others dropping dead in their tracks with no wound, has brought images of evil spirits lurking. Tales of ships swallowed by monsters of the deep, and of entire fleets that have disappeared without a trace, have created in their minds a world in which surviving the evils around them is by the grace of a power higher than their own. They are reluctant to mix with wrecked ships, where spirits of the dead crews might be lingering, to trouble the living.

Caleb led his men to the bow of the dead ship, where the bowsprit had been smashed away. Silent, reluctant, they carefully studied the outside hull on both sides of the splintered stump. The paint was peeled and faded, but the engraving in the heavy oak was intact. The name *Belle* was unmistakable.

"We found her," was all Caleb said before he led his men scrambling onto the tilted deck of the forward half of the ship. They saw the places where cannonballs had blasted the railings and the hatches, and musketballs had punched into the wood. The hatch covers had been ripped away, and they peered down into the blackness of the forward hold. It was flooded. They waded past the water that swamped the deck amidship, to the quarterdeck, where the passage down to the officer's quarters had been smashed by cannon shot, and then worked their way to the captain's compartment. The door was cracked, top to bottom, and hung inward at a deep angle, on one hinge. The small room inside was wrecked, with everything of value gone. They found the room where Adam had bunked, with his charts and navigation equipment, and it too had been sacked and smashed.

They climbed from the gloom back onto the deck, to the nearest hatch. The cover was gone, and the hold was filled with salt water. There was no way to go down to search for bodies, nor were there any signs of one. If men had died in the fight, they had gone to their graves in the sea.

Caleb turned to Young and Tunstall, standing on the tilted deck, sweating. "There are no longboats here. We've got to look on the beach."

They went ashore and divided the men. Caleb led his group south on the strip of white sand while Tunstall and Young worked their way north, walking slowly, heads turning from side to side searching for anything that would suggest a longboat had been there. Ninety minutes later they met back at the wreck of the *Belle*.

"See anything?" Caleb inquired.

Tunstall shook his head. "No sign."

"Is there anything else we can do here?"

"Nothing."

Within minutes they were back on the deck of the *Zephyr*, and Caleb gathered the crew on the quarterdeck. He pointed at the wreck of the *Belle* as he spoke.

"No sign of the crew, or the longboats. It makes sense that the crew, or what was left of them, took the longboats and tried for land. If they did, where are they, and how do we find them?" He studied the faces of the men and waited.

Abel Hedquist, aged, round-shouldered, craggy face wrinkled and burned brown by a life on the sea, was the first to speak. "I seen this before in these islands. If they got ashore and the British found 'em, they're in a British port right now, in a prison. The British will find out that the *Belle* is out of Boston, and they'll send a demand to the harbor master up there. We got a Boston crew from the *Belle* down here in prison because they was taken in the act of piracy. We'll hold 'em for ninety days and then hang 'em for pirates unless you want 'em back. If you do, deliver five thousand pounds British sterling to us here to pay for the damages they done and we'll consider letting them go."

Caleb turned to Young in disbelief. "The British would do that?"

Young bobbed his head. "They've done it before. So have the French. Legal piracy."

Both Tunstall and Young watched Caleb's eyes narrow and they could not miss the light that came into them, nor the purr in his voice as he spoke.

"We'll see about that. Where do we start? Which British port?"

Tunstall thought for a moment. "The two biggest ones close by are south of here, on the next big island."

"What name? The island?"

"Cat Island."

"Is that where you'd start looking?"

Tunstall looked at Young before he answered. "That's where I'd start."

Caleb said, "Chart your course, Mr. Tunstall."

Notes

For maps of the islands referenced in this chapter see Mackesy, *The War for America, 1775–1783*, page facing 227; National Geographic Society, *The National Geographic Picture Atlas of Our World*, pp. 64–65; and see also the description of the Bahamas, including the fact there are no fresh water rivers, the water is clear and blue-green in color.

For an explanation of spanker sails, jib sails, and the detail of ships of sail as referenced in this chapter, see Jobe, *The Great Age of Sail*, pp. 2–155.

CHAPTER XIX

★ ★ ★

*M*iles Young climbed from the hold of the *Zephyr*, dropped the cover banging on the hatch, and walked barefooted toward the tiny quarterdeck of the small schooner, with the sun hammering down from directly overhead, and a strong, blistering east wind at his back, blowing his long hair and moving his dark beard. He wore nothing but a pair of frayed gray cotton pants that reached just below his knees. From his waist up and his knees down, he was burned brown. He moved on the smooth, worn deck with the easy, rolling gait of men who had learned the rise and the fall and the roll of the deck of a ship running with the wind. He took the four steps up to the quarterdeck two at a time and stopped where Caleb and Nathan Tunstall were standing next to the helmsman and the big wheel that controlled the ship, holding a chart down in the wind while they pored over the markings.

Caleb spoke without looking up. "How do we stand?"

Young looked at the written list he had made belowdecks in the commissary and answered, his British accent prominent, and his fourteen years of training as a midshipman and first mate in the British navy limiting him to as few words as possible.

"Two days fresh water, four days flour, four days salt fish, one day salt beef, no potatoes, no carrots. All rotted. We can eat fish from the sea for a while, and maybe get coconuts or bananas from one of these islands for a little milk and meat and fruit, but we can't get fresh water unless we stop to resupply in the next few days. This heat sucks water out of a man. We've got to have fresh water."

Caleb considered for a moment, then spoke to Tunstall.

"How far?"

Young hunched over the chart with them to watch Tunstall trace a course with his finger.

"We're here, about center in the Windward Channel. One of the few good passages from the Atlantic to the Caribbean." He shifted his pointing finger. "Here, about thirty-five miles to the east, is Haiti. French. Their biggest port is St. Nicholas, right here. The eastern half of the island is Hispaniola. Some call it Saint Domingo. Santo Domingo. Spanish, not French." Again he shifted his finger. "Here, about thirty-five miles west of us, is Cuba. Spanish. No regular ports here on the east end but a lot of little coves and inlets where ships put in for water or fruit or tubers." He made a circular motion with his hand. "This whole spread of islands is called the Greater Antilles." He moved his hand south and west. "We're headed here to Jamaica, dead ahead. In the Caribbean. British. Their biggest harbor is here, on the leeward side. Called Port Royal. The town of Port Royal—what's left of it—is here, and across the harbor, here, is Kingston."

Caleb studied the chart and repeated the question. "How far?"

"The harbor? From here, a little over three hundred miles. We've got to go around the southeastern tip of the island, here, then back west about fifty miles, here."

Both Caleb and Young peered at the chart and the markings Tunstall had made in the past fifteen days, carefully charting their headings, and identifying the eight islands among the hundreds of the Bahamas, great and small, where they had dropped anchor in a few scattered, tiny ports and harbors. They had gone ashore to inquire in the squalor-ridden villages about a missing crew from a ship named the *Belle*, out of the port of Boston in the state of Massachusetts, far to the north in the United States. Some of the natives had rolled their white eyes in their black faces and shook their heads, while others shrugged and turned away. A missing ship crew? From America? The islands were steeped in wrecked ships and missing crews from every port in the civilized world. One more from America meant almost nothing.

Caleb, stripped to the waist, scratched at his three-week's beard and looked at Young. "You think Port Royal is the next place to look? Not Haiti or Cuba?"

Young shrugged. "Who knows? It makes sense to me. We found the *Belle* in the Bahamas, and they're British. We never found the longboats. I think the crew got off the ship before she wrecked. If they did, there are a lot more British ships in the Bahamas than either French or Spanish, so the chances are strong that a British ship picked them up. If it was a British ship, they would most likely put them ashore at some British port in the Bahamas. We've been there and no one's seen them. So where would a British ship be heading if not in the Bahamas? A French port in Haiti? A Spanish port in Cuba?" He shook his head. "They'd be heading to a British port, and the biggest one in the Caribbean is right there." He pointed. "Port Royal on Jamaica island."

Caleb turned to Tunstall. "Your opinion? Do we go there looking?"

The navigator ran his hand through his blowing hair and slowly shook his head. "I don't know. Young's been down here more than me. Maybe the longboats sank and the crew with them. Maybe the French have them, or the Spanish, but I doubt it. I don't think either of them want to risk trouble with the United States, at least not right now. That leaves the British. If the crew survived up in the Bahamas, then Young's reasoning is the best chance we've got. If the British have them at Port Royal under authority of their Orders in Council, they could be holding them in a prison, waiting for the United States to meet their demand that we pay to get them back. But, who knows?"

Caleb stared long and hard at the chart before he spoke.

"What does Port Royal amount to?"

Young shook his head and blew air. "The port? Pretty big. Deep water. The town? Bad. A hundred years ago, pirates everywhere. A big earthquake hit sometime in the 1690s and sank about half the town into the Caribbean, along with half the people. That's when Kingston started to grow across the bay. Hurricanes finished what the earthquake didn't.

Had another earthquake about ten years ago. What's left is old buildings and sugar and rum and bad women and taverns and people of mixed blood from all over the world, mainly slaves or their descendants. In one hour you can find twenty men down there who'll cut anybody's throat for a pint of rum. Bad."

Caleb asked, "Are we likely to get hit by a hurricane?"

"Not likely. Maybe a squall. A storm. They come any time. Hurricane season down here is in the fall. October, November."

"If we go there, what flag do we fly?"

"British. England still claims Jamaica."

For a time Caleb peered over the bow of the ship as though he could see Jamaica and the Port. He broke it off and said, "We go on. If we don't find something at Port Royal we better decide whether we keep looking or turn back. There are too many islands down here—thousands—and we can't keep this up forever." He paused for a moment. "It sounds like Port Royal could be trouble. We better have a plan. We'll have to work it out with the crew."

For two days and two nights the little schooner sped on, first west until Bartolo sighted the windward side of the island of Jamaica, then south, around the tip, then back nearly due north, keeping the coastline in the distance. The crew went about their daily duties with few words, constantly raising their eyes to peer ahead, searching for sails. After evening mess they gathered in the empty hold of the small ship with Caleb, Young, and Tunstall, and under yellow lantern light worked into the night in the give and take of creating a simple plan to get into Port Royal, find the missing crew if they were there, and get out.

In the two days, they sighted thirteen ships flying British colors, and four flying French and Spanish, but none approached, nor did the *Zephyr* pause to approach them. On the morning of the third day, with the rising sun caught bright in the sails, Bartolo's voice rang out from overhead.

"Port Royal. Starboard. Three miles."

Caleb turned to Young. "Get below with your two men. You know what to do with the seacocks."

Young spun, called the two men assigned to him, and disappeared down the main hatch.

Caleb called to the men waiting on the ropes in the rigging. "Furl all sails except the topsails on the mainmast. We're going in slow." He turned to Tunstall. "Give the helmsman a course to get us in through the channel."

With the seacocks in the main cargo hold wide open, tons of sea-water roared in with Young and his two men clinging to the heavy support timbers that reached from the hull to the main deck overhead to keep from being knocked off their feet, and every man on the ship felt it begin to settle in the sea. Young waited until the water reached above his knees before he bawled orders, and the three of them spun the wheels that closed the valves. The black waters settled, and Young and his two men quickly climbed the narrow wooden ladder up to daylight, and out onto the main deck. The two men slammed the hatch cover into place while Young called to Caleb on the quarterdeck, "Finished."

The *Zephyr* had settled in the water, from all appearances carrying a load in her cargo hold.

With Tunstall pointing and giving commands to the man holding the big wheel, the little schooner cautiously squared with the broad mouth of the harbor and slowly entered. Caleb stood at the bow with the crew at both railings, studying everything ahead. A small, stone light-house stood on each side of the harbor entrance, and not thirty yards inside they could not miss seeing two British men-o'-war, one to port, the other to starboard, about one hundred yards distant, each with forty-eight gunports, twenty-four on each side. The muzzle of a thirty-two pound cannon gleamed in each open port. On deck were seamen dressed in the red and white uniforms of the British military, half of them watching the little schooner. In the crow's nest of each gunboat was a man with a telescope, studying every detail of the *Zephyr.*

Caleb glanced at Young and a silent communication passed between them. If everything went wrong in the next twenty-four hours, they would have two British warships—forty-eight cannon at near point-blank range—to beat to get out of the Port Royal harbor alive. They accepted it and turned back to memorize the lay of the harbor.

There were no wharves nor docks on the waterfront, only the remains of a few black, rotting pilings thrusting out of the water at random angles near the shore where the busiest docks in the Caribbean had once been, before earthquakes and hurricanes destroyed them. Ships of all sizes and designs, and in various conditions of repair or disrepair, were at anchor in the deep water that reached within twenty yards of the town streets, some of which sloped down to disappear beneath the harbor waters where the convulsions of nature had sunk nearly half the town. The buildings facing the harbor were old, unpainted, irregular in order, some with walls cracked, roofs caved in. On the dirt streets, jammed among the buildings wherever they could find space, were small, makeshift stands made of old, weathered, driftwood planks, or cast-off barrels, heaped with near-worthless trinkets and bits of broken, discarded jewelry, small images carved from palmetto sticks, bits of cloth, bottles of all colors and shapes, green bananas, rusted knives with broken blades, old, rusted, useless calipers and compasses and other naval navigation equipment from wrecked or captured ships—anything that could be gathered from the trash heaps behind the town or from the refuse thrown from the ships—all for sale. In the squalor and stench, barefooted men and women wearing shapeless, dirty, frayed clothing stood nearby, with tiny children running unclothed and older children in tattered shirts and pants wandering about, waiting to pounce on the next seaman or stranger that passed, to hawk their collection of worthless wares for anything they could get.

Most ships flew the British Union Jack. Some flew no colors at all. The harbor was crisscrossed with longboats and old, battered barges manned by sweating black men dressed in ragged pants that had no belts, moving freight and people between ship and shore.

Caleb pointed, and the helmsman angled to starboard and held her steady until Caleb called up to crewmen waiting on the topsail spar, "Furl 'em," and then to two men waiting at the anchor, "Drop anchor." The *Zephyr* slowed and settled, then stopped as the anchor hit the water and sank to seize the sandy bottom. They were positioned at the right side of the harbor, alone, ninety yards from the nearest ship, which was an ancient, fat freighter with a dirty, ragged Union Jack fluttering from the top of the mainmast. The two gunboats were nearly two hundred yards behind them, commanding all who passed in or out of the harbor. Five hundred yards ahead and to their left, at the west edge of the ramshackle town, was the large, lone, square, two-storied stone building with the great double doors open and the British flag flying from a thirty-foot flagpole mounted on the roof. Red-coated soldiers moved in and out on the business of the day.

For a time the crew of the *Zephyr* stood at the rails, apprehensive, watching in the breeze, waiting to see if anyone would come inquiring, but no longboat came angling toward them through the maze of watercraft. Caleb checked his watch—half-past seven o'clock under a blazing morning sun—and asked Young, "Do they send out someone to see who we are?"

Young shook his head. "I've been here three times. There's no harbormaster." He raised his arm to point at the big building over a quarter-mile distant. "They expect you to report to that building after you go ashore so they know if you're peaceful or pirate, and to pay your harbor dues before you leave. If you don't, they collect the dues with those two gunboats back there."

Caleb straightened and spoke quietly. "We'll see about that." He turned to the crew. "It's time. You all know the plan?—what you're to do?"

Heads nodded.

They launched the two longboats, and two crewmen stayed behind on the ship while the others took their places on the plank seats of the undulating longboats, shoved the oarlocks into the mounts, dropped the oars into the slots, and began the rhythmic stroking toward shore. They were sun-browned, bearded, wearing the long-sleeved, striped cotton shirts, and the cotton pants of ordinary seamen, and sandals fashioned from sail canvas. All except Young, Tunstall, and Caleb. With his British accent and knowledge of the ways of British officers, Young was dressed in a loose, white cotton shirt closed with a tie at the throat, dark trousers, white socks, and black, square toed shoes with brass buckles. He carried a small packet of documents wrapped in oilskin, some of which were fictitious, with forged signatures. Young was the one who would do the talking with the British authorities in the big building. Caleb and Tunstall were dressed in long-sleeved white shirts, open at the throat, dark trousers, white stockings, and worn, buckled shoes. Caleb had a leather purse filled with coins stuffed into his pants pocket.

They threaded their way through the mix of barges and anchored ships, dragged the bows of the longboats onto the sand and tied them to an old, tilted piling at water's edge. The crew scattered in all directions, instantly surrounded by poverty-stricken natives who grasped at their sleeves and burst into a dialect that was a mix of at least three languages, begging them to buy the priceless treasures heaped on the old driftwood planks and broken barrelheads. Young turned left, drew a deep breath, squared his shoulders, and with Caleb and Tunstall on either side, said simply, "Ready?"

"Let's go."

They marched west, down the most poverty-stricken, worst waterfront they had ever seen, walking toward the British command building from which the red-coated military maintained an ironfisted control of Port Royal. A detachment of sweating regulars were quartered in the building, which, with the two huge men-o'-war at the mouth of the harbor, kept the peace in what otherwise would become a sanctuary for every crime and sin known to mankind. The three men ignored the natives clamboring around them, tugging at their sleeves, thrusting broken objects in their faces, and marched on, past the last of the derelict buildings at town's edge, to the large stone structure. Young did not slow. He kept his chin high and thrust forward in the finest tradition of a proud British officer as he led Tunstall and Caleb to the big, brass-studded doors of the building where two pickets, one with yellow corporal chevrons on his red sleeve, the other with those of a sergeant, stopped them.

The sergeant, sweating in his woollen uniform, studied them for a moment, suspicion plain on his face.

"Your business?" His proper British accent was prominent.

Young's answer was amiable, perfunctory. "Captain Miles Young. I command the schooner that anchored in your harbor this morning. The *Zephyr.*" Young's British accent was just as authentic and prominent as that of the sergeant. He paused for a moment before he continued. "Our business is to resupply with water and provision and locate a ship. The *Belle.* She was to be here two days ago. She is not in your harbor."

"Your papers?"

Young quickly unrolled the oilskin wrapping, selected one, and handed it to the sergeant. "My commission as an officer in the Royal British Navy."

The sergeant studied the document for a moment, read the date—October, 1779—and the signature—Admiral Sir George Rodney—and recognized both as authentic. It was Admiral Rodney who had been assigned by the British Parliament to command British naval operations in the West Indies in 1779. His reputation in the Caribbean as a competent officer was well remembered. The sergeant handed the commission back to Young.

"These men with you?"

"My first mate, Caleb Dunson, and our navigator, Nathan Tunstall."

The sergeant studied the two for a moment before he pushed the heavy door inward. "Go to the second office on the left."

Young half-bowed. "Thank you, sergeant," and led his first mate and navigator down the hall to the door marked "REGISTRAR." He pushed through the door into a square room with a large desk and a wispy, gray-haired, uniformed officer behind it, hunched over a ledger, silently mouthing words as his finger moved across the page. The thin man flinched at the sound of the door, peered over his spectacles at Young, then Caleb and Tunstall, and spoke in a high, breathy voice.

"Who are you?"

"Miles Young. Captain of the *Zephyr.* We anchored in your harbor this morning."

"You here to register?"

"We're here looking for a ship that's overdue, and we need water and provisions. Do we need to register for that?"

The little man nodded brusquely. "You do. You're British?"

"Yes."

"Papers?"

Young handed him his commission, and the nervous little man laid it on his desk, flattened it, and carefully mouthed the words as his finger moved on the lines.

"Admiral Rodney, eh? Gone now. You still in the navy?"

"No. A private shipping company."

"What port?"

"Nova Scotia."

"Papers?"

Young drew a second document from the oilskin packet and laid it before the little man. On its face, it was a declaration designating the *Zephyr* to be a British vessel claiming Nova Scotia as its homeport. In fact, it was the best forgery Young and Tunstall and Caleb could make, hunched over Young's small table in his quarters on the *Zephyr*, six nights earlier. Young's face was a mask of indifference, while Tunstall and Caleb glanced casually about the plain, austere, stone-walled room, from all appearances bored, waiting to get the nuisance of paperwork behind them.

The little man scanned it quickly and handed it back, then squared his open ledger before him and reached for his quill. Young watched him make the entry and lay his quill back in its place. "You come back here before you leave the harbor and pay your harbor fees. Understand?"

"I do. Could I inquire something, sir?"

A look of mild irritation crossed the thin, long face. "What is it?"

"The ship we're looking for is the *Belle*. Heard anything about her? Or her crew? We need to deliver our cargo to her."

The man leaned back in his chair. "We're holding what's left of two crews, waiting for their homeport to claim them and pay damages."

Caleb did not move. Tunstall wiped at perspiration with his sleeve. "Crews from which ships?"

The registrar shrugged. "Don't know. Not my department."

"How can we find out?"

"Ask the jailer. At the building behind this one."

Young stood. "Do I sign anything? Or get anything showing I've been here?"

"You get a receipt before you sail. If you don't, you'll have trouble leaving the harbor."

"Thank you." Young wrapped his papers back into the oilskin and walked back out into the hall with Caleb and Tunstall silently following. They stepped back out into the sunlight with the wind rising, blowing their hair, relieved they had gotten past the registrar. Young came to a stop, and for a moment he shaded his eyes and peered east, then turned to Caleb.

"Weather's coming. A squall. Or a storm. From the windward side. The Atlantic. I can smell it."

With the wind in his face, Caleb peered east, searching. "How soon?"

"Evening. Tonight. Could give us trouble getting out, if we try it tonight."

For several seconds Caleb stood still, staring at the dirt, unseeing. "The tides are with us tonight. We have to go. Let's move."

He led them past the back of the building to a great open area of dirt, packed hard by the stiff soles of British military shoes worn by men during drill. To their left, where the open drill field met the thick tangle of jungle, a small detachment of sweating men, four per rank, five ranks, were marching to the bellowed commands of a sergeant. Young stopped for a moment, then raised his arm to point to an ancient, low, moss-covered stone building at the far end of the drill field. There were no windows, and the single door was of black, rusted iron hung on great iron straps.

"That has to be the prison," Young said quietly. "Looks like a dungeon from two hundred years ago. Do we go down and ask?"

Without a word Caleb led them across the drill field and banged on the iron door, then stepped back with Tunstall to let Young do the speaking. Twenty seconds later the sound of a heavy bolt sliding on the inside came through the iron, and the door groaned open. A sickening stench rolled out and the three men clamped their mouths shut and breathed light as they faced a filthy, bearded, surly civilian whose shirt would not close around his belly. He glowered at the three of them and his jowls shook as he demanded, "What do you want?" The words were in English, but with a strong accent none of the three recognized.

Young hooked a thumb over his shoulder. "The registrar said you have some men held here."

"You got papers?"

"The registrar already looked at our papers. He sent us here."

Disgust was thick in the gutteral voice of the heavy man. "Release papers. You got to have release papers."

Young said, "Where do we get release papers?"

"The registrar. Don't come back 'til you got 'em."

The man started to close the door, and Caleb stepped past Young to jam his hand against it. "The registrar said you could tell us who you've got in there. You have men from a ship named the *Belle?*"

The little pig-eyes flashed with anger. "Get papers."

Caleb dropped his hand, and the heavy door clanged shut. They heard the inside bolt slam into place, and for a moment they stood there, pondering what to do next.

Caleb broke the silence. "The registrar sends us here and the jailer sends us back. Forget it." He turned to Young. "Did you see anything inside?"

"Only a light at the far end of the hall. I heard voices, but not words."

Caleb said, "Come on," and Young and Tunstall fell in behind him as he walked across the front of the building, then down the side, along the back wall, and up the remaining side to the front. There was no window in any of the old, dark, weather-stained, mold and moss-covered walls, and no other door. Each wall had been cracked by earthquakes, and the cracks were filled with flora from the thick jungle, which came within twenty feet of the back wall.

Caleb stopped in front of the building for a few moments, studying the roofline. "Has to be a flat roof, and there has to be an open court-yard in the center. Those walls are two feet thick, at least."

Tunstall looked at Caleb, skeptical. "What are you suggesting?"

"Nothing, yet. Let's go find the crew."

They strode back across the barren drill field with the wind rising, blowing dust, and they squinted their eyes until they were past the large building, back into the streets of the squalor-ridden town. It was five minutes past ten o'clock when the last of the crew returned to the long-boats in which they had arrived, and Caleb gathered them around.

"Find anything?"

A grizzled seaman with a gray beard stepped out. "This." He handed Caleb a navigator's compass. The glass was shattered, the needle twisted and bent, useless. Carefully Caleb turned it over, and froze. Etched in the back of the instrument, in beautiful cursive scroll, was the name "Adam Dunson."

Caleb raised his eyes. "Where?"

"Waterfront. An old man. With junk on a blanket on the ground."

Caleb studied the instrument for another moment, then asked, "Anything else? Anybody?"

A younger man with a blonde beard and a deep southern drawl spoke up. "A woman said she saw British longboats bring in ten, twelve men. About a month ago. Marched 'em down to the British building."

"She see 'em leave?"

The young seaman shook his head. "Says they're most certain still there, in a prison."

A third seaman called Pike, soft-spoken with deep-set eyes, spoke up. "I asked about the *Belle*. An old man—blind—can't talk—has some things. Wanted money before he'd show. I didn't have enough."

"Where is he now?"

Pike pointed with a bony finger. "Down there. Not far. Has some things in a box."

Caleb paused only long enough to gauge the rise in the wind coming in from the east, with the scent of rain. Then he turned to Young. "Take the crew and locate where the British dock their longboats, and meet me back here soon." He gestured to the soft-spoken Pike. "Show me the blind man."

Young and the crew walked to their left, along the waterfront, peering at the harbor traffic, looking for British longboats that had to be tied along the shore, or close to it. Caleb followed Pike to their right, into the rank smells and grime, pushing past people of every color who stepped before them with baubles and worthless trinkets to sell or barter. In the rubble of an ancient building destroyed by a forgotten earthquake, they found the old, thin, wrinkled, black blind man, seated, rocking back and forth on a small, broken water keg. He wore one filthy, tattered garment that reached from his shoulders to his ankles. His bald head shone in the sun, and his mouth was drawn into an habitual, toothless grin. His eyes were wide open, their lenses long since covered with the gray film of the sightless. Beside him was a makeshift table of slabs of driftwood. On it were bottles of colored glass, a bit of a broken necklace chain made of copper, some square, bent, iron nails, frayed cord, and other scraps of useless things. He turned his head toward Caleb and Pike as they approached.

Caleb studied the old derelict for a moment before he spoke. "Old man, I am looking for some men from a ship named the *Belle.* I am told you know something of them."

The old head bobbed. The grin held.

"What can you tell me?"

The man thrust out an emaciated hand, and with a finger of the other hand tapped the palm.

Caleb asked, "How much?"

The old man held up five misshapen fingers.

Caleb drew the leather purse from his pocket and rattled it. "Tell me first. Then I pay."

The old head shook, and the hand showed the five fingers again.

Patiently Caleb counted out five shillings, then took the withered hand in his and dropped them into the palm, one at a time. He did not release the hand.

"Five shillings. Tell me what you know."

With his free hand the old man reached beneath the driftwood table-top and drew out a wooden box, weathered, warped by being in seawater too long. Caleb motioned, and Pike picked it from the ground and opened it. Inside were knives, forks and spoons for the officer's mess of a ship. On the back of each was the stamped inscription, "*Belle.*"

Caleb, still holding the old, gnarled hand, asked, "Where did you get this?"

The old head did not turn as the free arm raised, and pointed down the waterfront, toward the great stone British headquarters building.

"The British? You got this from the British?"

The head bobbed.

"When?"

The hand held up four fingers.

"Four? Four what? Four weeks? Four weeks ago?"

The head nodded once.

"How did you get it? Did you buy it?"

The old head remained motionless, and Pike said, "Most likely stole it."

Caleb glanced up. "Blind? How could a blind man steal it?"

"Paid someone. Look around you."

Caleb folded the withered fingers over the five silver pieces and released the hand. Instantly the old man softly felt the face of each coin, and then shoved them inside his tunic.

Caleb said, "Let's go," and Pike tucked the wooden box under his arm and followed.

Within twenty minutes the remainder of the crew had returned to the two longboats that had brought them ashore. They gathered around Caleb and Pike as Pike opened the box, and the men stared at the steel utensils stamped *Belle*, then turned to Caleb, waiting.

"An old blind man says he got this from the British headquarters building about four weeks ago. If he did, I think some of those men in that prison down there are from Adam's crew."

Young said, "Most likely."

Caleb looked into the eyes of his crew. "This is what we came down here for. Tonight we get them out. You all know we have a blow and rain coming in from the east, over those mountains, and it will likely hit before we finish. We've got to get into the prison and out with men while British regulars are guarding them. No way to tell how bad it will get. Anyone wants to stay out of this, speak now. You can stay on the *Zephyr*, and no one will fault you."

No one moved or spoke.

"All right. Anyone know where to get fresh water for the *Zephyr*? And salt meat? Fruit? Vegetables?"

A voice called, "British headquarters building. They got a commissary. You have to pay."

Caleb tossed the leather purse to Tunstall. "When we're through here, take the men assigned to you and buy enough to get us back to Boston. Get it out to the ship."

Caleb turned to Young. "You found the British longboats?"

Young pointed. "West. Sixteen of them. Tied to pilings on shore."

Caleb paused to order his thoughts. "We'll take the rest of the crew in our longboats and get back to the *Zephyr* and start pumping the hold. Get her ready for the run. Soon after dark, we'll bring ten kegs of gunpowder and two grappling hooks and all meet back here. Everyone clear?"

All heads nodded.

Caleb looked at them one more time. Every man present had been in mortal combat many times. None had illusions about what cannon and musket could do to a man, yet none of them hesitated. Their faces were sober, eyes narrowed, shining a light that said they were relishing the desperate notion of sailing into a British port and bringing imprisoned Americans out. Some were grinning when the two crews separated, one to buy supplies, the other to get their ship ready for the run.

By midafternoon Caleb and the men on the *Zephyr*, stripped to the waist and sweating in the hold, had worked the handles of the two-man bilge pumps to push two feet of water back out into the sea. In the mounting wind, the little schooner was riding higher, straining at her anchor chain, dancing on the incoming tides. By four o'clock Tunstall was alongside with a great barge, his crew, and four extra hired men, transferring forty barrels of fresh water and ten barrels of salt beef onto the rolling deck of the ship. By six o'clock, Caleb's men had emptied the hold of seawater, stored the pumps below deck, wiped their dripping faces with their shirts, pulled them on, and were back on deck, where Tunstall's crew was transferring the last load of fresh water, salt fish, green bananas, and sweet potatoes from the barge onto the schooner. Tunstall paid the four hired men, who counted their coins and climbed down the net back to their barge and were gone.

By seven o'clock the food and water were stored below in the hold. The tides had reached their high-water mark and were just beginning to recede when the crew lowered a longboat into the wind-ruffled harbor, and Caleb climbed down with grappling hook and rope coiled over one shoulder, and set out for shore alone. By eight o'clock, in oncoming dusk, with the wind starting to sing in the rigging, the men had finished evening mess. By half-past eight, in deep twilight, Caleb was back on deck with the grappling hook, and the crew gathered around, quiet, waiting.

Caleb spoke to Tunstall. "I'll need a lantern and parchment and something to write with."

Twenty seconds later Tunstall set a lantern on a hatch cover and laid paper and a piece of lead beside it. Caleb squared the paper, picked up the long, thin piece of lead, and began.

"I was on the roof of the prison. This is how the British installation down there lays."

The crew watched intently as Caleb drew a large rectangle, then an open field, then a smaller square behind, with yet a smaller square inside. His voice was steady, contained. "We've gone over this before, but I want no mistakes."

His finger moved on the paper as he spoke. "This big rectangle is the administration building. Behind is the drill field. This smaller square is the prison. Here, in the center, is an open courtyard about twenty yards square. Four soldiers carried a kettle of soup or stew and some bowls from the front of the building across the courtyard to the back section, and were inside for maybe ten minutes. When they came out the kettle was empty. They had to be feeding the prisoners. Judging by the amount in the kettle, there must be about fifteen men in there. There's one door into the place, right here, where the prisoners are kept. No windows."

He paused for a moment to let the men study the drawings and understand what he had said, then moved on.

"We're going to use grappling hooks and ropes to get into that open courtyard and blow the door where the prisoners are,"—he tapped the drawing—"then get them out, over the wall, and back to our longboats that will be tied alongside the British longboats. Going in, we leave two men and three kegs of gunpowder in front of the administration building, and they stop anyone who might come out the front door to get us. When we're out, we get into our longboats and as many British longboats as we need, blow the rest of them, and get on out here to the ship. Those who are assigned to stay here will have the cannon mounted with the muzzles on the rails, angled upward, and they have to be ready to get us on board and unfurl the sails to make our run for the mouth of the harbor. Does every man here know his assignment?"

He looked every man in the eye. "Aye, sir."

"Are we agreed on the plan?"

"Agreed."

Without a word Caleb pointed, and all hands went below decks to emerge with ten, twenty-pound barrels of gunpowder, twenty-five feet of waterproof fuse, three folded pieces of sail canvas, three small metal boxes with smoldering tinder inside, and two grappling hooks with thirty feet of rope secured through the eyes. They stacked the barrels and grappling hooks along the rails next to the twelve cannon, still concealed under canvas. Caleb assembled the crew on the pitching deck and shouted to be heard above the mounting wind.

"Tunstall, when I and my men are in our longboats, hand the

gunpowder and grappling hooks down to us. We should be back in about ninety minutes if everything goes right. If it goes wrong, give us an extra half hour, then take the *Zephyr* out of the harbor and back to Boston. Any questions?"

"None."

"Let's move."

With the first great drops of slanting rain splattering on the crew and the deck, Caleb and ten picked men went over the rail and down the net into the bobbing longboats. Tunstall and his six men on the ship's deck lowered the ten kegs of gunpowder on ropes, then the length of fuse and the grappling hooks. The men in the loaded, pitching longboats rammed their oars against the hull of the schooner to shove themselves away, then jammed them into the oarlocks and heaved into them, pulling for shore, soaked, the wind-driven rain pounding on their backs, dripping from their beards and noses. The few lights still burning in the town were but faint blurs across the harbor. All barges and longboats had long since tied up at the shoreline; only the anchored ships remained on the heaving water in the harbor.

Caleb was crouched in the bow of the leading boat, peering ahead, shouting orders above the wind to the seaman on the tiller, while the trailing boat followed close behind. They picked their way to the westerly end of the town, located the British longboats bucking against the ropes that tied them to the old, decaying pilings, tied their two longboats alongside, and lowered themselves into the churning, waist-deep water to form a line from the boats to the shore. In the darkness, they passed the powder kegs from one man to the next until all ten kegs were on the beach, then the grappling hooks and coiled ropes, and finally the fuses. The soaked, dripping men waded ashore to streets that were vacant with but few lights scattered and dim in the driving rain. It took two trips to move all ten kegs of gunpowder down to the big British administration building. They left two men hovering over three of the kegs they had leaned against the front wall of the big structure. It took two more trips for the remaining seven men to move the other seven kegs across the muddy morass of the drill field to the side wall of the prison, a low, black blur against the jungle. Strong arms swung the grappling hooks on the ropes and heaved them over the top of the low wall, then jerked back hard until they caught. Two men climbed the ropes to the roof while others tied the first two barrels to the end of the ropes, and those on top pulled them sliding up the wall, released the rope, and dropped it back for the second two barrels, then the last one. Finally, those waiting in the mud climbed to the roof. They trotted to the far side, set the grappling hooks, and two men went over the edge, sliding down the ropes to the muck of the black, vacant courtyard. Five minutes later all seven barrels of gunpowder and all seven men were in the mud. Without a word they left the ropes hanging from the grappling hooks, each picked up a barrel of gunpowder, and they divided. Three went left to set their powder kegs five feet from the door into the front section of the building where the British soldiers were billeted, and they hunched over the kegs, waiting. Caleb and the other three seized the remaining four kegs of gunpowder and trotted splashing through the mire to the low rear wall of the courtyard. Caleb stopped at the big iron door into the dungeon and set his powder keg against the doorjamb, where the great bolt was held in place on the inside. He helped the other three men position their kegs on top of his, then banged on the door with the butt of his belt knife. There was no sound from the inside, and he banged again, stopped, put his ear against the wet, black iron, and listened as the faint sound of a pounding fist came through.

Caleb shouted, "Can you hear me? Hit the door twice if you can hear me."

The fist struck the door twice.

"Get back. Get away from the door. We're setting gunpowder. Get back! Do you understand? Hit the door twice if you understand."

Again the fist struck the door twice, then stopped.

Caleb turned and gave hand directions to his men. One man used the butt of his belt knife to knock the bung from the lowest barrel, set a two-foot length of fuse and step back. The second man unfolded the canvas and held it shielding the barrels from the rain while the third man crouched beneath it and drew out the tinderbox. He raised the lid, blew gently until flames came licking, then lowered it and held the fuse to the fire until it sputtered and caught. The man holding the canvas tucked it around the gunpowder and the sputtering fuse, and all four backed away fifteen feet to flatten themselves against the wall, heads turned away from the door and the gunpowder. Ten seconds later the night was shattered by a blast that blew flame outward halfway across the courtyard and sent a concussion wave slamming into the far wall. Burning bits and pieces of the kegs lay over the entire courtyard, and the smoke was still swirling in the rain when Caleb reached the heavy iron door. It was blown inward, still hanging at an angle by one hinge. He plunged into the black, reeking stench, "Get out, get out! Now! Move!"

Dark, bearded shapes, wearing only tattered pants came barefooted, cautious at first, then crowding while Caleb called "Adam Dunson" over and over as they passed him in single file to pick their way past the blown door and the smoke and burning shards of the kegs. The ninth man answered, "Caleb, is that you?" and Caleb seized his arm for one brief moment. "Are you all right?"

"Yes."

Caleb shoved him on. "Keep moving."

Sixteen dark shapes moved past him, out into the driving rain in the courtyard, where the three men with Caleb stopped them, held them in a group, and waited while Caleb, still inside, shouted, "Anyone else here? Speak up or be left behind!" There was no answer, and Caleb dodged past the iron door into the rain, and pointed. "Follow my men to the ropes on that wall, and wait. Move!"

His three men led the sixteen prisoners through the rain at a sprint, splashing through the morass of the courtyard, and Caleb came behind, slower, peering through the rain toward the front section of the old, decaying building, hunting in the darkness and the rain for his three men hunched over their three kegs of gunpowder, waiting for the British soldiers to burst from their quarters, muskets in hand. As he watched, the door swung open, a shaft of yellow lamplight leaped out into the courtyard to dissipate in the rain, followed by British regulars in various stages of dress and undress. They came uncertain, hesitant, bent forward, peering into the rain and the darkness, groping to understand what was happening.

Instantly Caleb's three men in front of them spread their canvas to shield against the rain, opened their tinderbox, set and lighted their fuses, dropped the canvas over the barrels, spun, and ran toward the group waiting at the wall while Caleb shouted to those around him, "Get down. Get down." They all dropped to their knees as the gunpowder in front of the barracks blew. Flame leaped eighty feet in the air. The shock wave inside the small courtyard threw four British regulars backwards into their barracks, and sent others rolling, skidding in the muck, all of them stunned, disoriented, unable to know what to do. Not one had fired a shot.

The concussion jolted Caleb's group, heads down and hunched low, passed over them, bounced off the wall, and was lost in the wind and rain. Instantly Caleb was on his feet. "Get to those ropes and onto the roof."

Eager hands seized the knotted ropes and seasoned seamen went up hand over hand, onto the rooftop, where they spun and waited for the next man to clamber over the edge. Caleb was the last man up, and the instant he heaved himself rolling onto the roof, his men jerked the ropes up, disengaged the grappling hooks, ran to the far side of the roof, reset the grappling hooks, and threw the ropes over into the wind and rain, and the black abyss below.

In less than four minutes all twenty-five men were in the mud, flattened against the outside wall of the ancient prison, and Caleb led them out onto the muddy morass of the drill field at a run, directly toward the side wall of the great Administration building. They were halfway past the wall when flames at the front of the building leaped into the storm, and then they heard the "whump" of the exploding gunpowder, and felt the tremor in their feet. They were twenty feet from the corner when Caleb's two men appeared before them, and Caleb did not break stride. With these men following, he angled left, down toward the waterfront where their longboats were tied beside the sixteen belonging to the British.

"Get aboard," Caleb shouted, and the men leaped into the first four longboats, onto the seats, slammed the oarlocks home, and shoved the oars down. In seconds they were turning the boats, and Caleb shouted to the two men standing among the British longboats.

"Blow them!"

The men shielded their tinderboxes, lit their fuses, and leaped from the boats, to pound along the beach sixty feet to Caleb's waiting long-boat and dive inside while the men with the oars strained to turn the boat and head out into the black, choppy, storm-tossed harbor. They had only gone fifteen feet when the first musket ball came whining over their heads from the shore, and they flinched and ducked, then continued their strokes. Four more musket balls came whistling before the gunpowder in the two longboats blasted, and for one brief moment the entire storm-ridden harbor was lit in vivid detail before it was plunged back into blackness and howling wind. Of the fourteen British longboats, six were blasted to bits, four were sinking with shattered hulls, and the last four were adrift in the storm.

Caleb turned toward the mouth of the harbor, straining to see the *Zephyr*, and the two British gunboats guarding the entrance. Within three minutes the blur of lights appeared on the deck of the nearest gunboat, and at the same moment, on the deck of the *Zephyr*, twisting in the wind, fighting her own anchor chain. Caleb wiped at the rain running from his hair down his face and eyes and into his beard to judge speed and distance and murmured, "It's going to be close!"

The longboats turned to come alongside the *Zephyr*, banged into her hull, and all the men leaped to the net strung over the railing. Within two minutes all were aboard, and Caleb shouted to Young, pointing, "Hoist the anchor and unfurl the mainsail. Take a heading straight for that gun-boat!"

Men hit the rope ladders up to the spars, walked out on the swinging hawsers, and jerked the knots that freed the sails. The canvas dropped, then caught in the wind, and the men on the lower spars grabbed them flapping and tied them down while men threw their weight into hoist-ing the anchor from the harbor floor. Instantly the little schooner leaped forward, running with the wind and tide, and the helmsman spun the wheel to bring her around on a course that would bring her into a collision dead center amidships on the nearest British gunboat.

"Man the cannon!" Caleb shouted, and men jerked the lids from the budge barrels, filled the ladles, and rammed gunpowder down the muzzles of the cannon, set on the ships railing, angled sharply upward. They shoved the wadding down, then dropped the cannonballs rattling down the barrels, and lighted the linstocks to hold them smoking beneath the cannon barrels away from the whipping rain. Caleb ran to the bow of the ship and peered forward at the three bare masts of the gunboat, thrust upward into the blackness, and the deck, twelve feet above that of the *Zephyr*. He turned to shout at the helmsman.

"Steady as she goes. When I say hard to port, turn as sharp as you can."

"Aye, sir."

He called to the four cannon crews on the starboard side of the racing schooner. "On my command, fire all guns."

"Aye, sir."

Running nearly due west with the wind, with her cargo hold almost empty, the little schooner was rolling, bucking, plowing through twelve foot waves, skimming on top of lesser ones. With the howling wind at his back, drenched, wind blowing wild, Caleb watched the bigger ship looming up black and he was aware that Young and Adam were beside him, wide-eyed, making their own calculations of speed and distance. At the last moment Caleb spun and shouted, "Hard port!"

The words were not out of his mouth when the helmsman spun the wheel and the little schooner leaned to starboard as she swung to port, deck slanted close to thirty degrees, with the crew clinging to hatches and ropes to keep their balance, waiting for the grinding shudder when the bowsprit of the *Zephyr* would hit the bigger ship and shatter, and then the much smaller schooner would plow into the side of the gunboat.

The swinging bowsprit missed the hull of the British warship by inches, and the starboard railing was less than a foot from the oak hull of the gunboat when the little schooner straightened and continued her swing to port. On board the gunboat, the gunnery commander was shouting orders to his men, and suddenly realized that his cannon were too high to come to bear on the smaller schooner. He could not depress the muzzles to fire downward. His only chance was to hope his cannon-balls would hit the masts close enough to their center to blast them in two.

He had raised his arm to give the command to fire when Caleb, directly alongside, shouted to his six guns on the starboard side, "FIRE!" The smoking linstocks hit the touchholes, the powder caught, and the six guns blasted upward in the darkness. They caught the hull of the larger ship just below the gunports on the second deck, shattered the wood, and continued upward.

No one on either ship expected what happened next.

One smoking cannonball knocked a British gunner backward, sprawling, sliding, and he lost the smoking linstock clutched in his hand. It slid across the deck to the budge barrel of the next gun crew, where grains of black gunpowder were scattered, and a few caught, then more, and then the budge barrel exploded. The blast knocked the budge barrel of the next gun crew rolling, powder spilling in piles on the deck, and it caught and exploded. Burning gunpowder sprayed thirty feet in every direction. Within five seconds, half a dozen open budge barrels exploded to blow most of the cannon of the second deck through the gunports into the sea. The upper deck was raised nearly a foot, and flames shot upward through the cracks. Fire swept through the second deck, then up to the first, and suddenly the entire harbor was a kaleidoscope of light and shadow as the ship burned in the wind and rain.

For three seconds the crew of the *Zephyr* stood stock-still on the deck of their little schooner, bucking in the storm, drenched, staring in wide-eyed disbelief at the holocaust on the big ship, and then Caleb shouted, "Man your stations! Unfurl all sail! We're not clear yet."

With all their canvas out, drenched, and stretched to its limits by the howling storm, the little ship was flying. With Caleb and Adam at the bow shouting directions, the helmsman picked their way through the ships and barges and longboats at anchor, rising and falling on the tides, pitching in the wind and rain, while the two brothers in the bow of the ship strained to see the two lighthouses that marked the entrance to the harbor.

Adam's arm shot up, pointing. "There! Starboard! One hundred yards."

All heads turned to see the glimmer of light to their right, then turned to peer left, searching for the lighthouse at the far extreme of the harbor entrance, but in the rain there was nothing. Caleb turned to Tunstall.

"Where's the channel?"

Tunstall shouted, "Port. Over one hundred yards," and the helmsman corrected to port and held the little ship quartering before the wind, roaring in from the east.

"Steady as she goes!"

The lighthouse to their right faded and disappeared as they moved to their left, and Caleb looked at Tunstall, concerned, inquiring.

Tunstall shook his head and Caleb heard the determination in his voice. "We'll make it."

Tunstall counted slowly to sixty, then shouted, "Starboard, thirty degrees." The ship leaned to port for the correction, and then steadied, running once again with the wind. One minute became five, and Tunstall nodded to Caleb. "We're clear of the harbor. Deep water. We made it. Any wounded? Lost?"

"None."

"What course do you want to go home?"

"What choices do we have?"

Three minutes later Caleb, Tunstall, Adam, and Young were crowded around the table in Tunstall's cramped quarters, wiping at the water in their hair and beards and clothes as Tunstall unrolled a chart. The room was rolling, pitching, creaking, as Tunstall dropped his finger to the parchment, yellow in the undulating light of the swinging lantern.

"We can go back the way we came in, here, at the Windward Channel. To do that we move west about 150 miles, then correct to due east to hit the channel. We'll be sailing directly into the wind." He moved his finger back to where he started and continued. "Or, we can run west from where we are for about 200 miles, then north nor'west about four hundred miles through the Yucatan Channel here, then turn back east nor'east around Cuba, through the Straits of Florida, here, back north about 150 miles past the Bahamas, then correct east by nor'east about fifty miles, and straight north home."

Caleb reflected for a moment. "Which do you recommend?"

Tunstall did not hesitate. "The second route. The wind is with us the first 300 miles, and there isn't a ship in that harbor that can catch us. The storm will pass, and the winds will be favorable most of the rest of the way. We've got enough provisions to see us clear through."

"Set your course."

Caleb turned to Adam. "How many men in your crew were in that prison?"

"Nine, including me."

"The others? Captain Rittenhouse?"

Adam shook his head. "Gone. Cannon and musket fire."

"The other seven? What ship?"

"The *Primrose*. American. Taken by pirates, like us."

"Will you get a list of all their names, and the home port of the *Primrose*? We'll need to notify the owner."

"Yes."

Later, after steaming bowls of hot beef soup had settled the crew and their rescued cargo, Adam rapped on the door of Caleb's quarters.

"Enter."

Adam pushed through the door into the small room and stood facing his brother in the yellow light of the lantern, swinging with the pitch of the ship. He laid a piece of paper on the tiny table.

"That's the list you asked for."

Caleb picked it up to scan it. "The *Primrose* is out of Charleston?"

"Yes."

"I'll see the owner gets notice."

Adam said, "The men asked me to tell you. They didn't have much hope of ever seeing home again. They're grateful. They wanted you to know."

Caleb nodded but said nothing.

"I'm grateful."

Caleb dropped his eyes for a moment. "It had to be done."

"Not many shipping companies would have tried it. Not what you did."

Caleb shrugged and a hint of a smile flickered. "It wasn't Dunson & Weems that sent me."

Adam's eyes widened. "Who did?"

Caleb held a straight face. "Mother. She said I was to get down here and bring you home. No nonsense about it."

For a moment Adam gaped, and then he chuckled, and then both brothers laughed. The levity held and then faded, and Adam looked his brother in the eyes. For a moment they were seeing into each other's heart, and Adam knew, and he said nothing as he turned and walked back into the narrow, low gangway leading back to the hold where his shipmates were spreading their blankets.

Notes

For the detail of the location, history, and the conditions of Port Royal, Jamaica, as they appear in this chapter, see Pawson and Buisseret, *Port Royal, Jamaica,* chapters 1–5.

British Admiral Sir George Rodney was appointed by England to command the West Indies in the 1779–1780 time frame. See Mackesy, *The War for America, 1775–1783,* pp. 320–21.

CHAPTER XX

★ ★ ★

*N*athaniel Gorham drew back the window curtain of his room on the second floor of the boardinghouse on Ninth Street just south of Spruce, unlatched the window, and swung it outward, hoping against hope for a breeze from the Delaware River, less than one mile to the east. None came in the dead, hot, humid, eight o'clock morning air that gripped Philadelphia.

For a time he stared down at the morning traffic moving north toward Market Street, gathering himself for the strain of serving another day on the dais in the insufferably hot East Room of the Statehouse. Another day that would become a blur with those that had come before and would come after, of intense concentration to hold the delegates within the parliamentary procedures without which they would become deadlocked in verbal wars over factional quarrels. His forehead was drawn down, eyes narrowed, as he watched the buggies and carriages and the pedestrians hurrying to and from homes and boardinghouses and offices, caught up in their midweek business. He let his thoughts run.

The fight between the big and the little states is fomenting—coming back again for the third time—soon—the vote yesterday didn't kill it—it could wreck the convention—I wonder what will come of it—how they'll handle it.

He sighed and walked to the small table in the corner to look once more at the morning's newspapers. He sat to smooth the morning *Herald*, and read:

"Whatever measure may be recommended by the Federal Convention, whether an addition to the old Constitution or the adoption of a new, it will in effect be a revolution in Government, accomplished by reasoning and deliberation; an event that has never occurred since the formation of society and which will be strongly characteristic of the philosophic and tolerant spirit of the age."

A wry smile flickered. *It will be a revolution in government, that's certain enough, but it's not quite so certain that it will be accomplished by reasoning and deliberation.*

He set the *Herald* aside and picked up the *Gazette.*

"It is agreed, says a correspondent, that our Convention are framing a wise and free Government for us. This Government will be opposed only by our civil officers who are afraid of new arrangements taking place, which will jostle them out of office. . . . In the meantime, the people are desired to beware of all essays and paragraphs that are opposed to a reform in our Government, for they all must and will come from civil officers or persons connected with them."

He dropped the newspaper back on the table, shaking his head. *A wise and free government? We don't even know what it will look like when we finish— If we finish. And as for being opposed only by our civil officers, right now half the committee opposes the other half!*

A knock at the door brought him around.

"Yes, come in," he called. The door opened, and the sparse, gray-haired owner of the boardinghouse stood in the doorway with a folded document in his outstretched hand.

"A letter for you. Just delivered."

"Thank you." Gorham accepted the folded document and broke the seal as the man left and closed the door. Gorham stood in the middle of the room and looked first at the signature of the letter. Nathan Dane, serving as a representative in the federal Confederation Congress convened in New York City. Gorham puzzled for a moment at why his friend and colleague, with whom he had served in Congress, would be writing him from New York.

My Dear Friend:

I wish the officers of Congress and members not engaged in the Convention would return to New York. I do not know how it may be in the Southern States, but, I assume, the present state of Congress has a very disagreeable effect in the Eastern States. The people hear of a Convention in Philadelphia, and that Congress is done sitting, etc. Many of them are told, it seems, that Congress will never meet again. Dr Samuel Holten says he saw several sober men who had got an idea that the people were to be called on to take arms to carry into effect immediately the report of the Convention, etc. I see no help for men's being so absurd and distracted; but those things have a pernicious effect on the industry, peace, and habits of the people.

Are not the printers imprudent to publish so many contradictory pieces about the proceedings of your body, which must be mere conjecture? You know many people believe all they see in the newspapers, without the least examination . . .

Gorham sat on the edge of his bed to read the letter once again, then raised his head in startled amazement. *Congress is in trouble because of this convention? People up in the eastern states think Congress will never convene again?—that we intend sending in the army or the militia to force a new government on them by musket and bayonet? Ridiculous! Who's responsible for this?*

He rose, angry, shaking his head. *Newspapers and gossipmongers that print such lies ought to be held accountable on charges of treason! They know that people tend to believe things that are in writing—the power of the press—and they use it to get gain at the price of dividing and damaging the country!*

He laid the letter on his desk, drew out his watch to check the time, and let his temper cool while he reached for his cravat and finished dressing. He preferred to walk the four blocks to the Statehouse, partly to gather himself for what the day would bring in the East Room, and partly to admire the pride and care that was so manifest in the orderliness of the streets of Philadelphia.

He made his way through the loose dirt maintained in the streets surrounding the Statehouse, into the hall leading to the East Room, nodding his greetings to other delegates who were now familiar to him, for better or worse. He stood in the small line of those gathered at the door and waited his turn for Joseph Fry to admit him, entered the East Room, and took his place at his desk. At ten o'clock George Washington took the dais, and the assembly quieted as he called them to order and referred to his ledger.

"Gentlemen, it is proposed that today we not resolve into the Committee of the Whole. Rather, as a convention we will consider and have a report on those resolutions already established by the committee."

Gorham drew a breath of relief and let it out slowly and relaxed at his desk as Washington continued.

"We shall now address the first resolution."

The words were still echoing in the hall when Oliver Ellsworth of Connecticut was on his feet.

"I move the first resolution be amended to read as follows, namely, 'that the Government of the United States ought to consist of a supreme legislative, executive, and judiciary.' This slight alteration would drop the word *national* and retain the proper title, 'The United States.'" He cleared his throat, then said, "It would be highly dangerous not to consider the Confederation as still subsisting. I also wish the plan of the Convention to go forth as an amendment to the Articles of Confederation, since under this idea the authority of the legislatures could ratify it. If they are unwilling, the people will be unwilling too." Again he paused, and for a moment stared down at his desk, pondering his next words. "I do not like these conventions. They are better fitted to pull down than to build up constitutions."

For a brief moment there was surprised silence, followed by open mutterings at the subtle attempt to appease those who did not want a national government ruled by the big states. Washington called them back to order, and Gorham declared from his desk, "I second the motion of Mr. Ellsworth."

Edmund Randolph from Virginia rose and Washington recognized him.

"I do not object to the change of the expression 'national,'" Randolph announced, "but I do give notice that I do not support it for the reasons given by Mr. Ellsworth, particularly that of getting rid of a reference to the people for ratification."

A voice said, "Call for the vote."

Jackson polled the delegates in turn, and the motion passed easily. The word "national" was deleted from all resolutions in the work done thus far by the committee of the whole.

Washington studied the daily agenda for a moment and continued. "We'll take up the next resolution. That the legislature ought to consist of two branches."

John Lansing of New York sat in his chair squirming, agitated, and then came to his feet. "The true question here is whether the convention will adhere to, or depart from, the foundation of the present confederacy. In short, our present government is founded on the Articles of Confederation, which provide for a congress that is of one, not two, houses. I repeat the two questions that have previously been before us. Does this convention have competent powers to eliminate the Articles of Confederation and the Congress which now serves as the basis for our government? And, is the mind of the people such that they will tolerate the abandonment of the government we now have and with which they are familiar?"

Lansing paused, drew a deep breath, and continued his now all-too-familiar disgorging of every conceivable reason that neither the convention nor the committee of the whole, had power to obliterate the Articles of Confederation, nor entertain any notions of a new legislature with two separate chambers—a senate and a house of representatives. Hot, irritated delegates bit down on their need to stand and shout: "We've heard all this before—let's move on!" but the rules of the convention and the strict control exercised by Washington would not allow it. They sat and suffered as Lansing rambled on for half an hour, finally bringing his harangue to a close.

"Will anyone say the states will ever agree to abolishing the only government they have ever known and supporting a new one that is without precedent in the history of the world? I am absolutely convinced that the new government now under consideration is utterly unattainable. It is obvious that no one can foresee what will come to pass between the general government and the state governments. One, or the other, must fall, and be absorbed in the whole."

He was in the act of sitting down when George Mason of Virginia rose, jaw firmly set, eyes blazing, and Washington recognized him.

Mason wasted no time. His voice rang echoing. "I did not expect this point would have to be reagitated!"

Washington raised a hand high and Mason clamped his mouth closed, waiting while Washington took a moment to let tempers cool in the hot room. A few eyes wandered to the windows, closed, drapes drawn, wishing fervently they could be flung open to catch any breath of air, regardless of the fact that with any fresh air would come swarms of Philadelphia's infamous and notorious stinging flies. On the balance, there were some days that stinging flies were preferred to the insufferable heat and the tedium of the debate. Washington spoke with finality. "Be it remembered, gentlemen, that the Committee of the Whole is a parliamentary device which provides opportunity for discussions that are not final nor binding on anyone. The work of the committee is advisory only, subject to proper action of the convention. Debate on any issue is not closed until the committee is dissolved. Matters considered by the committee and voted on yesterday may be reopened by any delegate tomorrow, for any purpose. Let us continue. Mr. Mason, you have the floor."

Mason, a fellow Virginian to Washington, brought himself under control and proceeded, hot, voice ringing as he piled argument upon argument against those just delivered by Lansing.

"Is it not true that this convention has met at a time in history when all the ordinary cautions *must* yield to the overpowering public need?

Have we forgotten that the commissioners sent by the Confederation Congress to Great Britain to forge the peace treaty signed in 1783 had boldly cast aside the limitations given them by Congress, and attained an honorable and happy peace, and by so doing had raised to themselves a monument more durable than brass? Can it be thought that the people will *ever* grant power of both the purse and the sword to one single institution?—one congress with one chamber only? Will the people ever consent to a marching army coming to collect taxes?"

He paused to compose himself and then finished. "To make myself clear beyond any possibility of being misunderstood, I absolutely do not suggest that the states relinquish their sovereignty. Nor do I suggest that there is less a need to establish a general government to deal with all matters beyond the authority of any single state. To create a government that recognizes both is not an insurmountable thing."

Mason sat down, breathing hard, and Luther Martin of Maryland rose and plowed into his discourse.

"I take this occasion to agree with Mr. Mason as to the importance of state governments. I will support them at the expense of the national government . . . there is no necessity for two branches in Congress, but should such necessity exist, the congress we now have can be divided into two branches. . . . When the thirteen states separated from Great Britain they chose to establish their new government under the Articles of Confederation, with one congress and thirteen separate sovereign states, and the thirteen states cannot now grant part of their sovereignty to a new national government without dissolving their own governments—and further, any system of a national court system would be inconsistent with state sovereignty."

Martin quieted, and Roger Sherman of Connecticut rose to support John Lansing's fervent speech against the creation of a congress composed of a house of representatives and a senate.

Sherman finished his lengthy statement, and James Wilson of Pennsylvania shoved his spectacles back up his nose and stood to deliver his all-too-familiar, rambling remarks that once again reached back into the long-forgotten histories of Amphyctyonic and Achaean, Swiss,

German, and Austrian history to absolutely prove the necessity of a congress with a house and senate.

Sweating, growing visibly irritable, weary of the harangues that were now before them for the third time, the convention postponed further proceedings to vote on the proposition of John Lansing. Did the convention want the new congress to be a single chamber institution as it was under the Articles of Confederation?

Ayes. Connecticut, New York, New Jersey, Delaware.

Nays. Massachusetts, Pennsylvania, Virginia, North Carolina, South Carolina, Georgia.

Four in favor, six against, one state divided. The new congress would not be a single chamber institution. Lansing's dissertation and the five hours of repeat debates he had triggered had failed for the third time, and there were many who dearly hoped it was the last.

The Delaware delegation requested that the remaining issues of the day be postponed until tomorrow, June twenty-first, and a weary convention gratefully rose when Washington adjourned for the day.

The following morning, the delegates took their seats, Washington called the convention to order, and the delegates took a deep breath before they bit into the gritty and widely scattered details that danced around the issue they all knew was at the core of their debate. The stand-or-fall battle was going to be between those who doggedly hung with the Articles of Confederation and those who had forsaken them for a new government, and that issue was inexorably, one day at a time, coming to the surface. Until it finally did, they continued with the lesser issues.

What was the true nature of federalism? Johnson, Wilson, and Madison discoursed on the subject for hours.

On what foundations should the house of representatives be based? General Pinckney, Hamilton, Mason, Rutledge, Wilson, and King were kind enough, and long-winded enough, to leave no doubt on the subject.

Thursday blended into Friday, then Saturday, while the delegates hammered at the peripheral issues one at a time. Sunday brought a day of blessed relief from the grinding debates, and Monday and Tuesday, June twenty-sixth and twenty-seventh brought the delegates back to the East Room to endure more heat from both Philadelphia and the debates that addressed more fringe issues while carefully avoiding the explosive one in the center of it all. They gathered their strength and took the small issues one at a time.

What is the true nature of representation? Randolph, Dickinson, Ellsworth, Wilson, Madison, Hamilton, Sherman, and Mason each obligingly shared their wisdom on the question, which left the convention a bit more muddled and divided than when they started.

More critically, what are the causes, and the cures, of corruption in legislatures? Madison, Rutledge, Mason, King, Wilson, Sherman, and Gerry offered their views, covering every temptation known to mankind and the general fallibility of the human race.

What is the use, structure, and tenure of the senate to be? Both General Pinckney and his cousin Charles Pinckney, with Gorham, Wilson, Ellsworth, Williamson, Mason, Read, Madison, Sherman, Hamilton, and Gerry felt inspired to enlighten the convention with their well-considered thoughts, notwithstanding the sour and dour glares of those who disagreed.

How much compensation should a congressman be paid? And who should pay them, the new national government, or the states? Ellsworth declared that the states should decide that for themselves, while Gorham stoutly took issue, claiming that the compensation should be equal throughout, and that Congress should set their own wages. Madison defined the dilemma but did not resolve it when he argued that if congressional salaries are paid by the states, the congressmen will become dependent on, and obliged to, the states; however, allowing Congress to pay itself might be even worse! So, Madison concluded, let Congress set its own base amount for wages, and then index it against a dependable commodity, like wheat, so that the wage could rise or fall with the general fortunes of the country. Almost no one agreed and it was only concluded that the wages of congressmen should be "adequate."

How old should a man be to serve as a congressman? Wilson argued against any age limitation. Mason reasoned that they ought to be at least twenty-five, since he could recall that his own political opinions at age twenty-one were both naïve and dangerous. Wilson lost, and Mason won. The minimum age for congressmen became twenty-five.

Young Charles Pinckney, the twenty-nine-year-old dandy from the prominent South Carolina Pinckneys, dressed in his silks and satins and lace, found occasion to blast a sizeable hole in Alexander Hamilton's recommendations that the new constitution and government should follow the pattern of England. *"Never!"* declared young Pinckney. "The people of the United States are perhaps the most singular of any we are acquainted with. . . . A system must be suited to the habits and genius of the people it governs. What makes Americans so different from the rest of the world is their spirit of equality. Among Americans, there are fewer distinctions of fortune and less of rank than among the inhabitants of any other nation. Every freeman has a right to the same protection and security, and a very moderate share of property entitles them to the possession of all the honors and privileges the public can bestow."

Pinckney's pronouncements caught many by surprise, coming as they did from a man not yet thirty years of age. But Pinckney's credentials included the fact he had voluntarily left wealth and leisure to fight in the ranks during the shooting war and, notwithstanding the wealth of his family, had served and survived in South Carolina politics to become a champion of the common man. He had paid his dues, and when he spoke, the delegates listened.

Through all the verbiage and dramatics and the heat and the frayed nerves, with Washington on the dais conducting the business with the delegates sitting as a convention, decisions were made that were fast becoming final.

The new congress would be two chambers: the House of Representatives and the Senate.

Members of the House of Representatives would be elected by the people.

Members of the Senate would be elected by the state legislatures.

Members of the House of Representatives would have a two-year term.

Members of the Senate would have a six-year term, with one-third of the members to be replaced at two-year intervals.

The morning of Wednesday, June twenty-seventh dawned as sweltering as the previous few days had been, and the traffic in the prim streets of Philadelphia was no more nor less than the day before. The large hallway in the Statehouse saw the same judges and lawyers disappear into the Supreme Court chambers, and those conducting the affairs of the State of Pennsylvania hurrying from one office to another with papers in their hands.

Yet, there was a sense in the depressing heat that something was to happen in the East Room that day that none would forget as long as they lived. The delegates were all seated and Washington was stepping onto the dais before it hit them. They were through with the prologue, finished with all the peripheral details. They could no longer continue the dance around the ugly question that they had pushed into the background. Ominous, deadly, it would no longer remain buried. Today was the day the monster demanded to be unshackled and turned loose on the floor of the convention for the debate and the vote that could, and likely would, rip the entire convention into two irreconcilable factions and forever end the dream of a united America. Washington called the convention into session and within seconds after he opened the floor for issues and debate, John Rutledge of South Carolina laid it open.

"I move that the resolution of the committee of the whole which involved the most fundamental points, that is to say, the rules of selecting members of the House of Representatives and the Senate, be reopened for further consideration."

He peered about, gauging the reaction of the delegates. Their eyes were bright, faces set; they were ready, even anxious for the battle that would for all time end this unbearable waiting. A few picked up papers and were in the act of rising when the voice of Luther Martin brought all heads around to stare at him in surprise.

Luther Martin of Maryland was seen by every other delegate as an unending surprise, often brilliant, articulate, but with thought sequences that were disconnected, confusing, often baffling. None could feel a close kinship to the man, since they never knew what to expect of him. Born on a small New Jersey farm in approximately 1748, he managed to make his way to Princeton College and graduated with honors in 1766. He taught school in Maryland for several years before entering the practice of law, to become a brilliant, although at times radical, lawyer. Along the way he had become addicted to strong drink, which had caused his face to take on a permanent ruddy cast. Stories were legendary and rampant of his appearances in court, obviously under the influence of liquor, to argue his cases brilliantly, and most often with resounding success. Some doubted that he could have done half so well had he been stone sober. Through political connections and his considerable reputation as a lawyer, he was appointed Attorney General of Maryland, then sent to Congress in 1784 and 1785, where he impressed his colleagues with two things: his astounding capacity to absorb strong drink and his powerful oratory. When appointed to attend the Grand Convention in Philadelphia, at least two of his fellow Maryland delegates, Daniel Carroll and Daniel of St. Thomas Jenifer, were less than happy to learn he would be with them.

Surprised, Washington straightened in his chair for a moment before he spoke. "Mr. Martin of Maryland has the floor."

Within minutes it was obvious that Martin had braced himself with a healthy dose of medicinal brandy before arriving at the East Room. In the first half hour, his thoughts were disconnected, rambling, irrelevant. In the next half hour the other delegates could not relate what he was saying to the issue before the convention. Nor did the rules allow any delegate to interrupt when another had been given the floor and was speaking. One hour became two, then three, as Martin rambled on. The other delegates, who in the previous days had at least shown a modicum of respect for others no matter how violently they might disagree with them, could no longer bear Martin's oration. They turned stony eyes toward him, both unable and unwilling to hide their disgust.

More than three hours had passed before Martin, fatigued by the heat and his own fervent disgorging, concluded, and then brought open groans from almost every man in the room when he announced he sought leave to continue his sermon in the morning.

Washington took note of the request and adjourned for the day.

The following morning, Thursday, June twenty-eighth, Washington reluctantly gave the floor once again to Luther Martin. Emanating the scent of fine brandy, Martin resumed his ramblings where he had left them, and for more than three more hours again held forth. The other delegates were close to revolt when he finally exhausted his random thoughts and his voice, and sat down.

The essence of his six-hour diatribe, spread over most of two days, could have been delivered in five minutes: It was his opinion " . . . that the general government ought to protect and secure the state governments. The cornerstone of a federal government is equality of votes. States may surrender this right, but if they do their liberties are lost. If I err on this point," he declared, "it is the error of the head, not of the heart."

As for the Virginia plan, already approved by the committee of the whole seventeen days earlier, but not by the convention, his position was simple:

"I would not trust a government organized on the Virginia plan for all the slaves of Carolina or the horses and oxen of Massachusetts!"

He emerged from it all as a wildly radical spokesman for the small states, committed to the principle that all states, small and large, must have equal voting power in the new congress.

When Martin finally sat down, Benjamin Franklin stirred in his chair, opened his eyes, rubbed his legs, and looked about, watching intently, waiting, knowing that the convention was about to be plunged into the vortex. Madison, his jaw set, blue eyes narrowed, sat as tall as he could, studying the faces of the delegates who supported his beloved Virginia plan, and those who opposed it. Washington straightened in his large, straight-backed chair on the dais, scanned the room, and waited for someone to make the motion that would bring the entire convention face-to-face with the deadly question.

John Lansing of New York stood. "I move that this convention reverse the action taken by the committee of the whole as regards accepting the Virginia plan."

Jonathan Dayton of New Jersey quickly called, "I second the motion."

The time had arrived. The issue that threatened the union of the United States was squarely before the men who must decide, and there was none among them who misunderstood the pivotal moment history had placed on their shoulders. Were the small states to have equal voting power with the large states? Each had made it clear that they would likely walk out of the convention if their position were not adopted.

Dayton continued, "I am greatly anxious that the question might not be put until tomorrow, since Mr. Livingston of New Jersey has been kept away on necessary business, not to return until tomorrow. Lacking his presence, the New Jersey representation is suspended for the day. It would be desirable to wait until we can have the benefit of the New Jersey vote."

Hugh Williamson of North Carolina rose. "If the states are equally sovereign now, and each parts with equal proportions of such sovereignty, they will remain equally sovereign. I see no harm in that for the small states, and wish someone would arrive at a solution for it. May I also remind this convention that new states will soon be forming to the west of us, and they will be small states, poor, unable to meet their financial obligations. And they will be joining the small states in congress."

Madison could remain seated no longer. He rose, was recognized by Washington, and delivered once again, with power and reason, the essence of his prior lengthy, masterful discourse in support of the Virginia plan. The representation of the individual states in the new congress must be on the basis of population. No need to fear the three large states—Virginia, Pennsylvania, and Massachusetts—whose combined populations could control Congress. Their interests lay in their commerce, and with Massachusetts based on fish, Pennsylvania on flour, and Virginia on tobacco, their various interests would prevent any thoughts of any political collusion to control the other states.

Madison sat down, and James Wilson rose to give a resounding endorsement to Madison's position, together with his own observations that the fears of the small states ran in the face of the history of small boroughs in England, which never suffered at the hands of the larger ones.

The tension in the hall was becoming charged. No one had changed his position, nor had any even hinted at a willingness to hunt for a compromise. Worse, none could see that a compromise was possible. It was much to be compared with a compass: could north ever be compromised with south, without destroying both?

Roger Sherman, the accomplished politician, rose and slowly, emphatically, with clipped words and phrases that concealed his anger, laid it out:

"The question is not what rights naturally belong to men, but how they may be most equally and effectually guarded in society. And if some give up more than others in order to obtain this end, there can be no room for complaint. To do otherwise, to require an equal concession from all, if it would create danger to the rights of some, would be sacrificing the end to the means. The rich man who enters into society along with the poor man, gives up more than the poor man. Yet with an equal vote he is equally safe. Were he to have more votes than the poor man in proportion to his superior stake, the rights of the poor man would immediately cease to be secure."

He paused to scan the faces of the other delegates as they digested the plain logic of his argument, then, with a raised fist and a voice that rang, finished:

"This consideration prevailed when the Articles of Confederation were formed and ought to prevail now!"

It was as though the air in the sweltering East Room were charged with electricity. Every man sat tense, focused, silent, waiting, unsure what to do, fearful they were watching the convention preparing to fracture and disband, and with it the unraveling of the dream of America. William Few of Georgia trembled at the realization that the rupture of the union was taking place before their eyes.

The sound of a chair sliding on the floor brought their heads around, and every eye in the room widened at the sight of Benjamin Franklin struggling to rise on his crippled, eighty-one-year-old legs. Silence gripped the room as Franklin straightened, lifting first one supporting hand, then the other, from his desk, and he stood tall, facing Washington.

Washington's voice sounded too loud in the dead quiet. "Mr. Franklin?"

Franklin's jowls moved for a moment as he pursed his mouth, and then the old man began:

"Mr. President. The small progress we have made after four or five weeks close attendance and continual reasonings with each other—our different sentiments on almost every question, several of the last producing as many noes as ayes, is methinks a melancholy proof of the imperfection of the human understanding. We indeed seem to feel our own want of political wisdom, since we have been running about in search of it. We have gone back to ancient history for models of government and examined the different forms of those republics which having been formed with the seeds of their own dissolution now no longer exist. And we have viewed modern states all round Europe, but find none of their constitutions suitable to our circumstances."

He paused to order his thoughts, then went on, his voice steady:

"In this situation of this assembly, groping as it were in the dark to find political truth, and scarce able to distinguish it when presented to us, how has it happened, sir, that we have not hitherto once thought of humbly applying to the Father of Lights to illuminate our understandings? In the beginning of the contest with Great Britain, when we were sensible of danger, we had daily prayer in this room for the divine protection. Our prayers, sir, were heard, and they were graciously answered. All of us who were engaged in the struggle must have observed frequent instances of a superintending providence in our favor. To that kind of providence we owe this happy opportunity of consulting in peace on the means of establishing our future national felicity. And have we now forgotten that powerful Friend? Or do we imagine that we no longer need his assistance? I have lived, sir, a long time, and the longer I live, the more convincing proofs I see of this truth."

The old man leaned forward, and with every fiber of his being declared, *"That God governs in the affairs of men. And if a sparrow cannot fall to the ground without his notice, is it probable that an empire can rise without his aid?"*

No one dared move.

"We have been assured, sir, in the sacred writings, that 'except the Lord build the house, they labor in vain that build it.' I firmly believe this; and I also believe that without his concurring aid we shall succeed in this political building no better than the builders of Babel. We shall be divided by our little partial local interests; our projects will be confounded; and we ourselves shall become a reproach and a bye word down to future ages. And what is worse, mankind may hereafter from this unfortunate instance, despair of establishing governments by human wisdom and leave it to chance, war, and conquest."

The entire convention sat mesmerized, humbled.

Franklin finished. "I therefore beg leave to move that henceforth prayers imploring the assistance of heaven, and its blessings on our deliberations, be held in this assembly every morning before we proceed to business, and that one or more of the clergy of this city be requested in that service."

With simple dignity the old man pulled his chair forward, and slowly, painfully settled his ailing body onto it, then raised his face to Washington, and for the first time, other delegates dared look about.

Never had they seen the expression they saw now in George Washington. The dignity remained, but shining through it was a joy and a radiance that held men staring. With feelings akin to fear they glanced about the room. Strong men with strong opinions on both sides of the issue that were ripping the convention apart sat staring, humbled, chastened, diminished. No one knew or cared how long they sat thus, struggling to understand how they had forgotten the true roots of their country, while the words "endowed by our creator" pounded through their minds like a chant.

Finally Roger Sherman said, "I second the motion."

Time passed before some suggested concern that the motion had come too late in the convention, that such a practice might cause some citizens to worry that conditions inside the East Room had reached desperation. Others said it was a mistake they had not begun the entire convention with the rule of daily prayer, and that it is never too late to correct an error. Hugh Williamson of North Carolina raised the hard fact that the convention did not have one penny to pay a clergyman for such services.

Then Edmund Randolph of Virginia stood. "I move that a sermon be preached at the request of the convention on the fourth of July, the anniversary of our independence, and thenceforward prayers be used in the convention every morning."

Benjamin Franklin raised a hand but did not stand. "I second the motion." Efforts were made to postpone the vote, and the session was adjourned without the vote being taken. Some were anguished, but others understood that taking the vote would have been desired, but not necessary. The good had already been accomplished by the elder statesman. The simplicity and power and rightness of his words had seized every man in the room by the nape of his neck, as it were, and hauled him involuntarily from the tangle of human debate and frailty back to face the basic truths on which the United States had been conceived and born. None would ever forget the feeling that surged in their hearts and spread to fill the room as Washington brought the business of the day to adjournment.

Talk among the delegates was subdued as they filed out of the room into the hallway and made their way to their separate quarters. None pretended the rupture between the small and large states was healed. To the contrary, they knew the final clash was yet coming, and few expected the union to survive. Still, as they sat at their supper tables, and paced in their rooms past midnight, running hands through rumpled hair, mumbling to themselves, desperately inventing and discarding ways to avoid the horrors of disunion, the words of their elder statesman, and the awesome power that had filled the East Room for those few moments, rose in their minds and breasts to fill them, mellow them, soften them. It occurred only to a few of the thoughtful ones that somehow a subtle shift was in the making. Some who had sworn they would never concede to the opposition were now searching for a way to give a little, take a little—to compromise. They struggled on through the night, and it rode them like a cruel master as they made their way to the Statehouse and silently gathered in the East Room the sultry morning of Friday, June 29, 1787.

In charged silence, Washington called the convention to order. "We return to the pending issue of how shall the House of Representatives be selected? By one vote in each of the states, or by the vote of the people?"

William Samuel Johnson of Connecticut rose immediately. "The controversy must be endless whilst gentlemen differ in the grounds of their arguments. Those on one side consider the states as districts *of people* composing one political society. Those on the other consider them as so many political societies, with no reference to the people. The fact is, that the states do exist as political societies, and a government is to be formed for them in their political capacity, *as well as for the individuals composing them.*"

Eyes narrowed in thought at the notion that the states served a dual role—one for the state, the other for the people.

Nathaniel Gorham rose. "The states as now confederated have no doubt a right to refuse to be consolidated, or to be formed into any new system. I wish the small states, which seem most ready to object to any system which deprives them of equality with the large ones, would consider which are to give up most, they or the larger ones."

He paused and calculated his next words before he uttered them. "A rupture of the union would be an event unhappy for all, but surely the large states would be able to take care of themselves and make connections with one another should such a rupture occur. The small states would be the ones that would suffer, and therefore should be most interested in establishing some general system for maintaining order. Consider the condition Delaware would face should a separation of the states occur. Would she not lie at the mercy of Pennsylvania? Consider that Massachusetts was once three colonies—Old Massachusetts, Plymouth, and Mayne. Those three small provinces found their salvation in merging into one—Massachusetts as we know it. The situation was repeated when Connecticut and Newhaven merged to become Connecticut. Should not the smaller states represented in this convention find the resolution of their problem in the same principle? Combine and merge to achieve equality with the larger ones?"

The faces of the delegates from the small states did not change, nor did their resolve. Oliver Ellsworth of Connecticut sensed the firming of positions and rose to state simply, "I do not despair. I yet trust that a good plan of government will be devised and adopted."

Again, neither faction changed.

Elbridge Gerry, the Grumbletonian from Massachusetts, stood, the expression on his face suggesting his breakfast had consisted of six sour pickles.

"We never were independent states—not now, and never can be, even on the principles of the confederation. The states are intoxicated with the idea of *sovereignty*. I was a member of Congress at the time the federal articles were framed, and I was all too keenly aware then of the injustice of allowing each state, large or small, an equal vote. I approved it then under the pressure of public danger and the obstinacy of the smaller states, but my approval was much against my own better judgment." His voice rose in angry emotion. "The present confederation is dissolving. The fate of the union will be decided by this convention! I lament that instead of coming here like a band of brothers, belonging to the same family, we seem to have brought with us the spirit of political negotiators."

Satisfied he had delivered his dire predictions and roundly chastised the entire convention, he seated his sparse frame on his chair, lower lip thrust out defiantly.

Luther Martin stood. The expression on his flushed face suggested his breakfast had consisted of a quart of strong Madeira wine at the Indian Queen Hotel. Low groans were heard from other delegates who feared that he was embarking on another two-day odyssey through the history of the world and a rehearsal of political thought reaching back to Moses in the Book of Exodus in the Old Testament.

To their profound amazement and gratitude, Martin was brief. "The language of the states being sovereign and independent was once familiar and understood. Now it seems strange and obscure. May I remind us all of the simple language in the Articles of Confederation." He raised a document and read the pertinent sections of the Articles, looked about, and sat down amid sighs of relief.

Washington waited a few moments, the room became still, and he put the question. "On the motion that the House of Representatives shall be elected by popular vote of the people and not by rule of one vote for each state, Mr. Jackson, proceed."

Jackson nodded and took the votes.

Ayes. Massachusetts, Pennsylvania, Virginia, North Carolina, South Carolina, Georgia.

Nays. Connecticut, New York, New Jersey, Delaware.

Maryland. Divided, no vote.

Six in favor, four against. One divided. The Virginia plan had won the battle in favor of the large states on election of members to the new House of Representatives. In the charged silence, heads swiveled as the large state delegates guardedly glanced at the faces of those from the small states, apprehensive, fearful of what might become their exodus from the East Room. Almost nothing was said, and no one moved. Then Oliver Ellsworth of the small state of Connecticut stood, and the entire room silenced. Washington recognized him, and Ellsworth's voice was firm and steady.

"I move that the rule of suffrage in the Senate be the same as that established by the Articles of Confederation. That is, one vote for each state. I am not sorry that the vote just passed has determined against this rule in the House of Representatives, but since we are partly national and partly federal, it is consistent that if the House is to be elected by popular vote of the people, then the Senate ought to be elected on the basis of one vote for each state."

It caught the delegates by surprise, and they leaned back, collecting their thoughts. Washington sensed the mood, and the timing, and declared, "The motion of Mr. Ellsworth is noted and will be taken up tomorrow morning, Saturday, June thirtieth. We stand adjourned for the day."

A somber delegation rose and walked out of the East Room into the big corridor, then out of the building into the heat of the late afternoon sun, conflicted, torn, mentally and emotionally exhausted from two weeks of intense, fruitless searching for an answer to the single issue they had feared most from the beginning. Every man knew that Ellsworth's closing motion was the last desperate stand of the small states to save themselves from the large ones. Further, they knew that the three delegates from Connecticut had put the same motion before the convention again and again, first by Sherman on June eleventh, and again on June twentieth, then by Johnson on June twenty-ninth, and now by Ellsworth. And each time the patient efforts of the Connecticut men had fallen to the power of the larger states.

By the time the delegates sat to their supper tables, most of them had sensed that tomorrow there would be no quarter asked, and none given, in a battle to the death. By midnight, most were still sitting hunched at their desks, or casting misshapen shadows on the walls as they paced the floors in the yellow lamplight of their quarters, caught in the impossible bind of either giving up that which they could not give up, or watching the United States broken to pieces.

Dawn broke hot, and some were perspiring as they walked down the corridor to the East Room, where Joseph Fry admitted them, then closed the doors and took his position. Washington called the convention to order and declared, "The first order of business is the motion of Mr. Ellsworth of Connecticut, that each state have one vote in the Senate."

The first man on his feet was David Brearly of New Jersey. "I respectfully move," he exclaimed, "that the President of this convention immediately write to Governor Sullivan of New Hampshire, urging the attendance of the delegates from that state."

The ploy was all too transparent. Brearly, and the small states, wanted one more small state added to their number before the final vote could be taken.

Rutledge, King, and Wilson hotly condemned the whole idea, and the motion was soundly defeated.

Washington moved on. "Having disposed of Mr. Brearly's motion, we now return to Mr. Ellsworth's motion regarding representation in the Senate."

He had no sooner said it than James Wilson of Pennsylvania was again on his feet. His demeanor was charged with emotion, his voice loud, ringing. "Can we forget for whom we are forming a government? Is it for men, or for the imaginary beings called states? A government founded on a principle by which a number of states containing a minority of the people can control those containing a majority can be neither solid nor lasting! Every man in this new government must have equal voting power!"

King rose hot. "Any reform would be nugatory if we should make another congress of the proposed senate." He paused, took a deep breath, and cut loose. "I am convinced of the obstinacy of the small states, and I consider that we are already ground asunder, sacrificed to the phantom of state sovereignty." There were open gasps from the small state delegates, and he paused for a moment before finishing. "I am amazed that when a just government founded on a fair representation of the *people* of America is within our reach, we should renounce the blessing from an attachment to the ideal freedom and importance of *states!* I repeat. Are we creating a government for *people*, or for *states?*"

Madison, ever levelheaded, conciliatory, but firm in his commitment to the Virginia plan, took the floor. "I find no reason for the small states to fear a combination against them of the large states from the north and from the south, because the states are divided into different interests. Not by their difference of size, but of circumstance, partly from climate differences, but principally from the effects of having or not having slaves."

Few were prepared for the slavery issue to again rear its ugly head, and chairs creaked as startled men moved, and murmured, and then settled. Madison continued in his soft, cultured voice.

"In a word, the differences do not lie between large and small states. It lies between the northern and the southern states."

Again men moved and murmured, then quieted.

"As regards the Senate, I suggest that voting power in the southern states could be augmented by granting those states the right to increase their vote by giving them authority to cast votes equal to three-fifths of the total number of slaves."

The small state delegates stiffened, and Jonathan Dayton of New Jersey came to his feet, finger thrust upward, voice too loud. "Declamation has now replaced argument! Gentlemen, I consider the proposed system of the larger states to be a novelty, an amphibious *monster which can never, never be accepted by the people!*"

Large state delegates looked at each other in surprise. Some were in the act of rising when Gunning Bedford of tiny Delaware sprang to his feet. All pretense of holding back was abandoned as he plunged in.

"There is no middle ground between a perfect consolidation and a mere confederacy of the states. The first is out of the question, and in the latter they must continue, if not perfectly, at least equally sovereign. If political societies possess ambition and avarice, and all the other passions which render them formidable to each other, ought we not to view them in this light here, and now?"

He stopped and leaned forward, palms flat on his desk, stiff arms supporting his upper body.

"Will not the same motives operate in America as elsewhere? If any gentleman doubts it let him look at the votes! Have they not been dictated by interest? Ambition? Are not the large states evidently seeking to aggrandize themselves at the expense of the small?"

Again he stopped, straightened, and waited for his words to strike home before he continued. "They think no doubt they have right on their side, but self-interest has blinded their eyes! Look at Georgia. Though a small state right now, she looks forward to the prospect of soon being a large one, and has shown her ambition by voting with the large states. Consider South Carolina and North Carolina. Two small states with the same ambitions as Georgia. Can any man here say honestly that an inequality of power will not result from an inequality of votes? Give the opportunity to any government, and ambition will not fail to abuse it. The whole history of mankind proves it. No matter what arguments are offered to justify granting larger states more power, the result will be the same. The smaller states will be ruined! Will the smaller states ever agree to the proposed degradation they are now facing?"

He paused to order his thoughts and bring his raging emotions under control, and then he delivered the most explosive conclusion yet heard in the East Room. His voice was under control, his words plainly spoken, not as a threat, but as a simple statement of fact.

"You of the larger states say you never will hurt or injure the lesser states." He drew a breath, looked the larger state delegates in the eye, and said simply, "I do not, gentlemen, trust you."

There was an audible intake of breath by the large state delegates. They were men of substance, experience, influence, reputation, and they had just been accused of being untrustworthy.

Bedford did not hesitate. He locked eyes with them, drew a breath and concluded with measured words. "If you possess the power, the abuse of it could not be checked. We small states have been told by you, with a dictatorial air, that this is the last moment for a fair trial in favor of a good government. But the large states *dare not dissolve the confederation. If you do, sooner than be ruined, the small states will find some foreign ally of more honor and good faith who will take us by the hand and do us justice!* If we solemnly renounce your new project, what will be the consequence? You will annihilate your federal government, and ruin must stare you in the face."

There it was! Finally, finally, the breach had been called out in raw, blunt, abrasive, unmistakable terms. If Bedford was right, the small states were prepared to walk out before they would become the pawns of the larger states, to enter into an alliance with a foreign power to protect themselves, regardless the fact that the United States would cease to exist! These were the words that the larger states had feared from the beginning, yet now that they were ringing off the walls, not one man was ready—or willing—to hear them. They sat there, minds reeling, sick in their hearts that they had not found a solution to the issue that was wrenching the convention to pieces.

King rose, angry, offended, to strike back at the humiliation Bedford had heaped upon him and the other large state delegates. His arm shot up, finger pointing directly at Bedford. "I protest the intemperance and the vehemence indulged in by Mr. Bedford. He has declared himself ready to turn from our country and seek the protection of some foreign power. I am grieved beyond expression that such a thought has entered into Mr. Bedford's heart. I am more grieved that such an expression has dropped from his lips. I cannot excuse it, except possibly that he was overcome with passion, however misplaced. For myself, whatever might be my torment, I would *never* turn to a foreign power for relief."

King sat down, breathing heavily, face flushed, anger leaping from his eyes.

Washington raised a hand, and in an instant the hall fell silent. No man in the room dared confront, or challenge, George Washington.

He spoke with calm deliberation. "Gentlemen, we are adjourned for the day. We will meet Monday morning, July second, ten o'clock A.M. Remember your oath of secrecy."

The waking hours of Sunday were spent by weary delegates in caucuses, venting their anger, cooling, probing, slowly coming to understand that one side, or the other side, or both sides, would have to yield, to compromise, to meet in the middle, to avoid the unthinkable disunion of the United States. None wished to ponder their fate if they were to report to the thirteen states that they had not only failed to create the new government they had dreamed of, but they had succeeded in wrecking the United States.

Monday morning saw them gathering at the Statehouse, staring straight ahead, saying nothing. Joseph Fry admitted the last of those who arrived and closed the door.

Scant notice was taken of the absence of some of their number, since from time to time, one delegate or another would be absent for a short while to take care of a business crises at home, or a family illness, or even a short but much needed visit. Alexander Hamilton had returned to New York, convinced his contribution to the entire proceeding was meaningless since his New York colleagues Robert Yates and John Lansing repeatedly combined to override him.

Washington called the convention to order, and the secretary, William Jackson, noted the absences. William Pierce of Georgia had gone to New York to attend the Confederation Congress for a short period and to fight a duel for which Alexander Hamilton was to be his second. William Few of Georgia was not present, for reasons not yet known, but Abraham Baldwin and William Houstoun were present, giving Georgia two of her four delegates. Daniel of St. Thomas Jenifer of Maryland was simply late in arriving. James McHenry of Maryland was at the bedside of his dying brother, and John Mercer and Daniel Carrol were not due to arrive for the convention for another fourteen days, thus, the single remaining delegate from Maryland was Luther Martin. Jackson looked up at Washington and certified there was a quorum of eleven states present. The vacant chairs were largely ignored.

There was strain in Washington's voice as he declared, "The convention will now proceed with the vote on Mr. Ellsworth's motion for each state having one vote in the Senate."

The tension in the room was like something alive, unbearable on the shoulders of each delegate. All they had done in the stifling heat of the East Room since the twenty-fifth day of May, and all their dreams of a new government for the United States, and their terrible fear they were going to force a disunion of the states, came down to what would happen in the next five minutes. No one, not one man, could now help or hinder. Washington, Franklin, Madison, Morris, Gerry, King, Wilson— all sat helpless, able only to wait for the country to stand or fall. Words and voices seemed distorted, strange, as Jackson called for the vote.

Connecticut. Aye.
Massachusetts. Nay.
Pennsylvania. Nay.
New York. Aye.

Virginia. Nay.

New Jersey. Aye.

Maryland. Aye.

North Carolina. Nay.

South Carolina. Nay.

Delaware. Aye.

In dead silence the delegates realized there were five states for, five states against—a tied vote—a deadlock! Neither side had won! It was Franklin who suddenly sat straight up, aware of what had caused it. The tardiness of Daniel of St. Thomas Jenifer and the absence of James McHenry, John Mercer, and Daniel Carroll, all of Maryland, left only Luther Martin to cast the Maryland vote, and with his habitual morning imbibing of brandy or strong wine under his belt, he had voted "Aye."

All eyes swiveled to the Georgia delegation, the only state which had not yet voted, and the heart went out of all the small states. From the beginning, Georgia had voted with the large states, looking forward to the time they would be among them, able to dominate the small ones. With William Few and William Pierce absent, there were but two delegates left, Abraham Baldwin and William Houstoun. Both had consistently voted with the large states.

Jackson called, "William Houstoun. How do you vote?"

Houstoun's voice came loud. "Nay."

Jackson marked his record and raised his head. "Abraham Baldwin. How do you vote?"

Few men were breathing in the terrible tension.

Abraham Baldwin was not a native Georgian. He was a transplanted Connecticut Yankee. The son of a learned blacksmith of North Guilford, he had graduated from Yale College, become a minister, served four years as a chaplain in the Continental Army, read the law, and become a successful lawyer. Then, in 1784, anxious for new adventures, he left for Augusta, Georgia, where he served in the Georgia legislature and was elected to the Confederation Congress. A confirmed bachelor, his reputation for hard work, common sense, and a good nature made him the most prominent delegate from Georgia, albeit one who thought much and spoke seldom. True to the commission issued to him by his adopted state to attend the Grand Convention, he had steadfastly voted with the larger states.

Baldwin studied Jackson for several seconds of deep thought, then said, "I vote aye."

Half the large state delegates partially raised from their chairs, shocked, stunned beyond words, certain there had been a monstrous error.

Startled, Jackson's head thrust forward and he exclaimed, "Aye? Does Abraham Baldwin vote aye?"

The calm, studied answer came back. "Yes. I vote aye."

Washington and Franklin sat wide-eyed, unmoving for one moment, struggling to accept what had happened. With the vote tied, five to five, Abraham Baldwin, a confirmed large state supporter, had voted for the small states! With his vote of aye, and Houstoun's vote of nay, Georgia was divided. Houstoun and Baldwin had cancelled each other! Georgia had not broken the tie. Neither side had won! The Union had survived. The small states had lived to fight another day!

The room filled with the outburst from the small state delegates. On the dais, Washington grasped the fact that the astonishing results of the vote had subtly shifted the momentum. It was now the large states who were on the defensive, trying to recover from the shock of the vote that had robbed them of certain victory. Washington let the din roll on for a time, watching the large state delegates like a hawk, fearing they might burst into some demonstration.

Slowly the room quieted, and when he could be heard, Oliver Ellsworth stood and waited until Washington recognized him.

"I respectfully move that a committee composed of one man from each state be appointed to create a compromise which will be acceptable to both the large and the small states."

Both Madison and Wilson rose to condemn any such notion, but failed. The motion was approved by a resounding majority.

Washington flattened both palms on his desk. "The motion passes. Agreeable to all, the committee will be appointed by ballot."

Ballots were cast, Jackson counted them, and the committee was announced. From the large states, Gerry, Franklin, Mason, William Davies, and Rutledge. From the small states, Ellsworth, Yates, Paterson, Bedford, Martin, and Baldwin.

For a moment Washington studied the eleven men. *The committee favors the small states! Those chosen from the large states will tend to compromise!* The expression on his face did not change as he inquired, "Is there anything else?"

"Yes, Mr. President. This is July second. May I suggest that it would be much in the interests of this convention to reward ourselves with a brief respite? Tomorrow is July third, and Wednesday is July fourth. Might we adjourn until July fifth, to give the newly appointed committee time to deliberate, and to celebrate the anniversary of the signing of the Declaration of Independence?"

Those nearest saw the immense relief and the tiny smile that flickered on Washington's face.

"This convention is adjourned until ten o'clock on July fifth."

It was later, in the privacy of his own library in his home at Franklin Court, that Benjamin Franklin sat sipping hot chocolate, reflecting on the unbelievable results of the day. For several terrifying moments the very existence of the United States had hung by a single tenuous, tiny thread. One vote—a single vote—from a man dedicated to the forces that would have destroyed the convention and the country—had abandoned his declared loyalty and saved both. What had caused it? Why had Abraham Baldwin breached his own commission to vote with the small states? What was in his mind?

A slow smile crossed the wrinkled, jowled face of the old man. *What was in Baldwin's mind? I doubt he will ever say. We'll likely never know. Odd how such things happen. Some delegates absent, some tardy, and the United States survives because one man changes one vote. It seems to me that man rose above himself—saw his place in history—and answered the call. Like sparrows that fall and nations that rise. Odd.*

He smiled again and squinted one eye to gingerly sip at his steaming chocolate.

Notes

The material appearing in this chapter is taken from the following:

Moyers, *Report from Philadelphia*, pages named Wednesday, June 20, 1787, through Monday, July 2, 1787.

Warren, *The Making of the Constitution*, pp. 233–65.

Bernstein, *Are We to Be a Nation?* pp. 161–67.

Farrand, *The Records of the Federal Convention*, pp. 334–521.

Berkin, *A Brilliant Solution*, pp. 103–12.

Rossiter, *1787: The Grand Convention*, pp. 182–92.

Farrand, *The Framing of the Constitution of the United States*, pp. 91–98.

The descriptions of the individual delegates, such as Nathaniel Gorham, Luther Martin, Abraham Baldwin, and others, including photographs of paintings of most of them, are found in Rossiter, *1787: The Grand Convention*, pp. 79–159, as well as in other texts too numerous to list.

The reader is again reminded that the lengthy speeches given by Madison and Franklin on the subject of prayer, and others, are much abbreviated, since the full text would be far beyond the limits of this book. However, this writer has attempted to preserve the essence of those speeches, and any inaccuracies or failures are mine.

CHAPTER XXI

★ ★ ★

*S*omething in the Grand Convention had changed in the two days since its adjournment on July second. It was in the air like the first faint scent of blossoms in the spring, or of fresh rain coming when there are yet no clouds in the sky. It was in the eyes and the faces of the delegates as they came steadily to the Statehouse on Thursday, July fifth.

It was true they had taken the two days to turn their backs on the insufferable heat of the closed room and the hostile standoff between the large and small states that had all but wrecked the convention. They had joined the Philadelphians in their raucous celebration commemorating the creation of the Declaration of Independence. The delegates had vented their pent up anger and frustration by mixing in the great parades and the demonstrations and spending the evenings at outdoor restaurants and taverns that abundantly flourished in the cool breeze of the Delaware River waterfront. The Indian Queen Hotel and the City Hotel were jammed with guests dressed in costumes, and the din and merriment reached far into the night with fireworks that lit up the entire city and brought exclamations from its citizens as they danced in the lighted streets. On July fourth, the churches had been filled, and the clergy had thumped the pulpit soundly as they assured their enthusiastic congregations that the Almighty himself had raised up this nation for his own divine purposes, and had smiled most graciously upon Philadelphia, his favorite city.

But with all the patriotic hubbub behind, a concerned George Washington felt the subtle shift in the East Room as he walked first to his table on the floor of the convention, and then on to the dais to take his chair as president. Whatever was in the air had not yet taken form and shape and definition, but it was there. Something was different.

For a moment Washington remained standing, silently studying those who had polarized the large states from the small to the brink of destroying America. Madison and Morris, leaders of the large states, were both at their tables, passive, saying little, gesturing not at all. Bedford, outspoken champion of the small states, wore the expression of a man devoid of concerns as he set his table in order. Franklin had his chair somewhat back from his desk, moving his feet, face drawn in discomfort.

Washington knew, as did nearly everyone on the floor, that some time during the two-day hiatus, the committee appointed late in the afternoon of July second to invent a compromise—slanted as the committee was in favor of the small states—had found time to meet and thrash out a proposal to be presented on the floor as the first order of business. Strong rumor had it that it was Franklin who had finally laid it out to the committee, plain and simple. Neither side was going to get all it wanted. Both had to give something. Compromise or fail. Then he had set out three very simple propositions that would fit within those boundaries. What they were remained unknown to the delegates.

Washington sat down, the room quieted, and he gestured to Secretary Jackson to call roll. There was mild surprise when it was discovered that Oliver Ellsworth of Connecticut was absent with illness, and that his place on the eleven-man committee had been filled by his Connecticut colleague, Roger Sherman.

Washington continued, "Is the committee prepared to make its report?"

Elbridge Gerry, thin, sharp features cast in an habitual frown that suggested indigestion, rose. "I have been appointed to speak for the committee."

Washington nodded. "Proceed."

"The committee recommends three propositions."

The room quieted, and men leaned forward, listening intently.

"In the House of Representatives there should be one representative for every forty thousand inhabitants in each state."

There was a rustle as men moved, and Gerry continued.

"The House of Representatives shall have the power to originate all bills for raising or appropriating money and for fixing salaries, not to be altered or amended by the second branch."

There was quiet murmuring, then silence as the convention waited for the committee's solution to the final and most critical issue. How was the Senate to be selected? It was the Gordian knot that until that moment had confounded them.

Gerry concluded. "That in the Senate, each state shall have an equal vote."

For one brief moment no one spoke or stirred, and then chairs creaked as men straightened and stared down at their tables while they struggled to grasp the meaning of what they had heard.

Selecting the House of Representatives according to population would favor states with larger numbers, clearly a blow to smaller states with less.

Selecting the Senate on the basis of one from each state would give the small states equal footing with the larger—a major blow to the large states.

Each, the large states and the small, had gained something, and each had lost something.

Washington glanced at Franklin, sitting back, fingers laced across his considerable paunch, mouth puckered thoughtfully, eyes squinted as he looked and listened to those around him.

Gerry paused to let the murmuring subside, and the blank look to disappear from the eyes of the delegates, then spoke again.

"As for myself, I urge you to accept the compromise, but I must frankly state that many of us on the committee—myself included—have objections to some particular parts of it. My reasons for urging its acceptance are simple. Unless a compromise takes place, a secession will occur.

The small states will disassociate from the union. If we do not come to some agreement among ourselves, some foreign sword will probably do the work for us."

Gerry stopped and sat down while his sobering words hit home.

George Mason of the large state of Virginia came to his feet. All eyes were on this man whose gifted judgment and model history carried the respect of every delegate present. There was not a sound as his voice rose with unprecedented passion, and he delivered the statement that reached to the core of every man.

"Accommodation is the object. It could not be more inconvenient to any gentleman in this convention to remain absent from his private affairs than it is for me." He paused and leaned forward, finger thumping his table as his voice rang off the walls. "But I would bury my bones in this city rather than expose this country to the consequences of a dissolution of this convention without anything being done!"

George Mason! Owner of the great estate of Gunston Hall, state of Virginia! One of the richest and most powerful. In his own right and in his own circles, almost as impressive as Washington. A key figure in the drafting of the Virginia Constitution and the Virginia Bill of Rights! A leader of the cause of the large states, now placing higher value on preserving the union than on winning the struggle against the small states!

Mason sat down, and for a moment no one moved.

Then Paterson rose and declared the proposal took too much from the small states and sat down. Instantly Madison was on his feet, blue eyes alive, words spaced for emphasis.

"If I must have the option between justice and gratifying the majority of the people, or of conciliating the smaller states, I must choose justice and the majority! It is vain to purchase accord in this convention on terms which would perpetuate discord among our constituents. This convention ought to pursue a plan which will bear the test of examination, and which will be espoused and supported by the enlightened and impartial part of America."

He paused, ordered his thoughts, and went on.

"I do not believe that Delaware and other smaller states will bid defiance to the remainder of the union."

The arguments wore on into the day with the snarl of opinions becoming worse as the summer heat inside the room increased. But from the dais, Washington sensed it. That "something" that was changing was the delegates. They had somehow grasped the place they were carving out in history. They could remain obdurate and wreck the union, or they could compromise and save it. Give. Take. Be satisfied. Move on. They were learning, but they were learning slowly and with great pain.

He adjourned for the night, and the following morning, July sixth, saw a glimmer of hope when the first motion placed on the floor was for the appointment of a special committee to address the question of fixing the ratio of votes for members in the House of Representatives to one seat for each forty thousand inhabitants. A ballot was taken, and five men took on the thorny problem: Gouverneur Morris, Gorham, Randolph, Rutledge, and King.

The next issue before them was the wisdom of granting the power over the money to the House of Representatives, and to them only.

The battle-weary delegates took a deep breath and launched into it, and the arguments piled on top of each other.

Gerry insisted the House of Representatives must hold the purse strings of the country because they were most responsible to the people. After all, in the states of Delaware, Maryland, Massachusetts, New Hampshire, New Jersey, South Carolina, and Virginia, the state constitutions vested the money power in the House of Representatives, and they were doing well.

Butler of South Carolina stoutly declared that giving the sole power of the purse strings to the House of Representatives was a form of discrimination against the Senate that decent men would not tolerate. If the Senate was to be degraded by lack of trust in their ability to handle the purse strings, or at least their share of it, then good men would not run for the Senate, but for the House instead.

King and Madison were adamant. Since the Senate would be generally

a more capable set of men, it would be wrong to disable them from giving their wisdom to the handling of the money of the new nation.

With weariness riding the delegation, the issue of which chamber of
the Congress would control the money came to a vote in the late afternoon. The East Room fell silent as the results were posted.

Ayes, five: North Carolina, Connecticut, New Jersey, Delaware, and
Maryland. Nays, three: Pennsylvania, Virginia, and South Carolina.
Massachusetts, New York, and Georgia, all divided—no vote.

It had been decided. The purse strings of the new nation would be
exclusively in the hands of the House of Representatives. Washington
adjourned the convention for the night.

Saturday morning, July seventh, the delegation once more plunged
into the morass of conflicting opinions from which they seemed unable
to retreat. As the day wore on, they tested the waters by proposing that
they take a preliminary vote to determine whether the proposition of one
vote for each state in the Senate should even remain as part of the report
of the eleven-man committee.

"This is the critical question," Gerry declared, "and while I am
opposed to the provision as a separate question, I would rather agree to
finding out now if we are at an impasse, or finding out later after we have
squandered more time. A government short of a proper national plan
would be preferable to one with such a plan that would cause discontent
among some states."

Sherman rose in support, and Wilson rose in opposition.

The vote was called, and Jackson recorded the results.

Ayes, six.

Nays, three.

Two states divided, with no vote.

The issue would remain in the report for further debate and final
vote. The small-state delegates began to breathe once again.

The convention adjourned until Monday morning, July ninth, to
gather and fall silent as they listened intently to the report of the committee of five who had been assigned the delicate problem of proposing
the number of representatives each state should have in the new House

of Representatives. Gouverneur Morris rose to represent the committee, and with a sheet of paper in hand delivered the results. The other delegates sat at their tables, quills in hand, scratching out the names and the numbers as they were announced.

New Hampshire, two.

Massachusetts, seven.

Rhode Island, one.

Connecticut, four.

New York, five.

New Jersey, three.

Pennsylvania, eight.

Delaware, one.

Maryland, four.

Virginia, nine.

North Carolina, five.

South Carolina, five.

Georgia, two.

By this proposal, there would be fifty-six men in the new House of Representatives.

"However," Morris continued, "as the present situation of the states may probably alter in both wealth and the number of inhabitants, the legislature should be authorized from time to time to augment the number of representatives."

Sherman rose. "On what principles or calculations are these numbers based? It does not appear to correspond to any rule, or any plan previously adopted by congress."

Gorham responded. "Some provision of this sort was necessary in the outset. The number of blacks and whites with some regard to supposed wealth was the general guide. Fractions of numbers were not considered. We did not follow the rule of one representative for every 40,000 inhabitants for two reasons. First, that with growth, there would soon be too many representatives, and second, if western states are admitted to the union in sizeable numbers, they would soon outvote the Atlantic states."

Gouverneur Morris rose. "This report is little more than a guess. We attempted to create it in light of the realities now existing, as we saw them."

Then William Paterson of New Jersey stood, and both Washington and Franklin focused on him. It was Paterson who had in previous debate at the convention made it known that he could not abide considering the slaves in any calculations dealing with electing members of the new congress.

"I consider the report of the committee, which is based on estimates of what the future will bring, to be too vague. New Jersey is against it. I can regard Negro slaves in no light other than property. They are not free agents, have no personal liberty, no means to acquire property, and in fact are themselves nothing more than property."

He paused in the dead silence, aware he had reopened one of the most delicate issues of the entire convention, and then he went on.

"What is the true principle of representation? It is a process accepted by all to send a few men to a forum where their political business can be handled, because the people themselves are either too numerous, or too widely scattered, to meet themselves. And, if such a meeting of the people were actually to take place, would the slaves be allowed to vote? No! Why then should they be represented in the new national congress?"

He stopped to consider his last remarks before he delivered them. "I am against counting the slaves in any manner when determining the voting power for seats in the new congress because it will encourage more slave trade. May I remind you, that the Confederation Congress, which has failed us, were admittedly ashamed to use the term *slaves* in their business, and to avoid it, used a description. *Other persons.*"

The arguments would not cease.

Once again, the motion was made to deliver the whole conflicted matter to another committee, one man from each state in the East Room, for them to reconsider the report from the first committee that was now under fire, and to report their findings based on the arguments heard that day.

The new committee was appointed, and the convention adjourned for the day.

Tuesday morning, July tenth, Rufus King of Massachusetts stood when Washington called for the report of the new committee. King read the report, then laid the copy on the desk of Secretary Jackson, and Jackson read it again, loud, slow.

The House of Representatives shall consist of sixty-five members, as follows:

Rhode Island and Delaware, one each.

New Hampshire and Georgia, three each.

New Jersey, four.

North Carolina, South Carolina, and Connecticut, five each.

Maryland and New York, six each.

Massachusetts and Pennsylvania, eight each.

Virginia, ten.

There was no letup in the disputes, and motions ran rampant. Half the states moved to get a larger number of representatives than the report gave them, and to take them from other states if necessary. None could understand the basis on which this new proposal was made. Yesterday it was fifty-six members in the House of Representatives, and today it is sixty-five! What accounted for the gain of nine new members?

In the late afternoon, with frustration coming close to anger, it was finally proposed that the whole mess be given back to the original committee of eleven, with the request that they furnish the convention with an explanation of the principles on which the latest set of numbers came to rest.

The motion was defeated, ten votes to one.

Paterson prepared a chart showing the total population of each state, and the proportion of slaves in each, to prove the number sixty-five was based on fact. It was ignored.

Brearly prepared his own chart, which resulted in a total of ninety delegates being the correct number. His chart was discarded.

Madison insisted the number of representatives ought to be doubled.

Sherman recommended the total should not exceed fifty.

All proposals became lost in a hopeless muddle of populations, wealth, slaves, conflicting claims, and rising tempers.

It was then made known that the two remaining delegates from New York, Robert Yates and John Lansing were leaving the convention with no intention of returning. Alexander Hamilton, the third member of the New York delegation had left weeks earlier. The reasons Yates and Lansing were leaving, which left no one representing New York? They thought the convention was exceeding its authority; that it was not practical to establish a government intended to reach all parts of the United States; and that any such government could only destroy the civil liberties of its citizens.

Few could remember a more somber closing when Washington adjourned for the day. Nor did any know that when he reached his quarters in the Robert Morris mansion, Washington sat down for a long time, head bowed, shoulders slumped, in utter despair. It was later in the evening that he took up his quill and poured out the despondency and fears that were tearing his heart in a letter to his former aide and long-time friend, Alexander Hamilton, in New York.

"When I refer you to the state of the counsels which have prevailed at the period you left this city, and add that they are now, if possible, in a worse train than ever, you will find but little ground on which the hope of a good establishment can be formed. In a word, I almost despair of seeing a favorable issue to the proceedings of our convention, and do therefore repent having had any agency in the business. The men who oppose a strong and energetic government, are, in my opinion, narrow-minded politicians. . . . The apprehension expressed by them, that the people will not accede to the form proposed, is the *ostensible,* not the *real* cause of opposition. . . . The proper question ought nevertheless to be: Is it or is it not the best form that such a country as this can adopt? If it be the best, we must recommend it. . . . I am sorry you went away. I wish you were back. The crisis is equally important and alarming, and no opposition, under such circumstances, should discourage exertions till the signature is offered."

Washington, the man with a will of steel, lost in hopeless despair?

Repentant of ever having associated with the Grand Convention? The man who had alone borne the revolution on his shoulders for eight harsh years? Sick in his heart?

Only Washington would ever know the feelings that rode him that night. Did his thoughts reach back to the early months of 1778 when he and his army were camped a short twenty-six miles from Philadelphia, along the frozen banks of the Schuylkill River at the place called Valley Forge, sick, emaciated, freezing, starving to death? Three thousand of them dead and buried in five months, rather than fail their country. Was it all lost? Those terrible, black days, wasted? Eight years of struggle against odds that would have crushed a lesser man—all for nothing?

Wednesday, July eleventh, the insoluble snarl worsened and the debate with it. What duty should be placed on the House of Representatives to police itself on a regular basis to be certain growing states, and new states, got their fair share of representatives? How often should such duty be exercised? Yearly? When needed?

Butler and Pinckney thumped their desks when they declared that the slaves ought to be included in the voting equally with the whites, and that the three-fifths recommendation be stricken from the record.

Gerry declared that the three-fifths rule was the highest figure that would even be considered. Mason agreed that slaves were valuable to the states where they provided labor, and ought to be in the mix, but not equal to whites. Three-fifths was acceptable.

Paterson again hotly stated his opinion that slaves are nothing beyond property and ought not be included in the debate at all.

Gouverneur Morris rose to declare that the people of his state— Pennsylvania—would rise up in revolt if they found themselves on the same footing as slaves!

William Davies of North Carolina sprang up, hot, loud. "Three-fifths is the least ratio North Carolina will tolerate! Anything less, and I will leave the convention."

The fear that the southern states would walk out as a block if they were abused by the slavery issue had been lurking in the minds of every delegate present, and with the threat now thrown down by Davies still ringing off the walls, hot heads cooled, and a sense of sanity settled among the delegates.

They reached a consensus. Slaves would be counted on the basis of three-fifths. But the document that declared it did not use the term *slaves.* They were instead included in *other persons.* The delegates could not bring themselves to endure the embarrassment of the use of the term *slaves.*

The other arguments raged on and blended into July twelfth, then Friday, July thirteenth, and Saturday, July fourteenth. Sunday, July fifteenth, forced both sides to take a step back and cool their ardor, and reflect on what they saw coming in the morning.

The morning of Monday, July sixteenth, 1787, broke still and hot, as had so many other preceding mornings, but there was not a man who failed to sense the electricity in the air as the convention gathered again in the East Room. It was like something alive, raising the hair on their arms. They took their places and Washington called them to order.

"The first order of business is the question of representation in the Congress. Mr. Secretary, read the proposal."

Jackson read slowly and loudly, tracking with his finger on the written document.

"Representation in the House of Representatives shall be a total of sixty-five, subject to adjustment as needed in the future, which sixty-five shall be apportioned among the various states according to the numbers previously assigned."

He paused for a moment and then went on. "The House of Representatives shall be vested with the power of originating bills related to money, with no interference from the Senate."

Never had the room been so silent as when he read the last proposal:

"Each state shall have two senators in the Senate, each senator with an equal vote."

All that had gone before, beginning with the first shot fired on the small, beautiful green at Lexington the morning of April 19, 1775, was but prologue. The next three minutes would see the United States stand, or fall. It all came down to this.

Jackson called for the vote.

Massachusetts. Divided.

Connecticut. Aye.

New Jersey. Aye.

Pennsylvania. Nay.

Delaware. Aye.

Maryland. Aye.

Virginia. Nay.

North Carolina. Aye.

South Carolina. Nay.

Georgia. Nay.

With held breath the delegates counted the votes, and counted again.

Five ayes.

Four nays.

Massachusetts divided, no vote. Had Massachusetts not been divided—if either Gerry or Strong, who voted aye, had not done so, but had voted no with King and Gorham, the proposal would have deadlocked and failed, and the United States would have ceased to be. By the paper-thin margin of one vote, the United States would stand. The delegates from the large states sat dejected, shoulders slumped, eyes glazed, grasping for what to do.

Edmund Randolph of Virginia stormed to his feet, nearly out of control in anger. "I wish this convention to adjourn that the large states might consider the steps proper to be taken in the present solemn crisis."

Gasps were heard throughout the hall. Adjourn? Simply stop and go home? Finish nothing? Abandon the Grand Convention?

Whatever Randolph had in mind, it was William Paterson who jerked out of his seat and turned directly to Randolph, voice hot, too loud, too accusing, and in two sentences threw down the challenge to Randolph.

"I think, with Mr. Randolph, that it is high time for the convention to adjourn, that the rule of secrecy ought to be rescinded, and that we be allowed to go to our constituents and tell them exactly what has just happened, and by whom. I second Mr. Randolph's motion with all my heart!"

Randolph recoiled and fumbled to recover some sense of poise. For three seconds that seemed an eternity he tried to formulate something—anything—that would not result in his becoming the man that history would never forget as the one who tried to destroy America. He raised one hand defensively and his voice was shaking.

"No, no, I am sorry my meaning was so readily and strangely misinterpreted. I never meant an adjournment *sine die*. I had it in view merely to adjourn until tomorrow in order that some conciliatory experiment might, if possible, be devised, and that if the small states should continue to hold back, the larger states might then take such measures as might be necessary."

For whatever reason, Mr. Randolph did not mention one such measure.

The vote for adjournment until tomorrow, July seventeenth, passed, Ayes, seven, Nays, two, one state divided.

Washington watched the men arrange their tables and walk out, some talking, others silent as they tried to understand the significance of what had happened in the few explosive minutes the convention was in session. States that had been ready to dissolve the United States had stayed the course. They had risen above themselves to accept the vote. Randolph had fired the last, lone shot, and then backed down.

The morose, sick feeling that had crept into Washington's heart lifted. He gathered the papers from his desk on the dais and raised his head once more to watch the delegates.

They have learned. That is what has been different the past several days—in the air. They were learning. They have risen above themselves—above selfish interests—above lust for power. Give and take. Compromise.

He tucked his papers under his arm and descended to floor level, and walked steadily down the aisle, and out into the great corridor.

Notes

The events, dates, persons, times, places, and speeches appearing in this chapter are taken from the following sources:

Berkin, *A Brilliant Solution,* pp. 107–12.

Warren, *The Making of the Constitution,* pp. 271–312.

Bernstein, *Are We to Be a Nation?* pp. 168–72.

Moyers, *Report from Philadelphia,* pages named Thursday, July 5, 1787, through Monday, July 16, 1787.

Farrand, *The Framing of the Constitution,* pp. 96–112.

Rossiter, *1787: The Grand Convention,* pp. 186–92.

Farrand, *The Records of the Federal Convention,* Volume 1, pp. 509–606; Volume 2, pp. 1–20.

Again the reader is reminded that the speeches and the proceedings have been abridged because it is impossible to include all that was said and debated in this work. Some speeches have been modified to make them more understandable today. Every effort has been made to preserve the intent and meaning of the speeches and debate, and any errors are those of this writer.

The very morose letter written by George Washington to Alexander Hamilton, in which Washington expressed despair and a feeling of repentance at even being part of the convention, is found in Warren, *The Making of the Constitution,* p. 284. The part appearing herein is nearly verbatim. It is the only instance where this writer has encountered such deep despondency in a document written by Washington.

The Atlantic, North of the Bahamas
Mid-July, 1787

CHAPTER XXII

$\mathcal{T}$he sameness of the days on the *Zephyr* became a blur as she plowed steadily north from her passage through the Straits of Florida, under a great yellow sun pounding heat down from the heavens during the days, and a velvet black dome overhead at night, spread with an eternity of stars that seemed so close the crew on the deck could almost reach up and stir them. Thirty-four men on board the tiny schooner were far too many; too much idle time on such a small vessel could all too quickly lead to trouble. Thus it was that from the break of dawn following the night they had shot their way out of Port Royal in a howling storm, Caleb had set four daily shifts that left no man with time on his hands. The deck had been soapstoned twice, all sails repaired, the cannon dismantled, cleaned, wrapped in canvas, and stored against the railings to appear as deck cargo, and all compartments below decks cleaned until they were spotless. The pants and shirts of the seamen were mended, beards and hair trimmed. Utensils in the galley had been rubbed with clean sand until they shone. All ropes and hawsers on the decks were coiled, and the anchor chain had been scraped of all barnacles.

They had flown the British Union Jack from the mainmast until they were clear of the Bahamas and out into the Atlantic, and then they raised the stars and stripes as they sped north, ninety miles off the East Florida coast. For the first three days they had a twenty-four hour watch on the stern of the ship and in the crow's nest, telescopes in hand, watching south for any vessel flying the British flag that appeared to be in pursuit. There were none. They had seen ships with flags from three continents, but none had approached them. The fourth day they relaxed the vigil and reverted to the standard watch of two men on deck and one in the crow's nest. They did not think there was a British ship in the Bahamas or the Caribbean that could catch the *Zephyr* in the open waters of the Atlantic.

In the glaring midmorning heat, Bartolo descended the rope ladder from the crow's nest, and Pike made the sixty-foot climb, telescope in hand, to stand in the tiny cylinder while he scanned the horizon for sails and studied the clear waters off the bow for sandbars and coral reefs that appeared on no charts. The sails were tight and the little vessel cut a twenty-foot curl hissing as she sped north on seas only slightly ruffled by a steady southeast wind, to leave a white wake more than one hundred yards behind her stern.

Onboard the men went about the dullness of their duties, sometimes grinning for no reason, and humming, and occasionally bursting into a snatch of a sea shantey or a church hymn learned in their childhood. The spirit among them seemed to be a mix of well-being, and pride. Leaving Boston, few had expected to find themselves in the infamous Port Royal harbor on the island of Jamaica in the middle of the Caribbean Sea. And none had dreamed that under the cover of a wind-driven cloudburst they would open a British prison with four kegs of gunpowder, liberate six-teen Americans, blow fourteen British longboats to splinters, and escape the harbor by blasting the second deck out of a British man-o'-war, to leave her burning and sinking in the storm.

American soil was ninety miles to the west. If the winds held they would pass St. Augustine in the dusk of evening, and the great seaport of Savannah, Georgia, not long before dawn. From there, north and west past the Carolinas, the Chesapeake, Delaware Bay, New York, Cape Cod, and home. There was magic in the word, and the crew on the *Zephyr* was feeling good.

Up in the private little world of the crow's nest, Pike raised his tele-scope and slowly turned from north to west, studying the flat line where the blue sky met the blue-green sea, and there was nothing. He continued his turn past south, then east, and back to north. There was not a sail in sight. He lowered his telescope and for a moment glanced down at the men on the deck below. He was raising his head when something in the sea fifty yards ahead and to starboard caught his eye, and he paused, hand raised to shield out the sun, trying to find it again, and then it was there, and he recognized it and recoiled.

"*Man in the water,*" he shouted, "*fifty yards ahead, to starboard!*"

Within seconds most of the crew was crowded along the bow railings, squinting against the sun-glare on the water, searching, and they saw it and for a moment stood in silence. A black body clad only in a loincloth was bobbing face down in the water, arms outspread.

Young shouted, "Spill the sails! Ready with a longboat!"

Seasoned men were in the rigging in less than one minute, turning the sails away from the wind, and the little ship was slowing as the body passed less than thirty feet from the staboard side.

"Slave," Tunstall murmured.

Two minutes later a longboat was in the water, and as the *Zephyr* settled and stopped, the dead body was lifted limp and dripping and laid in the bottom of the longboat. The four men swung the boat around and brought her back alongside the schooner and lifted the corpse high to waiting hands that laid the body on the deck. With the crew gathered in a silent circle, staring at the dead black man, the ship's surgeon knelt beside the body, thrust two fingers under the jaw, and closed his eyes to concentrate. After a few moments, he shook his head, then briefly examined the body before standing and backing away.

Kneeling beside the corpse, Caleb looked up at the surgeon. "How long has it been in the water?"

"Not long. Maybe a day."

Caleb inspected the dead man. Short, blocky build, muscular, broad nose, thick lips. The scalp was split and the crown of the skull was caved in. The scarred wrists and ankles were raw from iron shackles. The back was criss-crossed with long welts from a whip, some old and healed, some still open. The mouth was sagged open, and four front teeth were missing. The face was that of a forty-year-old man. Caleb was no stranger to death and violence, but when he rose his face was white. He spoke again to the surgeon.

"You see his head?"

"I saw it."

"Is that what killed him? Someone broke his skull?"

"Probably. If it didn't kill him, he would never have recovered from it."

"How old was he?"

"I'm guessing twenty-five. Maybe younger."

"Those scars on his back. How old?"

"The oldest? Fifteen years or thereabouts."

"They were beating him when he was ten?"

The surgeon nodded but stood silent, and Caleb continued.

"How did he lose the teeth?"

"Broken out. The stumps are still there."

Caleb's voice was quiet, and his eyes were like lightning as he concluded. "Have someone wrap him in canvas and get him belowdecks." He turned to Young. "He has to be from a slaver. I think she's ahead of us. What do you say?"

Young bobbed his head. "A slaver. Likely loaded at Santo Domingo, or Puerto Rico. Somewhere down there. Headed north. I'd expect Savannah, or Charleston. She's ahead of us."

Caleb cupped a hand to his mouth to call up to Pike, "Look sharp for more bodies, and for sails ahead of us."

"Aye, sir."

He turned to Tunstall. "Are we in waters usual to ships carrying cargo?"

"One of the main routes. If you're asking will that slaver hold this course, my guess is yes, or close to it."

"Then so do we. Tell the helmsman."

Tunstall turned and walked back to the helmsman.

Caleb spoke to the silent crew. "Put out all canvas. Spankers, jib, all of it."

Within minutes the little ship was cutting a thirty-foot curl, leaving a two-hundred yard white-water wake, both masts creaking under the strain of all sails full and tight. The crew went about their duties by habit while they peered north with the image of the dead black man bright in their minds. At one o'clock Bartolo took his second shift in the crow's nest. Shortly before two o'clock his excited voice rang out.

"Man in the water, fifty yards dead ahead!"

After they recovered the body, the crew on deck lifted it aboard, and the four in the longboat climbed the net back onto the schooner. They left the longboat in the water, tied alongside, riding light behind the curl. Minutes later Bartolo's arm shot up again, pointing.

"Man in the water, eighty yards ahead, to port!"

By half-past three in the afternoon, with the sun past its zenith, they had the bodies of five black slaves on board, wrapped in canvas, stored belowdecks. Four were men. One was a woman. Each showed the swelling and bruises on their wrists and ankles from iron shackles, and fresh scars and fresh welts on their backs from whippings. The crew moved through their duties mechanically with the growing feeling they were entering into something evil, something to be feared, something that could bring judgments down on their heads. They remained silent, peering ahead for sails.

Young motioned to Caleb and led him to his cramped quarters. "What's your plan if we catch the slaver?"

Caleb's face was a blank, his voice subdued, eyes points of light. "I don't know yet."

Young raised a warning hand. "Slavery is legal. The law says if we interfere with a ship engaged in lawful trade we can be charged with piracy. Hanged."

"I know that."

Young came directly to it. "Do you plan to do something about the slaver if we find it?"

"Maybe."

"You want to get all thirty-four of us hanged?"

"No."

In that moment Young saw something in Caleb's eyes, and he asked, "You have a personal stake in this?"

Caleb took a deep breath. "About eight years ago I was a prisoner of war in a British prison in South Carolina. I broke out and made a run. British pickets had me caught. A slave came out of nowhere and we swung a cannon around and fired it at them and we made it to the woods. His name was Primus. We came home on a ship where my older brother was captain. We came onto a slaver that had been demasted by a storm. They were throwing slaves overboard, some dead, some alive. We stopped the ship, and I went into the hold with my brother."

Caleb stopped and Young saw the sick look and then the rise of outrage come into Caleb's face as he continued.

"There was two feet of water in the hold. Blacks were down there, living in their own waste and filth. No one could lay down, or even sit down. The stink . . . " He stopped to swallow as the images came back, grotesque, inhuman. "More than a hundred, dead and dying. Sickness, starvation. Mothers with babies in their arms, both dead." His voice faltered and he paused for a moment. "We took that ship away from the crew and sailed it to port, and we used money from the war chest to buy wagons and horses. None of the slaves could speak English, so Primus and I took the ones that were still alive up to Nova Scotia and left them. Primus stayed. It was the best we could do for them. They built their own settlement. They may still be there, but I doubt it. I think as soon as they could they sold everything and bought passage on a ship back to Africa. I hope they did. I hope they're home. I hope Primus made it."

Caleb tilted his head forward to stare downward for a time, and it was Young who broke the silence.

"You intend doing the same thing if we catch this slaver?"

"Probably."

"And what of the law?"

Caleb's voice rose. "Whose law? Man's law that says slaves are property, like an ox. What about nature's law that says no man has the right to make another his slave? Which is right? Man's law, or nature's?"

Young stood silent, awed by the passion in Caleb, and Caleb went on.

"We told the British to give us our freedom, and we had to fight

them for six years to get it. Now, another six years have passed, and what
we're doing to those black men is a hundred times worse than what the
British were doing to us! If we catch that slaver, I don't think I'll hesitate. I think I'll take the ship away from the crew and do what I can for
the slaves."

Young waited until Caleb brought himself under control before he
answered.

"The law is the law. You better tell the crew if you intend to break it.
They have a right to choose if they want to be part of it."

"I will when the time comes."

The cooks were just beginning evening mess when the call came
from the crow's nest. *"Sails ahead. Maybe six miles, ten degrees off starboard."*

Within minutes every man on board the *Zephyr* was crowded against
the railings at the bow of the ship, hands raised to shield out the sun
while they strained to see the sails, still invisible except to the man in the
crow's nest with the telescope. Minutes passed while they stood still,
searching, and then one hand shot up, pointing.

"There! Dead ahead."

It was there. The slightest irregularity on the flat horizon.

The small schooner held her course and kept her canvas full, and she
knifed through the water as though with a will of her own, gaining on
the distant speck with every passing minute. At two miles the shout came
down from the crow's nest, "She's flying the Spanish flag."

Tunstall murmured, "She has to be from Santo Domingo."

Young turned to Caleb. "You intend telling the men? Now's the
time."

Caleb turned far enough to speak to the entire crew. His voice rang
out.

"If that is a slaver, I intend taking the ship away from the crew. We'll
put them in longboats and they can make it to the Florida coast. I'm
taking the ship on north, maybe as far as Canada. I intend setting the
cargo free."

He stopped to look into the faces of crew. Some were wide-eyed,
startled. Most were an expressionless, blank. Caleb went on.

"It will be an outright act of piracy. We could be hanged. If any of you do not want to get into this, say so now. You can go belowdecks until this is over as proof you refused to take part. No one can fault you for choosing not to break the law. Make up your minds. If you want to stay clear of it, go belowdecks before I start the action and stay there until it's over. Does everyone understand?"

Men looked to their right and left, and there was murmuring, and then quiet.

Caleb looked directly at the crew. "You're sure, then? It could mean trouble."

He waited again, but no one moved to go below.

Caleb turned to Tunstall. "Hold this course and bring us up about eighty yards from their starboard side."

Tunstall nodded and Caleb turned to Young. "Pass out muskets to every man. Get pistols for you and me and Tunstall and Adam. Get the cannon mounted and loaded. Two on each side with cannonballs, four with grapeshot. Get the muzzles on the rails."

"Aye, sir."

The crew swarmed over the cannon to uncover them, mount the barrels on the carriages, and ram the powder then the wadding then the cannonballs and grapeshot down the muzzles. They rolled them forward, lifted the barrels, then rolled them the last foot to leave the muzzles resting on the railings, angled upward. Finished, they picked up their muskets and walked the rolling deck back to the bow to watch the ship ahead growing larger with every passing minute. Caleb and Adam each shoved two pistols into their belts while they watched the crew, waiting, but none of them chose to go belowdecks.

Young spoke to Caleb. "What flag are you going to fly?"

Caleb reflected for a moment. "Spanish." A moment later he shook his head. "No, American. Leave it up there."

The gap between the two vessels shortened and then they were passing the stern of the heavy, three-masted freighter with the name *Angelique* carved in beautifully scrolled cursive beneath the windows of the captain's quarters. Her crew stood at their starboard rail, startled, staring down in near total disbelief at a schooner one-third their size flying the American flag, with twelve cannon mounted and apparently loaded, and gun crews standing beside them with smoking linstocks and muskets. Less than eighty yards separated the two ships.

The *Zephyr* spilled half her sails and slowed to keep pace with the heavy, more cumbersome freighter, and the captain of the larger ship used his horn to shout in broken English with a heavy Castillian accent, "Who are you? What is your purpose?"

Caleb raised his horn. "We are the *Zephyr.* American. *Angelique,* what is your cargo?"

There was anger in the voice of the squat, bearded captain. "That is not your concern! Declare your intentions!"

Caleb's voice boomed. "We have five dead bodies below. Four men, one woman. African. We believe they belong to you. If you are a slaver, declare yourself!"

The Captain on the freighter barked orders to his crew, and the men on the *Zephyr* stood in silence while they watched muskets and bayonets being rapidly passed out to the seamen on the railing of the larger ship. The Spanish crew measured gunpowder down the barrels and used their ramrods to seat the wadding and then the musketball, and then brought them to bear on the crew of the schooner. The voice of their captain rolled across the water.

"We declare nothing. Withdraw or we will assume you a pirate and fire on you."

Caleb's voice was paced, loud, disciplined. "Fire when you will. Our cannon are loaded with grape- and solid shot. This crew has muskets."

The armed crew on the larger ship glanced at each other, and the muzzles of their muskets wavered. More than half of them lowered their gun barrels as they stared down at the six cannon, muzzles angled upward. Too well did they know that if three or four of them were loaded with grapeshot, most of the crew on the *Angelique* would be blown halfway across the deck of their ship in the first blast.

For twenty seconds that seemed endless, both crews stood to their guns, the Spanish with their muskets, the Americans with their cannon and muskets, while the two ships plowed on in the heat of the late after-noon with the wind quartering in from the east, blowing hot through their hair and beards. Then the outraged voice of the Spanish captain reached across the gap.

"You are in an act of piracy."

The determination in Caleb's voice could not be mistaken. "You have ten seconds. Declare your cargo."

Every man on both ships was counting seconds, and then the Spanish captain shouted, "Our cargo is legal. You have no right—."

Caleb turned to the first gun crew. "Put one through their mainsail."

The gun crew adjusted the muzzle slightly, the smoking linstock dropped, the powder at the touchhole caught, and the big gun roared and bucked. The ball punched through the mainsail nearly dead center to leave a black, ragged hole as the big ship plowed on. The great cloud of white gunsmoke was swept aside by the speed of the two vessels, and when it cleared only the captain was standing at the rail of the larger ship. The entire crew had backed away from the muzzles of those big guns on the smaller ship. Caleb pointed at the captain.

"Declare your cargo. Five seconds."

The captain was shaking with rage as he bellowed, "Africans. Africans."

"We're coming alongside. Order your men to lay down their mus-kets and get back against the port rail."

The captain shook his fist and thundered, "I have your name. I have your name. You will be hunted down and hanged for this piracy."

"Lay down those muskets, or the blood of your crew is on your hands. Five seconds."

The captain turned and shouted orders in Spanish. His crew laid down their muskets and backed away, waiting his next command.

Caleb turned to Tunstall and the helmsman. "Bring us alongside," and then to Young, "Get the grappling hooks."

The little schooner veered to port, then to starboard to come along-side the heavier ship, and the grappling hooks arced over the five feet of dark Atlantic seawater that separated the two vessels to catch the railing of the *Angelique*, a full eight feet higher than the deck of the *Zephyr*. The crew of the small schooner pulled the hawsers tight and looped them over the cleats, and the sides of the two ships slammed together.

Caleb shouted to the captain, "Spill your sails and drop anchor. We're coming aboard." He turned to Young. "I'll take ten men. You stay here with the others and keep muskets on their crew. We'll collect their guns. If any of them go after them first, shoot."

Young licked dry lips and said, "Aye, sir."

Caleb spoke to Adam, standing to his right. "Keep your pistols where you can get to them. Pick nine more men with muskets and get ready to follow me."

"Aye, sir."

The Spanish captain shouted orders to his men and half of them scrambled into the rigging while Caleb ordered twelve of his own men up into the spars of the *Zephyr*, and within minutes both ships had emptied their sails and slowed to a stop. The anchor chain of the *Angelique* rattled and the two-thousand pound black iron hook hit the water and disappeared. The two ships were dead in the water, lashed together as one.

Caleb did not hesitate. With Adam and his nine men he climbed the hawsers binding the two ships together and dropped over the railing to the deck of the *Angelique*. The captain, short, barrel-chested, swarthy face twisted in fury, faced him fifteen feet away. His voice shook as he jerked an arm up, finger pointing at Caleb like a saber, and spoke.

"I have ships! They will hunt you down. You will hang! You and every man with you."

Caleb drew a pistol and held it at his side, loose and easy. "Adam, gather their muskets and get them on board the *Zephyr*."

While Adam and his men gathered the weapons and passed them over the starboard rail to waiting hands on the *Zephyr*, Caleb spoke to the captain. "I'm sending two men belowdecks. If any of your crew does anything we don't understand, you're the first one to be shot. Tell them."

The blocky man was trembling, face an ugly snarl, nearly out of control. "I will not!"

Caleb shrugged, cocked his pistol and brought it to bear on the third button of the captain's tunic. "On the count of five."

The only sound on the *Angelique* was the wind in the rigging while the crew silently counted to four before the captain shouted his orders to his men. Then he turned on Caleb and declared, "There is disease in the hold. Dysentery. Go down if you will."

Caleb gestured to Adam. "You know the smell of dysentery?"

"Yes." No man could ever forget the thick smell of the rotted linings of a man's stomach in his discharge, and every man who had served in an army from the dawn of time knew that dysentery had killed far more soldiers than grapeshot and cannon and bayonet.

"Take one man and go down into the hold. If you smell dysentery, come back out quick. If not, take a look."

"Aye, sir."

With one man following, Adam opened the small doors beneath the quarterdeck, paused to set his teeth against the stench that rolled out, then disappeared into the blackness. Caleb watched, expecting him to reappear within seconds, but one minute became two.

On the *Zephyr*, Tunstall was watching the Spanish crew like a hawk. Their dress, the sullen, dark look of pure hatred in their swarthy faces, their beards, and the rings in their ears. A strange look came into his face and he turned to look at Young, who wore the same puzzled expression.

Sounds came from the hold, and Adam and his man came from the blackness back onto the deck to stand erect, faces turned upward as they fought to breathe deeply of the clean, fresh air. Caleb waited, then asked, "Dysentery?"

Adam shook his head. "No. Starvation. They're about half-dead from starvation. Down there in their own filth. In chains. Some dead. Dying." He stared at the captain, unable to believe one human being could do to another the things he had seen in the twilight of the hold beneath their feet.

Caleb took two steps forward, and the muzzle of his pistol was less than three feet from the captain's chest when he asked, "You starved them?"

The captain was loud, defiant, defensive. "Rebellion. They rebelled. Without food they are too weak to rise up."

"The one with the crushed skull we found in the water?"

"Their leader."

"The other four we found?"

"They stirred them up."

"What port are you from?"

There was the slightest hesitation before the captain growled his answer. "Carenage."

Caleb had never heard of Carenage, but his expression did not change as he pointed. "Take me to your quarters. Now."

Caleb gestured and Adam followed the two men through the door into the small but ornately decorated quarters of the captain, where Caleb dragged the ship's war chest from beneath the captain's bunk.

He pointed to the huge iron lock. "Open it."

"I do not have the key."

Caleb shoved the muzzle of his pistol against the captain's throat. "Find it."

Thirty seconds later the lock was lying on the table and the heavy black hinges groaned as Caleb lifted the thick lid of the oak chest. Inside were six large leather pouches of gold French coins, a copy of the manifest, a list of the crew with their signatures, and the familiar insurance papers. With them was a contract for the purchase of the slaves by a man named Hairston in Charleston, South Carolina, from a French company named LeBlanc in Bordeaux, France. The ship to carry the slaves was the *Angelique*, whose home port was listed as Bordeaux.

For a moment Caleb pondered, then dropped the papers back into the chest and dropped the lid banging. He set the lock back in the hasp but did not close it, stuffed the key into his pocket, and grasped the thick iron handle on one end of the chest while Adam took the other. With the captain ahead of them, they climbed the five steps up the narrow passage back onto the deck, where the summer sun was casting long shadows eastward as it settled toward the western skyline.

The two brothers set the chest thumping on the deck, and Caleb called to Tunstall and Young. "Bring all the men and come over here."

The entire remaining crew of the *Zephyr* climbed onto the deck of the big freighter and faced Caleb, waiting.

He gestured to Young and Tunstall, then the chest. "Take a look at the papers inside. Tell me what's wrong."

Young slipped the lock from the hasp, opened the chest, and lifted out the papers. For a full minute he studied them, face drawn in puzzlement, then handed them to Tunstall, and waited while Tunstall peered at them.

Caleb spoke. "This man said his home port was Carenage. Where is Carenage?"

Tunstall's answer was instant. "An island in the Lesser Antilles called Saint Lucia. More than fifteen hundred miles southeast of here. French."

Caleb nodded. "I think those papers say the home port of this ship is Bordeaux, France, not Carenage. The company selling the slaves is LeBlanc, and this ship is the *Angelique.* All French. Not Spanish." He pointed upward. "This crew speaks Spanish and they fly the Spanish flag. Put it all together, and what have we got?"

For the first time the captain showed the faintest hint of fear, panic. Caleb watched him lick at his lips, and start to speak, then fall silent. To Caleb's left he saw the Spanish crew, wild-eyed, making calculations of how many would survive if they tried to cover the twenty-five feet between them and the Americans while the Americans were firing at point-blank range.

Caleb did not hesitate. "If your men are thinking resistance, you're the first one down. *Tell them!*"

The captain looked into Caleb's eyes and called orders to his men, and they settled, but the look of brazen defiance did not leave their faces.

Without moving Caleb spoke once more to Tunstall and Young. "What do those papers tell us?"

Suddenly Young's head jerked up, wide-eyed in stunned surprise as the truth broke clear in his mind. He pointed and blurted, "This crew stole this ship! They're pirates!"

Instantly the Spanish crew bolted for the Americans and the captain made a lunge for Caleb. Caleb and Adam fired their pistols in the same grain of time and the captain went down backwards. A dozen muskets from the *Zephyr* blasted and the first six of the running Spanish seamen tumbled and lay still or writhing on the deck. Those running behind sprawled over the fallen bodies and slowed, staring into the muzzles of fifteen more muskets and bayonets, and they retreated back to the port railing, hands raised high. It was over in less than ten seconds.

In one motion Caleb shoved the empty pistol into his belt and drew the other one, cocked it, and called out, "Anyone else?"

All heads shook.

Caleb spoke to Adam. "Get our surgeon over here."

Five minutes later the surgeon rose from the body of the captain. "Dead. All seven of them."

For one strange moment every man who could see them stared at the dead bodies, each unexpectedly caught up in the eternal mystery—how one moment a man is a living, feeling thing, and the next moment all that made him a man is gone. The lifeless, useless dead corpses were there before them, and they would be sewed inside a canvas sack and dropped into the sea and soon forgotten. But in the instant of death, what had left the body? From whence had it come? Where had it gone? Or was it nothing? All just a monstrous, meaningless, cruel prank played by random chance of pointless laws that follow no plan, no master, nothing? Each saw what he wanted to see in the death of the seven men and made a silent explanation that satisfied himself, and shifted his feet, and looked at Caleb, waiting.

Caleb reached to jerk the large key ring from the belt of the dead captain and gestured to Young. "Have some men move these bodies up on the quarterdeck—away from here."

Young gave orders, and men moved the bodies while others held their muskets on the Spanish crew, hands still in the air, crowded against the far railing. With their eyes never leaving the Spanish crew, Caleb gathered Young, Tunstall, and Adam around him, drew a deep breath, and asked, "Where do we go from here?"

Young answered. "You were going to put this Spanish crew in long-boats for the mainland." He shook his head. "We can't do that. They're pirates."

Caleb looked him full in the face. "So what do we do?"

Adam spoke up. "Put them in chains belowdecks, where the slaves are. Take them on to Boston and turn them over to the maritime commission. Notify the owner of this ship. Let him come claim it."

Caleb turned to his brother. "What about the slaves?"

Adam thought for a moment. "Take them on north to Canada."

"What do we tell whoever owns them?"

"The truth. Pirates took them from the owner and we took them from the pirates. If they want to file a claim, let them."

Tunstall broke in. "Let's get to Boston and lay this all out with Matthew and Billy and Tom. They have a stake in this—a big one."

Caleb looked into the faces of each of the three men and saw agreement. "Boston," he said. "I'm going to get the slaves up on deck and feed them, and those Spaniards are going to be chained down in the hold in the stink and filth for the night. The slaves can sleep on deck. Tomorrow the Spaniards are going to clean out the hold and they're going to stay chained down there the rest of the voyage with the slaves, and the slaves won't be shackled. Are we in agreement?"

All three heads nodded.

"All right." Caleb tossed the dead captain's keys to Adam. "Take about ten men and get the leg irons off the slaves and get them up here on deck. Move slow, and be careful they understand you've come to help." He turned to Young. "Get enough of our men with muskets to move this Spanish crew into the hold and put the shackles on them. Hoist the anchor and get the sails filled. It will be full dark soon and we need to be under way. Then take some of our crew into the galley of this ship and start the evening mess, enough for the Spaniards and the slaves. Get our evening mess going on the *Zephyr*."

Adam led ten men down into the blackness of the hold while Caleb and the others held their muskets on the Spanish crew. Minutes passed before Adam stepped back onto the deck, gasping for clean air, leading the first of the slaves. In the fading light they came, wearing tattered loin cloths, eyes white and wide in their dark faces, thin, bent over, bones and joints too big, some with bellies bloated from hunger. They stood on the deck, cowering, waiting to be clubbed and thrown overboard. The Americans looked at them and then lowered their faces and set their teeth before they raised them again, battling to control the rise of anger that came choking. The others stumbled up the stairs onto the deck—ninety-three of them—and Adam's men brought up the remaining eleven dead. Five men, one woman, and two boys and three girls who had not yet reached their fourteenth year.

While the men in the galleys of the two ships prepared the evening mess, the sailmakers sewed the bodies inside their canvas bags and moved them to the port railing of the *Angelique*. Under starlight the Americans herded the Spanish pirates at bayonet point down the narrow staircase into the hold and locked the leg irons above their ankles. Back on deck, in lantern light, they brought out six kettles of stew and hardtack and sat the slaves down in rows. They passed out wooden bowls and spoons, and ladled smoking chunks of salt beef and potatoes into the bowls while the slaves peered up, eyes wide and white in the starlight, unable to believe what they were seeing. They set the spoons on the deck and raised the bowls to blow on them and then brought them to their open mouths and used their fingers to push the chunks in as fast as they could chew and swallow. Some turned their heads to wretch, then tried to wipe it from the deck to swallow it again. They wolfed down the hardtack and picked every crumb from the deck. They did not know how to ask for more, so they held up their bowls in silence, eyes begging, and the Americans went down the rows a second time, filling them again.

They opened two barrels of fresh water, and the slaves dipped it with their bowls and drank, dipped again, drank, and dipped a third time. The Americans sat them again in rows, and the galley crews served the seamen on the decks of the two ships. They had scarcely begun to spoon the hot stew into their mouths when a low moan came from the slaves, and then, beneath the faint starlight, the rumble of primitive voices came in a rhythmic chant that stopped every man on the ship.

They did not know how long the thrilling, gutteral voices continued, nor did they understand the words. They only knew they were hearing something primal that reached to their very core and left them changed somehow. The Africans fell silent as suddenly as they had begun, and the white men finished their supper mess.

It was shortly before midnight that they all, Americans and Africans, stood to the port rail of the big ship with bowed heads, peering at the twenty-three sealed canvas bags. By lantern light, Adam read the Twenty-Third Psalm, and then the Lord's Prayer. Caleb nodded, and one by one, the deceased were placed on two boards balanced on the railing. Strong hands lifted one end of the board, and the remains slid into the night. They heard the sound as the bags hit the water, but they could not see them slip beneath the surface and disappear. Once again the sound of the African voices drifted outward, and their hands made the signs and their feet padded in rhythm on the deck as they said farewell to their own. Only then did Caleb give orders, and lukewarm stew and hardtack were taken into the stench of the hold to feed the captive Spanish pirates.

Blankets were passed out to the Africans and for a time they stood confused, unable to understand what they were to do. It was only when the Americans draped a blanket about the shoulders of one of them, and then sat him on the deck that they all sat down, and some laid down, covered with the blankets.

On Caleb's orders the anchor was hoisted, the hawsers binding the two ships together were loosened, the sails unfurled, and set to capture the night wind. The little schooner separated from the freighter, and with Young in command of the *Angelique* and Tunstall charting her course by the stars, and Caleb in command of the *Zephyr* with Adam as his navigator, and the thirty American seamen divided between them, the larger ship started north with the smaller one trailing, their wakes white in the starlight.

It was well past one o'clock in the morning when a knock came at Caleb's door. He was seated at his small table, back to his bunk. Deep weariness had settled in as he called, "Enter."

The door opened and Adam ducked to enter through the low, narrow door and took a seat on a stool in one corner of the cramped quarters, facing his brother. For a moment the two sat quietly in the yellow light of the single lamp on Caleb's table.

Adam broke the silence. "Long day. A lot happened."

Caleb studied his younger brother but said nothing. Adam looked down at his hands and began working them together slowly, thoughtfully.

"We killed seven men."

Caleb leaned forward, forearms on the table. It had not occurred to him that Adam had never been in a kill-or-be-killed fight before, never spilled blood, never taken life. Caleb felt a stab in his heart and searched for words.

"There was. . . . It had to be done. There was no other way. I wish you hadn't been there."

Adam looked up. "It's all right. I'm all right."

"It's never all right. That captain had to be killed, but it's never all right. I wish I could take that memory out of your mind, but I can't. It will always be there. You'll see it in your dreams tonight. Tomorrow night. It will become a familiar thing, but it will never be all right. I wish I knew how to stop it."

Adam saw the pain and the need in his brother, and he stared at his hands for a moment before he spoke again.

"I came here to tell you. You did right today. You did right."

Caleb slowly shook his head. "I broke half a dozen laws of the sea. I could be hanged for some of what I did."

Adam spaced his words. "I was afraid that's what you'd be thinking."

Caleb straightened in his chair, seeing something in his younger brother he had never suspected. He waited and Adam finished.

"You did the right thing. The rest of it doesn't much matter. When we get to Boston, I'll tell them. I'll tell them."

Adam stood and for one moment the two brothers looked into each other's eyes, and then Adam turned and walked back out the door into the night.

Notes

The characters and events in this chapter are fictional.

For maps of the islands and the ports mentioned herein, including the island of Saint Lucia, Port Carenage, the Lesser Antilles, and the several countries that laid claim to the islands, see Mackesy, *The War for America, 1775–1778,* pp. 3, 226.

For a thorough study of the slave trade, including the ships involved, the inhuman treatment of the slaves, the routes and ports, see Herberts, *The Atlantic Slave Trade,* all chapters.

Boston

Late July, 1787

CHAPTER XXIII

★ ★ ★

*M*atthew Dunson turned the key in the lock and pushed open the door with the sign above that read: DUNSON & WEEMS SHIPPING. The high rift of cirrus clouds in the eastern half of the blue heavens were flaming with reds and pinks and golds from a sun just rising, and the familiar smell of the salt sea and the sounds of the gulls and men working on the Boston docks were all around him, but unseen, unheard, unnoticed.

Shoulders hunched and head tilted forward, he closed the door, hung his tricorn on the rack of pegs on the front wall, and walked through the silent room to his desk. He dropped a freshly printed newspaper on the desktop and slumped into his chair, smothered in the crosscurrent of too many responsibilities, too many details, and too little time, while his thoughts ran, unchecked.

Caleb and Adam. The Zephyr. *Overdue. Gone far too long. Where are they? Sunk? In a British prison? Dead? Captured? If the* Zephyr *is sunk, we've got to file the insurance claim, but if we do, what do we declare as her business at the time she was lost? The insurance policy is limited to ships that are lost "during the regular course of the business." For Dunson & Weems, the "regular course of business" is carrying goods on ships for customers, not taking an armed schooner and a volunteer crew into hostile waters to find lost employees. And what of the crew? How long do we wait before we presume them dead or in prison, and hire new seamen to replace them? What do we tell Mother if Adam and Caleb don't come back? Two sons, lost?*

He shuddered and pushed it away, and his thoughts ran on.

What of the convention in Phildelphia? The newspaper says "GRAND CON-VENTION IN PHILDELPHIA CONTINUES." More than two months. What's gone wrong? Are they deadlocked? Beaten? Failed? He straightened and smoothed the newspaper, read again the brief single-column article, then shoved the newspaper away, fighting frustration that bordered on anger as his thoughts continued. *The fate of the United States hanging in the balance, and they are hiding behind their veil of secrecy, doing things known only to them and the Almighty. If they fail, what becomes of America? At least two separate countries, maybe three. And if that happens, what becomes of Dunson & Weems Shipping? Do the middle and southern states put tariffs and restrictions on their harbors that will stop the trade from the northern states? Will we lose the markets? If we do, what's left to us? The Caribbean trade belongs to the British and French and Spanish. Does Dunson & Weems go bankrupt?*

He could remain seated no longer, and rose, agitated, pacing. He glanced at Caleb's desk, conspicuous because Tom had cleared everything from the top and put it into the drawers, then pushed the chair into its well, ten days earlier. Matthew would never have supposed that a cleared desktop could become a thing so foreboding, so ominous.

He started at the sound of the front door opening, and peered at the black silhouette that entered and became Billy as the door closed. Billy paused to hang his tricorn next to Matthew's.

"You're here early," Billy said.

Matthew sat back down in his chair. "Can't sleep. Too much happening."

Billy walked back to stand at the corner of Matthew's desk. "Too much," he said quietly, "and too heavy." He paused for a moment. "If Caleb and Adam are gone. . . . " He slowly shook his head and did not finish the thought.

There was an edge to Matthew's voice. "I'll wait about five more days, and then I'm going down there looking. I have to know, one way or the other. Mother has to know."

Billy let a little time pass before he answered. "If you do, you'll have to let go of the convention in Philadelphia for a while."

Matthew nodded. "And that leaves you with this office to run. You and Tom." For a moment he stared at his desktop. "It seems like you've carried this office almost from the beginning. That shouldn't be."

Billy shrugged. "We'll manage."

"For how long? You didn't bargain for that load when we started. You can't keep it up forever. "

"Forever's a long time. Things are bound to change."

Matthew snorted. "Change for the better or worse? Lately there's been more worse than better."

A wry smile flitted on Billy's face. "And we're still here. One day at a time. One foot in front of the other." He broke off speaking and walked to his desk. "I have a month-end statement to finish."

Both men looked up as the front door opened, and old Tom entered, round-shouldered, slightly stooped, gray hair prominent in the early morning sunlight. He spoke as he hung his hat on the peg.

"Heard any more from Caleb or Adam? The *Zephyr?*"

Matthew answered, "Nothing. You?"

"Nothing," Tom answered. He walked to his desk and set a jar of apple cider on it, then sat down facing three stacks of documents. "Never lets up. The paperwork." He paused to study Matthew for a moment. "You all right? You don't look like it."

Matthew's face was drawn, scowling. "Too much gone wrong. Adam. Caleb. A ship wrecked. Another missing. The convention in Philadelphia. Too much."

Tom reached for a paper form. "About finished with the insurance papers on the *Belle.* Got to get the final figure on the dollar value of the cargo." He raised his eyes to Billy. "You got that figure yet?"

Billy shook his head. "Have it finished today."

Tom tipped his head forward and peered over his spectacles at Matthew. "Stay busy. These things work out better if you stay busy."

Matthew drew a deep breath. "We'll see."

The three men settled into the routine of their work. Talk was scant as they concentrated on the detail of contracts, insurance claims, payments received, payments made, crewmen gone, crewmen to be hired, food for the commissaries of their ships, tariffs, ships logs to be stored, records of ship repairs, schedules for dry-docking the ships to scrape the barnacles and crustaceans from the hulls.

The heat inside the closed office built. At midmorning Tom opened the jar of cider and they stopped for five minutes to share a tepid drink from wooden cups. Billy walked to the front of the office while Matthew went to the back, to leave both doors standing open. The familiar sounds of the waterfront came strong, and a light easterly wind moved through, hot and sultry. It did not cool the office but it cleared out the stagnant air.

The three men loosened their collars and rolled their shirtsleeves back two turns and had settled back into the paperwork when the sound of footsteps at the door brought their heads up to see two men enter. For a moment all three in the office sat transfixed, and then Matthew jerked to his feet, voice rising as he exclaimed, "Adam! Caleb! You're back!"

Matthew came up the aisle at a trot with Billy and Tom behind. Matthew seized Adam by the shoulders to study him, head to toe. "You're all right?"

Adam grinned. "I'm fine."

Matthew reached to grasp Caleb's hand. "You're all right?"

"No," Caleb said. "I'm dead. Got killed in the fight down there."

Matthew chuckled and Caleb grinned and the others laughed. Never in his life had relief flooded through Matthew as it did at that moment. In that instant of having his two brothers before him, safe, unharmed, his only thought was *Thank the Almighty.*

Billy seized Adam roughly and hugged him for a moment as a little brother, and then shook Caleb's hand. Tom shook their hands, and for a moment they stood there, not knowing where to start or what to say.

Matthew brought it to a focus. "The *Zephyr?*"

Adam hooked a thumb over his shoulder. "Tied up at our dock. She's sound. And we brought another."

"The *Belle?*"

Adam shook his head. "Not the *Belle.* She's gone. Wrecked. Pirates."

Matthew and Tom and Billy sobered. "The crew?"

"Lost all but nine. They're with us."

"Captain Stengard?"

"Dead. Cannon fire. We were hit by pirates," Adam said.

The three men fell silent for a little time as they accepted the loss of their men and the ship. Matthew went on. "You said you brought another ship?"

Caleb answered. "Yes." He cleared his throat. "We got one down there with the *Zephyr.* French. Named *Angelique.* We, uh, we . . . took her."

Matthew's face drew down. "Took her? Piracy?"

Caleb shifted his feet. "Not exactly. Well, matter of fact, yes. We took her like pirates. She was a slaver, and we found these dead bodies in the sea, and we tracked her down and boarded her. Turned out she had already been taken by pirates, so we took her away from the pirates."

Billy shook his head, fighting a grin. "Here we go. You're holding back something."

Adam took over. "We still have the slaves. And most of the pirate crew. We lost a few in the fight."

Matthew threw up his hands. "You pirated a slave ship that had already been seized by pirates, and you brought the slaves here with the pirate crew?"

Caleb pondered for a moment. "I think you got it."

Matthew pointed a finger. His eyes were pinpoints, and his voice too high. "Can you tell me what you expect to do with pirates and slaves in Boston?"

Caleb shrugged. "Young and Tunstall said you three would figure that out." He looked into Matthew's face with eyes innocent and trusting. "You'll do that, won't you?"

Tom burst into laughter.

Matthew ordered his thoughts and asked, "Where did you find Adam?"

"In a prison. British prison."

"Where?"

"Port Royal. Jamaica."

Matthew was incredulous. "You got him out of a British prison in Port Royal? How? How did you get him out?"

Caleb shrugged and answered nonchalantly, "Blew up the prison."

"You *what!?*"

"Well," Caleb said, searching for words, "it was an old prison. They needed a new one anyway."

Tom was holding his sides. Billy was shaking in silent laughter.

Matthew went on. "How did you get close enough to a British prison to blow it up?"

"Big storm. Bad night. We went over the walls with gunpowder. We got Adam and what was left of his crew out, and seven more of another crew."

"You . . . if you blew the prison, how did you get the *Zephyr* out of the harbor? They have a whole garrison of infantry down there, and gunboats at the harbor entrance."

Caleb continued in a calm, matter-of-fact tone of voice. "Blew about half the British infantry sliding in the mud—big storm, mud everywhere—and got to the longboats before they did. Blew up fourteen of their longboats and got our men into ours and two of theirs and out to the *Zephyr* before they figured out what was happening. We made a run for the harbor entrance and nearly rammed one of those big gunboats. Fired all six of our starboard cannon at one time. One of the balls touched off a budge barrel and others caught and blew out her second deck. I think she was sinking when we cleared the harbor." He paused, deciding if he had said it all, then finished. "Not much to it."

Matthew nearly foundered trying to stay with the speed of the story Caleb was spewing. "You sank a British man-o'-war? With that tiny little schooner out there?"

"Yes, I think that gunboat sank. Lucky shot, I guess."

Matthew's shoulders slumped. "You trying to start another war?"

Caleb pursed his mouth for a moment. "Well, no. I just went down to get my brother."

"You blew up a British garrison, along with some of their infantry, fourteen of their longboats, and sank a man-o'-war! Wars have been fought over less than that."

Caleb raised a hand in self defense. "Now, calm down, calm down. If they get mean about it, I'll tell them I'm sorry."

Tom guffawed. Billy leaned on his desk, face red as he fought for air.

Matthew went on. "How many men have you got out there, all told?"

"Well, let's see. Eighteen we left with, sixteen from the prison, and around twenty pirates in chains down in the hold of that slave ship. Somewhere near a hundred slaves."

"You got back with everyone safe?"

"That was the general idea, wasn't it?"

Matthew stopped, mind staggering with the wild story. He said quietly, "Caleb, you're insane."

Caleb shrugged. "It helps, when you work for Dunson & Weems."

Adam interrupted. "Matthew, we'd have died in that prison. Most of those slaves would have been dead if we hadn't taken that ship. Caleb did the right thing. I know there will be problems, but he did the right thing."

Tom brought himself under control and broke in. "You find the war chest on that slaver?"

Adam said, "Yes. We have it."

"What's her home port?"

"Bordeaux."

"Is her owner listed in the papers?"

"Yes."

"You took her from pirates?"

"We have about twenty out there in chains."

"Don't worry about it. You rescued a ship and a cargo from pirates. By the rules of the sea, if you return the ship to the owner, you have a legitimate claim for compensation. We can settle for delivering those slaves back to Africa where they came from, if that's what you want. Insurance will help cover the cost. The owner won't get all he bargained for in the sale of the slaves, but he'll get a lot more than he'd have gotten from the pirates and the insurance."

Caleb closed his eyes and rolled his head back. "I thought I was going to have to leave the country."

Matthew sobered and looked Caleb in the eye. "Adam's right. You did the right thing. Thank you."

For one moment something passed between the brothers, and the others stood in silent respect of it. Then Matthew glanced at Billy, and in that instant hope swelled in both their hearts as the unspoken acknowledgment came clear and strong, *Something's happened to Caleb . . . he's changing . . . coming back . . . coming home.*

Matthew broke it off and turned back to Caleb. "We'll take care of the ships. You two go home. Mother's frantic with worry."

Billy broke in. "You go with them. Kathleen needs to know."

Matthew looked at Tom.

Tom muttered, "Get out of here."

Matthew said, "I'll be back."

Tom answered, "Not today."

Matthew responded, "Tom, you come to Mother's tonight for supper. Billy, you bring Dorothy and Trudy. If I know Mother, she's going to prepare the fatted calf. Two of her sons were gone, and they have returned."

Caleb sighed. "More beef? I been eating salt beef for a month. Do you think Mother would consider cooking up some mutton?"

Note

All characters and events in this chapter are fictional.

Philadelphia
July 17, 1787

CHAPTER XXIV

*T*he razor-thin, five-to-four vote on the floor of the Grand Convention in Philadelphia on July sixteenth, which gave each state equal representation in the Senate, had been enough to keep the small states from walking out as they had threatened if the vote had gone against them, and saved the United States from self-destruction. But that was only the beginning of the earthshaking changes brought on by that pivotal event.

The delegates who were irrevocably sworn to the support of the large states—Madison, King, Wilson, and others—were rocked to their foundations. Their great dream of a new nation whose foundation was the popular vote of all the people was gone forever. If the new congress was not elected by the popular vote of all the people, regardless of their home state, could the new nation truly claim to be built on the foundation of equality for all its citizens? The value of having the House of Representatives elected by the vote of the people at large, and thus favoring the larger states, became meaningless when all states, large and small, had equal power in the Senate, and could stalemate the House at will. The large-state faction stood in silent shock the night of July sixteenth, unable to invent a way to recover from what they saw as a loss that was fatal to their very presence at the Grand Convention.

The loyal small-state supporters—Paterson, Dayton, Bedford—realized they had survived total annihilation by the five-to-four vote, the

375

slimmest margin possible. Though the vote could be seen as a victory for the small states, the thinking men realized it was not. It was just as devastating to the small states as to the large ones. If the small states had powers in the Senate equal to the large states, any advantage to the small states was utterly lost in the House of Representatives, where the large states had the greater power and could stalemate the Senate.

Both factions recognized that the thing they had created had no parallel in the history of the world. No country, no nation, had ever created a government on a split foundation, one-half controlled by the people, the other by states. The delegates had just taken the longest single step in nation-making, in the history of mankind, by creating a new kind of compound nation.

With both sides bewildered, groping, the voice of William Samuel Johnson joined with that of George Mason to clarify and soften what had been done. They reminded Paterson that America was, for many purposes, one political society composed of individuals, each of whom had the right to a voice in the government. They reminded Madison that the states, too, were political societies, each with their own interests to protect, and had an equal right to a voice in the government. And they concluded their advice with a summary that only slightly mollified both sides. "It is clear," they said, "that each, the people on the one hand, and the states on the other, are halves of a unique whole, and as such they ought to be combined so that in one branch the people are to be represented, and in the other, the states."

It was a solemn group that met in the opulence of the Indian Queen Hotel following the session of July sixteenth, to talk far into the night, as confused when they concluded as when they started. The following morning, July seventeenth, a subdued assembly of large-state supporters with a few small-state proponents in the mix met before the session in one last assault on the dilemma. The supporters of both extremes—large states and small states—declared that no good government could be built on the foundation of the compromise that was now before them. Some of the hard core, large-state supporters could find no way to retreat from their sworn positions and declared they were ready to push on without the intractable small-state faction, and once again, the threat of a split convention, and a fractured United States, appeared likely.

Cooler minds, however, prevailed. Less radical large-state proponents reasoned that it was probable that there was merit in yielding to the compromise, however imperfect and exceptionable it might be, as it was now agreed on by the convention as a body.

It was then that a strange spirit stole among the delegates, and the answer came. The problem was not to find a solution to the dilemma. The core problem was *to learn to live with the compromise!*

And learning to live with it was a hard road indeed!

The groaning and mumbling faded and died, and the delegates paused to face the facts of who they were. They were constitution-makers, here to create a new government. They pushed aside the fact they had nearly drowned in regional and political differences that had plunged them into brutal, vicious debate, and had come within a single vote of destroying themselves and their country in one stroke. They had survived, and they had learned to compromise, and they had created the beginnings of a government that was unique in all history. They looked at it, and they shifted their position and looked at it again from a different side, and yet another. Slowly the realization took form and substance in their hearts and minds. It is *American.* The best we could find in ourselves. Unique—like no other. It is ours. *American.*

With a new, growing, unspoken sense of purpose and unity, the delegates adjourned their ad hoc meeting and moved to the East Room. Washington called the convention to order, picked up the first piece of paper for the business of the day, and the delegates settled in as he read.

"Prior to adjournment yesterday, we had before us the issue of what powers should be vested in the new legislature. We shall continue. Mr. Secretary, would you read the provision previously adopted by the committee of the whole?"

Jackson bobbed his head, seized a paper, and stood.

"The legislature shall enjoy the legislative rights vested in Congress by the confederation, and moreover to legislate in all cases to which the separate states are incompetent or in which the harmony of the United States may be interrupted by the exercise of individual legislation."

Washington waited a moment for all delegates to catch up, then went on. "Debate is open." Pierce Butler stood and in his soft South Carolina drawl said, "It appears that the term *incompetent* requires some explanation, since what it implies may be open to debate."

Gorham responded, "The vagueness of the term is its virtue. We are now establishing general principles, to be extended hereafter into details which will be precise and explicit."

Butler sat down.

Roger Sherman stood. "I am disturbed at the possible encroachments on states' rights involved in these powers we are considering for the national legislature and, accordingly, I propose that the following change be made." He raised a paper and read.

"The national legislature be empowered to make laws binding on the people of the United States in all cases which may concern the common interests of the Union; but not to interfere with the government of the individual states in any matters of internal police which respect the government of such states only, and wherein the general welfare of the United States is not concerned."

James Wilson pushed his spectacles back up his nose and said loudly, "I strongly favor the proposal."

Gouverneur Morris's wooden leg hit the floor with a hollow thump as he stood. Large, paunchy, he shook his head. "I oppose Mr. Sherman's motion on the ground that there are cases in which the internal affairs of the states ought to be infringed and legislated upon by the national government, most notably to prevent the states from issuing their own paper money."

The vote was called for, and Mr. Sherman's motion died, eight states against, only two in favor. They moved on.

Gunning Bedford of Delaware took the floor. "I move that the powers of the national legislature be altered so as to read: 'To enjoy the legislative rights vested in congress by the confederation, and moreover to legislate in all cases for the general interests of the union, and also in those to which the states are separately incompetent, or in which the harmony of the United States may be interrupted by the exercise of individual legislation.'"

It took but one second for Roger Sherman to understand that this proposal gave the new national legislature more powers than any previous proposal, and he was on his feet in an instant, voice raised in alarm.

"This is a formidable idea indeed. It involves the power of violating all the laws and constitutions of the states, and of intermeddling with their internal affairs!"

A voice called, "Move for the vote."

"Seconded."

The vote was taken, and despite Sherman's protest, the motion passed, six votes in favor, two against. And among those voting in favor were the small states of New Jersey, Delaware, and Maryland. For a moment the large state delegates glanced at each other, startled that the three small states had voted in favor of granting these new, broad, sweeping powers to the new national government. It was the small states that had doggedly voted against the Virginia plan spawned by James Madison and Governor Edmund Randolph, howling their protest that it gave too much power to the new national government. Two days earlier they would have stormed and threatened at the proposal. Today? They had reversed themselves and shocked everyone in the East Room by joining hands with the large states!

For one moment Washington glanced about the room, aware something had changed. It took but a moment to understand that every delegate in the room had grasped the fact they had crossed the mountain in the vote of yesterday. The deadly collision between the large and small states that had threatened the very existence of the United States had come down to the historic vote, and America had survived. It was behind them. It was now on their shoulders to close ranks and move on. He picked up the next piece of paper, drew a deep breath, and resolutely read.

"It is proposed that the new congress be vested with the power to negative such state laws as are contravening in its opinion the Articles of Union."

The issue—the power in the national congress to negative and declare void any state law that Congress opined ran afoul of the Articles of Union—had first been argued on May thirty-first, and had been battered again on June sixteenth and June twentieth by the committee of the whole. Today it was before the convention for a final vote, if that were possible.

Once again Gouverneur Morris heaved his bulk from his chair, shook his head, and waved one hand. "Such a power in the national congress is likely to be terrible to the states. Worse, it will likely be a matter of utter disgust to them. They are jealous of their sovereignty and fearful of any institution vested with the power to override their own legislature."

Roger Sherman stood. "This proposal is unnecessary! The state courts will hold invalid any law contravening the authority of the Union, and since such a state law would not be valid or operative even if they did not hold it invalid, this proposal is superfluous."

The vote was called and taken. Three states aye, seven states nay. The entire proposal was resoundingly defeated, and James Madison had lost the second of his great dreams for a strong central government. The new national congress would not have the power to override state laws. Madison accepted his personal loss without a word.

Instantly Luther Martin of Maryland was on his feet, and Washington recognized him.

"I move," he declared, "that the following be approved." He plucked up a piece of paper and read:

"That the legislative acts of the United States made by virtue and in pursuance of the Articles of Union, and all treaties made and ratified under the authority of the United States, shall be the supreme law of the respective states, as far as those acts or treaties shall relate to the said states, or their citizens and inhabitants—and that the judiciaries of the several states shall be bound thereby in their decisions, anything in the respective laws of the individual states to the contrary notwithstanding."

For several seconds the room was gripped by silence as the delegates examined the proposal. Then their heads began to nod. It appeared that it was all there. The supremacy of the United States over the individual states, and the duty placed on the judiciary to enforce this supremacy.

"Call for the vote."

"Seconded."

"Mr. Secretary, take the vote."

It took but one minute to record the unanimous vote—Aye.

Washington glanced at the clock, then read from the next paper.

"It is proposed that the convention approve and adopt the proposal made by the committee of the whole that there should be an executive consisting of a single person, to be chosen by the national legislature."

A delegate stood. "I propose an amendment. Such executive shall be vested with two powers: one, to carry into execution the national laws; and two, to appoint to offices in cases not otherwise provided for."

Debate was perfunctory and limited before the vote was called and the proposal approved.

Washington again glanced at the clock, and then for a few moments those blue-gray eyes searched the faces of the delegates. He could not recall a day since the convention convened that rancor and acrimony had been less evident. Debate had been civil, differences of opinion respected, compromise quietly accepted. The convention had accomplished more on this day than any single day before. Something startling and fundamental had changed for the better, and he was reaching to define what it was.

He gathered his papers, and announced, "We stand adjourned until ten o'clock tomorrow morning."

Ten o'clock the morning of Wednesday, July eighteenth, saw the midsummer heat in Philadelphia at its worst, and the delegates at their desks, already wiping perspiration as Washington initiated the day's proceedings.

"The first matter to come before this body is the question of the judiciary branch of the proposed government. On June fourth this convention established one supreme tribunal. One supreme court. However, the issue of lesser courts was not resolved. The matter now before us is on the motion of Mr. Madison, seconded by Mr. Wilson, as follows: 'That the national legislature be empowered to institute inferior tribunals.' Debate is open."

In less than one minute the debate plunged into the prickly proposition that this convention must create a new level of national courts beneath the supreme court, which had power over all state laws and all state courts. While it appeared innocuous enough in concept, every man in the steamy room knew that the states had a near mortal terror of anything that would rob them of their sovereignty. Generations of living under a monarch who had absolute power over them—their property, their lives, their freedom—had instilled a loathing in their very bones for any person or any institution that rose above the power of a state to reign supreme within its own boundaries. Voting to establish one supreme court for the new national government had been one thing. Voting now to establish a series of lesser national courts with power over everything held dear by the states was quite another.

Pierce Butler of South Carolina rose. "I cannot see the slightest necessity for such a court system, since the state courts can certainly handle the affairs of their own states!"

Edmund Randolph, Governor of Virginia, took the floor. "The courts of the various states cannot be trusted with the administration of the national laws. With thirteen separate court systems attempting to interpret the national laws, it is clear and certain that in time, conflicting interpretations will result in chaos."

Luther Martin rose to agree. "The states will create jealousies and oppositions between the various jurisdictions."

Madison was on his feet. "If we do not establish courts at the national level, which are beneath the supreme court, it is only a matter of time until the appeals from state courts to the supreme court will be overwhelming. We must have intermediate courts at the national level with jurisdiction to receive and hear appeals from the state courts."

The arguments continued, firm but restrained, until the vote was called for. It was unanimous in favor. There would be a series of national courts, their number to be determined by the legislature.

Washington continued. "The next matter is the method of selecting judges for the courts. The resolution now before us provides that they shall be appointed by the national legislature. Debate is open."

A frowning James Wilson stood. "Unfortunately, experience has shown that when such appointments are made by a body of men with divergent views and interests, all too often the result is seriously lacking. Such appointments ought to be made by one person."

Randolph rose to oppose him. "I differ absolutely with my colleague," he declared. "Ten of the thirteen states have entrusted appointment of their judges to the legislatures, and they are doing well."

Rutledge stood, shaking his head. "I find it dangerous to vest so great a power in any one person."

A standoff was taking shape, and to avoid it, one delegate stood. "I move that we reconsider a prior motion of Mr. Madison. Simply stated, it was that the judges for the new national courts be appointed by the Senate, since each state has an equal voice in that branch of Congress."

Silence held for a moment before the call came, "Seconded."

"Call for the vote."

Secretary Jackson recorded the ayes and nays, and the motion passed. As of July eighteenth, 1787, judges in the new national court system would be appointed by the Senate.

Washington moved on. "The next matter is the jurisdiction of the various national courts."

Instantly the delegates braced for the debate that was coming. Three plans had already been presented, the first by Randolph of Virginia. His plan vested original jurisdiction in the lower national court system for piracies and felonies on the high seas, captures from an enemy, cases involving foreigners, national revenue, impeachment of national officers, and anything affecting the national peace and harmony. The second plan by Pinckney of South Carolina included treaties, the law of nations, trade and revenue, or any case wherein the United States was a party, as well as maritime matters. The third plan, from Paterson of New Jersey provided for only one national Supreme Court with appellate jurisdiction from all state supreme courts, basically on the same issues and matters presented by Randolph. To these, Madison added the clause that the jurisdiction of the national judiciary shall extend to cases involving laws passed by the national congress and any questions involving national peace and harmony.

Debate quickly bogged down in gritty arguments that reached into the most remote detail and it continued until one delegate stood, and the room became silent.

"Move for the vote on the plan of Mr. Randolph."

A relieved voice called, "Seconded."

Jackson recorded the vote, and the Randolph plan, as amended by Madison, was passed. There would be one supreme court, and a system of lesser courts at the national level, with jurisdiction as provided by Mr. Randolph and Mr. Madison.

Washington looked at the clock, then at the faces of the delegates, and announced, "We are adjourned until tomorrow morning."

There was no letup on July nineteenth, either in the sweltering Philadelphia heat, or the gritty detail of the convention agenda. Creating a new government for the United States was a grand idea when one spoke only in the abstractions of the glorious and idealistic principles on which it must be based. Who would take issue with the broad-stroke ideals of freedom, justice, harmony, peace, prosperity, happiness, and the checks and balances in a government that would forever protect the citizens from kings and monarchs and despotic institutions that would rob them of such precious things? The challenge did not lie in reciting the principles. The challenge lay in finding enough genius and endurance in this body of men to put together a government founded on the broad principles, but with a fabric of detail that would forever support them. And there was no blueprint, no model, no government since the dawn of time, to look to for guidance. Clearly, the devil was in the detail, and they were learning that the detail in creating a new government came in a gargantuan avalanche.

They collectively took a deep breath, set their teeth, wiped at the perspiration, and plowed on.

If the executive branch of the new government was to be but a single man, what qualifications should he have? What age? Who should select him?—the Senate?—the people by popular election? What should be his term of office? Should he be allowed to stand for reelection? And if so, how many times? Should he be subject to removal for good cause?—impeachment? Should he have the power to veto laws passed by the state legislatures that he might deem harmful to the national government? What checks and balances must be in place to keep a president from becoming a despot, as he surely would if unrestrained? The arguments multiplied and piled, one on top of another, first one, then another in opposition, then a third that was a blend of the first two. Gouverneur Morris could see no other course than electing the president by popular vote, or at least by the vote of the property owners of the various states, which appeared unworkable to some delegates and near suicidal to others. John Dickinson argued loudly for each state nominating its best citizen into a pool and letting the national congress elect the president from the thirteen-man pool; that proposal died instantly. Oliver Ellsworth of Connecticut campaigned for electing the president by the national legislature, with electors chosen by the state legislatures to take control whenever an executive sought reelection. James Wilson voiced his very low opinion of having legislatures elect the president by proposing that a group of national legislators be selected by drawing lots and letting them elect the president, following which Wilson quickly withdrew the notion, convinced he had delivered his message of contempt for the idea of having the legislatures elect the president.

The debates raged on with no end in sight. One sweaty day blended into the next, with no workable solution in sight. Few had expected the seemingly innocuous question of how to select a president to be such a thorny, stubborn thing. July twenty-third, the long-missing delegation from New Hampshire appeared for the first time. Nicholas Gilman and John Langdon walked into the East Room, took their places, and sat bewildered as others tried to explain all that had happened, and the current state of jumbled affairs. On that same day, James Paterson of New Jersey departed for home, not to return until September seventeenth, the day the newly approved constitution was signed.

In the midst of it, the delegates arose one morning to a newspaper article in the *Philadelphia Packet*, which at first struck fear into their hearts and then brought on great guffaws. The brief article said:

"So great is the unanimity, we hear, that prevails in the Convention, upon all great federal subjects, that it has been proposed to call the room in which they assemble, Unanimity Hall."

The fear that instantly seized their hearts was that some delegate had leaked information to a newspaper. All too well did they know that if the newspapers, and consequently the people in the thirteen states, learned of the hot, desperate struggles that had already transpired, and the head-on collision toward which the convention was speeding—the issue of slavery—they were doomed. It was only after a second or third reading that they realized nothing had been leaked to the newspapers. The article was but an uninformed foray—ill-advised—to make news where there was none.

Nevertheless, within days the story had appeared in every major newspaper in the country, while the delegates chuckled. Unanimity Hall? If there was ever a geographical location that did not deserve such a lofty characterization, it was the East Room in the Pennsylvania Statehouse during the Grand Convention. The delegates had their laugh, put the newspaper article behind them, and took a vote forbidding members of the convention to take copies of the resolutions already agreed to out of the East Room. Then they wiped at the sweat on their brows and struggled on.

A frustrated James Wilson examined all the conflicting proposals and shook his head. "I hope that a better method of election will yet be adopted."

But it was dour Elbridge Gerry who voiced the opinion of most delegates. "We seem," he declared with his usual acrid expression, "to be entirely at a loss on this head."

On July twenty-sixth, swamped with conflicting proposals for selecting the executive for the new government, weary to the point of exhaustion, the convention took two bold steps. First, they appointed a committee that was quickly styled the Committee of Detail, and dumped the snarled mess of conflicting proposals regarding the new executive onto them. The five-man committee included Rutledge of South Carolina, chairman; Randolph from Virginia; Ellsworth from Connecticut; Wilson from Pennsylvania; and Gorham from Massachusetts. Their specific charge was to prepare and report back to the convention, a rough draft of a constitution that conformed to the resolutions already passed. The Committee of Detail disappeared into their own secret huddle where they methodically laid out all conflicting proposals, organized them, and then selected Randolph to create the first rough draft of a constitution. Little of what they did in the privacy of their meetings was ever revealed; however, one scrap of paper was later discovered, which caught and crystallized the spirit that became the guiding star of the entire convention. It stated:

"In the draught of a fundamental constitution, two things deserve attention: I. To insert essential principles only, lest the operations of government should be closed by rendering those provisions permanent and unalterable, which ought to be accommodated to times and events; and 2. To use simple and precise language, and general propositions, according to the example of the several constitutions of the several states; for the construction of a constitution necessarily differs from that of law."

And, second, on the steamy morning of July twenty-sixth, a tired convention gratefully adjourned until August sixth, to give the newly authorized committee time to do its work. The delegates scattered. Some had their bags packed and were inside coaches leaving Philadelphia before the sun set, to return home to waiting wives and families, and business affairs too long neglected. Others, with homes too distant for travel in the ten-day reprieve, remained in the city to enjoy their leisure, lounging in the taverns and the open air restaurants that lined the Delaware River and visiting the theaters in the relative cool of the evening.

George Washington and Robert Morris saddled horses and rode northwest twenty-six miles to the place on the Schuylkill River called

Valley Forge, where the battered Continental Army had spent most of the winter of 1777–1778. Somber, thoughtful, Washington walked slowly through the neglected remains of the camp, with heart-wrenching memories alive in his mind at every step. Men dressed in tattered summer clothing, sick, starving, standing picket duty at midnight barefooted in the snow, the temperature nine degrees below zero, perhaps with only a felt hat beneath their feet to keep them from freezing to the ground. He came to the great plot of ground, overgrown with ten years of grass and Pennsylvania foliage, where three thousand of his men were buried in huge, unmarked graves—dead from freezing and starvation, and he stopped, and for a long time stood with his hat in his hand, head bowed. He was seeing his men as they were then, hollow-cheeked, sunken eyes, feet and legs blue and black, but refusing to leave—willing to die before they would abandon the dream. He settled his tricorn back onto his head and walked away with a burning in his chest.

We will finish it for you. We will make a nation. We will succeed.

Notes

The events, dates, persons, times, places, and speeches appearing in this chapter are taken from the following sources.

Bernstein, *Are We to Be a Nation?* pp. 172–74.

Berkin, *A Brilliant Solution*, pp. 116–130.

Warren, *The Making of the Constitution*, pp. 313–67.

Rossiter, *1787: The Grand Convention*, pp. 196–200. As the convention adjourned on July 26th for its hiatus until August 6, Robert Morris and George Washington made the horseback ride to Valley Forge where Washington spent time visiting all the familiar places from the Valley Forge affair in the winter of 1777–78, most of which were in ruins. Further, the quotation cited in this chapter wherein the Philadelphia newspaper *Pennsylvania Packet* referenced the East Room where the convention was meeting as "Unanimity Hall," appears and is quoted verbatim from page 203. The same quotation appears on pages 114–15 of Farrand, *The Framing of the Constitution of the United States.*

Farrand, *The Framing of the Constitution*, pp. 113–17.

Farrand, *The Records of the Federal Convention*, Vol. 2, pp. 21–128.

Moyers, *Report from Philadelphia*, pages named July 17, 1787–July 26, 1787.

The reader is again reminded that the speeches and proceedings have been necessarily abridged, since it is impossible to include them all in this work. Some speeches have been modified to make them more understandable today. Every effort has been made to preserve the intent and meanings of the speeches and debate, and any errors are those of this writer.

Also, much of the original thought in this chapter is to be credited to Max Farrand, as found in his masterful work, *The Framing of the Constitution of the United States.*

Boston

August 6, 1787

CHAPTER XXV

*I*n the hot, late afternoon Boston sun, Margaret Dunson spread her hand to lay it flat against one of the six stiff sheets still hanging from the clothesline in her backyard. It was Monday, and her gray, ankle-length wash-day dress and old leather shoes were still damp from the heavy labor of wash day in Boston.

Adam had remained at home in the early morning hours to set up the washtubs and the tripod, build the fire beneath the heavy kettle, and carry the first load of water before he had to go to the shipping office of Dunson & Weems. At noon Prissy had come dashing home from her work at the bakery for an hour before she ran back. It was Margaret who had kept the exhausting work going since dawn.

She closed her hand on the sheet and could feel the dampness that remained. *Another hour,* she thought. She walked to the root cellar, lifted the outer door, descended the steps to the lower door, and entered the cool gloom to pick a jar of apple cider from a shelf. For a moment she stood there in the twilight, on the cool earthen floor that John had covered with sand, wishing she could sit down for just ten minutes and do nothing. But wash day in Boston tolerated no such reprieve, and she climbed back up the stairs into the dead, humid heat of an August afternoon and walked steadily to the back door of the kitchen.

Through the open door she heard the faint sound of footsteps in the parlor, and as she entered, she called, "Brigitte? Is that you?"

"I'm home," came the answer.

"Did you get a copy of the law? From Harold Trumbull?"

"Yes, I have it." At twenty-nine years of age, by all the unspoken rules of Boston's high-nosed society, Brigitte was a spinster, consigned to employment at the women's clothing store the remainder of her life. She was also tall, beautifully formed, striking, with curls of auburn hair clinging to the light perspiration on her forehead, and as of recent days, betrothed. She walked into the kitchen as her mother, shorter, still attractive in her middle fifties, was setting the jar of apple cider on the cupboard.

"What does it say?"

"Pretty much what Reverend Olmstead told us."

Margaret gestured and the two walked into the dining room together and sat down at the long table, Margaret at the head, Brigitte to her left. Brigitte opened her bag and drew out a folded piece of paper with printing on one side, and laid it before Margaret.

"There it is."

Margaret flattened the paper on the tabletop and said, "Cool cider in the kitchen. Get a cup for both of us."

Brigitte walked to the kitchen to pour cider, and returned to set both cups, half-full, on the table. She sipped at hers while she sat silently, waiting. Margaret drank from her cup, then, following the printed lines with her finger, silently mouthing each word as she went, she read the document slowly, intently.

AN ACT FOR THE ORDERLY
SOLEMNIZATION OF MARRIAGES

Passed in the State of Massachusetts June 22, 1786.

A Justice of the Peace, or an Ordained Minister is authorized to perform marriages but only when the bride, or the groom, or both, reside in the town where such Justice of the Peace or Ordained Minister resides and performs his duties.

Prior to their marriage, the proposed bride and groom

must publish their intent to marry and shall do so by public announcement at three public religious meetings, on different days, not less than three days between, or, they may post in writing for the space of fourteen days, a written declaration of their intent to marry, in some public place.

Such publication having been completed, said bride and groom shall then obtain a written certificate signed by the town clerk in the town where they reside declaring that their intent to marry has been appropriately published according to the foregoing.

Upon delivery of such certificate to any Justice of the Peace, or any ordained Minister, they may then perform the marriage ceremony solemnizing the marriage of such bride and groom.

Margaret finished her cider, leaned back in her chair and said, "You and Billy will have to give public notice before you can get married. Is that what this says?"

Brigitte bobbed her head once. "That's what Harold said."

Margaret drew and released a great breath. "Is Billy coming over tonight after supper? To pick a day?"

"Yes."

"Well," Margaret said decisively, "this became law June twenty-second of last year. You can't get married until you've given public notice. You can give notice at church through Silas, or you can write it out and post it in a public place, whatever that means. Then you have to get a certificate from the city clerk saying you did it. The city clerk is Harold Trumbull. Is this what he told you?"

Brigitte nodded but remained silent.

Margaret ballooned her cheeks for a moment and then shook her head. "What's this world coming to? You can't just go get a license and get married anymore. You've got to publish it so the whole town knows it, and then prove you published it so the city clerk can issue the license. If you publish it, Silas sure ought to know it without getting a certificate from Harold to prove it." She shook her head. "What's it going to be next? You've got to get a certificate to have your babies? Will you have to publish notice of that in advance, too?"

Both women blushed and chuckled, and then Brigitte leaned forward, barely able to contain her laughter as she blurted, "Exactly what are you supposed say in that kind of a publication?"

For one moment the two women pondered the language that could appear in such a notice, and then both exploded into gales of laughter. It held until their faces were red, and tears were running down their cheeks, both unable to speak, or even to rise from their chairs. Eventually Margaret wheezed, "We ought to have whoever thought up this public notice idea tell us what we're supposed to say about having babies."

They lapsed back into their laughing seizure, wiping at the tears that were streaming, and Brigitte choked out, "How would he know? He's never had one."

Beyond control, neither of them heard the front door open, nor did they see the two men step through the dining room archway and stand there staring at the two hysterical women. Caleb and Adam stood wide-eyed, mouths hanging open, dumbstruck at the sight of their mother and older sister laughing as though they were demented, wiping at their red, tear-streaked faces. The two men waited until the uproar began to subside before Caleb spoke.

"It must have been good. What was it?"

Both surprised women turned to look at the men, and were instantly lost in laughter once more. Finally they brought themselves under control and Margaret said, "It's nothing. You wouldn't understand."

Caleb looked at Adam, then back at his mother. "Nothing? Nothing had you two about to fall off your chairs?"

Margaret wiped at her eyes with her apron. "Brigitte's getting married. She has to give notice."

Caleb's forehead drew down in puzzlement. "Oh! That's hilarious."

Adam said, "Are you talking about that new law? From last year?"

"Yes," Margaret answered, "you have to give public notice of your intent to get married."

"How are you going to do it? At church? Or by writing in a public place?"

Slowly the women came back to the business of the notice. "Well," Margaret said, "I suppose at church. Silas will do it." She turned to Brigitte. "What do you say?"

Brigitte shrugged. "At church."

Adam broke in. "Billy said he's coming over after supper to get all this settled."

Margaret leaned back to peer into the parlor at the clock on the mantel. "Forgot all about supper. Come on, Brigitte. Prissy's due home any time, and we've got to gather the sheets off the line and change clothes and get supper on the table. You boys go out and put the tubs and kettle away and then be sure there's enough kindling to keep the irons hot tomorrow. We've got a lot of ironing."

The front door opened as Margaret and Brigitte stood, and Prissy called, "I'm home."

Margaret answered, "We're in here. Your day all right?"

Prissy walked through the archway. "Good. All right. Is the wash done? Can I help with supper?"

Margaret gave the orders. "The wash is done. Change your clothes and help Brigitte gather the sheets. Fold them carefully so they don't wrinkle. I'll get supper."

No one questioned, no one challenged, as each went to their assignment. Since the nineteenth day of April 1775, when Tom Sievers had brought their father home from the fight at Concord mortally wounded and dying from a .75 caliber British musketball in his right lung, Margaret had carried the household on her shoulders. They had watched her hands become old and her shoulders round, and her face set and growing wrinkled from the work of both the woman of the house and the man, doing anything she could—washing, ironing, knitting, making meals for neighbors—to eke out enough money to pay the bills and doggedly maintain their independence. They had learned very early to take her orders in obedient silence and do the work well enough to receive her judgmental nod of approval. They were a team. If anyone failed, someone else had to pick up the load. The single exception was Caleb. Caught in the confused, bewildering time when the boy was trying to become the man, his world had been shattered when he had watched his father die, and he could not control the hot, bitter hatred for the British that had filled his soul. He could find no light in the war, and abandoned any belief in a God that could allow such pain for his mother, and his family, and himself. At sixteen he had left home to join the Continental Army with but one thought burning in his brain: *Make the British pay. Make them pay.*

It nearly broke Margaret's heart, to have young Caleb leave home, but she had no time to mourn. She had put the ache in a place in her heart and sealed it off in the hope that some day, some blessed day, her burdens in life would lift, and she would have time to go to that place to feel the pain, and sort it out, and begin to heal.

The shooting war had ended with the surrender of General Cornwallis and his eight thousand redcoated troops at Yorktown in October of 1781, but the headlong plunge of the country into near bankruptcy and the brink of civil war had given her no reprieve. She had found little time to reach inside herself for peace, and now she wondered if she could. She had stored so many things inside that it had become a habit she did not know if she could undo. She worried, but for now, there was wash to be gathered and kindling to be split and supper to prepare and a meeting with Billy Weems that would decide when her eldest daughter would marry.

Supper consisted of cold, sliced ham, home-baked bread, buttermilk, and fresh peaches. The women were clearing the table when a knock came at the front door, and Adam invited Billy in. The men sat in the parlor while Margaret and Prissy followed Brigitte to her room to help her fuss with her hair and set her thoughts in order. Then Margaret led them into the parlor, and the men stood.

Billy nodded. "Good evening." He was nervously twisting his tricorn in his hands, and for a moment looked like he wanted to say something else, but didn't know what it was.

"Good evening," Brigitte answered, smiling.

The three women sat down, and the men sat down, with Margaret seated between Brigitte and Billy. Adam and Prissy, the twins, were watching intently to learn how these affairs were conducted. Caleb leaned back in his chair with a casual, almost humorous, interest in how uncomfortable Billy was and the delicious joy the women were taking in the whole affair.

Margaret opened the business of the evening. "We're delighted that you could come, Billy."

"I'm happy to be here."

A hint of a smile played around Caleb's mouth.

Margaret saw little reason for the usual formality of circling the subject for a discreet amount of time before coming to it. After all, from the time any of the children could remember, Billy had been the extra member of the family, inseparable from Matthew, in and out of the Dunson home as though it were his own.

"I believe the time of engagement has been sufficient," she declared. "Is it time to talk about the marriage?"

Billy answered, "I think it is, that is, if Brigitte is in agreement."

Brigitte's eyes were shining. "I agree."

Margaret turned to Billy. "You're aware of the new law? About giving notice?"

"I've heard of it, yes."

"Have you thought about how you would like the notice to be given?"

"You mean at church or in writing at a public place?"

"Yes."

Billy paused for a moment. "I couldn't find the meaning of 'a public place.'"

Caleb cut in. "The jail. That's public. Very public."

Billy shifted uneasily in his seat, and Prissy stifled a giggle.

Margaret cast a disapproving eye on Caleb, and continued. "You and Brigitte should come to some agreement about giving notice. I thought it would be proper to have Silas do it at church."

Billy nodded. "I agree."

"Good." Margaret bobbed her head and went on. "Have you, uh, thought about when? When would be a good time?"

"I've thought about it. It seems to me Brigitte should be the one to decide," Billy said.

Caleb leaned forward, face drawn with intensity. "August of 1789. Two more years. That should be about right," he intoned.

Billy looked panic-stricken.

Margaret turned to Caleb with a perplexed look. "Will you be serious?"

Caleb's eyes opened wide in surprise. "What's wrong with 1789? No sense rushing into these things. They need to get to know each other first."

Prissy exclaimed, "They've known each other forever! Since before you were born!"

Caleb sobered and stared at the floor. "Oh!" he murmured, "I forgot."

Adam ducked his head, grinning.

Margaret raised one hand in frustration. "Brigitte, have you thought about when you would like this marriage to occur?"

Brigitte was trying to maintain a serious composure in the midst of the nonsense. "You and I talked about August thirty-first. That's a Friday."

Margaret turned back to Billy. "That's enough time for Silas to give notice and get the certificate from Harold."

Billy reflected for a moment. "That would be fine. It won't interfere with the business at the company."

"Then it will be Friday, August thirty-first. Where? At the church? At home?"

Brigitte answered. "Church. In the evening."

Billy nodded.

Margaret reflected for a moment. "Have you thought about where you'll live? Here? With Dorothy?"

Billy shook his head. "I spoke with Horatio Cutler today. He's decided to sell his home. With Druscilla gone, he's going to live with his eldest son in Harrisburg. I've made an appointment with him for next Friday. I thought Brigitte and I could go look at his home."

"The Cutler home near the Common?" Margaret asked.

"Yes."

"Oh," she exclaimed. "That's a good home, and the Common is a beautiful place. All the open grass."

Brigitte beamed. "A home of our own on the Common? Wonderful!"

"Well," Margaret said, "I think that concludes everything for now. You two had better go visit Silas. He'll need to start the notices Sunday."

Brigitte straightened in surprise. "Go see the Reverend now?"

"Now. He's expecting you. I told him."

Margaret rose from her chair, and the others rose and followed Billy and Brigitte to the front door. The family stood clustered outside in the afterglow of a sun now set, watching Billy and Brigitte walk through the front gate into the cobblestone street and turn right toward the church where the small, wiry, white-haired Silas Olmstead, who had been their spiritual guide since they could remember, lived with his ailing wife, Mattie, in the tiny quarters at the rear of the building. Billy and Brigitte walked steadily in the still, warm twilight, saying little, caught up in an unexpected sense of peace and rightness.

They walked across the grass past the front of the white church with the tall bell tower, to the side door, where Billy knocked and they waited until there was a stir inside and the door opened. The watery old eyes of Silas brightened when he saw them, and he thrust his wrinkled hand with the big knuckles forward to Billy.

"Billy and Brigitte! Margaret said you would be coming. What a joy. Do come in. Come in. Mattie's inside. Taken a chill, you know."

Billy gently shook the fragile hand, and Silas led them into the tiny parlor. Mattie was seated at one side with a worn, gray shawl around her narrow, pinched shoulders. She leaned forward and struggled to rise. Billy put a gentle hand on her shoulder. "Don't get up, Mattie. It's just us. It is good to see you."

There was gratitude in her eyes. "It is good to have you here," she said. Her voice was weak. "Silas said you would be coming." Through more than half a century of marriage, she and Silas had yearned and prayed for children that never came. To fill the void in their hearts, the two of them had become second parents to the children in their congregation.

Brigitte knelt beside her chair to look directly into her face. "Are you all right? Is there anything I can do?"

The wrinkled old face smiled. "I'm fine. Silas tries so hard."

Silas gestured to two straight-backed chairs. "Please be seated." They sat, and he took the only remaining chair in the plain room, facing them. Billy spoke.

"We wish to know if you could perform our marriage on the thirty-first day of this month. A Friday."

Mattie clasped her hands together beneath her chin. "Ohhhh! I've waited so long for this!"

Silas bowed his head in thought for a few moments. "I'm sure the church is free that day. What time?"

Brigitte said quietly, "In the early evening. Seven o'clock?"

"Yes, that will be fine," Silas said.

Billy broke in. "Could you make the announcement for the next three Sundays? I think that's what the law requires."

"Yes, I can. And I'll prepare the certificate. You can take it to Harold to get the license issued."

"That will be fine," Billy said.

Mattie broke in, eyes glistening. "Brigitte, do you have your wedding dress?"

"No. Mother and Prissy and I will sew it."

"Oh, I can hardly wait, " Mattie exclaimed. "You will be lovely. Just lovely."

Billy stood. "I think that finishes the business. We should go. Thank you."

Mattie interrupted. "You two come here for a moment. I need to hold you both."

They both came to her chair and bent low while the thin arms reached, and she held them close and kissed each of them on the cheek as though they were her own. They felt the slight tremor in the frail body, and they saw the distorted knuckles in the blue-veined hands, and the fingers that would never again lie straight. They kissed her on her cool cheek and they straightened and peered down at her for a moment while she clutched their hands to her breast.

"Come again soon," she pled. "Oh, please."

Brigitte smiled. "We will. I promise."

Silas followed them back to the door and they said their good-byes, and the small, round-shouldered man watched the two walk into the soft warmth of deep dusk and disappear.

Billy and Brigitte walked the crooked cobblestone street casually, greeting people as they passed, talking as best friends and sweethearts. Neither knew when it happened, but they found themselves holding hands, and Brigitte clutching his arm, glowing with excitement as they talked of the Cutler home, and the peculiar new law for obtaining their marriage license, and who would be at the wedding. All too soon they were at the gate into the Dunson yard, and then at the front door. Billy knocked and they entered to be met by the entire family.

"What did Silas say?" Margaret asked.

Brigitte grinned and her eyes shone, and there was color in her cheeks as she spoke. "We will be married the evening of Friday, the thirty-first. At seven o'clock."

Prissy covered her mouth with her hand, nearly trembling with excitement and anticipation. "Ohhh!" she exclaimed.

Margaret bobbed her head. "We have a lot to do, starting with your wedding dress." She looked at Billy. "We aren't supposed to speak of such things in front of the groom, but to me you're just Billy, and part of the family for the past thirty years. The groom part hasn't caught up with me yet."

Billy ducked his head to hide a tight grin. "To be honest, it hasn't caught up with me very much, either. This is a lot like marrying into my own family."

Caleb shook his head. "Be patient. It'll get worse."

Adam laughed out loud.

Billy reached for the door latch. "I had better get back home. Mother will want to know. And Trudy." He opened the door, and Brigitte stepped outside with him, and suddenly Caleb followed them and closed the door behind him. For a moment he stood there in the dim light, and then he reached to tenderly place the flat of his hand against the cheek of his sister who stood unmoving in surprise. He said nothing. He just stood with his hand touching her face, and she raised her hand to cover his. He dropped his hand to face Billy, and for a moment the two men looked into each other. They said nothing because words between them were not necessary as Caleb silently spoke of his deep love and respect for the strong, gentle man before him, and Billy silently promised he would spend his life trying to make Brigitte happy. Then Caleb opened the door and stepped inside, to leave the two alone in the cool of the evening and the dim, silvery light of the stars.

Twenty-five days. Three weeks and four days. Six hundred hours. In the two households—Dunsons and Weemses—Brigitte, Margaret, Prissy, Kathleen, Dorothy, and Trudy were counting the minutes while they worked and planned and talked. To the women, it simultaneously felt as though the day would never arrive and that it was arriving far too quickly. The contradiction never occurred to the women. They only knew the anticipation of the wedding, with all the fuss and preparation it thrust upon them, was one of the most delicious events in the life of any woman, and they savored every moment of it, hating that it would end on August thirty-first. At the same time, it seemed that August thirty-first was a time lost somewhere in the mists of the eternal future, never to arrive. The torture was exquisite, yet they reveled in it, loving every moment of preparation. Their world made perfect sense. To them.

The men observed the women scurrying about and listened to their unending buzz about trivialities that had scant meaning, no logic, and made absolutely no sense. Befuddled by the preparations, they looked at each other and shrugged and condescendingly tolerated the busyness while they went on with the real business of life—running a shipping business, innocently blind to the joy and inner fulfillment that was taking place all around them in the women.

The sewing of the wedding dress became the all-consuming project. They spent three days visiting every shop in Boston that had material in pure enough white and suitable to a wedding gown for Brigitte Dunson. For four days they pored over patterns, before deciding none of them was quire right. Brigitte's gown would have to have a certain simplicity yet elegance. It would need to be perfect, and they would design their own.

Then came the laying out of the silk on the big dining table, pinning their pattern to the cloth, and the careful tedium of using Margaret's shears to carefully make the cuts. And then the construction began. No one counted the hours Brigitte stood still while they hung and rehung the gown on her, adjusting pins, making tucks, standing back with their faces puckered while they fervently sought and corrected any defect that would detract from their creation. They worked with microscopic accuracy to attach the lace, sparingly, at the throat, and the wrists. They gathered together for hours with needles, making the tiny stitches while they chattered and giggled, and no one noticed or cared that the needlework lagged far behind the gossip and the talk.

The men—Matthew, Caleb, Adam, and Billy—had a shipping company to run, and though the world in which they moved made reasonable allowances for the interruptions represented by a marriage, even so great an event was not permitted to interfere with the real business that held the world together. There were contracts to be made and honored, ships and crews constantly at risk, exposed to the vagaries of the sea, constantly shifting tariffs and taxes, records, competition, and the never-ending drain of worry at the downward political and economic spiral that kept the United States teetering on the brink of destruction. If the men gathered in the maddening secrecy of the hot, sweaty, deadly battle going on in the East Room of the Statehouse in Philadelphia were to fail in this last attempt to save the union, only the Almighty knew how quickly, and how completely, the entire country would come to pieces. So the men of the Dunson and Weems families moved in the affairs of their practical, logical, sensible world, while the women tolerated them and moved on with their work of perpetuating the human race.

The women debated for fifteen days before they reached agreement. There would be no written announcements; the public notices posted by Reverend Olmstead would be sufficient. There would be no great feast for loved ones and friends following the wedding. That would come later in a housewarming sometime in September when the weather was cooler and the newlyweds had settled into their home near the Common.

On each of the three Sundays remaining in August, Silas stood in his pulpit in the white church as he had for more than forty years and formally announced the forthcoming marriage of Brigitte Dunson and Billy Weems, to take place at the church on the evening of Friday, August thirty-first. Each time, he paused while murmuring interrupted and the congregation craned their necks to peer at the two of them, sitting in their pews as they had since anyone could remember, smiling, beaming, blushing. The moment Silas concluded the benediction on the services, open talk erupted, and few people left until they had crowded around the two families on the grass in the churchyard to swamp them with congratulations and wish Brigitte and Billy a long and happy life together.

On the third Sunday, following the services, Silas delivered to Billy the certificate declaring that the required public notice had been given. On Monday, Billy and Brigitte visited the office of Harold Trumbull, Boston City Clerk, and left with the marriage license and Harold's beaming congratulations. That afternoon they met Horatio Cutler at the office of his attorney, where Billy made the necessary payment and they signed the purchase contract for the Cutler home near the Common.

The morning of August thirty-first brought a spectacular sunrise of high clouds shot through with reds and yellows and pinks, and a cool breeze ruffling the flags and the sails along the waterfront. The men were at the Dunson & Weems office by seven o'clock, and stayed through the day until five o'clock, when they turned it over to Tom Covington to close, and walked home in the unexpectedly cool late afternoon. During the day, the women disciplined themselves to perform the necessary household chores of making the beds and setting breakfast and the midday meals on the table, with each of them glancing at the mantel clock not less than fifty times. The thought of supper never entered their minds.

At 6:45 P.M. two shining coaches, each drawn by a pair of matched gray mares, stopped before the Dunson home, and Matthew stepped from one of the coaches into the street, through the gate, and quickly to the Dunsons' door. Margaret led Brigitte from the house, followed by Prissy, Dorothy, Trudy, Caleb and Adam, and they all followed Matthew back to the street, where he helped the five women into the first coach where Kathleen was waiting with young John seated beside her. The boy wore a dark woollen suit with a starched white shirt and tie, and a decided frown of disgust at being required to endure all the unnecessary, ridiculous stir surrounding the simple act of getting married. If people wanted to get married, why couldn't they just go see Silas and get married?

With the women and their gowns, all around him, John tugged at Kathleen's elbow. "Mother," he asked quietly, "can I go sit with the men?"

Kathleen reached for Matthew's hand. "Can John sit with you?"

Matthew looked at the pleading in the boy's eyes. "Come on," he answered, and the boy fairly leaped from the coach to seize his father's hand. The men entered the second coach, Matthew signaled, and the horses stepped out with their iron shoes ringing on the cobblestones as they moved through the familiar streets toward the church where Matthew had left Billy half an hour earlier. It seemed the ride had hardly begun when the drivers in their high-topped hats hauled back on the reins and whoaed the horses to a stop before the church. The men were on the ground before the coaches stopped rocking in their leathers and trotted to the coach ahead to open the doors and help the women down. They all paused while the ladies tugged to straighten their dresses, and for a moment the men studied Brigitte. They could not remember her ever being so radiant, so beautiful, so alive. Matthew offered his arm as the head of the Dunson family, Brigitte took it, and they led the procession up the cobblestone walkway to the doors of the church. Matthew opened the two doors, peered inside for a moment, located Billy standing before Silas at the front of the chapel, and once again took Brigitte on his arm. Silas raised one hand to signal to Matthew, and the procession walked steadily down the aisle. While hidden behind the organ, aged Ernst Steinhold pumped the bellows, while his wife, Kirsten, played "Praise God from Whom All Blessings Flow."

The chapel was filled with the friends and neighbors and loved ones Billy and Brigitte had known most of their lives. The westering sun set the stained glass windows high in the walls of the building afire, bathing the austere old room in a glow of every color in the rainbow. Radiant in her simple yet elegant wedding dress, Brigitte had not advanced fifteen feet down the aisle when the first subdued, discreet sniffling was heard. The two families took their places in their usual pews while Matthew walked forward to leave Brigitte standing shoulder to shoulder with Billy as the couple faced old Silas.

The organ quieted, the Reverend Olmstead raised a hand, and began in his high, reedy voice.

"We are gathered here this beautiful evening to join this man and this woman in holy matrimony according to the command of the Great Jehovah in the book of Genesis . . . "

Margaret swallowed hard and silently raised her handkerchief to wipe at the first tear. Dorothy's chin was quivering. Prissy and Trudy were wiping at tears and didn't know why.

" . . . marriage is according to the eternal plan. . . ."

Matthew studied Billy's back, with memories flashing. The two boys—Matthew serious, Billy steady—the young men who walked to war at Lexington and Concord with John Dunson—Billy shot and bayoneted—John dying—Matthew refusing to leave Billy—staying with him, sleeping beside his bed while he wasted and all but died—his slow recovery—both of them taking up arms against the British—the battles, Billy a lieutenant with the bull-strength to pick up an eleven-hundred pound cannon to save his sergeant the morning they stormed British Redoubt Number Ten at Yorktown—six years of endless fighting—somehow surviving—coming home—the shipping business they set up together—and now . . . the steady, common, plain-faced man he had loved from earliest memory, standing before Silas Olmstead to marry his sister. Matthew glanced at the floor and swallowed hard and raised his head once again.

" . . . who gives this woman to this man in holy matrimony . . . "

"I do." Matthew's words sounded too loud in the quiet of the room. Silas nodded and Matthew turned back to take his place beside Kathleen. Almost unobserved, he slipped his arm about her shoulder and drew her close while John looked up at his father with the silent question written all over his face. "When can we go home?"

" . . . if any man has reason against this marriage let him speak now or forever hold his peace . . . "

The only sound in the room was the quiet sounds of women working with their handkerchiefs.

" . . . you may exchange rings . . . "

Heads craned to watch Billy slip the beautiful wedding ring on Brigitte's delicate finger and Brigitte to work the large wedding band onto Billy's thick finger.

" . . . by the authority vested in me I pronounce you husband and wife . . . "

Prissy and Trudy stood on tiptoe, waiting.

"You may kiss your bride in the bonds of matrimony."

Both girls clapped their hands over their mouths and tears came as Billy tenderly bent forward to kiss his wife and Brigitte kissed him.

Old Silas could not resist. "You may kiss her again, if you've a notion."

Startled, Billy looked at him, and Silas gestured with his hand while laughter filled the chapel, and Billy kissed his sweetheart once more for the world to see.

Silas bowed his head and the room quieted while he petitioned the Almighty to grant the two newlyweds long and happy lives, filled with love and children. "Amen."

Ernst once again pumped the bellows and Kirsten played the organ while Billy offered Brigitte his arm and they walked together back down the aisle, with their families and then the congregation following them out into the cool of the evening. For a time they crowded about the couple, hugging Brigitte and pumping Billy's hand in congratulations. And then Matthew quietly took Billy's arm and led him and Brigitte to the waiting coach with the family following. He opened the coach door and Billy assisted Brigitte up the step, then followed her to take his seat beside her. Matthew gazed at them for several moments and they looked back at him, and then the rest of the family crowded around the open coach door with the congregation gathered behind. Margaret and Dorothy leaned in to seize the hands of their children, then backed away as Matthew closed the door and signaled the driver. The whip popped, the driver spoke, and the coach rolled forward. Half an hour passed before the crowd thinned, and Matthew and the family boarded the second coach, to deliver Dorothy and Trudy to their small home, before moving on to Margaret's home where the Dunsons all stepped down. Matthew settled the fare with the driver, and the family walked through the white picket gate to the front door and into the parlor.

Kathleen said, "That was beautiful. Just beautiful."

Margaret sighed. "It was. Beautiful." Suddenly her face clouded, and she could not hold herself in, and she covered her face with both hands and sobbed. Matthew stared at her in wonder, then looked at Kathleen, inquiring.

Kathleen threw her arms about Margaret and held her close, like a child. "It's all right. It's all right. He knows. He was there."

Matthew stared, unable to fathom his mother's tears, and Kathleen repeated, "John was there. He saw. He was there."

John! His father!

Kathleen stepped back and Matthew wrapped his trembling mother inside his arms and murmured, "He was there, mother. He was there. He saw it. I promise."

For a little time Margaret buried her face in his shoulder and shook with sobs. Then she stopped and stepped back and looked up at him, eyes red.

"I thought he was. I thought I felt him there."

"You did."

"Well," Margaret said, "we didn't even think about supper. Matthew, you and Kathleen will stay while we put something on the table, won't you?"

Twenty minutes later none noticed when Caleb slipped out the back door into the night. It was an hour later, when Matthew and Kathleen took John by the hand and started to leave that Margaret asked, "Where did Caleb go? That boy! Comes and goes just whenever he takes a notion. Won't tell a body—just disappears."

"Don't worry about him," Matthew said. "He can take care of himself."

"That may be so, but it still worries a mother."

It was just past midnight when Margaret heard the front gate open and close. She had been sitting alone for more than an hour in her rocking chair in the light of a single lamp, with Adam and Prissy asleep in their beds, lost in memories of Brigitte. The baby, the child, the adolescent, the grown woman, the married woman. She rose and walked to the front door to wait for the soft rap, and it came. She opened the door and stepped back to let Caleb enter. He went to the kitchen to dip water from the bucket, and drink, with her following.

"Are you all right?" she asked softly.

He nodded and put the dipper back into the wooden bucket.

"Where were you? I worried."

He shrugged, said nothing, and started toward the parlor, when she reached to take his arm.

"Can't you tell me where you were?"

For a few moments he looked into her eyes before he spoke.

"I was at the Cutler house. In the shadows of the yard. I waited until the windows were dark, and then I stayed for a time after. I didn't want anyone disturbing Billy and Brigitte on their wedding night."

He paused for a moment before he turned and walked toward his bedroom, leaving Margaret to stand in the dim light, stunned, and suddenly weeping again.

Notes

The persons and events in this chapter are fictional.

However, for an excellent map showing the open grassy area known as the "Common," as well as the street grid of the city of Boston and the wharves and docks of the Boston waterfront, in the 1780 time frame, see Freeman, *Washington*, the map facing page 229.

The essence of the rather strange Massachusetts law, passed June 22, 1786, requiring public notice either by announcement or posting in writing in a public place of the intent of a couple to marry, followed by a certificate that such notice has been made, appears in Ulrich, *A Midwife's Tale*, p. 139.

CHAPTER XXVI

★ ★ ★

*T*he Monday morning sun had cleared the eastern rim of the world far enough to promise another sweltering hot Philadelphia day, but not far enough for the banks and investment houses and law offices in the vital business district just west of the Statehouse to have unlocked their doors to morning traffic. The neat cobblestone-paved streets between the Delaware River waterfront to the east and Twelfth Street to the west echoed with the rumble of carts and wagons loaded heavy with fresh produce and cheeses from the thrifty Dutch farms surrounding the city.

In his room on the second floor of the Hartman boardinghouse, John Rutledge, one of the four delegates from South Carolina to the Grand Convention—white-haired, high, rounded forehead, solid chin and jaw—shrugged into his coat, tugged the sleeves straight, glanced at himself one last time in the mirror, walked out the door, down the stairs, and out into the bright sun. Born in 1739 to a middle-class family, by 1776, Rutledge's dedication and brilliance in the world of planting, law, and politics had gained him five plantations, a solid law practice, and established him as one of the first citizens in his home state. His record as a dedicated leader for the American patriot cause against English monarchy was unparalleled in the south, and the British repaid his efforts by confiscating and partially destroying all five of his plantations. At the close of the war he had been appointed presiding judge of the South

Carolina Supreme Court. When the call came for service in the Grand Convention in Philadelphia, South Carolina turned to him.

As he walked east toward the business district, he nodded a morning greeting to the few who acknowledged him in passing; his stellar life in South Carolina had done little to promote his recognition in Philadelphia. He stopped in the luxury of the Indian Queen Hotel foyer where James Wilson of Pennsylvania was waiting for him, and the two walked back into the street, and south the few blocks to a shop on Fruit Street with a small, neat sign in the window, DUNLAP & CLAYPOOLE, PRINTERS.

In the ten-day recess that was to end that morning, most of the other delegates had either journeyed home to resurrect their business affairs or to renew family ties or both, or they had remained in Philadelphia, trying to forget the sweltering East Room of the Statehouse and the tangled mass of confusion they had created in the two months of hot debate in that locked room, which at times seemed more akin to a prison than the hall in which the Grand Convention was convened. But the Committee of Detail, appointed on July twenty-sixth, and which included John Rutledge as chairman, with members Edmund Randolph of Virginia, James Wilson from Pennsylvania, Oliver Ellsworth from Connecticut, and Nathaniel Gorham from Massachusetts, enjoyed no such reprieve. As regards the qualifications of these five men, the consensus of the convention was that it would be difficult, perhaps impossible, to put together five men whose wisdom, clarity of thought, and dedication to purpose would rise to their level.

In the ten-day reprieve, John Rutledge skillfully kept them together, rapidly and systematically going over every document that might offer a part of the solution to the quandary that had brought the convention to a grinding halt. The committee had picked the Articles of Confederation to pieces, examined the discarded Pinckney plan and the Paterson plan, then half the constitutions of the various states, collecting a thought here, a principle there, a phrase, a word, that would fit somewhere in the puzzle.

Then they had piled the bundle on the desk of Edmund Randolph with the instruction: make sense of it and write the rough draft of a new constitution. With the other four looking over his shoulders, Randolph delivered.

John Rutledge had taken the Randolph rough draft with the ink scarcely dry and made a few recommendations in the margins, then passed the document to James Wilson, probably the most experienced, learned, and dedicated member of the committee. Wilson had risen above weariness and fatigue to create a new and corrected draft, which the committee dissected one line at a time, examined from every conceivable angle, approved it, and handed it back to Wilson. Thereupon Wilson had made the necessary corrections to create a smooth-flowing, simple, legally sound, and comprehensive document.

With John Rutledge at his shoulder, Wilson had approached the partnership of Dunlap & Claypoole, on Friday, August third, two businessmen who owned the Philadelphia newspaper the *Pennsylvania Packet*, which had most recently been made famous because of their article that dubbed the East Room of the Statehouse "Unanimity Hall." It was this company that had been previously selected to print other documents for Congress and had earned the trust of most men in the convention.

As Wilson and Rutledge entered the printing office, David Claypoole greeted them. "Good morning, gentlemen," he said, "may I be of service?" He glanced at the sealed document in Wilson's hands.

Wilson was amiable. "Good morning. Is Mr. Dunlap away?"

"New York. Attending congress."

Wilson laid the packet on the counter. "We are delivering to you a copy of a draft of a proposed constitution for the United States. This represents what has been accomplished by the Grand Convention since May twenty-fifth. We must have sixty copies of this by eight o'clock on Monday morning, August sixth. Three days from now."

Claypoole nodded but remained silent as Wilson continued.

"We trust you can do this with absolute secrecy. No one except you and your staff is to know what is written here. Can you agree to that?"

Claypoole nodded his head. "None. I'll handle it myself. I'll have it ready Monday morning."

Wilson looked at Rutledge, who nodded, and Wilson said, "Good. We'll want large margins on both sides for notes and corrections. I can't promise when you'll get paid, but one thing I can promise. If you are successful in this, we will notify your newspaper before anyone else, and you will have first release of this information to the public at large."

Claypoole nodded. "Agreed. I'll be waiting for you Monday morning."

Monday morning, August sixth, eight o'clock A.M., had arrived. Wilson stopped at the front door of the print shop, turned the handle, and walked in. David Claypoole was seated at his desk, waiting, and he stepped rapidly to the front counter to greet them. He still wore his large, dark, gray printer's apron, with heavy black gauntlets from his wrists to his elbows to protect his white shirt. His thin face showed a hint of pride. He laid a sealed box on the desk nearest the door.

"Here they are. Sixty copies. Seven pages each. Large margins. The billing is inside." He drew a document from inside his apron. "This is a copy for your examination."

For two minutes both Wilson and Rutledge studied the detail of the document. It was all there, just as Wilson's final draft had it. Wilson raised his eyes to Claypoole.

"Excellent. No one else knows of this?"

"No one. I did most of it myself. My father helped a little, but no one will ever learn of it from him."

Wilson offered the copy back to Claypoole, and Claypoole shook his head.

"You keep it. That is the only other copy, and we don't want the responsibility. Do with it as you wish. Oh, one more thing. We have sealed the printing plates in another box and have them in the vault. They will remain there until you either call for them, or tell us you no longer need them, and we'll disassemble them."

Wilson thrust out his hand. "Keep them safe for now. The day we finish, we will report to you here. Thank you."

With the box clutched under one arm, Wilson followed Rutledge back into the street, and the two hurried to the Statehouse, down the large, vacuous hall to the East Room, and Fry swung the door open for them to enter. They set the box on Wilson's desk, opened it, placed the sixty copies to one side, discarded the box, and waited for the other delegates to arrive. They came noisily after their ten-day reprieve and crowded around Wilson's desk, pointing, gesturing, inquiring about the stack of papers. At ten o'clock George Washington took his chair on the dais and the room quieted.

"The convention will come to order. Secretary Jackson will call the roll."

Jackson's roll call was perfunctory, and he turned to Washington. "A quorum is present, Mr. President."

"Thank you." Washington looked directly at John Rutledge. "Our first order of business is a report from the Committee of Detail. Mr. Chairman . . . "

Rutledge stood. "Mr. President, the Committee has reduced its efforts to a seven-page, printed draft of a proposal. I have sixty printed copies and I respectfully request permission to distribute them to the delegates."

Washington nodded. "Deliver the copies to Mr. Jackson's desk." He turned to look down at Jackson. "Carefully distribute the copies, one per delegate, and keep a record. All undistributed copies are to be delivered to this desk. Every copy must be accounted for."

"Yes, Mr. President."

The delegates quickly formed a line down the aisle, and Jackson systematically called their names and made a check mark on a paper as he handed out the documents. The remaining few copies were placed on the corner of Washington's desk on the dais, and within three minutes the only sounds in the room were pages being turned and the occasional scratch of a quill as notations were made in the generous margins on the printed pages.

Within ten minutes, the sound of the quills had ceased as the delegates began to grasp the reach and the depth of the twenty-three articles in the document. They recognized phrases and words and principles from the Articles of Confederation, the Virginia Plan, the New Jersey

Plan, Pinckney's work, Paterson's documents, the debates, some state constitutions, and a few from sources unknown. In even-handed, plain style, it was all there, simple, clear, uncluttered. Terms and designations that identified offices and governmental entities appeared—*President, Speaker, Congress, Senate, House of Representatives, Supreme Court.* Phrases that were at once simple yet comprehensive caught their eye—*We the people—state of the union—privileges and immunities, necessary and proper—vacancies—disabilities.* The internal workings of both houses of the new Congress were defined, with the procedures of the qualified veto power and the jurisdiction of the courts. The power of impeachment was granted to the House of Representatives, and the power to convict to the Supreme Court. The procedure by which new states would be admitted to the union was carefully described. The provisions went on and on.

Within half an hour the delegates understood that the Committee of Detail had produced a document that moved the entire convention a gigantic step forward on the long and twisted road of creating a new government. They had created a detailed, defined list of eighteen powers vested in the new national government, beyond which it could not go. Further, the document had denied certain powers to the states. States could not coin money, issue letters of marque and reprisal, make treaties, or grant titles of nobility. They could not print paper money, lay duties on imports, keep troops or ships of war in time of peace, declare war singly or in combination with any other state or states.

The result was that some of the hazy, ill-defined lines between the new national government and the state governments were clarified, but others remained, still fuzzy, yet to be resolved.

Further, the committee had intentionally left to the convention the issue of how many states would be required to ratify the new constitution, by leaving an open blank in the language of Article XXI:

"The ratification of the conventions of _____ states shall be sufficient for organizing this constitution."

The number that would eventually fill the blank was a matter of great speculation among the delegates, and it ranged from seven, a bare majority, to all thirteen states, although most reckoned that they would never require all thirteen states to ratify. Too well did they remember the infuriating roadblocks that the belligerent, stubborn Rhode Island had thrown in the way of progress under the Articles of Confederation, which required the agreement of all thirteen states on many of the critical votes.

But most significant, the Committee had attempted to neutralize the naked threat of Charles Cotesworth Pinckney of South Carolina, issued on July twenty-third. With eyes blazing, in a soft, steady voice, he had made it known that if the convention intended meddling with the issue of slavery, he and his delegation were prepared to walk out, and the business of nation-making would crash.

The Committee of Detail had addressed Pinckney's deadly pronouncement, and realized they could find no middle ground. The issue had to fall one way or the other—for or against slavery. They gambled.

"No tax or duty shall be laid by the legislature on articles exported from any state; nor on the migration or importation of such persons as the several states shall think proper to admit; nor shall such migration or importation be prohibited. No navigation act shall be passed without the assent of two thirds of the members present in each house."

The words were polite, innocuous, inoffensive in and of themselves. They were also transparent to every delegate. "Such persons" were the slaves. "Navigation act" was the tax to be paid upon the sale of "such persons." Slavery would be left as it was. The fuse was lit. The issue of slavery was yet to explode between most northern and southern states, and no one would know the outcome of the gamble taken by the Committee of Detail until the smoke had cleared and the wreckage was in view.

The delegates accepted it and moved on.

It was past eleven o'clock when the general consensus was voiced by one delegate who stood and was recognized.

"Mr. President, I respectfully move that we adjourn until tomorrow morning for purposes of having time to study the detail of this proposal."

Washington nodded his agreement. "We are adjourned until tomorrow morning, eleven o'clock. Punctuality is required."

The following morning brought a heat wave that held for days. The delegates were already perspiring when Washington called them to order.

"The first order of business is consideration of the report of the Committee of Detail. I presume each of you has acquainted himself with the provisions."

Pinckney stood. "I move that we adjourn into the committee of the whole for further debate." He had not anticipated the vitriolic response that came hot and loud.

Gorham was on his feet. "Some could not agree to the form of the government before the powers were defined, while others could not agree to the powers till it was seen how the government was formed. If we do not get past such things, I fear there will be no end to the delays and postponements."

Gorham sat down and Rutledge stood, eyes flashing. "I have had my fill of the tediousness of such proceedings!"

Oliver Ellsworth, with a faint cloud of snuff dust hanging in the air about his bald head, stood, chin thrust out defiantly. "We grow more and more skeptical as we proceed. If we do not decide soon, we shall be unable to come to any decision at all."

A voice rang out, "Call for the vote!"

The vote was three in favor, six against—two to one against the torment and the delay of starting the debates all over again in the committee of the whole.

Benjamin Franklin moved his legs, adjusted his spectacles, and looked about the room with eyes that saw and felt. *They're ready. Anxious. Impatient. No more delays. They've had a glimpse of the end of it, and they want it finished.*

Under the watchful and skilled eye of George Washington, they collectively took a deep breath and settled into the intense, tedious, mentally punishing work of taking the entire proposal of the Committee of Detail apart, one article, one paragraph, one line, one word at a time, and putting it back together.

They attacked the preamble first. "We, the people of the States of New Hampshire, Massachusetts, Rhode Island, . . . " Each state was named.

Gouverneur Morris shook his head. "Too many words. Cut it back. 'We the people of the United States . . . '" With his gift for power and simplicity in writing, he completed the preamble.

Move on.

Which citizens are to have the right to vote in the elections for the new national government? Persons who own land? Persons who own shops? Businesses? Persons with education? Whites? Blacks? Chinese? What is to be done about the fact that each state has its own qualifications for voters, and none of them are the same? What age must a person be to vote? And worst of all, what would the citizens of the separate states do if they suddenly discovered that the new qualifications for voters excluded them from voting in the national elections at all? Would there be a rebellion?

August eighth came, and the debate ground on with but one conclusion. Owing land would not be one of the requirements for voting in the new national government. Other issues were left undecided.

August ninth, hot, sweaty, the convention picked its way through the question of which government should control the times and places of the election for national offices. The states, or the new government? In his quiet, methodical logic, Madison persuaded them. If it is to be a national election, the national government ought to address the terms, or some of them. Further, should vacancies appear in congress, the governor of the state in question would be vested with the power to appoint a replacement.

The days came and went in a blur in the sweltering heat, with the delegates beginning to show the stress and strain. Debate became less lengthy, more pointed. Tolerance faded, replaced by bluntness. New leaders emerged. Gouverneur Morris lifted everyone with his wit that saw the convention through otherwise dark days. Benjamin Franklin sprinkled his well-chosen wisdom at crucial moments in snarled debates. Dickinson recovered some of the stature he had lost in a dull July. The men who had led the convention from the beginning—Madison, Wilson, King, Read, Mason, and others—held the debates to a high level of relevance and decision as they steadily plowed on.

What qualifications must a person have to become a congressman?

Senator? Thirty years of age, a citizen of the United States for nine years, and a resident in the state represented.

Representative? Twenty-five years of age, a citizen of the United States for seven years, and a resident of the state represented.

On Monday, August thirteenth, tempers flared and harsh words flew when the issue of which branch of congress, the House or the Senate, had the power to originate revenue bills. Most delegates thought that matter had been forever settled during the battle that resulted in the Great Compromise between the large and small states, at which time the power of raising revenue had been given exclusively to the House of Representatives, to soften the blow of granting the small states power in the Senate equal to the large states. To now rob the House of their bargain was treachery. The new vote, on August thirteenth, continued to favor the Senate, but one thing was certain: the convention had not seen the last of that issue.

What should be the pay for members of congress? The proposal before the convention was simple:

"The members of congress shall receive a compensation for their services, to be ascertained and paid by the state in which they shall be chosen."

"Ridiculous!" exclaimed King and Wilson. "If the states pay their representatives in the national congress, they are simply state employees, not national representatives! The very thought destroys the entire concept of a national government!"

The arguments raged. William Pierce of Georgia moved that "the wages should be paid out of the national treasury!" Oliver Ellsworth hotly disagreed. "The wages must be paid by the states, since the property in the various states differs so greatly!"

The vote was called, and the majority decided that the national treasury, not the states, should pay the national employees.

The next issue was handled in short order. How much should senators and representatives be paid?

Once again divergent views filled the chamber, ranging from "liberal compensation," to "no compensation at all," with the question posed and discarded, should the actual dollar amount be included in the constitution itself? The issue was resolved by amending the clause to declare that the wages would "be ascertained by law."

August fifteenth saw the convention reaffirm their previous vote, that the president of the United States should have veto power over laws passed by Congress, however, his veto power was subject to override by a two-thirds vote in both the House and the Senate.

From his place on the dais, Washington glanced down at Franklin, and a silent communication passed between the two men. *The checks and balances are slipping into place on every issue—no one branch of this new government will have unlimited power.*

The small, endless, thorny issues that demanded resolution continued amid the sweltering heat in the closed room, to grind at the resolve of the men who had no choice but to take them one at a time, word by word, harangue, argue, amend, vote, and move on.

What powers should Congress have?

Establish a uniform rule of naturalization; coin money; regulate the value of foreign coin; fix standards of weights and measures; establish post offices; appoint a treasurer; create courts below the Supreme Court; establish rules as to captures on land and water; define and punish piracies and felonies committed on the high seas, as well as counterfeiting the currency of the United States, and offences against the law of nations. What powers should Congress have regarding the army and the navy? Madison and young Pinckney made their proposal. Congress was to have power to raise and support armies and maintain a navy. The vote of the delegates agreed. Included was the power to make all laws that should be necessary and proper for carrying into execution all the foregoing powers, and all other powers vested by the new constitution, and that included the power to define treason and punish those found guilty of the heinous offense.

The morning of August twenty-second, Washington stared at the business of the day long and hard before he drew a resolute breath and called the convention to order.

"The debate on Article VII, Section 4 shall be resumed."

Slavery! The word did not appear in Section 4. What did appear were restrictions on taxes and the rights of navigation, which could essentially end the slave trade. If navigation laws struck at the right to carry "other persons" in commerce, and tax laws were strict enough, those who had an aversion to slavery could strangle the commerce of the southern states, which depended on slave labor for economic survival.

George Mason of Virginia came to his feet, eyes flashing, face flushed in anger. "This infernal traffic originated out of the avarice of British merchants. It was the British government that constantly undercut the attempts of Virginia to abolish it altogether. This issue does not concern just those states that are now importing slaves. It concerns the entire union! The effect of slavery on the United States is deplorable! Slavery discourages the arts and manufactures. It prevents the immigration of whites! Every master of slaves is born a petty tyrant!"

Madison was shocked. George Mason was himself a slave owner!

Mason paused and waited until the room was silent before he raised a hand, one finger pointed to heaven.

"Slavery brings the judgment of heaven on a country. As nations cannot be rewarded or punished in the next world they must be punished in this! By an inevitable chain of causes and effects, providence punishes national sins, by national calamities."

He stopped with his words ringing off the walls, and not one delegate moved or made a sound as they realized they had just received a prophecy from a man whom all considered both qualified and capable of delivering one.

Mason waited until the spell began to dwindle and then concluded.

"It is essential in every point of view, that the general government should have power to prevent the increase of slavery."

Young Charles Pinckney waited until murmuring broke the silence before he took his feet. He cleared his throat, and began.

"If slavery be wrong, it is justified by the example of all the world. In all ages, one half of mankind has been slaves." He paused while delegates glanced at each other. "If the southern states are left alone, they will probably voluntarily stop the importation of slaves. I would vote for such a proposal. However, any attempt by this convention to take away the right, as it is now proposed, will result in serious objections—perhaps fatal—to the constitution which we all wish to have adopted."

Young Charles's second cousin, Charles Cotesworth Pinckney came to his feet, and it was obvious he had no intention of being as gentle in his words as his young kinsman.

"If I and all of you sign this constitution and exert all our influence, it will be of no avail towards getting agreement from the citizens of South Carolina. South Carolina and Georgia cannot survive without slaves. Should this convention attempt to stop slavery by law, South Carolina will rebel. The importation of slaves will be in the best interest of the entire union. The more slaves, the more produce, the more consumption, and the more revenue. Take heed of the cost of eliminating slavery. It can split the union."

Nerves frayed raw from weeks of engaging in intense debate, fretting over endless details, and enduring insufferable heat, frustration, and mental exhaustion, finally gave way to hot anger.

John Rutledge jerked to his feet, voice loud, ringing. "If this convention thinks that North Carolina, South Carolina, and Georgia will ever agree to a plan that does not guarantee their right to import slaves, that expectation is nonsense! The people of those states will never be such fools as to give up so important an interest."

John Dickinson was speaking while he rose. "It is inadmissible—absolutely inadmissible—on every principle of honor and safety that the importation of slaves should be authorized to the states by this constitution. The true question is whether the national happiness will be promoted or impeded by the importation of slaves, and this question ought to be left to the national government, not to the states who are importing slaves."

John Langdon of New Hampshire spoke from his chair. "I cannot in good conscience leave it with the states to decide if they will traffic in slavery, when the clear opinion of this convention is to the contrary."

Roger Sherman of Connecticut stood. "A tax on slaves clearly makes them property! Not persons! Should the power be given to the national government to prohibit such a thing, that power ought to be exercised!"

The arguments raged on, back and forth, with the leaders dividing into two opposing camps that were without question preparing for a collision that could split the convention.

In desperation, a proposal was thrown out for consideration. Why not appoint a committee to study the matter and report? It was not that the proposal was so attractive, but that at that moment it was the last clear hope of saving all they had accomplished. The proposal was approved, nine votes to two, and one delegate from each state was appointed to the committee: Langdon, King, Johnson, Clymer, Dickinson, Martin, Madison, Williamson, the senior Pinckney, and Baldwin, with William Livingston of New Jersey as chairman.

Two days later, on Friday, August twenty-fourth, the atmosphere inside the sweltering room was charged with electricity when Washington took his place on the dais.

"Mr. Livingston, is the committee prepared to report?"

Livingston rose, and every eye was on him as he spoke. "We are." He picked several sheets of paper from his desk and walked steadily to the desk of William Jackson, the secretary, and laid them down, then returned to his desk.

Washington peered down at Jackson. "The secretary will read the report."

Jackson picked up the papers, perused them for a moment, and with the room in total silence, read.

"Strike out so much of the fourth section of the seventh article as was referred to the committee and insert, 'The migration or importation of such persons as the several states now existing shall think proper to admit, shall not be prohibited by the legislature prior to the year 1800—but a tax or duty may be imposed on such migration or importation at a rate not exceeding the average of the duties laid on imports.'"

For a moment no one breathed, and then there was the sound of breath being exhaled and murmuring broke out. There was no solution! The committee had solved the immediate problem by avoiding it for the next thirteen years! What would happen in thirteen years was for that generation to thrash out. In the meantime, if the convention voted in favor of the committee's proposal, they could move on with the detail of finishing their work.

The vote was called and Jackson recorded it. Seven in the affirmative, two in the negative. The bizarre proposal had passed! The last great barrier to their work was behind them. Relief was nearly a palpable thing as Jackson read the remainder of the committee's recommendations, and the votes were taken, up or down. With the slavery issue left a matter for future generations to solve, the flow was almost uninterrupted.

Monday, August twenty-seventh, the convention made short work of the new court system. There would be one supreme court, lower courts as needed, all to become the third branch of government, independent of and equal to the executive and the legislative branches. The judges? To be nominated by the President, with the advice and consent of the Senate, as a check on the President. Always, always, always, a check and a balance on any power granted to any part of the new government. And, to protect the supreme court judges from reprisals, they would serve for life, or during good behavior, and their compensation could not be reduced while they were serving.

What of the coin of the realm? Should Congress be authorized to print and circulate paper money? Too many of the delegates remembered the forty-two times the old Continental Congress, under the Articles of Confederation, had printed and circulated paper money, called Continental Dollars, until they were worthless. The worst epithet in common usage was to condemn a thing as not being worth "a continental." States had circulated their own paper money until the country was awash in it. The delegates would not soon forget that at one time, a pair of shoes in Virginia cost five thousand dollars. Yet, there was also the memory that the worthless money had saved the Revolution. It had paid for beef and muskets and flour for the army. But in the balance, the convention shuddered at the thought of paper money.

It was voted down. The coin of the realm would continue to be gold and silver, not paper.

Every delegate was aware of plans laid by ambitious men to reach westward to organize new states. It was no secret that Benjamin Franklin had already created a plan for a new state to be called Franklin. It was to be in the lush Tennessee River Valley, west of North Carolina, which had claimed the valley as her own. Three years earlier, the pioneers and settlers in that wilderness decided North Carolina was not looking out for their interests, so they declared their independence, elected a governor, set up their own militia, and provided for the collection of taxes to pay for their new state. Because no one had money, the taxes were collected in tobacco, fruit brandy, or beeswax. And, the new state of Franklin had recently sought acceptance as the fourteenth state in the foundling new union.

The dilemma was plain. If Franklin became the fourteenth state, what was to prevent other groups of disgruntled citizens from declaring their independence from a mother state and applying for admission into the Union? And, if they were admitted to the Union, should they have all rights of the other states previously admitted?

The answer was not long in coming. No state could be created from within the boundaries of an existing state without the consent of Congress, and, new states properly constituted would be admitted with all rights of all other states.

What of religion? The Puritans had come to this new land to worship the Almighty according to their own consciences. And they saw to it that those who disagreed left town, or were thrown in jail. In many states an oath was required of those elected to public office that they would worship according to the dictates of the church designated in that state. The delegates shied away from it; Thomas Jefferson despised the notion of a state-mandated religion. The convention dealt with that issue by providing the following mandate:

"No religious test shall ever be required as a qualification to any office or public trust under the authority of the United States."

Friday, the last day of August, the bone-weary delegates raised their heads and realized they were very close to the end of their incomparable odyssey. The Constitution was very nearly finished. With it came the recognition that creating it was one thing; establishing it as the foundation for the new government was quite another.

Washington called them to order and plucked up his daily agenda. "You will recall that on August sixth the Committee of Detail made its recommendation for ratification of the constitution as follows: 'Item XXI. The ratifications of _____ states shall be sufficient for organizing this constitution. Item XXII. This constitution shall be laid before the United States in congress assembled, for their approbation, and it is the opinion of this convention, that it should be afterwards submitted to a convention chosen in each state under the recommendation of its legislature, in order to receive the ratification of such convention."

Washington raised his head and cleared his throat. "Debate is open."

Luther Martin rose. "The Articles of Confederation were ratified by all thirteen states. It is unthinkable that this new constitution should be ratified by less."

Daniel Carroll of Maryland called, "Fill in the blank with the number thirteen! Unanimity will be essential to dissolve the existing confederacy, since all thirteen states ratified it."

Roger Sherman shook his head. "The hard practicality is that if all thirteen states must ratify, the new constitution is doomed, since Rhode Island has in its entire history never cooperated with the other twelve states on issues such as this. Nor has that state even sent delegates to this convention! Their vote will either be 'nay,' or no vote at all, which is also a 'nay.' I propose the blank be filled with the number ten."

Gouverneur Morris rose, his wooden leg thumping. "I move that we strike the requirement that the new constitution receive the approbation of Congress before being submitted to the state conventions. Rhode Island will have representation in Congress, and assuredly they will not lend their approbation. That being true, the constitution will never reach the people for their ratification."

"Second the motion."

The vote was unanimous in favor. The constitution would go directly to the Confederation Congress then in session, but not for debate, vote, or approbation. Only for them to acknowledge it and forward it on to state conventions, convened for the purpose of ratification by the people. The sole remaining issues were how many states would be required to achieve ratification, and, what would be the process for ratification?

James Wilson tilted his head to peer over his spectacles. "What is the problem? Seven states is a majority. Seven should be sufficient to ratify."

Edmund Randolph objected. "Seven is too narrow a margin. Nine is more respectable. It should be nine states."

The room quieted for a short time while the delegates pondered how Randolph had arrived at the number, nine. The answer came to most of them. Rhode Island would not ratify, which eliminated the number thirteen. Seven was a simple majority, but nine, a strong majority, seemed more appropriate for so important an issue.

The vote was called and recorded. The vote of nine states could ratify the constitution.

The last thorny question now lay before them. Who should ratify?

Elbridge Gerry stood, dour, face drawn down into its perpetual frown. "Ratification cannot be left to the people at large! Their ideas of sound government are the wildest in the world!"

Nathaniel Gorham disagreed. "Leave it to the legislatures, and the local politicians who benefit from the system as it is will find some way to block ratification, to protect their own self interests. It must finally be a matter for the people, not the politicians."

In succession, George Mason, followed by James Madison, rose to take the same position.

"Referring the plan to the authority of the people is essential. The legislatures have no power to ratify it. They are the mere creatures of the state constitution and cannot be greater than their creators. I consider the difference between a system founded on the legislatures only, and one founded on the people, to be the true difference between a league or treaty, and a constitution!"

Talk ceased. The issue was framed. The vote was called for and taken. The ratification of the new constitution would come from the people, in conventions held for that purpose in each state.

In short order the delegates handled the question of whether a state delegate could also serve as a national delegate. Too many remembered the corruption that had been brought about in England, when a man in a prominent political position was allowed to seek influence in other branches of the government, either for himself or his friends, with the result that a small clique of men enjoyed most of the power—to the downfall of the system. In the United States, that was not going to happen. State delegates could not at the same time be national delegates in any capacity. Checks and balances, always, always, always.

With the conclusion of the convention in sight, the delegates settled in to resolve the prickly question of how the President should be elected. That it was to be one man had already been decided. But how to pick that man? That was the question. The thought of granting pivotal powers to a single man made every delegate in the convention nervous, uneasy, for every man among them understood that nothing will corrupt a man more quickly or more completely than power, or the lust for it.

A proposed resolution of the problem came from the Committee on Postponed Matters and was reported on the floor of the convention by the chairman, Judge David Brearly of New Jersey. On September fourth, at the behest of Washington, Brearly laid out the work of the committee.

The President would serve for four years, with no restriction against reelection. He would be elected by the vote of electors equal in number to the Senators and Representatives from each state, and chosen by each state in a mode to be decided by that state. Should there be a tied vote, the Senate would decide. There would also be a new office, never before mentioned in the convention, titled Vice President, who would be ex-officio President of the Senate. The President must be at least thirty-five years of age, a natural born citizen of the United States, and a resident therein for at least fourteen years. He could be impeached by the House and tried and convicted by the Senate. He, the President, and not the Senate, was empowered to make treaties with the concurrence of two-thirds of the Senate. He would be vested with power to appoint judges and ambassadors, subject to advise and consent of the Senate, and to make treaties with foreign nations, also subject to the advise and consent of the Senate.

Portions of the Brearly proposal caught the convention by surprise. What was this new, cumbersome notion of electing people to elect the President? An electoral college? They recalled that James Wilson had earlier suggested a similar plan, but it had received little attention and no vote. The delegates wrestled with it, defined it, and tried to accept it. There had been no less than seven separate proposals for how to elect the President, and each of them were fatally flawed. At least twelve different votes had been taken in the past three months, and not one of the proposals had survived. The delegates shook their heads at this latest awkward proposal, then decided they needed more time, and returned it to the postponed matters agenda.

And what of the sweeping powers proposed to be vested in the President? One man. How long before "Mr. President" would become "Your Majesty"? Some delegates squirmed at the thought, while others faced the hard reality. If the new government was to be founded on three separate branches, the legislative, judicial, and executive, each empowered to check and balance the other, then the executive must be given its due. They came to a conclusion slowly, but surely. Give the president powers equal to those of the legislative and judicial arms of the government, and trust the people to get rid of despots who sought the presidency to corrupt it. It was a giant leap of faith in the common people, but the delegates accepted the concept, and moved on.

What was to be done with the Indians?—the natives who greeted the first whites to arrive only to find themselves steadily driven back, westward, steadily losing their land to the white man's voracious appetite for space. They had struck back the only way they understood, with raids and depredations on the white settlers, and had turned to making treaties and agreements with the Spanish for arms and ammunition. What was to be done to provide recourse and redress to the Indians for the wrongs done them by the western states, and to stop the sporadic, ongoing fighting? The answer was simple. They would have the status of a "foreign nation" and the right to treaty with them was given exclusively to the new government, to the exclusion of the various states. Few paid attention to the irony of seizing the land from those who had occupied it from ancient antiquity, and then declaring *them* to be the foreigners!

George Mason, Benjamin Franklin, George Washington, and others, had spent many hours pondering two harsh truths. No instrument of government created by men had ever been perfect, and, it was inevitable that time would bring changes in human affairs. What if the constitution was flawed? And what if changing times and thought made it obsolete? What was to be done?

The profoundly gifted George Mason of Virginia stated the solution with crystal clarity.

"The plan now to be formed will certainly be defective, as the Confederation has been found on trial to be. Amendments, therefore, will be necessary, and it will be better to provide for them in an easy, regular, and constitutional way, than to trust to chance and violence."

Instantly heads nodded in vigorous agreement, then stopped as thoughtful men asked the obvious questions. *How* is it to be amended, and *when?* If the process of amendment were made too easy, it would invite proposed amendments with every passing whim. If it were too difficult, the Constitution might be so rigid the people would reject it. Further, *who* could amend? The state legislatures? The new Congress? The delegates scratched their heads and cast about for answers.

Alexander Hamilton of New York called it out. "The state legislatures will not apply for amendments, except to increase their own powers. The national legislature will be the first to perceive the true need for amendment, and will be most sensible to the necessity of doing it."

The result? A compromise. *Another* compromise. The delegates had learned well that the art of creating new nations, and politics, is grounded on the principle of compromise.

James Madison made it simple. Both the national congress and the state legislatures could propose amendments to the Constitution, but no amendment would be effective until approved by three-fourths of the states. The clearer minds in the small states added one more provision—since each state had two senators, which gave the small states power in that branch of the new government equal to the large states, the small states wanted a guarantee that proposed amendments to the Constitution could not be adopted without the consent of the small states. The large states compromised once more. The guarantee was granted.

With minds swamped by their swift march through the last details of creating a new government, on Saturday, September eighth, the delegates realized the time had arrived to create the final draft of the Constitution. How to handle it? Appoint another committee, of course, this time to be called the Committee of Stile and Arrangement. Five men. William Samuel Johnson to serve as chairman, with Alexander Hamilton, Gouverneur Morris, James Madison, and Rufus King as committee members.

In the heat of the afternoon Washington spoke from the dais. "We stand adjourned until Monday morning, the usual hour."

While the other delegates gratefully took their leave of the hot, stale room, the five-man committee gathered for a time, to decide when they would meet, and where, to reduce the mind-boggling gathering of notes to an organized, understandable, simple document that would be suited to the highest and lowest intellects in the United States. As they stood huddled around the desk of William Johnson, Benjamin Franklin stalked slowly up the aisle, cane clicking on the floor with each step, to peer at the chair in which George Washington sat on the dais.

It was a large wooden chair, sturdy, straight backed, no-nonsense, with leather-padded arms, scant adornment, with one exception. The back of the chair was topped with a small rise on which appeared a carefully painted sun, the bottom half hidden as though by a distant skyline. The rays of the sun spread evenly across the back, reaching in all directions. Franklin stood before the chair, adjusted his spectacles, and leaned forward on his cane to examine the painting with great care before he nodded his satisfaction and slowly made his way out of the East Room.

Monday found the convention still locked in the give and take of small, insignificant details that spilled over through Tuesday, September eleventh. In the late afternoon, Washington announced, "We stand adjourned until tomorrow morning, the usual hour, at which time the Committee of Stile and Arrangement will make its report."

The final days were upon them. What would the last draft of their historic summer look like? What had the committee done with the draft delivered by the Committee of Detail on August sixth, and which had been added upon by the convention since that time with a disorganized collection of ideas on nation-making, the like of which the world had never seen? Only the five-man committee, and David Claypoole, who had printed several hundred copies of the work of the committee on four pages, one side only, knew the answer.

No day held the anticipation of the delegates like Wednesday morning, September twelfth, 1787, as they gathered once again in the muggy heat of the sealed East Room.

Washington took his seat on the dais. "The first order of business is the report of the Committee of Stile and Arrangement. Mr. Johnson, do you have the report?"

Johnson rose. "I do, sir." He held up the stack of printed documents. "Request permission to pass out a copy of the work to each member present."

"Granted."

Within minutes each delegate had a copy of the document spread on his desk, and leaned forward, locked in silence, with an intensity seldom seen during the convention while he slowly, thoughtfully read the document.

The preamble no longer named all thirteen states. Rather, it stated with simple dignity, "We the people of the United States . . . " The twenty-three articles of the prior draft of August sixth, which had covered seven printed pages, had been reduced to seven articles in language that was plain, simple, unmistakable, within the grasp of most Americans, and were complete on four pages. It flowed with an ease that bespoke a master craftsman, and it was soon understood that most of the genius in the document had flowed from the mind and quill of Gouverneur Morris.

Article One. All legislative powers herein granted shall be vested in a Congress of the United States. . . .

Article Two. The executive power shall be vested in a president. . . .

Article Three. The judicial power of the United States shall be vested in one supreme Court. . . .

Article Four. New states may be admitted by the Congress into this union. . . .

Article Five. The Congress shall propose amendments to this constitution. . . .

Article Six. This constitution shall be the supreme law of the land. . . .

Article Seven. The ratification of the conventions of nine states shall be sufficient for the establishment of this constitution.

Every man in the room would remember for the rest of his life the price that had been paid to create those four pages. The heat, the acrimonious debates, the two times the convention had exploded into a division between the north and the south that came within a whisper of destroying the United States altogether, the brutal words that had boiled over between avid opponents—they would never forget them. But now, they marveled at the skill with which the committee had removed all trace of the anger and the frustration and had set aside the animosities between north and south, large states and small, slaveholders and non-slaveholders. They read and reread the passages that anticipated and closed every door that might allow tyranny or corruption or conspiracy to creep into the new government, stunned by the simplicity and the thoroughness with which the convoluted, complicated provisions had been spelled out. The checks and balances were all in place, ensuring that no branch of the government or any inidividual could ever rise above another to become tyrannical.

And finally, the single provision that separated their new nation from any other in the world. The power of the government was vested in the people. The common people who ran the farms, and the shops, and fisheries. In the known history of the human race, no government had ever taken such a leap of faith.

For several minutes a hush held in the East Room. Every man present sensed a feeling in his soul that rose in his breast to hold him silent. What had they created? No one had gotten everything he had contended for, but everyone had gotten something. Some were satisfied with it, some disgruntled, a few disappointed. Some reckoned it was the work of fifty-five men who had reached inside themselves for the best they had. Others remembered the words of John Adams: "God is the great legislator of the universe."

Washington waited until the unexpected spirit ebbed before moving on. It was George Mason of Virginia who loudly stated what he conceived as being the one missing provision, without which the constitution would not be complete.

"The constitution is to be paramount to state constitutions and declarations of rights. For that reason, I wish the plan was prefaced with a bill of rights. And I would second a motion if made for the purpose. It would give great quiet to the people." Patiently Mason continued, "Freedom of speech, freedom of religion, the right to a fair trial, these and other liberties ought to be defined in a bill of rights. Eight state constitutions already have such guarantees. It should be one of the cornerstones of this new government."

Roger Sherman rose, thoughtfully tugging at his chin. "I am for securing the rights of the people where requisite. But the state declarations of rights are not repealed by this constitution. They are sufficient."

Murmuring was heard and questions quietly asked between the delegates. "Why is a bill of rights necessary? The states already have them, and the rights of the people are all protected by the document as it now stands."

The vote was called, and to the amazement and embarrassment of Mason, the vote was unanimous against any such bill. Even his native state of Virginia had voted against it. Any bill of rights would have to wait.

For the next two days the delegates scrambled to finish the housekeeping detail of adding a word here, changing a word there, deleting a word now and again. Debate was nearly non-existent in their overwhelming desire to finish their work and go home. Four months away from home, wives, business, and family, locked inside a sealed room in the heat of a Philadelphia summer, had been enough. At the close of the day of Saturday, September fifteenth, every man in the room fervently hoped all the delegates would sign the document when it was completed, but it was not to be. Three of their number loudly proclaimed their intent not to sign.

Edmund Randolph of Virginia startled them all. None could forget that on May twenty-fifth, it had been Randolph who had introduced the Virginia Plan, which had served as the framework for the entire convention, and the Constitution as it now existed. And now it was Randolph who exclaimed, "Am I to promote the establishment of a plan which I verily believe will end in tyranny? I will sign it only if this convention now approves a plan for a second convention, to give the people time to study this proposed constitution and to suggest amendments."

At Randolph's outburst, James Madison did not change expression, but the thought came to his mind, *he's shifted again—unstable thought processes.*

George Mason, a fellow Virginian, rose and shocked every man in the room. "I agree with Mr. Randolph." The delegates were remembering this same George Mason was the one who in July had declared he would rather bury his bones in Philadelphia than leave without a constitution. They were scarcely breathing as Mason explained. "This constitution has been formed without the knowledge or idea of the people. It is improper to say to the people, take this or nothing. It does not provide a means of stopping the heinous institution of slave trade, nor does it include a bill of rights! I would rather cut off my right hand than sign a constitution that could lead to a despotic government!"

The third dissenter was the grumbletonian, Elbridge Gerry of Massachusetts. In a ten-minute narrative he laid out his exceptions to the constitution, which included deep concerns about the sweeping powers granted to all three of the branches of the new government, the gray areas that left doubt as to intent and limits, and the shift of power from the states to the new national government. He could not in good conscience sign the instrument as it then stood.

The business of the day was finished, and Washington adjourned until the next business day.

Monday, September seventeenth, 1787, they met for the last time as colleagues in the convention that changed the world.

Washington called them to order and turned to the secretary. "Mr. Jackson will read the constitution as amended."

Silence held while Jackson read the four pages, slowly, steadily. He finished, turned to nod to Washington, and sat down.

Alexander Hamilton, the only delegate from New York who had returned to the convention to represent his state in the signing of the new constitution, stood.

"No man's ideas are known to be further from the plan than mine are known to be. Nonetheless, I rise to urge all to sign this instrument, as I will. I am convinced that if the public mind is properly instructed, it will rise to the challenge of nationhood and adopt such a solid plan." A thoughtful silence settled in the room as the brilliant Hamilton sat down.

The sound of Benjamin Franklin struggling to his feet brought every eye in the room to watch him stand, leaning on his cane. "Mr. President, respectfully I seek permission to address the convention." He held up a paper. "Mr. James Wilson who has been so accommodating in reading my remarks throughout the convention has kindly consented to read this one."

For a moment Washington studied the eighty-one year old man, famous the world over, among the wisest to be found. "Mr. Wilson may read the document."

For the last time, James Wilson pushed his spectacles back up his nose, took the paper from Franklin, and read.

"I confess that there are several parts of this constitution which I do not at present approve, but I am not sure I shall never approve them. For having lived long, I have experienced many instances of being obliged by better information, or fuller consideration, to change opinions even on important subjects, which I once thought right, but found to be otherwise. It is, therefore, that the older I grow, the more apt I am to doubt my own judgment, and to pay more respect to the judgment of others.

Thus, I consent, sir, to this constitution, because I expect no better, and because I am not sure, that it is not the best. On the whole, sir, I cannot help expressing a wish that every member of the convention who may still have objections to it, would, with me, on this occasion doubt a little of his own infallibility, and to make manifest our unanimity, put his name to this instrument."

For a time the delegates remained silent, aware that Franklin had given his last great effort to persuade Randolph, Mason, and Gerry to add their signatures to the new constitution. None of the three would raise their eyes to Franklin, and it was clear they would not change their minds. It was Franklin who turned to Washington and broke the awkward silence.

"Mr. President, I recommend that it would be in proper form to affix the words, 'Done in convention by the unanimous consent of the states present.'"

The subtlety of the wise old leader was apparent. If he could not persuade Randolph, Mason, and Gerry to sign the document and show the world the unanimity of all the delegates, at least he could add the prefix that would show the unanimity of all the states. Washington replied, "The prefix shall be added."

There was but one matter of business yet to be concluded. Nathaniel Gorham rose to his feet, and Washington recognized him.

"I move that the figure of 40,000 citizens per one representative in the House of Representatives is too high," Gorham exclaimed. "I request that figure be reduced to 30,000, to obtain a more acceptable representation per state in the House."

Washington surprised the entire convention by rising to his feet on the dais. No one moved as he spoke.

"I hesitate to seek a favor from this convention, but I believe Mr. Gorham to be correct. In my view, the figure of 40,000 citizens per one representative in the House of Representatives is too high. I concur that it ought to be reduced to 30,000 to give all states a more balanced representation. I ask for your consideration."

Washington had never made such request. Without one word of

debate, Gorham's motion was passed by a unanimous vote, and the amendment was inserted.

Franklin stood once more. "I move that the constitution now be signed by the delegates."

The vote was unanimous in favor of the motion.

Each delegate approached the secretary's desk in geographical order, took the quill, dipped it in the inkwell, and signed for his state. All states present signed. Randolph, Mason, and Gerry did not.

It was while the last of the delegates were at the desk that Franklin uttered his last remarks. Peering at the chair in which Washington sat on the dais, he gestured toward the small, delicate painting of the sun that capped the back of the chair, and spoke.

"I have often in course of this session, and the vicissitudes of my hopes and fears as to its issue, looked at that image behind the President, without being able to tell whether it is rising or setting. But now, at length, I have the happiness to know that it is a rising, and not a setting, sun."

The signing was completed, and the signers were standing grouped about the table on which the new constitution lay. Washington looked at the clock, and Jackson noted it was four o'clock in the afternoon when Washington resumed his place on the dais. The delegates quieted, and the tall man performed his final function as president of the convention.

"All matters properly before us having been concluded, I hereby dissolve this constitutional convention, *sine die.*"

It was finished. For a time the delegates gathered papers and personal things from their desks, and stood about in small groups, talking, not quite knowing what to do or say as they struggled to accept the fact their summer in the heat of a closed room in the Statehouse in Philadelphia was over. The battles and the tempers and the compromises were finished. Slowly they began to say their good-byes and walk out into the great hallway and into the streets, while their thoughts were of home and wives and families and other affairs too long neglected.

Among the last to leave was Benjamin Franklin, who made his way slowly, cane in hand, tapping on the hard floor as he moved down the long hallway toward the door out of the building. A woman whom he did not recognize stopped him and looked him in the eye.

"Dr. Franklin, what have you given us? A republic, or a monarchy?"

For a moment Franklin reflected, and then he spoke. "A republic. If you can keep it."

He smiled, nodded his farewell, and walked on out the door.

Behind him, a very thoughtful woman watched him leave, as she pondered his words. A republic. If you can keep it. A republic. Controlled by the voice of the people. Can the people lose a republic? How? How can the people lose a republic?

Notes

The events, dates, persons, times, places, and speeches appearing in this chapter are taken from the following sources.

Bernstein, *Are We to Be a Nation?* pp. 170–90.

Moyers, *Report from Philadelphia*, pages styled Monday August 6, 1787–Monday, September 17, 1787.

Warren, *The Making of the Constitution*, pp. 384–730.

Berkin, *A Brilliant Solution*, pp. 130–68.

Rossiter, *1787: The Grand Convention*, pp. 200–273.

Farrand, *The Framing of the Constitution of the United States*, pp. 124–95.

Farrand, *The Records of the Federal Convention*, Vol. 2, pp. 129–650.

Where possible, the speeches or comments of the various delegates as herein set out are verbatim, however, in many cases they have been abbreviated or the language has been changed slightly to make them more understandable today. Such abbreviations or changes, and any errors, are the sole responsibility of this writer.

The speech of Benjamin Franklin, which was read by James Wilson on the last day of the constitutional convention, wherein Franklin attempted to persuade the three delegates who refused to sign the finished instrument—Randolph, Mason, and Gerry—to change their position and add their names to the new constitution was much longer than reported herein. The portion appearing in this chapter is an abstract, which is hoped reaches the core of Franklin's remarkable address. For the entire speech, see Rossiter, *1787: The*

Grand Convention, pp. 234–35. For the condensed version, see Warren, *The Making of the Constitution,* p. 709.

The remarks made by Franklin as the last signers affixed their signatures to the constitution, regarding his conclusion that the sun painted on the back of Washington's chair was a rising sun, not a setting sun, are found in Rossiter, *1787: The Grand Convention,* p. 237. For a photograph of the chair, see the page facing page 318.

John Adams once referred to God as "the Great Legislator of the Universe." Bernstein, *Are We to Be a Nation?* p. 63.

Again, much of the original thought in this chapter is an outgrowth of the work of Clinton Rossiter as it appears in his work, *1787: The Grand Convention.*

Boston
September 21, 1787

CHAPTER XXVII

*T*he punishing heat of summer had mellowed into the warm days and cool nights of early fall. The patchwork of grainfields on the Boston peninsula and the mainland were changing from yellow to white, preparing for harvest, and the cornstalks were turning from green to brittle tan. Beady-eyed squirrels, wearing the beginnings of their long-haired winter coats, scolded all who invaded their world as they darted about seizing the acorns and seeds to test them for full maturity before stuffing them into their cheeks and then disappearing into the hollow trunks of oak trees to organize and store them against need in the approaching winter. Leaves on the trees that lined the streets and yards in Boston, and in the forests, were showing the first hint of their magic change from green to every color known to mankind. Summer was past, and winter was coming, but between the two seasons was the soul-satisfying time of reaping what had been sown, gathering into barns, filling root cellars, turning apples into barrels of cider, filling smokehouses with hams and bacons and strips of beef and fish, all the while watching the green world transform itself into a new fairyland, painted with hues so vivid they dazzled the beholder.

There was a spring in the stride of Adam Dunson as he pushed through the front gate of his mother's home into the crooked street and turned east toward Fruit Street and on to the office of Dunson & Weems. He made his way among farm carts with their two gigantic wheels, and the wagons, overloaded with the produce and cheeses and meat for the Boston markets that the sweat and faith of the farmers had wrested from mother earth. He watched the draft horses lean into their collars, their heads rising and falling with each plodding stride, and he tipped his hat to the ladies and called greetings to acquaintances with the exuberance of one whose world was good and right, at least for the moment. He was home. The mortal threat of dying in a British prison in Port Royal on the island of Jamaica was behind him. The family was safe, sound, strong. The shipping company was succeeding. With the harvest would come contracts for their ships to carry Massachusetts wheat and oats and cider and maple sugar south, and southern cotton and indigo on the return. Troubles would come as they always did, but for the moment, for this morning, the world was good.

He pushed through the front door of the Rose Inn with its engraved rose sign hanging from an arm above the door, and nodded to guests and acquaintances seated at tables, eating breakfasts of thick porridge, or eggs and ham, and steaming hot chocolate. He made his way through the buzz of talk and the rich aroma to the desk where Agnes Merryfield kept her ledgers of guests, bills, and business, and sorted and held the mail for the waterfront.

"'Morning, Agnes," Adam greeted.

Large, aproned, face as round as a melon, hair slightly awry, Agnes grinned back at him. Her two front teeth were noticeably gapped.

"'Morning." She pointed to a small bundle of mail set on a large package. "Got something there. From Philadelphia. A package. By special messenger."

A shadow of question flickered across Adam's face. "Philadelphia?"

"From James Madison."

For a moment a hush fell among those seated nearby and heads turned to peer at Adam as he reached for the package. It was addressed to Mr. Matthew Dunson, Esq., and in the upper left corner, in beautiful small scroll, was the name, James Madison.

Adam seized the few envelopes that were with the package, bobbed his head in thanks to Agnes, and hurried back onto the street. He broke into a trot as he followed Fruit Street to the waterfront, and he was breathing heavily when he burst through the office door of the shipping company. Matthew and Billy both jumped at the sound, and raised their heads from the work at their desks to peer at him as he strode down the aisle. He stopped at Matthew's desk and thrust the package forward as Billy came to his side, waiting.

"James Madison. Philadelphia," Adam blurted.

Matthew seized the package, used a scissor to cut the cord, and peeled back the wrapping. Inside was a three-page letter written in the small cursive of James Madison, and ten copies of the new, four-page constitution. For a moment Matthew sat frozen, staring, and then he exclaimed, "I'd heard they'd finished it, but this is the first time I've seen it!"

He snatched up the letter and closed out the world as he read. Billy and Adam each picked up a copy of the constitution and began to silently read while they walked to their own desks. Matthew read the letter a second time, then seized a copy of the constitution and for a time the three men remained in silence, each caught up in the profound simplicity of the document that had been born of the inspired genius of fifty-five men, who had shared a sweltering room for one hundred fifteen days through a scorching Philadelphia summer. The men were startled by the sound of the front door opening, and Tom Covington entering the room, eyes wide as they adjusted from the bright sunlight that flooded the waterfront. Round-shouldered, slightly stooped, Tom slowed at the sight of the three men seated at their desks all reading identical documents.

"Something happen?" Tom asked.

Matthew pointed. "A letter from James Madison, and copies of the new constitution."

Tom stopped short. "Madison? They got it printed?"

"Read it," Matthew said, and Tom took a copy to his desk, smoothed it, and started through it, silently mouthing each word. For a time the only sound in the office was the occasional whisper of pages being turned, and the unrelenting rumble of men handling freight and ships on the docks and wharves.

After a time, Tom straightened, wide-eyed, and tapped his copy with an index finger. "Never read anything like this in my life."

Matthew turned to look at him. "I thought they were sent to amend the old Articles of Confederation. This doesn't even mention them! This is a plan for a national government like none I've ever heard of, or dreamed! I feared they would give the ultimate power to someone who would soon look like a king, and we'd be back where we started in 1775. But they haven't! They've given the power to the people! The ordinary people! Farmers and merchants and mechanics, and those men out there on the docks. Think about it! The people are responsible for their own government—good or bad—they're responsible. They can vote corrupt men, or incompetent men, out of office. I can't believe it!"

Billy spoke quietly. "It's all there. Two governments. State and national. Freedoms spelled out. Powers defined and divided. I wonder how it will feel, being a citizen of two governments. Sounds odd when you say it."

Adam said, "I've read it twice, and it's too new, too radical. I can't yet grasp it. There are some in Massachusetts who will disgree with it, but still, it's like nothing I've ever seen. How did they do it? How did they get their minds to conceive of it, and write it?"

Matthew said, "If I understand it right, nine states have to ratify this before it becomes the law of the land. If that's true, we'd better take a little time and think it through. The first thing we need to do is be sure we understand the fundamentals of what this new constitution says. The second thing, we better digest that letter from James Madison. He identifies some states that he expects will ratify quickly, but there are others he fears will be trouble, and asks for help. I have contacts in all thirteen states, and it appears that now is the time we make use of them."

He paused, then added, "In the meantime, we've got a shipping company to run. I think we'd better get back to work. Read the constitution again two or three times, make notes, take it home tonight, read it again, and talk about it in the morning. In the meantime I'll leave the Madison letter here on the desk. Read it. I'll spend some time later today and tonight with my files of contacts and make some sort of plan to reach the ones in the states that are in doubt. We'll talk again in the morning. Anyone have some better ideas?"

Heads were shaking when the front door opened and Caleb walked in. "I got the crew organized for the *Penrod*. She can sail on tomorrow's tide. Sheldon Torres will be captain, and—"

He fell silent, eyes narrowed as he stared at the four men. "What's wrong? What's happened?"

Matthew gestured. "A letter from James Madison, and copies of the new constitution. It's finished. Read it."

Caleb walked to the desk and picked up the letter, then a copy of the constitution. "There was talk on the docks that it was finished. This is it? Four pages?"

Matthew nodded. "Four pages. Seven articles. Nothing like it in the world."

Caleb glanced at the others, silent, faces set, eyes boring in. "About fifty men in a room all summer? Four pages? That's all?"

Tom broke in. "Just read it."

Caleb glanced at the document. "From the look on your faces, this must be like the Bible."

Billy said quietly, "Close."

Matthew rose from his chair to face Caleb. "Before you came in we decided to spend some time with the letter and the constitution today and take them home tonight to study them some more. It takes nine states to ratify it, and Madison is asking for help. We'll be back in the morning to make a plan. Should we meet early? Seven o'clock?"

"Agreed."

Quietly, thoughtfully, the five men came back again and again to read the letter from James Madison. Ratification. Nine states. By noon all five men realized the four printed pages had turned their world upside down. They were entering a new era in the history of the world, and their lives would never be the same. Their fierce pride in being Bostonians, from the sovereign state of Massachusetts, would not change, but they sensed that soon, very soon, their pride in being Americans would come first. Americans. A new sovereign nation taking its rightful place among the other sovereign nations of the world, with a new government, the like of which no monarch, no king, had ever dreamed. The ultimate power of this infant nation was given to the care of common sense, the decency, the daring, the genius of the ordinary people! What king or monarch in the civilized world would believe it? What would they say? What would they do?

The office of Dunson & Weems handled the necessary business of the day, but in the minutes between, the room was filled with an intense silence while the five men went over the four printed pages again and again. With each reading they discovered a word, a phrase, a sentence, with meanings so profoundly deep that they had to pause and read it again and again to begin to plumb the depths of the wisdom of the men who had survived the sweltering summer in the East Room of the Philadelphia Statehouse, locked in fiery debate, and through the slippery, sometimes shady art of political compromise, had crafted a document unlike any other.

With the sun reaching for the treetops to the west, they checked their clock, locked the office door, and worked their way through the unending gather of men and freight on the docks. Tom moved north, and the other four together moved west, then separated—Billy toward Brigitte and their home near the Common, and Matthew, with his heavy files under his arm, to Kathleen, while Adam and Caleb walked on to the home of their waiting mother.

Kathleen met Matthew at the door with John at her side. She glanced at the files, then at the intensity in Matthew's eyes, and knew instantly something pivotal had occurred. She reached to peck him on the cheek, then asked, "Something happened?"

"A letter from James Madison. And copies of the new constitution." She stopped dead. "In truth? You have copies?"

He nodded. "I want you to read it and tell me what you think."

John's face clouded as he peered up at the two. "What's a constitution?"

Matthew paused for a moment before he looked his son in the eyes to answer. "It's a paper that says how we're going to have a new country."

A look of near terror crossed John's face. "I like it now. I don't want a new one."

Kathleen reached to touch his hair. "Not a new Boston. Or a new home. Just a way to make the one we have now a better one."

She looked at Matthew. "Ready for supper? I'll read the letter and constitution after."

Kathleen set the beef roast and condiments on the table, they took their places, and bowed their heads while Matthew offered grace. They ate with Matthew preoccupied, Kathleen respecting his need for quiet, and John shifting inquiring eyes from one to the other, knowing something he did not understand was going on, but unsure what it was. He never doubted his mother's word, but still . . . he did not want a new home or a new Boston.

Matthew and John helped clear the table, and Matthew dried the dishes while Kathleen washed. Matthew rose above his need to pore over his files and the constitution, and sent John to get the family Bible from its place in the library. The three of them sat at the dining table while Matthew read the parable of the good Samaritan. Then he turned to John.

"One more story. Which one do you choose?" There was no question which story was to be chosen. There were two that captured the boy's imagination beyond all others. Samson, and David and Goliath. They had read Samson only last night.

The boy's face lighted. "David. When that big giant was going to get him."

"Goliath?"

"Yes. Goliath."

With pauses, and emphasis, and a few words of his own added to increase the intensity, Matthew slowly and dramatically read the seventeenth chapter of the Book of First Samuel in the Old Testament. When the round stone from the brook struck Goliath in the forehead and his fall made the ground tremble, there was an extended "Ooooo" from

John, who sat mesmerized, wide-eyed as he saw it all in his mind. Then John asked the question he always asked, "How big is a cubit?" and Matthew answered as he always did. "Goliath was about nine feet tall." He raised his hand high over his own head. "More than that big."

John murmured, "Oooooo. How big was David?"

Matthew eyed the boy from head to toe for a moment. "About your size. Maybe a little taller. He was twelve."

John grinned, lost in the miracle.

Matthew asked, as he always did, "What do we learn from this story?" and John answered as he had been taught.

"Faith."

"In whom?"

"The Almighty. That's how David did it."

Matthew bobbed his head. "And now we're going to have enough faith to get you into bed."

With John in his nightshirt, the parents knelt at their son's bedside, and the boy bowed his head and clasped his hands beneath his chin to offer his evening prayers. When he finished, Kathleen tucked him in, trimmed the lamp, left the door partly open, and followed Matthew back to the dining room, where he sat down at the table, squared his files and papers in front of him, and handed two documents to Kathleen.

"Here's the Madison letter and the proposed constitution. Let me know your thoughts."

For half an hour the two sat at the table with the lamp casting its pale yellow light over the papers, Kathleen poring over the constitution while Matthew systematically laid out his files. Kathleen finished and sat back in her chair, hands resting for a moment on her extended mid-section.

Matthew saw her hands. "You all right?"

She nodded and shrugged. "Fine. The baby moves once in a while." She tapped the constitution. "I don't think I've ever seen anything like it. It all sounds so simple when you read it, but when you study it out, it's new. Am I right?"

Matthew leaned back in his chair. "Like nothing the world has ever seen. Read it again and notice how the framers have provided a system of overlapping checks and balances. They've made everyone, every institution, subject to scrutiny by someone else or some other institution. Congress can veto the President. The President can override a veto. The courts can correct the Congress or the President. Congress can make the laws, but the judiciary enforces them. Every office in the entire structure is bound by good behavior, including the President. Misconduct? They can be impeached. It's pure genius."

He paused and his eyes dropped to the table for a long moment before he continued. "And notice where the ultimate power comes to rest."

"The vote?"

Matthew nodded. "The vote of the people. The common people. Can you imagine what is going to happen in Europe when they find out we're putting our ultimate faith in the common people? Farmers, shop-keepers, merchants, mechanics, sailors? Think about it. Never in the history of the world . . ."

Kathleen slowly raised her hands to cover her mouth as she stared into Matthew's eyes, and for a long time they did not move while it broke clear in her mind what was happening. She lowered her hands and spoke quietly.

"We're changing history."

"Our own, and the world's."

She continued. "But before it becomes law, the constitution has to be ratified by the states. Is that right?"

"Nine."

"And that's why Madison wrote to you. That's why you have all those papers here tonight."

"Exactly."

"You're going to be right in the middle of it. It's going to be a battle. The last one. The big one."

"Starting tomorrow. Are you up to it? With the baby due in January?"

"What choice do I have? You do what you have to do. I'll be all right."

For a moment it flashed in Matthew's mind. *History will remember the men. But the women? When will they get their due?*

He drew a breath. "I'll be a while. Why don't you go on to bed? I have a little more to do with these files."

She nodded. "I'll leave the lamp up."

It was past one o'clock when Matthew's head drooped over his files, his eyes closed, and his breathing slowed. Minutes later he jerked awake, staring, trying to understand where he was. He turned down the lamp and made his way quietly down the hall to the bedroom, where he hung his clothes over a chair, pulled on his nightshirt, and quietly slipped into bed beside Kathleen. Her voice came softly in the darkness.

"You all right?"

He did not answer. He turned her until her back was toward him then drew her to him, wrapped inside his arms. She reached to take his hand in hers and moved it up beneath her chin, and closed her eyes, and they slept.

Dawn broke clear in a cloudless sky and by seven o'clock all five men were seated around Matthew's desk in the waterfront offices of Dunson & Weems. Outside the tides were going out and the gulls and grebes were cluttering the air with their arguments over the dead fish and refuse left behind. Stacked in front of Matthew were his files containing correspondence with political leaders in all thirteen states. He wasted no time.

"This is how I see it as of now. The constitution must be ratified by nine states. Each state is to convene a ratification convention on its own terms. There is no time limitation given." He held up Madison's letter. "Madison thinks the ratification will succeed, but he has no illusions about it. It's going to be a battle. He has identified the states he thinks will ratify quickly, and those he expects will resist."

Matthew stopped to pick his words. "Let's get our terms in order. The states that are friendly to the constitution we call ratification states. The states that oppose the constitution we call non-ratification states, or other states. Are we clear?"

The four men nodded, and Matthew went on. "Remember, three men at the convention refused to sign the finished constitution. Mason and Randolph of Virginia, and Gerry of Massachusetts. I say this to point out the fact that even among the men who did the work, there were those who disagreed. And it's certain there are states that are going to disagree."

He continued, "Madison says Pennsylvania is a pivotal state. Big, with a heavy population. September eighteenth, one day after the constitution was signed, Benjamin Franklin delivered a copy to the Pennsylvania Assembly and had it read before the legislatures and an audience that filled the gallery. Within two days every newspaper in Philadelphia had it printed."

He paused, then said, "It provoked two reactions. Ratification supporters were enthusiastic. The others believed it would destroy Pennsylvania's charter and constitution—eventually ruin the state and rob it of its power and authority. So the others met and planned an attack. As soon as the constitution was published statewide, they had newspapers everywhere publish articles claiming the convention in Philadelphia had exceeded its authority, warning that the Constitution would eliminate the state of Pennsylvania altogether, that the proposed Senate would become a body of aristocrats, and that the President would become a monarch. The opponents tried to sway the Quakers by claiming the Constitution approved slavery. There was no bill of rights. These articles pointed out the Constitution did nothing to guarantee the rights of the citizens, and they claimed that if this new constitution is approved, the entire revolution will have been fought in vain. Someone under the assumed name of 'Centinel' published eighteen newspaper articles in which he attacked the members of the convention personally, asserting that Benjamin Franklin was too old to know what was really going on and that George Washington had been duped by fast talking politicians."

"You think there's any truth to that?" Billy asked.

"Not according to Madison," Matthew said. "He was there through the whole thing, and he says Franklin knew exactly what was at stake. And as for Washington, Madison can't say enough good about the man."

Matthew went on, "This has all happened in the last few days, but the worst of it is happening right now. The Pennsylvania legislature is in its final days for the year, and the ratification supporters want to call a state ratifying convention before they adjourn. Adjournment is scheduled for September twenty-eighth. Six days. The others want a delay in appointing a ratifying convention—as much time as they can get. If they succeed, it will give them until next year to spread their attack."

Matthew turned to Caleb. "The *Penrod* sails with the tides today, headed south for Elks Head, at the top of the Chesapeake. With all canvas out, it can take one extra day to go up the Delaware to Philadelphia, and still make Elks Head on schedule. You can be in Philadelphia by late afternoon of the twenty-fourth."

Caleb straightened, knowing too well what was coming.

Matthew continued. "Any reason you can't make that trip?"

Caleb shrugged. "And do what?"

Matthew handed him a piece of paper. "Find this man. James Wilson. He's a lawyer. Give that paper to him. I've exchanged letters with him, and he knows me. He was one of the more powerful voices in the convention, and he's now a leader in the battle for ratification. He'll tell you everything you need to know, and maybe find a way for you to help."

Matthew stopped and all eyes were on Caleb while he folded the paper and slipped it into his pocket, deciding if he could be gone for a sustained period of time.

"I can go. I'll have to get some clothes from home and some money."

"Wait until we've finished here, then get your clothes. We'll get you some money. What time does the *Penrod* sail?"

"Ten o'clock. Two hours. A little over."

Matthew checked the clock. "We'll have you there on time." He picked up a second paper and handed it to Caleb. "Here's the name of a boardinghouse where I stayed in Philadelphia. I can recommend it. On Thirteenth Street, just off Market. Owned by a widow named Sarah Asher. Asher's Boarding. Call her Mother Asher." Matthew stopped to chuckle at the remembrance of the stocky little woman mothering him. "She'll take care of you."

Caleb glanced at the paper, read the brief information, and tucked it into his pocket with the other paper before he spoke to Matthew. "You need me to stay here for anything else?"

"Yes. You need to know what else is going to happen in the next few weeks." He turned to Billy.

"Madison thinks New Hampshire will be trouble. It started about twelve years ago. New Hampshire was the only province without a formal charter of incorporation, which means they did not have a legal government when the last governor appointed by King George—his name was John Wentworth—fled for his life in 1775. So delegates from the towns created an illegal provincial congress that took control. That congress drafted a constitution and made the congress the new house of representatives for the state. An argument broke out between the towns on the coast and those on the three major rivers—Piscataqua, Merrimack, and Connecticut—and the towns further inland, over claims that the coastal and river towns were getting rich at the expense of the inland settlements. The result was a move by some western towns to secede from the state of New Hampshire and become part of Vermont. As you know, Vermont is still an independent republic."

Matthew paused, gathered his thoughts, and went on. "There's more to it than that, but for our purposes, the essence of it is this. We have to make contact with a man over there who is powerful in politics. His name is John Langdon. He represented New Hampshire at the Constitutional Convention. He's strong for ratification. Last report, he was in Portsmouth, on the coast. Both Madison and I have exchanged correspondence with him, and he knows me."

Billy had not moved as he listened to Matthew. Now he shifted in his chair, settled, and Matthew went on.

"If I recall rightly, Eli Stroud and his family live somewhere in Vermont or New Hampshire."

Billy nodded but said nothing.

"Right now there are two factions over there that are tearing the state to pieces. One is on the coast, the other inland, in the mountains. I agree with Madison that if we can find a way to bring them together, ratification has a much better chance."

He stopped and Billy slowly began to nod his head. "The answer is yes. I can find Eli, and if you'll give me a letter of introduction, I can likely find Langdon. Is that what you had in mind?"

"Yes. The question is, are you willing? You'll be gone a while. Brigitte might not agree."

"I'll talk with her tonight. I think it will be all right. Is there any rush?"

"No. They haven't begun to appoint their ratification convention yet. It will take a little time."

"Let me talk with Brigitte."

Matthew nodded his approval, then moved on. "Madison warns that Massachusetts is a deep concern. Our governor, John Hancock, is a popular man, and he seems to be leaning away from ratification. It's because Elbridge Gerry refused to sign the Constitution. People know that, and it makes them uneasy. Worse, Samuel Adams has all but openly said he does not favor ratification, and he's another popular figure. As of right now, it is likely the majority sentiment in this state is against us."

Again Matthew waited while the other men shifted their feet and their weight, and settled back in their chairs.

"I'll do what I can with the problem here in Massachusetts. I'll need Adam to help." He exhaled a deep breath and concluded. "Those are the three states Madison thinks we can help with. Pennsylvania, New Hampshire, and Massachusetts."

He stopped, and several seconds passed before he turned to Tom.

"That is going to leave you with pretty much the whole load of the office on your shoulders. Can we get enough people hired to get you through it? Or is it too much?"

Tom squared his shoulders. "No, it won't be too much. There are people that have worked here before, and they're still around. Some of them will come help. It can be arranged."

Matthew spoke slowly, eyes boring into Tom's. "Sure?"

"Sure."

"All right. Just one more thing." He stopped and gestured at the files stacked on his desk. "We're taking a strong political stand in all this, and right now there are a large number of people on the other side of the ratification battle. If the battle gets hot enough, and people take exception to what we're doing, it's possible Dunson & Weems could suffer. Are we willing to accept that?"

For a time they all sat in thoughtful silence, weighing it out, forming a decision. It was Billy who broke the silence.

"The question isn't whether or not we hurt the company. The question is whether we're ready to let six years of war and six more years of watching this country go to pieces, come to nothing. I can't do that. I say, let's get on with it."

Matthew bobbed his head. "The rest of you?"

Caleb stood. "I'll go home and get some clothes. Can you get some money for me while I'm gone?"

Matthew looked at Tom, who drew a deep breath and rose from his chair. "There's about four old men I need to find. They helped me set up this business and run it. With two or three of them, we'll get through this."

Adam stood and leaned over Matthew's desk for the files. "Which ones of these will tell me what's happening in Massachusetts?"

Notes

The handwriting of James Madison, as described herein, was small, well-formed, and well-organized. For a sample of his handwriting, see Bernstein, *Are We to Be a Nation?* p. 151.

The names of the politicians, that is, John Wentworth, John Langdon, James Wilson, John Hancock, Samuel Adams, and others mentioned herein, their contributions to the revolutionary time period, their attitudes toward the ratification battle, and the attitudes of the states of Pennsylvania, New Hampshire, and Massachusetts, all as described herein, were taken in large part from Conely and Kaminski, *The Constitution and the States*, pp. 37–53, 113–30, 181–200.

In support, see Bernstein, *Are We to Be a Nation?* pp. 199–205; Warren, *The Making of the Constitution*, pp. 733–44; Berkin, *A Brilliant Solution*, pp. 169–79.

Over a period of time, a writer using the pen name "Centinel" did publish eighteen articles in Pennsylvania newspapers, attacking the constitution, criticizing Benjamin Franklin as too old to know what was going on at the constitutional convention, and demeaning George Washington as having been duped by fast-talking politicians. It was a common practice in the revolutionary times for writers who entered the political arena to disguise their true identity by using such peculiar pen names as "Centinel," or "Publius," as shall become apparent in later chapters of this volume. Conely and Kaminski, *The Constitution and the States*, pp. 49, 87, 88.

CHAPTER XXVIII

*I*n the warmth of a late September afternoon, Caleb stood on the porch of the large, square, two-storied home on Thirteenth Street in Philadelphia with the modest sign "Asher's Boarding" displayed in the well-kept front yard. In one hand he grasped the handle of the bag holding his clothes, and he had raised the other hand to knock on the door a second time when he heard quick steps inside. The handle turned, the door swung open, and he found himself looking down at a short, robust, gray-haired woman with large, shining blue eyes. She wore a light gray dress that reached her ankles, and was wiping her hands on her apron that showed splotches of flour. The sweet aroma of hot peach pies cooling in the kitchen reached out.

"Yes," the woman said, "is there something I can do for you, young man?"

"My name is Caleb Dunson. My brother recommended your boarding . . ."

She clapped both hands to her cheeks and exclaimed, "Matthew Dunson! Your brother is Matthew Dunson! I can see it as plain as plain in your face. He's taller, but there's that look about you. Oh, how is he? He's just the sweetest man. He was here—let me see—May, wasn't it? Oh, has it been four months? That long? He recommended you come here? Oh, that's just wonderful. You need a room? With the summer gone, all the conventions are past and done, and I have some rooms. Would you like the one he had? Upstairs in the corner? It's available. Is that why you're here?"

"Well, yes. I will need a room for about one week. Perhaps a few days longer. You have one then?"

"Oh, yes. Do come in. Supper's in the oven. We only have four other guests right now, but serving supper for one more will not be a problem. Do you like beef roast and potatoes? Peach pie? Oh, goodness, there I go again. Can't stop talking. Can you forgive me? My late husband, Horatio, said I talk too much. He was right, but what am I to do about it? Got it from my mother, you know. Do come in. Come in."

The parlor was clean and orderly, the carpet showed wear, and the paintings on the walls were ordinary, but there was the look of care and warmth. The little woman prattled on.

"Caleb? Did I hear your name is Caleb? My name is Sarah Asher. Like in the Old Testament. Abraham's wife. But you call me Mother Asher. Or just Mother." She pointed. "Right up those stairs, down in the corner, last room. Sheets are fresh. Down the hall is a washroom if you need it. Now you just take your bag right on up there and make yourself at home. I'll bring the key up directly. Caleb. That's a nice name. It's in the Bible, you know. I'll call you for supper. Six o'clock. We can talk then."

Caleb hesitated. "What's the price of the room, and when do you need to be paid?"

"The price? The same as for your brother. And don't worry about when to pay. We'll settle that when we talk."

Caleb obediently marched up the stairs with his bag in one hand and his hat in the other, battling the need to laugh. *When we talk? When who talks? So far it's one of us talking and the other one listening!*

Caleb entered the room and laid his bag on the bed, opened the window to let in fresh air, then sat on the bed. It was firm, comfortable, with a thick comforter and two snowy-white pillows. He walked to the window to look down at the intersection of Thirteenth and Market Streets, where the coach and foot traffic was heavy with people leaving the business district for their homes. He was listening to the noises of the city when the rap came behind him, and Mother Asher strode across the room.

"Here's your key. Towels and washcloth in the dresser. You can wash before supper if you like. Oh, it's good to have you here. Do you have other brothers or sisters?"

"Yes. Two sisters and another brother. Brigitte and Priscilla, and Adam. Prissy and Adam are twins."

"Twins! Five of you. Your mother must be so proud."

Caleb smiled. "She puts up with us."

"You tell her how fortunate she is. Well, I'd better get back down to the kitchen. I think the roast is about done. And I've got to get pickles out of the root cellar."

"Can I help with something?"

Her eyes widened. "How kind of you! No, I'll take care of it. I'll call up the stairs when it's time."

Caleb had washed and was again standing at the window, lost in his own thoughts when the call came up the stairs, "Supper is ready."

Mother Asher met him as he entered the dining room and pointed to his chair. There were two elderly married couples already seated, and she made introductions all around. Mr. and Mrs. Alexander Theophilus opposite Caleb, kindly, quiet, shy, and Mr. and Mrs. Ulysses Milwood beside him, portly, talkative. Mother Asher required they all bow their heads while she returned grace for the bounties of life, and the steaming bowls and platters began the rounds.

The beef roast was tender, the potatoes and condiments rich and pungent, the buttermilk strong, and the peach pie rare. Conversation was sparse, and when the meal was finished, Caleb excused himself and returned to his room. Mother Asher cleared the table, washed and dried the dishes, then climbed the stairs to rap on Caleb's door.

"Would you care to come down to the library for a while? We need to talk."

They sat facing each other in an orderly room with the maple bookshelves reaching from the floor to the ceiling, and an old, ornately carved desk near the stone fireplace. On the wall opposite the bookshelves was a painting of a square-jawed man with a fringe of white hair circling his head, bushy eyebrows, and a stern look.

"Horatio," Mother Asher said, pointing. "I miss him so." She turned to Caleb, and an unexpected intensity came into her face.

"Your brother was here for the convention, but they disallowed the public. The convention is finished, and the constitution has been published. I presume you're here to complete what your brother started."

Caleb sobered at the unexpected perceptions of Mother Asher. "To become law, the constitution has to be ratified by nine states. I'm here to follow the Pennsylvania ratification convention."

For a moment she studied her hands. "I see." She raised her eyes. "At this moment there is strong sentiment both for and against the new government. The legislature is divided. Things are not good."

"I know. I'm to find James Wilson. A lawyer. He was a delegate to the convention. Do you know of him?"

"James Wilson?" she exclaimed. "Oh, yes. A prominent man. Lawyer, politician. He favors the document, and he makes no apologies for it. Are you two acquainted?"

"No. Matthew knows him. They've exchanged correspondence. Where can I find him?"

"He has an office somewhere in the business district. Market Street, around Fourth or Fifth Street, I think. Either there, or attending court, or at the Statehouse with the legislature. He is very influential. Powerful."

"Do you know his appearance? What he looks like?"

She reflected for a few seconds. "I've only seen him once, at a distance. He's tall. Round-faced. And he wears spectacles. I remember the spectacles."

"That will help," Caleb answered.

"You were worried about paying me. We'll work that out when you leave. Is that agreeable?"

"Agreed."

"Well," she said, rising, "I imagine you have things you need to do to get ready for tomorrow. If you need anything washed or ironed, you tell me."

"Thank you. I will."

"Breakfast at eight o'clock. Porridge and ham and eggs."

"I'll be there."

The high rift of clouds that caught the morning sun were gone by eight o'clock, and the city was awash in bright, fall sunshine when Caleb took his place at the breakfast table. With bowed head Mother Asher returned thanks, then hurried into the kitchen for the platter of scrambled eggs and diced ham, still in the oven, then the pitchers of fresh apple cider. There was light talk as each took portions and ate. Caleb used a thick piece of fresh-baked bread to clean his plate, commended a blushing Mother Asher, and excused himself.

He strode east on Market Street, conscious that the streets were wide, orderly, tree-lined, and laid out in a square grid, with the named streets running between the Delaware River on the east, and the Schuylkill River on the west, while the numbered streets ran square with them. He passed through the business and financial district, impressed by the care and pride he saw reflected in neat signs, and the clean cobblestone sidewalks, and the well-kept storefronts. He stopped to ask a uniformed constable directions to the Statehouse and followed his instructions to the square, red-brick building. He entered the huge, vacuous hallway and asked directions from a man passing between two offices. He was directed upstairs, where he opened a door and entered the spectators' gallery, overlooking the floor of the Pennsylvania legislature, assembled. A dais dominated the room with a great, dark wooden desk and hardbacked chair for the president, a flag behind it, a desk and chair on one side for the secretary, and another one opposite for the sergeant at arms. There was scant frill or pretense; this was the place where the political battles were fought that moved the government of Pennsylvania.

The gallery was filling with Philadelphians from both factions, neither of which showed hesitation in voicing their opinions, for and against ratification. Caleb picked a place on the bench overlooking the gallery railing to watch the legislators enter the chamber and go to their desks for a moment, then gather in clusters to add to the growing undertone of talk, for and against the new constitution. At nine o'clock a man climbed the two stairs onto the dais, assumed his position behind the desk, and the legislators took their positions at their individual desks.

"The legislature will come to order." His words rang hollow in the large, sparse chamber. "The secretary will call roll."

The secretary droned out the names, and most were present. "Mr. Speaker, we have a quorum."

"We shall proceed with the business of the day," the speaker declared.

Caleb settled, listening and watching intently.

It was close to ten o'clock before they finished with the trivial house-keeping items on the calendar, and the speaker announced, "The next matter of business is the pending motion to call a state convention for ratification of the proposed constitution of the United States."

There was open comment in the crowded gallery, some calling for the convention, others condemning the proposition altogether. Caleb turned to peer at them for a moment, startled at the intensity he saw in most faces. He turned back and concentrated on the proceedings below.

The speaker continued. "Debate is open."

Four men sprang to their feet simultaneously, each speaking loudly to be recognized first. The speaker called out a name, three of them sat down, and the fourth launched into it.

"It is critical to the future of this state that we convene a ratification convention prior to our proposed adjournment date of September twenty-eighth. That is this Friday! Should we fail to do so, there is no predicting when, if ever, this state will ratify the constitution of the United States, and failure to do so will plunge this state into chaos and disasters that will remain so long as there is a Pennsylvania!" The man's voice was rising, filled with emotion, beginning to tremble. "What will our posterity say of us? That we considered the entire revolution as nothing? Twelve years of blood and turmoil and discord. Nothing? If it is the concensus of this august body that we not ratify the constitution, then so be it. But let us do it as men, in a fair vote, and not as cowards who shrank from the task and failed our state and our posterity by default!"

The man continued for a time before he sat down, and instantly half a dozen other men were on their feet, clamoring for recognition. The speaker uttered a name, and one man remained standing. He raised his voice to a near shout, with one finger thrust upward.

"Clearly, we are being urged—battered if you will—by those who would have this body make the fatal mistake of calling a ratification convention before we have even received the official statement of the United States Congress now convened in New York, that the constitution is completed, and that they are forwarding it to the several states to be considered for ratification, with their official authorization that we do so. Lacking that official authorization, we are not empowered to assemble a ratification convention. Any such convention would be an outlaw gathering, and no matter what the result, it would be illegal. Why are we even considering such ridiculous proposals? Until we have the authority to do so, we are wasting time with it! We have no choice! We must wait for authorization from the United States Congress in New York!"

Again the hall was filled with emotional outbursts from the gallery. Some citizens stood, fists raised in defiance. The speaker glared upward and boomed, "There will be order, or the sergeant at arms will clear the gallery." The people in the gallery resumed their seats and the chamber quieted.

The debate raged on, with Caleb listening intently, first to one side, then the other, all the while with his thoughts and questions running. *Who are the leaders on both sides? Why are the suppoters so anxious to call the convention, and why are the others so bent on postponing the whole thing? Which side has the most men on the floor down there? Who is "Centinel" and why is he so strongly opposed to ratification? What's his stake in all this?*

The noon recess did not cool things. The debate plunged on in the afternoon until Caleb leaned back, wearied, with a rising feeling of disgust at his first exposure to the business of politics. The clock on the wall behind the president had reached fifteen minutes past four before the president stood.

"We are adjourned until tomorrow morning, same time."

Caleb was the first on his feet in the gallery, and the first out the door. He walked rapidly to the staircase down to the second floor and took up a position near the door. Most of the legislators were still inside, gathered again into clusters, loudly proclaiming the virtues of their position and the lack of their opponents. Caleb waited until the speaker made his way through the press of men and confronted him at the door.

"Sir, I need some help. Do you know, is James Wilson in this building?"

The speaker's face showed no emotion as he quickly measured Caleb. "I don't believe I know you, sir."

"Caleb Dunson. Massachusetts. I was sent here to find James Wilson. I thought you might know how to find him."

"He should be in his law office right now. He appeared before the Supreme Court this morning, down on the first floor. It's likely he went back to his office."

"Could you direct me how to find his office?"

"Yes. On Market street at the corner of Fourth Street. Second floor. There will be a sign."

"One more thing. Who is the chief spokesman for the supporters in the assembly?"

"I think you're referring to George Clymer. He was here today."

Caleb nodded. "Thank you, sir."

The speaker returned the nod, and Caleb stepped aside to let him pass. Ten minutes later Caleb was opening the polished oak door on the second floor of a brick building at the intersection of Market and Fourth Streets. The unpretentious sign beside the door read JAMES WILSON, LAWYER. He entered the anteroom and faced a young man seated behind a moderately-sized, beautifully engraved oak desk. Framed on the wall to the right of the desk was a painting of George Washington, with other original engravings of Coke and Blackstone on the remaining walls. The hardwood floor was polished, the appointments excellent.

The young man, bespectacled, thin, pinched shoulders, long face, stood. "May I assist you, sir?"

"Is Mr. Wilson available?"

"He is in conference in his office."

Caleb handed him the folded paper signed by Matthew. "Could you deliver that to him?"

The young man unfolded the document, read it, then looked at Caleb. "You are the brother of Matthew Dunson?"

"Yes."

"Do I understand you are sent here to promote the ratification convention? For the new constitution?"

"Yes."

"If you'll take a seat, I'll let Mr. Wilson know you're here."

"Thank you."

Caleb sat in the quiet, aware of the scent of well-oiled furniture, and of the subtle feel of quality all around him. He shifted in the upholstered chair, impatient with his day of sitting on a hardwood bench in the gallery of the Pennsylvania State legislature for seven hours while hot, emotional arguments were thrown back and forth, repetition piled on repetition. He flinched when the clock on the beautifully sculpted mantel above the small stone fireplace chimed five o'clock, and within two minutes the door to his right opened and two men emerged, still engaged in conversation. One was average in build, the other taller, with a round face, round chin, round nose, jowls just beginning to sag, gray hair, and spectacles. The two walked to the door, said their good-byes, and the man with the spectacles turned to Caleb.

"Mr. Dunson, I presume?" He offered his hand, soft, thick-fingered, fleshy.

Caleb stood. "Right. Caleb Dunson. Are you James Wilson?"

"I am. Won't you come into my office?"

Caleb followed him into the office and waited while Wilson took his place behind his massive oak desk. It was stacked with organized piles of papers and law books. One wall was given to bookshelves filled with orderly rows of law books. A large painting of the city of Philadelphia was centered on the opposite wall. Behind Wilson was a brick fireplace with a carved mantel and a great clock.

"Please be seated," Wilson said, and Caleb sat in the upholstered chair facing the desk while Wilson sat down in his leather chair opposite him.

For a moment Wilson studied Caleb with the skilled eye of a lawyer and a politician who needs to know who he is facing. In the same brief time Caleb looked into Wilson, making his calculations of what the man was. Their unspoken impressions continued to build as they talked.

Wilson picked up the letter of introduction from Matthew, smiling, amiable, while his eyes were shrewd, probing. "Your brother indicates you're here to do what you can to assist in the ratification of the new constitution."

"Yes."

"Did you attend the legislative session at the Statehouse today?"

"Yes."

"What did you think?"

"Standoff. There are some things I would like to know about what I saw and heard."

"Can I be of help?"

"Who is George Clymer?"

Wilson did not hesitate. "It was my great privilege to serve with him at the constitutional convention. He was a fellow delegate from Pennsylvania. Great man. Very strong in support of ratification. Was he there today?"

"Yes, he was. He took a strong position for the new constitution. I was told I should talk with him."

"You should. No one is more acquainted than he with what is happening now."

"In the assembly, who has the majority? Supporters or non-supporters?"

"Supporters, but it is a close margin."

"Can you tell me why the others are so determined to delay convening a ratifying convention?"

Wilson took a breath and exhaled it slowly. "Let me give you a brief background. At one time the others controlled the legislature, but at the last election, control shifted to the supporters. The next election for legislators is October ninth. The others have met to plan their strategy, and they're desperate to postpone the ratification convention until after October ninth, in the hope that they can regain control of the legislature in the election. If they succeed, they intend voting down anything to do with a ratification convention, and if they are successful the constitution will most likely not be ratified in this state, at least not for a very long time."

Wilson stopped and watched Caleb's eyes until they showed understanding before he continued.

"The supporters have also met and planned their strategy. They are going to force a vote for a ratification convention before they adjourn this session, if they can. Right now they have the majority in the legislature, and it appears they might succeed."

Caleb interrupted. "If the supporters have the majority, why would they fail?"

Caleb saw the weariness of endless political and legal battles in Wilson's eyes as he responded.

"The others intend to argue that this legislature does not have authority to create a ratification convention because we have not yet received official documents from the national congress in New York stating they have examined the constitution and are forwarding it to all states for the ratification process. They claim that lacking congressional permission, we lack the authority to act."

Caleb nodded. "That's what I've been hearing all day. Is it true?"

Wilson pursed his mouth for a moment. "Arguably."

"There's no way to get the congress in New York to act?"

"I doubt it. They move at their own pace."

"If the national congress did send the documents you mentioned, what would happen next?"

"We in the supporting camp would make a motion in the legislature for the ratification convention."

"Could the opposition stop it?"

Wilson reflected for a moment before he answered. "Yes, they could. They could boycott the legislature. The legislature cannot vote unless they have two-thirds of the delegates present. If the non-supporters refuse to attend, and the supporters cannot muster a quorum, there can be no legal vote. That could happen. I don't know if they've thought of it yet, but we have."

"Do I understand this session is to end on Friday? September twenty-eighth?"

"That is correct."

Caleb leaned back, mouth rounded for a moment. "We've got a problem. This could be interesting."

The difference between the two men was emerging. Wilson had never borne arms, never killed in combat, never faced death, and was an intellectual giant, gifted in his grasp of human affairs, committed to what he thought to be right, fearless in his convictions, honest, straightforward. Caleb had never been in politics or law, had borne arms for more than four years, killed men, faced death a hundred times, had little patience with wasted time, knew no fear once his mind was clear, and had an inner need for action, even foolish action if that was all that was left to him. Each man sensed and silently acknowledged that they were near exact opposites, and each strangely respected the strength of the other. Instinctively they knew they could speak freely.

Caleb asked, "Do you have a plan?"

Wilson slowly shook his head. "Not yet. We're waiting for the papers to arrive from New York. If they don't get here, we'll have to do the best we can." He stopped and for a time sat with his fingers interlaced on his desk before him, eyes downcast in thought. Then he raised his head and continued.

"There's a second man you need to meet. Judge Thomas McKean. He is chief justice of the Pennsylvania Supreme Court. A great soul. He's dedicated to getting this constitution ratified in this state. Let me make an arrangement with you. If we do not hear from congress in New York by Thursday afternoon, I will have George Clymer and Justice McKean in this office at five o'clock. Can you be here?"

"I can."

"They've both corresponded with your brother Matthew, and if I tell them he has sent you, I believe they will come. Is it agreed?"

"Agreed."

Wilson leaned back. "Is there anything else for now?"

Caleb shook his head. "Not that I can think of. I want to thank you for taking time with me."

"It has been my pleasure. Your brother has certainly done his country a service."

"If something comes up in the meantime, may I come again?"

"Whenever necessary."

Wilson stood and walked Caleb out into the foyer, to the outer door and opened it. "If you need anything, just let me know."

Caleb reached to shake his hand. "Thank you."

He walked down the stairs into the bright sunlight of late afternoon on Market Street, and fell in step with the press of people leaving their offices. He worked his way west on the cobblestones toward Thirteenth Street, preoccupied, caught up in the dilemma of two opposing sides that had long since abandoned any hope of resolution of their differences and were locked in a hot, blind, emotional war from which neither would, nor could, retreat.

He ate his supper in near total silence, speaking only when spoken to, and excused himself under the worried eye of Mother Asher to go to his room. He opened the window and for a time stared unseeing at the dwindling Market Street traffic. He paced the floor for a time, and with dusk coming on, returned to the window to watch a man light the street lamps that transformed the city into a wonderland of light and shadow in the trees and on the buildings. It was late when he stripped off his shirt and shoes and lay on the bed to drift into a sleep filled with grotesque images of angry, shouting men shaking their fists at each other.

For two more days, Caleb sat in the observation gallery of the Pennsylvania legislature, listening again and again to arguments that did not vary. Pennsylvania *must* convene a ratification convention or be remembered forever as a state that failed the Revolution. No,

Pennsylvania can*not* convene a ratification convention until authorized by the congress now in session in New York.

On Thursday, September twenty-seventh, Caleb gritted his teeth, cursed all politicians, endured until the speaker adjourned the session for the day, and got out of the building into fresh air as quickly as he could barge his way through the crowd. Without a word he marched to the law office of James Wilson, where the thin young apprentice at the front desk admitted him into Wilson's private office. The door closed with Wilson facing Caleb, and two men on either side of his desk. Wilson took control, gesturing as he spoke.

"Mr. Dunson, may I present Mr. George Clymer of the Pennsylvania Assembly, and Mr. Justice Thomas McKean, Chief Justice of the Pennsylvania Supreme Court."

Caleb stepped forward to accept the extended hand of Clymer. "I am honored, sir."

Clymer was of average build, strength in his handshake, handsome features, strong chin. His eyes seemed to have a perpetual smile. "The honor is mine, Mr. Dunson."

Caleb turned to Justice McKean to shake his extended hand. McKean was the tallest of the three men facing Caleb. His face was long, his chin pointed, eyes serious, intense, and slightly sunken, mouth a straight line, face a mask without emotion.

"It is my honor to meet you, sir."

The judge bowed slightly without a change in his expression. "My pleasure, I assure you."

"Well," Wilson said, "shall we be seated? We have a few matters to discuss."

As they took their seats, Caleb glanced at the two men beside Wilson's desk. It was clear to him they had reservations about spending time here with a man half their age, from the state of Massachusetts. He ignored it.

Wilson turned to Clymer. "Would you care to share your plan, as you have just explained it to Justice McKean and myself?"

Clymer leaned forward, one forearm on the desk, intense, talking rapidly. "Tomorrow morning on the floor of the legislature I am going to propose resolutions calling for a state ratification convention. The papers have not yet arrived from New York, and it's clear there will be an uproar, but there is no other choice. We do have a majority of supporters in the assembly, but no one knows what the opposition will do. If they walk out—and they might—we will lack a quorum. Without a quorum we cannot make a legal vote. And that will be the end of it for now."

Clymer stopped, and Justice McKean interrupted. His voice was a monotone. "If they boycott the legislature—walk out—the president can order the sergeant at arms to go find them and bring them back. He has that authority."

Wilson leaned forward with his forearms on his desk. "If he can find them." Wilson was watching Caleb—his face, his eyes, the movements of his hands, his feet.

Caleb spoke up. "May I inquire, how many men do you have serving as sergeants at arms?"

Wilson's eyes were alive. "One."

"If he does find absent assemblymen, and he does order them to return, what's the penalty if they refuse?"

"If they're found in this state, they could face a fine, or even suspension for a period of time. If they cross the river into New Jersey, the sergeant at arms can do nothing. He lacks jurisdiction. But either way, we will still lack a quorum for the crucial vote."

For five seconds no one moved nor spoke. Caleb had his hands folded in his lap, and was staring down at them while he worked with his thoughts. He raised his head.

"Are you expecting a boycott?"

Wilson nodded his head twice but said nothing.

For a time the only sound in the room was the steady, rhythmic tick of the large clock on the mantel, and then Caleb spoke to Wilson. "We'll see about that."

Wilson was leaning forward, watching Caleb's face and eyes with a fierce concentration, and he saw it, there in Caleb's eyes. Caleb, the warrior. The man of action. Wilson eased back in his chair and spoke.

"You'll be there?"

"I'll be there."

Wilson glanced at Clymer and McKean. "Is there anything else we need to discuss today?"

Both men remained silent.

"Good," Wilson continued, and turned to Clymer. "Mr. Clymer, if things go ill for us tomorrow, would it be a good idea to come back here to talk it over?"

Clymer looked at McKean. "What do you say?"

McKean nodded but said nothing. In the entire interview, the expression on his face had not changed.

Wilson stood. "If we are successful tomorrow, the matter is concluded. If not, we will meet back here as soon as the legislature adjourns for the day."

The others stood, and as Caleb shook their hands, he saw it in the faces of both Clymer and McKean. Both were in question as to why they had been called to Wilson's office to waste valuable time talking with a man from Massachusetts who obviously had no grasp of politics, no standing to do anything with the Pennsylvania Assembly, and almost no conception of the breadth and depth of the crisis that was going to erupt tomorrow in the Statehouse.

Caleb made his way down the stairs onto Market Street and walked steadily through the crowd, sorting out his thoughts and reaching for conclusions. *Those men—Clymer, Wilson, McKean—will talk this thing to death—but they won't go past talking—finally, if talk fails, someone has to do something—even if its wrong, someone has to do something—and they won't do it because they're politicians.*

Mother Asher met him at the door, head thrust forward, hands clasped in front of her, face drawn in concern. "Caleb, you do not look well. Haven't looked right for two days. Come into the kitchen and have some cider. You need a minute to catch up."

Caleb stopped short and took stock of himself. She was right.

They sat in the kitchen together, sipping sweet cider, with Mother Asher chattering on about the weather, and her deceased husband, Horatio, and her sainted mother, and the secret she had discovered of how to make the flakiest pie crust in Philadelphia. Caleb listened and nodded from time to time and saw his own mother, Margaret, sitting opposite him, trying to lighten a load that had become too heavy. He finished his glass, set it on the table, and stood.

"That helped. Thank you."

Mother Asher rose to face him. "You look better. Now go on upstairs. I'll call you for supper."

With supper finished, over Mother Asher's protest, Caleb helped clear the table, and patiently dried the dishes as she washed and talked. Later, alone in his room, he sat in the shadows of deep dusk, sorting out his thoughts. *The sergeant at arms. Is that the answer? Maybe. Maybe. Tomorrow we'll know.*

He slept deeply, finished breakfast at half-past eight, and walked rapidly to the Statehouse in streets flooded with sunlight. He climbed the stairs to the gallery and watched the speaker take the dais at nine o'clock. The man quickly moved through the formalities of roll call and two perfunctory matters relating to the pay of the legislators, and with the entire floor waiting in hushed anticipation, moved into it.

"The next order of business is the question of convening a ratification convention to address the new United States constitution. The floor is open."

Before he finished speaking, half a dozen men were on their feet, including George Clymer, whose hand was raised high, and the instant the president's words stopped, Clymer's voice cracked out above the outburst.

"Mr. Speaker!"

"Mr. Clymer, you may proceed."

"I propose a resolution that this body appoint delegates to attend a convention at which the order of business will be ratification of the new constitution of the United States."

Instantly a din arose that drowned out all else that Clymer had to say. The president rose, his eyes narrowed in anger as he stared down the legislators, and then turned his face toward those in the gallery. Caleb was still seated, silent, not moving, waiting, watching, missing nothing.

"There will be order in this chamber," the speaker fairly shouted, "or I shall order the spectators cleared from this chamber and we shall then meet in closed session."

He waited until every person in the room was seated and quieted, then looked down at George Clymer. "Mr. Clymer, you may proceed."

"Thank you. I further propose a resolution establishing the place of such convention, the time it shall convene, and the compensation to be paid to the delegates."

Murmuring began, the speaker rose once again, and the room fell silent. George Clymer continued, once again enunciating with great emotion all the arguments the supporters had been so loudly proclaiming for the past four days. The Articles of Confederation were unquestionably a disaster; only the new constitution could restore peace and harmony, both within Pennsylvania and among the thirteen states; it was the product of the best minds of the times; if Benjamin Franklin and George Washington favored it, it was undoubtedly correct for the country. Delay would only heap acrimony on the glorious name of Pennsylvania if she did not take the lead in establishing the new government.

The opposition leaders rose, hot, loud, to proclaim the same arguments Caleb had heard from the time he arrived. Any such convention would be illegal, since it was mandatory that they receive proper authorization from the national congress in New York before they could legally proceed; Benjamin Franklin was feeble in his old age and did not know what he had signed; George Washington was a soldier, not a politician, and had been deceived by smooth-tongued supporters; it was only fair that time be allowed to let the people of Pennsylvania study the new document and decide for themselves.

A supporter rose and was recognized. "I move for the vote."

An outburst erupted, the speaker jerked to his feet, and the hall quieted. Caleb glanced at the clock. It was ten minutes before noon.

A voice called, "Second the motion."

Still on his feet, the speaker considered for a moment, then announced, "In view of the time, we will vote on the resolutions in the order they were proposed. The first vote will be whether or not we should approve the resolution calling for a ratification convention. The remainder of the proposed resolutions will be debated and voted on this afternoon. Is that clear?"

It was clear.

The speaker turned to the secretary. "Record the vote."

In the standard monotone, the secretary called the names of the delegates, each answering "Aye" or "No," according to his convictions, while the vote was posted on the board. Caleb watched as each mark was entered, counting. With but three votes yet to be called, it was clear the supporters had won. Murmuring began, and when the last vote was recorded, the room was once again drowned in applause from one side, and angry shouts of "illegal, illegal, illegal" from the other.

The speaker raised both hands for order, and waited while the chamber quieted before he announced, "We stand in recess until two o'clock this afternoon."

Any sense of courtesy was lost as the crowd in the gallery shoved and pushed to get out the door and down to the assembly floor to heap laurels on the heads of their representatives or condemnation on the heads of their opponents. Caleb made his way to the floor and stood to one side, watching, listening to the uproar, making calculations. *If these nonsupporters lose this afternoon, this could get ugly. Will they riot?*

It was past one o'clock when he made his way out into the sunshine and sat on a shaded bench, watching people hurry about on their business, wondering what the afternoon would bring, bracing for the worst. At two o'clock he took his seat, and with the gallery jammed to standing room only, the speaker called for order. The legislators took their seats, and instantly there was a gasp, and then dead silence.

Nineteen of the opposition were absent! Their chairs were conspicuously empty! Half of the supporters sprang to their feet, shouting blasphemies and threats against the others, and the word "boycott" echoed off the walls again and again. The speaker stood and pounded his desk with the flat of his hand until the chamber quieted. His face was flushed with anger as he growled out the words, "We are again in session. Mr. Secretary, call the roll."

The hush that filled the room was like a thing alive as the names of the nineteen absent non-supporters were called, only to echo off the walls unanswered. The secretary concluded, and the hush held as he made his count, and addressed the speaker.

"Mr. Speaker, we do not have a quorum."

"How many delegates must we have to bring this floor to a quorum?"

"Two, sir."

The speaker turned to the sergeant at arms. "I hereby direct you to do whatever is required to locate two of the absent legislators, and bring them to this chamber as quickly as possible. You are authorized to exert whatever force is justified. We will remain here until your return, no matter how long it takes. Am I clear?"

Mouths dropped open, and legislators and observers in the gallery stared. Such orders were seldom issued in the hallowed halls of the Pennsylvania legislature.

The sergeant at arms blanched, swallowed hard, and stammered, "Yes, sir." He stood stock-still for a moment, bewildered, wondering what to do next, and finally turned on his heel and nearly ran from the chamber.

The speaker announced, "We stand in recess subject to instant recall upon the return of the sergeant at arms."

Caleb stood, tempted to go down onto the floor to talk with George Clymer, but decided against it. Until the sergeant at arms returned, no one would know whether the boycott had succeeded in defeating the supporters. He went back to his seat and sat down, nervous, waiting.

Fifty minutes later the door behind the desk occupied by the sergeant at arms opened, and the man walked in. The instant Caleb saw him, he knew.

The secretary hurried from the hall to return with the speaker, and within two minutes every available legislator was seated at his desk, eyes locked onto the speaker as he stood on the dais.

"Mr. Sergeant at arms, make your report."

The man, tall, slender, gray-haired, looked at the speaker, licked at dry lips, started to speak, stammered, and continued.

"Mr. President, I was unable to locate even one of the absent legislators. I tried. I don't know what else to say."

All eyes went back to the speaker, waiting. For a time he stood there, eyes downcast, pondering. Then he raised his head and his voice came strong.

"We stand adjourned until tomorrow morning, September twenty-ninth, at nine o'clock."

It had been expected that the assembly would adjourn *sine die* that afternoon, September twenty-eighth! Talk filled the hall as the legislators accepted the fact they would be there at least one more day, and every person in the room knew that Saturday, September twenty-ninth, 1787, would be a day they would not soon forget.

For a time Caleb held his place in the gallery, listening to the arguments and acrimony that was mounting among the observers. The crowd thinned, and he pushed through the hallway out onto Market Street, and walked again to the corner of Fourth Street, up the stairs to the second floor of the brick building, and into the anteroom of the law firm of James Wilson. The eager young apprentice led him to the door to Wilson's office and Caleb walked in, where Wilson, George Clymer, and Thomas McKean were already gathered.

Wilson asked, "You were present at the assembly today?"

"I was."

"You know about the boycott?"

"I do."

Wilson gestured to Clymer and McKean. "We were just discussing what's to be done about it. Right at this moment, we can't reach a conclusion because we don't know what to expect in the morning. It's clear that Mr. Fitzsimons is going to send the sergeant at arms out at least one more time to try to bring in two more legislators, to get a quorum. If he succeeds, there will be no problem. If he fails . . ." Wilson did not finish the sentence, rather, a troubled look flitted across his face. Clymer shifted in his chair, and for the first time, McKean showed a hint of emotion in his face—a mix of frustration and anger.

Caleb interrupted. "Who is Mr. Fitzsimons?"

"Thomas Fitzsimons? He is the speaker in the legislature."

Caleb repeated the name silently to himself and went on. "If I heard it right, the sergeant at arms couldn't find even two of the absent legislators."

Clymer nodded. "That's right. I spoke with him just after adjournment."

"Does anyone know where they are?"

"Not at the moment."

McKean leaned forward. "I spoke with the mayor. He's going to have the constables search for them overnight."

Caleb's eyes narrowed. "Won't they expect that?"

McKean's eyes opened in surprise. "Probably. What else can be done?"

Caleb asked, "Does anyone keep a list of the legislators and where they're staying while the legislature is in session?"

Clymer answered. "Yes, but if a legislator wishes to not be found, he can simply take up a room elsewhere. Philadelphia has no end to inns and taverns with rooms available."

Wilson broke in. "I doubt we can do anything tonight. We'll just have to wait and see what tomorrow morning brings. It is still possible we can assemble a quorum. If not, we do what we can and move on."

Caleb looked at McKean. "Do you intend being at the session tomorrow morning?"

"I have considered it. I will likely be there."

Caleb turned to Wilson. "Will you attend?"

"Yes. In the meantime, I see nothing else to do but wait."

The men stood, shook hands as they said their good-byes, and Caleb walked out the door and down the stairs into the usual Market Street foot traffic with deep concern and grave doubts rising in his chest. He entered Mother Asher's parlor and climbed the stairs, searching for a plan, an answer, to what was rapidly becoming a disaster at the Statehouse. When Mother Asher called for supper, he sat at the table speaking only when spoken to, his mind struggling. He finished his meal, excused himself, and returned to his room. From his window he watched the men light the street lamps, and for a time was seized with a compulsion to walk back down to the business district, and then the waterfront, searching through the inns and taverns for the missing assemblymen. But he did not know what they looked like, or even their names. It was midnight before he stretched out on the bed and fell into a troubled, fitful sleep.

No one in Philadelphia knew of the small, wiry rider, weary and exhausted, who dismounted a deep-chested, jaded bay mare on the New Jersey side of the Delaware River while the morning star was still bright in the eastern sky, and led the horse clattering onto the ferry bound for Philadelphia, across the river. None knew that he had left New York thirty-six hours earlier, and changed horses four times on his mission to carry a packet of papers from the national congress in New York, southwest on New Jersey dirt roads, to the speaker of the Pennsylvania legislature. In the packet was a letter declaring that the national congress had officially reviewed the new constitution and authorized and recommended that ratification conventions be arranged by all thirteen states. With the letter were twelve copies of the new constitution.

The ferry docked on the Philadelphia waterfront, the rider mounted his mare once more, and raised her to an easy lope north on Market Street with her iron horseshoes striking sparks from the granite cobblestones. The morning star was fading when he reined her to a stop before the Statehouse. He dismounted, loosened the saddle cinch, led her to the nearest watering trough, and stood beside her, rubbing her neck as she sunk her muzzle into the clear water, and he heard the gugging sound as she sucked the water up the rings of her gullet.

She drank her fill, and he dipped water from the trough with his hand, drank, then led the horse to the nearest hitching rack to tie her, then sat down on the bench nearby to let the tension begin to drain from muscles, wound tight and set from two days in the saddle. He was still sitting on the bench when the sun rose, and the first people arrived to unlock the Statehouse and prepare the building for the business of the day. He followed a man to the front door and spoke to him while the man worked a large brass key in the lock.

"I have an express package from the congress in New York for the speaker of the Pennsylvania legislature. Is the legislature adjourned, or will he be here today?"

The man with the key saw the lines of weariness in the courier's face and the road dust collected on the wrinkled clothes. He glanced at the horse on the street, head down, lines of dried salt sweat gathered around the saddle and bridle.

"The session is still convened. He'll be here shortly. Can I deliver the package for you?"

"My orders are to deliver it to him by my hand."

"Would you like to come in? I can take you to his private chambers. You can wait there."

Shortly after eight o'clock, Mr. Fitzsimons walked down the great hall, leather heels clicking a steady cadence, and slowed as he came to the door to his chambers. He stopped before the little man who rose to meet him.

"Sir," Fitzsimons said, "are you waiting for me?"

"Are you the speaker of the legislature?"

"I am."

The man handed him the package. "I am Robert Clarington. I'm an express rider for the United States Congress in New York. I am under their orders to deliver this to you, sir."

Fitzsimons' eyes widened for a moment before he unlocked his door. "The congress in New York? Would you come inside and wait? I may have a message for you to carry back."

The spectators' gallery overlooking the floor of the assembly was jammed long before nine o'clock, with Caleb in his seat at one end of the front bench, near the exit door, nervous, apprehensive, watching the large clock on the wall behind the president's dais. The clock struck nine times, and the room fell silent in expectation of the speaker making his appearance, but he did not. It was five minutes past the hour when his door opened and he marched to the dais. Silence held while he spoke.

"We are now in session." He paused until the floor was silent before he continued. "I have received this morning a dispatch from the congress convened in New York."

Caleb nearly stopped breathing. Not a man on the floor moved.

"I have their letter before me, with twelve copies of the new constitution. The congress has officially given notice to all thirteen states that they have received and reviewed the new constitution of the United States and have recommended that all thirteen states convene conventions for purposes of ratifying it."

For a moment the only sound was the clock ticking, and then the room was filled with sounds, both cheering and booing.

Caleb's eyes closed and his head rolled back as relief flooded through his system.

Fitzsimons waited until the room quieted, then turned to the secretary. "Mr. Secretary, call roll."

The nineteen chairs that had been vacant during the Friday session, were still vacant; there was not a sound as the secretary called the roll, made his tally, and turned to the speaker.

"Sir, we are still two assemblymen short of a quorum."

Fitzsimons did not hesitate. "Very well. Mr. Sergeant at arms, you will immediately visit the office of the mayor to determine if they were able to locate some of the missing assemblymen overnight, and if they did so, you will bring at least two of those assemblymen here by whatever reasonable means necessary. Do you have any questions?"

"No, no, sir."

Fitzsimons bobbed his head. "We stand in recess subject to immediate recall upon the return of the sergeant at arms."

Caleb stood but remained at his bench while talk filled the chamber. It seemed that time was standing still while the legislators on the floor, and the spectators in the gallery gathered into small clusters, pointing, gesturing, exclaiming. Caleb studied the men below and located George Clymer. James Wilson and Judge McKean were not to be seen. They were not legislators, but did have political standing to be on the floor below. Caleb ran a nervous hand over his hair. *Where are Wilson and McKean? If they don't get a quorum down there, we'll need them. Where are they?* He looked again at the clock, then sat down to wait out the return of the sergeant at arms.

With the hands on the large clock just two minutes short of ten forty-five, the door behind the desk of the sergeant at arms burst open, and the man approached his desk, breathless, moving nervously. The secretary brought the speaker from his chambers, and he stepped up onto the dais.

"Mr. Sergeant at arms, make your report."

The man gathered his courage, faced Fitzsimons, and in the hushed silence, his voice came too high, his speech too fast. Caleb did not miss a word.

"Sir, a constable in the Mayor's office informed me two of the legislators have taken a room on the second floor of the Bellamy boardinghouse on Sixteenth Street, near Spruce. I went there. The hallway to the room was . . . filled . . . guarded . . . by three men. Large men. I was not allowed to reach the room. I returned to report that I was not able to bring the legislators."

Caleb came off his bench and bolted for the door. He took the stairs downward two at a time, and barged through the crowded hallway to the nearest door into the floor of the legislature, to face the doorkeeper. He stopped short and exclaimed, "I have got to talk with George Clymer. He's inside."

The doorkeeper shook his head. "You cannot enter while they're in session. You'll have to wait until—"

From inside the room came sounds of a rising tumult, and the doorkeeper turned to open the door to peer inside, then turned back to Caleb. "They just declared a recess. You can go on in."

Caleb pushed his way through the mix of men and sound to Clymer's desk, where two men were facing Clymer in hot, angered debate. Caleb paid no attention to them.

"Mr. Clymer, I've got to see you. Now!"

Clymer's face drew down in question. "Yes. What is it?"

"Are Judge McKean and James Wilson here somewhere?"

"In the chambers of the speaker. They're discussing what ought to be done."

"We need to see them."

"Now?"

"Now!"

With Caleb following, Clymer pushed his way through to a door near the dais and knocked. The door opened one inch, an eye appeared, and then it swung wide. Both men entered the room and Clymer spoke to Fitzsimons, explaining the purpose of the intrusion, and introducing Caleb and his purpose in being in Philadelphia.

Fitzsimons studied Caleb for a moment, shrewd eyes missing very little. "Is there something we can do for you, Mr. Dunson?"

"It appears you need two more assemblymen to make a quorum."

"Correct."

"What are the qualifications of a sergeant at arms?"

All four men stared at Caleb, caught by surprise. "Qualifications?" Fitzsimons shrugged. "Twenty years of age. Physically capable."

"They don't have to be a resident of this state?"

Fitzsimons looked at Judge McKean. "Not that I've ever heard. Judge, what do you say?"

"No residency requirement I know of."

Caleb continued. "Can you swear me in as a sergeant at arms?"

Fitzsimons suddenly leaned forward, forearms on his desk, face a blank. "What? What are you talking about?"

"Swear me in, and give me something in writing to verify it. I want the address of that boardinghouse. Bellamy. And the names of those two legislators. I'd like to try to bring them here."

Fitzsimons was incredulous. "You *what?*"

There was a strange look in Wilson's eyes as he interrupted. "Nothing to be lost by trying. Swear him in. Give him his chance."

Clymer and McKean both turned to look at Wilson as though he had taken leave of his senses, and Wilson returned their stares as he repeated himself. "Give him his chance! Unless any of you have a better idea."

Caleb left the building at a trot with a folded piece of paper signed by the speaker in his pocket, and the sergeant at arms puffing along behind, trying to keep up. Half a dozen men labored along behind, determined to see what was going to happen in the hallway at the Bellamy Boardinghouse.

With the sergeant at arms calling directions, they worked their way west, past the financial district, then the large, spacious homes, on to the section where the yards were neglected and the fences needed paint and some broken pickets replaced. They approached a two-storied house with paint peeling and a faded sign on a crooked post, and Caleb mounted the steps to the large porch and the front door two at a time. He knocked loudly and waited. The door opened, and a hunch-shouldered man with three-days' growth of beard stubble and rumpled hair stood before them, looking sour, irritated.

"If you're looking for a room, we're full." He reached to close the door, and Caleb stopped it with his foot. He unfolded the paper signed by Fitzsimons, thrust it forward, and said, "I am an authorized sergeant at arms from the Pennsylvania legislature. I have been sent here by the speaker to assist two of your boarders back to the legislature. Their names are Henry Pollard and Josephus Edmunds. I believe they are on the second floor. I am under orders to proceed. Now."

The man looked at the crowd behind Caleb, and Caleb saw the hesitation and turmoil in his face as he spoke. "There's men up there in the hallway. I don't want no trouble.

Caleb answered, "Neither do I."

He pushed past the man and with the crowd following, marched up the stairs and into the hallway. There was no question where the two assemblymen had taken refuge. Three men sat on chairs in the hallway, two on one side of a door, one on the other. At the sound and sight of Caleb and those behind him walking steadily down the hall, all three men stood and gathered together, shoulder to shoulder, in front of the door, silent, waiting.

Caleb was still twenty feet from the nearest one when the sergeant at arms grasped his coat sleeve and whispered, "The big one has a pistol in his belt. I saw it this morning."

Caleb walked steadily to them, stopped, and faced the biggest man, directly in front of the door. He estimated the man at six feet three inches, and two-hundred-forty pounds. Those beside him were both slightly smaller, but over six feet tall and above two hundred pounds. Their dress was of the streets, and their faces showed marks of many battles. Their eyes were dead, flat, without expression.

Caleb looked up into the face of the big man. "I am a sergeant at arms sent by the president of the Pennsylvania assembly. There are two men in this room, Henry Pollard and Josephus Edmunds. I'm under orders to bring them back to the Statehouse." He held up the Fitzsimons paper. "This is my authority, signed by the speaker of the legislature."

The big man ignored the paper and looked down at Caleb. An insolent grin flickered for a moment. "Those men aren't here." He pointed at the sergeant at arms who had flattened himself against the wall behind Caleb and was standing white-faced, frozen. "I told him the same thing this morning."

"Then why," Caleb asked, "are you standing here guarding an empty room?"

A quizzical look crossed the man's face, and then a darkness rose in his eyes. "That's none of your business."

Caleb ignored it. "If those men aren't in there, you won't mind letting us in, will you?"

The big man's face clouded. "Get away from here. Get away."

Caleb shook his head. "I can't do that."

The big man shifted his left foot forward with his right hand folded into a fist and Caleb read the moves perfectly. His left hand flicked up and out as his fist broke the big man's nose and his right hand sunk eight inches into the fleshy paunch. As the big man grunted and doubled over, Caleb's left hand struck just above the man's ear dropping him to his knees, stunned, unable to move or rise. The man to Caleb's left reached for Caleb's left arm and Caleb's right fist caught him flush on the point of the chin with every pound Caleb had, and the man was knocked over backwards, rolling, twitching for a moment, then lying still. The third man, to Caleb's right, threw up both hands and backed away, pasty-faced, muttering, "I'm out of this, I'm out of this." He turned and raced pounding down the hall and the stairs, and they heard the front door slam shut behind him. Less than ten seconds had passed from the time the big man had moved his foot to get braced to hit Caleb.

The sergeant at arms remained flat against the wall, eyes popping, and the crowd that had followed were bunched beside him, stunned, motionless, staring first at the two men on the floor, and then at Caleb, trying to make their minds accept what they had just seen.

Caleb tipped the big man off his hands and knees, onto his side, opened his coat, and jerked a pistol from his belt. He opened the frizzen to check the powder load, snapped it shut again, and thrust it to the sergeant at arms, who recoiled as though it were a snake.

"Take that," Caleb demanded, "and keep it pointed at these men until I'm back out here."

The sergeant at arms grasped the pistol with both shaking hands and pointed it down, with his back still flat against the wall. Caleb stepped to the door and knocked loudly. There was no answer, and no sound from inside. He knocked again and waited, but there was no response, nothing. He took one step back, and kicked hard with his right foot. The door jamb splintered and the door swung open.

Standing opposite the door, before a window at the far end of the room, were two men, one heavy, the other slight, both wide-eyed, white-faced. They had heard the sounds of a brief pitched battle in the hallway, and were now looking at one man facing them in a splintered doorway. In the hall behind him was a thin man holding a pistol with both hands, pointing it at one of their hired bodyguards who was lying on the floor, dazed, unable to rise to his feet. Caleb held up the paper.

"I take it you are Mr. Pollard and Mr. Edmunds. I have written orders from the speaker of the Pennsylvania legislature to escort you back to your desks at the Statehouse. You can come peacefully, or you can resist. Either way, you're coming. Your choice."

The men looked at the thin man with the pistol, and their hired bully helpless on the floor, and they swallowed hard before the heavy one stammered, "You can't do this . . . you've got no authority."

Caleb started across the room. "Tell that to the speaker of the legislature. Are you coming? Make your choice."

The two men hesitated for one second, then walked across the room, out into the hallway with Caleb following. They paused for a moment to stare down at the two men on the floor, one unconscious, the other still too dazed to stand, and then they looked at the pistol, and they walked down the hall, Caleb right behind.

In the twenty-five minutes it took to walk them back to the Statehouse, not less than fifty people fell in behind the entourage, the strangest anyone could remember seeing in Philadelphia. Two men marching shoulder to shoulder, followed closely by a man who watched them like a hawk, and behind him, an elderly thin man with a pistol, followed by a growing knot of excited men, who were talking loudly, pointing, expounding a story that was past belief.

The column walked through the doors of the Statehouse, down the big hallway, past the doorman, and onto the floor of the legislature, with the doorman standing stock-still, eyes bugging in disbelief. Caleb pointed, and the two delinquent legislators took their seats at their desks. Twenty supporters gaped, then came crowding around.

Caleb said, "Keep them here while I get the speaker."

He walked to the door, knocked, and was admitted by a secretary, who followed Caleb to face Fitzsimons seated behind his desk. Fitzsimons laid down his pen, looked carefully at Caleb, and said, "Well?"

"Pollard and Edmunds are at their desks. That should make a quorum."

Slowly Fitzsimons leaned forward. "What?"

"You've got a quorum."

Fitzsimons gaped. "How . . . is either of them harmed?"

"No."

"Then how did you . . ."

"Their bodyguards didn't fare so well."

Fitzsimons recoiled. "Dead?"

"No. They'll be fine by tonight."

Fitzsimons forced some sense of order to his thoughts and stood. "Enough of that. If they're here, let's get on with it."

Within ten minutes all the supporting legislators were at their seats, euphoric at the sight of Pollard and Edmunds in their chairs, knowing what was coming. The gallery was filled.

Fitzsimons took the dais and declared, "We are now in session. Mr. Secretary, take the roll call."

The names were called, the answers were taken, the secretary ran his tally, and turned to Fitzsimons.

"Sir, we have a quorum."

"We shall proceed with . . ."

A voice rang out, the president stopped in midsentence, and Pollard waved a hand. "Mr. President, I have urgent need to leave the floor. Five minutes. That's all I ask."

The man seated next to him battled a grin. "I believe he really does need to leave. I'll go with him to be sure he returns."

Fitzsimons stared, first at Pollard, then the volunteer next to him, and it dawned on him what would prompt a man to request permission to leave for just five minutes. Fitzsimons raised a hand to thoughtfully scratch beneath his chin for a few moments before he spoke.

"Mr. Pollard, it seems to me you've delayed this legislature long enough in the past two days. We're going to proceed with our business, and you will remain where you are until we are finished."

Muffled laughter was heard, which slowly dwindled, and Fitzsimons picked up the paper on which was written the agenda.

"First order of business. Having already voted to conduct a ratification convention, the question is, where shall it be held, and when?"

It would be held at the Statehouse, or at such other location in Philadelphia convenient and agreeable to the delegates, two weeks after the election of the delegates.

"When shall the delegates be elected?"

November sixth.

"How shall the delegates be compensated?"

They would be paid commensurate with the pay received by the legislators.

The president stared at his agenda for a few seconds to be certain there was no possible way for the furious non-supporters to claim error or impropriety in what had been done, and there was none. All matters necessary to convene the ratification convention had been completed under authority of the national congress at New York, and by a majority of the Pennsylvania assembly vote, with a quorum present.

It was finished.

Fitzsimons stood and the chamber quieted. "We stand adjourned, *sine die.*"

The supporting faction came to their feet in loud, heady talk at their resounding success, shaking hands, clapping each other on the back. Pollard nearly ran for the door and down the hall. Citizens in the gallery rose to call out their sentiments, both for and against the action just completed on the floor below them. Caleb stood, drew and released a great breath of relief, and made his way to the door. He walked down the stairs, to the door into the floor of the legislature, to find George Clymer. He found him huddled with Judge Thomas McKean and James Wilson, shaking hands, exclaiming, congratulating each other. Clymer saw Caleb approaching and turned to face him directly.

"Young man, need we say how grateful we are for your performance?" He seized Caleb's hand to shake it firmly and repeatedly. Clymer released his hand, and Wilson seized it to shake it, then McKean.

"Thank you," Caleb said. "Would it be possible to spend a minute with Mr. Fitzsimons?"

"Absolutely," Clymer exclaimed. He took Caleb by the arm, and with Wilson and McKean following, made his way to the chambers of the speaker. Inside, Fitzsimons came to his feet the moment they entered the door.

"Mr. Dunson, I'm not certain that any of us fully understands the value of what you did for us today. My hearty congratulations, sir, and my deepest thanks." He thrust out his hand to Caleb, who seized it.

Caleb said, "Mr. Fitzsimons, I need to be certain. Is the matter finished?"

Fitzsimons reflected for a moment. "I believe I had better not answer that. I am the speaker, and I have to remain unbiased in these things." He turned to Clymer. "Mr. Clymer, how would you answer that?"

Clymer was emphatic. "Absolutely! I give you my personal guarantee that Pennsylvania will ratify the constitution. The convention is set, the time, place, and compensation decided, and it was all done pursuant to instruction from the United States Congress convened in New York, and by majority vote of a quorum in the legislature. It is over. Finished. Complete. I will write your brother my letter saying so within the next two days."

Wilson cut in. "George, you might make mention that none of it would have happened, except for the service of this young man."

"By all means! By all means! We are in your debt, sir. Deeply in your debt."

Wilson turned to Caleb. "Would you care to share with us what happened at the Bellamy Boardinghouse?"

All four men turned, waiting in fascinated silence.

"Nothing, as to Pollard and Edmunds. There were three men in the hall blocking the door. Pretty big. I can see why your sergeant at arms came back empty-handed. I showed them the paper Mr. Fitzsimons signed for me. We had a brief discussion. They decided to let me enter the room. Pollard and Edmunds came peacefully enough."

Wilson shook his head, grinning. "No, you left something out. The brief discussion. I want to know about that."

Caleb looked at him for a moment, wiped at his mouth, and answered. "Three men were at the door. The big man, maybe six feet three inches, two-hundred-forty pounds, refused to let me in. He moved his left foot and balled his right fist to hit me. He got a broken nose and a lump over his left ear before he went down. The man to his right made a grab and he got hit on the chin. He went down. The third man left. In a hurry. I took a pistol from the belt of the big man while he was on the floor and gave it to your sergeant at arms. He held it on the two men while I entered the room—kicked the door open—and asked Pollard and Edmunds to come peacefully. They saw the pistol and two of their bodyguards on the hall floor, and came along without any trouble." He stopped for a moment, then finished. "Is that what you wanted to hear, Mr. Wilson?"

Fitzsimons and McKean and Clymer were standing like statues, spellbound, while a grin split Wilson's face. "That's what I wanted to hear, sir. You have no idea how badly I wanted to hear that."

Caleb said, "Your sergeant at arms still has that pistol, and it would be a nice thing to let him keep it. I should also warn you, when I kicked that door open, the jamb splintered. You may get a repair bill from whoever owns the Bellamy Boardinghouse."

Wilson chuckled. "I'll pay all damages personally. And I want to thank you for the privilege."

"My pleasure. Gentlemen, I appreciate your patience with me. I know I am a poor fit in your world. I'm glad it turned out in your favor."

Judge McKean found his voice. "It is we who are indebted to you, sir."

"Unless there is something further, I should go. I have to get to the waterfront to find a ship sailing for Boston, and I have to collect my things."

Wilson took him by the shoulder. "You tend to your business, son. If you ever come to Philadelphia again, I will be insulted if you don't come find me."

Caleb nodded to the four men, turned and walked out of the chamber, across the floor of the legislature, down the long hall, and out into the bright, warm late afternoon sun of Philadelphia.

It was later, when he was packing his bag, that he came across the folded paper signed by Fitzsimons. He unfolded it and read it.

"Dated this twenty-ninth day of September 1787. Know all men by these presents that I, Thomas Fitzsimons, Speaker of the Legislature of the State of Pennsylvania, have this date duly and regularly authorized Caleb Dunson as a Sergeant At Arms for said legislature."

For a time Caleb stared at the document, thoughts running, and then he folded it and carefully put it back in his pocket, with a grin forming.

A sergeant at arms for the Pennsylvania legislature. Matthew and Billy and Adam have got to see this. They aren't going to believe it. I can hardly believe it myself.

Notes

The Pennsylvania state legislature convened in Philadelphia in September 1787 to address the question of ratification of the new United States Constitution. At the time, the state was divided, some supporting ratification, some opposing. The supporters held a slight advantage in numbers in the legislature. The debate between the two interests occurred as described, including the slurs against Benjamin Franklin and George Washington. The boycott by nineteen non-supporters is historically factual as is the part played by George Clymer in the affair. The speaker, Thomas Fitzsimons, did in fact order the sergeant at arms to go find two of the absent non-supporters and bring them to the floor. He returned without them. They adjourned for one more day, to Saturday, September twenty-ninth. That night, almost as a miracle, an express rider sent by the United States Congress convened in New York arrived in Philadelphia carrying news that congress had received the new constitution, considered it, and had authorized all thirteen states to convene ratification conventions to act on it. The morning of Saturday, September twenty-ninth, the nineteen missing non-supporters again failed to appear. Again speaker Fitzsimons sent the sergeant at arms to bring them in, and again he failed. The record then states that "a mob succeeded in forcibly returning the necessary two seceding assemblymen, and the legislature completed its business."

The name of the supporting leader, George Clymer, is accurate, as are the names of Judge Thomas McKean, Chief Justice of the Pennsylvania Supreme Court, Thomas Fitzsimons who was speaker of the legislature, and James Wilson, one of the strongest men at the constitutional convention, and a powerful figure in the politics of Pennsylvania. The part played by Caleb Dunson in bringing the reluctant assemblymen back to their places in the legislature is fictitious.

For a concise and authoritative description of the above events, see Conely and Kaminski, *The Constitution and the States*, pp. 37–53. For a photograph of a painting of George Clymer, see p. 50; for Judge Thomas McKean, p. 52; for

James Wilson, p. 45. The name of Thomas Fitzsimons, speaker of the legislature, is found in Bernstein, *Are We to Be a Nation?* p. 203.

In support of the rather humorous scene of a "mob" hauling the two absent legislators from their boardinghouse back to the floor of the legislature, see Bernstein, *Are We to Be a Nation?* p. 203; see also generally pp. 199–207. See also Berkin, *A Brilliant Solution,* p. 183.

In support of the near miraculous arrival of the express rider sent by the United States congress in New York, see Conely and Kaminski, *The Constitution and the States,* p. 51, second paragraph.

CHAPTER XXIX

*I*ce hung ragged from the ropes in the rigging and the furled sails of every ship anchored in Boston harbor and tied to the docks, and rattled in the freezing wind that gusted raw and bitter from the Atlantic. With the wind ruffling their feathers, seabirds walked the ice that reached fifteen feet from the shore and prowled the ice-coated, black timbers of the wharf, hunting for anything they could snatch and swallow for food. The men loading and unloading the ships moved slowly, wrapped in heavy woollen coats with caps pulled low, and mittens or gloves on hands numb from the cold. They wore heavy scarves wrapped high, over their mouths and beards, and the wind whipped the vapor from their faces. White spots appeared on their cheeks, and they rubbed them, and kept working with the wooden cases and the barrels that moved the freight of the world.

In the frigid midmorning sun of a cloudless sky, Adam Dunson ducked as he leaned into the wind and held his tricorn on his head with one hand while he worked his way to the offices of Dunson & Weems. He opened the door and slammed it shut against the wind while those inside clutched at papers that moved. He walked through the scant warmth of the room to the desk where Billy and Tom were seated facing Matthew and dropped a flat package before his brother.

"From Madison," he said, and walked back to hang his hat and coat on the pegs near the door, before going to stand before the large, black stove at the rear of the office. He moved close and extended his hands flat toward the heat.

Matthew cut the string and opened the package, glanced at it, and put it aside. "More essays from 'Publius,'" he said. "They can wait for now." He called to Adam, "Anything else from the post?"

"No. Just the package."

"When you're ready, we're handling things you need to know."

Adam turned to drag the chair from his desk and take his place with Billy and Tom. He cupped his cold hands to his mouth to blow on them, then rubbed them briskly together and listened intently as Matthew referred to a large chart spread on his desk. On the chart were the names of all thirteen states, with Matthew's notations of when the ratification conventions were scheduled, where they were to be held, and the best information his unending correspondence with high political figures had produced concerning the likelihood of ratification. Beside the chart were two stacks of files, six inches deep. Following his chart with a finger, Matthew began, with the steady hum of the wind outside.

"As of now, Delaware has ratified the Consitution. A unanimous vote. That was December seventh. Pennsylvania ratified December twelfth with a vote of forty-six to twenty-three—two to one in favor. New Jersey was unanimous in favor December eighteenth. Georgia has probably ratified by now, but we won't know until we get the official notice. That makes four states that have ratified, and one of them— Pennsylvania—was critical. We had to have Pennsylvania."

He paused for a moment. "It looks like Maryland will be scheduling their convention sometime in April. We're still waiting on notice from the others."

He leaned forward over the chart. "You know that our state— Massachusetts—is another state we must have. Pennsylvania, Massachusetts, Virginia; three of the biggest and most powerful. The other states are watching. We've got to have all three." He paused, and Adam watched the concern come into Matthew's eyes for a moment before Matthew drew a deep breath and pointed to a map on the wall to his left.

"As of right now, it appears that the Massachusetts counties away from the coast—the farming counties—Middlesex, Bristol, Worcester, Hampshire, Berkshire—are against ratification. Strongly so. Maybe two to one against it." He shifted his pointing finger. "I estimate that the populated counties on the coast—Suffolk, Essex, Plymouth, Barnstable —all favor ratification, perhaps as much as four or five to one."

He placed both hands flat on the desktop. "Today is January third. Our ratification convention is scheduled for next Wednesday, the ninth. And as of right now, our people do not control the convention. Those against ratification do."

Billy and Tom shifted in their chairs but said nothing while Matthew continued.

"Madison said he received a letter from Rufus King that said our prospects of getting Massachusetts to ratify are gloomy. King represented Massachusetts at the big convention in Philadelphia and has worked hard for ratification since his return. One of our hard problems is that Elbridge Gerry was also at the Philadelphia convention, and Gerry refused to sign the finished constitution. Too many people wonder what's wrong with it that he would refuse, after he took such an active part in creating it. They think he should have been a delegate to the ratification convention, but he isn't. We know now that Samuel Adams is against ratification, and he has invited Gerry to attend the convention to answer questions as to why he refused to sign the constitution, and Gerry has accepted."

For a moment he glanced at the map on the wall. "Put it all together, and I think we're in serious trouble."

The front door opened and Caleb stepped in and forced it shut against the wind. He hung his heavy coat and tricorn on the pegs before he walked to the stove and backed toward it, hands behind him, watching the men at the desk. "Go on with it," he said. "I can listen from here."

Matthew asked Caleb, "Did you get the crew for the *Helene*?"

"Ready to go. Saturday."

Matthew nodded, then continued.

"You'll remember ten days ago we decided to approach Governor Hancock because he's popular, and one of the signers of the Declaration of Independence. He's well thought of by the citizens from the rural counties because he took up their cause after Shays' rebellion. I've talked with his office. I have an appointment with him tomorrow. I can tell you now, no one knows where he stands on ratification. He's too ambitious, too much the politician. I think he's waiting to see which side he thinks will win before he takes a position, and he'll go with that side. He wants to be reelected as governor, and there's speculation that he wants to be the first president of the United States, or at least hold some other high office in the national government. There are some delegates who are still unsettled in their views, and I think if we can get John Hancock to support us, he'll bring them along."

Caleb snorted and the four men at the table turned to look at him. "Nothing," he said. "Just thinking about politics and politicians, and Pennsylvania."

Billy smiled at the remembrance of the letter received from George Clymer that arrived in Boston one week after Caleb's return from Philadelphia. The letter had heaped praise on Caleb, but between the lines was a quiet message. The politicians Clymer, McKean, Wilson, and Fitzsimons together couldn't get a quorum into the convention room in the Philadelphia Statehouse to make the decisive vote for ratification. Caleb had done it in forty-five minutes.

Matthew went on. "The plan is to make him an offer. If he'll support ratification, we'll support him in his bid for reelection. And if he later runs for national office, we'll support him for president if Virginia fails to ratify. If Virginia ratifies, George Washington will be our president, and we'll support Hancock for vice president."

Adam asked, "Any idea how he'll accept that?"

"Not yet. But there's more. I know he favors creating a bill of rights, and making some other amendments to the Constitution as it now stands, and we'll agree to support some of those amendments. Maybe give him a few of our own. That will give him a way to tell the people that he has some amendments to improve the Constitution, and with the amendments, that it appears to be a good thing for this state."

Tom interrupted. "We decided to talk to Sam Adams, too. Anything come of it?"

Matthew nodded. "I talked with him. I don't know what to expect. He sounded like he was against us, but there was something about the way he talked that left the whole thing hanging. I can't guess what's in his mind."

For a few seconds they sat in silence, until Matthew said, "I think that's where we are for right now." He pushed the open package to Adam. "More writings by Madison and Hamilton down in New York. How many essays by 'Publius' does that make?"

"Close to thirty."

"Read these when you find time and tell me what they say. Did you spend some time with number ten? The one on factions?"

Adam nodded. "I did. It runs contrary to the thoughts of just about every political philosopher known. Madison proposes that diversity is a good thing, not bad. The more different views in a society, the better, since diversity will tend to prevent one view from becoming the view of all."

"I think he's right. Let me know what you find in these latest ones, and whether we should be sure they're published in the Boston newspapers, like some of the previous ones." He turned to Tom and Billy. "Are we finished?"

The front door burst open and they all turned to peer at the short, stout silhouette in the bright sunlight. Billy rose to his feet, concern in his face.

"Trudy! What are you doing on the waterfront? What's happened?"

Trudy pushed the door closed and turned to face the men who were gaping at her. She removed the thick shawl she had over her head and said, "Matthew, you better come. Doctor Soderquist is with Kathleen. It came on sudden. The baby is coming. Mother sent me."

Matthew leaped from his chair. "She was all right when I left this morning. Is there trouble?"

Trudy shook her head. "I don't know. I only know Doctor Soderquist said to get you there. Quickly."

Matthew sprang to the pegs by the front door. Grabbing his coat, he said, "Billy, take charge. I'll be back when I can."

He was still buttoning his greatcoat as he bolted through the door and onto the ice-slick wharf. He jammed his tricorn onto his head, and with the wind at his back sprinted toward Fruit Street, then on to the narrow street and the large home with the white picket fence. He shoved through the gate, hit the front door at a run, and barged into the parlor. It was vacant. He raced down the hall to the master bedroom, threw the door open, and stopped. In an instant Margaret was in front of him, both hands locked onto his coat, holding him. Her voice came firm, her authority clear.

"You go on back to the parlor. We'll take care of things here."

Behind Margaret, big, gray, shambling Doctor Walter Soderquist was hunched forward over the bed, partially blocking Matthew's view of his wife. Kathleen lay on her back, eyes clenched shut, perspiration shining, mouth clamped, and a thin, muffled moan coming from her throat. The comforter and sheet were thrown back, her knees high and separated. Doctor Soderquist had his coat off, shirtsleeves rolled up past his elbows, forehead covered with sweat while he worked with his hands. At the foot of the bed stood Dorothy Weems and Prissy, silent, still, mesmerized, watching the doctor's every move.

"Is she all right?" Matthew demanded. "Trudy said something was going wrong."

Margaret looked him in the eyes. "We'll take care of it. She will be all right. You shouldn't be here. Go on back to the parlor. We'll call you."

Soderquist glanced over his shoulder. "I've got to turn the baby a little. Now you go on out and we'll call you."

Margaret steadily moved him out the door and closed it, and Matthew stood in the hallway for a time, fighting the need to be inside the room with Kathleen, struggling with the unwritten rule against allowing the father, or any other man, into the room during delivery of a baby, the doctor being the sole exception.

He had reached the parlor and hung his coat and tricorn and was pacing back and forth when the front door slammed open and Adam came in, Caleb and Billy right behind. They were breathing hard from their run, and their faces showed the white spots of the beginnings of frostbite.

"What's happening?" Adam exclaimed.

"They're in the bedroom with her now. Dr. Soderquist said he has to turn the baby. Something's gone wrong."

Adam shook his head violently. "Did Dr. Soderquist say that?"

"No."

"Then let's not jump to conclusions. Dr. Soderquist would have told you if something was wrong."

Billy was working with his coat buttons when he spoke. "Who's back there with Dr. Soderquist?"

"Mother. Dorothy. Prissy."

Billy hung his coat. "Trudy's on the way. Dr. Soderquist knows what he's doing. The women will take care of it."

Matthew asked, "Is Tom back at the office?"

Caleb answered. "Yes."

The front door jerked open and Trudy entered, breathless. "Am I too late?"

Billy answered. "No. Things are happening back there right now."

Trudy was hanging her coat and shawl when Matthew stopped short. "Where's John?"

Adam answered, "Probably at school, where he belongs."

Caleb said, "This business of birthing babies goes on every day. Dr. Soderquist's delivered half the town of Boston. Let him take care of it."

Matthew took a deep breath and brought himself under control. "I know, I know," he said, "but I keep seeing Mary. Eli's wife. They lost her in childbirth."

Billy felt the pain once again. "Her lungs were bad. Pneumonia from the smoke from that fire. She'd have been all right if—"

From the hallway came the sound of a tiny voice raising a protest at having come from the warmth and comfort of the womb into the world of cold air and chilly hands that held the infant by the heels to whack it on the bottom and bring on the gasp that inflated the lungs. The men instantly turned to look at the archway, and the little voice gained strength as it wailed. Relief flooded through Matthew.

"It's here! Kathleen . . . I've got to see if she's all right." The others followed him down the hallway where he rapped on the door. Margaret opened it a crack and shook her head. "Not yet. We've got a few things to do before you come in."

"Is Kathleen all right?"

"She's fine. So is your daughter. Wait until we've had time to clean things up. I'll call you. Trudy, you come on in. You can help." Trudy slipped past Matthew into the room, and Margaret closed the door in Matthew's face.

Standing over Kathleen, Doctor Soderquist tied and clipped the umbilical cord, cleared some mucous from the baby's nose and mouth, then handed the infant to the women, who dried the newcomer and wrapped her in a thick towel. Margaret gazed into the baby's red and wrinkled little face. There was a thick growth of dark hair above the brown eyes, and the rosebud mouth was open wide as the little person wailed her grievance. Margaret held her for a time, then carefully placed her in Dorothy's arms as Prissy and Trudy gathered close to admire and coo at the newborn.

Doctor Soderquist's voice stopped them all. "Whoops! Get ready! We've got another one coming! *That's* what was giving us trouble."

The women gaped, and Margaret exclaimed, "Twins!" and then the room was filled with action. Prissy and Trudy gathered up the bloody sheets while the two mothers grabbed clean ones and Margaret raised Kathleen's midsection while Dorothy jammed them underneath her, and Margaret ran to the kitchen for a clean, fresh towel. Kathleen raised her head far enough to ask, "Twins?" and Dr. Soderquist answered, "You have a daughter, and number two will be here in about three minutes. Push."

In the hallway, impatient, fearful of why he was not being allowed into the bedroom, Matthew was reaching for the doorknob when the unmistakable sound of a second high, wavering voice reached through the door, and Matthew dropped his hand to stand stock-still for a moment with the other three men, wide-eyed in surprise.

"Two?" Matthew exclaimed. "Twins?"

Caleb jabbed a finger toward Adam, grinning. "It happens."

Another five minutes that seemed an eternity passed before the door opened and Margaret, beaming, glowing, stepped aside. "You can come in now."

Matthew stepped through the doorway with the three other men following, and slowed for a moment. Clean sheets covered Kathleen to her chin, and on the near side of the bed, wrapped in clean towels, were two tiny squirming infants, heads covered with dark hair, red faces wrinkled as they wailed in unison. Matthew walked to the bed and knelt, touching the two tiny heads in wonder, and then reached to lay his hand tenderly against Kathleen's cheek.

"Are you all right?"

Her eyes were weary, her voice thin. "Fine. Tired." She smiled. "We have twins."

"Twin girls," Margaret announced.

Walter added. "Identical twins."

Matthew turned to look up at the broad face. "Identical?"

"I can't tell them apart. I judge each to be about six and a half pounds. I tied a string on the ankle of the one that was born first, so we can keep the birth certificates straight. You two get the names to me as soon as you can. Matthew, you should hold your daughters for a minute and then you'll have to leave. The afterbirth is coming and then we've got to close the loin and wrap Kathleen."

"You're sure she's all right?"

"Fine. She just needs some rest. She'll start nursing tonight. Now you hold those two little people for a minute and then you and the rest of the men go on out."

With Margaret's help, Matthew took one in each arm, then gazed down at them, proudly studying their little faces, memorizing everything about them. After a few moments, he laid them back beside their mother, and once more leaned to tenderly touch her face. She saw the look in his face, and she held his hand against her cheek. Then he straightened and walked from the room with Billy, Caleb and Adam following him back to the parlor.

Billy said, "We three ought to get back to the office." He faced Matthew, the brother he had never had, and extended his hand. "I'm happy for you."

Grinning and expressing their congratulations, the others also shook Matthew's hand. Then they buttoned on their heavy coats, pulled their tricorns low, and made their windblown way back to the wharf, one mittened hand holding their hats as they hunched forward into the freezing wind.

With Dorothy and Margaret helping, Doctor Soderquist handled the afterbirth, then washed Kathleen completely, and wrapped her loosely in long, clean cotton strips, from her knees to well above her waist. He covered her with a fresh sheet and the great comforter, then laid the two infants beside her.

"There. We've got the loin closed, and you should be comfortable. When you're ready, nurse them. You'll likely want to have someone to help with the nursing. I'll send Henrietta Burns tomorrow. If you need me for anything, send Prissy or Adam, and I'll come."

He stopped beside the bed and looked down at Kathleen and there was a gentleness in his great, craggy face. "Two beautiful daughters," he said quietly. "You're blessed." He walked from the room, buttoned on his great coat, and nodded his good-bye to Matthew and the women before walking out the door with his bag in his hand.

Prissy brought John home from school, and Matthew took him into the bedroom to stand beside his mother's bed, staring at the two babes gazing about with eyes that could not see, working their tiny mouths and their fingers.

"They're so small," he said. "Was I that small?"

Kathleen reached to cup his chin in her hand. "Once. They'll grow. You'll have to help."

"Can I touch one?"

Kathleen smiled. "Just be very careful."

Cautiously he touched the nearest hand, and the fingers flexed and for a moment curled about his finger. He grinned at Kathleen. "She likes me."

"Of course she does. She's your sister."

"What's her name?"

"You'll have to help us choose. Two names."

Margaret glanced at Dorothy. "Well, the excitement's passed for now. We've got a bundle of wash to do and a supper to prepare."

Dorothy said, "I'll take the wash home and bring it back tomorrow."

Margaret nodded. "I'll get something on for supper. You and Trudy come back about six o'clock and eat with us."

The wind slowed in the late afternoon and died at sunset. With dusk settling, the first snowflakes came drifting, large and silent. By the time supper was finished and the women had gathered in the kitchen to wash and dry the dishes and fill the room with their excited chatter, the streets of Boston were white. Brigitte had forgiven the others for not getting her from her work and had gone into the bedroom half a dozen times to see the twins and watch while Matthew helped Kathleen sip at the thick, rich broth from the beef roast, and eat brown bread, and drink buttermilk.

Margaret gathered them in the dining room.

"I'll stay here for a few days. Prissy, you'll have to take care of our house and Caleb and Adam. Matthew, you and the men will be busy at the shipping office. I know you're supposed to visit with the governor tomorrow—John Hancock. Things will be fine here. Dorothy, bring the wash whenever you finish it. If we need anything, I'll send for you and Trudy. Will that be all right?"

"Of course."

"Then that's the plan. The day's over. Let's all go on about our business and let Kathleen and the babies have some rest."

Early the next morning, with snow still falling, Henrietta Burns arrived just as Matthew was leaving the house. She was to help nurse the twins and care for Kathleen in her confinement.

Walking in the quiet of the white wonderland, toward his meeting with John Hancock, Matthew carried beneath his arm his leather case filled with the documents and maps he thought might be needed to persuade the governor to support ratification of the Constitution.

He stopped inside the door of the Statehouse to shake the snow from his heavy cape and tricorn, then walked briskly to the governor's office and was seated for a few moments before being taken to the heavy door into the governor's office. He entered at the governor's invitation and walked toward a large desk covered with documents. Governor Hancock rose to meet him.

"Mr. Dunson. Nice to see you again. I understand you've been busy getting ready for the convention next week." Hancock reached to shake hands, smiling, cordial, eyes shrewd, calculating what Matthew would want of him. Everyone wanted something from the governor. Hancock coveted the power.

"Thank you, sir," Matthew replied. "I appreciate your time."

"Not at all. Please. Have a seat."

They had met three times previously, exchanged letters, knew at least in large part what the other was about. Hancock, average size, regular features, a Harvard graduate with a fortune gained from commercial enterprise and five times governor, saw no sense in the usual waste of time spent in dancing around issues. He leaned forward in his chair and came directly to it.

"What can I do for you?"

Matthew laid his leather case on his side of the desk. "It's possible we can do something for each other."

Hancock's expression did not change. He could not remember how many times he had heard those words in the world of politics. He waited, and Matthew did not waste time or words.

"The ratification convention convenes next Wednesday. You will attend, and those of us who support ratification of the new constitution will give you full support for president of the convention. In return, we ask that you consider giving your support to ratification."

Hancock's face was an inscrutable mask. Matthew continued. "We know that Sam Adams has invited Elbridge Gerry to attend the convention to answer questions about why he did not sign the document. We

don't know what Gerry will say. But whatever it is, your support of ratification will be helpful. Probably crucial."

Matthew sat back and waited. Hancock dropped his gaze to his
hands on his desktop and a few seconds passed.

"I'll have to think on that. You should know that I am among those
who share Mr. Gerry's concern that the constitution does not include a
bill of rights."

"I'm aware of that," Matthew said and waited, fully aware that the
game of politics was based largely on one's ability to know what parts of
a plan to reveal, and when. He had said enough; the remainder of what
he was prepared to give Hancock would wait.

When the governor did not respond, Matthew observed, "I think
Mr. Gerry will finally support ratification. He was a major contributor to
the document as it now stands, with or without a bill of rights, and when
the time comes, I think he'll support it."

Hancock smiled woodenly. "That could be. Time will tell."

They passed the necessary brief pleasantries, Matthew took his cue,
rose, picked up his leather case, shook hands with Hancock, and walked
back out into the snow-covered streets of Boston.

On Wednesday, January ninth, the Massachusetts convention convened and took up its business, but governor John Hancock was not
present. He had been stricken with a serious flare-up of gout and begged
to be excused; he would be in attendance as soon as possible. In the
meantime he wished them every success as they proceeded. Back hall
rumor was to the contrary. Some delegates whispered that Hancock had
not yet made up his mind as to which faction would win, the supporters
or the non-supporters, and until he made that determination, he would
continue to be absent. Hancock *had* to be on the winning side; much of
his consuming ambition for future political office depended on it.

Matthew sat in the gallery as the business of the convention proceeded, watching, making notes. Gerry appeared on schedule and sat
quietly, waiting to be questioned publicly about his refusal to sign the
document he had helped draft. He held his peace until Saturday, January
twelfth, when a delegate launched into an attack on the horrendous

debate held in May and June of 1787 in Philadelphia that had brought the entire constitutional convention to the verge of dissolving the United States, and had resulted in the pivotal compromise between the large and small states that saved the Union. Matthew watched Gerry squirm and control himself as long as he could, then rise and request permission to speak.

The hall fell silent until Francis Dana and other delegates sprang to their feet to loudly claim Gerry was out of order. In five seconds the chamber was locked in a verbal brawl that took the acting president minutes to quiet. To prevent further uproar, and perhaps violence, he loudly announced, "We stand adjourned until further notice."

Matthew stood, relieved and concerned at the same time. Would this rupture in the proceeding result in worse animosity between the two groups? At the same time, he knew that at that moment the opposition would win if it came to an immediate vote. Thus, the supporters needed all the time they could get to argue their case behind the scenes. With Sunday to give the delegates time to cool, he wondered what Monday would bring.

They reconvened on Monday, and the most obvious person in the convention was Gerry, not because he was present, but because he was not. Offended, humiliated, he had refused to return to the chamber for any reason, and he never did. Matthew listened to the opposition as they sensed victory, and watched as they mounted steady pressure to bring the issue to a final vote. Matthew's heart sank. With the opposition in the majority, they were succeeding, and there appeared to be no way to stop them.

Then Samuel Adams stood and was recognized. Sam Adams, the firebrand of the Revolution, who had not been hesitant to speak his views against ratification. Matthew leaned forward in his seat in the gallery, heart in his mouth, waiting for Sam Adams to deliver the death knell to the supporters.

Sam waited for quiet before he spoke. "Gentlemen, I sense these proceedings moving rapidly toward a conclusion. A final vote." Murmuring broke out and subsided. "It concerns me. The matter we have before us—the question of the newly completed constitution—is of weight. It merits thought and reflection. I wonder at the wisdom of rushing these proceedings for any reason, least of all political gain. I think we ought not to be stingy of our time. Given the purpose for which we are gathered, may I suggest we have the obligation to give the debate on the question of ratification its due."

Matthew straightened in surprise. *Sam Adams, who had been against ratification?—giving the supporters more time, rescuing them from the brink of defeat?* Matthew searched for an explanation, but could find none. He left the gallery and fairly trotted back to the office to try to invent a way to use the precious time to rally support. For three days he attended the convention sessions, seated in the gallery, listening, probing, seeking the answer. In the late afternoons he gathered knowledgeable persons at the office and sat in council with his people, arguing, scheming, searching. On Friday one of them brought a copy of the *Massachusetts Sentinel* newspaper, dated January twelfth, and read an article by an anonymous writer who styled himself as a "Republican Federalist." The man proposed ratification of the constitution, but with " . . . *proposed amendments . . .*"

Amendments! Matthew and Billy and Adam had talked of amendments before, and had prepared a few for John Hancock to consider when the time came. The time was now!

Hastily Matthew arranged a second meeting with Governor John Hancock, this time at the governor's home, bringing Adam along to serve as his silent support. With his case beneath his arm, he rapped on the door and was shown into the library where John Hancock rose from behind his desk to shake their hands. Ever the politician, the governor smiled broadly as Matthew introduced Adam.

"Governor, this is Adam Dunson, my youngest brother. Harvard graduate, professional navigator, and personal assistant in the effort to obtain ratification of the constitution."

Above the smile, Hancock's eyes were severe, probing, watching Adam. "It is my pleasure, Adam," Hancock said. "There is always room for a bright, educated young man. Won't you both be seated?"

Adam watched Hancock move, aware that there wasn't the slightest hint of gout in his legs. The luxurious appointments in the library and the wall covered with oak shelves and books on every subject were lost on Adam as he studied the governor. Matthew laid his case on the desk before him and waited for Hancock's invitation, and Hancock took his cue.

"I've been distressed that my health has prevented my attendance at the convention," he began. "I've been reading the daily journal of the proceedings. Interesting. I was surprised at Sam Adams. I presume you were too."

Matthew answered, "I think Mr. Adams has had a change of heart."

Hancock interrupted. "Sam? I doubt it. But who knows?"

Matthew read the message correctly. *Don't count on Sam just yet.* Matthew wasted no further time. He opened his case and drew out a handwritten document. There was a firmness in his voice as he spoke.

"I have here several—about eleven—proposed amendments to the constitution. They include some—many—of the guarantees the citizens have been asking for in the form of a bill of rights. Among them is an amendment providing that all powers not specifically delegated by the constitution to the general government, are reserved to the states. We were going to introduce these on the floor of the convention ourselves, but on reflection, we now offer you the opportunity of introducing them."

Matthew saw Hancock's eyes narrow for a split second, and then Hancock took the paper, and for thirty seconds he scanned it, closely, carefully, then laid it down. Both he and Matthew knew that some of the strongest arguments against the constitution were the feeling that it robbed the states of their sovereignty, and left the people with no bill of rights. The proposed amendments made a giant leap toward giving the people what they wanted.

"Interesting." That is all he said about them, and moved on. "Was there anything else?"

Again Matthew read the covert message. *You want my support. What else are you offering?*

Matthew eased back in his chair and said firmly, "Should the constitution be ratified and become the law of the land, we are prepared to discuss backing you for vice president of the United States."

Matthew stopped and for the first time he knew he had caught Hancock by total surprise.

Hancock repeated, quietly, thoughtfully, "Vice president."

Matthew cut in. "Vice president. Further, if Virginia does not ratify the constitution, we will discuss supporting you for president."

Hancock slowly eased back in his chair, and in his eyes were his visions of power and prestige, far beyond any office in the state of Massachusetts. President of the United States. How it stirred Hancock! For a time Matthew remained silent, watching Hancock. Adam did not move as he studied both men, caught up in the startling experience of seeing for the first time the real world of politics in action.

Hancock brought his reveries under control and leaned forward. "You've made an interesting proposal. I think I can agree to it. You do what you have suggested, and you'll have my support."

With no further exchange, it was done. It had taken less than eight minutes. Hancock drew and released a breath. "Is there anything else?"

"Yes. Are you aware of the meeting that was held just as the convention began? The one at the Green Dragon Tavern on Union Street in the North End?"

Hancock searched his memory. "I heard about it, but not the detail. Why?"

"Sam Adams is one of the representatives most trusted by the working men of Boston. They met at the Green Dragon to discuss the ratification. The crowd reached out into the streets. They decided to support ratification. Paul Revere was among them. He took the information to Sam Adams."

Hancock was fascinated. "Go on."

"Sam asked Revere one question. 'How many were there?' Revere answered, 'as many as the stars in the heavens.'"

Matthew paused to let the impact settle into Hancock, then went on.

"I think Sam Adams now intends supporting ratification."

Hancock's eyebrows arched. "Adams? Has he said so?"

"No, not in words. But rumor has it he is saying it quietly to his constituents."

Hancock stood. "We'll see. In the meantime I want to study those proposed amendments. Keep me advised as this thing moves."

The battle inside the convention chamber continued, with Matthew watching, listening, waiting every day. On Wednesday, January thirtieth, Governor John Hancock made his first appearance, his gout miraculously cured at the same instant he perceived which side was going to win the ongoing fight. On January thirty-first he took the floor and the room became silent in anticipation.

"My fellow delegates, I rise to propose some amendments to the constitution as it is now written, which we can pass on to the national congress for their consideration. Included in these proposed amendments is a bill of rights, and a reservation of all powers to the states, unless specifically granted to the new national government."

Loud comment broke out and then quieted, and Hancock went on.

"My motive in presenting this to you is simple. I support ratification of the new constitution, and with these amendments it is my hope to pave the way for the adoption of a form of government that may extend its good influence to every part of the United States and advance the prosperity of the whole world."

Applause filled the chamber.

Sam Adams then took the floor. "I move that the amendments, which are in fact conciliatory propositions, be taken under consideration. For those of us who are still undecided, may I suggest that this plan—the Massachusetts plan—is the best way of dealing with any misgivings."

Comment rose and he paused and waited for silence before he finished. "Should Massachusetts fail to ratify, I can see repercussions through the nation that will lead to the breakup of the union, and I tremble at the consequence."

Matthew leaned back, aware that the actions of Hancock and Adams had changed the entire course of the convention, away from the opposition, in favor of the supporters of ratification of the constitution. He leaned forward to peer down at the floor, waiting for the hot attack that he knew was going to come from the opposition. Some rose, angry, to renew their condemnation of the constitution.

Then, Matthew watched in stunned silence as three dedicated men of the opposition rose to declare they had changed their position. The actions of Governor John Hancock, followed by Sam Adams, had persuaded them that ratifying the Constitution, with the proposed amendments, was clearly the best course for the state of Massachusetts. Chief among the three was a brilliant, articulate young lawyer from Andover, William Symmes, who shocked the opposition as his words rang out.

"I refuse to apologize for switching sides, for in so doing I stand acquitted of my own conscience. I hope and trust I shall be so acquitted by my constituents, and I know I shall before God!"

Matthew watched the opponents on the floor disintegrate into loud confusion. A delegate sprang to his feet.

"I move for immediate adjournment."

The sure knowledge flashed in Matthew's mind. *They're desperate. Trying to adjourn to avoid a vote that will defeat them!*

Another voice rang out. "Second the motion."

The vote was taken, the tally posted, and the motion was defeated. There would be no delay during which the frantic opposition could rally their people.

Adams sensed an opportunity and once again took the floor. "I propose further conciliatory amendments." He read a list. The debate went on for a time before it became obvious the newly arrived amendments were not favored, and Adams withdrew them.

Debate continued, the opposition desperately trying to stall, the supporters steadily pushing forward. One by one the obstacles were cleared, and on February sixth, 1788, true to his commitment, Governor John Hancock took the floor.

"I rise to suggest that we have completed our duty. Debate has been energetic and thorough, all pending motions have been resolved in favor of a conclusion to the issue now before us, and I recommend we proceed to a vote on the issue of ratification of the new constitution, with the proposed amendments."

"Second the motion."

The tension in the chamber was palpable. Matthew sat with his chart, making marks as the vote was taken.

Of the 401 communities in the commonwealth of Massachusetts that were eligible to send representatives to the convention, forty-six had failed to send any at all. The rural counties of Middlesex, Bristol, Worcester, Hampshire, and Berkshire, as expected, had voted against ratification, 128 votes against, 60 votes in favor. The urban coastal counties of Suffolk, Essex, Plymouth, and Barnstable, also as expected, had voted in favor of ratification, 100 in favor, 19 against.

Quickly Matthew added the columns that included all the counties, and for a moment closed his eyes in heady relief. The constitution had been ratified by a total vote of 187 in favor, 168 against. A margin of only nineteen votes.

He put his papers back in his leather case, rose from his place in the gallery, and walked briskly out into the frigid, clean air and the bright Massachusetts sun, striding toward Fruit Street and the offices of Dunson & Weems where his people were waiting.

We had to have Massachusetts, and we got it!

Notes

The delegates who supported ratification of the Constitution understood they would need the support of Pennsylvania, Massachusetts, and Virginia, three of the largest states, to succeed. The Massachusetts supporters also knew that the opposition held a majority in their home state. Of the 401 communities authorized to send delegates to the ratification convention, forty-six did not send representatives, as described. The parts played by John Hancock and Samuel Adams, as represented here are historically accurate, as are the political strategies employed by both factions. The portrayal of Hancock as a politically motivated man, along with his feigned illness, is factual. The description of Elbridge Gerry's refusal to account for his reservations to the Massachusetts convention was as described—he had been offended and never again took part in the debates. January twelfth, the *Massachusetts Sentinel* newspaper included an article by "A Republican Federalist" who favored ratification if certain amendments were included in the constitution, including a bill of rights, and others, but debate continued to run strongly against the supporters in the convention. The other events described in this chapter, leading to ratification by Massachusetts convention are based on the historical record, including Paul Revere's declaration that the number of working men who supported ratification were "as many as the stars in the heavens." Adams and Hancock were both heavily impressed. On January thirtieth Hancock did in fact attend the convention for the first time. On January thirty-first he rose to propose the amendments he had received from the supporters, as his own, according to their understanding. Sam Adams then rose in support of Hancock's proposal. Three opposing delegates rose to state they had changed their position, and now favored the constitution, with the amendments. Strongest of the three was William Symmes, a very articulate lawyer, who added his explanation that he made no apologies for changing sides, since in so doing he stood " . . . acquitted of my own conscience . . . my constituents . . . and . . . before God." The die was cast. Debate moved on, Adams added a few amendments of his own that were not favored, and on February sixth, 1788, the vote was taken with the result being as described, including the narrow margin of victory.

For support, see Conely and Kaminski, *The Constitution and the States,* pp. 113–30. See also Bernstein, *Are We to Be a Nation?* pp. 207–8; Rossiter, *1787: The Grand Convention,* pp. 287–89; Berkin, *A Brilliant Solution,* pp. 183–85; Warren, *The Making of the Constitution,* p. 819.

The description of how doctors, midwives, and wet nurses handled the births of babies as described in this chapter is accurate. See Ulrich, *A Midwife's Tale,* pp. 165–97, particularly page 176.

CHAPTER XXX

★ ★ ★

*A*dam Dunson sat hunched forward at his desk in the rising midmorning Boston heat, impervious to the sounds of the waterfront that came through the partially open door of the Dunson & Weems office as he concentrated for the third time on essay number 51. The document was dated February 6, 1788, and had appeared in *The New York Packet* on February 8 in a series of essays written by the fictional "Publius" in an ongoing effort to persuade New Yorkers of the merits of the new constitution. The first essay had been dated October 27, 1787, and had been printed in *The New York Packet* and *The Daily Advertiser* on October 30. Essay number 80 had been published May 28, 1788, and more, yet unpublished, were to follow. The authors had followed the tradition of presenting their works to the public under the assumed name of some ancient philosopher or figure in an attempt to present their thoughts in an unbiased posture. But some knew that "Publius" was in reality Alexander Hamilton, James Madison, and John Jay, trying to gain converts for ratification of the Constitution by using the Roman "Publius," who had led his countrymen to a republican form of government to replace the tyranny of the Etruscan Kings. The three anonymous conspirators had pooled their collective genius in their essays, to examine every principle of government known to man and to carefully explain how the best of these principles had been brought together in the new constitution. Adam, and hundreds of other students of law and philosophy, had quickly perceived the essays were the most profound documents they had ever seen, of their kind.

Adam raised his head and called to Matthew, behind him, "Have you studied number 51?"

For a moment Matthew searched his memory. "About the separation of powers?"

"Yes."

"Great document."

"Brilliant! Separate the powers of government and force each to check the other. Have you read number 15?"

"Yes, but I don't remember what it was about."

"An analysis of the reasons the Articles of Confederation failed. So simple. Hard to understand why people are still arguing the issue."

Matthew said, "Protect that file of essays. They're going to be valuable."

"They are now," Adam exclaimed. "I've never seen logic and reason so simple and yet so—"

The partially open front door swung wide, and all four men in the office turned to look. Matthew was the first to recognize the stocky figure standing in the doorway, holding a bag filled with clothing.

"Billy!" he exclaimed. "You're back."

Billy Weems nodded. "I'm back."

"How are you? When did you get in?"

"I'm fine. Got in just now. Haven't been home yet. Thought I better come here first to make a report."

All four men were on their feet, waiting.

"New Hampshire ratified," Billy said. "June twenty-first. Five days ago. Fifty-seven to forty-seven. We won."

Matthew's eyes closed and his head rolled back for a moment. "The ninth state! The Constitution is now the law of the land!"

Billy set the bag on his own desk. "They were number nine? I didn't know. I lost track up there."

"South Carolina was number eight. Ratified on May twenty-third.

New Hampshire has the honor of ushering in the new United States Constitution!"

Billy shook his head in wonder. "We didn't know."

Caleb interrupted. "You been gone long enough. What is it? Eight weeks?"

Billy grinned at him. "Eight weeks this trip. Six weeks last January. It's been a while."

Old Tom pointed. "Sit down there at your desk. You've got time to tell us at least the essentials of what went on up there. We've heard some pretty unusual things."

Billy said, "It got unusual a few times."

Matthew asked, "How did you travel home?"

"Walked part of the way. Caught a freight wagon coming right onto the waterfront. Got here five minutes ago."

"Brigitte doesn't know you're here?"

"Not yet. I thought I should give you the news first."

"Want to take time to tell us some of it?"

Billy shrugged. "Where do you want to start? You know I was up there in January and February with Eli, on snowshoes. Those people up in those river valleys—Merrimack, Connecticut, Piscataqua—are a pretty independent, pretty hardheaded lot. They're suspicious of any form of strong centralized government. Eli and I found that out at that first convention in Exeter last winter. They were going to vote against ratification right then and there, but we were able to get them to adjourn and put off any vote until June. If they had gone ahead, New Hampshire would have rejected the new form of government."

Tom broke in. "What happened between then and the vote five days ago? What changed?"

Billy chuckled. "Just about everything happened."

Caleb asked, "Like what?"

Billy sat down in clothes that showed dust and roadwear. Weariness showed in his face. "At Exeter, we found out we were in trouble. We knew the majority of people up there were opposed to the constitution, but they were watching Massachusetts to see what it would do. Eli knows most of the leaders up there, and they know him. We went to John Langdon and John Sullivan for help. Langdon is a rare man—strong reputation in politics. Maybe you remember that he commanded militia back at the Saratoga fight in '77. He was a delegate to the Philadelphia Convention."

Billy paused, remembering the battle on the Hudson River that had turned the Revolutionary War in favor of the rebel Americans. He and Eli had led the do-or-die charge against the Breymann Redoubt and been there to witness the surrender of the vaunted British general John Burgoyne. He set the images aside and went on.

"Sullivan is the president of New Hampshire. President or governor, whichever they call it. He was also a general in the war. And both Langdon and Sullivan are strong for the Constitution and the new government. They agreed to help, and they brought others with them—influential men, such as Gilman, Livermore, and West. Gillman was also a delegate to the Philadelphia Convention."

Billy paused for a moment to order his thoughts. "They helped us put together a plan, and things got interesting in a hurry. We urged all the supporters to get to the convention early and as soon as a quorum was there, force an election of the chairman and set some rules that would help get the meeting postponed if it would help." Billy smiled. "It worked. Our people got there earlier than the opposition, and they voted Josiah Bartlett to be chairman. Bartlett was one of our leaders. That afternoon the opposition arrived, and again the next morning, and they had a clear majority, but they were too late. We already had the chairman and the rules we wanted in place."

Billy shook his head and grinned. "It angered the opposition, and when debate opened on the ratification question, I never heard such language. Eli was there, standing quietly to one side with that long Pennsylvania rifle of his and his tomahawk in his belt, or I think we might have had a riot right there in the convention. We were taking a count every day, and the opposition was doing the same, to decide if we had enough strength to stand up to a vote, but we didn't."

Billy shifted in his chair. "Then something happened I can't explain.

Eleven of the opposition came to Langdon in private and said they had been told by their constituents to vote against ratification, so they had to do it, but that they didn't feel good about it. So if it became necessary, Langdon would ask for an adjournment of the convention, and propose one later to be held at Concord, sometime in June, and they would support the motion for adjournment at Exeter. By then we knew they had the majority, so Langdon made the motion for adjournment, and those eleven men voted for it, along with our people. The final count was fifty-six in favor, fifty opposed. The Exeter convention was finished. That was in late February."

Matthew interrupted. "What happened between then and June?"

Billy shook his head in wonderment. "Things I never would have dreamed. The newspapers were filled with articles from both sides, and I never saw such things in writing. Then both sides went out into the little towns that were to send delegates to the June convention in Concord, and started making promises and deals with just about everybody, to get support. A man named Benjamin Bellows somehow got to be the delegate from Walpole, and rumor was that he secretly changed the record of the votes to do it! The town of Hopkinton held a special election so they could tell their delegate he was not bound to vote against ratification. In Boscawen, the citizens drew up a petition that declared the recent election was illegal, and started over. Things got a bit testy, and we sent Eli with his rifle and tomahawk to be sure no one got hurt." He shook his head. "There's something about that tomahawk."

Old Tom laughed out loud, and the others grinned. Billy went on.

"Anyway, before the June convention, we counted six delegates who had changed from the opposition to our side. Then the time came for New Hampshire to elect its new governor, and Langdon was voted in. In his inaugural address, he spared no words. He gave a spellbinder speech that left no doubt—New Hampshire would ratify the Constitution, or it would pay a high price in poverty and internal troubles.

"We convened at the North Meetinghouse in Concord on June eighteenth. Our people got there first—of the one hundred thirteen gathered on that first day, ninety were ours. We got the rules we wanted, and by the time the opposition showed up the next day, the debate was in progress. The opposition found out we had a slight majority, and I never saw such twisting and turning to adjourn, or postpone, or do anything to avoid a vote. It didn't work. The vote was taken June twenty-first. I tell you now, we thought it would come out very close to a tie, but when the tally was made, we won by ten votes. Caught everyone by surprise."

Billy stopped speaking for a moment, then said, "One more thing. We heard that Virginia was getting close to a vote at about the same time. Our people wanted to be the ninth state if we could, so New Hampshire would go down in history as the state that ushered in the Constitution and the new government of the United States. The secretary at the convention reported the vote as having been final at 1:00 o'clock P.M., just in case Virginia ratified later that same day. Have you heard anything from Virginia about their vote?"

Matthew shook his head. "Nothing. I know they were expecting a vote sometime in the past few days, but no news yet."

Billy leaned back and rubbed tired eyes with the heels of his hands. "Well, that's about the nub of it. There's more in the detail, but that will come later." He put his hands on his knees, then stood. "I think I'd better go on home."

They saw it in his eyes. He wanted to see Brigitte. He had been gone too long.

Matthew stopped him. "How are things with Eli?"

Billy looked directly into his face. "Good. You should see the respect they have for him over there. He could have about any public office he wanted, where he lives. And Laura? Do you remember Mary? How she looked? The beauty in her face?"

"I remember."

"Sometimes when you look at Laura, you'd swear you were looking at Mary all over again. That girl is special. Worships her father. And both of them—Eli and Laura—made me promise to bring their greetings. They'll be coming to see us sometime this summer."

"We owe that man. Did you tell him that?"

"I did. One more thing I should tell you. The Ohio River Valley is just opening for settlement. Eli took some time to go look. He says he might consider going. New country, free land, opportunity. It's tempting."

Matthew pointed to the door. "Go on home to Brigitte. She's been counting days."

Billy picked up his bag from his desktop and walked to the door with the four men following. They watched him walk rapidly through the men and the freight and the ships on the waterfront, hurrying toward Fruit Street and home. For a moment Matthew watched his back as it disappeared in the crowd. *Langdon, Sullivan, Madison, Hamilton, Jay, Jefferson, Washington—the big names. History will remember the big names. But Weems, Stroud—the little people who stood up and made it all happen? Who will remember them? Who?*

With an ever-quickening step Billy walked away from the waterfront toward the Commons and Brigitte. He saw the picket fence and the yard, and the square house, and his heart leaped. He pushed through the gate, and to the door, and it opened, and she was there. She threw her arms about him and he dropped his bag and wrapped her to him, and he felt the tremor of a sob in her, and they stood for a time, clinging to each other, lost in the silent flow and exchange, give and take, that was the foundation of their lives.

Notes

The essays Adam Dunson is reading in this chapter were written by James Madison, John Jay, and Alexander Hamilton, who followed the custom of the day by writing them under an assumed name, in this case, "Publius." They were published in many New York papers, and then in newspapers in all thirteen states. There were 85 in all, the first published October 27, 1787, the last published May 28, 1788. The essays were collected and became known as "The Federalist" papers, and remain today probably the most comprehensive and authoritative expositions on political thought of the revolutionary time period. See Cooke, *The Federalist*, pp. 3–595. For an authoritative analysis of the key essays and an explanation of the process, see Bernstein, *Are We to Be a Nation?* pp. 230–42.

Billy Weems's narrative in this chapter includes the basic facts of the ratification process that occurred in New Hampshire. The dates of the conventions, with the several delays and incidental events are accurately stated, along with the participants named as being the leaders, with John Langdon and John Sullivan, both of whom eventually served a term as governor, and had commanded soldiers in the war, chief among those seeking ratification of the Constitution.

New Hampshire was in fact the ninth state to ratify, thus becoming the state that secured the Constitution for the United States. Four days later, June 25, Virginia ratified, to become the tenth, and one of the most important states, to approve the new constitution.

For full detail, see Conely and Kaminski, *The Constitution and the States,* pp. 181–200; Berkin, *A Brilliant Solution,* 185–86; Rossiter, *1787: The Grand Convention,* pp. 289–90.

For a schedule showing the order in which the states ratified and the dates on which each ratified, see Warren, *The Making of the Constitution,* pp. 819–20.

EPILOGUE

Y ou can all come to the table now," Margaret called.

The men rose from their chairs in the library of the Dunson home, while the women came from the kitchen to gather in the dining room, where the table was set with glowing white linen, china, and silver. Talking stopped as they waited for the matriarch to speak.

"It just seemed right," she began, "to bring us all together for this supper. We have a new country, with a new constitution and a new government, and everyone in this room is partly responsible." For a moment her chin quivered. "I talked with John about it last night, and he said he'd be here, and I believe he is."

She paused to clear her throat and regain control. "Anyway, Matthew, you sit at the head of the table. Kathleen, you there on his right. Billy and Brigitte, next, then Prissy. I'll sit at the far end, opposite Matthew. Adam, you and Caleb and Dorothy and Trudy sit up that side. John, you squeeze in between your mother and father. Kathleen, are the twins all right? Louise and Linda?"

"In your bedroom asleep."

They all saw the soft glow in Margaret's eyes as she said, "Those little darlings. Well, enough of that. Take your places and kneel beside your chairs. Matthew, you return thanks."

They knelt, and Matthew waited for quiet before he clasped his hands and bowed his head. "Almighty Father of us all. Our hearts are full as we gather here to share the bounties of thy goodness to us. We thank thee for this new nation raised by thy hand, and the blessings of freedom and liberty that are ours. We beseech thee to guide us in preserving it to our posterity. We thank thee for the fruits of the earth that are prepared for our table and seek thy blessings upon it, and upon us to turn it to good. Most of all, we thank thee for each other and the bonds that bring us together. May we never forget. Amen."

For a moment a hush held, and then Margaret rose. "All right, you women help bring it in from the kitchen."

They came with steaming platters of meats and smoking bowls of vegetables, and condiments and sauces in crystal dishes, and warm bread on plates, and pitchers of cider, buttermilk and water. Talk flowed while the food was passed around and plates were filled. Quietly, almost unnoticed, an unexpected feeling came creeping among the men. Matthew glanced at Billy, then at Caleb, and he saw it in their faces. Memories were beginning to flow. Bright images from days long ago were passing before their eyes. They ate the food, and they smiled and laughed as the chatter continued, but they were seeing things hidden from the others.

April 19, 1775—Concord—the blasting of muskets and cannon—Billy down with a British musketball and bayonet through his side that should have killed him—John Dunson down with a great gout of blood on his back, dying from a musketball in his right lung—

"Matthew, please pass the cider."

June 17, 1775—the fight across the bay at Charlestown—Bunker Hill, Breed's Hill—the terrible carnage of redcoated British regulars slaughtered as they climbed toward the guns of the Americans dug in—

"Billy, did you have any trouble with the Indians in New Hampshire?"

March 4, 1776—the Bahamas—blowing the doors on the British arsenals to capture their cannon and gunpowder to bolster a failing American army—

"Kathleen, did I hear the twins awake in the bedroom?"

August 27, 1776—Long Island, New York—the destruction of the Continental Army by General William Howe with his regulars and the German Hessian mercenaries—the sick retreat—the beating absorbed at White Plains—the disaster at

Fort Washington—the wild disintegration of the Continental Army—the run across New Jersey—Washington's crossing of the Delaware—the camp of beaten, sick, starving Americans at McKonkie's Ferry—

"Matthew, are you all right?"

December 26, 1776—Trenton—the brutal fight in the blizzard—the killing or capture of the entire command of Hessian mercenaries—their commander, Colonel Rahl? dead—

"Give me the platter. I'll get more roast beef from the oven."

January 3, 1777—Princeton—shattering the British garrison under command of Colonel Mawhood—

"Could I have one more slice of bread?"

Eli Stroud—more Iroquois warrior than white—fearless—read the forest like a book—wanting to learn more about Jesus and George Washington—

"Have you been to visit Silas and Mattie lately? She seems to be getting better."

The summer of 1777—Americans losing the battle of Brandywine Creek—the stand-or-fall fight at Saratoga on the Hudson River—the American victory over British general Gentleman John Burgoyne—his surrender—the shock experienced by King Louis XVI of France when Benjamin Franklin made the report—the decision of the French to enter the war on the American side—

"Caleb, tell us again about Pennsylvania. That boardinghouse thing."

December 19, 1778—Valley Forge—an army sick, starving, naked, freezing, dying, five hundred each month—the German officer Baron Friederich von Steuben—the miracle of training the Continental Army—

"Mother, is there any more gravy?"

July 1779—the heartrending treason of Benedict Arnold—how could it be?— how could it be?—

"John, sit straight and use your fork."

September 23, 1779—twelve miles off the coast of England—the Bon Homme Richard *and the* Serapis*—the sea battle at night—John Paul Jones—"I have not yet begun to fight"—Tom Sievers up in the rigging—shot—dying in Matthew's arms—*

"Be careful with those china bowls."

August 16, 1780—South Carolina—Camden—American general Horatio Gates abandoning his command—the terrible loss in the fight with the British—

"We need more butter."

October 7, 1780—South Carolina—the battle at King's Mountain—the British scattered, beaten—

"I'll go to the root cellar for more butter."

January 17, 1781—South Carolina—Cowpens—General Dan Morgan—the hated British commander Banastre Tarleton—the American riflemen, including Caleb and Primus, cutting down the redcoated regulars with their Deckhard rifles—the British shattered, running—

"I'll clear some of the dishes away and we'll serve dessert, if you're ready."

September 5, 1781—the French and British fleets—Chesapeake Bay—the battle—the British retreating south, beaten—General Cornwallis and his army land-locked at Yorktown—the siege—storming Redoubt Number Ten—Sergeant Alvin Turlock—burned and hurt by a cannon blast—Billy carrying him out for help—the British surrender—the end of the war—the treaty—

"Prissy, you come help bring in the saucers for dessert."

Matthew turned to Kathleen. "I'll go check on the twins."

Margaret and Prissy brought the warm fruit cobbler from the oven, and scooped it onto waiting saucers. For a time no one spoke, lost in the sweetness of Margaret's dessert. Some took second helpings, and a mel-lowness settled over the table as they talked and sipped at cider and but-termilk and laughed and gossiped about everyone they knew in Boston. It was Brigitte who finally stood.

"I can't remember a better evening. I just loved it. Mother, we're going to help with the dishes."

Margaret pointed her finger. "I can do that."

"I know that. We're still going to help."

Margaret shook her head. "Where *did that girl* get such indepen-dence?"

Everyone laughed, and the other women stood, and began gathering the dishes.

Deep dusk had settled when they gathered at the door and Matthew and Billy put on their coats. Matthew looked at Billy and Caleb, and a silent communication passed between them while the women hugged everyone. Brigitte and Kathleen tied their bonnets in place, and with the twins in the baby carriage and Matthew holding John's hand, they walked to the front gate. Billy and Brigitte and Matthew and Kathleen and John stopped at the front gate to wave at those framed in the light of the doorway and walked into the cobblestone street.

The heavens were alive with an eternity of stars. There was no breeze, and the evening air was still warm from the heat of the day as they walked together, caught up in their own thoughts. They stopped near Fruit Street and stood for a moment in the quiet of the town that had been theirs since birth.

Matthew looked at Billy, and for a moment the two men locked eyes in silence. Neither knew the words, nor did they try, nor did it matter. Kathleen hugged Brigitte, and the two couples separated toward their separate homes.

Later, in her own kitchen, Kathleen quietly called for Matthew who was in the library. There was no answer, and she removed her shoes to walk silently to the door. It was open, the room dark. She looked down the hall, where a faint light glowed beneath their bedroom door. Softly she opened the door. Matthew was inside, on one knee beside the cradle in which the twins lay sleeping. He turned from gazing at their sleeping faces, to look up at her, then back at the babies. She came to the bed and sat down, waiting, watching, sensing something was happening between her husband and their two children.

Minutes passed before Matthew rose and took his place beside her on the bed, and she turned to look into his face. He nodded toward the twins, and his voice was a whisper.

"What have we given them? I mean this country. What have we given them?"

"A new land. New government."

"That, and maybe more. Freedom. Liberty. The right to decide. They will grow up in a land like no other."

"I know."

Matthew did not continue for a time, and then he went on. "It will demand a price. The right things always do. Tonight, at Mother's, I was thinking about the price that has been paid to give all this to them. Thirteen years of blood and heartache and fear and struggle."

Kathleen nodded but remained silent.

"What price will they have to pay to keep it all?"

"I don't know."

He sighed. "Well," he whispered, "only time will tell." He waited for a moment, then said, "I think I should go make a report to father. Would you mind?"

"You go. He'll want to know."

She followed him to the door, and waited while he put on his tricorn. She reached both arms around his neck and peered into his face. "I love you." He drew her close and kissed her. "I love you. I won't be long."

He walked slowly, thoughtfully in the familiar streets, into the graveyard near the church, on to the modest headstone with the name JOHN PHELPS DUNSON engraved upon it. He removed his tricorn, and went to one knee, holding his hat in his hand.

"Father, there are some things I need to say. The fight we started there at Concord, it's finished. We have our freedom. A new constitution. A new land. Liberty. The right to choose. This new country is like nothing you ever knew, at least while you were here with us. It's hard to believe that the whole thing has been given to the common people. Like you, and me, and Billy. No king. No monarch. We choose our leaders now, and we have the power to get rid of them if they do wrong. I wish you were here. I wish you could see all this."

He stopped and for a moment touched his hat before he continued.

"It was not without cost. Your life, Tom Sievers, thousands of others. Was it worth it? I hope with all my heart it was worth it. Oh, how we missed you. How we missed you." He stopped, and for a few moments wiped at his eyes.

"Mother's fine, but I think you know that. Don't worry about Caleb. He's changing. He's coming back. And Adam? Fine boy. Brigitte and Billy are married. I've never seen either of them so happy. Prissy's a beautiful young lady. Some young man will come to the door soon, asking for her.

Our shipping business is doing well. Young John is going to be a lot like you, and the twins—Louise and Linda—are healthy and beautiful."

He paused to gather his thoughts. "I think that's about all for now. I hope that I've done what I should have after you left us. No one could really take your place at the head of the family, but I tried."

He stood. "Anyway, I thought I should come tell you how it all came out. We finished the war and we won it. We have a new land, a new constitution, a new government, and I believe now the fight is going to be to keep it. The fight between good and evil. A shooting war comes and it goes, but the war between the good and the bad—it never ends. I promise I'll do all I can to keep what you fought for, Father. What you died for. I promise."

He did not know what else to say, so he turned and started away. A faint breeze stirred in the darkness, and he stopped to look back for a moment, then he smiled, and turned back toward home, Kathleen, and the children.

Note

The characters depicted in this chapter are fictitious but represent the common American people of that generation, to whom we owe so much.

BIBLIOGRAPHY

Berkin, Carol. *A Brilliant Solution: Inventing the American Constitution*. New York: Harcourt, Inc., 2002.

Bernstein, Richard B. *Are We to Be a Nation? The Making of the Constitution*. Cambridge, Mass.: Harvard University Press, 1987.

Compton's Encyclopedia. 26 vols. Edited by University of Chicago. Chicago: F. E. Compton Company, 1974.

Conely, Patrick T., and John P. Kaminski, eds. *The Constitution and the States*. Madison, Wis.: Madison House, 1988.

Cooke, Jacob E., ed. *The Federalist*. Middletown, Conn.: Wesleyan University Press, 1961.

Earle, Alice Morse. *Home Life in Colonial Days*. Stockbridge, Mass.: Berkshire House Publishers, 1992.

Farrand, Max. *The Records of the Federal Convention*. 3 vols. New Haven, Mass.: Yale University Press, 1911.

Freeman, Douglas Southall. *Washington*. New York: Simon & Schuster, 1995.

Herberts, Klein. *The Atlantic Slave Trade*. New York: Cambridge University Press, 1999.

Higginbotham, Don. *The War of American Independence: Military Attitudes, Policies, and Practice, 1763–1789*. Boston: Northeastern University Press, 1983.

Jobé, Joseph, ed. *The Great Age of Sail*. Translated by Michael Kelly. New York: Crescent Books, 1967.

Mackesy, Piers. *The War for America, 1775–1783*. Lincoln, Nebr.: University of Nebraska Press, 1992.

Moyers, Bill. *Moyers: Report from Philadelphia: The Constitutional Convention of 1787*. New York: Ballantine Books, 1987.

National Geographic Society Picture Atlas of Our Fifty States. Contributions by Bettie Donley, Diane S. Marton, and Maureen Palmedo. Washington, D.C.: National Geographic Society, 1978.

Outhwaite, Leonard. *The Atlantic: A History of an Ocean*. New York: Coward-McCann, 1957.

Pawson, Michael, and David Buisseret. *Port Royal, Jamaica*. Oxford: Clarendon Press, 1975.

Rossiter, Clinton. *1787: The Grand Convention.* New York: Macmillan, 1966.

Ulrich, Laurel Thatcher. *A Midwife's Tale: The Life of Martha Ballard, Based on Her Diary, 1785–1812.* New York: Vintage Books, 1991.

Warren, Charles. *The Making of the Constitution.* Boston: Little, Brown and Company, 1929.

Special Acknowledgments

*D*r. Richard B. Bernstein of Brooklyn, New York, with his internationally recognized expertise in the history of the Revolutionary War time period, has been indispensable in the writing of this work. Over the past seven years, he has read every word of all eight volumes, made endless corrections to preserve the historical integrity of the story, and been available at all times, day and night, when needed. He is a rare person, a monumental historian, and a trusted friend.

Harriet S. Abels, distinguished author and noted educator, graciously accepted this writer as a student more than fifteen years ago. She performed the work of a master in making something from almost nothing. She has faithfully read, edited, rearranged, and corrected every manuscript of this series of books, and in the process has proven to be a great soul, dedicated to her work, and has become a lifelong friend.

Without the contributions of these two, this work would never have been completed.